Sartor Resartus

THE NORMAN AND CHARLOTTE STROUSE EDITION OF THE WRITINGS OF

Thomas Carlyle

Sartor Resartus

THE LIFE AND OPINIONS OF
HERR TEUFELSDRÖCKH
IN THREE BOOKS

Mein Vermächtniss, wie herrlich weit und breit!
Die Zeit ist mein Vermächtniss, mein Acker ist die Zeit.

Introduction and Notes by
Rodger L. Tarr

Text Established by
Mark Engel and Rodger L. Tarr

University of California Press

BERKELEY   LOS ANGELES   LONDON

University of California Press
Berkeley and Los Angeles, California

University of California Press, Ltd.
London, England

© 2000 by
The Regents of the University of California

Library of Congress Cataloging-in-Publication Data

Carlyle, Thomas, 1795–1881.
    Sartor Resartus: the life and opinions of Herr Teufelsdröckh in
three books / introduction and notes by Rodger L. Tarr; text
established by Mark Engel and Rodger L. Tarr.
        p.   cm. — (The Norman and Charlotte Strouse edition of
the writings of Thomas Carlyle)
    "Committee on Scholarly Editions, an approved edition, Modern
Language Association"—T.p. verso.
    Includes bibliographical references and index.
    ISBN 0-520-20928-1 (alk. paper)
    1. Philosophers—Germany—Fiction.   2. Philosophy—Fiction.
I. Tarr, Rodger L. II. Engel, Mark. III. Title. IV. Series: Carlyle,
Thomas, 1795–1881. Works. 1993.
PR4429.A2T37   2000
824'.8—dc21   91-3100
                                                             CIP
Printed in the United States of America

9 8 7 6 5 4 3 2 1

The paper used in this publication meets the minimum requirements
of American National Standard for Information Sciences—Permanence
of Paper for Printed Library Materials, ANSI Z39.48-1984. ∞

CONTENTS

ILLUSTRATIONS

Following page cxxviii

PREFACE

SARTOR *Resartus* is Thomas Carlyle's most enduring and most widely read work. Yet to date there has been no reliable edition, providing both an accurate text based on modern textual principles and full annotation. The now out-of-print editions edited by Archibald MacMechan (Ginn, 1896), J. A. S. Barrett (Black, 1897), James Wood (Dent, 1902), William S. Johnson (Houghton Mifflin, 1924), and Charles F. Harrold (Odyssey, 1937) offer valuable, though incomplete, annotation. All are based upon flawed texts. A more recent edition as part of *A Carlyle Reader* by G. B. Tennyson (Random House, 1969) contains a valuable general preface but no annotation. The "World's Classics" edition (Oxford, 1987), edited by Kerry McSweeney and Peter Sabor, contains very brief annotation. Both the *Reader* and the "World's Classics" editions are also based upon flawed texts. The so-called standard edition, the Centenary Edition (Chapman and Hall, 1896), has no annotation and is rife with errors.[1] The Strouse Carlyle Edition seeks to redress the faults and inadequacies of previous editions and to present a critical text based upon a full collation of all source texts with any claim to Carlyle's authorial or editorial participation.

To establish an accurate text the editors have devised an integrated system for the computer-assisted production of the edition, based on the CASE (Computer Assistance to Scholarly Editing) programs.[2] The application of electronic technology in every stage of the editorial process, from the collection of evidence through the final typesetting of the text and apparatus, permits a high level of accuracy, while leaving all decisions requiring editorial judgment in the control of scholars. (A valuable byproduct of the use of computer technology throughout the project has been the creation of a machine-readable archive of Carlylean texts, textual apparatus, and annotation.) The text is preceded by a discussion of the evidence and editorial principles used to establish it, and a full textual apparatus is appended, including a list of all emendations of the copy-text and a complete collation of authoritative versions, keyed to the present text by page and line number. To facilitate reading, we present Carlyle's work as clear text, without editorial or reference symbols.

[1] See the Note on the Text, pp. cxxvi–cxxvii below.
[2] For a description of the CASE programs, see Shillingsburg, *Scholarly Editing in the Computer Age*, 128-46.

ix

The historical introduction is intended to elaborate the significance of the work for Carlyle's era and to suggest its importance for our own, as well as explaining its origin and biographical context. By providing a full critical and explanatory annotation, the editors hope to assist the contemporary reader in negotiating Carlyle's densely referential prose. A tissue of quotation from varied and disparate sources intertwined with the historic events of Victorian life, Carlyle's art weaves together multifarious references and allusions, which we have sought, wherever possible, to identify, gloss, and translate. The editors hope that the explanatory annotation, like the critical text, will provide the basis for new readings and new interpretations, foundations on which readers of the present and future may build the often-changing structures of cultural analysis. We have resisted the temptation to impose our own readings, offering instead the essential materials for interpretation, hoping thereby to approximate Carlyle's own ideal book, in which the reader is "excited . . . to self-activity."[3]

The materials of the edition, both on paper and in electronic form, have been added to the Norman and Charlotte Strouse Collection of Thomas Carlyle, housed in Special Collections, University Library, at the University of California, Santa Cruz. In recovering the impact of the original Carlyle and making his work accessible to readers of the present and the future, this edition fulfills the central purposes of the Strouse Collection, which has been our inspiration, base of operations, and invaluable resource. In recognition of their inestimable service to Carlyle studies, the edition is dedicated to Norman and Charlotte Strouse.

This work would not have been possible without the assistance of many people and institutions. Their contributions can only imperfectly be acknowledged by brief mention here.

Funding for the edition was provided by research grants from the University of California, Santa Cruz, for which we must thank Chancellors Robert Sinsheimer, Robert B. Stevens, and Karl S. Pister; Academic Vice Chancellors Kivie Moldave, Isebill V. Gruhn, and Michael Tanner; Deans Michael Cowan, Gary Lease, and Geoffrey Pullum; and the Committee on Research of the Academic Senate. Other University officers who have aided the project, providing facilities and administrative support, include Assistant Vice Chancellor Daniel G. Aldrich III; University Librarian Alan Dyson; Janice Crooks and Richard W. Jensen of the Academic Vice Chancellor's office; Robert E. Jorgensen, Cindi Smith, Terri Ediger-Hamerly, and Kathie

[3] *Sartor Resartus*, 1.4.22.

Kenyon of the office of the Dean of Humanities; and Peggy M. Hathcock and Joan A. Houston of the Humanities Business Office.

Our funding was supplemented by generous contributions from private patrons including Lou and Isabell Bartfield, Donald and Emily Clark, Wendell B. Coon, Donald D. Cummins, Ruth Engel, Mrs. Fred C. Foy, Dr. James D. Hart, Frederick B. Henderson, Stephen G. Herrick, Alan and Judy Levin, Dean and Jane McHenry, Charles M. Merrill, Gurden Mooser, and of course Norman Strouse.

Rodger Tarr wishes to express his gratitude to the National Endowment for the Humanities and the Fulbright Commission who funded the research for his *Thomas Carlyle: A Descriptive Bibliography* (1989), which provided the basis for this edition. He also wishes to thank Illinois State University, in particular the former Dean of the College of Arts and Sciences, Virginia L. Owen; the former Chair of the Department of English, Charles B. Harris; the current Dean of the College of Arts and Sciences, Paul Schollaert; and the current Chair of the Department of English, Ronald Fortune, who in divers ways provided funds not only for this edition, but for the Strouse Edition as a whole. Illinois State University also provided much-needed research and travel funds.

Rodger Tarr further wishes to express his personal debt to the many scholars who have contributed markedly to this edition. He is especially grateful to his old friend and mentor K. J. Fielding, Emeritus Saintsbury Professor of English Literature, University of Edinburgh, who painstakingly read and offered suggestions for the Introduction and the Notes. He is grateful in kind to Anne Skabarnicki, Royal Military College of Canada, and to the late Clyde de L. Ryals, Duke University, who read and contributed to the notes. Ian Campbell, University of Edinburgh, provided important information. John Hruschka, Pennsylvania State University, helped check the notes against the sources and offered stimulating suggestions. Robert Hirst, General Editor of the Mark Twain Project, University of California, Berkeley, offered splendid advice on how to proceed with the unique printer's proof of the 1841 edition. Carol Anita Tarr patiently read multiple drafts.

Rodger Tarr also wishes to express his profound debt to the many librarians who participated in this edition. Rita B. Bottoms, University Archivist and curator of Special Collections at UC Santa Cruz, and her staff Carol Champion, Paul S. Stubbs, Irene Crawley Berry, and Paul Machlis, the keepers of the Strouse Carlyle Collection, provided invaluable assistance, as did the Reference staff including

Margaret N. Gordon, Alan Ritch, and Deborah Murphy. Jerry James, Humanities Bibliographer emeritus, was the rock upon which much was built. The reference librarians of the Beinecke Library, Yale University, and the Houghton Library, Harvard University, were instrumental in making their collections available. The librarians of the British Library, National Library of Scotland, and the University of Edinburgh Library are herewith acknowledged for their many kindnesses. The same acknowledgment is given to the librarians of Oberlin College, Hamilton College, the University of Georgia, and the University of South Carolina, the last now the owner of the Rodger L. Tarr Carlyle Collection, used extensively in this edition. In addition, grateful use has been made of the rich resources of institutions including the National Trust, Carlyle House, the British Museum, the National Portrait Gallery, the University Library, Cambridge, and the Trinity College Cambridge Library. Permission to quote from unpublished correspondence or to use illustrations from their collections was graciously granted by the National Library of Scotland, University of Edinburgh Library, British Library, Pierpont Morgan Library, University of California, Santa Cruz, Yale University, Duke University, and Harvard University.

Finally, Rodger Tarr wishes to acknowledge Peter L. Shillingsburg, Lamar University, who shared with us the CASE programs developed under his supervision for the Thackeray Edition of which he is the general editor, and who provided textual wisdom. David Nordloh, Indiana University, the textual advisor for this edition, is honored for his unwavering support, infinite patience, and unparalleled sense of humor. G. B. Tennyson, most valued friend, freely gave repeated encouragement and witty appraisal. David J. DeLaura, University of Pennsylvania, and the late Carlisle Moore, University of Oregon, mentors both, stood faithfully, always there to assist. Thanks also to Craig Fata for helping with the Works Cited and Irene Taylor for her inputting of Carlyle's Index. Jerry and Jan James, Santa Cruz, California, offered their home and comfort for an oft-weary sojourner. Thanks also to G. Ross Roy, University of South Carolina, who nurtured an antiquarian spirit. Matthew J. Bruccoli, University of South Carolina, provided, unwittingly, the example to bring this project to fruition. For her work on the Index, special acknowledgment is given to Louise Freeman-Toole; and for his tireless work as a researcher, specific recognition goes to Brent Kinser. And special recognition is given to Zoë Sodja at UC Santa Cruz, for her expert, patient work in preparing the camera-ready copy.

Our work has been assisted by the genuine collaboration of the members of the Editorial Board and the Advisory Board, who are listed facing the title page of this volume. These scholars traveled to Santa Cruz for a series of organizational meetings, participated in the formulation of policies for the edition, and read and commented on various stages of the manuscript. We must mention in particular the assistance of K. J. Fielding of the University of Edinburgh who, together with his colleagues Ian M. Campbell of Edinburgh and the late Clyde de L. Ryals of Duke University, made available to us the essential resources of their ongoing project to publish the Collected Letters of Thomas *and Jane Welsh Carlyle.* Carlyle biographer Fred Kaplan of the City University of New York prepared the Chronology of Carlyle's Life that appears on pp. xv–xix.

Mark Engel also wishes to thank Peter L. Shillingsburg of Lamar University, who was appointed our inspector by the Committee for Scholarly Editions of the Modern Language Association, and who functioned in that capacity as our advisor as well as our judge. Other scholars who have assisted our work include Michael J. Warren, UC Santa Cruz; Scott Cook, San Jose State University; and especially Joel J. Brattin of Worcester Polytechnic Institute.

Mark Engel is also grateful for the help of many of the libraries and librarians already mentioned, including the staff of UCSC Special Collections, as well as the staff of the Morgan and Houghton Libraries. For the loan of their Hinman Collator, we must thank Donald Kunitz and John Skarstad of Special Collections, Shields Library, University of California, Davis.

Our use of computer technology in all stages of the project has of course required the assistance of many programmers and consultants who are to us as heroes in their arcane skills and technical competence. Peter Shillingsburg and his indispensable CASE collation programs have already been mentioned. Rob Strand of the University of California, Santa Cruz Computer Center modified the original CASE programs so that they could be run on a CMS-based IBM mainframe. Much of the pre- and post-collation processing of the text and collation lists was done on the UC Santa Cruz campuswide unix-based mainframe system, while typesetting and layout was done on Macintosh personal computers in the edition office. James Ganong, programmer extraordinaire, designed our system and wrote magical filter programs that make it possible for us to move our complex text files freely among the CMS, unix, and Macintosh platforms. Noah Kaplan, besides assisting James Ganong with the unix programming, showed endless patience in carrying out the tedious experimentation needed to make everything work. In addition we must thank Daniel Wenger, former computing director of the Division of Humanities of UC Santa Cruz, and the staff of Computer and Telecommunications Services, especially emeriti Assistant Vice Chancellor Alan Schlenger, User Services Manager Dennie Van Tassel, and Senior Data Analysis Consultant James P. Mulherin.

We have had the support throughout of our publishers, the University of California Press, and must mention in particular our sponsoring editors, Dr. Jack R. Miles and William J. McClung, our project editor Sheila Levine, editor Laura Driussi, design assistance from Czeslaw Jan Grycz, Jeanne Sugiyama, and Steve Renick, and editorial assistance from Marilyn Schwartz, Douglas Abrams-Arava, and our acute copy editor Nancy Evans.

Among the many who have labored valiantly on this book are Henrietta Brown, Rebecca Levy, Zoë Sodja, Heidi Swillinger, Joan Tannheimer, and Nona Williams of the UCSC Document Publishing and Editing Center, supervised by Cheryl VanDeVeer, and Betsy G. Wootten of the UCSC Kresge College Services to Academic Staff office. Our own yeoman staff of clerical and research assistants has included Pam Dunn, Elizabeth Jones, Rosemarie Milazzo, Marc Moskowitz, Mary Kate St. Clair, Erik Trump, and Hesper Wilson.

The Strouse Carlyle Edition is administered by the Dickens Project, a multicampus research group of the University of California. Our special thanks go to its past and present staff including Joanna Rottke, Dorene Blake, Tom Graves, and T. Lark Letchworth—and notably Linda Rosewood Hooper, who gave us indispensable assistance with production and layout—and its director, John O. Jordan, without whom our list of heroes would not be complete.

All of those mentioned here have made this volume better than it would have been without their help; none is responsible for any errors that may remain.

— Murray Baumgarten
Editor-in-Chief

CHRONOLOGY OF CARLYLE'S LIFE

1795 Thomas Carlyle born on December 4 in Ecclefechan, Scotland.

1801 Jane Baillie Welsh born in Haddington, near Edinburgh, on July 14.

1806 Carlyle enrolls as a day student at Annan Academy.

1809 Begins his education at the University of Edinburgh.

1813 Enrolls in Divinity Hall to fulfill his parents' expectation that he will become a minister.

1814 Leaves the university and returns to Annan Academy as mathematics tutor.

1816 Meets Edward Irving, a teacher and minister. Begins teaching in parish school in Kirkcaldy near Edinburgh.

1817 Tours the Highlands and western Scotland with Irving. Writes articles, letters to newspapers, and occasional poems on scientific and philosophic subjects.

1819 Moves to Edinburgh.

1820 Does translations from the French; writes a series of encyclopedia articles.

1821 Irving introduces him to Jane Welsh. Carlyle takes a well-paid position, arranged by Irving, as a private tutor to Charles and Arthur Buller.

1822 Has a conversion experience in Leith Walk, near Edinburgh, in which he commits himself to the primacy and importance of work, rather than belief or theology, as the essence of personal self-definition. With his brother John's help, he translates Legendre's *Elements of Geometry*.

1823 Translates Goethe's *Wilhelm Meister* (1824) and expands an article on Schiller into *The Life of Schiller* (1825).

1824 Beginning in June, makes an extended visit to London. A guest of the Buller family and the Irving circle, he is introduced to London literary society, including Coleridge and Charles Lamb.

1825   Translates various German authors, and falls strongly under the influence of Goethe.

1826   Marries Jane Baillie Welsh on October 17. Begins an autobiographical bildungsroman, the unfinished *Wotton Reinfred*.

1827   Francis Jeffrey, editor of the *Edinburgh Review*, becomes his patron and family friend. Jeffrey publishes a series of Carlyle's review-essays, mainly on German literature and culture, which initiate his Scottish and English reputation. *German Romance* published in four volumes.

1828   Unsuccessful efforts to find suitable employment. Carlyles move to Craigenputtoch, a remote farm near Dunscore.

1828–29 Publishes "Burns" and "Signs of the Times" in the *Edinburgh Review* and articles on German literature in the *Foreign Review*.

1830   "On History" published in *Fraser's Magazine*. Begins *Sartor Resartus*.

1831   In London for an extended visit, he renews contact with the Buller-Irving circle, begins a friendship with John Stuart Mill, and unsuccessfully tries to find a publisher for *Sartor Resartus*. "Characteristics" published in the *Edinburgh Review*.

1832   Death of his father, James Carlyle. Thomas writes a substantial memoir of him, later included in *Reminiscences* (1881). Carlyles return to Craigenputtoch.

1833   *Sartor Resartus* is published serially in *Fraser's Magazine* from November 1833 to August 1834. Encouraged by Mill, he begins to write about the French Revolution ("The Diamond Necklace"). In August, Emerson visits Carlyle at Craigenputtoch, the beginning of a lifelong friendship. Carlyle gives thought to emigrating to America.

1834   The Carlyles move to 24 Cheyne Row, London, their residence for the remainder of their lives. Edward Irving dies. In September, Carlyle begins to write *The French Revolution*.

1835   In March he is forced to begin *The French Revolution* again when the only copy of the manuscript (one-third completed) is accidentally destroyed while in the keeping of John Stuart

Mill. Meets Southey and Wordsworth, and becomes friends with John Sterling. In the next five years his circle of London friends expands to include Leigh Hunt, Harriet Martineau, Erasmus Darwin, Monckton Milnes, John Forster, Dickens, Thackeray, Tennyson, FitzGerald, and Browning.

1836   *Sartor Resartus* first published in book form in Boston.

1837   Gives seven public lectures on German literature beginning in May. *The French Revolution* is published.

1838   Course of twelve lectures on European literature. *Sartor Resartus* is published in book form in London. With Emerson's help, *Critical and Miscellaneous Essays* is published in Boston.

1839   Six lectures on the revolutions of modern Europe. *On Chartism* published. Plays a formative role in the creation of the London Library.

1840   Delivers six lectures on heroes. Spends the summer in Scotland, henceforth an annual practice, and considers writing a biography of Cromwell.

1841   *On Heroes, Hero-Worship, and the Heroic in History* published.

1842   While visiting the Bury St. Edmunds area, he conceives the idea for *Past and Present.*

1843   *Past and Present* published.

1844   John Sterling dies.

1845   *Oliver Cromwell's Letters and Speeches* published.

1847   Emerson visits England and spends time with the Carlyles.

1848   Carlyle meets Sir Robert Peel, whom he admires and whose leading role in the repeal of the Corn Laws he has supported.

1849   Carlyle tours Ireland with his friend Gavan Duffy and finds English policies substantially responsible for the condition of Ireland. Writes his *Reminiscences of My Irish Journey,* published posthumously in 1882. Anger and despair about political and cultural conditions in Britain expressed in reviews and essays, including "Occasional Discourse on the Negro Question," published in *Fraser's Magazine.*

1850   Publishes *Latter-Day Pamphlets*, a series of eight satirical essays on the condition of modern Britain. Ruskin visits Carlyle for the first time and soon becomes a disciple. Friendships with a younger generation of intellectuals and writers, including William Allingham and John Tyndall.

1851   *Life of John Sterling*. In the fall, he visits Paris, accompanied by Robert and Elizabeth Browning. Begins to consider Frederick the Great as a subject for a biography.

1852   In the late summer, travels to Germany for the first time, visiting sites associated with Luther, Goethe, and Frederick the Great.

1856   Completes the writing of the first two volumes of *Frederick the Great*.

1857–58 *Collected Works* (the Uniform Edition) published in sixteen volumes.

1858   First two volumes of *Frederick the Great* published. In late summer, makes a second visit to Germany to complete a survey of sites associated with Frederick.

1863   Jane Carlyle's health deteriorates. Volume 3 of *Frederick the Great* is published.

1864   Volume 4 of *Frederick the Great* is published.

1865   Completes *Frederick the Great;* volumes 5 and 6 are published. In November he is elected Lord Rector of Edinburgh University.

1866   On April 2, Carlyle delivers his "Inaugural Address" in Edinburgh. On April 21, Jane Carlyle dies of a stroke. Carlyle writes a biographical and autobiographical memoir of Jane and another of Edward Irving, both later included in *Reminiscences*. In the fall Carlyle joins the Governor Eyre committee whose purpose is to defend Eyre against the charge that his suppression of the Jamaican slave revolt (1865) was too harsh.

1867   Writes brief memoirs of Southey, Wordsworth, and William Hamilton. In August, he publishes a satiric attack on the Reform Bill of 1867, "Shooting Niagara: And After?" The essay also attacks environmental pollution. Ruskin and Carlyle become estranged.

1868–69 Works sporadically at a selected edition of Jane's letters, then decides to postpone publication.

1869 A second edition of the *Collected Works* (the Library Edition, thirty volumes) begins publication. In March, he has an interview with Queen Victoria.

1870 Publishes a letter in the *Times* strongly supporting Germany in the Franco-Prussian War.

1871 Turns over to James Anthony Froude some personal papers and manuscripts, particularly Jane's letters, in effect appointing Froude his biographer and Jane's editor. In 1873 he gives Froude most of the remaining documents. His right hand becomes palsied, making it difficult for him to write.

1872 He dictates *Early Kings of Norway* (1875), but finds dictation an unsatisfactory way of writing.

1873 Carlyle's portrait is painted by Whistler.

1874–75 Enters the controversy about the authenticity of a portrait of John Knox and dictates an essay, "Portraits of John Knox" (1875).

1875 His eightieth birthday in December is the occasion for an international celebration, with gifts, honorary degrees, testimonial letters, and an engraved gold medallion. He declines Disraeli's offer of a title.

1875–76 Publishes two letters in the *Times* opposing Disraeli's policy of support for the Turks against the Russians.

1879 Visits Scotland. With the death of his favorite younger brother John, he has outlived most of his family and personal and professional friends.

1881 On February 5, Carlyle dies at Cheyne Row. He is buried on February 10 next to his parents in the churchyard at Ecclefechan.

INTRODUCTION

I. BACKGROUNDS AND IMPULSES

THE STAGE

Sartor Resartus is among the most imaginative, ingenious works ever written, and also among the most difficult to understand. It is one of those books where an appreciation of style is necessary for an appreciation of content. Through his foregrounding of style, Carlyle is able to explore philosophical ambiguities that would otherwise be difficult to express. At every juncture method informs content and content method. As the text unfolds, signs turn to allusions and allusions to discourse, only to return to signs. The language of paradox conflates with the language of irony, which in turn leads to a density of expression that frequently baffles even the most astute reader. A contemporary reviewer, choosing anonymity, called it a "heap of clotted nonsense," and suggested that at least one sentence could be read "backwards or forwards" with much the same effect. A modern critic, G. B. Tennyson, opines, partly in jest and partly in imitation: "One could call it paratactic, periphrastic, parasynthetic, hypotypotic, paraenetic, paraleptic, parenthetic, paradoxical, occasionally paralogic, and no doubt more. Many would be content to add paralytic."[1] There is little doubt that such ambiguity of expression is intentional on Carlyle's part. Majestically humorous like *Don Quixote*, outrageously satirical like *Candide*, and bitingly ironic like *Tristram Shandy*, *Sartor Resartus* attempts to embrace all that is of value in belles lettres, past and present.[2] It also bodies forth in the manner of a

---

[1] See "[*Sartor Resartus*]." *Sun*, April 1, 1834, 2; and G. B. Tennyson, "*Sartor* Called "*Resartus*," 242, the latter of which remains the most insightful discussion of the peculiarities and the influences of Carlyle's style. Not surprising, Carlyle's style has been the subject of considerable debate. During the nineteenth century it became known as Carlylese, and resulted in a host of imitators and parodists. There are a number of informed shorter studies which has led, inevitably, to computer analyses of Carlyle's use of words, phrases, and sentences: see R. L. Oakman, "Carlyle and the Machine: A Quantitative Analysis of Syntax in Prose Style"; and Robert Cluett, "Victoria Resarta: Carlyle Among His Contemporaries," the latter of whom uses graphs, tables, and statistics to conclude that "no man . . . has written English awkwardlier" (178).

[2] The humor in *Sartor Resartus* depends of course on reader perception. In many respects it is literal, following the conventions of Augustan satire, although tempered appreciably by Romantic aesthetics. Yet it is also figurative

biblical prophecy, and in consequence focuses on transcendence, if not always the transcendental. It rejects cultural paradigms which are formed in custom and which end in stasis. The impulse is palingenetic, and the philosophy "perpetual metamorphoses" (174).

Sartor Resartus is not just the "tailor retailored"; it is the text tailored, and the context retailored, as metaphor builds upon metaphor and allusion fosters allusion. Paradox inevitably invites paradox. The light of Plato clashes with the darkness of Milton; the order of Shakespeare with the discord of Byron; the despair of Swift with the optimism of Goethe; the cynicism of Hobbes with the idealism of Fichte. Carlyle's purpose is Blake's purpose: to reshape the enduring texts of the past into an intellectual prophecy for the future. To accomplish this end, he fuses genre to genre. Sartor Resartus is a novel anti-novel, guided by figurative language and informed by paradoxical relationships.[3] It is a fictive narrative while a parody of didactic fiction; it is a complex of structures similar to a mathematical tract while a challenge to the Newtonian systems of cosmos; it is a formal essay while an inventive discourse; it is a veiled autobiography

---

and relies on a recognition of the complex allusions which are often dependent on or enhanced by the use of irony. For discussions of Carlyle's use of humor, see Waldo H. Dunn, "The Centennial of Sartor Resartus"; Tennyson, "Sartor" Called "Resartus," 273-83; and Richard J. Dunn, "'Inverse Sublimity': Carlyle's Theory of Humour." For discussions of Carlyle's use of irony, see Jacques Blondel, "Vision et ironie dans Sartor Resartus"; Janice L. Haney, "'Shadow-Hunting': Romantic Irony, Sartor Resartus, and Victorian Romanticism"; and Anne K. Mellor, "Carlyle's Sartor Resartus: A Self-Consuming Artifact," Romantic Irony. Carlyle's linguistic deviltry is intertextual and extends even to his revisions, as in the following emendation: "Ach, mein Leiber!" [Oh, my stomach!] is the exclamation as Teufelsdröckh leaves the coffee-house on Wahngasse [Dream-Lane] in Weissnichtwo [Know-Not-Where]. The language is changed, in the 1849 edition and all subsequent editions, to a less humorous address: "Ach, mein Lieber" [Oh, my friend!].

[3] John Holloway, The Victorian Sage , 36-37, is astonished by Carlyle's use of figurative language, particularly metaphor: Sartor Resartus "displays not merely its use, but its creation. . . . [Carlyle] develops a figurative language that becomes more and more esoteric; and the developments do not occur in isolation, but interconnect and sometimes fuse." Carlyle's claim that Sartor Resartus is a "sort of Didactic Novel" has resulted in debate on whether it was intended as fiction and thus whether it belongs to the genre of the novel. For discussions of Carlyle's relationships to and attitudes toward fiction, see Carlisle Moore, "Thomas Carlyle and Fiction: 1822–1834"; George Levine, "Sartor Resartus and the Balance of Fiction"; Tennyson, "Sartor" Called "Resartus," 173–85; and Rodger L. Tarr, "'Fictional High-Seriousness': Carlyle and the Victorian Novel."

while an intentional fragmentation of biography; and, it is a social manifesto while eschewing political dogma. *Sartor Resartus* defies labeling. It is everything and nothing, declarative and interrogatory, a sort of cornucopia of intellectual philosophy—in Carlyle's own words, "Nonsense."[4]

THE IMPETUS

The history that brought Carlyle to this threshold of "Nonsense" is not particularly complicated. He was educated under the stern eyes of Calvinist parents of the conservative Burgher sect, but as a young man broke from their confining values and set his sights on the philosophic world of inquiry instead of the Masonic world of trade. At the University of Edinburgh he studied theology and law, and rejected both. The study of mathematics brought him little contentment, even though later he was to translate, with the assistance of his brother John, Adrien Marie Legendre's *Éléments de géométrie*. A pivotal year in Carlyle's intellectual development was 1819, when he came under the influence of German literature and philosophy. Goethe soon became his literary father and personal mentor. By the mid-1820s, he was fully committed to the German tradition. In 1824, he translated Goethe's *Wilhelm Meisters Lehrjahre*; in 1825, he wrote the *Life of Schiller*; and, in 1827, he translated German fiction under the title *German Romance*. He even began a history of German literature, but was forced to abandon the project when he could not find the support of a publisher. The poetry he composed during this period was largely inspired by German idealism, as was the fiction, especially the unfinished novel, *Wotton*

---

[4] *Two Note Books*, 176. In many respects *Sartor Resartus* anticipates the so-called literature of nonsense in the Victorian period, most notably that written by Lewis Carroll. At the semiotic level there is much in common between *Sartor Resartus* and *Alice in Wonderland*, and also *Through the Looking Glass*. Among other things, each uses language to create language; each uses mathematics to refute mathematics; and each mirrors reality to form a new reality. When Carlyle called his work "Nonsense," he could not of course have realized or approved the specific tradition that was to develop. What he did sense, however, was that literature needed a new, refreshing focus, one that would release the writer from the conventions of the past. Presenting sense as nonsense and nonsense as sense opened up new avenues appropriate to his multi-level meta-discourse. See Keith Hughes, "*Sartor Resartus* and Nonsense." Carlyle's penchant for disguising mathematical narrative in the language of semiotics is discussed by Carlisle Moore, "Carlyle: Mathematics and 'Mathesis,'" who concludes, "The very germination of *Sartor* was largely in mathematical terms . . ." (89).

Reinfred. His many essays and criticisms were also written from this perspective.[5] The influence of German culture upon his psyche cannot be overestimated, although it is sometimes overstated. Kantian and post-Kantian philosophy became a part of his life during the crucial period leading up to and during the composition of *Sartor Resartus.* Thus, whether he was writing a review of the French Voltaire, or the Scot Burns, or the German Richter, or the English Johnson, he was doing so from a decidedly German point of view. His social essays, like "Signs of the Times," are no different. *Entsagung* (renunciation) is at the heart of his aesthetic.[6]

This is not to say that Carlyle ignored his British contemporaries. In fact, as the "Explanatory Notes" in this edition attest, he was thoroughly familiar with the British writers of his age. The poets, Wordsworth, Coleridge, and Byron, and to a lesser extent Shelley, and the essayists, Hazlitt, Lamb, and Macaulay, were always at his side, and were kept there in part by Jane Welsh whom he married in 1826. And, of course, there were other looming images from the immediate past. The philosophers Locke and Hume, the historians Gibbon and Robertson, the poets Gray and Burns, and the essayists Pope and Johnson were favorites and are representative of his extensive knowledge of eighteenth-century thought. His acquaintanceship with the novels of the period is no less impressive. Add to this his reading of the French encyclopædists like Diderot and Montesquieu, the essayists like Voltaire and Montaigne, and the philosophers like Descartes and Rousseau, and the dimensions of Carlyle's eclecticism are evident. The influence of the *encyclopædic* tradition is found not

[5] For a complete detailing of Carlyle's writings, including a full description of the lifetime editions and publishing history of *Sartor Resartus,* see Rodger L. Tarr, *Thomas Carlyle: A Descriptive Bibliography.* See also *The Collected Poems of Thomas and Jane Welsh Carlyle.*

[6] *Entsagung,* taken from Goethe's autobiographical *Dichtung und Wahrheit* [*Fiction and Truth*], is a difficult term to define beyond the usual conception of renunciation. Carlyle's use of the term seems to embrace a more personal self-renunciation, followed by an equally personal self-revelation. The general subject of the influence of German literature and philosophy upon Carlyle has resulted in a host of important short studies on specific influences, too numerous to list here. See G. B. Tennyson, "The Carlyles," 96–100; and Rodger L. Tarr, *Thomas Carlyle: A Bibliography of English-Language Criticism, 1824–1974,* passim. To date, the most thorough studies on the subject are Charles F. Harrold, *Carlyle and German Thought: 1819–1834* , Tennyson, *"Sartor" Called "Resartus";* and E. M. Vida, *Romantic Affinities: German Authors and Carlyle;* and a provocative one of lesser length by Ruth apRoberts, *The Ancient Dialect: Thomas Carlyle and Comparative Religion,* especially 1–72.

only in *Sartor Resartus*, but in his own encyclopædia articles written
for David Brewster's *Edinburgh Encyclopædia* in 1820–1823. Carlyle
was widely read in a number of modern foreign languages.[7] His pro-
ficiency in Latin extended to medical and scientific treatises, and his
knowledge of Greek, though less than Latin, was adequate for reading. He read Dante and Cervantes in the original as well as in translation. He also took a special interest in linguistics, and was particularly proud of his knowledge of Norse dialects. Thus, as he came to
write *Sartor Resartus*, Carlyle was, at least in his reading, a Renaissance man.

THE HERITAGE

The intellectual heritage of *Sartor Resartus* is a complex of interweav-
ings that is often difficult to fathom. The work is an "Essay on
Metaphors," or so Carlyle once claimed.[8] However, such a designation is in itself confusing, for the reader is then trapped in elusive
definitions of what is metaphor, or what is metaphorical. Designations like essay or tract are just as meaningless as calling it, as often
is done, non-dramatic philosophical prose. For one thing it is deftly
dramatic, and for another it is repeatedly poetic, if not mythic.[9] *Sartor*

[7] The extent of Carlyle's reading through the composition of *Sartor Resartus*
has been treated by Hill Shine, *Carlyle's Early Reading to 1834*; Rodger L.
Tarr, "Thomas Carlyle's Libraries at Chelsea and Ecclefechan"; and in the
notes and indexes to *The Collected Letters of Thomas and Jane Welsh Carlyle*,
vols. 1-7.

[8] *Two Note Books*, 142.

[9] *Sartor Resartus*, especially the opening chapters of Book II, is more autobiographical than even Carlyle was prepared to admit. His biographer, James
A. Froude, *Thomas Carlyle: A History of the First Forty Years of His Life*,
through misquotation left the impression, too often accepted, that the biographical portions of *Sartor Resartus* were, in Carlyle's words, "symbolical
myth all," a statement which in fact applies to only a certain moment in the
work. Froude's misstatement was discovered and corrected by John Clubbe,
ed., *Two Reminiscen*ces, 49. Yet Tennyson, *"Sartor" Called "Resartus,"*
cautions against reading too much of Carlyle's life into *Sartor Resartus*. He
seems certain that it is not a "literal autobiography," although he concedes
that "Teufelsdröckh's biography can be broadly denominated a
Bildungsroman [life novel] or *Entwicklungsroman* [developmental novel],
or . . . even a *Künstlerroman* [art novel]." These designations are suggestive, and to a large extent true, but they do not adequately address the fact
that a number of incidents in *Sartor Resartus* are directly traceable to Carlyle's
life. The issue is not whether *Sartor Resartus* is autobiographical; rather the
issue is just how much of it actually is. The notes to this edition, aided
considerably by the *Collected Letters* which were not available to Tennyson,

Resartus defies confining designations, and perhaps, at least from its Romantic context, that *is* its point. Carlyle drew deeply from the "epics of nonsense," where reality is often indistinguishable from fantasy, created by Rabelais' *Gargantua and Pantagruel*, Cervantes' *Don Quixote*, Swift's *Gulliver's Travels*, Voltaire's *Candide*, and, most dramatically, Sterne's *Tristram Shandy*. Yet his sources extend beyond these proto-texts to the more remote and arcane. He anticipated early in composition the necessarily sophisticated nature of his audience, and quickly turned *Sartor Resartus* into an intellectual chess match in which the author's expressions anticipate the readers' impressions. Carlyle, in effect, demands reader response by having the fictive editor manipulate both text and context.[10] The final irony is that, in spite of its apparent dogmatism, *Sartor Resartus* does not pretend to contain any ultimate truth, evidenced formally by the question mark that ends the text. Carlyle is a Romantic addressing theory, not a Victorian promulgating fact. *Sartor Resartus* may very well be a prophecy, but it is a prophecy firmly situated in Romantic discourse.

---

suggest that significant parts of the opening chapters of Book II are autobiographical. Thus to Tennyson's desigxnations might be added *Selbstbiographie* [autobiography]. *Wotton Reinfred* and "Illudo Chartis" represent Carlyle's earlier attempts at fictive autobiography.

[10] The relationship of the reader to the text is especially crucial in dealing with the ambiguities raised by the style. The possibilities of ironic interplay between writer and reader are myriad. The reader must not only sort through Carlyle's style, but also that of his imaginary editor, who edits a selection of imaginary manuscripts communicated to him by an imaginary intermediary, who claims to have secured them from an imaginary writer. The narrative intrigues of *Don Quixote* and *Tristram Shandy* no doubt served as the immediate sources for Carlyle's narrative deceptions. See Lee C. R. Baker, "The Open Secret of *Sartor Resartus*," who provides an overview of the issue and concludes that Carlyle's intent was to recreate a "romantically ironic vision" for his reader (235). See also J. Douglas Rabb, "The Silence of Thomas Carlyle," who argues that Carlyle uses reader participation as a narrative device, and Steven Helmling, *The Esoteric Comedies of Carlyle, Newman, and Yeats*, who argues that Carlyle subverts reader assumptions through "ironic, parodic, and self-consciously difficult esoteric comedy" (37). M. H. Abrams, *Natural Supernaturalism*, feels that the circuitous narrative style leads to a "classic description of social and cosmic alienation" (310), and Chris R. Vanden Bossche, *Carlyle and the Search for Authority*, argues it is formed upon a "crisis of authority" (40). G. B. Tennyson, "The Editor Editing, The Reviewer Reviewing," views Carlyle's style as more deliberately mapped: the "mature Carlyle . . . is virtually always Carlyle the Reviewer, Carlyle the Translator, Carlyle the Editor, and not infrequently all in one" (44).

The method used to advance discourse in *Sartor Resartus* is allusion. Indeed, it might be called "The Book of Allusions." The reader must look at the text as if it were a tapestry in the making. Cords must be connected to cords; knots must be tied, only to be retied. The text challenges the reader to string together discordant allusions (sartor) and thereby to (re)weave transcendent harmony (resartus). Its beauty, if not truth, is curiously dependent upon the reader's own cultural heritage. Repeatedly, games are played with perception(s). The reader is constantly maneuvered: miss an allusion and miss the immediate point; pretend to grasp the allusion and miss the final point. *Sartor Resartus* is not meant to be understood; it is, rather, a fragment to be experienced, much like Coleridge's "Kubla Khan." It is a complex of meaning(s) skillfully condensed to tease the reader, to paraphrase Keats, beyond thought. Within this framework it questions the very nature of epistemology by creating a mythic cosmology bounded only by the reader's ability to recognize the boundless immensity of language. Language is its cornerstone, metaphor its prop, and myth its universe. Each and all, however, are (inter)dependent upon the tapestry of allusion.

Why, then, did Carlyle declare it "Nonsense"? Even though this declaration, elusive in itself, was made in the privacy of Carlyle's Journal, it holds the key to approaching the text. *Sartor Resartus* is an epistemological experiment, where phenomenon blends into noumenon, fact becomes fiction, and life fades into dream. Time and Place attenuate in the face of miracle. Despair becomes dependent upon Hope. In this dialectical world, buttressed by allusion, writer and reader are separate, yet never separated. *Sartor Resartus* anticipates by fifty years the Symbolist Movement, and by 150 years the cult of the absurd prominent in post-modern fiction and drama. Its inviting ironies are most dramatically broadcast in the name of its hero: Diogenes Teufelsdröckh, often translated God-Born Devil's-Dung. It is a work of its time and before its time. Composed at a remote farm named Craigenputtoch, near Dunscore, in Dumfriesshire, Scotland, *Sartor Resartus* rekindled the dying flame of Romanticism by keeping transcendental hope alive in a world rushing toward existential despair. Part-mystical and part-evangelical, and never wholly fathomable, it was to have a profound impact upon the shaping of socio-moral philosophy, not only in Great Britain and America, but throughout the English-speaking world.

THE LEGACY

The influence of *Sartor Resartus* in Great Britain was immediate, although not immediately evident. Defenders of the great tradition, befuddled by its linguistic antics and philosophic discordances, offered disapprobation. However, the young intellectuals, most notable among them Charles Dickens, were drawn by its magnetism. Dickens quickly became Carlyle's champion. Carlyle's influence upon Dickens is difficult to overstate. His devotion to *Sartor Resartus* is apparent throughout his works. The idiom of *Pickwick Papers*, the clothes philosophy of "Meditations in Monmouth Street" and *Oliver Twist*, the satire on education in *Dombey and Son* and *Hard Times*, the conversion pattern in "A Christmas Carol" and *David Copperfield*, the ridicule of dandyism in *Bleak House* and *Hard Times*, and the vocabulary of contempt in *Our Mutual Friend* are but examples of its pervasive influence. In *The Uncommercial Traveller*, Dickens refers directly to the language of Teufelsdröckh. In like manner, other novelists of the period turned to *Sartor Resartus* for guidance and insight. Charles Kingsley was so impressed that he created a Carlylean philosopher-hero for both *Yeast* and *Alton Locke*. Mrs. Gaskell depends upon Carlylean moral injunctions in *Mary Barton* and *North and South*, as does Benjamin Disraeli in *Sybil*. As David Masson observes, by the 1840s Carlyle's "name was running like wildfire through the British Islands and through English-speaking America, . . . specially among the young men." Kathleen Tillotson concurs, pointing out that the social novel would not be the same if it were not for Carlyle. Harriet Martineau, herself an advocate of *Sartor Resartus*, said it is Carlyle who "most essentially modified the mind of his time." The indelible influence continued unabated after mid-century. Anthony Trollope toyed with *Sartor Resartus* in *The Warden*, and George Meredith turned to the emblem of the tailor in *Evan Harrington*. George Eliot relied heavily on *Sartor Resartus*, especially in *Adam Bede, The Mill on the Floss*, and *Middlemarch*. Eliot's own testimony to Carlyle's enduring impact is evidence enough. In 1855, she likened Carlyle to an oak sowing acorns: "The character of his influence is best seen in the fact that many of the men who have the least agreement with his opinions are those to whom the reading of *Sartor Resartus* was an epoch in the history of their minds."[11]

[11] Articles on the influence of *Sartor Resartus* upon Dickens are too numerous to mention. For two representative, but not exhaustive book-length studies, see Michael Goldberg, *Carlyle and Dickens*, and William Oddie,

The poets of the period were no less immune to the spirit of *Sartor Resartus*. Its "New Mythus" is found in Alfred Tennyson's *In Memoriam*, its prophecy in "Locksley Hall," and its metaphor in "Maud." Robert Browning employed its theory of symbol in *Sordello*, its ironic humor in *The Ring and the Book*; its transcendental vision in "Fra Lippo Lippi," its philosophy of Wonder in "Transcendentalism," its defiance in "Childe Roland," its retailoring theme in *Bishop Blougram's Apology*, its clothes and martial metaphors in "How It Strikes a Contemporary," and its narrative strategies in *Red Cotton Night-Cap Country*. Matthew Arnold adopted its conversion pattern in *Empedocles on Etna*, and debated its aesthetic in "The Scholar-Gypsy." Arthur Hugh Clough's *The Bothie* has been described as *Sartor Resartus* in rhyme. The influence of *Sartor Resartus* on the prose writers was equally dramatic. Carlyle's "Philistine" enjoys a prominent role in Arnold's "The Function of Criticism" and *Culture and Anarchy*. Ruskin's hauntingly beautiful *Praeterita* speaks silently of *Sartor Resartus*. In his *Autobiography*, John Stuart Mill remembers reading *Sartor Resartus* with "enthusiastic admiration" and "keen delight." T. H. Huxley, who, like Mill, was startled by Carlyle's metaphysics, confesses that *Sartor Resartus* brought him "redemption." The list of testimonials is endless. In a review of Browning's poetry in 1868, J. H. Stirling stops in mid-thought to say of Carlyle: "[He] has swept through the souls of a generation, with a power possessed in an equal degree by no other Englishman that ever lived."[12]

Dickens and Carlyle: The Question of Influence. For Kingsley, Gaskell, and Disraeli, see Maria Meyer, *Carlyles Einfluss auf Kingsley*, and Louis Cazamian, *Le Roman social en Angleterre*. For Eliot, see Alicia Carroll, "'The Same Sort of Pleasure': Re-envisioning the Carlylean in *The Mill on the Floss*," and Rodger L. Tarr, "Dorothea's 'Resartus' and the Palingenetic Impulse of *Middlemarch*." For overviews, see David Masson, *Carlyle Personally and in His Writings*, Harriet Martineau, *History of England*, and Kathleen Tillotson, *Novels of the Eighteen-Forties*. See also George Eliot, 1035.

[12] For Tennyson, see De Witt T. Starnes, "The Influence of Carlyle upon Tennyson"; William D. Templeman, "Tennyson's 'Locksley Hall' and Thomas Carlyle"; Robert A. Greenberg, "A Possible Source of Tennyson's 'Tooth and Claw'"; George O. Marshall, "An Incident from Carlyle in Tennyson's 'Maud'"; Charles R. Sanders, "Carlyle and Tennyson"; Clyde de L. Ryals, "The 'Heavenly Friend': The 'New Mythus' of *In Memoriam*"; and Michael Timko, *Carlyle and Tennyson*. For Browning, see Richard D. Altick, "Browning's 'Transcendentalism'"; Charlotte C. Watkins, "Browning's 'Red Cotton Night-Cap Country' and Carlyle"; Glen Omans, "Browning's 'Fra Lippo Lippi'"; Frederic E. Faverty, "The Brownings and Their Contemporaries"; Susan H. Aiken, "On Clothes and Heroes: Carlyle

The power of *Sartor Resartus* continued as the century came to a close. Thomas Hardy recast its "Wandering Jew" metaphor in *Jude the Obscure* and its dialectic in *Tess of the D'Urbervilles*. Joseph Conrad used its transcendental argument in *Lord Jim* and its fire metaphor in "Youth." D. H. Lawrence turned to its phoenix metaphor in his call for social regeneration, James Joyce, who once described Carlyle as one of those "giants" who held "empire over the thinking world in modern times," employed its cryptic language in *Ulysses* and responded to its theory of art in *Finnegans Wake*. Virginia Woolf adapted its concept of perpetual metamorphoses in *To the Lighthouse* and *Orlando*. These are but examples and do not consider the influence of *Sartor Resartus* upon non-English writers as diverse as Charles Baudelaire and Miguel de Unamuno, or Jorge Luis Borges and Yukio Mishima. Baudelaire was intrigued by its "Philosophie du costume." Unamuno boldly used its ideas and adopted its style in *Amor y pedagogía*. Borges barely disguised his use of its narrative intrusions in "Pierre Menard, Author of the *Quixote*." Mishima adapted its transcendence. That a copy of *Sartor Resartus* sits atop one of *Paradise Lost* in Paul Gauguin's 1889 portrait of Meyer de Hann is ample acknowledgment of its importance.[13]

However, the most immediate and most pronounced impact of *Sartor Resartus* began in Boston in the 1830s. The young intellectuals of New England had already been reading Carlyle's reviews and essays with the hope of finding a new light, what they called the "new way." When *Sartor Resartus* reached New England, Ralph Waldo Emerson claimed that a "new thinker had been let loose upon the

---

and 'How It Strikes a Contemporary'" and "Bishop Blougram and Carlyle." For Arnold, see Kathleen Tillotson, "Matthew Arnold and Carlyle"; and David J. DeLaura, "Arnold and Carlyle." For Ruskin, see Charles H. Kegel, "Carlyle and Ruskin: An Influential Friendship"; Donald R. Swanson, "Ruskin and His 'Master'"; and George A. Cate, intro., *The Correspondence of Thomas Carlyle and John Ruskin*. For Mill, see Murray Baumgarten, "Mill, Carlyle, and the Question of Influence."

[13] For Conrad, see Stanley Renner, "*Sartor Resartus* Retailored? Conrad's *Lord Jim* and the Perils of Idealism." For Lawrence, see Edward Alexander, "Thomas Carlyle and D. H. Lawrence." For Woolf, see D. G. Mason, "Woolf, Carlyle, and the Writing of *Orlando*"; and C. Anita Tarr, "Getting to the Lighthouse: Thomas Carlyle and Virginia Woolf." For Unamuno, see Peter G. Earle. "Unamuno and the Theme of History"; and James D. Earnest, "The Influence of Thomas Carlyle upon the Early Novels of Miguel de Unamuno." For Baudelaire, see Bernard Howells, "Heroïsme, Dandysme et la 'Philosophie du Costume': Note sur Baudelaire et Carlyle."

planet."[14] Carlyle was, to a large extent, the entranceway to German idealistic philosophy. And, what the New Englanders soon learned was that Carlyle did not mirror German thinking; he expanded it. His work was not a reflection, but instead a refraction. *Sartor Resartus* was its own prism.

1836 was a pivotal year for *Sartor Resartus* in America. Nathaniel L. Frothingham wrote a lengthy article for the *Christian Examiner* which captures the essence of the enthusiasm in Boston. Frothingham asserts that *Sartor Resartus* is a "singular production," although "very odd" in its message and style. This review of the 1836 Boston edition, the first trade printing, makes little mention of Emerson's famous "Preface," which is extravagant in its caution, warning readers not to be offended by the "masquerade" and the "occasional eccentricity," but to enjoy the "frequent bursts of pure splendor" and "purity of moral sentiment." The Boston *Sartor Resartus* was an immediate success, selling out 500 copies, which resulted in a second edition in 1837, and a third edition in 1840. As Frothingham before him, William Gilmore Simms in the lead article for the *Southern Literary Journal* in March of 1837 issues a note of caution about its "extremely odd tissue of fiction," but in the end declares it a "singular book" with a "rich vein of humour." The specific impact of such declarations from leading journals in both the North and the South is in the end difficult to measure. However, there is no doubt whatsover that *Sartor Resartus* became the foundational text of the American Transcendental Movement.[15]

Sartor Resartus also led to one of the most important literary friendships in the nineteenth century. Emerson, already an accomplished critic, came immediately under Carlyle's sway, not always in agreement, but always in sympathy. As Kenneth M. Harris notes, it was through Carlyle's lens that Emerson came to Coleridge and Kant and finally to the nebulous philosophy called Transcendentalism. It would be wrong, of course, to attribute everything transcendental to Carlyle, especially since Carlyle himself was uneasy with the term and often wondered why it was so lavishly ascribed to him. In *American Notes*, Dickens observes, somewhat in amazement and somewhat in jest, that Carlyle is considered the "Father *in absentia*" of the Transcendental Movement. In any event, the early work of Emerson cannot be properly read

[14] Quoted in Froude, *Life in London* 1: 289.
[15] See William S. Vance, "Carlyle in America before *Sartor Resartus*"; Ralph W. Emerson, "Preface" to *Sartor Resartus*, iii-v; and [William G. Simms], "Carlyle's *Sartor Resartus*."

without the knowledge that *Sartor Resartus* was its spiritual and linguistic foundation. *Divinity School Address* would be different if not for
Carlyle's call for the new mythus, *Nature* if not for Carlyle's appeal for
a new social fabric, and "The Over-Soul" if not for Carlyle's clothes
philosophy. Emerson was Carlyle's most prominent translator, a gift of
considerable circumstance in the light of the dancing iridescence of
Sartor Resartus. What is more important, however, is that through
Emerson's determination and loyalty Carlyle became a familiar presence to American readers.[16]

The American host that followed *Sartor Resartus* was diverse. Lydia
Maria Child and Margaret Fuller, leaders of the growing Feminist
Movement, were entranced by Carlyle. The former turned to *Sartor
Resartus* for "spiritual food"; the latter spoke of Carlyle as a "bene-
factor." Meanwhile, the youthful Louisa May Alcott, under the stern
tutelage of her father Bronson Alcott, was being exposed to Carlylean
tropes, which were later to make their way into *Little Women.* Similarly, the maturation of Emily Dickinson—a portrait of Carlyle hung
over her writing desk—owes a great deal to the truncated metaphor,
ironic wit, and linguistic oddity of *Sartor Resartus.* In 1847, Henry
David Thoreau refers to *Sartor Resartus* as the "sunniest and most
philosophical" of Carlyle's works. Not surprisingly, Thoreau's own
Walden pays tribute to Carlyle's theories of self-help and narrative
art. Herman Melville was not far behind. As he came increasingly to
distrust his language of romance represented by novels like *Typee* and
Omoo, Melville turned to Carlyle to re-energize his style. The result
was immediate and enduring: *Moby-Dick* became Melville's Carlylean
window to the future. Nathaniel Hawthorne, having little sympathy
for Transcendentalism, was less impressed, satirizing the heirs of *Sartor
Resartus* in the "The Celestial Railroad" and *The Blithedale Romance.*
Edgar Allan Poe was less oblique than Hawthorne. Employing his
pleasure principle, he dismissed *Sartor Resartus* as a "personal *reductio ad absurdum.*"[17]

---

[16] See Kenneth M. Harris, *Carlyle and Emerson: Their Long Debate*, 6. For an
excellent overview of Carlyle's influence upon the Transcendental Movement, see Joseph Slater, intro., *The Correspondence of Emerson and Carlyle*,
3-43. See also Leon Jackson, "The Social Construction of Carlyle's New
England Reputation, 1834-1836."

[17] See Margaret Fuller, "A Picture of Mr. Carlyle"; Henry D. Thoreau, "Thomas Carlyle and His Works"; and Edgar A. Poe, "Marginalia." For Child,
see Rodger L. Tarr, "Emerson's Transcendentalism in L. M. Child's Letter
to Carlyle." For Thoreau, see Sharon L. Gravett, "Carlyle's Demanding

Hawthorne and Poe were not representative of nineteenth-century opinion, however. For the most part, Carlyle was lionized, made larger than life by what he called his "little Book." The influence of *Sartor Resartus* upon American literature is so vast, so pervasive, that it is difficult to overstate. In 1838, from the then frontier of Columbus, Ohio, J. J. J. [Isaac Jewett] writes in the *Hesperian* that the purpose of *Sartor Resartus* is "to teach . . . to awaken . . . to inspire." The diversity of its impact upon nineteenth-century American intellectuals is reflected in the empathic language of Walt Whitman who appropriated its noumenal perspective in *Leaves of Grass*, and who wrote upon learning of Carlyle's death in 1881: "The way to test how much he has left us all were to consider, or try to consider, for the moment the array of British thought, the resultant and *ensemble* of the last fifty years, as existing to-day, *but with Carlyle left out*. It would be like an army with no artillery." Mark Twain's use of Carlyle's clothes metaphor in *Pudd'nhead Wilson* and *Huckleberry Finn* stands as later proof of Whitman's assertion. Sarah Orne Jewett was so impressed with Carlyle's presence that she penned a fictive visit of Carlyle to America, where he lectured to his disciples in Boston. In 1891, Willa Cather, who used the narrative structures of *Sartor Resartus* in *The Professor's House*, pronounced Carlyle a "Giant among Lilliputians."[18]

By the turn of the century, *Sartor Resartus* was a required text in many American schools. T. S. Eliot, notoriously anti-Romantic, read it while a student at Harvard University. Eliot's first London lecture, now lost, was on *Sartor Resartus*. "The Love Song of J. Alfred Prufrock" is in both language and statement a response. And, if its influence can be found in Eliot, then surely Ezra Pound is not far distant. To what extent Carlyle's transcendental manifesto has weaved its way into twentieth-century American literature has yet to be fully considered. More recently, its philosophy has been traced in Ernest Hemingway's fiction, and there seems little doubt that Isaac Bashevis Singer was intimately acquainted with Carlyle's midrashic Teufelsdröckh. Nevertheless, there has yet to be a thorough study on the relationship of *Sartor Resartus*

Companion: Henry David Thoreau." For Melville, see James Barbour and Leon Howard, "Carlyle and the Conclusion of *Moby-Dick*."
[18] See J. J. J. [Isaac Jewett], "Thomas Carlyle"; Walt Whitman, "The Dead Carlyle"; and Willa Cather, "Concerning Thomas Carlyle." For Jewett, see Rodger L. Tarr and C. Anita Tarr, ed., "'Carlyle in America': An Unpublished Short Story of Sarah Orne Jewett." For Cather, see Meredith R. Machen, "Carlyle's Presence in *The Professor's House*."

to literary movements and theoretical constructions. Thus, just where the intertextual threads will manifest themselves next cannot be easily predicted, although it is certain that continuing acknowledgment of its ever-expanding fabric is inevitable.[19]

THE VOICES

This legacy, which extends beyond individual influence to the very theory of literature, is only suggestive, but does raise the question of why *Sartor Resartus* was so appealing. What was the "New Mythus" it created? What was the force that made it so popular that 69,000 copies had been sold by 1881?[20] A substantial body of scholarship argues that Carlyle's instincts were German, and that the young minds of the Victorian reformation were eager to hear its new message. The argument is simply put: understand *Sartor Resartus* and you will understand the resulting strain of idealism in Victorian letters. Such claims are compelling, but in the end not fully accurate. The drawing of direct comparisons to Goethe, to Schiller, to Kant, to Schlegel, to Novalis, to Herder, to Jacobi, among others, too often suggests a shared cultural homogeneity. It is true, of course, that in *Sartor Resartus* Carlyle repeatedly quotes directly, echoes openly, and paraphrases freely the German idealists. He luxuriates in the paradoxes of Richter;

---

[19] For Hemingway, see Roger Asselineau, "Hemingway, or 'Sartor Resartus' Once More." For the importance of *Sartor Resartus* in the late nineteenth-century Aesthetic Movement, see Ruth apRoberts, "Carlyle and the Aesthetic Movement." For suggestive studies on the intersections of *Sartor Resartus* and post-modern theory, see Geoffrey H. Hartman, "Carlyle, Eliot, and Bloom"; L. M. Findlay, "Paul de Man, Thomas Carlyle, and 'The Rhetoric of Temporality'"; J. Hillis Miller, "'Hieroglyphical Truth' in *Sartor Resartus*: Carlyle and the Language of Parable"; and Wolfgang Iser, "The Emergence of a Cross-Cultural Discourse: Thomas Carlyle's *Sartor Resartus*."

[20] This claim is made on the front cover of the large-wrapper edition published by Chapman and Hall in 1881. Previously the publisher claimed 35,000 sold by 1872. These figures are cumulative, and do not represent the earlier sales by James Fraser of London and James Munroe of Boston, nor the many editions subsequently published by other firms. Regrettably, the actual publishing records have been destroyed. Yet it would be safe to estimate that by Carlyle's death in 1881, some 80 to 90,000 had been sold, and this does not include the German and Dutch lifetime printings. *Sartor Resartus* was also the featured first volume in the Library Edition and the People's Edition, in 1869 and 1871, which gives some idea of the value and the importance Carlyle gave to it. See Rodger L. Tarr, *A Descriptive Bibliography*, 35–48, 451.

he bows to the seedfield of Goethe; and he revels in the tropes of Fichte. Without doubt, German philosophy and letters exercised a powerful influence upon the aesthetic and the locution of *Sartor Resartus*, but it is misleading to assert that Carlyle was the "Voice of Germany in Britain."[21] Writing about German literature and espousing German dogma are quite different. Indeed, to a large extent, Carlyle did not understand the Germans, even though he was among the most learned German scholars of his time. He freely admitted his sometime bewilderment, sometime wonder, at the confusing turns in German philosophy. Coleridge's misunderstandings, which shaped in part Carlyle's readings, confused the issues even more. The point to be made here is that there is a vital difference between cultural understanding and professed discipleship. The grand ideas that Carlyle gathered directly from Germany, particularly from Goethe, and indirectly through the Romantics, especially Coleridge, represent more general professions of faith than specific articles of confederation. What he found in Germany was a spirit of idealism that enabled him to recast, if not cast away, the harsher realities of his Calvinist heritage.

On the other hand, the role that Calvinism plays in *Sartor Resartus* is difficult to overstate. Carlyle's Burgher upbringing and his attempts to reconcile himself to it comprise the foundations of his work. The daunting presence of God and Kirk was an everyday reality to Carlyle's mother and father, sisters and brothers; and, like Burns before him, Carlyle revered the belief while holding the institution suspect. *Sartor Resartus* is a classic expression of crisis in faith. Carlyle was torn between acceptance and rejection. To accept the tenets of Calvinism was impossible, yet to reject them was equally impossible. Just before the composition of *Sartor Resartus*, he considered testing his notions of theology by writing a biography of Luther. Indeed, as his Journal indicates, it was the thoughts on Luther that led to the "Thoughts on Clothes." Although the Luther project was finally abandoned, its consideration is symptomatic of Carlyle's reforming spirit. Calvinism

[21] See G. B. Tennyson, "Carlyle as Mediator of German Language and Thought," 266. See also Charles F. Harrold, *Carlyle and German Thought*; and Hill Shine, intro., *Carlyle's Unfinished History of German Literature*. On the other hand, Tennyson's general point that throughout his life Carlyle kept his pen in the well of German literature is beyond dispute. In no manner, however, does such devotion lead to the misguided assertion that Carlyle was the 'Spiritual Father' of fascism as argued by Philip Rosenberg, *The Seventh Hero*. For a retrospective on the notion that Carlyle was a proto-fascist, see Murray Baumgarten, *Carlyle and His Era*.

need not be rejected, but instead should be reformed. The "Old" should be assimilated by the "New." *Sartor Resartus* documents this passage from the "Old Faith" to the "New Mythus," and interestingly enough Carlyle accomplishes this passage by relying on the central source of his frustration, the Bible. He quotes the Bible more than any other single work. His interest in the Bible is, however, less historical than prophetic. As a composer of metaphors, he is suspicious of the literal. The historical traditions surrounding Christ he found enigmatic and finally destructive.[22] Carlyle's vision of Christ is much closer to the tormented persona found in Richter's existential *todten Christus* than to the resurrected persona advanced by Kirk orthodoxy.[23] Tradition, what Blake termed Ratio, represented by Calvinism contradicted *Entsagung*, a viewpoint Emerson was to re-

---

[22] The subject of Carlyle's religion has produced and will continue to produce endless diversity of opinion. Charles F. Harrold, "The Nature of Carlyle's Calvinism," thinks Carlyle is a Transcendentalist; Basil Willey, *Nineteenth-Century Studies*, sees him as an "escaped" (106) Puritan; G. B. Tennyson, *Carlyle and the Modern World*, 25, opts for Theist; Philip Rosenberg, *The Seventh Hero*, 49, settles on Pantheist; and Chris R. Vanden Bossche, *Carlyle and the Search for Authority*, 30, echoing F. D. Maurice, argues for Theocratist. For a more radical view of Carlyle's relationship to Calvinism, see Morse Peckham, *Victorian Revolutionaries*, 83-84, who sees Carlyle's battles with his religion as a deep-seated psychological trauma, an apocalypse in faith, what he calls the "Carlylean terror." Earlier, in *Beyond the Tragic Vision*, 185-86, Peckham argues that Carlyle departed from his Calvinist heritage because he came to believe that "all men are divine" through the "power of self." Such a position, Peckham concludes, left Carlyle outside the Kirk hunting for meaning in an increasingly "insane" universe. For a more centralist view, see Ian Campbell, "Carlyle's Religion: The Scottish Background," who concludes that Carlyle's belief is formed on "rational inquiry" (5). For a more progressive view, see Eloise M. Behnken, *Thomas Carlyle: "Calvinist Without the Theology,"* who argues that Carlyle charts the increasing trend in the nineteenth century away from orthodoxy toward "humanism and secularism" (132). David J. DeLaura astutely frames Carlyle's more aesthetic attitudes in the period after *Sartor Resartus* in "Carlyle and Arnold: The Religious Issue."

[23] J. P. Vijn, *Carlyle and Jean Paul: Their Spiritual Optics*, provides a thorough commentary on the influence of Richter on Carlyle's religious/theological sensibilities. Vijn also sees connections forward to Jungian psychology, particularly to Jung's position that "Life, so called, is a short episode between two great mysteries, which are one" (118). It needs to be said, however, that as much as Jung echoes Carlyle, Carlyle echoes Blake through Johann Lavater that life is a grain of sand in the ether of eternity, much of which resonates in Emanuel Swedenborg's mystic reflection that God is at once nothing and all. The intertextual connections finally overwhelm.

state a short time later in the *Divinity School Address*. Carlyle saw the
Bible as a seedbed of inspiration, but always as a book of theology in
need of perpetual revision.

Carlyle's view of other literatures was equally reverential. Homer
and Virgil were at his fingertips, and his general knowledge of classical literature and philosophy is remarkable for someone not formally
trained in the discipline. The works of Shakespeare and Milton were
constant inspirations, and he was able to quote them verbatim. His
allusions to other writers from the Renaissance, especially Spenser and
Bunyan, display a similar mastery of text. *Sartor Resartus* is a com-
pendium of divers literatures. The English Neo-Classicists are especially influential. The style and the language of *Sartor Resartus* owe
an immense debt to Swift, particularly to *A Tale of a Tub*. The sarcastic wit of Pope and Johnson is everywhere, as are allusions to the
novels of the time, but especially to Goethe's *Sorrows of Young Werther*
and to Sterne's *Tristram Shandy* which served, in many respects, as
prototypes. The allusions to Romantic literature are equally numerous and varied. Carlyle is comfortable with such divergent talents as
Coleridge and Burns, Wordsworth and Shelley, Byron and Southey. A
vital complement to his keen sense of literature is his keen sense of
historical periodicity within the larger framework of historical movements.[24] Allusions to contemporary as well as to past events abound.
And, of course, the richness of Carlyle's heritage can be found in
what he wrote or translated prior to and during the composition of
Sartor Resartus. He alludes to his own work regularly, including his
translations of Goethe's *Wilhelm Meisters Lehrjahre* and the short
fiction under the title *German Romance*. He also quotes from his
biography *The Life of Schiller* and from his unfinished novel *Wotten
Reinfred*. Likewise, his numerous essays and reviews serve as invaluable commentaries for his "Book of Allusions."

[24] *Sartor Resartus* represents, in part, that crucial tension in Carlyle between
immediate historical event and remote historical tradition. *Sartor Resartus*
is a document of its time as much as it is a reflection on its time.
Teufelsdröckh is a social radical as well as a philosophical radical, as is
evident, for example, in his sympathies for the social idealism of Saint-
Simon. See Hill Shine, *Carlyle and the Saint-Simonians*; and K. J. Fielding,
"Carlyle and the Saint-Simonians (1830–1832): New Considerations." Ralph
Jessop, *Carlyle and Scottish Thought*, sees *Sartor Resartus* standing in "radical opposition" (195) to the materialism and skepticism advanced by Scot-
tish Enlightenment philosophy.

THE FRAME

Any attempt to discuss the subject(s) of *Sartor Resartus* invites controversy. It is not a book easily defined, and as suggested above,
definition depends on the readers' confidences. To pretend full understanding and to presume final exegesis are tantamount to an intellectual confidence game. It is impossible to provide the "Key to All
Mythologies" for *Sartor Resartus*. Those most intimate with it admit
its frustrations; those least intimate with it hold on to its memorable
clichés. It is often claimed, for example, that the answer to the work
lies in the dogmatic declarations from the chapter in Book II "The
Everlasting Yea," which include: "Close thy *Byron*; open thy *Goethe*";
"Love not Pleasure; love God"; "*Do the Duty which lies nearest thee*";
and "Work while it is called Today; for the Night cometh, wherein no
man can work." The acceptance (or rejection) of such aphorisms
makes the readers' tasks easier, until one asks, "Does Carlyle mean to
abandon Byron for Goethe?"; or "Is there finally a qualitative difference between the love of pleasure and the love of God?" To the Old
Testament mind (Sartor), the answer is "Yes" to these and other
questions of faith. However, to the New Testament mind (Resartus),
the answers are not so clear. Skeptics inevitably turn away from the
implied privilege of the "Yea" and toward the ethereal chapter in
Book III, "Natural Supernaturalism," where life becomes a dream,
and the miracle of transcendence is manifest. *Sartor Resartus* is like
that; it confronts the readers' sensibilities. The Classical mind demands closure and finds it in the central chapters of Book II, the now
famous trilogy "The Everlasting No," "Centre of Indifference," and
"The Everlasting Yea." Here the Kantians see Kant, the Goetheans
Goethe, the Newtonians Newton. On the other hand, the Romantic
mind rejects such security of understanding and jumps forward to the
palingenetic Book III, where the emphasis is not upon sensual closure
but upon spiritual awakening. Here the "New Mythus" lies; here
Transcendentalism properly begins.[25]

---

[25] Richard E. Brantley, *Coordinates of Anglo-American Romanticism*, sees a
"creative tension" between "empiricism and evangelicalism" (1) and traces
such tension to John Wesley and Jonathan Edwards. Similarly, Michael
Timko, *Carlyle and Tennyson*, argues that Newton's empirical *Principia*
gave Carlyle "firm support for believing in God's handiwork" until the
reading of Kant's transcendental *Kritik der reinen Vernunft* [*Critique of
Pure Reason*] introduced him to "natural supernaturalism" (24-30). The
threads that separate empiricism and evangelicalism and transcendentalism
comprise the aesthetic of *Sartor Resartus*.

Further, critical perspective is inextricably linked to the structures inferred. Any framework of explanation that suggests that *Sartor Resartus* is dualistic in structure misses the (inter)dependence of the "Old" and the "New." Important as binary structures are to the presentation, each cannot, in Carlyle's mythus, survive without the other. "Old" and "New" are not separate, but instead intersect like circles forever superimposed upon each other. *Sartor Resartus* is, in philosophic structure at least, Neo-Platonic; it survives on the belief that thought and action are expressions of cyclical continua. Narrative is linear; action is solid. The very structure involves the superimposing of Book upon Book, Chapter upon Chapter, Sentence upon Sentence, Word upon Word. Carlyle writes and devises in triads: Book I (The Nature of Clothes) interlocks with Book II (The Life of Teufelsdröckh), and Book II with Book III (The Clothes Philosophy); or Book I (Vesture) interlocks with Book II (Body), and Book II with Book III (Spirit); or Book I (Editor Presents) interlocks with Book II (Editor Edits), and Book II with Book III (Editor Interprets).[26] The implication of this schema is that the center, through implied tension, holds the essence of what came before and what comes after, while at the same time it is the bridge that connects both. Thus, unity is accomplished, a unity suggested in the Coleridgean triad/pentad:

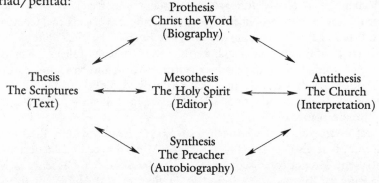

Prothesis
Christ the Word
(Biography)

Thesis   Mesothesis   Antithesis
The Scriptures   The Holy Spirit   The Church
(Text)   (Editor)   (Interpretation)

Synthesis
The Preacher
(Autobiography)

[26] See Tennyson, *"Sartor" Called "Resartus,"* 155–93, who works out in detail this interlocking structure, and then relates it to the style and the substance of the book. See also Gerry Brookes, *The Rhetorical Form of Carlyle's "Sartor Resartus,"* who challenges Tennyson's fictive models and holds that the book is structured as a persuasive essay. Brookes's opening chapter contains a very useful commentary on a number of short studies on the structure of *Sartor Resartus.* See also Rodger L. Tarr, "The Manuscript Chronology of *Sartor Resartus.*"

This triadic/pentadic structure is also similar to that of Hegel where Thesis and Antithesis result in Synthesis, only to reform and to begin again.

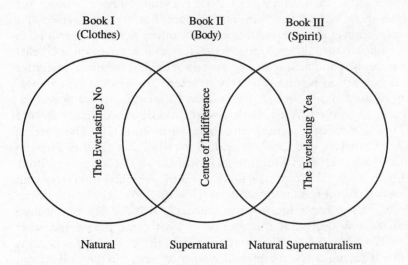

The chapters in *Sartor Resartus* are often set in triads as well, the most notable example being: "The Everlasting No" leads to "Centre of Indifference" which culminates in "The Everlasting Yea." The same holds true within chapters, such as "Natural Supernaturalism," which is its own conflation of the distinct Natural World and the Supernatural World. Triads within syntactical patterns also abound, as in the expression "high, silent, meditative Transcendentalism" in the chapter "Reminiscences."

Yet, as similar as the structure of *Sartor Resartus* is to Platonic dialogue, it is also remarkably similar to Midrash, located in hermeneutic and exegetical discourse. *Sartor Resartus* can be seen as a collapsing of the dialectics found in Hellenism and Hebraism from which emerges a universal Transcendental Christianity. Midrash is implied in the name Diogenes Teufelsdröckh: his given name identifies him with the Hellenistic tradition and his surname with his Hebraistic heritage. Carlyle's hero is a distillation of the intellectual traditions of the German professor and the rhetorical traditions of the rabbi. The academic title *D.u.J.*, *Doctor utriusque Juris*, is transposed to *J.U.D.*, suggesting the German *Jude*, or Jew, thus implying that Teufelsdröckh is not merely a Jew, but a learned Jew, or rabbi. Structurally, if not philosophically, Teufelsdröckh is linked to Moses: he is found as a baby in a basket (65) and later becomes a "wandering spirit" (216) who leads his reader through the modern wilderness of "Nescience" (169) into the "new Mythus" (144). Further, Teufelsdröckh's close association with rabbinical erudition is found in the quasi-cabalistic equations that appear throughout *Sartor Resartus*: the "Rule of Three" (97) and the "grand-climacteric" (104) are examples. But the clearest examples of Teufelsdröck's Hebraistic learning are found in the characterization of the "*Adam-Kadmon*" as "Primeval Element" (28) and the use of the phrase "'the true SHEKINAH is Man'" as "GOD'S-PRESENCE" (51). Finally, within the context of midrashic discourse, the reader becomes the third participant, the host in whom the discourse is integrated and developed. This tripartite structure of commentary, counter-commentary, and integration follows closely the intertextual pattern of scriptural commentary found in Midrash. Like Midrash, *Sartor Resartus* displays an obsession with the connections within and among texts: Teufelsdröckh often quotes from or alludes to ten or more sources in a single paragraph; the Editor then struggles with the disordered scraps of Teufelsdröckh's papers; and the Reader is left to negotiate the meaning, in effect adding quotations and allusions to the tapestry of the discourse. Without the Reader, working in concert with Teufelsdröckh and the Editor, the thread snaps, and the discourse fails.[27]

On the other hand, as much as the foundation of *Sartor Resartus* is triadic, the imagery and metaphor used to express that structure is dualistic. God and creation are light, Satan and chaos dark. Fire is the destroyer and the preserver. Diogenes is surnamed Teufelsdröckh. Sartor is called Resartus. The examples are literally endless. That Carlyle consciously employed dualistic framing is beyond argument; that Carlyle should be called a dualist is yet another matter. He was, in fact, not a philosophic dualist. Indeed, his basic disagreement with Calvinism rests on his belief that Good and Evil, for example, are not easily defined, much less easily divided. Carlyle, like Coleridge before him and Hawthorne after him, was uneasy with definition and bifurcation. Like Blake's "Lamb" and "Tyger," Carlyle's opposites are extensions of one another. "Creation and destruction," as Carlyle says, "proceed together" (180). Light and dark are forever blending, not separating. Order and chaos are manifestations of the same uni-

---

[27] See John Hruschka, "Carlyle's Rabbinical Hero: Teufelsdröckh and the Midrashic Tradition."

verse. The result is an intriguing philosophy that articulates Classical dimension through the use of Romantic binary. The problem is that such conflation is difficult to understand, particularly for the reader whose perspective is outward-in rather than inward-out. It is easy enough to appreciate the surge and the wane of the Eolian Harp, but not so easy to understand its intermittent silence. Yet that is precisely what *Sartor Resartus* demands. It is a lute marked by its silence, that point where surge and wane are indistinguishable. Thus, when confronted with seemingly dualistic urgings, such as "Close thy *Byron*; open thy *Goethe*," the reader must understand that Carlyle does not mean that one should cease reading Byron and begin reading Goethe. Such simplifications confuse dualistic structure and triadic discourse, not to mention the philosophies of Byron and Goethe.[28] Life, to Carlyle, was a matter of emphases, not exclusions. Dual (linear) excludes; Triad (cycle) includes. Life is a "perpetual metamorphoses." 'Sartor' is extended by 'Resartus.'

II. WRITINGS AND REVISIONS

THE WRITING OF "THOUGHTS ON CLOTHES"

Carlyle's first acknowledgment that he was about to embark on the subject that eventually was to become *Sartor Resartus* is in a letter to his brother Dr. John Carlyle, September 18, 1830: "I am going to *write something of my own*; I have sworn it."[29] He had of course written 'things of his own' previously: the celebrated *Life of Schiller*, the unpublished autobiographical fiction *Wotten Reinfred*, the short story "Cruthers and Jonson," and a number of poetic experiments are but examples. Yet he was still known primarily as a translator and historian of German literature in particular, and a reviewer and critic of belles lettres in general. Late in 1829, while researching his projected life of Luther, Carlyle records in his journal that he is considering a more creative work, noting the "Prodigious influence of metaphors! Never saw into it till lately. A truly useful and philosophical work would be a good *Essay on Metaphors*. Some day I will write one!"[30] And, as the philosophic nature of the entries for the next year

---

[28] See Charles R. Sanders, "The Byron Closed in *Sartor Resartus*," who documents that no finality was intended in this expression: "Not all of Byron was shut out; not all of Goethe was invited in" (104).

[29] *Letters* 5:164.

[30] *Two Note Books*, 142.

in his Journal attests, Carlyle had begun the long process of creating
Sartor Resartus.

Carlyle was determined to establish himself as a creative artist. In
June of 1830, he urges himself on: ". . . *im Teufel's Namen*, get to
thy work then!"[31] In August he writes of man as "A pitiful hungry
biped that wears breeches," and on September 28 he declares: "I am
going to write—Nonsense. It is on 'Clothes.' Heaven be my com-
forter!"[32] He then enters a long passage on the virtue of Silence
("Speech is human, Silence is divine"), which was to become one of
the focal statements in the chapter "Symbols." The ambivalence of
Carlyle's position, as he worked himself from despair toward hope, is
reflected in a letter to his mother Margaret on October 10: "I study
not to get too *wae* [depressed]; but often I think of many solemn and
sad things, which indeed I do not wish to forget. . . . Why should we
fear? Let us *hope*; we are in 'the Place of Hope,' our Life is a Hope."[33]
Carlyle quotes here what he was later to attribute to Teufelsdröckh
who in "The Everlasting No" says, the world of man is "emphatically
the 'Place of Hope'" (121), clearly indicating that this chapter in
Book II was one of the first written. Caught up in this spirit of hope,
Carlyle adds regarding his manuscript: "For the last three weeks I
have been writing by taskwork again, and get along wonderfully well:
what it is to be I cannot yet tell, whether a Book or a string of
Magazine Articles; we hope, the former; but in either case, it may be
worth something."[34]

The work on the manuscript progressed so well that on October 19
Carlyle was able to report to John that he was "writing with impetuosity. . . . What I am writing at is the strangest of all things: begun as
an Article for *Fraser*; then found to be too long (except it were divided
into two); now sometimes looking almost, as if it would swell into a
Book. A very singular piece, I assure you! It glances from Heaven to
Earth & back again in a strange satirical frenzy whether *fine* or not
remains to be seen. Whether Fraser will get the offer of it or not I
know not. . . . *Teufelsdreck* (that is the title of my present *Schrift* [Work])
will be done (so far—50 pages) tomorrow."[35] Assuming the manuscript was written on foolscap, Carlyle would have written at this point
approximately 25,000 words, which is the approximate length of Book

[31] *Two Note Books,* 156.
[32] *Two Note Books,* 163, 176.
[33] *Letters* 5:171.
[34] *Letters* 5:171.
[35] *Letters* 5:175–76.

II, excluding the final chapter, "Pause," part of which was added later. Certainly, by this time in October, Carlyle was consumed with the completion of Book II, and no doubt had completed the pivotal chapters, "The Everlasting No," "Centre of Indifference," and "The Everlasting Yea." The intensity of the language in his Journal and in his letters points toward a personal catharsis. In a letter to Goethe, October 23, he discusses the "'high meaning of ENTSAGEN' [renunciation]," and concludes that "the blessedness of Life is not in Living, but in Working well."[36] Each of these concepts is a foundation of the epiphanic "The Everlasting Yea." Later in the same letter to Goethe, he reports that his partly written history of German literature has not been received favorably by prospective publishers, and that "Meanwhile I have been engaged a little in other more ambitious enterprizes: but whether the result may be a Book, or only a pair of Magazine Essays I cannot yet predict. . . ."[37] What these letters to John and Goethe indicate is that Carlyle, virtually from the outset, held hope that "Thoughts on Clothes" would be book-length rather than an article or articles. Whatever the case, he writes in his Journal October 28 that the manuscript is completed: "Written a strange piece 'On clothes': know not what will come of it."[38]

By early November, however, the idea that "Thoughts on Clothes" would make a book seems to have been abandoned. In a letter to John on November 12, Carlyle is firm in his plans to commit the manuscript to *Fraser's Magazine*: "I wrote to William Fraser about his Magazine, and that Teufelsdreck paper of mine, which I have now resolved not to make a Book of; but, if I have opportunity, two *Articles*, and the germ of more."[39] Near November 24 he records in his Journal that the decision to send the manuscript to *Fraser's Magazine* was, in part at least, financially motivated: "Sent away the *Clothes*; of which I could make a kind of Book; but cannot *afford* it. Have still *the* Book *in petto* but in the most chaotic shape."[40] The language of this passage is a bit cryptic, but what might be concluded here is that Carlyle sent "Thoughts on Clothes" (Book II), while at the same time having already undertaken additional writing, perhaps the beginning of what is now Book I. By mid-December the decision to commit the manuscript to book-length is about to be made, and

[36] *Letters* 5:177–78.
[37] *Letters* 5:180.
[38] *Two Note Books*, 177.
[39] *Letters* 5:190–91.
[40] *Two Note Books*, 178.

Carlyle confidently writes to John on December 19: "*Mein Acker ist die Zeit* [Time is my seed-field]." This quotation is from Carlyle's translation of Goethe's *Wilhelm Meisters Wanderjahre*, and it figures prominently in the opening of Book I, Chapter II, of *Sartor Resartus*. Then, after complaining about Fraser's dilatoriness, Carlyle adds: "Hang them! I *have* a Book in me that will cause ears to tingle; and one day out it must and will issue."[41]

THE WRITING OF *TEUFELSDRECK*

By the outset of the new year, Carlyle made what seems to have been an inevitable decision to withdraw "Thoughts on Clothes" from *Fraser's Magazine*, which he faulted for its "scurvy remuneration. . . . It is also a frothy, washy, punchy [flabby], dirty kind of Periodical. . . ." In this letter to John, on January 21, 1831, Carlyle irrevocably changes the textual history of *Sartor Resartus*: "I have a serious commission for you (trouble, as usual) grounded on these facts. Will you go to Fraser and get from him by all means my long Paper entitled *Thoughts on Clothes*. . . . Get it from him, unless it is absolutely printed: the rest [other manuscripts] he can keep, . . . but of this . . . I have taken a notion that I can make rather a good *Book* of it, and one above all likely to produce some desirable impression on the world even now. Do thou get it, my dear Jack, read it well over thyself, and then say what thou thinkest."[42]

What is suggested here is that Carlyle, if not having actually written beyond the manuscript "Thoughts on Clothes," has in fact thought beyond it. His vision of *Sartor Resartus* in larger format came at "Templeland one morning . . . the *germ* of it rose above the ground. 'Nine months,' I used to say, it had cost me in writing."[43] The nine months, actually eight, referred to here are from January to early August of 1831. Part of the additions to the manuscript are described in the above letter to John: "I can devise some more Biography for Teufelsdreck; give a second deeper part, in the same vein, leading thro' Religion and the nature of Society, and Lord knows what. Nay that very 'Thoughts,' slightly altered w*d* itself make a little volume first (which would encourage me immensely) could one find any Bookseller, which however I suppose one cannot."[44]

---

[41] *Letters* 5:200, 202.
[42] *Letters* 5:215.
[43] *Reminiscences*, 82.
[44] *Letters* 5:215.

The suggestions here are once more cryptic. When Carlyle says that he means to "devise some more Biography," it seems logical to assume that he is speaking of the first five chapters of Book II, which examine in detail Teufelsdreck's fictional history. Yet the subject of "Religion and the nature of Society" is now the specific topic of Book III, Chapter II, which further belies any notion that *Sartor Resartus* was written in the sequence in which it now appears. Clearly, significant alterations were to be made in "Thoughts on Clothes," which must have included a rearrangement of various chapters. At this point the manuscript now called *Teufelsdreck* was born. Carlyle then closes his letter to John by suggesting the possible future direction the manuscript might take: "Whether it were worth while to show Fraser the Manuscript (for I think he has not read it) and take counsel with him; or still rather to show Edward Irving it (whose friendliness and feeling of the True, widely as it differs from him, I know) do thou judge. I fear perfect *anonymity* is now out of the question; however swear every one to secrecy, for I mean to speak fearlessly if at all."[45]

In the end Carlyle relinquished any desire for anonymity; for, even though *Sartor Resartus* was not signed in *Fraser's Magazine*, he obviously permitted Fraser to expose his identity in the craftily written and carefully worded portrait of him just before the work was to appear. And, as this passage suggests, Carlyle gave John a major role in the development of the manuscript.

The road to the completion of *Teufelsdreck* was a rocky one. In a letter to Goethe, January 22, Carlyle is circumspect: ". . . I am working at another curious enterprise of my own, which is yet too amorphous to be prophecied of."[46] In a letter to his mother Margaret, February 1, he is even less definite, saying that he is "hovering about the materials of a Book, which I have so long talked of: one day or other it *must* out."[47] Meanwhile, John retrieved from Fraser the manuscript "Thoughts on Clothes" and wrote to Carlyle on January 31: "I have got your papers from Fraser. Those thoughts on Clothes must not be given to him. I have read them very hastily over, & my impression is that they contain a great deal, & if put into a somewhat more acceptable shape would doubtless produce a great impression at present. The first part seemed too long & too German. . . ."[48] Just what part is "too German" is a mystery. Certainly he could mean the

---

[45] *Letters* 5:215–16.
[46] *Letters* 5:220.
[47] *Letters* 5:226.
[48] *Letters* 5:229n.

first five chapters of Book II, where the emphasis is placed on Teufelsdreck's Germanic heritage. Or, the comment could apply to the opening chapters, or any combination thereof, of what is now Book I, or for that matter a great part of Book III. That the manuscript is "too German" seems to lead nowhere, for such a description could apply to any part of *Sartor Resartus*.

On February 7 Carlyle acknowledges in his Journal that "Thoughts on Clothes" has been secured by John, which effectively ends the history of that manuscript: "Sent to Jack to liberate my *Teufelsdreck* from Editorial durance in London, and am seriously thinking to make a Book of it. The thing is not right, not *Art*; yet perhaps a nearer approach to Art than I have yet made. We ought to try. I want to get it done; and then translate *Faust*, as I have partially promised to Goethe. Thro' *Teufelsdreck* I am yet far from seeing my way; nevertheless materials are partly forthcoming."[49] On February 10 Carlyle responds to John's letter of January 31: "My plan is . . . to get some kind of *financial* work for myself, to keep house with, and in the mean time to labour at my Teufelsdreck Book, and bring it up to London in my pocket so soon as it is ready. . . . I am a little comforted by your view of *Teufelsdreck*, which agrees with my own." Carlyle then says that it is "indifferent" to him whether Irving or anyone else reads the manuscript: "They can throw no new light on the business; and I believe, myself, that possibly I may make something of the work, and therefore shall try. It is full of dross, but there is also metal in it, and the thing still lives and produces with me."[50] Even though distressed about the declining health of Goethe and the failure of his *Literary History of Germany* to find a publisher, Carlyle is positive in his commitment to *Sartor Resartus* as a book. Its completion is now uppermost in his mind.

On February 26 Carlyle writes to John that the "*Teufelsdreck Ms.*" is now in his possession. This acknowledgment was in response to John's most revealing letter of February 12: "I did not care to show the MS ['Thoughts on Clothes'] to William Fraser, for he is not to be calculated upon in any undertaking, and will not tell you clearly & plainly what he thinks. He is indeed full of kindness & very ready to oblige; but there is a want of courage about him. . . . He esteems you highly, & says that he 'never began to think at all till he read your writings.'"

---

[49] *Two Note Books*, 183.
[50] *Letters* 5:230–32.

John continues by telling Carlyle that he had taken the manuscript to Irving to read, and then reports Irving's reactions:

> He *'perfectly agreed with you in what you had said about religion & the state of society,'* & wished much it were in his power to talk largely with you of these matters. You had shown great power, & copiousness & 'learning.' The MS might be altered & expanded into a book likely to produce a great & salutary impression at the present time. The character of Teufelsdreck,—the meaning of which name, by the way, he seemed to have no conception of—he thought was very graphically & 'humourously' drawn. He submitted, at the same time; that there was perhaps too little action in proportion to the machinery employed; that the preliminary matter of the first chapter was too long; that you seemed to have poured out the rich flood of your thoughts, without caring whether the reader might feel it possible to keep pace with you, or bear the load of ideas you were heaping upon him. All these deficiencies were attributable to your having written for the Magazine. More subdivisions, more resting points, might make the work more acceptable & effectual.

Irving's reactions, which are of course in part John's, are the first substantial criticisms extant of the manuscript. As if to reinforce the precautions of Irving, John then adds: "As to my own opinion, it is substantially the same as Irving[']s. I think you have materials enough for a book that w*d* make a great impression, if you could work these materials into a more light & easy form, & give them more life & action. Could anything like a story be made? It is the thing w*d sell* best & take most effect. . . . I do not believe it would be possible to find any bookseller to undertake publication of a first volume ['Thoughts on Clothes']; but if the whole were finished I do not think it would be difficult to find one on advantageous terms,—indeed I sh*d* engage to find one myself."[51]

The opinions of Irving and John, one his valued friend and the other his trusted brother, no doubt had a significant impact upon the

[51] *Letters* 5:233-34n.

future content of the manuscript. And, equally important, it now seems certain from Irving's reference to *"religion & the state of society"* that at least a part of the chapter "Church Clothes" (Book III, Chapter II) was originally a part of the manuscript "Thoughts on Clothes." Further, John's wish for more "life & action" may eventually have been realized in the most autobiographical and most fictionalized chapters of *Sartor Resartus*, Book II, Chapters I–V.

Whatever subsequent patterns of composition finally materialized, it now seems apparent that all three books of the present text of *Sartor Resartus* were represented in some manner in the manuscript "Thoughts on Clothes." In the eventful letter to John, February 26, Carlyle promises to spare no effort: ". . . I purpose seriously inclining heart and hand to the finishing of *Teufk*—if indeed he be finishable!" He asks John to thank Irving for the *"right* faults kindly indicated," and then concludes: "I will make the attempt!"[52] By March 4, Carlyle apparently has made significant progress toward revision and expansion as indicated in a letter to John, whom he hopes to join shortly in London: "Yes, I compute that before the long days are done, I shall have realised two things: finished my prodigal son *Teufelsdreck*, and got Fifty pounds into my pocket. . . . [S]urely we shall have space to find a Publisher for Devilsdreck, and look around also. . . ."[53] Later in the letter he renews his promise to John: "Thus I see a busy summer before me, and therefore no unhappy one. Teufelsdreck I *hege und pflege* [nurture], night and day. . . . *Teufk* is not the *right* thing yet, but there is a kind of life in it, and I *will* finish it."[54] By March 15 the struggle to complete the manuscript has not abated. In a letter to his mother Carlyle vents his frustrations and hopes: "Meanwhile you will rejoice to learn, my dear Mother, that I am actually working with all diligence at that same *Book* I have talked so long about! Ask no account of it, for it is indescribable: however, I think it may *do*, and be not altogether unworthy of doing. I mean to finish it . . . this summer; and try London with it in the beginning of Winter."[55] Two days later Carlyle complains to John about "having *nerves*, at present, and little talent for sleep—owing to *Teufelsdreck* partly," yet a few lines later he is able to report that he has been "writing *Teufelk*, after considerable meditation, and have even the First and Second Chapters down *perfect*, and think it will make a kind

[52] *Letters* 5:237.
[53] *Letters* 5:243.
[54] *Letters* 5:244.
[55] *Letters* 5:247.

of *Werke* [Book]!"[56] Here again another part is added to the puzzle of composition. If it is assumed that Carlyle is not rewriting into fair copy, a procedure unlikely at this juncture, then it is clear that the opening of Book I was written after most of Book II. Further, Carlyle's verification here that he has completed the first two chapters of Book I, and from the context it would seem 'new' chapters, then it can be safely inferred that Book I, Chapters I–II, were not a part of the original manuscript "Thoughts on Clothes." Such a theory is supported by the next letter to John on March 27: "Teufelsdreck advances, slowly yet sure; sometimes I am in hope that it will really do; at all times, determined that it shall be finished. . . . Chapter 4*th* is about concluded. Much must be added; something omitted: were I once rightly on fire, I should defy all things."[57] Since Carlyle is almost certainly referring to Chapter IV of Book I, the evidence is mounting that a substantial part if not the whole of Book I was written after Book II.

The spirited progress Carlyle is making toward completion now seems not to be seriously interrupted. On March 29 he describes his pace to his mother: "For myself I am dashing away at my *Book*, and determined to have it done and printed."[58] On April [5?] or [12?], he again writes to his mother: "As for myself I am struggling forward daily with my Book, and hope to be done sometime in June . . . ; and sometimes *hope* my Book will *not* be a Dud."[59] The projection here that he cannot complete the manuscript before June (it was finally completed in late July) suggests that there is a substantial part left to do, which would include a considerable part of Book III. Yet by April 18 Carlyle reports to John: "*Teufelsdreck* advances steadily . . . ; the *third part* of him is *finally* on paper; under good hopes."[60] For the first time it is disclosed that there will be a "*third part*" to *Sartor Resartus*, and this part must surely be Book III. Thus, it can now be inferred that the writing of most if not all of Book I preceded Book III, and that the writing of most if not all of Book II preceded Book I. Still, any notion of a final copy remained uncertain, as evidenced in a letter to his mother on May 17: "For myself I have resumed my task, and this day accomplished two clear pages,—which indeed is little, yet a thousand times more than Nothing. I too (like the Old

[56] *Letters* 5:249–50.
[57] *Letters* 5:253.
[58] *Letters* 5:258.
[59] *Letters* 5:261.
[60] *Letters* 5:264.

Mare) am in jeopardy, yet hope I may get thro'. The Book *must* be written, if I continue living; the buying and reading of it does not depend on me."[61] It is important to note that in his metaphorical language Carlyle has documented the projected word-length of the pages of the now-lost manuscript: 1000 words for two pages, or 500 words per page, which in turn verifies that he was using foolscap.

With the coming of June, the progress toward completion became naggingly slow. On June 6 Carlyle writes to John: ". . . I am daily busy with *Teufelsdreck*, which I calculate on finishing early next month. But like James Brown, 'I write dreadfully slow.' It will be one of the strangest volumes ever offered to the English world, whether *worth* anything is another question. At all events, I determine to finish it, and bring it up to London in my pocket during this very session of Parl*t* (if I can). . . ."[62] June quickly passed into July, and the frustration mounted. On July 7 Carlyle reports to John: "I now *see thro* Teufel., write at him literally night and day; yet cannot be done within, say, fifteen days. . . . As to the Teuf*k* itself, whereof 122 solid pages lie written off, and some forty, above half ready are to follow, I cannot pretend to prophecy. . . . Sometimes I think it goodish, at othertimes bad; at most times, the best I can make it here. A strange Book all men will admit it to be: partially intended to be a True Book I know it to be. *Nous verrons* [we shall see]. It shall be printed, if there is a possibility."[63] Aside from the confirmation of the autobiographical truths contained in the work, Carlyle has also established the present and the proposed length of the manuscript. Considering his own projection of 500 words to the page, Carlyle would have written by this point approximately 61,000 words. The average word count in *Fraser's Magazine* is 620 words per double-column page, which would put him past the middle of Book III, assuming that the chronology is now firmly established. Whether he actually wrote forty more pages to complete the manuscript is problematic. If he did, the approximate length of the manuscript would be 160 pages, or 80,000 words. This approximation coincides with the printed version in *Fraser's Magazine* which is some 80,000 words.

By July 12 Carlyle is approaching the end, and hopes to be with John in London by the beginning of August to present the manuscript to a publisher. He has even gone so far as to secure a note to the publisher Longmans through Macvey Napier. On July 12 Carlyle

[61] *Letters* 5:275.
[62] *Letters* 5:283.
[63] *Letters* 5:297.

writes to John: "I am struggling forward with Dreck, sick enough, but not in bad heart. I think the world will nowise be enraptured with this (medicinal) *Devil's Dung*; that the critical republic will cackle vituperatively or perhaps maintain total silence: *à la bonne heure* [well and good]! It was the best I had in me; what God had given me, what the Devil shall not take away." Carlyle then adds regarding the manuscript itself: ". . . I am so far back with my 'Chapter on Symbols.' I am at the 132*nd* page: there may be some 170; but much of it is half-written."[64] What is significant here to the establishing of the chronology is that Carlyle acknowledges that he is reworking an already written "Chapter on Symbols," which must certainly have been in the original manuscript "Thoughts on Clothes."

The urgency to complete the manuscript and to be in London by the beginning of August is evidenced in a letter to John on July 17: "I am labouring at *Teufel* with considerable impetuosity and calculate that unless accidents intervene, I may be actually ready to get under way about the end of the month. But there will not be a minute to lose. I sometimes think the Book *will* prove a kind of medicinal Assafoetida [sic] for the pudding Stomach of England, and produce new secretions there. *Iacta est alea* [The die is cast]! I will speak out what is in me. . . . I must to my *Dreck*, for the hours go: *Gott mit Dir* [God be with you]!"[65] The language here suggests that Carlyle has yet to complete his manuscript, although it seems likely at this point that he is now rewriting rather than creating additional chapters, except of course for the last chapter "Farewell," part of which must have been written near the end of the composing process. Two days later, on July 19, Carlyle expresses his good health to his mother, and then paraphrases from "The Everlasting No," saying that he is "very high in the humour, and defiant both of the Devil and the World. I think I have look[e]d into the *worst* that is in them both; and, thro' God's grace, no longer fear it."[66] It is in these days of late July, and in this mood of defiance, that Carlyle finished his manuscript. By August 4 he was on his way to London, and the long hunt for a publisher for *Teufelsdreck* was about to begin.[67]

---

[64] *Letters* 5:303–04.
[65] *Letters* 5:305.
[66] *Letters* 5:309.
[67] *Two Note Books*, 191.

THE HAWKING OF *TEUFELSDRECK*

Carlyle arrived in London on August 10, and immediately set out to find a publisher. Because of previous contacts John Murray was first on the list, principally at the recommendation of Francis Jeffrey who alerted Murray to Carlyle. Carlyle describes what transpired in a letter to Jane on August 11, explaining that he took "counsel" of Jeffrey: "He tho*t* Murray (in spite of his radicalism) would be the better publisher [than Longman?]; to him accordingly he gave me a line saying that I was a genius and would like become eminent; further that he (Jeffrey) would like well to confer with him about that Book. I directly set off with this to Albemarle Street; found Murray *out*; returned afterwards and found him *in*, gave an outline of the Book . . . , stated also that I had nothing else ado here but the getting of it published, and was above all anxious that his decision should be given soon. He answered that we would begin this very afternoon; that on Wednesday next he would give me an answer. I then went off; despatched my *Teuf*k with *your* tape round him; agreeing to all their stipulations: on Wednesday I am to go there and get an answer of my *Ms*." The influence of Jeffrey was considerable. In a Journal entry, August 11, Carlyle writes of his meeting with Murray: "A tall squinting man; not of the wisest aspect; seems to know me, and smiles on my description of *Dreck* (the dog! I fear he will make me *greet* on it yet): the favour of the Ministry, through Jeffrey's interest, buoys me up with him."[68] There was then hope that an agreement would be quickly reached, as Carlyle continues to Jane: "Of the probable issue I can form no conjecture: only Murray seemed to know me; and I daresay is very anxious to keep well with Ministry, so will risk what he dare."[69] The formal letter to Murray is dated August 10: "I here send you the Ms; concerning which I have, for the present, only to repeat my urgent request that no time may be lost in deciding on it. At latest next Wednesday I shall wait upon you, to see what farther, or whether anything farther, is to be done. In the mean while, it is perhaps unnecessary to say that the whole business is *strictly confidential*; the rather as I wish to publish anonymously."[70]

The wish for anonymity is not altogether clear, especially since Carlyle had not published a book anonymously since his translation, the *German Romance*, in 1827. Nevertheless, the sense of urgency is

[68] *Two Note Books*, 194.
[69] *Letters* 5:318–19.
[70] *Letters* 5:315.

apparent, an urgency brought on not so much by an arrogance of manner but by the often-expressed concern for personal finances.

Murray was, however, to prove disappointing on all accounts. The reform agitation was affecting the sales of all publishers, and Murray was not immune. Carlyle seems to have sensed the problem facing his manuscript, and in a letter to Goethe, August 13, he is not sanguine: "I have come hither chiefly to dispose of the Piece which I lately described myself as writing. Whether or how I shall succeed seems questionable: for the whole world here is dancing a Tarantula Dance of Political Reform, and has no ear left for Literature."[71] Insofar as the publication of *Teufelsdreck* was concerned, Carlyle's words proved to be prophetic. Murray was unusually dilatory, blaming it on family matters when in truth he was looking for a way to decline without insulting the testimony of Jeffrey. Carlyle was persistent, which made the whole course of events all the more embarrassing. Two days after communicating his uneasiness to Goethe, Carlyle was more blunt with Jane: "If Murray fail me (as Wednesday will probably show) I have calculated that it will hardly be worth while to take up time with offering these people [Longman] *Dreck*; but that I must try some other course with him." Carlyle then becomes gloomier: "*I hope not at all*; therefore hardly think that Murray will accept (so *lucky* were it); and am already looking out what I can for other resources in the *worst* issue. Dreck shall be printed if a man in London will do it: if not with, then without 'fee or reward.'"[72] Carlyle is not suffering from persecution here, but rather he is confronting realistically the situation facing him. His initial enthusiasm was waning. There is now talk of subvention, even failure, which explains perhaps his perfunctory assessment to his mother that he had put his "Manuscript into the hands of the chief Bookseller here, and am to learn how he feels about it the day after tomorrow."[73]

Whether intentionally or not, Murray's dilatoriness continued, for between Monday and Tuesday he seems to have communicated to Carlyle that he needed more time. On Tuesday, August 16, Carlyle wrote to Allan Cunningham, "My Scriptory ware still lies in the scales, which way inclining I cannot say, except in the spirit of a Prophet that ever prophecyeth *evil*. On Saturday I shall perhaps know more."[74] However, on Wednesday, August 17, Carlyle kept his origi-

[71] *Letters* 5:327.
[72] *Letters* 5:328.
[73] *Letters* 5:334.
[74] *Letters* 5:335.

nal appointment with Murray, but as he reports to Jane later in the day: "The Dog of a Bookseller gone to the country. I leave my card with remonstrances and pressing inquiries *when*. The Clerk talks of 'Mr Murray writing you, Sir': I will call again tomorrow morning, and make M[urry] speak to me, I hope."[75] On Thursday morning Carlyle again went to Murray, and this time found him in but with little result: "This morning, I returned again to Albemarle Street: the Bookseller was first denied to me, then showed his broad one-eyed face . . . ; and my Manuscript—lay still unopened! I reminded him, not without emphasis, of the engagement made, and how I had nothing else to do here, but see that matter brought to an end: to all which he pleaded hard in extenuation, and for 'two or three days' farther allowance. I made him *name* a new day: 'Saturday first'; then I am to return and hear how the matter stands." At this point Carlyle is worried about "longer delays," followed by "final rejection." He then reports that he has made an unsuccessful attempt to see James Fraser to inquire about the "dim schemes" he had for *Fraser's Magazine*.[76]

Throughout Carlyle seems always to have depended on Fraser, even though he once abruptly recalled "Thoughts on Clothes" from the firm. Also, it is apparent that Carlyle was considering serialization, for the once article-length "Thoughts on Clothes" had now become the book-length *Teufelsdreck*. With *Fraser's Magazine* as a recourse if all else failed, Carlyle remained confident in the face of mounting odds. In a letter to his brother Alexander, on August 18, he concludes: "My book is taking its own course, if I look not to it: the 'trade' is said to be at the lowest ebb &c; but all that does not discourage me a whit."[77] Some of this stated confidence is of course bravado; Carlyle most assuredly was concerned that he could come away from London without a publisher. Jane read his passions well, and in a lengthy letter on August 18 appealed to Carlyle's increasingly fragile ego, reassuring him from distant Craigenputtoch that he had the full support of his friends, not the least of whom is Jeffrey who assured her "that he 'will *do what he can for the book* but fears its extravagance and what will be called its affectation.'" Almost resentful of Jeffrey's concerns, Jane adds: "Let him not tro[u]ble his dear little heart overmuch—Dreck is *done for* already and no Bookseller or body of booksellers, no discerning public—can *undo* him—not the Devil himself can undo him—If *they* will not publish him—

---

[75] *Letters* 5:339.
[76] *Letters* 5:341.
[77] *Letters* 5:344.

bring him back and *I* will take care of him and read him and admire
him—till we are enabled to publish him on our own account—"[78]
Meanwhile, Carlyle wrote to Murray on August 19 to request a
"short meeting at any the earliest, hour that suits your convenience."[79]
Murray disappointed Carlyle again, admitting that the manuscript
had not been read and pleading for more time, an additional month,
to consider it. By this time Carlyle certainly must have realized that
his hope in Murray was dashed, and thus he turned to James Fraser
who, as Carlyle writes to Jane on August 22, "would publish the
Book for me, on this principle: If I would give *him* a sum not exceed-
ing £150 sterling!"[80] Jeffrey counseled against such an arrangement,
and Carlyle said that he would "'wait to the end of Eternity first.'"
Rejecting outright Fraser's offer to publish with a subvention, Carlyle
was once more forced into the streets of London to look for a publisher. His description to Jane of his sojourn is illustrative and revealing:

> Spurning at Destiny, yet in the mildest terms taking
> leave of Fraser, I strode thro' these streets, carrying
> Teuf*k* openly in my hand, *not* like a gentleman. I
> took a pipe and glass of water, and counsel with myself.
> I was bilious and sad. . . . Having rested a little, I set
> out again to Longmans to hear what they had to
> say. . . . I describe Teufelsdreck; bargain that they are
> to look at it themselves; and send it back again in two
> days; that is tomorrow. . . . Meanwhile I keep look-
> ing out on all hands, for another issue. Perhaps I
> shall have to march thro' the whole squad of scoun-
> drels, and try them all. *A la bonne heure* [Well and
> good]! I have a problem which *is* possible: either to
> get Dreck printed, or to ascertain that I *cannot* and
> so tie him up and come home with him. So fear
> nothing. . . . Teuf*k* is in his place and his time here
> grows stronger the more I see of London and its
> philosophy: the Doctrine of the *Phoenix*, of *Nat.
> Supernaturalism* and the whole Clothes Philosophy
> . . . is exactly what all intelligent men are wanting.[81]

[78] *Letters* 5:345–46.
[79] *Letters* 5:348.
[80] *Letters* 5:353.
[81] *Letters* 5:354.

Carlyle was willing to continue his now grueling search for a publisher. Later in the above letter to Jane he confirms this willingness: "I go with *Dreck* (in the *worst* issue) to Jeffrey next morning and also get a frank [appraisal]—."[82] On August 24 he reports the dismal news to Jane that Owen Rees, partner of Longman, who had recently rejected his *History of German Literature*, also declined: "My *Ms* is returned, as I expected: Rees says 'notwithstanding the high ability' &c &c they decline the article. This was Tuesday morning: an hour afterwards I had it over to Jeffrey's, who I daresay has never looked on it. . . ." Carlyle had expected as much when he wrote in his Journal on August 13: "Shall I try them [Longman] with *Dreck* if Murray fail? *Schwerlich* [Hardly]!"[83] Meanwhile, Jeffrey promised that he would intervene again "'this week,'" but Carlyle now realized that Jeffrey could be of little aid. He then went to William Fraser, editor of the *Foreign Review*, to have him "work on other quarters of the Trade; chiefly to reconnoitre for tho' unspeakably willing, he can do nothing more. . . . He talks of grand possibilities: but I believe in nothing."[84] On August 26 Carlyle writes to his mother, "The business of the Book proceeds but crabbedly: the whole English world, I find, has ceased to read Books of late. . . . The manuscript is at present in Jeffrey's hands, whence I expect to receive it in some two days, with favourable or at worst unfavourable judgement. . . . Little money, I think, will be had for my work: but I will have it printed if there be a man in London that will do it, even without payment to myself. . . ." Yet Carlyle sees that he might have to "tie a piece of good *Skeenyie* [packthread] about my Papers, stick the whole in my pocket, and march home again with it, . . . and I can wait till better times."[85] In the next several days the prospects did not change. On August 29 he tells Jane "so fast is my Paper waning. Of History indeed there is little to be told: slowly, slowly does the business of poor *Dreck* get along let me push it as I may."[86]

However, Carlyle's spirits were buoyed, this time by the efforts of William Fraser who intervened with the publishers Colburn and Bentley. As Carlyle wrote to Jane on August 29: "Fraser, who was to sound Colbourn [sic] about *Dreck*, had never called, and did not call: not till the next day came a Letter . . . stating that the Puff-

[82] *Letters* 5:356.
[83] *Two Note Books*, 196.
[84] *Letters* 5:362–63.
[85] *Letters* 5:367-68.
[86] *Letters* 5:374.

Publishers were prepared to consider my Manuscript as soon as might be."[87] Carlyle was of course unable to approach Colburn because Jeffrey still had the manuscript and had other plans: "Inquiring for Teufel*k* as I was privileged to do, the Critic professed that he had 'honestly read' 28 pages of it (surprising feat!) that he objected to the dilatoriness of the introductory part (as *we* both did also), and very much admired the scene of the sleeping City: farther that he would write to Murray that very day . . . to appoint a meeting with him, and if possible attain some *finish* with that individual at least. He (Jeffrey) would look thro' the Book farther in the interim &c &c. Alas! What could I do, but consent to let him *have* that 'other week.'"[88] Jeffrey did write to Murray on August 28, and presumably met with him "on the subject of my friend Carlyle's projected publication."[89] Jeffrey's willingness to intervene personally with Murray brought relief, as Carlyle expresses in a letter to Jane in early September: "The Book as you see I need not torment myself *so* much with pressing forward; we shall be here to see it thro'—'or publish it on our own account, my love.'"[90] Meanwhile Jane continued, on September 1, her litanies of encouragement: "And Jeffrey admired the sleeping city—Thank him for nothing— He would have been the dullest of mortals if he had not—My beloved Dreck! my jewel of great price! The builders despise thee; but thou wilt yet be *brought out with shouting* and I shall live to see thee in thy place—All these discouragements do but increase my confidence—as a candle burns brighter for being snuffed—for Dreck is imperishable, indestructible as the substance of the four elements— and all Booksellerdom all Devildom cannot prevail against him!"[91]

On September 4 Carlyle was able to report the startling news to Jane: *Teufelsdreck* had survived the latest round with Murray, no doubt the result of Jeffrey's influence. A tentative offer was extended by letter on September 3: "Murray will print a small edition (750 copies) of *Dreck*, on the half-profits system (that is I getting *nothing*, but also *giving* nothing) after which the sole Copyright of the Book is to be mine. . . . A poorish offer, Goody; yet perhaps after all, the best I shall get. Better considerably than *my* giving £150 [Fraser's offer] for the frolic of having written such a Work!" Carlyle, however, was still

---

[87] *Letters* 5:375.
[88] *Letters* 5:376.
[89] *Letters* 5:376n.
[90] *Letters* 5:388.
[91] *Letters* 5:392–93.

not convinced that Murray was offering the best deal. Half-profits would bring Carlyle only half of the profit after Murray's expenses. Thus, he tells Jane that they will still attempt to strike a deal with Colburn, even though Jeffrey has made the commitment to Murray: "I mean to set off tomorrow-morning to Colburn and Bentley (whom Fraser has prepared for me), and ascertain whether they will pay me *anything* for a first edition: unless they say about £100, I will prefer Murray; unless they look like saying something of that sort, they shall not even see the Article for a week which is the time they require." It is of interest to note that Carlyle continues to refer, on occasion, to the manuscript as an "Article," a result no doubt of "Thoughts on Clothes," but also because he may now be giving thought to some type of serialization if all else fails. He concludes by reminding Jane of the "consummate knaves" at Colburn's: "I hate knaves, but still need money. Murray *wished* me to try elsewhere."[92] On Monday Carlyle met with a representative of Colburn whom he describes as a "coarse muddy, greedy character," who "hinted at the *sole* object of Publisher's being money," and who explained the "difference between talent and popularity." Carlyle was displeased and disbelieving. Clearly Murray now held the key to the publishing of *Teufelsdreck*: "I will . . . make an attempt to see Murray tomorrow morning; . . . I mean to close with him, and have done. The offer is not so bad: 750 Copies for the task of publishing poor Dreck, and the rest of him *our own*."[93]

However, the day before writing his formal letter of acceptance to Murray's terms, Carlyle tried Longman one more time, but in his letter to Macvey Napier on September 5 he reported that Rees of Longman, Rees, and Company declined once again, principally because the "Public has ceased to buy Books."[94] And, on this same day, Carlyle learned that Colburn also was not interested. If the manuscript were to be published as a book, Murray was the only prospect left. Thus, on Tuesday, September 6, Carlyle wrote to John Murray accepting, saying that he was "very anxious to have [Murray] as a Publisher, and to see my Book put forth soon."[95] The earlier problem of Murray's inaccessibility remained, however. Carlyle was suspicious of Murray's resolve, a matter he confided to Jane on September 8: "The history of *Dreck* still sticks simply where it was. The Colburns, on Monday night, as I predicted, will not act; . . . next morning I went over to

[92] *Letters* 5:399.
[93] *Letters* 5:400–01.
[94] *Letters* 5:402.
[95] *Letters* 5:403.

Murray; as usual, could not see him; left a Letter saying that I was *ready* for such an engagement, and eager that it should be *soon*; and there the matter still lies."[96] Carlyle was determined to "*press* the matter forward with an incessant shouldering," but was now convinced that it was "less and less likely" that the printing of the manuscript would result in any remuneration: "thank God that we have been able to write it, and to write it *gratis*!"[97] Carlyle's acknowledgment, here and elsewhere, of Jane's part in the writing of the manuscript is not mere salutation, and seems ample evidence that she took an active role in its formulation, which in part at least accounts for her passion regarding the progress of *Teufelsdreck*. As Carlyle was to say later, *Teufelsdreck* was written "under the eye of the Flower of Haddington!"[98]

By September 11 Carlyle's misgivings about Murray were deepening. Murray had not answered his letter of acceptance and the worst was assumed. Carlyle had expected it, and his letter to Jane expresses more resignation than indignation: "*Dreck* again lies tied together in my trunk; and for aught I see may lie some time: I have written and travelled to Albemarle Street, but never once succeeded in getting a glimpse or a word of the Pontiff [Murray]. . . . Nay, if Murray will not say something reasonable, *Dreck* shall take his ease where he is: some one will by and by print him, if he be wanted in the world: that we have written him is still a kind of comfort."[99] On the same day, without knowing the Murray circumstance, Jane writes about their decision to leave the "barren heath" of Craigenputtoch, feeling that their isolated residence there might adversely affect Carlyle's future negotiations: "Yet let it not be forgotten that at Craigenputtoch you have written Teufe[l]sdreck—yes the candle sometimes burns its way *thro'* the bushel—but what a waste of light!"[100] Such letters were a boon to Carlyle, especially since the fortunes of *Teufelsdreck* seemed to be changing. Murray was finally cornered by Carlyle and in such a position agreed to publish the manuscript, as he describes to Jane on Wednesday, September 14: "The Dog was standing on the floor when I entered, and could not escape me! He is the slipperiest, lamest, most confused unbusinesslike man I have seen. Nevertheless poor *Dreck* was in a few minutes settled, or put on the way of settlement:

[96] *Letters* 5:404.
[97] *Letters* 5:404–05.
[98] *Letters* 5:429.
[99] *Letters* 5:415–16.
[100] *Letters* 5:423.

I got a line to his printer [William Clowes] . . . ; found him; expounded to him; and finally about two in the afternoon saw *Dreck* on the way to the Printing Office, and can hope to get the first page of him tomorrow! Perhaps a week may elapse (perhaps less, so *exceedingly* irregular is Murray) before we be fairly under steady way: after which a month or so will roll it all off my hands, and Dreck will lie in sheets till his hour come. Murray speaks of the 'beginning of the year' for Publication. . . ."[101]

On Thursday Carlyle assures Jane that he is to see the printer again regarding the disposition of the manuscript: ". . . I shall require one or more personal discussions before we get fairly afloat, and *Dreck* . . . is not come yet." Clowes failed to keep the date as promised, and Carlyle's mood once again swings toward the negative: "The Printer has failed of his hour; let him now wait for *me*." In the afternoon he fluctuates between despair and hope: "No Teufelsdreck, no Hope or tidings of such has arrived. No matter; really it is no matter at all; there will be time enough."[102] In a letter to his mother, September 19, he complains about the adverse impact the reform agitation has had on the publishing world, and then says that he was "obliged to *give* my poor Book *away* (that is the first Edition of it; whether there will ever be a second is to try for), and am even glad to see it printed on these terms," and he looks forward to "superintend[ing] the printing of our 'bit [small] Book'. . . ." In a postscript to this letter to his mother Carlyle writes, "My Book is fairly *at Press*."[103] On the same day, he is able to report to Jane: "The best news I can tell you today is that *Dreck* is fairly getting into types. As you will see by that snip of a 'specimen page,' which I inclose here, to gratify your pretty eyes. I know not what will become of the Book: . . . I did my best."[104]

However, after writing to Jane about the much-awaited progress of the printing, the unexpected news arrived from Murray. In a letter written on September 17 Murray sent a short but pointed note: "Your conversations with me, respecting the publication of your MS, led me to infer, that you had given me the *preference* and, certainly not, that you had, already, submitted it to the greatest publishers in London—who had declined to engage in it. Under these circumstances, it will be necessary for me also to get it read by some literary

---

[101] *Letters* 5:429.
[102] *Letters* 5:430–32.
[103] *Letters* 5:436, 438.
[104] *Letters* 5:440.

friend before I can in justice to myself engage in the printing of it."[105]

Murray's concern is mere pretense, for he most assuredly would have known that Carlyle had tried to find other publishers, particularly since he had recommended that Carlyle do so. Clearly Murray never wanted to publish the manuscript and had now arrived at a formal excuse not to. After all, why would he need to find a reader when the learned and influential Francis Jeffrey had already served in that capacity? Carlyle was fully aware of the deception by Murray, and wrote a considered response on September 19. He first assures Murray that his firm was given preference; he then acknowledges that he had taken the manuscript to Longman, but only after Murray had released it for the first time; and finally he says "that if you mean the Bargain, which I had understood myself to have made with you, unmade, you have only to cause your Printer who is now working on my Ms., to return the same without damage or delay, and consider the business as finished."[106] Carlyle's response is unusually magnanimous under the circumstances, even though he does not acknowledge that he had shown the manuscript to Colburn and discussed it with Fraser, among others. There is no doubt: Murray simply did not want to publish it, and was willing at this point to incur the displeasure of Jeffrey. His commitment and Carlyle's feelings were not of final concern.

Acutely disappointed and feeling betrayed, Carlyle was less temperate in his description of the affair to Jane on September 23: ". . . [I]t is my (I know not whether painful or pleasant) duty to tell you that the Printing of *Teufelsdreck* which I announced as commencing, and even (in my Scotsbrig Note) sent you a specimen of, has altogether stopt, and Murray's Bargain with me has burst into the air. The man behaved like a Pig, and was speared perhaps not without art; Jack [John Carlyle] and I at least laughed that night *à gorge deployée* [with splitting sides], at the Answer I wrote his base *glar* of a Letter: he has written again in much politer style, and I shall answer him . . . 'sharp but mannerly.' The truth of the matter is, now clearly enough: Dreck cannot be disposed of in London at this time." Yet Carlyle adds, ". . . I shall give Murray perhaps another chance, if he be eager for it."[107] On September 24 Murray wrote to Carlyle a mildly apologetic, certainly opportunistic, letter, stating that he had only wished

[105] *Letters* 5:441.
[106] *Letters* 5:442.
[107] *Letters* 5:444.

to be given the same right of "perusal" as Longman, a frank admission on Murray's part that he had not read the manuscript before his commitment to Carlyle. In spite of Murray's untenable position, Carlyle was again unusually temperate in his response written on the same day. In it Carlyle offers to release Murray from "all engagement or shadow of engagement," and then suggests that if Murray desires to re-examine the manuscript (a liberal interpretation of Murray's letter) that he should "expect some higher remuneration for a work that has cost me so much effort, were once it fairly examined." Carlyle then completely seizes the initiative and informs Murray he expects a "quite new negotiation, if you incline to enter on such: I shall then see whether the limited extent of my time will allow me to wait yours." If this is all unacceptable, Carlyle then demands his "Papers be returned with the least possible delay."[108] Murray was no doubt annoyed if not angered by Carlyle's epistolary maneuvers, given strength by the presence of John and the impending arrival of Jane in London.

Murray still wanted out of any agreement, stated or implied, but was being careful, no doubt because of the looming shadow of Jeffrey. Carlyle, on the other hand, was clearly desperate and was willing to seek any agreement that would not compromise his dignity. The arrival of Jane in London on October 1 must certainly have improved his spirits. Still, it was at this juncture that the manuscript was most vulnerable. Carlyle had abandoned manuscripts of this size before; there was now little to keep him from doing the same again. In these darkest days of October 1831, it was entirely possible that *Teufelsdreck* would suffer the fate of its predecessor, the autobiographical novel *Wotten Reinfred*. Remarkably, it was Murray's dilatoriness that perhaps saved the manuscript from the oblivion of the trunk, or worse. For whatever reasons, Murray was slow in returning the manuscript he had already rejected. On October 4 Carlyle was forced to ask Murray "to engage in a new treaty" (a word choice not lost on Murray), or "to have the *Ms.* forthwith returned."[109] On October 6 Murray responded to this entreaty with yet another blow to Carlyle's already fragile ego. He had sent the manuscript to a "Gentleman in the highest class of Men of Letters," and the recommendation was not to publish it in its present form. The gentleman was not, as once assumed, John Gibson Lockhart, editor of Murray's *Quarterly Review*, but the Rev. Henry Hart Milman, a trusted contributor to the journal.

[108] *Letters* 5:446–47.
[109] *Letters* 6:4.

Milman's evaluation, later printed by Carlyle in an edited and truncated form in the "Testimonies of Authors," is not altogether unkind, even though he apparently did not see the opening chapter(s). Milman found Carlyle's thought, language, and style "completely Germanized." He lamented that a writer with such "cleverness and knowledge" should write something that was so "strange and fantastic," and concluded by wondering whether it might indeed be a "translation."[110]

Carlyle responded to Milman's evaluation and Murray's letter of rejection, [6 October], in a cordial manner, which in itself speaks to the issue of Carlyle's courtesy through the whole matter with Murray: "I have received the *Ms.*, with your Note, and your friend's criticism; and find it all safe and right . . . [and] join cordially in the hope you express that, in some fitter case, a closer relationship may arise between us."[111] Jane was less kind in her letter to Carlyle's mother, [6 October]: "They are not going to print the book after all—Murray has lost heart lest it do not take with the public and so like a stupid ass as he is has sent back the manuscript[.] The *deevil* may care it *shall* be printed in spite of Murray some time and in the meanwhile it is not losing any of its worth by lying." Carlyle then adds: "As for the Bookseller's refusal of my Book I care not a doit for it: I know what is wrong and what is right in the Book without his counsel; I will have it printed one day too: nay if it is *not* to be printed at all, I can still live and rejoice."[112] However, Carlyle's temper did flare in a letter written to John two weeks later on October 21. He acknowledges receiving "a 'Criticism' from some altogether immortal 'Master of German Literature,' to me quite unknown; which Criticism (a miserable, Dandiacal, *quodlibet* [any thing whatever], in the usual vein) did *not* authorize the Publication in these times . . . ; thus *Dreck* may perhaps be considered as postponed *sine die* [for an indefinite period]."[113]

Meanwhile, Carlyle, seemingly content that he had done what he could with the manuscript, was now willing to wait until conditions improved in the publishing business. On October 10 he records in his Journal: "*Teufelsdreck*, after various perplexed destinies, returned to me, and now lying safe in his box. There must he continue, till the

---

[110]The discovery that Milman was the reader for Murray was made by Thomas C. Richardson, "John Murray's Reader and the Rejection of *Sartor Resartus.*"
[111]*Letters* 6:6.
[112]*Letters* 6:9–10.
[113]*Letters* 6:28–29.

Book-trade revive a little; if forever, what matter? The Book contents
me little; yet perhaps there is material in it: in any case I did my
best."[114] The sentiment was the same to his brother Alexander on
October 15: "My poor *Book* . . . cannot be printed at present; for this
plain reason, all Bookselling is *at an end*, till once this Reform Bill of
theirs be passed. . . . I have locked up my Manuscript here beside me;
and mean to let it lie at least till next month before making any
further attempt."[115] On October 17, in a letter to William Graham,
Carlyle continues to attribute the failure to sell the manuscript to the
crisis over the Reform Bill: "No Bookseller will so much as look at
a Manuscript for the last five months; all trade in Books is utterly
asleep. . . . I have locked up my poor Bundle of Papers, and do not
mean to speak about them, for some weeks; not at all, if times do not
alter. . . ."[116] By November 10, he perceives a slight change in the
mood of publishers, and he writes to his mother: "My *Book* still lies
quite safe in the Drawer, and I doubt must lie till Reform-Bill work
is over: however, I think of beginning a new set of trials soon among
the Booksellers, for there are some slight symptoms of Trade beginning to stir in that quarter again. At the same time one must not
hawk a Manuscript, or the Blockheads begin to think it is nothing
worth."[117] Carlyle's memory, recorded in the *Reminiscences*, of the
failure to find a publisher for *Teufelsdreck* is a bit more sour:

> The beggarly history of poor *Sartor* [*Teufelsdreck*]
> *among the Blockheadisms* is not worth recording, or
> remembering. . . .—In short, finding that whereas I
> had got £100 (if memory serve) for *Schiller* six or
> seven years before [1825], and for *Sartor* "at least
> *thrice* as good," I could, not only, *not* "get [£200],"
> but even get no "Murray" or the like to publish it on
> "half-profits" (Murray, a most stupendous object to
> me; tumbling about, eyeless, with the evidently strong
> wish to say "Yes *and* No,"—my first signal experi-
> ence of that sad human predicament),—I said, "We
> will make it *No*, then; wrap up our MS.; wait till this
> 'Reform Bill' uproar abate; and see. . . ."[118]

[114] *Two Note Books*, 201.
[115] *Letters* 6:16.
[116] *Letters* 6:21.
[117] *Letters* 6:39.
[118] *Reminiscences*, 83.

Later in the *Reminiscences* Carlyle writes with a certain compassion that Murray's "position was an impossible one, position of a poor old man endeavouring to answer 'Yes *and* No!' I had striven and pushed, for some weeks, with him and others. . . . I, with brevity, demanded my poor Manuscript from Murray; received it with some apologetic palaver (enclosing an opinion from his Taster, which was subsequently printed in one edition), and much hope etc. etc.; locked *it* away into a fixity of silence for the present . . . and decided to send for the Dear One [Jane]. . . ."[119]

The attempt to find a publisher did not end with Murray, for the record indicates that Carlyle continued to try to advance the cause of the manuscript. He lent it to his friends to read with the expectation that their criticisms might offer flame to an otherwise damp fire. Most notable among these friends was John Stuart Mill, who had seen it at least once before and seemed quite willing to read it once again. In a letter to John on November 13 Carlyle says that he has lent Mill "*Teufelk* to read; which wonderful Book I am again cautiously bestirring myself to get printed. . . ."[120] However, mixed with cautious hope is always an element of despair, as evidenced in a letter to Napier on November 26: "All manner of perplexities have occurred in the publishing of my poor Book; which perplexities I could only cut asunder, not unloose: so the Ms like an unhappy Ghost still lingers on the wrong side of Styx; the Charon of Albemarle Street [Murray] durst not risk it in his *sutilis cymba* [stitched-together boat]; so it leaped ashore again. Better days are coming. . . ."[121] On December 4, Carlyle writes to Alexander, "I am again among the Booksellers with my Manuscript: but have yet got nothing fixed; not even my first *refusal*." The postscript, written the next day, is not as optimistic: "My Manuscript, as I expected, *refused* [by Tilt]! I make other trials, and care not a *rush*."[122] On December 17, Carlyle tells Napier that he might have to "stick my own little Book in my pocket again, after all;"[123] and, on December 20, Carlyle sums up the situation to John: Charles Tilt and David Bogue "got sight of the Book; and as I from the first could have sworn he would, returned it with compliments. I have now given it to Dilke [Charles Wentworth Dilke of the *Athenaeum*] to look over and see what he advises: if he advise *nothing*, I see not that there is anything

[119] *Reminiscences*, 335-36.
[120] *Letters* 6:49.
[121] *Letters* 6:58.
[122] *Letters* 6:62–63.
[123] *Letters* 6:66.

further to be attempted here, but tie the Papers up again and take them home." Carlyle then adds, "I have also written to Tait," William Tait of Edinburgh who had published the *German Romance*. "We shall do what we can. [William] Glen read the *Ms* . 'with infinite satisfaction'; John Mill with fears that 'the world would take some time to see what meaning was in it': 'perhaps all Eternity,' I answered."[124] On December 21 the appraisal of the situation to Alexander remains the same: "There is still not the faintest outlook for *Teufelsdreck*, more especially till the Reform Bill get out of the way. . . ."[125]

It is clear then that during the month of December Carlyle did everything he could, without success, to find a publisher. He used every advantage, every friend, every influence—the result was always the same—rejection. At the outset of the new year, 1832, it was apparent that the publication of *Teufelsdreck* was a dead matter. Carlyle's frustration is recorded in his Journal in an entry on January 10: "*Dreck* unpublished, to all appearances unpublishable. One Tilt of Fleet-street (a triviality) 'glanced over it,' then 'regretted' &c. Dilke had no light to throw on the business, and I think will have none: the MS at this moment in the hands of Charles Buller. Glen, Mill and he have all read it; apparently, not without result: it was *intended* for such, therefore seems not wholly *verfehlt* [a failure]. As for the publication of it, I grow indifferent about the matter; indeed the whole concern is becoming unimportant to me. . . . We can wait,—forever."[126] His letter to John, also January 10, contains what now has become the usual news. The publishers are frightened; the young intellectuals are enthusiastic: "With *Teufelsdreck* I believe I can do nothing: I took it back from Dilke last Saturday, who could give me no light but a sort of dull London fog, or darkness visible . . . ; and now it lies in the hands of Charles Buller, who seemed anxious to see it. My chief comfort is in the effect it appears to produce on young *unbestimmt* [undecided] people like him: Glen was even asking for a *third* perusal of it."[127] To Alexander on January 14 he confides, "My Book, I think, *cannot be printed* at this time . . . ,"[128] a conclusion which is repeated to his mother and to John in letters begun on January 22, on the occasion of the death of his father.[129]

[124] *Letters* 6:70–71.
[125] *Letters* 6:74.
[126] *Two Note Books*, 233–34.
[127] *Letters* 6:87.
[128] *Letters* 6:91.
[129] *Letters* 6:96–97, 109.

MAKING *TEUFELSDRECK* TEUFELSDRÖCKH

The intervening months before the Carlyles finally left London on March 24 were especially eventful. Carlyle's father died on January 22; Goethe on March 22. There seemed to be no opportunity for the manuscript. Yet, in spite of the repeated shocks, the Carlyles remained remarkably cheerful. On July 17 the subject of the manuscript resurfaces in a letter to Johann Peter Eckermann: "I have some thoughts of taking it to Edinburgh this winter, and there printing it at my own charges."[130] Carlyle repeats this determination to John on July 31: "I have some thought that we shall see [ourselves] in Edinburgh this winter; printing of *Dreck* and what not." Carlyle then adds that he hopes to save £100, to "clear Edin*r*, and even print *Dreck*. Or *Dreck* can lie unprinted, till the means *be* lent me."[131] The thought that he might have to pay for the publication of *Teufelsdreck* now seems to be expected. In the meantime, much needed moral support continued to filter in from the young intellectuals of London, this time from Adolphus Bernays who, in a letter to Carlyle on August 17, asks: "[W]ho der Teufel is Teufelsdreck, & where you have aufgegabelt [seized upon] this odd book of his?"[132]

More than two years have now passed since Carlyle began the writing of what was first called "Thoughts on Clothes" and then *Teufelsdreck*. Many revisions and emendations were made along the way, but still no one wanted to publish it. And the Carlyles were not in a financial position to do so themselves. John Carlyle, himself not a person of means, offered in a letter on August 31 to lend the monies for subvention: "Of Teufelsdreck in its present shape I read enough to know that it cannot fall to the ground, but contains Truth which must tell sometime or other. . . . It treats the most important of subjects & deserves all consideration before any step is taken with it that is irretrievable."[133] Carlyle gracefully declined in a letter on October 17: "As to the printing of *Teufelsdreck*, it lies over for better insight; shall not be attempted, at all events, till I have money of *my own*, to pay the piper."[134] The acknowledgment here that the manuscript needs further revision is important to the textual history of *Sartor Resartus*, and in fact belies Carlyle's teasing claims made nearly

[130] *Letters* 6:189.
[131] *Letters* 5:195, 197.
[132] *Letters* 6:216n.
[133] *Letters* 6:268n.
[134] *Letters* 6:248.

forty years later that he did not revise once *Teufelsdreck* was completed. In his annotations to Friedrich Althaus's biographical sketch of him, Carlyle notes: "Not a letter of it altered; except in the *last* and *first* page, a word or two![135] As for the previous desire for anonymity and John's questioning of it, Carlyle responds: "As to the *anonymity* of *Teufelsk*, it is an *aesthetic* objection, not a prudential one. . . . Nay, could I be sure of the world's knowing the Book to be mine, it would answer me better. But we shall see the Book, after all, is little other than a *dud*; what I most want is to be rid of it."[136]

The manuscript is not mentioned in the letters now extant until January 27, 1833, when in a letter to Alexander, Carlyle relays the now-predictable complaint: "Literature all is as dull here as it could possibly be: my old Manuscript is lying by me quiet; there is no likelihood of its being printed this winter, for I have not the Cash just ready and it is a thing that can wait. I do not think of vexing my soul with *Booksellers* about it or any other thing again,—so long as I can help it."[137] That Carlyle was unable to place the manuscript is certain enough, but that he left it untouched in his drawer is questionable. Indeed, it is at this point, the beginning of 1833, that the manuscript might have been transformed into its present structure, save obvious later alterations he would make to bring it into shape for serialization in *Fraser's Magazine*. As previously noted, John's broad hint, in August of 1831, that the manuscript still needed revision, and Carlyle's acknowledgment of that point in October, suggest that *Teufelsdreck* was to go through at least one more transformation. Teufelsdreck the name was to be revised to "Teufelsdröckh"; *Teufelsdreck* the book was to become *Sartor Resartus*. On February 10 in a letter to John, Carlyle hints that he is going to make changes in the manuscript: "*Teufelsdreck* cannot see the light this summer, tho' I remain determined to spend a sixty pounds on him, when convenient: also, most probably, neither now nor at any other time will I treat again with Booksellers about such a matter. . . . Teufel*k* (whom by the by I mean to call Teufels*dröckh*) is worth little, yet also *not* worth nothing; I fancy there are from four to five hundred young men in the British Isles, whom he would teach many things; and sure enough, they, and not the *fire*, shall have him."[138] The positive tone of this letter suggests that Carlyle was willing to make what changes were necessary

---

[135] *Two Reminiscences,* 74.
[136] *Letters* 6:248.
[137] *Letters* 6:308.
[138] *Letters* 6:317.

in order to sell the manuscript. Indeed, it is likely that he has already been thinking about serial publication in *Fraser's Magazine*, whose Tory proclivities made it a suitable venue for Carlyle's radical subject. In the absence of a manuscript, however, the degree of alterations is hypothetical, yet all evidence clearly suggests that it was significant, including the possibility of the reordering and the addition of chapters to fit the serial format.

Whatever work Carlyle now had to do on the manuscript, it was given impetus by a new direction his fortunes took. He was already a well-known reviewer and essayist, and in fact was beginning to develop a following among the young, and often radical, intellectuals. He was now convinced that there was an audience for his work, as evidenced this time in a letter to his mother on February 13: "Henry Inglis has had my Book reading (the Manuscript one), and returns it with a most extatic exaggerated Letter; wherein this is comfortable, that he *has* seized the drift of the Speculation. . . . There are perhaps many such in this Island, whom it may profit; so that I can stand by the old resolution to print at my own risk, so soon as I have £60 to spare, but not till then."[139] Carlyle's faith in the manuscript, now under revision, was renewed; hope was restored. In a letter to Leigh Hunt, February 28, he quotes from the manuscript that the world is a *"Place of Hope."*[140] This mood is carried over in a letter to his mother on March 16: ". . . [T]he *Book* can hardly be printed this season, but one ought to be content. I really am rather content. . . ."[141]

There is a two-month silence before the progress of the manuscript is mentioned again. On May 17, Carlyle writes to John that he has made the decision to commit the manuscript to serialization: "My chief project for the summer is to cut Teufelsdreck into slips, and have it printed in Fraser's Magazine: I have not proposed it to him yet, and must go warily to work in that, for I have spoiled such things already by want of diplomacy. It will be worth almost £200 to me that way, and I shall get rid of it. . . ."[142] Carlyle has come to realize that the focus of the publishing world has changed dramatically. Increasingly, publishers were aiming at a mass audience. Carlyle's new awareness is reflected in his lengthy and revealing proposal to Fraser on May 27:

[139] *Letters* 6:325.
[140] *Letters* 6:337.
[141] *Letters* 6:344.
[142] *Letters* 6:388.

Most probably you recollect the Manuscript *Book* I had with me in London; and how during that Reform hurlyburly, which unluckily still continues and is like to continue, I failed to make any bargain about it. The Manuscript still lies in my drawer; and now after long deliberation I have determined to slit it up into stripes, and send it forth in the Periodical way; for which in any case it was perhaps better adapted. The pains I took with the composition of it, truly, were greater than even I might have thought necessary, had this been foreseen: but what then? Care of that sort is never altogether thrown away; far better too much than too little. I reckon that it will be easy for the Magazine Printer to save some thirty or forty complete Copies, as he prints it; these can be bound up and distributed among my Friends likely to profit thereby; and in the end of all we can *re*print it into a Book proper, if that seem good. Your Magazine is the first I think of for this object; and I must have got a distinct negative from you before I go any farther. Listen to me, then, and judge.

The Book is at present named "Thoughts on Clothes; or Life and Opinions of Herr D. Teufelsdröckh D. U. J."; but perhaps we might see right to alter the title a little; for the rest, some brief Introduction could fit it handsomely enough into its new destination: it is already divided into three "Books," and farther into very short "Chapters" capable in all ways of subdivision. Nay some tell me, what perhaps is true, that taking a few chapters at a time is really the profitablest way of reading it. There may be in all some Eight sheets of *Fraser*. It is put together in the fashion of a kind of Didactic Novel; but indeed properly *like* nothing yet extant. I used to characterize it briefly as a kind of "Satirical Extravaganza on Things in General"; it contains more of my opinions on Art, Politics, Religion, Heaven Earth and Air, than all the things I have yet written. The Creed promulgated on all these things, as you may judge, is *mine*, and firmly *believed*: for the rest, the main Actor in the business ("Editor of these sheets" as he often

calls himself) assumes a kind of Conservative (tho'
Antiquack) character; and would suit *Fraser* perhaps
better than any other Magazine. The ultimate result,
however, I need hardly premise, is a deep religious
speculative-radicalism (so I call it for want of a better
name), with which you are already well enough acquainted in me.

There are only five persons that have read this
Manuscript: of whom two have expressed themselves
(I mean convinced me that they *are*) considerably
interested and gratified; two quite *struck*, "overwhelmed with astonishment and new hope" (this is
the result I aimed at for souls worthy of hope); and
one in secret discontented and displeased. William
Fraser is a sixth reader, or rather half-reader; for I
think he had only got half-way or so; and I never
learned his opinion. With him, if you like, at this
stage of the business you can consult freely about it.
My conjecture is that *Teufelsdröckh*, whenever published, will astonish most that read it, be wholly
understood by very few; but to the astonishment of
some will add touches of (almost the deepest) spiritual interest, with others quite the opposite feeling.
I think I can practically prophecy that for some six or
eight months (for it must be published without interruption), it would be apt at least to *keep the eyes* of
the Public on you.

Such is all the description I can give you, in these
limits: now what say you to it? Let me hear as soon
as you can; for the time seems come to set these little
bits of Doctrine forth; and, as I said, till your *finale*
arrive, I can do nothing. Would you like to see the
Ms. yourself? It can come, and return, by Coach for
a few shillings, if you think of that: it will of course
want the Introduction, and various other "O. Y.'s"
that will perhaps be useful. I need not remind you
that about shewing it to any third party (as I have
learned by experience) there is a certain delicacy to
be observed: I shall like to hear from you first. Write
to me, therefore, with the same openness as I have

done to you; we shall then soon see how it lies between us.[143]

This letter is important not only as a statement on the past history
of the manuscript, but also serves as a prophecy of its future. Carlyle's
frank admission about the past problems with the manuscript, in part
already known to Fraser but here formally acknowledged, provides in
itself a realization that the subject could at best appeal to a narrow
audience. Carlyle's own readers were, in varying degrees, perplexed;
he could expect no more from any future audience. The fact that he
was willing to commit the manuscript to serialization, "to slit it up
into stripes," is in itself a register of Carlyle's own lack of certitude.
Still, he was willing, willing not only to cut it up but also to edit
further the already edited work. The whims of the fictional "Oliver
York," in fact William Maginn, the editor of *Fraser's Magazine*, must
be satisfied. Carlyle experienced a difficult lesson, one that was to
remain with him the rest of his career: the artist and his art were, in
the end, dependent upon a fickle, often crass publishing world.

Exactly how much editing and rearranging took place before the
manuscript was ready for *Fraser's Magazine* is, in the absence of the
manuscript, impossible to determine. What does seem likely, however, is that Carlyle made more than just incidental changes to satisfy
James Fraser. For example, the "brief Introduction" proposed might
in fact be the idiosyncratic opening chapters, which serve as a microcosm for the larger work. Further, the addition of references to *Fraser's
Magazine* and to Oliver Yorke in particular could not have been made
without transitional alterations to the original text. And, of course, it
goes without saying that when Carlyle "slit" the text he had to make,
at the very least, further changes in the original. It is little wonder
that his fictional editor is so familiar with the vagaries and nuances of
editing. Just what Fraser's and Maginn's roles were in this editing is,
regrettably, not known, for their responses to Carlyle's entreaties also
have not survived. However, it seems certain that by June a contract
was entered into, because in the June issue of *Fraser's Magazine*
appeared a pencil drawing of Carlyle by Daniel Maclise and a description of Carlyle by Maginn. The description is revealing, for it is a
parody of the subject, style, and language of *Sartor Resartus*: "Here
hast thou, O Reader! the-from-stone-printed effigies of Thomas Carlyle,

[143] *Letters* 6:395–97.

the thunderwordoversetter of Herr Johann Wolfgang von Goethe,"
whose translations (creations) are "so Teutonical in raiment, in the
structure of sentence, the modulation of phrase, and round-about,
hubble-bubble, rumfustianish (*hübble-bübblen, rümfustianischen*), roly-
poly growlery of style, so Germanically set forth, that it is with difficulty
we can recognize them to be translations at all." Maginn pretends to
be referring to Carlyle's earlier work, particularly his translations, but
it is clear from the context that he is imitating the soon-to-be-seri-
alized *Sartor Resartus*, which of course means that Maginn had pre-
viewed all or a significant portion of the manuscript. Yet after all the
false starts, anything that needed to be done now seemed incidental
to Carlyle. On June 25 he assures his mother the manuscript will
"require a very little sorting"[144] to bring it into shape for publication.

The actual editing of the manuscript was to take no more than
three months, for the first installment began in the November-De-
cember number of *Fraser's Magazine*. By July 18 Carlyle seems to
have completed most of the work, including the adoption of a new
title, as he writes to Mill: "*Teufelsdröckh*[,] under the whimsical title
of *Sartor Resartus*, is to come out piecemeal in *Fraser's Magazine*: I
am heartily glad to get my hands washed of the thing; which I now
look upon not without a tincture of abhorrence: nevertheless what is
written may stand written; I did it as I could."[145] Mill's qualified
response on September 5 provides a picture of the immediate reception *Sartor Resartus* was to receive as it began to appear in serialization: "About . . . that Teufelsdreck, by the way, it has frequently
occurred to me of late to ask of myself and also of you, whether that
mode of writing between sarcasm or irony and earnest, be really
deserving of so much honour as you give it by making use of it so
frequently. I do not say that it is not good: all modes of writing, in
the hands of a sincere man, are good, provided they are intelligible.
But are there many things, worth saying, and capable of being said
in that manner which cannot be as well or better said in a more direct
way? The same doubt has occasionally occurred to me respecting
much of your phraseology, which fails to bring home your meaning
to the comprehension of most readers so well as would perhaps be
done by commoner and more familiar phrases. . . ."[146]

Mill's pre-publication evaluation of the style of *Sartor Resartus*
was not meant to be unkind and was not taken so by Carlyle, who

[144] *Fraser's Magazine* 7 (1833):706; *Letters* 6:407.
[145] *Letters* 6:414–15.
[146] *Letters* 6:449n.

responded on September 24: "You are right about my style; your interrogatory is right. I think often of the matter myself; and *see* only that I cannot yet see. Irony is a sharp instrument; but ill to handle without cutting *yourself.*" Carlyle then identifies his problem as one of perceived audience: "I never know or can even guess what or who my audience is, or whether I have any audience: thus too naturally I adjust myself on the Devil-may-care principle."[147]

III. RECEPTION AND RESULTS

THE IMMEDIATE RECEPTION

Carlyle realized what Mill and others previously sensed in their readings of the manuscript: *Sartor Resartus* would face a skeptical readership. They were not wrong. Except for the young radical intelligentsia, the immediate audience found little of value in the rarefied life of Herr Teufelsdröckh in spite of the fictional relationship he shared with Don Quixote and Tristram Shandy, among others. Carlyle himself could only think he had failed. In his Journal for October 28, he writes: "*Teufelsdröckh* to begin appearing this month in *Fraser*. Poor Teufel*k* I have got a kind of pitying love for him, much otherwise as I feel his shortcomings, his worthlessness."[148] In a letter to Leigh Hunt the following day, Carlyle is very nearly glum: "A cynical Extravaganza of mine is indeed beginning to appear in *Fraser's Magazine*, and will continue there till you are all tired of it. . . ."[149] On November 18 he reports in passing to John that he is "correcting the second Fraction of *Teufelsd*k," which would be the proof for Book I, Chapters V–XI, to appear in the December number. It is of course likely that at this juncture Carlyle is making substantive changes in proof as he further adapts the work to serialization. Here again, however, this is only conjecture, founded upon Carlyle's known working habits, for the proof, like the manuscript seems not to have survived. Nevertheless, Carlyle's expectation remains negative, as he continues to John: "*Teufelsdröckh*, as was hinted, is coming out, in *Fraser*; going 'to pot' probably, yet not without leaving me some money, not without making me quit of him."[150] On December 24 in a letter to John, Carlyle pretends indifference: "*Teufel*k is coming

---

[147] *Letters* 6:448-49.
[148] *Letters* 7:29n.
[149] *Letters* 7:29.
[150] *Letters* 7:39, 41.

regularly out in *Fraser*, with what effect or non-effect I know not, consider not. . . ."[151]

By January of 1834, the reaction to the first two installments of *Sartor Resartus* was coming in to Fraser's office, and it was not favorable. On January 21 Carlyle reports to John: "James Fraser writes me that Teufelsdreck meets with the most unqualified disapproval; which is all extremely proper. His payment arrives, which is still more proper."[152] It is interesting to note that Carlyle is being paid as the installments appear. Since Carlyle received only £82.1.0 for the whole, he would be receiving approximately £10 per installment for the eight monthly installments, a remuneration that could not possibly cover what he already had invested in it. Yet a month later, on February 25, Carlyle expressed some satisfaction to John: "I corrected the *fourth* Paper of it lately; and found some pages of it *gelungen* [well done]; a great comfort to me."[153] The fourth installment would be Book II, Chapters V–VII, published in March. The correcting of proof continued, apparently without event, a fact reported to John on March 27: "I will send the *Teufelk* wo irgend moglich [whenever possible]. It goes on; and Fraser complains still that the world complains. The last two Papers [February & March, Book II, Chapters I–VII] I call goodish. Tandem sit finis [at last I am to finish]!"[154] On April 18, however, Carlyle's mood was to change. He complains to Hunt about the state of the manuscript and the reception of the published numbers: ". . . [A]s for the unhappy *Sartor* none can detest him more than my present Self; there are some ten pages rightly *fused* and harmonious; the rest is only *welded* or even agglomerated, and may be thrown to the swine."[155] Carlyle's irritation is understandable. His original article, "Thoughts on Clothes," was by choice turned into a book named *Teufelsdreck*, which then by commercial necessity was serialized, however improved, under the name *Sartor Resartus*. On April 28 he complains to Henry Inglis that the public is receiving the work with "fixed ba[yonets]. Little wonder."[156]

To complicate matters, the Carlyles decided to move from Craigenputtoch to London. Carlyle arrived in London on May 13, and Jane followed in June, and all this time the remaining proofs of

---

[151] *Letters* 7:61.
[152] *Letters* 7:81.
[153] *Letters* 7:108.
[154] *Letters* 7:125.
[155] *Letters* 7:133.
[156] *Letters* 7:139.

Sartor Resartus had to be seen to. Four days later in a letter to Jane, Carlyle says that immediately upon arriving in London he "corrected the Proofsheet of *Teufelk* (which I found at Dumfries), and left it at Fraser's (whom I did not see, then or since). . . ."[157] The proof in question is no doubt the sixth installment, Book III, Chapters I–V, published in June. During this trying period of house-hunting, the reception in Britain continued to be negative, as he points out in a letter to Jane on May 21: Fraser complains that "*Teufelk* beyond measure unpopular; an oldest subscriber came in and said, 'If there is any more of that d—d stuff, I will &c. . . .'"[158] In his annotations to Friedrich Althaus's biographical sketch of him, Carlyle recalls the scene in larger detail: "Fraser's Public liked the *Johnson* so much . . . that he was willing to accept *Sartor* in the slit condition; had it so (probably on cheaper terms), went on with it obstinately till done,— tho', from his Public, he had a sore time with it: 'What wretched unintelligible nonsense!' 'Sir, if you publish any more of that d——d [stuff], I shall be obliged to give up my Magazine!' and so forth, in the whole world (so far as could be learned) only two persons dissentient, 1° a certain man called *Emerson*, in Concord Massachusetts, and 2° a certain Irish Catholic Priest, Father O'Shea of Cork . . . writing to him, each for himself, 'So long as any thing by that man appears in your Magazine, punctually send it me.' So that Fraser conceived a certain terror, if also a certain respect, of my writings & me; and knew not what to do,—beyond standing by his bargain, with an effort."[159]

By July the long task of editing and correcting proof was over. Carlyle's relief at being rid of the experience and his contempt for those who displayed displeasure at his efforts are graphically stated in a letter to Inglis on July 8: "The *Teufel* Manuscript, be the Heavens thanked, is now all but finished: loud, earnest, universal has been the disapproval of it. *A la bonne heure* [Well and good]! The critical world of London, whereunto shall one liken it? To the *bug* world of the same city; blind, fetid, poisonous, ineradicable: a million individual bugs you scald and crack, but there in its foul glory bugdom flourishes and has flourished."[160] On July 22, Carlyle writes to John that his editorial journey is now at an end: ". . . [T]he last *Teufelsdröckh*

---

[157] *Letters* 7:150.
[158] *Letters* 7:175.
[159] *Two Reminiscences*, 74–75.
[160] *Letters* 7:239–40.

is in next No, and there I calculate we shall *stop* finally short."[161] Just what Carlyle means by "*stop* finally short" is not clear. It is entirely possible that Fraser has asked him to lengthen the manuscript to fit the requirements of serialization. Certainly Chapter X, "The Dandiacal Body," of the last number, which is inordinately long and somewhat chaotic, might be an example of Carlyle's attempt to lengthen the manuscript. In fact, it is possible that this chapter is from previously rejected material, here put in to satisfy Fraser.

By August 5, Carlyle was able to speak in the past tense about the publication of *Sartor Resartus*, this time in a letter to William Graham: "A singular rhapsody written long ago at Craigenputtoch has at length worked itself out piecemeal thro' *Fraser's Magazine*: I hope to send it you stitched together and legible some six weeks hence. . . ."[162] On the same day Carlyle writes to his mother: "My former Book, that came out thro' *Fraser*, is happily at last all printed within these last days: I hope to send you . . . a full Copy of it about the beginning of next month by the Dumfries Bookseller. You will have leisure to peruse it and consider it; and finding it very *queer*, may not find it altogether empty and false. It has met with next to no recognition that I hear of in these parts; a circumstance not to be surprised at, not to be wept over. On the other hand, my American Friend [Emerson] . . . sends me a week ago the most cheering Letter of thanks for it . . . , and bids me go on in God's name, for in remotest nooks, in distant ends of the Earth, men *are* listening to me and loving me."[163] After having read the first four numbers, Emerson wrote to Carlyle on May 14, praising him for "Sartor Resartus for whose light, thanks evermore."[164] The full copy Carlyle refers to in his letters to Graham and his mother is the privately printed copy—58 copies in all—that Fraser bound in wrappers from the magazine sheets after renumbering the pages and providing a title page. These copies were in addition to the £82.1.0 paid Carlyle. Carlyle was later to recall that "poor *Sartor* got passed through *Fraser*, and was done up from the *Fraser* types as a separate thing, perhaps about fifty copies being struck off,—I sent six copies to six Edinburgh Literary Friends; from not one of whom did I get the smallest whisper even of receipt. . . ."[165]

[161] *Letters* 7:245.
[162] *Letters* 7:255.
[163] *Letters* 7:258-59.
[164] *Correspondence of Emerson and Carlyle*, 98.
[165] *Reminiscences*, 395.

In the absence of support from Edinburgh, Carlyle turned to America
and his disciple Emerson. On August 12 he writes to Emerson expressing his unqualified debt for Emerson's support:

> You thank me for *Teufelsdröckh*: how much more
> ought I to thank you for your hearty, genuine tho'
> extravagant acknowledgement of it! Blessed is the
> voice that amid dispiritment stupidity and contradic-
> tion proclaims to us: *Euge* [well done]! Nothing was
> ever more ungenial than the soil that poor Teufels-
> dröckhish seedcorn has been thrown on here; none
> cries, Good speed to it; the sorriest nettle or hemlock
> seed . . . had been more welcome. For indeed our
> British periodical critics, and especially the public of
> Fraser's Magazine . . . exceed all speech; require not
> even contempt, only oblivion. Poor Teufelsdröckh!
> Creature of mischance, miscalculation, and thousand-
> fold obstruction! Here nevertheless he is, as you see;
> has struggled across the Stygian marshes, and now, as
> a stitched Pamphlet "for Friends," cannot be *burnt*,
> or lost—before his time. I send you one copy for
> your own behoof; three others you yourself can per-
> haps find fit readers for. . . . From the British side of
> the water, I have met simply *one* intelligent response
> [that of Father O'Shea].[166]

On August 18 Carlyle forwarded a private copy to Mill and enclosed another for Harriet Taylor without substantive comment. Ten
days later he writes to Alexander: "We have finished off *Teufelsdröckh*,
last month; he [Fraser] paid me for it honestly what he bargained for;
he made me up 50 [58] complete copies, most of which I have
dispersed far and wide. . . . The thing is not worthless; you will get
something out of it, in the winter time, and at all events, a remembrance of your Brother and his old Life (for it was written the last
summer we were together), which will be dear to you."[167] And, on
September 1, fully four years after he began the writing of *Sartor
Resartus*, he writes to ask his mother whether the family has received
their copies of the book, and in the letter he encloses Emerson's

<hr>

[166] *Letters* 7:264.
[167] *Letters* 7:281.

testimonial with the request that it not be circulated for that is "wretched vanity."[168]

As 1834 came to a close Carlyle had little time to reflect upon the publishing history of *Sartor Resartus*, for he was already fully at work on the manuscript of *The French Revolution*. Yet there were moments when his guarded vanity broke, when he wished for more for the work now buried in the pages of *Fraser's Magazine*. On October 28 he writes to John in Rome: ". . . I will only add that a *Teufelsdröckh* is on its way to Rome for you. . . . As for Teufelsdröckh I think he rather meets with approbation and recognition in the bound up shape: had the thing come out as a Book, it might perhaps have done something; yet, after all, so questionable a production is probably 'just as well' in its actual middle-state of published and unpublished; it cannot be *lost* now, by fire or accident; afflicts nobody, and is ready if ever wanted."[169] What Carlyle could not possibly have anticipated was that *Sartor Resartus* was already "wanted," not in Britain but in New England where it was quickly becoming the Bible of the new Transcendental Movement. In 1834, no less than five reviews of the newly published American edition of *The Life of Friedrich Schiller* (Boston, 1833) appeared in New England journals; all given impetus by the arrival in installments of *Sartor Resartus*. On March 12, 1835, James Fraser was asked to send "50 or 100 copies" to America, which of course he was unable to do.[170] On May 13, in a letter to Emerson, Carlyle expressed shock at the "astonishing reception of Teufelsdr[ö]ckh in your New England circle. . . . As for Fraser, however, the idea of a New Edition is frightful to him; or rather, ludicrous, unimaginable. Of him no man has inquired for a *Sartor*. . . ."[171] Carlyle's astonishment is partly because of Emerson's report that there was a movement underway to begin a journal to be titled *The Transcendentalist*, and further there was hope that Carlyle would come to America to edit it.[172] In October the influential *North American Review* published the first important review of *Sartor Resartus*, an appreciative commentary by A. H. Everett who declares the "little volume"

[168] *Letters* 7:285.
[169] *Letters* 7:325–26.
[170] *Letters* 8:117n.
[171] *Letters* 8:119.
[172] *Correspondence of Emerson and Carlyle*, 119, 125.

to be of "quaint and singular form," containing "a great deal of deep thought, sound principle, and fine writing." In a letter to his mother on December 24, Carlyle calls Everett's review "good natured, rather stupid," and in a Journal entry he calls it "very insignificant; say inane"[173] Carlyle clearly did not know how to handle such praise, even though he grudgingly admitted the "Yankees" are a "good sort of people." In spite of any uneasiness, Carlyle's position as the prophet of the "New Philosophy" was confirmed, and his name became synonymous with the palingenetic impulse spreading throughout America.

By 1836, the call had gone out in America to make *Sartor Resartus* readily available, for until this time it could only be read in imported copies of *Fraser's Magazine* or in the privately printed copies, four in all, sent by Carlyle to Emerson. With the sponsorship of Emerson, who provided one of his copies to be used as the printer's text, Charles Stearns Wheeler set out to edit, with a short preface by Emerson and with the assistance of Le Baron Russell, the first trade edition. In late May of 1836, Carlyle writes to Mill that he has received a copy of the first American edition, and in a Journal entry, June 1, he writes: "Edition of Teufelsdröckh, very prettily printed, from Boston. . . . How curious; almost pathetic!"[174] The first major review of this edition, by Nathaniel L. Frothingham, appeared in September in the *Christian Examiner*, and was wholly laudatory, even though it was forecasted that "it will not be read through by a great many readers, nor be liked by all its readers." It is "chiefly prized," says Frothingham, for its "philosophic, spiritual, humane cast of thought. . . . It soars away far beyond the theories of Utilitarian calculators. . . . It is spirit." In a letter to John on March 21, 1837, Carlyle says Frothingham's review "pleased me very much, tho' it would have been very vain to believe it all. It *was* here and there a kind of idealized image of me however, and had more true perception and appreciation than all the other critiques laudations and vituperations I had seen of myself."[175] The first American edition apparently sold out quickly, for it was soon determined that a second was needed. In 1837, a second edition was printed by the publisher Munroe. This edition also sold rapidly. On November 5, 1836, Carlyle writes to Emerson that he welcomes the "prospect of your *second* Teufelsd*h*:

[173] *North American Review* 41 (1835):454–82; *Letters* 8:278n.
[174] *Letters* 8:350n.
[175] *Christian Examiner* 21 (1836):74–84; *Letters* 9:175.

the *first* too is now in my possession. . . . It is a beautiful little Book; and a Preface to it such as no kindest friend could have improved."[176] On November 20 Carlyle reports to his mother that the first American edition is "altogether sold: poor *Teufelsdröckh!* Mill declares he is going to review it here."[177] On December 2, 1836, Carlyle acknowledges to John that he has received a "new copy of *Teufelk*," presumably another of the first edition. And, on January 28, 1837, he writes Mill: "As you take an interest in Teufelsdröckh, it will be good news to hear that they are printing a second edition of him in America;— of 1000, the first having only been 500. I even heard some whisper of an Edition coming out here by and by."[178] Regrettably, Mill did not carry out his plans to review *Sartor Resartus*, and the first British edition of 1838 hinted at here was more than a year away.

The popularity of *Sartor Resartus* in America cannot be overestimated. On February 13, 1837, Carlyle acknowledges to Emerson that he has heard from George Ripley that a "new edition of a thousand copies of Sartor is now in press; every copy (500) of the first edition being sold. . . . You can, probably, form but a faint conception, on your side of the water, of the earnestness with which a true voice is welcome here, by those who recognize it; the greater, as such voices are seldom heard among us. . . ."[179] When Carlyle actually saw the 1837 edition, he was disappointed with the number of errors in printing.[180] Nevertheless, an indication of the book's popularity is found in the effusive praise of the anonymous reviewer, perhaps William Gilmore Simms, of the *Southern Literary Journal*, who in the March issue declares the work "singular," an "extremely odd tissue of fiction, with which the author has seen fit to interweave his jewels of thought."[181]

However, in Great Britain, in spite of the efforts of Harriet Martineau, who twice imported copies from America, the "poor rag" or "poor orphan,"[182] as Carlyle called it, languished, even though it gained the attention of young intellectuals like Charles Dickens who artfully rewove its fabric into *Pickwick Papers* and *Oliver Twist*. The general opinion is perhaps best represented by the words of James Currie, "What's ta use on 't? naebody can tell what he

---

[176] *Letters* 9:84.
[177] *Letters* 9:86–87.
[178] *Letters* 9:130.
[179] *Letters* 9:138n.
[180] *Letters* 10:103.
[181] Simms, 1.
[182] *Letters* 9: 139.

would be at."[183] Carlyle held no illusions about its popularity in Britain, as he admits in a letter to John on January 12, 1835: "Thousand thanks for the good you get of *Teufel!* A few such voices are real *votes*, and outweigh all the babble or no-babble that is, was, or will be."[184] In a letter to Alexander on January 29, Carlyle expresses hope that it might be printed as a book in England to give it "another chance. I feel pret[ty] much inclined to believe that had it been published in that fashion at first, it might actually h[ave] *done*. Several persons do more than like it."[185] Not surprising, Carlyle's Burgher mother was among those who "never said anything" about *Sartor Resartus*.[186] On May 12 Carlyle writes to his mother that the "good Yankees seem smit with some strange fatuity about me; which will abate in good time. Fraser . . . has no hope that an Edition of the Book would sell here: so they [the Americans] must just provide *themselves* with copies, these worthy souls."[187] Carlyle's hope that *Sartor Resartus* might soon find a permanent place among the intellectuals of England was not buoyed when in early June he received through John a lengthy, and often critical, appraisal from John Sterling who was a favorite of the Carlyles. Carlyle personally held Sterling's opinions in the highest esteem, so much so that he printed the letter, with minor excisions, in his *Life of John Sterling* (1851). Carlyle introduces the letter by saying that it "much entertained me, in various ways. It turns on a poor Book of mine, called *Sartor Resartus*; which was not then even a Book, but was still hanging desolately under bibliopolic difficulties, now in its fourth or fifth year, on the wrong side of the river, as a mere aggregate of Magazine Articles; having at last been slit into that form, and lately completed *so*, and put together into legibility."

Sterling's objections are predictably conservative: he finds the style is too "Rhapsodico-Reflective"; the language "overly barbarous"; the choice of diction and the inverted syntax somewhat "grotesque"; the allusions "bewildering"; and, most important, the choice of a German professor, who apparently does not believe in God, as the hero not "judicious." Yet he appreciates fully the "genius and moral energy" of the book. Cautiously negative and always humble, Sterling's letter, May 29, remains the foremost contemporary analysis of *Sartor*

---

[183] *Letters* 8:6n.
[184] *Letters* 8, 12.
[185] *Letters* 8:62.
[186] *Letters* 8:82.
[187] *Letters* 8:116–17.

Resartus. Carlyle's response, June 4, is marked by compassion and discretion, a tone set in a Journal entry on June 1: "Letter from John Sterling criticising *Teufelk*; the spirit of it, the language of it: some truth in the censure; to which I have replied in friendly temper." However, a follow-up letter from Sterling apparently displeased Carlyle, as he continues in his Journal: "*Another* letter from him yesterday in enforcement of his views (on style): *das wirds zu lang*: I made it into matches."[188]

Jane Carlyle was equally kind, writing to Sterling herself on June 4: "Far from being offended by your des[s]ertation on the Sartor I think it is the best that has been said or sung of him. Even where your criticism does not quite fall in with my humble views, I still love the spirit of the critic."[189] Carlyle was less charitable to Sterling in a letter to John on June 15: "Let me mention only that Sterling has sent me . . . a vituperative expostulatory criticism on Teufelk of *thirteen pages*; that the Americans have sent an order for '50 or a hundred copies' of the same poor Book, and could only get three (and threaten to reprint it); finally that these surprising Yankees invite me in really pressing terms to come over to them this very winter, and 'lecture' on *any* subject, with assurance of success!"[190]

The difference in response to *Sartor Resartus* in America and Britain was dramatic. Sterling's letter in many ways represents the misgivings of the British audience which, for the most part, was not receptive to Carlyle's Germanisms in spite of their British context. On the other hand, in America the commitment to Carlyle's transcendental philosophy was overwhelmingly positive. The contrast is no more markedly stated than in the letter of George Ripley, an Unitarian minister of Boston, who on June 1 wrote to Carlyle in elegiac terms, hailing the "deep wisdom" and "mystic sayings" of *Sartor Resartus.* Carlyle was, to Ripley, "a gifted Teacher of Humanity."[191] Ripley's letter is indicative of a growing following among American readers, a circumstance most certainly given impetus by Emerson's unfailing devotion to Carlyle. On August 10 in a letter to John, Carlyle says that Ripley's devotional is "full of the most enthusiastic estimation; really a good feeling ill-expressed, struggling for expression: . . . his Letter gave me no comfort at the time, it seemed so overdone; but it does now

[188] *Life of John Sterling* 108–14; *Letters* 8:134n.
[189] *Letters* 8:139.
[190] *Letters* 8:149.
[191] *Letters* 8:185–87n.

occasionally some, when I think of it."[192] On September 10 he wrote
to his mother that the Ripley letter made him "blush."[193] In spite of
Emerson's many assurances, Carlyle was understandably unsettled by
the reaction to him in America: how was it that his *Sartor Resartus*
was virtually ignored at home, but enjoyed such popularity on a
distant continent, a place known only to him as "Yankeeland"?

Meanwhile, Harriet Martineau, the social reformer and writer, on
her own initiative set out to make *Sartor Resartus* popular in London
circles. Carlyle was surprised, and grateful. On July 17, 1837, Jane
writes to Carlyle: "I expect we shall have Sartor running the round
of the journals presently: for Harriet Martineau has absolutely set up
a thriving trade on that sole singular item! She has imported . . . a
houseful of copies, which she is selling off at fifty per cent! the profits
(I understand) being considered as pertaining to you."[194] By December Carlyle's growing reputation, built largely on the enormous success of *The French Revolution*, led James Fraser to propose *Sartor
Resartus* be published as a book in Britain. In a letter to John on
December 12, Carlyle writes, somewhat incredulously: "But one of
the most conclusive literary signs I have met with for years occurred
last week: James Fraser sent for me to propose printing *Teufelk.* . . .
Not so long ago . . . He shrieked literally at the very hint of it. And
now he is willing, nay eager; there even seemed to lie *money* in him,
if I could bring it out."[195]

Fraser's belief in the market value of Carlyle's books was, however,
short lived. By April of 1838, Fraser was attempting to extricate
himself from the offer to publish *Sartor Resartus*. He was concerned
that *The French Revolution* was not selling as it should: of the 1000
copies printed of Carlyle's history, 250 were unsold. On April 12
Carlyle writes to John: ". . . I saw Fraser lately, and frightened him
much; without result. He had been behaving in a knavish way about
that *Teufelsk*; clearly knavish."[196] Carlyle's confidence in Fraser was
delivered yet another blow when he learned that Fraser, without his
permission, had been selling copies of *Sartor Resartus*, presumably
extra copies he had made when he ran off the fifty-eight copies for

[192] *Letters* 8:185.
[193] *Letters* 8:203.
[194] *Letters* 9:247.
[195] *Letters* 9:365.
[196] *Letters* 10:64.

Carlyle for private distribution. In a letter to William Graham on May 10, Carlyle is blunt: "Nay the scamp has found a set of *Teufelsdröckhs* (you know the pamphlet, worth about six-pence) which lay rotting in his cellar as 'd——d stuff'; and sells them directly for five shillings each!" Any consideration for the royalties owed Carlyle did not seem to concern Fraser. The number of copies Fraser sold this way cannot be determined, but were apparently enough to raise Carlyle's ire, as he continues to Graham: "I have checked the five-shillings 'Teufel' however, and will do another thing or two in regard to that matter. Hang it!"[197]

What Carlyle did was to seek other publishers in London for *Sartor Resartus*. When Fraser learned what Carlyle was doing, he immediately offered again to publish the work, this time at "half-profits." Carlyle was justifiably irritated and decided, partly out of spite, to turn elsewhere. In a letter to his mother on June 12, he outlines his future plans: ". . . Fraser I say *drew up* all of a sudden, and was quite determined that *he* would go either on the 'half-profits' system or not at all. Whereupon I said to myself, 'Not thou, O Fraser, not thou but another; *any* other is preferable to thee!' So I walked over, and made a half-profits bargain with 'Saunders and Otley,' a Bookselling house of far better character than Fraser's. . . . *Teufelsdröckh* accordingly is actually at press; and I can hope to give my Mother an English copy of him in regular shape before long. Poor fellow, he has had a sore struggle to get out here, some seven years or more. . . . Good luck to him we will say;—tho' perhaps he is no great shakes after all, poor fellow!"[198] Saunders and Otley published 500 copies, including for the first time the "Testimonies of Authors." They required a subscription list of 300 copies, which Harriet Martineau among others helped to collect. Saunders and Otley did not, however, publish the essays, which were finally published by Fraser in 1839, from the sheets of the first American edition of James Munroe. The proof sheets for *Sartor Resartus* were quick in coming, evidenced by Carlyle's letter of June 13 to Alexander: ". . . [T]he first Proof of *Teufelsdröckh* has actually come to hand and been corrected: it will make a nice enough Book, which I hope to shew you soon. 'I am glad he is going to get published, poor beast,' said Jane. And so am I too, 'poor beast': he has had a sore fight for it. . . . And now he is actually getting up; and will breathe, and live as long as is appointed him; a day, or a year and day, that is of no

---

[197] *Letters* 10:74.
[198] *Letters* 10:96.

moment; simply *as long as it is given him*, which is just the *right* longness."[199]

Carlyle was also pleased with what he perceived as the financial benefit of having *Sartor Resartus* published in England, even though as he writes to Emerson on June 15 he computes the half-profits plan "generally to mean equal partition of the oyster-*shells*, and a net result of *zero*. But the thing will be economically useful to me otherwise. . . ."[200] On July 6 Carlyle reports the progress of printing to his sister Jean Carlyle Aitken: "*Teufelsdröckh* will be printed out I expect in about a week; . . ."[201] but the next day he complains to Sterling, "The Printer lingers sadly with the last leaves of *Teufelsdröckh*."[202] On July 14 he writes to John: "I corrected the proofsheets of *Teufelsdröckh*. . . . [It] is to be published *today* (I suppose); Saunders & Otley are my men; Fraser cut a little too close, last time we talked, so I am off with him." Carlyle then laments that "*Teufelk* was little other than a weariness to me," and then claims, "There is no change in *Teufk* from the genuine Fraser Copy; a few pages called 'Testimonies of Authors' stand by way of Preface, beginning with John Murray and his *Taster* . . . , and ending with Emerson's Preface to the Yankee edition; it gives covertly a history of the poor Manuscript & publication, and embraces the wisest and stupidest, the worst and best, that can be said of it."[203] The actual date of publication was apparently delayed, for on July 18 Carlyle writes to John, "*Teufelsk* is not out yet to my knowledge. . . ."[204] On July 26, however, Carlyle writes to his mother that *Sartor Resartus* has finally been published: ". . . *Teufelsdröckh* [is] fairly at last in the shape of a Book! They have got it out finally, after long delays. . . . It is not a pretty volume, not at all finely done off; but on the whole I care next to nothing at all about it, or about what comes of it. . . . The present edition is small; the sale will not be great."[205]

Carlyle's pretense that the publication of *Sartor Resartus* means little to him is just that—pretense. He fought seven years to have it published, and without doubt the Saunders & Otley volume—published handsomely in boards like *The French Revolution*—was a tri-

---

[199] *Letters* 10:101.
[200] *Letters* 10:104.
[201] *Letters* 10:113.
[202] *Letters* 10:116.
[203] *Letters* 10:121-22.
[204] *Letters* 10:126.
[205] *Letters* 10:131.

umph for him. Nevertheless, in characteristic fashion he continued to distance himself from the publication, telling John on July 27 that "nothing can be more indifferent than I am to the fate of the whole matter. . . . [T]he volume is one of the shabbiest as to getting up,— printed by Clowes in the cheap fashion my Conduit St*t* men are used to."[206] Jane felt otherwise, and in a letter to Carlyle on September 9 she writes that the Saunders & Otley *Sartor Resartus* is "quite beautiful."[207] Whatever aesthetic judgments might be made about the physical appearance of the work, the problem of availability surfaced immediately. Since 300 of the 500 copies were distributed by subscription, this left only 200 available to booksellers throughout Great Britain. On September 15 Carlyle complains to Jane that there seems to be "no copy" available in Edinburgh since the local seller "had never heard of it," a fact which brought Carlyle to a defense of his work: "Depend on it, . . . all these vague things they tell thee about Sartor, are mere vague blarney;—and think further that we will not care a strand whether they are or not. No; a certain fair Critic long ago among the peatbogs [Jane at Craigenputtoch] declared Sartor to be a 'work of genius'; and such it is and shall continue tho' no copy of it should sell these hundred years."[208]

The reviews of the 1838 edition were not as negative as Carlyle seemed to expect. The *Metropolitan Magazine* declared Carlyle to be "one of the deepest thinking and most original minded writers of the present day," and then defended the "odd and crabbed style" of *Sartor Resartus* "because we are wearied to death with the trim and measured sentences of the mass of modern writers." The *Monthly Review*, though less enthusiastic about the style, was unqualified in its praise of the aesthetics of the book: "In a word the work forms a most curious romance, partly biographical, but chiefly sentimental and philosophical,—beautiful fancies and valuable truths being, in the quaintest manner possible, yet often happily and forcibly, brought out." The reviewer concludes the lengthy review by calling *Sartor Resartus* an "extraordinary book, so full of a new system built upon a new subject of philosophy." *Tait's Edinburgh Magazine* was more circumspect, suggesting that what seems to be a translation might in fact be what the "English call a *hoax*, and the Yankee a *hum*." However, the reviewer retreats to the authority of the *North American*

---

[206] *Letters* 10:135.
[207] *Letters* 10:171.
[208] *Letters* 10:178-79.

Review, which has discovered that "Professor Teufelsdröckh is about as real a personage as Tristram Shandy's father, Captain Gulliver, or Don Quixote," and then concludes, "We can, no more than the English translator, promise . . . permanent popularity in England; but this we can promise: those who can *taste* him, will not easily forget his race." The *Edinburgh Review*, the influential organ of Francis Jeffrey, saw fit only to announce its publication; while *The Globe* newspaper gave it this legitimacy: "Neither Mr. Carlyle's Lectures, or any other of his writings, as far as we know, have attracted half the notice and admiration which has attended this production." Through it all the Americans remained faithful, as evidenced by J. J. J. [Isaac Jewett] of the Columbus, Ohio, *The Hesperian*, who chastises the bookseller in London who thought Carlyle "'mad,'" and reminds the British that they have "failed to properly appreciate one of the most original minds, that has yet developed itself into the nineteenth century." Of *Sartor Resartus* Jewett claims:

> The tendency of the work is to elevate the spiritual into its rightful throne, above the material; to render cant, and shams, and all untruths detestable; to teach a reliance on self, not on outward circumstances, for the means of earthly well-being; to awaken thought on themes most vital to the human interest; and to inspire them with solemnity, in presence of the mysterious world wherein they live. It abounds in humour, pathos, generous philanthropy, and purest moral sentiment. It is not written to gratify the wants of the age, but, so far as it can, to spiritualize those wants. Its designs are magnanimous, elevated, Christian: to their accomplishment are brought a strength of intellect, a boundlessness of illustration, a brilliancy of fancy, and an intense earnestness of endeavor, which through no other work in the English language have, of late years, been manifested. (20)

Although it is unlikely that Carlyle ever read this testimonial by Jewett, he could not possibly have wished for more for his "poor little Book."[209]

[209]See *Metropolitan Magazine* 23 (September, 1838): 1–5; *Monthly Review* 147 (September 1838): 54–66; *Tait's Edinburgh Magazine* 5 (September 1838): 611–12; [Alexander H. Everett], "Thomas Carlyle." *North Ameri-*

From this point in 1838 until the publication of the second edition in 1841, there is little mention of *Sartor Resartus* in Carlyle's letters or in the journals and newspapers of the day. Carlyle was, however, not without readers. *The French Revolution* continued to be popular and went into a second edition of 1500 copies, published by James Fraser in 1839. *Chartism*, the prophetic warning to the leaders of British domestic politics, drew considerable attention upon its publication in December of 1839, so much so that a second issue of 1000 copies was published in April of 1840. Fraser also issued an edition of 260 copies of the *Critical and Miscellaneous Essays*, the sheets from the very popular American edition published by James Munroe in 1838–1839. Then, there were the lectures delivered in May of 1840, which were published in an edition of 1000 copies under the title *On Heroes, Hero-Worship, & The Heroic In History* in June of 1841. In fact, it was the publication of the lectures which gave impetus to the second English edition of *Sartor Resartus*. On January 26 Carlyle writes to John: "In the course of last week I bargained with Fraser for my Lecture-Book. £75 the dog would give no more; but he also gives a £75 for a thousand *Sartors*, the edition of that being run out too: so we go on printing *both*, with all imaginable velocity. . . ."[210] In a letter to his mother on January 26, Carlyle expresses amazement that he was able to get anything for *Sartor Resartus*: "I did not calculate on getting anything at *present* for *Teufelsdröckh*. . . . Poor Teufelsdröckh, it seems very curious that money should lie even in him! They trampled him into the gutter at his first appearance; but he rises up again, finds money bid for him."[211]

The printing of the second edition was not without its trials. On February 5 he reports to John that he has been having troubles with

---

can *Review* 41 (October 1835): 454–82; *Edinburgh Review* 68 (October 1838): 266; *The Globe* September 14, 1838, quoted in the *Letters* 10:184; *Hesperian* 2 (November 1838): 5–20. The first English edition was reviewed one year later by John Sterling, "Carlyle's Works." *London and Westminster Review* 33 (October 1839): 52–59, who praises *Sartor Resartus* with much the same qualifications cited in his previously quoted letter to Carlyle, and then concludes by comparing Carlyle unfavorably to his mentor Goethe: Carlyle is like "the hot spring of Iceland, boiling among snows and blasted rocks," and Goethe like "a sunny river flowing from distant hills." Sterling seemed unable to forgive the radical, often contentious, spirit of *Sartor Resartus*. It is interesting to note that John Stuart Mill, as editor, appended a disclaimer at the end of Sterling's review.
[210] *Letters* 13:24.
[211] *Letters* 13:28.

Saunders & Otley, who seem to think they have the rights to the second edition, but that the printing for Fraser "goes on, and with great rapidity. Him I print according to the printed copy [1838 edition], and correct only with pencil, a *comma* or so in the page."[212] On February 6 Carlyle reports to his mother: "My Proofsheets keep me in a perpetual whirl of swift occupation. Two Books going on at once, and the Printers using all speed! But already we are almost as good as half done. By the end of the month I expect we shall have it entirely off our hands."[213] On February 12 Carlyle writes to Henrietta Maria Stanley that he is "up to the throat in Proofsheets."[214] Yet on February 15 Carlyle waxes poetic to Geraldine Jewsbury: "The other Book is your old friend *Sartor*, which they are reprinting. It is strange, and other than joyful for the most part, to look back upon your *Self* of ten years ago! Good part of this Book I find to be true; but it all lies at a distance from one's *Here*,—so visible, so inaccessible, in the 'transparent prison' of the Past."[215] On February 18 he tells his mother that he is "kept in a perpetual *Kippitch* [confusion] with the Printers at present. But they are getting on very swiftly and well; both the Books are *two-thirds* done. . . ."[216] And, on March 2 he is able to report to John Sterling: "*Sartor* and the Hero-*Lectures* are both printed, and away from me. With great pleasure I bequeath them both to the Prince of the Power of the Air [Satan]. . . ."[217] However, on March 7 he writes to his brother James that *Sartor Resartus* will probably "come out this very day."[218] The book was actually published on March 9, as Carlyle writes to John: "The Hero-book is not an ugly little volume: *Teufelk* is still better."[219] On March 10 Carlyle complains to his mother that Fraser is stingy with the author's copies: "Fraser the dog allows me only 12. . . . You have all copies of *Sartor*, have you not? This is a much prettier one; but the same otherwise."[220]

However physically attractive the second edition of *Sartor Resartus* might have been, that quality did not affect the reviews of it. Except for brief trade publication notices, it was ignored by the periodical

---

[212] *Letters* 13:30.
[213] *Letters* 13:32.
[214] *Letters* 13:33.
[215] *Letters* 13:35.
[216] *Letters* 13:38.
[217] *Letters* 13:48.
[218] *Letters* 13:51.
[219] *Letters* 13:54.
[220] *Letters* 13:58.

press. Instead immediate attention was given to the controversial *Heroes and Hero-Worship*. That is not to say that *Sartor Resartus* did not sell, for it did; but it did not have the freshness of the lectures, and hence its sales were moderate. A contributing problem was the house of Fraser itself, which was experiencing financial difficulties, and finally was sold in 1842 to the firm of George Nickisson which in turn went out of business in 1847. Sensing the demise of Fraser and Nickisson, Carlyle signed on with Chapman and Hall for *Past and Present* in 1843, and remained with that firm throughout the rest of his life. *Sartor Resartus* faded from memory as the task of editing *Oliver Cromwell's Letters and Speeches*, published in 1845, became a priority. In the meantime, *Sartor Resartus* continued to enjoy significant support in America. James Munroe issued a third edition in 1840. In 1844, it was republished by the New York publisher, Saxton & Miles; and then reissued in this format by Munroe in 1846 and 1856, and again in 1866, by Munroe's successor James Miller. The American market was so lucrative that in 1846, Carlyle through Emerson authorized Wiley and Putnam of New York to publish an edition of *Sartor Resartus* containing Carlyle's imprimatur. Wiley reissued the book in 1847, and in 1848 Harper and Brothers bought the Wiley plates and published in one volume *Sartor Resartus, Chartism,* and *Past and Present*. Harper reissued this edition ten times during Carlyle's lifetime, which in itself attests to his enduring popularity America.

The third English edition was published with little fanfare by Chapman and Hall in 1849 (actually December 9, 1848), and went out of print with even less notice. Carlyle was most concerned with the new edition of *Oliver Cromwell's Letters and Speeches*, and apparently did little with *Sartor Resartus*, although it is clear that he did provide Chapman and Hall with a corrected copy. In 1855, the first German edition was published by Otto Wigand of Leipzig, translated with an introduction by A. Kretzschmar. The fourth English edition, part of the *Uniform Edition* of the first Collected Works by Chapman and Hall, was published in 1858. This edition is noteworthy because it was edited by Carlyle's friends Henry Larkin and Vernon Lushington, who added the "Chapter Summaries" at the beginning of each chapter and the indexes, as well as reading proof. Carlyle, who was overwhelmed at the time with the writing of *Frederick the Great*, did not play a significant role in this edition, although it is clear that he authorized the work.

In 1869, the *Library Edition* was published by Chapman and Hall. Carlyle exercised some control over this edition, particularly with re-

gard to format and appearance. He was also annoyed by the suggestion
that the capitalization in *Sartor Resartus* be regularized. In a letter to
the printer Charles Robson, May 11, 1868, he writes, "That *abolition*
of Capitals . . . will never do; abolition quasi-total, which in many
places considerably obscures the sense (or comprehensibility in reading): much better let the thing stand as it is than *so*.—I cannot myself
undertake to read the Book with an eye to Capitals; tho' I have tried
passages of it;—you shall have a *fresh* Copy, marked by me here &
there."[221] Carlyle was also intent on restoring the "Testimonies of
Authors," as originally published in the 1838 edition. In a letter, June
30, 1868, to Jean Carlyle Aitken, he asks if anyone in the family has
a copy of this "Preface . . . satirically called '*Testimonies of Authors*.'"[222]
On January 11, 1869, Carlyle writes to his brother John that Chapman
and Hall will publish *Sartor Resartus* on "Friday 15th," and that Robson
is already printing volumes 7–8: "sent me *8* sheets Saturday last, which
is as much as I want weekly."[223] From these letters it is clear that
Carlyle took an active interest in the Library Edition and in the text of
Sartor Resartus in particular. To this expensive edition, which sold
more than 3500 copies, he also added the so-called "Author's Note"
on the genesis of the text:

> This questionable little Book was undoubtedly writ-
> ten among the mountain solitudes, in 1831; but,
> owing to impediments natural and accidental, could
> not, for seven years more, appear as a Volume in
> England;—and had at last to clip itself in pieces, and
> be content to struggle out, bit by bit, in some cou-
> rageous *Magazine* that offered. Whereby now, to
> certain idly curious readers, and even to myself till I
> make study, the insignificant but at last irritating
> question, What its real history and chronology are,
> is, if not insoluble, considerably involved in haze. To
> the first English Edition, 1838, which an American,
> or two Americans had now opened the way for, there
> was slightingly prefixed, under the title '*Testimonies
> of Authors*,' some straggle of real documents, which,
> now that I find it again, sets the matter into clear

[221]MS Pierpont Morgan Library.
[222]MS National Library of Scotland.
[223]MS National Library of Scotland.

light and sequence;—and shall here, for removal of idle stumbling-blocks and nugatory guessings from the path of every reader, be reprinted as it stood.[224]

In 1871, *Sartor Resartus* was published as the lead volume, as it had been in the Library Edition, of the People's Edition of the Collected Works. Carlyle had little to do with this edition, even though he did make a few substantive changes. He was by this time a venerated author, and the sales figures for *Sartor Resartus* reflect his popularity. By July of 1871, for example, 30,000 copies of the People's Edition had been sold; and by 1872, 35,000 copies. By 1881, the year of Carlyle's death, Chapman and Hall claimed that in excess of 69,000 copies were in print. With the publication of the People's Edition and its numerous reissues in Great Britain and in America, the formal printing history of *Sartor Resartus*, in Carlyle's lifetime, comes to a close. It can now be safely said that it was one of the largest, if not *the* largest, selling works in Carlyle's canon, a fitting tribute to a Romantic discourse which, to paraphrase from Psalms, was once rejected by the London publishers only later to become a cornerstone of Victorian philosophy.

[224] *Author's Note of 1868.* Library Edition.

NOTE ON THE TEXT

THE text of *Sartor Resartus* that we present in this volume is a critical
or reconstructed text. In general, it follows the readings of the work's
first publication and earliest extant version, the 1833–34 serialization
in *Fraser's Magazine*, which was of course typeset from Carlyle's
handwritten manuscript, now lost.[1] However, we have emended that
text in many places to incorporate revisions found in later versions,
where we have reason to believe that such revisions were ordered or
intended by the author.[2] It is incumbent on us to offer an account of
this procedure and to share with both scholars and general readers
the evidence and the reasoning on which it is based. The best way
both to describe the evidence we have collected and to explain the
use we have made of it is to present a brief narrative history of the
vicissitudes of the text following its first publication.

Some of the evidence for that history is external to the various
versions of the text itself (e.g., Carlyle's correspondence and other
relevant biographical data), but the principal source of evidence for
the history of the text is the various extant versions of the work. To
assemble this evidence, we collated the *Fraser's Magazine* text of
1833–34 against the eight subsequent versions of the work published during Carlyle's lifetime with his at least nominal participation, as well as against the remarkable surviving marked proofs for
the 1841 edition.[3] The complete record of variants found in the

---

[1] See Introduction, pp. liii–lxxv above.

[2] The complete list of Emendations of the Copy-Text, i.e., readings where
the present text differs from that of the *Fraser's* serialization, is found in the
Textual Apparatus, pp. 489–501 below.

[3] Five copies of the *Fraser's Magazine* serial version were compared on a
Hinman Collator to establish a baseline text (Copy A: Newberry Library;
Copy B: Illinois State University Library; Copies C and D: Tarr Carlyle
Collection, University of South Carolina Library; Copy E: Strouse Carlyle
Collection, University of California, Santa Cruz Library). No hidden printings were found. The editions we collated against this baseline text include
the privately printed reprint of 1834 (Tarr A5.1, Tarr Carlyle Collection),
the first British trade edition of 1838 (Tarr A5.4, Tarr Carlyle Collection),
the British "Second Edition" of 1841 (Tarr A5.6, Tarr Carlyle Collection),
the authorized American edition of 1846 (Tarr A5.8.a, Tarr Carlyle Collection), the British "Third Edition" of 1849 (Tarr A5.9, Tarr Carlyle Collection), the Uniform Edition of 1858 (Tarr D2, Mills College), the Library
Edition of 1869 (Tarr D5, Oberlin College), and the People's Edition of
1871 (Tarr D9, Tarr Carlyle Collection). We also collated the first American trade edition of 1836 (Tarr A5.2, Tarr Carlyle Collection), although,

versions we judged to be relevant to Carlyle's development of the text is given in the Historical Collation, pp. 541–605 below.

To summarize the results of that collation, we found that the British publications form a linear stemma in which each subsequent version was based on the immediately previous version and was in turn the basis for the immediately succeeding version. (We will explain the relation to this stemma of the 1836 and 1846 American editions, which we also collated, at the appropriate points in our narrative.) Each subsequent version contains many textual variants from its predecessor, and most of these new readings in each version were followed in all later editions.

These variants can be seen as falling into the following categories: (*a*) Every authorized re-publication after the 1833–34, except the last lifetime edition in 1871, contains new readings that by their nature can be explained only as the result of revisions made, or at least authorized, by Carlyle himself. (*b*) Every published version, including the initial serialization, contains a few obvious typographical errors, inadvertent failures of the typesetters to reproduce their copy accurately. Most such errors, but not all, were detected and corrected in the next succeeding edition, that is, the next time the work was set in type. (*c*) A large intermediate class of variants in every new edition—including individually minor but cumulatively significant alterations in such matters as spelling, capitalization, and punctuation—cannot be assigned with any degree of confidence either to Carlyle's revision or to typesetter's error. And for many such variants, there is a third available explanation: that someone at the printing house—either the typesetter or the in-house proofreader—may have made the change deliberately and without consulting the author. Printers apparently considered themselves authorized to correct, to modernize, or simply to improve the "mechanical" aspects of the text, such as spelling, capitalization, and punctuation, according to their best understanding of the then-current rules of "style," perhaps as enunciated in a house printer's manual.[4]

---

as the collation proved, it does not contain authorial variants nor does it figure in the stemma of lifetime authorial editions. For complete bibliographic descriptions of these various editions, see Tarr, *Bibliography*, 35–48, 447–51.

[4] A number of such manuals from nineteenth-century London printing houses survive, but not from any of the printers with whom Carlyle worked. See Philip A. Brown, *London Publishers and Printers c. 1800–1870* (London: British Library, 1982).

To those familiar with the procedures of modern publishing, where a professional copy-editor is generally interposed between author and printer and where typesetters are constrained to follow every detail of the manuscript as prepared by the copy-editor, it may be surprising to learn that the case was otherwise in the nineteenth century and before. Professional copy-editors did not then exist; typesetters worked from handwritten manuscripts or from a previous edition revised, if at all, by the author's marks in it. Such copy was bound to contain errors of various kinds (and standards of correctness change over time). Typesetters were expected to correct such "errors" as they came to them. Printers considered it part of their job to present an author's words in the most correct, up-to-date spelling, punctuation, and typographical style. (It is assumed that printers never deliberately altered the actual *wording* of the author's text.) Printing was a craft, but, because printers had to be highly literate to perform this editorial function, it aspired to recognition as a learned profession. Thus the printer functioned somewhat as an editor does today, except that printers who were responsible for editing "on the fly" as they set type would have felt entitled to make silent emendations on their own authority, rather than interrupting their work to send queries to the author, as a modern editor might feel obliged to do in doubtful cases. The problem for the historical editor is further complicated when authors corrected proof themselves, as Carlyle did for at least the first three London printings of *Sartor Resartus*. In reading proofs, all aspects of the text must be attended to, since the object is to find and to correct errors of any kind in the new typesetting, and we know from the surviving 1841 proofs that as a proofreader Carlyle was capable of concerning himself with the smallest textual details.

As literary historians, we are primarily interested in what our author wrote, and only secondarily in what his readers read. It is thus our unavoidable task to disentangle, as far as possible, the various contributions of author and printer to the published text. But often the situation presented to the editor by a variant in one of Carlyle's published texts (other than the 1841 *Sartor Resartus*) is that while it is clear enough that someone made the change deliberately, and often clear enough why the change was thought an improvement, it is impossible to say who did it, author or printer. (Examples are given in the discussions of the various lifetime editions below.) In such cases, the choice is between following a revision that may well not have been authorial, and following the reading of the *Fraser's Magazine* copy-text, which was at least based on the author's manuscript.

We choose to record the fact of the variant in our textual apparatus but in our reconstructed text to follow the earlier reading. We thus create a version in which, within the limitations of the evidence, the readings we have followed are as close as possible to what Carlyle, at some point in the history of the text, intended them to be, though we have undoubtedly failed to include many genuinely but undetectably authorial minor revisions.

Although no critical text can be considered final or definitive—since in preparing one useful, readable version it is necessary to use editorial judgment as to which variants represent authorial revision and should be accepted as emendations—we can claim that our text, when combined with the material in the textual appendix, constitutes a complete, and we believe accurate, record of all authoritative versions of the work. A different approach to scholarly editing, more interested in literary works as they were published and read in their social and historical context, would suggest that we ought to have chosen one of the published editions and reproduced it without emendation.[5] We have preferred to create a text that combines readings from nearly all of the extant authoritative versions in order to eliminate, as far as possible, the interference of Carlyle's printers, but we have recorded and preserved all of those interventions in our textual apparatus, and an interested scholar can reconstruct the exact text of any of the collated versions by consulting the Historical Collation.

The critical text that we have thus constructed is presented as "clear text"; that is, no editorial symbols or other indications of variants or emendations appear on the page. No attempt has been made to reproduce non-textual design features (typeface, lineation, pagination, etc.) of any of the source texts. Running heads were variously treated in the lifetime editions; we have generally followed the pattern of the 1838 first British trade edition. Other extra-textual materials, such as the "Testimonies of Authors" introduced in 1838, the "Summary" introduced in the 1858 Uniform Edition, and Carlyle's

---

[5] The logic of this position would imply that an editor should choose to reproduce the published edition that is most interesting from a social or historical point of view, or to put it another way, the edition that is most implicated in social analyses or historical narratives. But whether such a choice could meaningfully be made and defended must depend on the history of each work to be edited, especially its publishing history. In the case of *Sartor Resartus*, it is far from obvious which of the lifetime editions could be considered most influential, or most typical, or otherwise most historically interesting.

note on the genesis of the text introduced in the 1869 Library Edition, are included as appendices following the text proper.

The 1833–34 *Fraser's Magazine* serialization

Sartor Resartus was first published, in eight serial parts, in *Fraser's Magazine* between November 1833 and August 1834.[6] Since no manuscript material is known to exist, this serialization constitutes the earliest extant form of the text, and we have selected it as the copy-text for the present edition.

In choosing this version as our copy-text, we do not mean to suggest that we believe it to be in every detail an accurate copy of Carlyle's manuscript. Indeed, in two sorts of cases we are able to infer that the readings of some later version are closer to what Carlyle must have written (or intended to write): First, when we find that the *Fraser's* text has had imposed on it an identifiable, idiosyncratic *Fraser's Magazine* "house style" contrary to Carlyle's normal usage, and that this style was reversed in 1838, in the next edition to be supervised by Carlyle, we are justified in concluding that the manuscript must have been more like the 1838 edition than like the *Fraser's* text in that respect. The most clear-cut example of such a "house style" having been imposed on *Sartor Resartus* is the system of quotation marks that *Fraser's Magazine* employed, a minor but pervasive feature of the text: the magazine consistently used double inverted commas as ordinary quotation marks and single inverted commas to mark quotations within quotations, the same as the modern American style, as used, for example, in this essay. But beginning with the 1838 edition, all later authorized editions of *Sartor Resartus* follow the modern British practice of using single inverted commas as ordinary or "outside" quotation marks and doubles to mark embedded or "inside" quotations, with the exception of one Carlylean idiosyncracy which will be described below. The use of quotation marks in all editions beginning with 1838 presumably represents the system that Carlyle used in the manuscript. Second, when we find apparent typographical errors in the *Fraser's* text that were corrected in later

---

[6] The parts are: Book I, Chapters I–IV (November 1833, 8:581–92); Book I, Chapters V–XI (December 1833, 8:669–84); Book II, Chapters I–IV (February 1834, 9:177–95); Book II, Chapters V–VII (March 1834, 9:301–13); Book II, Chapters VIII–X (April 1834, 9:443–55); Book III, Chapters I–V (June 1834, 9:664–74); Book III, Chapters VI–VIII (July 1834, 10:77–87); Book III, Chapters IX–XII (August 1834, 10:182–93).

editions, we can infer either that the typesetter slipped (e.g., "lit lemechanism" for "little mechanism" at 86.31,[7] corrected in 1834) or on the other hand that the typesetter misread the manuscript or perhaps Carlyle's pen had slipped (e.g., "dusk" for "dust" at 108.9, corrected in 1838; "required" for "acquired" at 128.24, not corrected until 1858; and "Zodaical" for "Zodiacal" at 189.12, corrected in 1838). In such cases, the author's original intention can be determined (with more or less certainty) to have been different from the reading found in the copy-text. But no doubt there are more inaccuracies in the copy-text than these, which must forever go undetected, unless the manuscript be found, because they were more plausible or more negligible than these relatively obvious ones and either they were never corrected in any edition or their corrections cannot be distinguished among the mass of unattributable revisions in editions other than 1841.[8]

Carlyle corrected the proofs for the *Fraser's Magazine* serialization himself.[9] The manuscript or the proofs may also have had the attention of the magazine's editor, William Maginn, whose editorial pseudonym (*nom de crayon bleu*) was Oliver York, and who ostensibly contributed a footnote (on p. 10 of the present edition), which is signed "O.Y." and which was retained in all editions. Again, since we lack any earlier version against which to collate the *Fraser's* text as it was finally published, we are unable to detect any changes that may have been made in proof, whether by Carlyle or others.

THE 1834 REPRINT

After the printing of the final installment in the August 1834 issue of *Fraser's Magazine*, the typesetting of all the parts was assembled, rearranged, and used to print at least fifty copies[10] of the *Fraser's*

---

[7] Numbers in this form refer to page and line numbers in the present edition. See the Textual Apparatus at the corresponding place for the details of the variants thus referred to in this textual essay.

[8] The surviving 1841 proofs allow us confidently to attribute *all* 1841 variants either to the author or the typesetter, as explained below.

[9] See Introduction, pp. lxxv–lxxviii above.

[10] Just how many copies of the reprint were produced is open to question. On August 28, 1834, Carlyle wrote to his brother Alexander that Fraser "made me up 50 complete copies, most of which I have dispersed far and wide" (*Letters* 7:281). However, four years later in 1838 Carlyle complained that Fraser had been flogging additional copies of the reprint at 5s. per copy without Carlyle's permission (*Letters* 10:74).

typesetting in book form for private distribution, bound in grayish brown unprinted wrappers. A legend in gothic type on the title page reads "Reprinted for Friends from Fraser's Magazine." James Fraser is listed as publisher, and the date is given as 1834; according to the printer's colophon on page ii, the reprint, like *Fraser's Magazine* itself, was "printed by J. Moyes, Castle Street, Leicester Square." The text fills 107 pages, in the same two-column format, with 62 or 63 lines per column, as used in the magazine.

Inspection discloses that there was no extensive resetting of type; the line-breaks, for example, are the same throughout both texts (except at 196.4–5; see below). The column- and page-breaks are the same in both magazine and reprint through the first serial part, but at the end of Book I, Chapter IV, where the magazine page had two less-than-full-length columns, each of 46 lines, leaving room for two inches of white space and a hairline rule to signal the end of the serial installment, the reprint has two full-length columns, beginning Chapter V in the middle of the second column. From that page until the end of Book I, therefore, the column- and page-breaks in the two printings do not correspond. They are again synchronized on the first page of Book II, which begins a new page in both printings, but both columns on the second page of Book II are a line longer in the magazine than in the reprint, so column- and page-breaks are out of correspondence from there until the end of Book II. Although Book III also begins a new page, its first page is two lines shorter in the reprint than in the magazine, so its column- and page-breaks never correspond. We can only speculate on why all this extra work was undertaken for the sake of a small number of reprints. Clearly there was an effort to erase obvious signs of the book's serialized origins, but that does not explain why the layout of the first serial parts of Books II and III should have been altered.[11]

---

[11] Another indication that an effort was made to eliminate traces of the book's prior serialization is found in the resetting of the first lines of three chapters (Book II, Chapter VIII and Book III, Chapters VI and IX). *Fraser's Magazine* printed the first word of each serial part flush left in small caps (except that the first word of Book I, Chapter V was indented, no doubt inadvertently), while the reprint tried to restrict the use of flush-left small caps to the first word of each book (in both cases the printer seems to be following a rule of style that calls for a block paragraph and small caps whenever a section of text begins a new page). There are five part-breaks in the serialization that are not also divisions between books. Two of these were not reset for the reprint because the first words are As (at 27.1) and For (101.1), where the small caps are not conspicuous (and the As at 27.1

Even though the type was not reset, there are ten textual variants in the 1834 reprint,[12] only three of which seem to have been deliberate on anyone's part (the 1833 typo "lit lemechanism" was fixed at 86.31; the extra leading between paragraphs at 185.35 was lost when the reprint layout called for a page-break at that point, and was never restored; and two lines were reset at 196.4–5, fixing a tight line by bringing down the "vul-" in "vulgar" to the next line and making room for it, in part, by changing "Woollen-Hulls" to "Woolen-Hulls," a spelling change that persisted in British editions until 1869, when the 1833 spelling was coincidentally restored). The other seven variants can all be explained as the result of broken or worn type; five of these are either at ends of lines (i.e., edges of columns) or on the first line of a new column in the reprint, places where wear and breakage would be most liable to occur. Although only one of the 1834 variants, the fixing of the 1833 typo, represents a deliberate revision of the text, either by Carlyle or the printers, nevertheless six of the ten variants were followed in the 1838 and subsequent editions and five persisted through all lifetime editions. This fact proves that the 1838 edition was set from a copy of the 1834 reprint, probably a copy marked with revisions by Carlyle himself, rather than from the original magazine parts.

THE 1836 AMERICAN EDITION

As recounted in the Introduction (pp. lxxx–lxxxii above), the first trade-book edition of *Sartor Resartus* was published in Boston in 1836 by the firm of James Munroe and Company at the instigation

---

had already been indented). But in two of the other three cases, the first words are THOUGH (127.1) and HERE (196.1), where the small caps are obvious, and these lines were reset for the reprint. Also reset was the line beginning with As at 176.1, which was indented.

To complete this aspect of our narrative, though the issues are not strictly textual but rather a matter of typographic design: in the 1838 trade edition each chapter begins a new page and begins with a word in small caps, flush left. This pattern was followed in each subsequent British edition through 1849. In the collected editions of 1858 and 1871, only new books begin new pages, but each chapter still begins with a word in small caps and a block paragraph; the more deluxe collected edition of 1869 reverts to the style of the trade editions. We have followed the design of the 1838 edition in this respect.

[12] At 10.2, 59.8, 75.10, 86.31, 121.35, 125.27, 140.26, 140.27, 185.35, and 196.5.

of Ralph Waldo Emerson. The text was edited by Charles Stearns Wheeler with the assistance of Le Baron Russell, who asked Emerson to write a preface. Emerson did not oversee the actual editing. Although the text was apparently based on Emerson's personal copy of the 1834 reprint, now in the Houghton Library, Emerson scholars doubt whether the editorial markings in this copy are in Emerson's hand. In any case, the marks order no revisions more significant than lower-casing many of Carlyle's irregular capitalizations, nor do they account for many of the variants in the 1836 edition as published.[13] The printer's colophon reads: "Cambridge Press: Metcalf, Torry, and Ballou." Five hundred copies were published in April of 1836, and were sold at $1 per copy.

Since Carlyle took no part in the publication of the 1836 Boston edition, and since collation proves that it was not the basis for any subsequent authorized edition (though it was the basis for several pirated American editions), its variants have no relevance to our narrative and have not been reported in our textual apparatus. However, the text of the "Preface of the American Editors" in this edition, written but not signed by Emerson, was included by Carlyle in its entirety, attributed to "New England Editors," as the fourth and final item in the "Testimonies of Authors" (see Introduction, pp. lxxx–lxxxii above) which Carlyle attached as a preface to the editions of 1838, 1841, and 1849, and as an appendix to the editions of 1869 and 1871 (pp. 219–26 in the present edition).[14] The other three sections of the "Testimonies of Authors," as entitled by Carlyle, are: "I. Highest Class, Bookseller's Taster," which quotes a few words from the "reader's evaluation" letter of H. H. Milman to the publisher John Murray and from Murray's letter of rejection to Carlyle (see Introduction, pp. lxiii–lxiv above); "II. Critic of the Sun," from a review in the *Sun* newspaper of April 1, 1834, of the *Fraser's Magazine* publication of *Sartor Resartus*; and "III. North American Re-

---

[13] See Tarr, *Bibliography*, 37–41. The single page from Emerson's copy photographically reproduced in Tarr (*Bibliography*, 37) shows fifteen changes marked (between 75.7 and 76.37 of the present edition), all of them the lower-casing of capitalized nouns. All fifteen of these lower-casings were followed in the 1836 Boston publication, and thirty more words were lower-cased in the same passage as published

[14] The "Testimonies" were omitted from the 1858 Uniform Edition, perhaps because in that first collected edition of Carlyle's works *Sartor* and *On Heroes* were combined in a single volume, with new summaries and indexes of both.

viewer," a long extract from the *North American Review* of October 1835. See Appendix A.

THE 1838 FIRST BRITISH TRADE EDITION

In July of 1838 *Sartor Resartus* was first published as a trade edition in England by the firm of Saunders and Otley. The printer was William Clowes and Sons; 500 copies were published, and were sold at 10s.6d. per copy.[15] Collation discloses that there are approximately 440 textual variants between the 1838 edition and the 1834 reprint that served as its printer's copy. The possible explanations for these variants include: (*a*) Carlyle's revisions marked in the printer's copy (we infer but cannot prove that he ordered such revisions); (*b*) the typesetters' failure to reproduce their copy exactly, either inadvertently or deliberately; (*c*) Carlyle's revisions marked on the proofsheets, which he personally corrected. Since we have no documentary evidence for earlier stages of the text of this edition, unlike our situation given the surviving proofs of the 1841 edition (see below), our only basis for assigning a particular 1838 variant to one or another of these categories must be the nature of the variant itself.

To illustrate this point, let us begin by considering some examples of variants that seem clearly to have been introduced by the author, whether marked as revisions in the printer's copy or on the proofsheets (without either document, it is impossible to say which). Although Carlyle wrote to his brother John that "there is no change in *Teufk* from the genuine Fraser Copy" other than the addition of the "Testimonies of Authors,"[16] there is evidence of occasional authorial revision throughout. For such changes as "at least" to "at heart" (64.12, perhaps a correction of a misreading of the manuscript by the *Fraser's Magazine* printer), "new" to "mad" (120.5), "recks" to "boots" (122.22), "Orpheus" to "Orpheus, or Amphion" (193.15), and "brush" to "sponge" (215.31), no other explanation is nearly as plausible as authorial revision: they are not likely to have been typographical errors,[17] nor are they the sort of "corrections" from an unfamiliar to a clichéd expression that printers might introduce in the

---

[15] See Tarr, *Bibliography*, 42–44, and the Introduction, pp. lxxxv–lxxxix above.
[16] *Letters* 10:121–22, TC to John Carlyle, July 14, 1838.
[17] But some of the surprising erroneous changes of wording in the 1846 American editions of *On Heroes* and *Sartor* warn us to be wary of assuming too easily that any change is deliberate, much less authorial; see the discussion of the 1846 *Sartor* American edition of *Sartor* below.

course of setting type, either accidentally or believing themselves to be correcting an error in their copy. These therefore are examples of variants that seem clearly the result of Carlyle's own editorial activity. On this kind of internal evidence, we have felt justified in attributing about a tenth of the new variants in 1838 to authorial revision and accepting them as emendations of our text.

Examples in this edition of variants that are obvious typographical errors include *inter alia* the memorable "furred breasts" for "furred beasts" at 44.1, as well as "met" for "meet" (34.33), "Sarmacand" for "Samarcand" (131.38), and "very" for "every" (217.8). Of these examples, all but "Sarmacand" were noticed and corrected by the typesetters of the 1841 edition, and Carlyle himself corrected "Sarmacand" in the proofs for that edition. There were other errors that were not detected in 1841 and were only corrected in later editions (e.g., "inuendoes" for "innuendoes" at 138.33 was not corrected until the 1849 edition).

The 1838 trade edition also contains a large number of variants that, while apparently deliberate, may well not have been authorial. For example, although the text of *Sartor Resartus*, in all editions, is even more richly encrusted with capitalized nouns than is usual for Carlyle—perhaps in honor, imitation, or even parody of its Germanic sources and topics—nevertheless there is a trend toward lower-casing that begins in 1838 and continues through all lifetime editions. The evidence of the 1841 proofs shows that, at least in that edition, both the printer and the author participated in furthering this trend, though both did so only occasionally and unsystematically. Similarly, every edition beginning with 1838 reveals spelling changes apparently intended to modernize and regularize Carlyle's idiosyncratic and archaic orthography, in parallel with the evolution of the conventions of British orthography in the course of the nineteenth century. There are also many minor variants in punctuation in every edition beginning with 1838, likewise altering the eighteenth-century flavor of "rhetorical" punctuation increasingly in the direction of a more modern, "syntactic," rule-bound style of punctuation. Again, the 1841 proofs disclose that in that edition some of these changes of spelling and punctuation were introduced by the printers during typesetting, while some were ordered by Carlyle in proof.

Another feature of the 1838 trade edition, already referred to, is a change in the system of quotation marks used as house-style in *Fraser's Magazine*, or rather two changes. First, with a few exceptions all double inverted commas in *Fraser's Magazine* become single inverted commas and vice versa in 1838, the normal modern British system.

In our editing of *On Heroes*, we found that in all authorized editions of that work Carlyle used an idiosyncratic system of quotation marks, not characteristic of his normal practice: He clearly intended single and double quotes to represent different types of quotation, although it is not easy to infer the distinction he was making. In the "Note on the Text" of *On Heroes* we wrote, with a regrettable lack of clarity, that single quotation marks are used in that work "to indicate common expressions or implied speech" while double quotes "indicate fictional or actual speech or dialogue" (ciii). A better approximation to the rule might be to say that in *On Heroes* double quotes mark quoted *speech*, while single quotes mark quotes from written sources, though not without puzzling exceptions.[18] What is indubitable is that some distinction was intended; this is proved by the remarkable faithfulness with which the different quotation marks were reproduced in all lifetime editions of *On Heroes*, including the authorized American edition of 1846. (A somewhat similar system

[18] For an example that forcibly conveys the difficulty of drawing the distinction Carlyle intended, a single paragraph in the first lecture of *On Heroes* contains the following uses of quotation marks:

> You have heard of St. Chrysostom's celebrated saying, in reference to the Shekinah, or Ark of Testimony, visible Revelation of God, among the Hebrews: "The true Shekinah is Man!" Yes, it is even so: this is no vain phrase; it is veritably so. The essence of our being, the mystery in us that calls itself "I,"—ah, what words have we for such things?—is a breath of Heaven; the Highest Being reveals himself in man. This body, these faculties, this life of ours, is it not all as a vesture for that Unnamed? 'There is but one temple in the Universe,' says the devout Novalis, 'and that is the Body of Man. Nothing is holier than that high form. Bending before men is a reverence done to this Revelation in the Flesh. We touch Heaven when we lay our hand on a human body!' (10.33–11.6).

It is difficult to see any difference between the quotation from Chrysostom and that from Novalis that would call for a different style of quotation marks. Also, the phrase

> the mystery in us that calls itself "I,"

may be contrasted with

> We call that fire of the black thunder-cloud 'electricity,' (9.4–6)

which occurs on the preceding page, without disclosing any obvious reason for the differing treatment of the quoted word.

may have been used in "Mirabeau" [1837]. See the forthcoming Strouse Edition volume of Carlyle's *Historical Essays*.) In the case of *Sartor Resartus*, beginning with the 1838 edition, the first edition whose typesetting was supervised by the author, we find that the predominant distinction expressed by the use of single and double quotation marks was the conventional one between "outside" and "inside" quotations, a distinction often called into play in *Sartor Resartus*, which contains many long "quotations" from the contents of the six Paper Bags. This distinction was the only one observed in the *Fraser's Magazine* house style of quotation marks, so for the most part the only changes in 1838 were the global substitution of single for double quotes and vice versa. However in one passage in the 1838 and subsequent editions the double quotes of the *Fraser's* text marking normal, "outside" quotes were retained.

We have not reported these global changes in the Historical Collation. The reader should be aware that all quotation marks in the text and apparatus are represented in the 1838 style. Only exceptions to the rule are reported. In other words, in the apparatus the symbols ' and ' must be understood to mean "double inverted commas until revised to single inverted commas in 1838" unless otherwise noted.

The second change in the treatment of quotations in the 1838 edition presents a different editorial problem. In 1838 and all subsequent lifetime editions, for all quotations that extend over more than one line of text, a left quotation mark—single or double according to context—is inserted at the beginning of each line of the continuing quote. (This stylistic device, which results in each continuing line of a quote being indented by the width of a quotation mark, is the apparent ancestor of our contemporary style of treating long quotations by indenting them from both margins while omitting any quotation marks. It has an advantage over our current style in that it clearly marks long quotations that extend over an entire page; when using the modern style, if there is no text on the page that is not indented, the indentation may not be obvious. Its disadvantage is that it is typographically ugly and odd-looking, at least to our unaccustomed eyes.) Since much of the text of *Sartor Resartus* is composed of just such long quotations, this device is a visually prominent feature of all lifetime editions beginning with 1838. It confronts us with a difficult choice: We could argue that since this style was at least acceptable to Carlyle, and was perhaps even his preference for *Sartor*, and since it can at times be helpful in orienting the reader among the various voices and levels of embedded quotation of which *Sartor* is composed, we should reproduce it in our edition. With some regret, we have decided that the typographic treatment of long quotations is finally a typographic rather than a textual issue, and that page after page with columns of quotation marks at the left margin would be simply too odd, too typographically unappealing, and too distracting for a contemporary reader's edition. The *Fraser's Magazine* printing made no attempt to distinguish long quotations, other than the normal left quotation mark at the beginning of each paragraph within quotations. We have followed our *Fraser's* copy-text in this respect.

THE 1841 "SECOND EDITION"

In the same months, January to early March 1841, during which Carlyle was completing the manuscript of *On Heroes* and reading the proofs for its first edition, he was also proofreading the so-called Second Edition of *Sartor Resartus* (evidently counting the first British trade issue of 1838 as the first edition). Both volumes were published by James Fraser, and printed by "Robson, Levey, and Franklyn" of 46 St. Martin's Lane.[19] Only two pages of proof for the first edition of *On Heroes* survive,[20] but the complete set of proofsheets for the 1841 *Sartor Resartus*, with corrections in Carlyle's hand, was folded, trimmed, and put into a contemporary binding similar to that of the published edition. This unique document has been acquired by the Strouse Carlyle Collection.[21] We foresee that it will be of great interest to students of nineteenth-century printing practice, and its occasional candid marginalia constitute an important addition to our knowledge of Carlyle as author and maker of books. We hope in the future to make the document available in a facsimile edition.

For our present purpose, however, the significance of these proofs lies in the direct evidence they provide concerning the extent and character of the collaboration between author and printer in revising the text for the 1841 edition (and, by implication, indirect evidence of the extent of that collaboration for other editions). This single document gives us two additional versions of the text: first, the 1841 text as initially typeset, the typesetting from which the proofsheets

[19] For Carlyle's long association with his printer Charles Robson, see "Note on the Text," *On Heroes*, xc–xci.
[20] Reproduced as plate 3 in *On Heroes*, and discussed in the "Note on the Text," *On Heroes*, lxxxvii.
[21] These unique proofs were found by K. J. Fielding through an Edinburgh bookseller and were acquired from the dealer by Rodger L. Tarr, who then sold them to the University of California, Santa Cruz.

were pulled; second, that text as revised by Carlyle's marked corrections. Since the printer failed to make two such corrections (at 111.5 and 155.8), the 1841 edition as finally published constitutes, strictly speaking, yet a third version of the text. In our Historical Collation, these three versions are identified by the symbols "41U" ("uncorrected") for the 1841 proofs as typeset but not corrected, "41R" ("revised") for the corrections marked on the proofs in Carlyle's hand, and "41" for the "Second Edition" as published.

The circumstance that Carlyle apparently did *not* mark revisions in the printer's copy *prior* to the 1841 typesetting means that we have documentary evidence attributing every new variant that appears in the "Second Edition" either to authorial revision or to the independent activity of the typesetters. It is obvious from collation that the printer's copy for the 1841 edition was a copy of the 1838 trade edition, since the 1841 proofs reproduce nearly all of that edition's new variants. However, many further new variants were introduced in the 1841 typesetting (41U), most of which were not corrected by Carlyle in his proofreading and so were transmitted into all later versions of the text. Whether any of these variants that first appear in the 1841 proofs could represent authorial revision depends on whether Carlyle could have ordered such revisions in a marked printer's copy, his only earlier opportunity to have done so.[22]

Carlyle's correspondence, especially his frequent letters to his mother and brother, gives a detailed account of his literary activity for the period in question. There is no mention in these letters that he spent any time preparing a copy of the 1838 *Sartor Resartus* with marked revisions for the printers. The weeks preceding the March 1841 publication of the *Sartor* "Second Edition" were filled with intense work, mostly focused on the first edition of *On Heroes*, published simultaneously.[23] We first hear of the plan for a new edition of *Sartor* in a letter to Carlyle's brother on January 26:

> In the course of last week I bargained with Fraser for
> my Lecture-Book [*On Heroes*]. £75 the dog would

---

[22] We can dismiss the possibility of an earlier round of proofreading as an opportunity for earlier authorial revision. The proofs as we have them contain too many obvious typographical errors to have been subjected to a prior set of corrections, and there was neither time nor financial incentive for such another complete proofreading. Also, Carlyle would certainly have complained in his letters about so much extra work.

[23] See "Note on the Text," *On Heroes*, lxxxviii–xc.

give me no more; but he also gives a £75 for a thousand *Sartors*, the edition of that being run out too:
so we go on printing *both*, with all imaginable velocity; and I am to have £150 for the two. We must be
content. "4 sheets of each, 8 of both" are to come to
me every week *credat Judaeus!* I am very busy *revising* the Lectures; am now thro' the First. I design to
make few changes. In five or six weeks I may fairly
expect the quit of the concern;—free for another.[24]

In other words, although the printers have already begun setting
type for both works, Carlyle is still working on the manuscript of
On Heroes. ("*Revising* the Lectures" means revising the *manuscript*,
not the proofs, of the lectures on heroes. Carlyle has still not received the first proofsheets of either book on January 27, but he has
finished his "revisal" of the second lecture.[25]) There is no mention
of revising the printer's copy of *Sartor Resartus*, nor would we
expect it. The new edition of *Sartor* was purely a manufacturing
concern—the 1838 edition had "run out" and more copies were
needed—whereas *On Heroes* was being published for the first time,
from a manuscript with which Carlyle was not completely satisfied,
and the letters make clear that it was exclusively with the text of *On
Heroes* that he was wrestling.

By February 5, he was heavily revising *On Heroes* in proof:
"Proofsheets have much occupied me. We are now far into the second
Lecture: the First needed very heavy correction; paragraphs to be
added &c."[26] He was simultaneously correcting the *Sartor Resartus*
proofs as well, but this was a less dramatic business, as shown both
by the absence of specific references to it in the letters and by the lack
of major revisions in the *Sartor* text. By mid-February, "both the
Books are *two-thirds* done,"[27] "nearly done" on February 24,[28] and
both were "printed, and away from me" by March 2, after something

---

[24] *Letters* 13:24, TC to John A. Carlyle, January 26, 1841.
[25] *Letters* 13:27, TC to John A. Carlyle, January 27, 1841.
[26] *Letters* 13:29, TC to John A. Carlyle, February 5, 1841.
[27] *Letters* 13:32, TC to Margaret A. Carlyle. The editors of the *Collected
Letters* infer a date of February 6 for this letter, but on the assumption that
the work of proofing the two volumes proceeded at a fairly constant pace,
this date cannot be correct. The chronology strongly suggests a date closer
to February 16.
[28] *Letters* 13:46, TC to John Stuart Mill, February 24, 1841.

over four weeks of work, leaving the author-proofreader in a state of collapse "under the frightfullest despotism of Influenza."[29]

The evidence of the correspondence therefore strongly supports the hypothesis that none of the variants in the initial typesetting of the 1841 *Sartor Resartus* represents authorial revision in the printer's copy: both the positive evidence that Carlyle was "very busy" preparing the first edition of *On Heroes* from the moment the new edition of *Sartor* was first proposed, and the negative evidence that the letters do not mention preparing revised copy before the *Sartor* typesetting, although Carlyle habitually kept his mother and brother well informed about all his literary work. The evidence from collation is consistent with this hypothesis. Collation discloses no variants in the 1841 typesetting that are unambiguously authorial, in the sense that the change in 1838 from "Orpheus" to "Orpheus, or Amphion" is unambiguously authorial. There are eleven points in 41U at which the words or word order have been altered from the 1838 reading, alterations which are not obvious typographical errors and to which Carlyle did not object in his 41R proofreading,[30] but these can all be explained either as less-obvious errors (e.g., "especially" for "specially" at 106.4,[31] "yet in all darkness" for "yet all in darkness" at 109.5, or "tiresome" for "toilsome" at 151.27, none of which was corrected in proof or in any subsequent lifetime edition) or as "regularizations," typesetters' corrections of apparent usage errors (e.g., "who" for "that" at 121.38; Carlyle made the same correction himself in proof twice more, at 127.21 and 168.28). One such change, "what is to be looked for" for "what is it to be looked for" at 185.27, seems to be a necessary correction of an error in the 1833–1834 text, and we have accepted it as such, but it does not prove that the 1841 typesetters had the guidance of an authorially revised printer's copy, nor does the correction of the German spelling of "*die auszurottende Journalistic*" to "*Journalistik*" at 96.37, though it does suggest a typesetter with some knowledge of German.[32] This complete absence from the 41U text of any unambiguously authorial revisions is strong evidence that

[29] *Letters* 13:48, TC to John Sterling, March 2, 1841.
[30] At 37.23, 106.4, 109.5, 121.38, 123.3, 142.25, 145.33, 151.27, 165.26, 185.27, and 201.20, not counting self-evident typographers' errors like "disco-coloured tin breeches" at 72.35, "spirit" for "principle" at 99.37, or "to in hemp" for "to die in hemp" at 142.24, all of which Carlyle corrected in proof.
[31] Carlyle corrected the same mistake at 200.2.
[32] Many other errors in German spelling and usage remained uncorrected until 1858; see the discussion of the 1858 Uniform Edition below. It is

Carlyle made no revisions before typesetting, especially when it is considered that examples of such unambiguously authorial variants can be found in every other authorized lifetime edition (including 41R) except the last, as we will show.

It follows that new variants attributed in the Collation to "41U" are entirely the responsibility of the various typesetters who worked on the 1841 edition, whereas variants marked "41R" are indisputably authorial, and these two categories between them completely account for all new variants found in the 1841 edition as finally published. It is worth describing these two categories in some detail. The text of the 1841 *Sartor Resartus* as published contains approximately the same number of new variants from its 1838 printer's copy as the 1838 trade edition did from its 1834 printer's copy.[33] As it happens, about half of these are attributable to Carlyle's markings in the surviving proofs; the other half must be attributed to Carlyle's printers.

The kinds of variants in these two categories overlap to a significant extent. Both the printers and Carlyle as proofreader made roughly the same numbers of changes in spelling (including hyphenation), punctuation, and capitalization. The 1841 proofs are a compelling demonstration that the relation between Carlyle and his printers was a real collaboration in the project of publishing a "correct" text. For example, both 41U and 41R continue the trend toward lower-casing Carlyle's irregular capitalizations begun in 1838; the typesetters of

---

perhaps worth observing that if the 1841 proofs had not survived, the assumption on which our editorial policy is based—that printers did not except in unusual circumstances alter the wording of an author's text— would have required us to conclude that about half of the eleven variants listed in note 30 above were presumptively authorial. They are not dramatically different in kind from the eighteen changes of wording that Carlyle did in fact order in proof (at 29.1, 55.8, 59.7, 73.37, 84.15, 114.3, 119.13, 127.21, 138.30, 143.12, 143.26, 157.17, 168.28, 169.19, 190.7, 192.31, 203.34, and 218.29), some of which we might *not* have accepted as authorial. For example, without the evidence of the 1841 proofs we might well have decided that the more probable explanation for the change (in 41U) from "in this matter" to "in this manner" at 165.26 was authorial revision, whereas given the 1841 proofs we can be fairly confident that the true explanation is typographical error. Conversely, we might have questioned whether the change (in 41R) from "the far stronger Force of Man" to "the far stranger Force of Man" at 55.8 were not a typographical error if we did not have the revision in Carlyle's own hand.

[33] This tally of course does not consider the global change in the style of quotation marks in 1838.

41U lower-cased 32 of them, and then Carlyle lowered 28 more in
41R. On the other hand, 41U added nine new capitals, and 41R added
four more. Likewise, both 41U and 41R wrestle with *Sartor*'s idiosyncratic spelling: The word "waggon," spelled thus, occurs four times
in both the *Fraser's* and the 1838 editions. In 41U, the first two of
these (at 29.12 and 49.16) were changed to "wagon" while the latter
two (at 130.11 and 132.29) were set as "waggon"; Carlyle then
marked the latter two to be changed in 41R. (The question arises
whether "waggon" was an affectation of *Fraser's Magazine* style, or
on the other hand whether Carlyle's revisions to "wagon" in 41R
were a mere acceptance, for the sake of editorial consistency, of the
typesetters' changes on earlier pages, rather than a change in his own
preferred orthographic style. See Discussion of Editorial Decisions at
29.12, page 508 below.) For another example, Carlyle constructs
superlatives in -*est* on adjectives ending in -*ful* in seven places in
Sartor ("frightfullest" three times, "pitifullest" twice, and "painfullest" twice). In the *Fraser's* text, the *l* is always doubled; in 1838, the
first of the seven instances is spelled "frightfulest" while the others
follow copy; in 41U both the first and the second instance are spelled
"-fulest"; in 41R Carlyle marked the fourth through seventh to be
changed to "-fulest," so only the third instance had two *l*'s in 41 as
published; in 1849, the next British edition, all but the fifth and sixth
are "-fulest"; finally, in 1858 and after, all seven are restored to
"-fullest."[34] Here again, we see Carlyle, in marking the 1841 proofs,
apparently remembering the choices that the 41U typesetters had
made earlier in the book, and seeming to care more about achieving
consistency than about imposing his own preferred spellings.

Carlyle makes this attitude explicit in a marginal query to his
printer on page 106 of the 1841 proofs (see plate 10). Carlyle drew
a line over "forever" (at 70.15 of the present edition) and wrote in
the margin:

[fo]r ever (? in
[th]is volume?
[I] always write it as one word: in the Lectures you print it
[a]s one; but here?)

Carlyle is querying the printer whether the marked instance of "forever" ought not to be spelled as two words. He is correct that "in the
Lectures" (*On Heroes*), whose first edition was being proofed at the

---

[34] The variants are at 83.31, 102.8, 123.15, 146.13, 152.25, 167.18, and
203.26.

same time as this edition of *Sartor Resartus*, all thirty-five occurrences of "forever" are printed as one word in all lifetime editions. On the other hand, of the sixteen occurrences of "forever" in *Sartor*, the 41 proofs had it spelled as two words fourteen times, only twice as one word.[35] Three questions arise: First, if Carlyle preferred it as one word, why didn't he fix the twelve instances of "for ever" that he left alone in 1841, whereas if he didn't care, why did he fix the two instances that he did mark? Second, what does he mean by "in this volume?" and "but here?"? What is different about *Sartor Resartus* that would call for different spelling conventions from those being followed in *On Heroes*, if that is what he means? Third, what did the printer reply to this query, if anything? This instance of "forever" as one word, the occasion for this marginal note, was left alone, in spite of the implication in Carlyle's query that they should consider changing it, but Carlyle marked instances set as two words eight pages earlier and ninety-one pages later to be printed as one word, without further marginal comment, and this was done. Whereas, as we have said, twelve other instances of "for ever" as two words were left alone.

One plausible explication of this marginal comment is, "I have noticed that in this volume, unlike *On Heroes* and my own preference, 'forever' is often printed as two words. I marked one instance of this to be closed up eight pages ago, having let a few others go by earlier, but here I find a case where it's already one word. Ought we to take the trouble to be consistent about this, one way or the other, and is it the established style of this volume to use 'for ever'?" To which the printer's tacit reply was, "No, both are acceptable, and it would be too much trouble to reread the proofs looking only for 'for ever's to be changed to 'forever' or vice versa." (Consistency was not achieved until 1858, when someone—Carlyle had editorial "assistants" in the

---

[35] In the *Fraser's* text, "forever" occurs five times, "for ever" eleven times. In 1838, three of the five "forever"s were changed to "for ever," leaving fourteen "for ever"s and two "forever"s. In the 41U proofs there were no changes. In Carlyle's 41R proofreading, he changed two of the then fourteen "for ever"s to "forever," including one of the three new "for ever"s from 1838, leaving twelve "for ever"s and four "forever"s. In both 46 and 49, three of the twelve "for ever"s remaining from 41 were changed to "forever," and 49 changed two more that were not changed in 46, so that there were seven "for ever"s and nine "forever"s in 49 as published. All seven remaining "for ever"s were changed to "forever" in 58, and all sixteen remained "forever" through 71. For the record, the sixteen loci are 3.13, 12.21, 19.8, 43.2, 65.8, 70.15, 107.5, 125.33, 126.3, 126.15, 185.2, 185.8, 185.11, 190.15, 192.23, and 213.28.

preparation of the 1858 edition, as explained below—made them all "forever.") If this interpretation is correct, then the answer to the second question is probably that what was special about *Sartor Resartus*, in this instance, is that its text still bore traces of the "house style" of *Fraser's Magazine* or its printers, which may have preferred "for ever,"[36] whereas *On Heroes* was being set fresh from Carlyle's manuscript, where, as he says, he always wrote it as one word. In short, Carlyle, speaking in this marginal note in his character of editor, seeking the editorial desideratum of consistency, is asking his printer whether, given that *Sartor* is already full of "for ever"s, they shouldn't make this one "for ever" as well. Since this was not done, we may take it that the printer was not willing to take a suggestion as an order and make extra work for himself, but left well alone except in the two other places where Carlyle specifically marked a change. For us, on the other hand, Carlyle's explicitly stated authorial preference is our command, so we have decided to follow the 1858 edition in these cases, printing "forever" as one word throughout.

Carlyle was a dutiful but not an infallible proofreader. Several typographical errors, and many typographers' emendations, escaped him (the most significant are included among the changes of wording in 41u discussed above and listed in note 30). Although he thrice scolded the printers for inaccuracy by writing "Copy!" (i.e., "Follow your copy more carefully!") in the margins of the proofs,[37] he allowed many more changes, apparently indistinguishable, to pass without objection.[38] Contrary to the implication of those marginalia, we do not believe that Carlyle habitually read proof "against copy." An example of Carlyle's revisions in proof also illustrates his fallible proofreading: The name "Shakespeare" occurs three times in *Sartor Resartus*, spelled thus in all editions before 1841. In *On Heroes*, first printed in 1841, the name is spelled "Shakspeare" at all seventy-two of its occurrences in all lifetime editions. In the 1841 *Sartor* proofs, Carlyle marked two of the instances of "Shakespeare" to be changed to "Shakspeare" (at 182.1 and 212.4) but failed to mark the third in-

---

[36] The *OED* lists "forever" as "the phrase *for ever*, written as one word" and characterizes it as "Now chiefly U.S."

[37] At 40.4 and 40.14, both cases of commas added where no comma should be, and, more mysteriously, at 104.3, where a colon had been set instead of a semicolon.

[38] Commas are added, deleted, or moved sixty-five times in 41u; Carlyle corrected nine of these changes in proof. Semicolons are changed to colons fourteen times; Carlyle reversed three of these in proof.

stance (at 196.16, midway between the other two), which remained "Shakespeare" until 1858.

In general then, our text does not include the new variants found in 41U, with exceptions like "*Journalistik*" and "what is to be looked for" discussed above, but of course we have generally followed Carlyle's marked revisions in the 41R proofs, although we have made exceptions at a few points where we are confident that Carlyle's revisions were entirely prompted by changes made by the 41U typesetters rather than by changes in his own authorial preference.[39]

THE 1846 AMERICAN EDITION

In the spring of 1846, Carlyle entered into a comprehensive agreement with Wiley and Putnam, the New York publishers, to publish all of his books in America.[40] George Putnam himself was in London, where he negotiated the contract with Carlyle personally. Since many of Carlyle's works were already available in America in pirated versions, the marketability of the Wiley and Putnam editions would depend on their special status as having been authorized, corrected, and revised by Carlyle himself. Accordingly, all of Carlyle's books published by Wiley and Putnam in 1846, including editions of *On Heroes* and *The French Revolution* as well as *Sartor Resartus*, contain the following "Imprimatur" on the verso of their title pages:

> This Book, "[TITLE]," I have read over and revised into a correct state for Messrs. WILEY & PUTNAM, of New York, who are hereby authorised, they and they only, so far as I can authorise them, to print and vend the same in the United States.
>
> THOMAS CARLYLE.
> *London, June* 18, 1846.

Carlyle did in fact prepare printer's copies of these books "for the American people,"[41] marking his desired revisions in copies of the most recent British edition of each work, though none of these printer's copies are known to have survived. In the case of *On Heroes*, it

---

[39] These exceptions are all explained in the Discussion of Editorial Decisions, pp. 503–34 below.

[40] The Wiley and Putnam *Sartor*, according to its colophon, was produced by "C. A. ALVORD, PRINTER, / COR. JOHN AND DUTCH STS." and "T. B. SMITH, STEREOTYPER, / 216 WILLIAM STREET."

[41] TC to Edward Chapman, April 28, 1846 (*Letters* 20:182).

happened that Carlyle's London publishers, Chapman and Hall, wanted
to print a new edition of that work themselves in 1846, so Carlyle
prepared a second printer's copy for the London printers, transcrib-
ing his revisions from one copy into the second. On June 15 Carlyle
wrote to George Putnam, "I have had two of the books, *Sartor* and
Heroes, carefully revised for your printer. Copies for him are now in
readiness precisely identical with those that our English printer will
bring out."[42] In our editing of *On Heroes*, therefore, the fact that
both 1846 editions, the New York Wiley and Putnam edition and the
London Chapman and Hall edition, were set from "precisely identical" printer's copies allowed us, by considering points at which identical new readings appear in both texts, to reconstruct many of the
revisions that Carlyle must have marked in those "identical" printer's
copies, revisions which we accordingly adopted as emendations in our
text of that work.[43]

There was no new British edition of *Sartor Resartus* in 1846, but
the assertion in Carlyle's June 15 letter to Putnam that he had prepared two "precisely identical" printer's copies of *Sartor* as well as of
On Heroes suggests the possibility that the second marked copy of
Sartor might have been saved to be used as the printer's copy of the
next British typesetting, which did not occur until the "Third Edition" in 1849.[44] In fact, collation discloses a pattern of 79 identical
new variants in both the 1846 American and 1849 British *Sartor*,
including identical changes of wording as well as parallels in the usual
alterations of spelling, punctuation, capitalization, and the like, similar to the pattern found in the collation of the two 1846 editions of
On Heroes. Thus for each such parallel new variant in both of these
editions of *Sartor Resartus*, we must consider, as we did in editing *On
Heroes*, whether the best explanation for the correspondence of the
two texts is the coincidental independent activity of the New York
and London typesetters or rather whether the improbability of such
a coincidence means that the revision in question must have been
ordered by Carlyle in the parallel printer's copies. For most such
variants (fifty-nine of them, in our judgment), the latter explanation

---

[42] TC to G. P. Putnam, June 15, 1846 (*Letters* 20:203).
[43] See "Note on the Text," *On Heroes*, xcv–xcviii.
[44] Carlyle wrote to Edward Chapman about the possibility of a new edition
of *Sartor* on August 31, 1848: "Robson," Carlyle's regular printer after
1841, "has a corrected Copy of the Book" (*Letters* 23:101). There can be
little doubt that this was the other "precisely identical" copy of the 1841
Sartor that had been prepared in 1846.

seems more likely, and these have been adopted as emendations of the present text. Twenty of them, however, for various reasons seem to us credibly coincidental and have not been adopted.[45]

Notable among the changes of wording found in both the 1846 American and the 1849 British *Sartor* are the fifteen places where the word "must" has been replaced by a paraphrase (e.g., "have to").[46] Carlyle had made this kind of change once before, in marking the 1841 proofs (at 119.13), but none of the other 111 occurrences of the word "must" in the *Sartor* text were altered in any other lifetime edition. (Of the 131 instances of "must" in the first edition of *On Heroes*, only one was ever altered, and that single change occurred simultaneously in both 1846 editions of that work.)

However, Carlyle's "Imprimatur" notwithstanding, there are many more variant readings in the 1846 Wiley and Putnam *Sartor Resartus* than can be accounted for by our reconstruction of the changes Carlyle ordered in its printer's copy.[47] Since Carlyle took no further part in the preparation of this edition, almost none of the variants not paralleled in the 1849 British edition can be considered authorial.[48]

---

[45] In the list of emendations, pp. 489–501 below, which indicates the source text in which each emendation first appeared, those variants whose authority derives from their parallel appearance in the 1846 American and the 1849 British *Sartor* are marked "46 & 49." Parallel variants that we have not accepted as emendations are listed and explained in the Discussion of Editorial Decisions, pp. 503–34.

[46] At 41.9, 66.27, 67.13, 70.18, 87.8, 96.28, 103.24, 116.32, 122.16, 166.23, 172.6, 181.11, 192.17, 202.4 and 215.6.

[47] The Historical Collation records 437 variants in the 1846 American edition, coincidentally very nearly the same number of new variants as occurred in each of the 1838 and 1841 editions.

[48] The inevitable exception, in this case, is the correction of "Shakespeare" to Carlyle's post-1841 preferred spelling of "Shakspeare" at 196.16, making it consistent with the other two instances at 182.1 and 212.4 that had been marked in 41R. Either the 1846 New York typesetter alertly corrected this on his own initiative, or it was marked in the two printer's copies but missed by the 1849 London typesetter, or it was marked in the American printer's copy but Carlyle failed to transcribe the change into the British printer's copy. It is perhaps relevant that there is also a single indubitably authorial variant in the 1846 British *On Heroes* that is not present in the 1846 American edition of that work (at *On Heroes*, 135.2; see Discussion of Editorial Decisions, *On Heroes*, 436), suggesting that Carlyle's transcription of his revisions from one copy of *On Heroes* into the "precisely identical" copy may have been imperfect, which in turn supports the possibility that his transcription of his *Sartor* revisions was similarly imperfect.

There are nearly seventy points at which the wording or word order have been altered, all of which must be considered typographical errors. Some of these errors are fairly severe and make nonsense of the passages in which they occur (e.g., "died" for "dyed" at 38.24, "Sighs" for "Sights" at 73.25, "fair" for "far" at 74.18, "policy" for "police" at 74.26, "abandoned fruit" for "abundant fruit" at 83.25, "unfriendly" for "unfriended" at 92.30, "Too" for "Two" at 134.35, "Psyche clothes himself" for " . . . herself" at 151.15, "fearful" for "fateful" at 178.23, and "For" for "Nor" at 217.13), though none is quite as inexplicable as the worst of the errors in the Wiley and Putnam edition of *On Heroes* of the same year (e.g., "picture" for "piece" or "sudden" for "certain").[49]

THE 1849 "THIRD EDITION"

In January 1849, a "Third Edition" of *Sartor Resartus* was published in London by Chapman and Hall, Carlyle's British publishers since the death of James Fraser in October 1841.[50] In addition to the seventy-nine points at which this edition agrees with the 1846 Wiley and Putnam edition in differing from their common 1841 printer's copy, discussed above, the "Third Edition" text contains some two hundred new variants of its own, i.e., readings not found in either the 1841 "Second Edition" or the 1846 American edition. None of these is unambiguously authorial. The only changes of wording are probably typographical errors ("seered" for "seared" at 67.20, not corrected until 1871; "quiet" for "quite" at 113.20, not corrected until 1869; "grows" for "goes" at 121.15, not corrected until 1869; and "men" for "man" at 160.5, never corrected). The spelling of the name "John Balliol" is twice changed to "Baliol" (see Discussion of Editorial Decisions at 177.30). The bulk of the variants are in punctuation; the trend toward lower-casing Carlyle's irregular capitalized nouns is unsystematically continued.

This absence of authorial revisions not also found in the 1846 American edition strongly argues that Carlyle's participation in this edition was limited to his preparation of its printer's copy in 1846.

---

[49] See "Note on the Text," *On Heroes*, xcviii.
[50] "PRINTED BY ROBSON, LEVEY, AND FRANKLYN, / Great New Street, Fetter Lane."

The 1858 "Uniform Edition"

In 1857 and 1858, Chapman and Hall published the first collected edition of Carlyle's works, the "Uniform Edition," in sixteen volumes, again printed by "Robson, Levey, and Franklyn." *Sartor Resartus*, bound together with *On Heroes* as Volume 6, was published in 1858.[51] The coincidences between this edition of *Sartor Resartus* and of its companion work *On Heroes* are remarkable; the editing of the two works was "uniform" indeed. The text of *Sartor Resartus* occupies the first 182 pages of Volume 6; the text of *On Heroes* the next 183 pages. Both texts contain very similar numbers of new variants (just over five hundred). In both approximately 320 of these new variants are added hyphens, of which most (about 260 in *On Heroes*, 220 in *Sartor*) join verbs and following prepositions (e.g., "shut-out" at 9.22, "stood-up" at 13.1, and so on). Another odd coincidence is that the single occurrence of the word "unison" in each work is changed to "harmony" in this edition (at 94.36 in *On Heroes*, 97.14 in *Sartor*).

This notable consistency of editing is surely not unrelated to the editorial assistance in preparing the "Uniform Edition" that Carlyle received from members of his coterie of hero-worshipping young men: Vernon Lushington and Henry Larkin certainly, and perhaps also Alexander Gilchrist and Joseph Neuberg.[52] One or more of these assistants created a "Summary" and an Index for each work.[53] A letter from Carlyle to Vernon Lushington on October 5, 1857, suggests that Lushington was responsible for at least the first draft of the Summary and Index for both *On Heroes* and *Sartor Resartus* :

> I have got duly, by the two Installments, the *Lectures* and *Sartor* (the latter this morning); with their *Summaries* and *Indexes*, and Corrected Text,—all Complete, and in the perfect order I am used to from you. The *two* Corrections to each vol. I have thankfully adopted;—Sartor, in the railway, had swallowed his "markers"; but by dextrous shaking I have just

---

[51] See "Note on the Text," *On Heroes*, xcix–c.
[52] For Larkin, Gilchrist, and Neuberg, see Kaplan, *Thomas Carlyle*, 414–16; for Lushington, see K. J. Fielding, "Vernon Lushington," 16.
[53] The 1858 "Summary" of *Sartor Resartus* will be found in an appendix to the present text, pp. 227–36 below, and may be compared with the "Summary" of *On Heroes*, 213–21 in the Strouse Edition.

made him render them again: in both passages the
Commentator indisputably *right*,—as in all other
points when I have yet got up on him. The Summaries & Indexes seem excellent, so far as I examine;
and I do not mean to give you any more bother
about them. I beg you to believe me very grateful. . . . [54]

Since both Summaries and Indexes had to refer to the 1858 pagination and thus could only have been prepared from proof pages, we
may take it that the "Corrected Text" was the corrected proofs, corrected presumably by Lushington. We cannot speculate as to the "*two*
Corrections to each vol.*" but the phrase does not exclude the possibility that the proofs had been extensively corrected throughout
(including added hyphens) by Lushington, who put bookmarks only
in the two places in each work where he needed to query Carlyle
about suggested alterations, no doubt changes in wording. On the
same day, Carlyle wrote to Henry Larkin,

If you call tomorrow or any day (no hurry), I have
got Mr Lushington's *Sartor & Heroes*, with *Summaries* &c; wh^h I wish you to take charge of, and carry
away with you. The *Text* is perfect: of the *Summaries
& Indexes* I know not that there is anything whatever
*im*perfect; but I desire you to *examine*, and bring
them to a conformity (in any point you may find
needing it) with *your own* honest productions and
wise methods in that kind. [55]

This participation of third parties other than author and printer,
for the first time in the textual history of *Sartor Resartus* since William Maginn in 1833, means that we must be suspicious of such
global changes as the addition of those hundreds of hyphens. However, other global changes in the 1858 *Sartor* seem to us authorial for
various reasons, not necessarily in the sense that Carlyle was personally responsible for marking the revisions before or after typesetting,
but in the sense that they are expressive of Carlyle's intentions for the
text. For example, someone, not necessarily Carlyle, achieved consistency in the spelling of "forever" as one word in 1858, but we have

[54] National Library of Scotland, Acc. 9348.
[55] MS Huntington Library.

Carlyle's own assertion of his preference in this matter in the marginal notation on the 1841 proofs.

This is also the place to mention a pattern of revisions in *Sartor*'s frequent use of German words and phrases. Some of these revisions are corrections of errors in German spelling and usage. The early editions of *Sartor Resartus* are full of such errors, which are gradually corrected from edition to edition. Not all of these corrections occurred in 1858—similar corrections are found in both earlier and later editions—but more of them happened in 1858 than in any other edition.[56] For example, "Old Leischen," the name of Teufelsdröckh's housekeeper in the early editions, must always have been meant to be "Lieschen" (at 18.36, 19.9, 19.19, and 217.4) but did not become so until 1858. Umlauts are supplied where missing, or deleted where superfluous, in 1858 at 36.14, 70.5, 102.4, and 150.32; the same kind of correction had been made once before, at 20.6 in 1846 and 1849. "*Lieber*" was "*Leiber*" at 17.15 until 1846 and 1849; "*verteift*" was "*vertieft*" at 58.13 until 41υ; and "*Wohlgeboren*" was misspelled "*Wohlgebohren*" at 216.37 and 217.12 until 1858. "*Journalistik*" at 96.37, corrected in 41υ, has already been mentioned.

Other revisions in Carlyle's German seem to represent not corrections so much as authorial changes of mind. For example, the optional intensifier "*doch*" was inserted in "*Wo steckt doch der Schalk?*" at 13.15 in 1869. Where such variants seem to be corrections of errors, we feel obliged to adopt them regardless of who may have actually made the correction or when; where they seem to represent authorial revision, we of course adopt them for that reason. It follows that all German variants, from whatever edition, have been accepted as emendations.[57]

---

[56]We speculate that at least some of these corrections may be due to the editorial participation, in some capacity, of Joseph Neuberg, a native German speaker. Neuberg had discovered a number of factual errors in *On Heroes* in the course of making a German translation of it in 1852 and pointed them out to Carlyle in a series of letters, with the result that many of these errors were corrected in the 1852 Fourth Edition of that work. See "Note on the Text," *On Heroes*, xcviii–xcix.

[57]There are also a couple of points at which French words are misspelled in early editions: "*Esprit des Lois*" was misspelled "*Loix*" at 27.2 until 1869, and "*L'âge d'or*" ("the golden age") was misspelled "*L'age d'or*" ("the golden plough") at 174.36 until 1858.

THE 1869 "LIBRARY EDITION"

The next authorized resetting of *Sartor Resartus* was published in 1869 as Volume 1 of the "Library Edition" (Chapman and Hall, 1869–71), though a letter from Carlyle to his printer, quoted below, proves that work on it had already begun as early as May 1868. The text of the "Testimonies of Authors" that had been omitted from the 1858 edition was restored, though as an appendix rather than a preface, and preceded by a new introductory passage of two paragraphs. As explained in the Introduction, p. xciii above, Carlyle had to ask his family if anyone had a copy of one of the earlier editions of *Sartor Resartus* that contained the "Testimonies," last published twenty years previously.

The Library Edition *Sartor* text was obviously based on that of the Uniform Edition, but differs from it at about five hundred points. These variants are quite miscellaneous, but they include revisions that can only be explained as authorial. (As with the 1838 edition, we cannot be sure whether these revisions were ordered before or after typesetting; we do know that Carlyle corrected the proofs for this edition,[58] and it is also possible that he had prepared a marked copy of the Uniform Edition for the printers.) The changes of wording found in the Library Edition run the gamut from the clearly authorial (e.g., "all the Journals of the Nation" for "the whole Journals of the Nation" at 9.8, the addition of "*doch*" at 13.15 mentioned above, "Thou thyself" for "Thou too" at 54.17, "never or seldom" for "nowise" at 84.19, and the addition of "(*Schaam*)" at 162.13) to the clearly erroneous ("the place of wages of Performance" for "the place and wages of Performance" at 86.6, and "should I speaks" for "should I speak" at 212.3).

The Library Edition versions of both *Sartor Resartus* and *On Heroes* (published as Volume 12 in 1870) show "a similar pattern of minor changes of wording" throughout.[59] Examples from *Sartor* include ten instances of moving the "not" in negative questions from its more normal position after the subject pronoun to a more rhetorically distinctive position before it ("does not she?" for "does she not?" at 56.12, "does not there" for "does there not" at 98.1, "have not I" for "have I not" at 132.15, and other precisely analogous examples at 132.31, 137.12, 140.26, 156.28, 176.20, 177.6, and 194.24).

---

[58]See the letter from John Carlyle to Charles Butler quoted below in the discussion of the 1871 People's Edition.
[59]"Note on the Text," *On Heroes*, c.

These inversions are unmistakably authorial, quite unlike the inversions found in the 41u typesetting, which are either changes in the direction of a more normal word order such as typesetters might make inadvertently or deliberately (e.g., "*This thou shalt do*" for "*This shalt thou do*" at 123.3) or obvious mistakes (e.g., "yet in all darkness" for "yet all in darkness" at 109.5, mentioned above, but also "every with" for "with every" at 6.28, and "ti" for "it" at 109.35).

Of the other variants in the Library Edition, seventy-six are lower-casings of remaining irregular capitals. These are not evenly distributed through the text. The first quarter of the book averages 0.79 lower-casings per page in this edition, the second quarter 0.24 per page, the third quarter 0.13 per page, the fourth quarter 0.24 per page. A letter from Carlyle to his printer Charles Robson, May 11, 1868, may be relevant to this uneven distribution:

> That *abolition* of Capitals . . . will never do; abolition quasi-total, which in many places considerably obscures the sense (or comprehensibility in reading): much better let the thing stand as it is than *so*.—I cannot myself undertake to read the Book with an eye to Capitals; tho' I have tried passages of it;—you shall have a *fresh* Copy, marked by me here & there.[60]

Carlyle is evidently objecting to the frequent lower-casing in the first quarter of the book. It seems likely that the letter was written in the course of his proofreading, objecting to changes that the printers had made in the early sheets, and that it had the effect of reducing the frequency of such changes as typesetting proceeded. (Another possibility is that someone other than Carlyle had prepared a marked printer's copy to which he was objecting prior to typesetting. This makes more sense of the words "you shall have a *fresh* Copy," but would not explain the odd distribution of the changes that were made. The truth may lie in some combination of these scenarios, perhaps that the letter was written during proofreading and that Carlyle was offering to provide a new printer's copy for the remaining typesetting as an alternative to his having to restore capitals that had been lowered on the proofsheets.) Despite Carlyle's expressed fondness for his meaningful capitals, there are over 150 words that were capitalized in the first printing of *Sartor Resartus* but are lower-cased in the last lifetime edition (1871). Of these, we can attribute sixteen to

[60] MS Pierpont Morgan Library.

Carlyle's own unsystematic revision, mostly based on his corrections marked in the 1841 proofs, and he may well have been responsible for a handful of the unattributable remainder. But many of these lower-casings do indeed "considerably obscure the sense" of the passages in which they occur.[61]

THE 1871 "PEOPLE'S EDITION"

On May 20, 1871, Thomas's brother John Carlyle, who lived nearby and was a daily visitor, wrote to their friend the American financier Charles Butler (1802–1897) reporting on Thomas's activities:

> He has got the whole of his works published in what is called the "Library Edition" of thirty volumes; corrected the final proofs himself, making no alterations at all, only rectifying errors wherever he could discover any. A "People's Edition" in the same number of volumes has been begun, but he has no charge of it at all, the printers merely having to follow the Library Edition which is stereotyped.[62]

The last authorized publication of *Sartor Resartus* in Carlyle's lifetime was as volume 1 (1871) of the People's Edition of 1871–74, and its many reprints that continued to be produced at least through 1901. The People's Edition was clearly based on the Library Edition, preserving most of its punctuation and spelling, but it is a complete resetting, not using the "stereotyped" plates of the Library Edition, contrary to the implication in John Carlyle's letter. The type in the People's Edition is considerably smaller, and the lineation and pagination do not correspond.

There are no variants in the 1871 *Sartor Resartus* that suggest authorial revision. The few changes of wording all look like either typographical errors (e.g., "lead" for "led" at 85.12, "justice" for "justness" at 121.3, "that" for "than" at 156.31, and "handbreaths" for "handbreadths" at 189.1) or typographers' regularizations ("positions" for "position" at 18.10).

We might mention at this point the phenomenon of migrating hyphens, since the results of that process all accumulate in this edition. Consider a not untypical example of migrating hyphens:

---

[61] For examples, consider in context the variants at 11.25, 29.11, 31.26, 50.36, 55.30, 55.34, 185.32, 214.21, and 216.29.
[62] MS University of Edinburgh Library.

71.22   fire-clad bodyguard   33
         fire-/clad bodyguard   58
         fireclad body-/guard   69
         fireclad body-guard   71

In the typesetting of the 1858 edition, the hyphen in "fire-clad," which had occurred "in line" in all previous editions, happened to fall at a line break. The 1869 typesetter then mistook the 1858 line-end hyphen for an optional hyphen such as printers are allowed to introduce for the sake of line spacing. Since the line break in the 1869 edition did not fall at that point, the typesetter omitted the hyphen, but introduced one at his line-end in "body-/guard." The 1871 typesetter in turn mistook that hyphen for a genuine, non-optional hyphen, so in the course of the last three lifetime editions the hyphen migrated from "fire-clad bodyguard" to "fireclad body-guard." Such mistakes can be found in every oblique edition of *Sartor Resartus*. Over fifty hyphens appear and disappear in this way from edition to edition, introducing what amount to unintended changes of spelling. They prove that no one was checking the proximate printer's copy against any earlier version of the text. That Carlyle was aware of this problem is shown by his marginal instructions on page 101 of the 1841 proofs: The printer had broken a line at the hyphen in the compound "pap-fed" (66.32), and Carlyle marked it and wrote in the margin next to it, "this word in line; with hyphen"; that line and the preceding one were accordingly reset. However at other locations in the text, the 41u typesetting, like every other new typesetting, both misinterprets line-end hyphens in its printer's copy and introduces its own ambiguous line-end hyphens that were misinterpreted in subsequent typesettings.[63]

THE "CENTENARY EDITION"

The posthumous Centenary Edition of Carlyle's Collected Works, edited by H. D. Traill (London: Chapman and Hall, 1896–99), which has served as the standard edition for purposes of scholarly reference, was based on the "last lifetime edition," the 1871 People's Edition. As we discovered when we collated the Centenary Edition text of *On*

---

[63] The two lists of hyphenated compounds in the Textual Apparatus, pp. 535–40 below, respectively present our resolutions of ambiguous hyphens that occurred at line-ends in the *Fraser's* copy-text and of those that occur at line-ends in the present text.

Heroes for the initial volume in this series, Traill's edition actually followed a late, undated reprint of the People's Edition, incorporating some of its distinctive typographical errors while committing many egregious new ones, and arbitrarily imposing a new set of revisions of spelling and punctuational style.[64] Although we did not collate the Centenary Edition of *Sartor Resartus*, examples of its flaws such as "star-doomed" for "star-domed" at 194.3 show that it is not more reliable than the Centenary Edition of *On Heroes*. We stand by the conclusion we reached in our editing of *On Heroes*, that the Centenary Edition, "the edition of Carlyle's works that has been most respectfully and generally used," is "textually the worst."[65]

NOTE ON THE TITLE

The first serial part of the *Fraser's Magazine* publication is headed, "SARTOR RESARTUS. / IN THREE BOOKS." followed by the couplet from Goethe (see Notes, p. 246 below), a short rule, and "BOOK I." Subsequent parts print "SARTOR RESARTUS." and "IN THREE BOOKS." on the same line, separated by an em-space, and omit the quotation from Goethe and the short rule. The second part has the subhead "*Chapters V. to XI.*" while all the other parts have "BOOK II." or "BOOK III." below the main title. The title page of the 1834 private reprint similarly reads, "SARTOR RESARTUS. / IN THREE BOOKS." (see Tarr, *Bibliography*, 35). But in 1838, in the first British trade book edition, the title on the title page reads, "SARTOR RESARTUS: / THE / LIFE AND OPINIONS / OF / HERR TEUFELSDRÖCKH. / IN THREE BOOKS." below which the Goethe quotation appears between short rules. The same wording (and lineation) of the title is found in the 1841 "Second Edition," except that the colon after "SARTOR RESARTUS" is changed to a semicolon. In the 1849 "Third Edition," the semicolon reverts to a colon and the title is thus identical with the 1838 edition.

    In the Uniform Edition of 1857–58, as explained above, *Sartor* is bound together with *On Heroes* as Volume 6. The title page of that volume therefore reads, "SARTOR RESARTUS / (1831). / LECTURES ON HEROES / (1840). / BY / THOMAS CARLYLE" (the dates presumably representing the dates of composition), but there is a half-title page on which the complete title appears: "SARTOR

---

[64] For the details see "Note on the Text," *On Heroes*, cii–ciii.
[65] "Note on the Text," *On Heroes*, ciii.

RESARTUS: / THE / LIFE AND OPINIONS OF HERR TEUFELSDRÖCKH. / IN THREE BOOKS." with the Goethe couplet beneath. In both the Library Edition of 1869–71 and the People's Edition of 1871–74, *Sartor* has Volume 1 to itself. In both, the title on the title page has the same wording, punctuation, and lineation as in the Uniform Edition. "Goethe" is added to the couplet to identify its source, and "[1831.]" appears below the Goethe quotation.

The title of the present edition follows the wording, obviously authorial, that appears in all lifetime British editions after 1838. Our title page omits the punctuation in the title, in conformity with contemporary book design principles.

Yours faithfully,

T. Carlyle

PLATE 1. Sketch of Carlyle from *Fraser's
Magazine* (1833).

GALLERY OF LITERARY CHARACTERS.

No. XXXVII.

THOMAS CARLYLE, ESQ.

HERE hast thou, O Reader! the-from stone-printed effigies of Thomas Carlyle, the thunderwordoversetter of Herr Johann Wolfgang von Goethe. These fingers, now in listless occupation supporting his head, or clutching that outward integument which with the head holds so singular a relation, that those who philosophically examine, and with a fire-glance penetrate into the contents of the great majority of the orb-shaped knobs which form the upper extremity of man, know not with assured critic-craft to decide whether the hat was made to cover the head, or the head erected as a peg to hang the hat upon;—yea, these fingers have transferred some of the most harmonious and mystic passages,—to the initiated, mild-shining, inaudible-light instinct—and to the uninitiated, dark and untransparent as the shadows of Eleusis—of those forty volumes of musical wisdom which are commonly known by the title of *Goethe's Werke*, from the Fatherlandish dialect of High-Dutch to the Allgemeine-Mid-Lothianish of Auld Reekie. Over-set Goethe hath Carlyle, not in the ordinary manner of language-turners, who content themselves with giving, according to the capacity of knowingness or honesty within them, the meaning or the idea (if any there be) of the original book-fashioner, on whom their secondhand-penmongery is employed; but with reverential thought, word-worshipping even the articulable clothing wherein the clear and ethereal harmony of Goethe is invested, Carlyle hath bestowed upon us the *Wilhelm Meister*, and other works, so Teutonical in raiment, in the structure of sentence, the modulation of phrase, and the roundabout, hubble-bubble, rumfustianish (*hübble-bübblen, rümfüstianischen*), roly-poly growlery of style, so Germanically set forth, that it is with difficulty we can recognise them to be translations at all.

Come, come, some reader will impatiently exclaim,—quite enough of this! A whole page of imitative Carlylese would be as bad as the influenza. In human English, then, Thomas Carlyle,—like Dionysius, of Syracuse, among the ancients; and Milton and Johnson among the moderns,—formerly instilled the prima stamina of knowledge into the minds of ingenuous youth; but for some years past has retired from what Oppian calls, or is supposed to call (see Bayle *in voce*), feeding the sheep of the muses, to the rural occupations of a Dumfriesshire laird, in a place rejoicing in the melodious title of Craigenputtock, an appellation which must have delighted his ear, from its similarity in harmonious sound to the poetical effusions of the bards he loves. Here he occupies his leisure hours in translating Goethe, or in corresponding with the *Edinburgh Review*, or *Fraser's Magazine*, the *Morning Post*, or the *Examiner*,—in all, donner-und-blitzenizing it like a north-wester. To his credit be it spoken, he gave a Christian and an honourable tone to the articles of the *Edinburgh;* but he came too late. The concern was worn out and gone, and not even Carlyle could keep it from destruction, particularly when he was associated with Thomas Babbletongue Macaulay, whose articles would swamp a seventy-four. He has a more congenial soil in *Regina*, where he expounds, in the most approved fashion of the Cimbri and the Teutones, his opinions on men and things, greatly to the edification of our readers. Of his contributions to the forty-eight feet of diurnal or septimanal literature which are set before the industrious eyes of the readers of newspapers, we know nothing.

He is an honourable and worthy man, and talks the most unquestionable High Fifeshire. Of our German scholars, he is clearly the first; and it is generally suspected that he has an idea that he understands the meaning of the books which he is continually reading, which really is a merit of no small magnitude, particularly when we consider that nobody ever thinks of publishing a translation from the German without prefixing thereto a preface, proving in general in the most satisfactory manner that his predecessors in the work of translation made as many blunders as there were lines in the book, and that of the spirit of the original they were perfectly ignorant. Even-handed justice is sure to bring back the chalice to his own lips, and he receives the same compliment from his successor.

PLATE 2. William Maginn's description of Carlyle in *Fraser's Magazine* (June 1833).

PLATE 3. Gallery of Literary Characters from
Fraser's Magazine. Carlyle, with the curly
front lock, is fifth from the right of the
standing figure.

PLATE 4. Sketch of William Maginn, editor of
Fraser's Magazine, "Oliver Yorke" in *Sartor
Resartus.*

SARTOR RESARTUS.

IN THREE BOOKS.

———◆———

Reprinted for Friends from Fraser's Magazine.

Mein Vermächtniss, wie herrlich weit und breit!
Die Zeit ist mein Vermächtniss, mein Acker ist die Zeit.

LONDON:

JAMES FRASER, 215 REGENT STREET.

———

M.DCCC.XXXIV.

PLATE 5. Title page of privately printed 1834
edition. Tarr Carlyle Collection, Cooper
Library, University of South Carolina.

SARTOR RESARTUS;

THE

LIFE AND OPINIONS

OF

HERR TEUFELSDRÖCKH.

IN THREE BOOKS.

Mein Vermächtniß, wie herrlich weit und breit!
Die Zeit ist mein Vermächtniß, mein Acker ist die Zeit.

LONDON:

SAUNDERS AND OTLEY, CONDUIT STREET.

M.DCCC.XXXVIII.

PLATE 6. Title page of the first English trade
edition of 1838. Tarr Carlyle Collection,
Cooper Library, University of South Carolina.

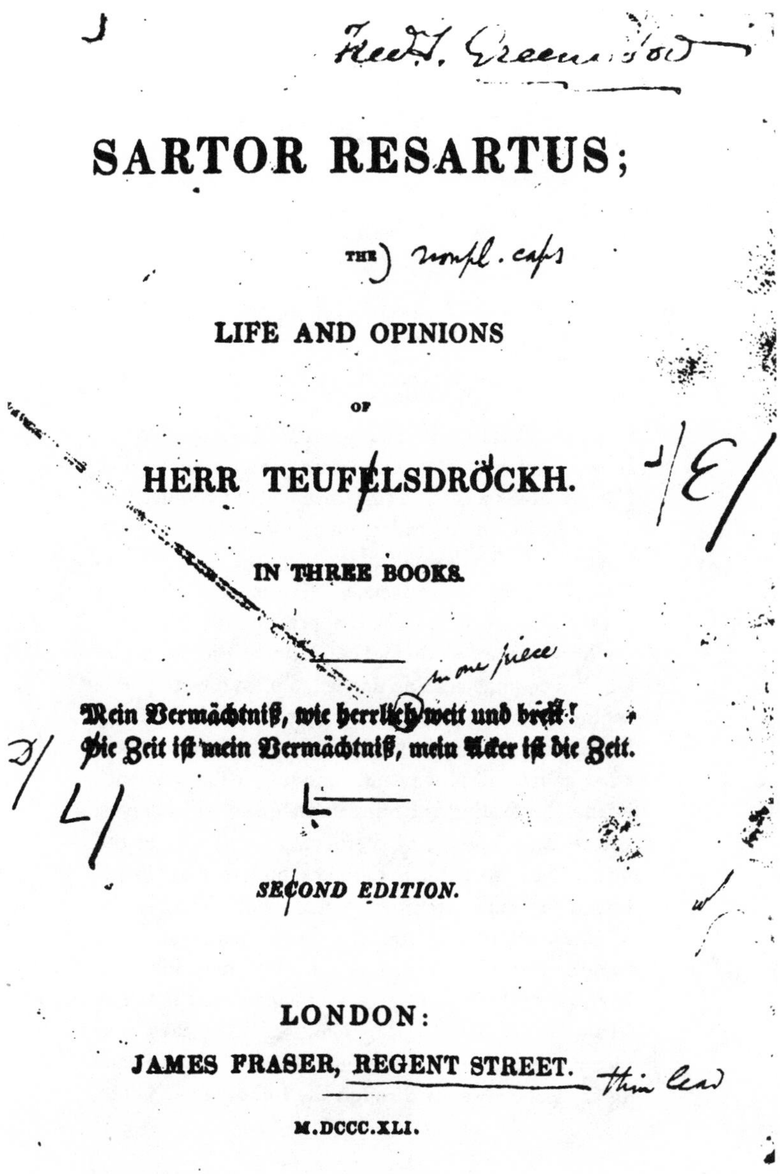

SARTOR RESARTUS;

LIFE AND OPINIONS

OF

HERR TEUFELSDRÖCKH.

IN THREE BOOKS.

Mein Vermächtniß, wie herrlich weit und breit!
Die Zeit ist mein Vermächtniß, mein Acker ist die Zeit.

SECOND EDITION.

LONDON:

JAMES FRASER, REGENT STREET.

M.DCCC.XLI.

PLATE 7. Title page of the 1841 printer's
proof. Strouse Collection, University Libraries,
University of California, Santa Cruz.

CHAPTER VIII.

THE WORLD OUT OF CLOTHES.

IF in the Descriptive-Historical Portion of this Volume, Teufelsdröckh, discussing merely the *Werden* (Origin and successive Improvement) of Clothes, has astonished many a reader, much more will he in the Speculative-Philosophical Portion, which treats of their *Wirken*, or Influences. It is here that the present Editor first feels the pressure of his task; for here properly the higher and new Philosophy of Clothes commences: an untried, almost inconceivable region, or chaos | in venturing upon which, how difficult, yet how unspeakably important is it to know what course, of survey and conquest, is the true one; where the footing is firm substance and will bear us, where it is hollow, or mere cloud, and may engulf us! Teufelsdröckh undertakes no less than to expound the moral, political, even religious Influences of Clothes; he undertakes to make manifest, in its thousandfold bearings, this grand Proposition, that Man's earthly interests 'are all hooked and buttoned 'together, and held up, by Clothes.' He says in so many words, 'Society is founded upon Cloth;' and again, 'Society sails through the Infinitude on Cloth,

PLATE 8. Corrections in Carlyle's hand and the compositors' signatures for the inner and outer formes in the 1841 printer's proof. Strouse Collection, University Libraries, University of California, Santa Cruz.

the Bag *Libra*, on various Papers, which we arrange
with difficulty, ' dwelt Andreas Futteral and his wife;
' childless, in still seclusion, and cheerful though
' now verging towards old age. Andreas had been
' grenadier Sergeant, and even regimental School-
' master under Frederick the Great ; but now, quit-
' ting the halbert and ferule for the spade and prun-
' ing-hook, cultivated a little Orchard, on the produce
' of which he, Cincinnatus-like, lived not without dig-
' nity. Fruits, the peach, the apple, the grape, with
' other varieties came in their season ; all which An-
' dreas knew how to sell : on evenings he smoked
' largely, or read (as beseemed a regimental School-
' master), and talked to neighbours that would listen
' about the Victory of Rossbach ; and how Fritz the
' Only (*der Einzige*) had once with his own royal
' lips spoken to him, had been pleased to say, when
' Andreas as camp-sentinel demanded the pass-word,
' " *Schweig Du Hund* (Peace, hound !)," before any
' of his staff-adjutants could answer. " *Das nenn*
' *ich mir einen König*, there is what I call a King,"
' would Andreas exclaim : but the smoke of Kuners-
' dorf was still smarting his eyes."

' Gretchen, the housewife, won like Desdemona
' by the deeds rather than the looks of her now vete-
' ran Othello, lived not in altogether military subor-
' dination ; for, as Andreas said, " the womankind
' will not drill (*wer kann die Weiberchen dressiren*) :"
' nevertheless she at heart loved him both for valour
' and wisdom ; to her a Prussian grenadier Sergeant

CHAPTER II.

IDYLLIC.

',Happy season of Childhood!' exclaims Teufelsdröckh: Kind Nature, that art to all a bountiful
' mother; that visitest the poor man's hut with au-
' roral radiance; and for thy Nurseling hast provided
' a soft swathing of Love and infinite Hope, wherein
' he waxes and slumbers, danced-round (*umgäukelt*)
' by sweetest Dreams! If the paternal Cottage still
' shuts us in, its roof still screens us; with a Father
' we have as yet a prophet, priest and king, and an
' Obedience that makes us Free. The young spirit
' has awakened out of Eternity, and knows not what
' we mean by Time; as yet Time is no fast-hurrying
' stream, but a sportful sunlit ocean; years to the
' child are as ages: ah! the secret of Vicissitude, of
' that slower or quicker decay and ceaseless down-
' rushing of the universal World-fabric, from the
' granite mountain to the man or day-moth, is yet
' unknown; and in a motionless Universe, we taste,
' what afterwards in this quick-whirling Universe is
' forever denied us, the balm of Rest. Sleep on,
' thou fair Child, for thy long rough journey is at
' hand! A little while, and thou too shalt sleep no

PLATE 10. Note in Carlyle's hand in the 1841 printer's proof.
See Note on the Text, p. cxiii. Strouse Collection, University
Libraries, University of California, Santa Cruz.

with aimless speed. Thus must he, over the whole
surface of the Earth (by foot-prints), write his *Sorrows of Teufelsdröckh;* even as the great Goethe, in
passionate words write his *Sorrows of Werter,*
before the spirit freed herself, and he could become
a Man. Vain truly is the hope of your swiftest
Runner to escape from his own Shadow!' Nevertheless, in these sick days, when the Born of Heaven
first descries himself (about the age of twenty) in a
world such as ours, richer than usual in two things,
in Truths grown obsolete, and Trades grown obsolete,—what can the fool think but that it is all a
Den of Lies, wherein whoso will not speak Lies and
act Lies, must stand idle and despair? Whereby it
happens that, for your nobler minds, the publishing
of some such Work of Art, in one or the other dialect, becomes almost a necessity. For what is it
properly but an Altercation with the Devil, before
you begin honestly Fighting him? Your Byron
publishes his *Sorrows of Lord George,* in verse and
in prose, and copiously otherwise : your Bonaparte
represents his *Sorrows of Napoleon* Opera, in an all-
too stupendous style; with music of cannon-vollies,
and murder-shrieks of a world ; his stage-lights are
the fires of Conflagration ; his rhyme and recitative
are the tramp of embattled Hosts and the sound of
falling Cities.—Happier is he who, like our Clothes-
Philosopher, can write such matter, since it must be
written, on the insensible Earth, with his shoe-soles
only ; and also survive the writing thereof!

PLATE 11. Substantive corrections in Carlyle's hand in the 1841
printer's proof. Strouse Collection, University Libraries,
University of California, Santa Cruz.

ambrosial joy as of over-weariness falling into sleep, lay down his pen. Well does he know, if human testimony be worth aught, that to innumerable British readers likewise, this is a satisfying consummation; that innumerable British readers consider him, during these current months, but as an uneasy interruption to their ways of thought and digestion, not without a certain irritancy and even spoken invective. For which, as for other mercies, ought he not to thank the Upper Powers? To one and all of you, O irritated readers, he, with outstretched arms and open heart, will wave a kind farewell. Thou too, miraculous Entity, that namest thyself YORKE and OLIVER, and with thy vivacities and genialities, with thy all-too Irish mirth and madness, and odour of palled punch, makest such strange work, farewell; long as thou canst, fare-*well*! Have we not, in the course of Eternity, travelled some months of our Life-journey in partial sight of one another; have we not lived together, though in a state of quarrel?

THE END.

LONDON:

PRINTED BY ROBSON, LEVEY, AND FRANKLYN,
46 St. Martin's Lane.

PLATE 12. Substantive corrections in Carlyle's hand and compositors' signatures in 1841 printer's proof. Strouse Collection, University Libraries, University of California, Santa Cruz.

PLATES 13a and 13b (*opposite*). Regency dandies in costume.

PLATE 14. Sketch of Goethe from *Fraser's Magazine*.

Sartor Resartus

THE LIFE AND OPINIONS OF
HERR TEUFELSDRÖCKH
IN THREE BOOKS

By Thomas Carlyle

Mein Vermächtniss, wie herrlich weit und breit!
Die Zeit ist mein Vermächtniss, mein Acker ist die Zeit.

BOOK I.

CHAPTER I.

PRELIMINARY.

CONSIDERING our present advanced state of culture, and how the Torch of Science has now been brandished and borne about, with more or less effect, for five thousand years and upwards; how, in these times especially, not only the Torch still burns, and perhaps more fiercely than ever, but innumerable Rush-lights and Sulphur-matches, kindled thereat, are also glancing in every direction, so that not the smallest cranny or doghole in Nature or Art can remain unilluminated,—it might strike the reflective mind with some surprise that hitherto little or nothing of a fundamental character, whether in the way of Philosophy or History, has been written on the subject of Clothes.

Our Theory of Gravitation is as good as perfect: Lagrange, it is well known, has proved that the Planetary System, on this scheme, will endure forever; Laplace, still more cunningly, even guesses that it could not have been made on any other scheme. Whereby, at least, our nautical Logbooks can be better kept; and water-transport of all kinds has grown more commodious. Of Geology and Geognosy we know enough: what with the labours of our Werners and Huttons, what with the ardent genius of their disciples, it has come about that now, to many a Royal Society, the Creation of a World is little more mysterious than the cooking of a Dumpling; concerning which last, indeed, there have been minds to whom the question, *How the apples were got in*, presented difficulties. Why mention our disquisitions on the Social Contract, on the Standard of Taste, on the Migrations of

3

the Herring? Then, have we not a Doctrine of Rent, a Theory of
Value; Philosophies of Language, of History, of Pottery, of Apparitions, of Intoxicating Liquors? Man's whole life and environment
have been laid open and elucidated; scarcely a fragment or fibre of his
5   Soul, Body, and Possessions, but has been probed, dissected, distilled,
desiccated, and scientifically decomposed: our spiritual Faculties, of
which it appears there are not a few, have their Stewarts, Cousins,
Royer Collards: every cellular, vascular, muscular Tissue glories in its
Lawrences, Majendies, Bichâts.
10   How, then, comes it, may the reflective mind repeat, that the
grand Tissue of all Tissues, the only real *Tissue*, should have been
quite overlooked by Science,—the vestural Tissue, namely, of woollen
or other Cloth; which Man's Soul wears as its outmost wrappage and
overall; wherein his whole other Tissues are included and screened,
15   his whole Faculties work, his whole Self lives, moves, and has its
being? For if, now and then, some straggling broken-winged thinker
has cast an owl's-glance into this obscure region, the most have soared
over it altogether heedless; regarding Clothes as a property, not an
accident, as quite natural and spontaneous, like the leaves of trees,
20   like the plumage of birds. In all speculations they have tacitly figured
man as a *Clothed Animal;* whereas he is by nature a *Naked Animal;*
and only in certain circumstances, by purpose and device, masks himself in Clothes. Shakespeare says, we are creatures that look before
and after: the more surprising that we do not look round a little, and
25   see what is passing under our very eyes.
        But here, as in so many other cases, Germany, learned, indefati-
gable, deep-thinking Germany comes to our aid. It is, after all, a
blessing that, in these revolutionary times, there should be one country where abstract Thought can still take shelter; that while the din
30   and frenzy of Catholic Emancipations, and Rotten Boroughs, and
Revolts of Paris, deafen every French and every English ear, the German
can stand peaceful on his scientific watch-tower; and, to the raging,
struggling multitude here and elsewhere, solemnly, from hour to hour,
with preparatory blast of cowhorn, emit his *Höret ihr Herren und*
35   *lasset's Euch sagen;* in other words, tell the Universe, which so often
forgets that fact, what o'clock it really is. Not unfrequently the Germans have been blamed for an unprofitable diligence; as if they struck

into devious courses, where nothing was to be had but the toil of a
rough journey; as if, forsaking the gold-mines of Finance, and that
political slaughter of fat oxen whereby a man himself grows fat, they
were apt to run goose-hunting into regions of bilberries and crowber-
ries, and be swallowed up at last in remote peat-bogs. Of that unwise   5
science, which, as our Humorist expresses it,

> 'By geometric scale
> Doth take the size of pots of ale,'

still more, of that altogether misdirected industry, which is seen vigorously thrashing mere straw, there can nothing defensive be said. In   10
so far as the Germans are chargeable with such, let them take the
consequence. Nevertheless be it remarked, that even a Russian Steppe
has Tumuli and gold ornaments; also many a scene that looks desert
and rock-bound from the distance, will unfold itself, when visited,
into rare valleys. Nay, in any case, would Criticism erect not only   15
fingerposts and turnpikes, but spiked gates and impassable barriers,
for the mind of man? It is written, 'Many shall run to and fro, and
knowledge shall be increased.' Surely the plain rule is, Let each con-
siderate person have his way, and see what it will lead to. For not this
man and that man, but all men make up mankind, and their united   20
tasks the task of mankind. How often have we seen some such adventurous, and perhaps much-censured wanderer light on some outlying,
neglected, yet vitally momentous province; the hidden treasures of
which he first discovered, and kept proclaiming till the general eye
and effort were directed thither, and the conquest was completed;—   25
thereby, in these his seemingly so aimless rambles, planting new standards, founding new habitable colonies, in the immeasurable circumambient realm of Nothingness and Night! Wise man was he who
counselled that Speculation should have free course, and look fearlessly towards all the thirty-two points of the compass, whithersoever   30
and howsoever it listed.

Perhaps it is proof of the stinted condition in which pure Science,
especially pure moral Science, languishes among us English; and how
our mercantile greatness, and invaluable Constitution, impressing   35
a political or other immediately practical tendency on all English

culture and endeavour, cramps the free flight of Thought,—that this,
not Philosophy of Clothes, but recognition even that we have no
such Philosophy, stands here for the first time published in our language. What English intellect could have chosen such a topic, or by
5   chance stumbled on it? But for that same unshackled, and even sequestered condition of the German Learned, which permits and in-
duces them to fish in all manner of waters, with all manner of nets,
it seems probable enough, this abstruse Inquiry might, in spite of the
results it leads to, have continued dormant for indefinite periods. The
10   Editor of these sheets, though otherwise boasting himself a man of
confirmed speculative habits, and perhaps discursive enough, is free
to confess, that never, till these last months, did the above very plain
considerations, on our total want of a Philosophy of Clothes, occur
to him; and then, by quite foreign suggestion. By the arrival, namely,
15   of a new Book from Professor Teufelsdröckh of Weissnichtwo; treating expressly of this subject; and in a style which, whether understood
or not, could not even by the blindest be overlooked. In the present
Editor's way of thought, this remarkable Treatise, with its Doctrines,
whether as judicially acceded to, or judicially denied, has not re-
20   mained without effect.

'*Die Kleider ihr Werden und Wirken* (Clothes, their Origin and
Influence): *von Diog. Teufelsdröckh, J.U.D. etc. Stillschweigen und Co^gnie.*
Weissnichtwo, 1831.

'Here,' says the *Weissnichtwo'sche Anzeiger*, 'comes a Volume of
25   that extensive, close-printed, close-meditated sort, which, be it spoken with pride, is seen only in Germany, perhaps only in Weissnichtwo:
issuing from the hitherto irreproachable Firm of Stillschweigen and
Company, with every external furtherance, it is of such internal quality as to set Neglect at defiance.' * * * 'A work,' concludes the well
30   nigh enthusiastic Reviewer, 'interesting alike to the antiquary, the
historian, and the philosophic thinker; a masterpiece of boldness,
lynx-eyed acuteness, and rugged independent Germanism and Philanthropy (*derber Kerndeutschheit und Menschenliebe*); which will not,
assuredly, pass current without opposition in high places; but must
35   and will exalt the almost new name of Teufelsdröckh to the first ranks
of Philosophy, in our German Temple-of-Honour.'

Mindful of old friendship, the distinguished Professor, in this the
first blaze of his fame, which however does not dazzle him, sends

hither a Presentation Copy of his Book; with compliments and enco-
miums which modesty forbids the present Editor to rehearse; yet
without indicated wish or hope of any kind, except what may be
implied in the concluding phrase: *Möchte es* (this remarkable Treatise)
auch im Brittischen Boden gedeihen!   5

CHAPTER II.

IF for a speculative man, 'whose seedfield,' in the sublime words of the Poet, 'is Time,' no conquest is important but that of new Ideas, then might the arrival of Professor Teufelsdröckh's Book be marked with chalk in the Editor's calendar. It is indeed an 'extensive Volume,' of boundless, almost formless contents, a very Sea of Thought; neither calm nor clear, if you will; yet wherein the toughest pearl-diver may dive to his utmost depth, and return not only with sea-wreck but with true orients.

Directly on the first perusal, almost on the first deliberate inspection, it became apparent that here a quite new Branch of Philosophy, leading to as yet undescried ulterior results, was disclosed; farther, what seemed scarcely less interesting, a quite new human Individuality, an almost unexampled personal Character, that, namely, of Professor Teufelsdröckh the Discloser. Of both which novelties, as far as might be possible, we resolved to master the significance. But as man is emphatically a Proselytising creature, no sooner was such mastery even fairly attempted, than the new question arose: How might this acquired good be imparted to others, perhaps in equal need thereof; how could the Philosophy of Clothes, and the Author of such Philosophy, be brought home, in any measure, to the business and bosoms of our own English nation? For if new-got gold is said to burn the pockets till it be cast forth into circulation, much more may new Truth.

8

Here, however, difficulties occurred. The first thought naturally was to publish Article after Article on this remarkable volume, in such widely-circulating Critical Journals as the Editor might stand connected with, or by money or love procure access to. But, on the other hand, was it not clear that such matter as must here be revealed and treated of might endanger the circulation of any Journal extant? If, indeed, all party-divisions in the State could have been abolished, Whig, Tory, and Radical, embracing in discrepant union; and all the Journals of the Nation could have been jumbled into one Journal, and the Philosophy of Clothes poured forth in incessant torrents therefrom, the attempt had seemed possible. But, alas, what vehicle of that sort have we, except *Fraser's Magazine*? A vehicle all strewed (figuratively speaking) with the maddest Waterloo-Crackers, exploding distractively and destructively, wheresoever the mystified passenger stands or sits; nay, in any case, understood to be, of late years, a vehicle full to overflowing, and inexorably shut! Besides, to state the Philosophy of Clothes without the Philosopher, the ideas of Teufelsdröckh without something of his personality, was it not to insure both of entire misapprehension? Now for Biography, had it been otherwise admissible, there were no adequate documents, no hope of obtaining such, but rather, owing to circumstances, a special despair. Thus did the Editor see himself, for the while, shut out from all public utterance of these extraordinary Doctrines, and constrained to revolve them, not without disquietude, in the dark depths of his own mind.

So had it lasted for some months; and now the Volume on Clothes, read and again read, was in several points becoming lucid and lucent; the personality of its Author more and more surprising, but, in spite of all that memory and conjecture could do, more and more enigmatic; whereby the old disquietude seemed fast settling into fixed discontent,—when altogether unexpectedly arrives a Letter from Herr Hofrath Heuschrecke, our Professor's chief friend and associate in Weissnichtwo, with whom we had not previously corresponded. The Hofrath, after much quite extraneous matter, began dilating largely on the 'agitation and attention' which the Philosophy of Clothes was exciting in its own German Republic of Letters; on the deep significance and tendency of his Friend's Volume; and then, at length, with great circumlocution, hinted at the practicability of conveying 'some

knowledge of it, and of him, to England, and through England to the
distant West;' a Work on Professor Teufelsdröckh 'were undoubtedly
welcome to the *Family*, the *National*, or any other of those patriotic
Libraries, at present the glory of British Literature;' might work revo-
5　lutions in Thought; and so forth;—in conclusion, intimating not
obscurely, that should the present Editor feel disposed to undertake
a Biography of Teufelsdröckh, he, Hofrath Heuschrecke, had it in his
power to furnish the requisite Documents.

As in some chemical mixture, that has stood long evaporating, but
10　would not crystallise, instantly when the wire or other fixed substance
is introduced, crystallisation commences, and rapidly proceeds till the
whole is finished, so was it with the Editor's mind and this offer of
Heuschrecke's. Form rose out of void solution and discontinuity; like
united itself with like in definite arrangement; and soon either in
15　actual vision and possession, or in fixed reasonable hope, the image
of the whole Enterprise had shaped itself, so to speak, into a solid
mass. Cautiously yet courageously, through the twopenny post, application to the famed redoubtable OLIVER YORKE was now made: an
interview, interviews with that singular man have taken place; with
20　more of assurance on our side, with less of satire (at least of open
satire) on his, than we anticipated;—for the rest, with such issue as
is now visible. As to those same 'patriotic *Libraries*,' the Hofrath's
counsel could only be viewed with silent amazement; but with his
offer of Documents we joyfully and almost instantaneously closed.
25　Thus, too, in the sure expectation of these, we already see our task
begun; and this our *Sartor Resartus*, which is properly a 'Life and
Opinions of Herr Teufelsdröckh,' hourly advancing.

Of our fitness for the Enterprise, to which we have such title and
30　vocation, it were perhaps uninteresting to say more. Let the British
reader study and enjoy, in simplicity of heart, what is here presented
him, and with whatever metaphysical acumen, and talent for Meditation
he is possessed of. Let him strive to keep a free, open sense; cleared from
the mists of Prejudice, above all from the paralysis of Cant; and directed
35　rather to the Book itself than to the Editor of the Book. Who or what
such Editor may be, must remain conjectural, and even insignificant:*

---

*With us even he still communicates in some sort of mask, or muffler; and,
we have reason to think, under a feigned name! — O.Y.

it is a Voice publishing tidings of the Philosophy of Clothes; undoubtedly a Spirit addressing Spirits: whoso hath ears let him hear.

On one other point the Editor thinks it needful to give warning:
namely, that he is animated with a true though perhaps a feeble
attachment to the Institutions of our Ancestors; and minded to de-   5
fend these, according to ability, at all hazards; nay, it was partly with
a view to such defence that he engaged in this undertaking. To stem,
or if that be impossible, profitably to divert the current of Innovation, such a Volume as Teufelsdröckh's, if cunningly planted down,
were no despicable pile, or floodgate, in the Logical wear.   10

For the rest, be it nowise apprehended that any personal connexion
of ours with Teufelsdröckh, Heuschrecke, or this Philosophy of Clothes,
can pervert our judgment, or sway us to extenuate or exaggerate.
Powerless, we venture to promise, are those private Compliments
themselves. Grateful they may well be; as generous illusions of friend-   15
ship; as fair mementos of bygone unions, of those nights and suppers
of the gods, when lapped in the symphonies and harmonies of Philosophic Eloquence, though with baser accompaniments, the present
Editor revelled in that feast of reason, never since vouchsafed him in
so full measure! But what then? *Amicus Plato, magis amica veritas;*   20
Teufelsdröckh is our friend, Truth is our divinity. In our historical
and critical capacity, we hope, we are strangers to all the world; have
feud or favour with no one,—save indeed the Devil, with whom as
with the Prince of Lies and Darkness we do at all times wage internecine
war. This assurance, at an epoch when Puffery and Quackery have   25
reached a height unexampled in the annals of mankind, and even
English Editors, like Chinese Shopkeepers, must write on their door-
lintels, *No cheating here,*—we thought it good to premise.

CHAPTER III.

To the Author's private circle the appearance of this singular Work on Clothes must have occasioned little less surprise than it has to the rest of the world. For ourselves, at least, few things have been more unexpected. Professor Teufelsdröckh, at the period of our acquain-
5 tance with him, seemed to lead a quite still and self-contained life: a man devoted to the higher Philosophies, indeed; yet more likely, if he published at all, to publish a Refutation of Hegel and Bardili, both of whom, strangely enough, he included under a common ban; than to descend, as he has here done, into the angry noisy Forum, with an
10 Argument that cannot but exasperate and divide. Not, that we can remember, was the Philosophy of Clothes once touched upon be- tween us. If through the high silent, meditative Transcendentalism of our Friend we detected any practical tendency whatever, it was at most Political, and towards a certain prospective, and for the present
15 quite speculative, Radicalism; as indeed some correspondence, on his part, with Herr Oken of Jena was now and then suspected; though his special contributions to the *Isis* could never be more than sur- mised at. But, at all events, nothing Moral, still less any thing Didactico- Religious, was looked for from him.
20   Well do we recollect the last words he spoke in our hearing; which indeed, with the Night they were uttered in, are to be forever re- membered. Lifting his huge tumbler of *Gukguk*,* and for a moment

---

*Gukguk is unhappily only an academical—Beer.

lowering his tobacco-pipe, he stood up in full coffeehouse (it was *Zur Grünen Gans*, the largest in Weissnichtwo, where all the Virtuosity, and nearly all the Intellect, of the place assembled of an evening); and there, with low, soul-stirring tone, and the look truly of an angel, though whether of a white or of a black one might be dubious, pro-   5
posed this toast: *Die Sache der Armen in Gottes und Teufels Namen* (The Cause of the Poor in Heaven's name and ——'s)! One full shout, breaking the leaden silence; then a gurgle of innumerable emptying bumpers, again followed by universal cheering, returned him loud acclaim. It was the finale of the night: resuming their pipes;   10
in the highest enthusiasm, amid volumes of tobacco-smoke; trium-phant, cloudcapt without and within, the assembly broke up, each to his thoughtful pillow. *Bleibt doch ein echter Spass- und Galgen-vogel,* said several; meaning thereby that, one day, he would probably be hanged for his democratic sentiments. *Wo steckt doch der Schalk?* added   15
they, looking round: but Teufelsdröckh had retired by private alleys, and the Compiler of these pages beheld him no more.

In such scenes has it been our lot to live with this Philosopher, such estimate to form of his purposes and powers. And yet, thou brave Teufelsdröckh, who could tell what lurked in thee? Under those   20
thick locks of thine, so long and lank, overlapping roof-wise the grav-est face we ever in this world saw, there dwelt a most busy brain. In thy eyes, too, deep under their shaggy brows, and looking out so still and dreamy, have we not noticed gleams of an ethereal or else a di-abolic fire, and half fancied that their stillness was but the rest of   25
infinite motion, the *sleep* of a spinning-top? Thy little figure, there as in loose, ill-brushed, threadbare habiliments, thou sattest, amid litter and lumber, whole days, to 'think and smoke tobacco,' held in it a mighty heart. The secrets of man's Life were laid open to thee; thou sawest into the mystery of the Universe, farther than another; thou   30
hadst *in petto* thy remarkable Volume on Clothes. Nay, was there not in that clear logically-founded Transcendentalism of thine; still more, in thy meek, silent, deepseated Sansculottism, combined with a true princely Courtesy of inward nature, the visible rudiments of such speculation? But great men are too often unknown, or what is worse,   35
misknown. Already, when we dreamed not of it, the warp of thy remarkable Volume lay on the loom; and silently, mysterious shuttles were putting in the woof!

How the Hofrath Heuschrecke is to furnish biographical data, in this case, may be a curious question; the answer of which, however, is happily not our concern, but his. To us it appeared, after repeated trial, that in Weissnichtwo, from the archives or memories of the best-informed classes, no Biography of Teufelsdröckh was to be gathered; not so much as a false one. He was a Stranger there, wafted thither by what is called the course of circumstances; concerning whose parentage, birth-place, prospects or pursuits, Curiosity had indeed made inquiries, but satisfied herself with the most indistinct replies. For himself, he was a man so still and altogether unparticipating, that to question him even afar off on such particulars was a thing of more than usual delicacy: besides, in his sly way, he had ever some quaint turn, not without its satirical edge, wherewith to divert such intrusions, and deter you from the like. Wits spoke of him secretly as if he were a kind of Melchizedek, without father or mother of any kind; sometimes, with reference to his great historic and statistic knowledge, and the vivid way he had of expressing himself like an eye-witness of distant transactions and scenes, they called him the *Ewige Jude*, Everlasting, or as we say, Wandering Jew.

To the most, indeed, he had become not so much a Man as a Thing; which Thing doubtless they were accustomed to see, and with satisfaction; but no more thought of accounting for than for the fabrication of their daily *Allgemeine Zeitung*, or the domestic habits of the Sun. Both were there and welcome; the world enjoyed what good was in them, and thought no more of the matter. The man Teufelsdröckh passed and repassed, in his little circle, as one of those originals and nondescripts, more frequent in German Universities than elsewhere; of whom, though you see them alive, and feel certain enough that they must have a History, no History seems to be discoverable; or only such as men give of mountain rocks and antediluvian ruins: that they have been created by unknown agencies, are in a state of gradual decay, and for the present reflect light and resist pressure; that is, are visible and tangible objects in this phantasm world, where so much other mystery is.

It was to be remarked that though, by title and diploma, *Professor der Allerley-Wissenschaft*, or as we should say in English, 'Professor of Things in General,' he had never delivered any Course; perhaps never been incited thereto by any public furtherance or requisition. To all

appearance, the enlightened Government of Weissnichtwo, in founding their New University, imagined they had done enough, if 'in
times like ours,' as the half-official Program expressed it, 'when all
things are, rapidly or slowly, resolving themselves into Chaos, a Professorship of this kind had been established; whereby, as occasion   5
called, the task of bodying somewhat forth again from such Chaos
might be, even slightly, facilitated.' That actual Lectures should be
held, and Public Classes for the 'Science of Things in General,' they
doubtless considered premature; on which ground too they had only
established the Professorship, nowise endowed it; so that Teufelsdröckh,   10
'recommended by the highest Names,' had been promoted thereby
to a Name merely.

Great, among the more enlightened classes, was the admiration of
this new Professorship: how an enlightened Government had seen
into the Want of the Age (*Zeitbedürfniss*); how at length, instead of   15
Denial and Destruction, we were to have a science of Affirmation and
Re-construction; and Germany and Weissnichtwo were, where they
should be, in the vanguard of the world. Considerable also was the
wonder at the new Professor, dropt opportunely enough into the
nascent University; so able to lecture, should occasion call; so ready   20
to hold his peace for indefinite periods, should an enlightened Government consider that occasion did not call. But such admiration and
such wonder, being followed by no act to keep them living, could last
only nine days; and, long before our visit to that scene, had quite died
away. The more cunning heads thought it was all an expiring clutch   25
at popularity, on the part of a Minister, whom domestic embarrass-
ments, court intrigues, old age, and dropsy soon afterwards finally
drove from the helm.

As for Teufelsdröckh, except by his nightly appearances at the
Grüne Gans, Weissnichtwo saw little of him, felt little of him. Here,   30
over his tumbler of Gukguk, he sat reading Journals; sometimes con-
templatively looking into the clouds of his tobacco-pipe, without
other visible employment: always, from his mild ways, an agreeable
phenomenon there; more especially when he opened his lips for speech;
on which occasions the whole Coffeehouse would hush itself into   35
silence, as if sure to hear something noteworthy. Nay, perhaps to hear
a whole series and river of the most memorable utterances; such as,
when once thawed, he would for hours indulge in, with fit audience:

and the more memorable, as issuing from a head apparently not more
interested in them, not more conscious of them, than is the sculp-
tured stone head of some public Fountain, which through its brass
mouth-tube emits water to the worthy and the unworthy; careless
5   whether it be for cooking victuals or quenching conflagrations; indeed, maintains the same earnest assiduous look, whether any water
be flowing or not.

To the Editor of these sheets, as to a young enthusiastic Englishman, however unworthy, Teufelsdröckh opened himself perhaps more
10   than to the most. Pity only that we could not then half guess his
importance, and scrutinise him with due power of vision! We enjoyed, what not three men in Weissnichtwo could boast of, a certain
degree of access to the Professor's private domicile. It was the attic
floor of the highest house in the Wahngasse; and might truly be called
15   the pinnacle of Weissnichtwo, for it rose sheer up above the contiguous roofs, themselves rising from elevated ground. Moreover, with its
windows, it looked towards all the four *Orte*, or as the Scotch say, and
we ought to say, *Airts:* the Sitting-room itself commanded three;
another came to view in the *Schlafgemach* (Bed-room) at the opposite
20   end; to say nothing of the Kitchen, which offered two, as it were,
duplicates, and showing nothing new. So that it was in fact the speculum or watch-tower of Teufelsdröckh; wherefrom, sitting at ease, he
might see the whole life-circulation of that considerable City; the
streets and lanes of which, with all their doing and driving (*Thun und*
25   *Treiben*) were for most part visible there.

'I look down into all that wasp-nest or bee-hive,' have we heard
him say, 'and witness their wax-laying and honey-making, and poison-
brewing, and choking by sulphur. From the Palace esplanade, where
music plays while Serene Highness is pleased to eat his victuals,
30   down the low lane, where in her door-sill the aged widow, knitting
for a thin livelihood, sits to feel the afternoon sun, I see it all; for,
except the Schlosskirche weathercock, no biped stands so high.
Couriers arrive bestrapped and bebooted, bearing Joy and Sorrow
bagged up in pouches of leather: there, topladen, and with four swift
35   horses, rolls in the country Baron and his household; here, on timber
leg, the lamed Soldier hops painfully along, begging alms: a thousand carriages, and wains, and cars, come tumbling in with Food, with
young Rusticity, and other Raw Produce, inanimate or animate, and

go tumbling out again with Produce manufactured. That living flood, pouring through these streets, of all qualities and ages, knowest thou whence it is coming, whither it is going? *Aus der Ewigkeit, zu der Ewigkeit hin:* From Eternity, onwards to Eternity! These are Apparitions: what else? Are they not Souls rendered visible; in Bodies, that took shape, and will lose it; melting into air? Their solid pavement is a Picture of the Sense; they walk on the bosom of Nothing, blank Time is behind them and before them. Or fanciest thou, the red and yellow Clothes-screen yonder, with spurs on its heels, and feather in its crown, is but of To-day, without a Yesterday or a To-morrow; and had not rather its Ancestor alive when Hengst and Horsa overran thy Island? Friend, thou seest here a living link in that Tissue of History, which inweaves all Being: watch well, or it will be past thee, and seen no more.'

'*Ach, mein Lieber!*' said he once, at midnight, when we had returned from the Coffeehouse in rather earnest talk, 'it is a true sublimity to dwell here. These fringes of lamplight, struggling up through smoke and thousand-fold exhalation, some fathoms into the ancient reign of Night, what thinks Boötes of them, as he leads his Hunting Dogs over the Zenith in their leash of sidereal fire? That stifled hum of Midnight, when Traffic has lain down to rest; and the chariot-wheels of Vanity, still rolling here and there through distant streets, are bearing her to Halls roofed in, and lighted to the due pitch for her; and only Vice and Misery, to prowl or to moan like nightbirds, are abroad: that hum, I say, like the stertorous, unquiet slumber of sick Life, is heard in Heaven! Oh, under that hideous coverlid of vapours, and putrefactions, and unimaginable gases, what a Fermenting-vat lies simmering and hid! The joyful and the sorrowful are there; men are dying there, men are being born; men are praying,— on the other side of a brick partition, men are cursing; and around them all is the vast, void Night. The proud Grandee still lingers in his perfumed saloons, or reposes within damask curtains; Wretchedness cowers into truckle-beds, or shivers hunger-stricken into its lair of straw: in obscure cellars, *Rouge-et-Noir* languidly emits its voice-of-destiny to haggard hungry Villains; while Councillors of State sit plotting, and playing their high chess-game, whereof the pawns are Men. The Lover whispers his mistress that the coach is ready; and she, full of hope and fear, glides down, to fly with him over the

borders: the Thief, still more silently, sets-to his picklocks and crow-
bars, or lurks in wait till the watchmen first snore in their boxes. Gay
mansions, with supper-rooms and dancing-rooms, are full of light and
music and high-swelling hearts; but, in the Condemned Cells, the
5 pulse of life beats tremulous and faint, and bloodshot eyes look out
through the darkness, which is around and within, for the light of a
stern last morning. Six men are to be hanged on the morrow: comes
no hammering from the *Rabenstein?*—their gallows must even now
be o' building. Upwards of five hundred thousand two-legged ani-
10 mals without feathers lie round us, in horizontal position; their heads
all in nightcaps, and full of the foolishest dreams. Riot cries aloud,
and staggers and swaggers in his rank dens of shame; and the Mother,
with streaming hair, kneels over her pallid dying infant, whose cracked
lips only her tears now moisten.—All these heaped and huddled to-
15 gether, with nothing but a little carpentry and masonry between
them;—crammed in, like salted fish, in their barrel;—or weltering,
shall I say, like an Egyptian pitcher of tamed Vipers, each struggling
to get its *head above* the others: *such* work goes on under that smoke-
counterpane!—But I, *mein Werther*, sit above it all; I am alone with
20 the Stars.'
      We looked in his face to see whether, in the utterance of such
extraordinary Night-thoughts, no feeling might be traced there; but
with the light we had, which indeed was only a single tallow-light,
and far enough from the window, nothing save that old calmness and
25 fixedness was visible.
      These were the Professor's talking seasons: most commonly he
spoke in mere monosyllables, or sat altogether silent, and smoked;
while the visitor had liberty either to say what he listed, receiving for
answer an occasional grunt; or to look round for a space, and then
30 take himself away. It was a strange apartment; full of books and
tattered papers, and miscellaneous shreds of all conceivable substances,
'united in a common element of dust.' Books lay on tables, and
below tables; here fluttered a sheet of manuscript, there a torn hand-
kerchief, or nightcap hastily thrown aside: ink-bottles alternated with
35 bread-crusts, coffee-pots, tobacco-boxes, Periodical Literature, and
Blücher Boots. Old Lieschen (Lisekin, 'Liza), who was his bed-maker
and stove-lighter, his washer and wringer, cook, errand-maid, and
general lion's-provider, and for the rest a very orderly creature, had

no sovereign authority in this last citadel of Teufelsdröckh; only some once in the month, she half-forcibly made her way thither, with broom and duster, and (Teufelsdröckh hastily saving his manuscripts) effected a partial clearance, a jail-delivery of such lumber as was not Literary. These were her *Erdbeben* (Earthquakes), which Teufelsdröckh dreaded worse than the pestilence; nevertheless, to such length he had been forced to comply. Glad would he have been to sit here philosophising forever, or till the litter, by accumulation, drove him out of doors: but Lieschen was his right-arm, and spoon, and necessary of life, and would not be flatly gainsayed. We can still remember the ancient woman; so silent that some thought her dumb; deaf also you would often have supposed her; for Teufelsdröckh and Teufelsdröckh only would she serve or give heed to; and with him she seemed to communicate chiefly by signs; if it were not rather by some secret divination that she guessed all his wants, and supplied them. Assiduous old dame! she scoured, and sorted, and swept, in her kitchen, with the least possible violence to the ear; yet all was tight and right there: hot and black came the coffee ever at the due moment; and the speechless Lieschen herself looked out on you, from under her clean white coif with its lappets, through her clean withered face and wrinkles, with a look of helpful intelligence, almost of benevolence.

Few strangers, as above hinted, had admittance hither: the only one we ever saw there, ourselves excepted, was the Hofrath Heuschrecke, already known, by name and expectation, to the readers of these pages. To us, at that period, Herr Heuschrecke seemed one of those purse-mouthed, crane-necked, clean-brushed, pacific individuals, perhaps sufficiently distinguished in society by this fact, that, in dry weather or in wet, 'they never appear without their umbrella.' Had we not known with what 'little-wisdom' the world is governed; and how, in Germany as elsewhere, the ninety and nine Public Men can for most part be but mute train-bearers to the hundredth, perhaps but stalking-horses and willing or unwilling dupes,— it might have seemed wonderful how Herr Heuschrecke should be named a *Rath*, or Councillor, and Counsellor, even in Weissnichtwo. What counsel to any man, or to any woman, could this particular Hofrath give; in whose loose, zigzag figure; in whose thin visage, as it went jerking to and fro, in minute incessant fluctuation,—you traced rather confusion worse confounded; at most, Timidity and physical

Cold? Some indeed said withal, he was 'the very Spirit of Love embodied:' blue earnest eyes, full of sadness and kindness; purse ever
open, and so forth; the whole of which, we shall now hope for many
reasons, was not quite groundless. Nevertheless, friend Teufelsdröckh's
5 outline, who indeed handled the burin like few in these cases, was
probably the best: *Er hat Gemüth und Geist, hat wenigstens gehabt,
doch ohne Organ, ohne Schicksals-Gunst; ist gegenwärtig aber halb-
zerrüttet, halb-erstarrt,* 'He has heart and talent, at least has had
such, yet without fit mode of utterance, or favour of Fortune; and so
10 is now half-cracked, half-congealed.'—What the Hofrath shall think
of this, when he sees it, readers may wonder: we, safe in the stronghold of Historical Fidelity, are careless.

The main point, doubtless, for us all, is his love of Teufelsdröckh,
which indeed was also by far the most decisive feature of Heuschrecke
15 himself. We are enabled to assert that he hung on the Professor with
the fondness of a Boswell for his Johnson. And perhaps with the like
return; for Teufelsdröckh treated his gaunt admirer with little outward regard, as some half-rational or altogether irrational friend, and
at best loved him out of gratitude and by habit. On the other hand,
20 it was curious to observe with what reverent kindness, and a sort of
fatherly protection, our Hofrath, being the elder, richer, and as he
fondly imagined far more practically influential of the two, looked
and tended on his little Sage, whom he seemed to consider as a living
oracle. Let but Teufelsdröckh open his mouth, Heuschrecke's also
25 unpuckered itself into a free doorway, besides his being all eye and all
ear, so that nothing might be lost: and then, at every pause in the
harangue he gurgled out his pursy chuckle of a cough-laugh (for the
machinery of laughter took some time to get in motion, and seemed
crank and slack), or else his twanging, nasal *Bravo! Das glaub' ich;* in
30 either case, by way of heartiest approval. In short, if Teufelsdröckh
was Dalai-Lama, of which except perhaps in his self-seclusion, and
god-like Indifference, there was no symptom, then might Heuschrecke
pass for his chief Talapoin, to whom no dough-pill he could knead
and publish was other than medicinal and sacred.
35   In such environment, social, domestic, physical, did Teufelsdröckh,
at the time of our acquaintance, and most likely does he still, live and
meditate. Here, perched up in his high Wahngasse watchtower, and
often, in solitude, outwatching the Bear, it was that the indomitable

Inquirer fought all his battles with Dulness and Darkness; here, in all probability, that he wrote this surprising Volume on *Clothes*. Additional particulars: of his age, which was of that standing middle sort you could only guess at; of his wide surtout; the colour of his trousers, fashion of his broad-brimmed steeple-hat, and so forth, we might report, but do not. The Wisest truly is, in these times, the Greatest; so that an enlightened curiosity leaving Kings and such like to rest very much on their own basis, turns more and more to the Philosophic Class: nevertheless, what reader expects that, with all our writing and reporting, Teufelsdröckh could be brought home to him, till once the Documents arrive? His Life, Fortunes, and Bodily Presence, are as yet hidden from us, or matter only of faint conjecture. But on the other hand, does not his Soul lie enclosed in this remarkable Volume, much more truly than Pedro Garcia's did in the buried Bag of Doubloons? To the soul of Diogenes Teufelsdröckh, to his opinions namely on the 'Origin and Influence of Clothes,' we for the present gladly return.

CHAPTER IV.

CHARACTERISTICS.

IT were a piece of vain flattery to pretend that this Work on Clothes entirely contents us; that it is not, like all works of Genius, like the very Sun, which, though the highest published Creation, or work of Genius, has nevertheless black spots and troubled nebulosities amid its effulgence,—a mixture of insight, inspiration, with dulness, double-vision, and even utter blindness.

Without committing ourselves to those enthusiastic praises and prophesyings of the *Weissnichtwo' sche Anzeiger*, we admitted that the Book had in a high degree excited us to self-activity, which is the best effect of any book; that it had even operated changes in our way of thought; nay, that it promised to prove, as it were, the opening of a new mine-shaft, wherein the whole world of Speculation might henceforth dig to unknown depths. More specially it may now be declared that Professor Teufelsdröckh's acquirements, patience of research, philosophic and even poetic vigour, are here made indisputably manifest; and unhappily no less his prolixity and tortuosity and manifold inaptitude; that, on the whole, as in opening new mine-shafts is not unreasonable, there is much rubbish in his Book, though likewise specimens of almost invaluable ore. A paramount popularity in England we cannot promise him. Apart from the choice of such a topic as Clothes, too often the manner of treating it betokens in the Author a rusticity and academic seclusion, unblamable, indeed inevitable in a German, but fatal to his success with our public.

22

Of good society Teufelsdröckh appears to have seen little, or has mostly forgotten what he saw. He speaks out with a strange plainness; calls many things by their mere dictionary names. To him the Upholsterer is no Pontiff, neither is any Drawing-room a Temple, were it never so begilt and overhung: 'a whole immensity of Brussels carpets, and pier-glasses, and or-molu,' as he himself expresses it, 'cannot hide from me that such Drawing-room is simply a section of Infinite Space, where so many God-created Souls do for the time meet together.' To Teufelsdröckh the highest Duchess is respectable, is venerable; but nowise for her pearl-bracelets, and Malines laces: in his eyes, the star of a Lord is little less and little more than the broad button of Birmingham spelter in a Clown's smock; 'each is an implement,' he says, 'in its kind; a tag for *hooking-together;* and, for the rest, was dug from the earth, and hammered on a stithy before smiths' fingers.' Thus does the Professor look in men's faces with a strange impartiality, a strange scientific freedom; like a man unversed in the higher circles, like a man dropped thither from the Moon. Rightly considered, it is in this peculiarity, running through his whole system of thought, that all these short-comings, over-shootings, and multiform perversities, take rise: if indeed they have not a second source, also natural enough, in his Transcendental Philosophies, and humour of looking at all Matter and Material things as Spirit; whereby truly his case were but the more hopeless, the more lamentable.

To the Thinkers of this nation, however, of which class it is firmly believed there are individuals yet extant, we can safely recommend the Work: nay, who knows but among the fashionable ranks too, if it be true, as Teufelsdröckh maintains, that 'within the most starched cravat there passes a windpipe and weasand, and under the thickliest embroidered waistcoat beats a heart,'—the force of that rapt earnestness may be felt, and here and there an arrow of the soul pierce through. In our wild Seer, shaggy, unkempt, like a Baptist living on locusts and wild honey, there is an untutored energy, a silent as it were unconscious strength, which, except in the higher walks of Literature, must be rare. Many a deep glance, and often with unspeakable precision, has he cast into mysterious Nature, and the still more mysterious Life of Man. Wonderful it is with what cutting words, now and then, he severs asunder the confusion; sheers down, were it furlongs deep, into the true centre of the matter; and there not only

hits the nail on the head, but with crushing force smites it home, and
buries it.—On the other hand, let us be free to admit, he is the most
unequal writer breathing. Often after some such feat, he will play
truant for long pages, and go dawdling and dreaming, and mumbling
5 and maundering the merest commonplaces, as if he were asleep with
eyes open, which indeed he is.

Of his boundless Learning, and how all reading and literature in
most known tongues, from *Sanchoniathon* to *Dr. Lingard*, from your
Oriental *Shasters*, and *Talmuds*, and *Korans*, with Cassini's *Siamese*
10 *Tables*, and Laplace's *Mécanique Céleste*, down to *Robinson Crusoe* and
the *Belfast Town and Country Almanack*, are familiar to him,—we
shall say nothing: for unexampled as it is with us, to the Germans
such universality of study passes without wonder, as a thing com-
mendable, indeed, but natural, indispensable, and there of course. A
15 man that devotes his life to learning, shall he not be learned?

In respect of style our Author manifests the same genial capability,
marred too often by the same rudeness, inequality, and apparent want
of intercourse with the higher classes. Occasionally, as above hinted,
we find consummate vigour, a true inspiration: his burning Thoughts
20 step forth in fit burning Words, like so many full-formed Minervas,
issuing amid flame and splendour from Jove's head; a rich, idiomatic
diction, picturesque allusions, fiery poetic emphasis, or quaint tricksy
turns; all the graces and terrors of a wild Imagination, wedded to the
clearest Intellect, alternate in beautiful vicissitude. Were it not that
25 sheer sleeping and soporific passages; circumlocutions, repetitions,
touches even of pure doting jargon, so often intervene! On the whole,
Professor Teufelsdröckh is not a cultivated writer. Of his sentences
perhaps not more than nine-tenths stand straight on their legs; the
remainder are in quite angular attitudes, buttressed up by props (of
30 parentheses and dashes), and ever with this or the other tagrag hanging from them; a few even sprawl out helplessly on all sides quite
broken-backed and dismembered. Nevertheless, in almost his very
worst moods, there lies in him a singular attraction. A wild tone
pervades the whole utterance of the man, like its keynote and regu-
35 lator; now screwing itself aloft as into the Song of Spirits, or else the
shrill mockery of Fiends; now sinking in cadences, not without melodious heartiness, though sometimes abrupt enough, into the common pitch, when we hear it only as a monotonous hum; of which

hum the true character is extremely difficult to fix. Up to this hour we have never fully satisfied ourselves whether it is a tone and hum of real Humour, which we reckon among the very highest qualities of genius, or some echo of mere Insanity and Inanity, which doubtless ranks below the very lowest.   5

Under a like difficulty, in spite even of our personal intercourse, do we still lie with regard to the Professor's moral feeling. Gleams of an ethereal Love burst forth from him, soft wailings of infinite Pity; he could clasp the whole Universe into his bosom, and keep it warm; it seems as if under that rude exterior there dwelt a very seraph. Then   10 again he is so sly and still, so imperturbably saturnine; shews such indifference, malign coolness towards all that men strive after; and ever with some half-visible wrinkle of a bitter sardonic humour, if indeed it be not mere stolid callousness,—that you look on him almost with a shudder, as on some incarnate Mephistopheles, to   15 whom this great terrestrial and celestial Round, after all, were but some huge foolish Whirligig, where kings and beggars, and angels and demons, and stars and street-sweepings, were chaotically whirled; in which only children could take interest. His look, as we mentioned, is probably the gravest ever seen: yet it is not of that cast-iron   20 gravity frequent enough among our own Chancery suitors; but rather the gravity as of some silent, high-encircled mountain-pool, perhaps the crater of an extinct volcano; into whose black deeps you fear to gaze: those eyes, those lights that sparkle in it, may indeed be reflexes of the heavenly Stars, but perhaps also glances from the region of   25 Nether Fire!

Certainly a most involved, self-secluded, altogether enigmatic nature, this of Teufelsdröckh! Here, however, we gladly recall to mind that once we saw him *laugh;* once only, perhaps it was the first and last time in his life; but then such a peal of laughter, enough to have   30 awakened the Seven Sleepers! It was of Jean Paul's doing: some single billow in that vast world-Mahlstrom of Humour, with its heaven-kissing coruscations, which is now, alas, all congealed in the frost of Death! The large-bodied Poet and the small, both large enough in soul, sat talking miscellaneously together, the present Editor being   35 privileged to listen; and now Paul, in his serious way, was giving one of those inimitable 'Extra-harangues;' and, as it chanced, On the Proposal for a *Cast-metal King:* gradually a light kindled in our

Professor's eyes and face, a beaming, mantling, loveliest light; through those murky features, a radiant ever-young Apollo looked; and he burst forth like the neighing of all Tattersall's,—tears streaming down his cheeks, pipe held aloft, foot clutched into the air,—loud, long-continuing, uncontrollable; a laugh not of the face and diaphragm only, but of the whole man from head to heel. The present Editor, who laughed indeed, yet with measure, began to fear all was not right: however, Teufelsdröckh composed himself, and sank into his old stillness; on his inscrutable countenance there was, if any thing, a slight look of shame; and Richter himself could not rouse him again. Readers who have any tincture of Psychology know how much is to be inferred from this; and that no man who has once heartily and wholly laughed can be altogether irreclaimably bad. How much lies in Laughter: the cipher-key, wherewith we decipher the whole man! Some men wear an everlasting barren simper; in the smile of others lies a cold glitter as of ice: the fewest are able to laugh, what can be called laughing, but only sniff and titter and snigger from the throat outwards; or at best, produce some whiffling husky cachinnation, as if they were laughing through wool: of none such comes good. The man who cannot laugh is not only fit for treasons, stratagems, and spoils; but his whole life is already a treason and a stratagem.

Considered as an Author, Herr Teufelsdröckh has one scarcely pardonable fault, doubtless his worst: an almost total want of arrangement. In this remarkable Volume, it is true, his adherence to the mere course of Time produces, through the Narrative portions, a certain shew of outward method; but of true logical method and sequence there is too little. Apart from its multifarious sections and subdivisions, the Work naturally falls into two Parts; a Historical-Descriptive, and a Philosophical-Speculative: but falls, unhappily, by no firm line of demarcation; in that labyrinthic combination, each Part overlaps, and indents, and indeed runs quite through the other. Many sections are of a debatable rubric, or even quite nondescript and unnameable; whereby the Book not only loses in accessibility, but too often distresses us like some mad banquet, wherein all courses had been confounded, and fish and flesh, soup and solid, oyster-sauce, lettuces, Rhine-wine and French mustard, were hurled into one huge tureen or trough, and the hungry Public invited to help itself. To bring what order we can out of this Chaos shall be part of our endeavour.

CHAPTER V.

'As Montesquieu wrote a *Spirit of Laws,*' observes our Professor, 'so could I write a *Spirit of Clothes;* thus, with an *Esprit des Lois,* properly an *Esprit de Coutumes,* we should have an *Esprit de Costumes.* For neither in tailoring nor in legislating does man proceed by mere Accident, but the hand is ever guided on by mysterious operations of   5
the mind. In all his Modes, and habilatory endeavours, an Architectural Idea will be found lurking; his Body and the Cloth are the site and materials whereon and whereby his beautified edifice, of a Person, is to be built. Whether he flow gracefully out in folded mantles, based on light sandals; tower up in high headgear, from amid peaks,   10
spangles and bell-girdles; swell out in starched ruffs, buckram stuffings and monstrous tuberosities; or girth himself into separate sections, and front the world an Agglomeration of four limbs,—will depend on the nature of such Architectural Idea: whether Grecian, Gothic, Later-Gothic, or altogether Modern, and Parisian or Anglo-Dandiacal. Again,   15
what meaning lies in Colour! From the soberest drab to the high-flaming scarlet, spiritual idiosyncrasies unfold themselves in choice of Colour: if the Cut betoken Intellect and Talent, so does the Colour betoken Temper and Heart. In all which, among nations as among individuals, there is an incessant, indubitable, though infinitely com-   20
plex working of Cause and Effect: every snip of the Scissors has been regulated and prescribed by ever-active Influences, which doubtless to Intelligences of a superior order are neither invisible nor illegible.

27

'For such superior Intelligences a Cause-and-effect Philosophy of Clothes, as of Laws, were probably a comfortable winter-evening entertainment: nevertheless, for inferior Intelligences, like men, such Philosophies have always seemed to me uninstructive enough. Nay, what is your Montesquieu himself but a clever infant spelling Letters from a hieroglyphical prophetic Book, the lexicon of which lies in Eternity, in Heaven?—Let any Cause-and-Effect Philosopher explain, not why I wear such and such a Garment, obey such and such a Law; but even why *I* am *here*, to wear and obey any thing!—Much, therefore, if not the whole, of that same *Spirit of Clothes* I shall suppress, as hypothetical, ineffectual, and even impertinent: naked Facts, and Deductions drawn therefrom in quite another than that omniscient style, are my humbler and proper province.'

Acting on which prudent restriction, Teufelsdröckh has nevertheless contrived to take in a well-nigh boundless extent of field; at least, the boundaries too often lie quite beyond our horizon. Selection being indispensable, we shall here glance over his First Part only in the most cursory manner. This First Part is, no doubt, distinguished by omnivorous learning, and utmost patience and fairness: at the same time, in its results and delineations, it is much more likely to interest the Compilers of some *Library* of General, Entertaining, Useful, or even Useless Knowledge than the miscellaneous readers of these pages. Was it this Part of the Book which Heuschrecke had in view, when he recommended us to that joint-stock vehicle of publication, 'at present the glory of British Literature?' If so, the Library Editors are welcome to dig in it for their own behoof.

To the First Chapter, which turns on Paradise and Fig-leaves, and leads us into interminable disquisitions of a mythological, metaphorical, cabalistico-sartorial and quite antediluvian cast, we shall content ourselves with giving an unconcerned approval. Still less have we to do with 'Lilis, Adam's first wife, whom, according to the Talmudists, he had before Eve, and who bore him, in that wedlock, the whole progeny of aerial, aquatic, and terrestrial Devils,'—very needlessly, we think. On this portion of the Work, with its profound glances into the *Adam-Kadmon*, or Primeval Element, here strangely brought into relation with the *Nifl* and *Muspel* (Darkness and Light) of the antique North, it may be enough to say that its correctness of deduction, and depth of Talmudic and Rabbinical lore have filled perhaps not the worst Hebraist in Britain with something like astonishment.

But quitting this twilight region, Teufelsdröckh hastens from the Tower of Babel, to follow the dispersion of Mankind over the whole habitable and habilable globe. Walking by the light of Oriental, Pelasgic, Scandinavian, Egyptian, Otaheitean, Ancient and Modern researches of every conceivable kind, he strives to give us in compressed shape (as the Nürnbergers give an *Orbis Pictus*) an *Orbis Vestitus;* or view of the costumes of all mankind, in all countries, in all times. It is here that to the Antiquarian, to the Historian, we can triumphantly say: Fall to! Here is Learning: an irregular Treasury, if you will; but inexhaustible as the Hoard of King Nibelung, which twelve waggons in twelve days, at the rate of three journeys a day, could not carry off. Sheepskin cloaks and wampum belts; phylacteries, stoles, albs; chlamydes, togas, Chinese silks, Afghaun shawls, trunk hose, leather breeches, Celtic philibegs (though breeches, as the name *Gallia Braccata* indicates, are the more ancient), Hussar cloaks, Vandyke tippets, ruffs, fardingales, are brought vividly before us,—even the Kilmarnock nightcap is not forgotten. For most part too we must admit that the Learning, heterogeneous as it is, and tumbled down quite pell-mell, is true concentrated and purified Learning, the drossy parts smelted out and thrown aside.

Philosophical reflections intervene, and sometimes touching pictures of human life. Of this sort the following has surprised us. The first purpose of Clothes, as our Professor imagines, was not warmth or decency, but ornament. 'Miserable indeed,' says he, 'was the condition of the Aboriginal Savage, glaring fiercely from under his fleece of hair, which with the beard reached down to his loins, and hung round him like a matted cloak; the rest of his body sheeted in its thick natural fell. He loitered in the sunny glades of the forest, living on wild fruits; or, as the ancient Caledonian, squatted himself in morasses, lurking for his bestial or human prey; without implements, without arms, save the ball of heavy Flint, to which, that his sole possession and defence might not be lost, he had attached a long cord of plaited thongs; thereby recovering as well as hurling it with deadly unerring skill. Nevertheless, the pains of Hunger and Revenge once satisfied, his next care was not Comfort but Decoration (*Putz*).

Warmth he found in the toils of the chase; or amid dried leaves, in his
hollow tree, in his bark shed, or natural grotto: but for Decoration he
must have Clothes. Nay, among wild people, we find tattooing and
painting even prior to Clothes. The first spiritual want of a barbarous
5   man is Decoration; as indeed we still see among the barbarous classes
in civilised countries.

'Reader, the heaven-inspired melodious Singer; loftiest Serene
Highness; nay thy own amber-locked, snow-and-rosebloom Maiden,
worthy to glide sylphlike almost on air, whom thou lovest, worshippest
10 as a divine Presence, which indeed, symbolically taken, she is,—has
descended, like thyself, from that same hair-mantled, flint-hurling
Aboriginal Anthropophagus! Out of the eater cometh forth meat;
out of the strong cometh forth sweetness. What changes are wrought,
not by Time, yet in Time! For not Mankind only, but all that Man-
15 kind does or beholds, is in continual growth, re-genesis and self-
perfecting vitality. Cast forth thy Act, thy Word, into the ever-living,
ever-working Universe: it is a seed-grain that cannot die; unnoticed
to-day (says one) it will be found flourishing as a Banyan-grove (perhaps, alas, as a Hemlock-forest!) after a thousand years.
20   'He who first shortened the labour of Copyists by device of *Movable
Types* was disbanding hired Armies, and cashiering most Kings and
Senates, and creating a whole new Democratic world: he had invented
the Art of Printing. The first ground handful of Nitre, Sulphur, and
Charcoal drove Monk Schwartz's pestle through the ceiling: what
25 will the last do? Achieve the final undisputed prostration of Force
under Thought, of Animal Courage under Spiritual. A simple invention
was it in the old-world Grazier,—sick of lugging his slow Ox about
the country till he got it bartered for corn or oil,—to take a piece of
Leather, and thereon scratch or stamp the mere Figure of an Ox (or
30 *Pecus*); put it in his pocket, and call it *Pecunia*, Money. Yet hereby did
Barter grow Sale, the Leather Money is now Golden and Paper, and
all miracles have been out-miracled: for there are Rothschilds and
English National Debts; and whoso has sixpence is Sovereign (to the
length of sixpence) over all men; commands Cooks to feed him,
35 Philosophers to teach him, Kings to mount guard over him,—to the
length of sixpence.—Clothes too, which began in foolishest love of
Ornament, what have they not become! Increased Security, and

pleasurable Heat soon followed: but what of these? Shame, divine Shame (*Schaam*, Modesty), as yet a stranger to the Anthropophagous bosom, arose there mysteriously under Clothes; a mystic grove-encircled shrine for the Holy in man. Clothes gave us individuality, distinctions, social polity; Clothes have made Men of us; they are threatening to   5 make Clothes-screens of us.

'But on the whole,' continues our eloquent Professor, 'Man is a Tool-using Animal (*Handthierendes Thier*). Weak in himself, and of small stature, he stands on a basis, at most for the flattest-soled, of some half square-foot, insecurely enough; has to straddle out his legs,   10 lest the very wind supplant him. Feeblest of bipeds! Three quintals are a crushing load for him; the Steer of the meadow tosses him aloft, like a waste rag. Nevertheless he can use Tools, can devise Tools: with these the granite mountain melts into light dust before him; he kneads glowing iron, as if it were soft paste; seas are his smooth highway,   15 winds and fire his unwearying steeds. Nowhere do you find him without Tools; without Tools he is nothing, with Tools he is all.'

Here may we not, for a moment, interrupt the stream of Oratory with a remark that this Definition of the Tool-using Animal, appears to us, of all that Animal-sort, considerably the precisest and best?   20 Man is called a Laughing Animal: but do not the apes also laugh, or attempt to do it; and is the manliest man the greatest and oftenest laugher? Teufelsdröckh himself, as we said, laughed only once. Still less do we make of that other French Definition of the Cooking Animal; which, indeed, for rigorous scientific purposes, is as good as   25 useless. Can a Tartar be said to Cook, when he only readies his steak by riding on it? Again, what Cookery does the Greenlander use, beyond stowing up his whale-blubber, as a marmot, in the like case, might do? Or how would Monsieur Ude prosper among those Orinocco Indians who, according to Humboldt, lodge in crow-nests, on the   30 branches of trees; and, for half the year, have no victuals but pipe-clay, the whole country being under water? But on the other hand, show us the human being, of any period or climate, without his Tools: those very Caledonians, as we saw, had their Flint-ball, and Thong to it, such as no brute has or can have.   35

'Man is a Tool-using animal,' concludes Teufelsdröckh in his abrupt way; 'of which truth Clothes are but one example: and surely if we consider the interval between the first wooden Dibble fashioned by man, and those Liverpool Steam-carriages, or the British House of Commons, we shall note what progress he has made. He digs up certain black stones from the bosom of the Earth, and says to them, *Transport me, and this luggage, at the rate of five-and-thirty miles an hour;* and they do it: he collects, apparently by lot, six hundred and fifty-eight miscellaneous individuals, and says to them, *Make this nation toil for us, bleed for us, hunger, and sorrow, and sin for us;* and they do it.'

CHAPTER VI.

ONE of the most unsatisfactory Sections in the whole Volume is that *on Aprons.* What though stout old Gao the Persian Blacksmith, 'whose Apron, now indeed hidden under jewels, because raised in revolt which proved successful, is still the royal standard of that country;' what though John Knox's Daughter, 'who threatened Sovereign 5 Majesty that she would catch her Husband's head in her Apron, rather than he should lie and be a Bishop;' what though the Land-gravine Elizabeth, with many other Apron worthies,—figure here? An idle wire-drawing spirit, sometimes even a tone of levity, approaching to conventional satire, is too clearly discernible. What, for example, 10 are we to make of such sentences as the following?

'Aprons are Defences; against injury to cleanliness, to safety, to modesty, sometimes to roguery. From the thin slip of notched silk (as it were, the Emblem and beatified Ghost of an Apron), which some highest-bred housewife, sitting at Nürnberg Workboxes and Toyboxes, 15 has gracefully fastened on; to the thick-tanned hide, girt round him with thongs, wherein the Builder builds, and at evening sticks his trowel; or to those jingling sheet-iron Aprons, wherein your other-wise half-naked Vulcans hammer and smelt in their Smelt-furnace,— is there not range enough in the fashion and uses of this Vestment? 20 How much has been concealed, how much has been defended in Aprons! Nay, rightly considered, what is your whole Military and Police Establishment, charged at uncalculated millions, but a huge

scarlet-coloured, iron-fastened Apron, wherein Society works (uneas-
ily enough); guarding itself from some soil and stithy-sparks, in this
Devil's-smithy (*Teufels-schmiede*) of a world? But of all Aprons the
most puzzling to me hitherto has been the Episcopal, or Cassock.
Wherein consists the usefulness of this Apron? The Overseer (*Episcopus*)
of Souls, I notice, has tucked-in the corner of it, as if his day's work
were done: what does he shadow forth thereby?' &c. &c.

Or again, has it often been the lot of our readers to read such stuff
as we shall now quote?

'I consider those printed Paper Aprons, worn by the Parisian Cooks,
as a new vent, though a slight one, for Typography; therefore as an
encouragement to modern Literature, and deserving of approval: nor
is it without satisfaction that I hear of a celebrated London Firm
having in view to introduce the same fashion, with important extensions, in England.'—We who are on the spot hear of no such thing;
and indeed have reason to be thankful that hitherto there are other
vents for our Literature, exuberant as it is.—Teufelsdröckh continues: 'If such supply of printed Paper should rise so far as to choke
up the highways and public thoroughfares, new means must of necessity be had recourse to. In a world existing by Industry, we grudge
to employ Fire as a destroying element, and not as a creating one.
However, Heaven is omnipotent, and will find us an outlet. In the
meanwhile, is it not beautiful to see five million quintals of Rags
picked annually from the Laystall; and annually, after being macer-
ated, hot-pressed, printed on, and sold,—returned thither; filling so
many hungry mouths by the way? Thus is the Laystall, especially
with its Rags or Clothes-rubbish, the grand Electric Battery, and
Fountain-of-Motion, from which and to which the Social Activities
(like vitreous and resinous Electricities) circulate, in larger or smaller
circles, through the mighty, billowy, stormtost Chaos of Life, which
they keep alive!'—Such passages fill us who love the man, and partly
esteem him, with a very mixed feeling.

Farther down we meet with this: 'The Journalists are now the true
Kings and Clergy: henceforth Historians, unless they are fools, must
write not of Bourbon Dynasties, and Tudors and Hapsburgs; but of
Stamped Broad-sheet Dynasties, and quite new successive Names,
according as this or the other Able Editor, or Combination of Able
Editors, gains the world's ear. Of the British Newspaper Press, perhaps

the most important of all, and wonderful enough in its secret constitution and procedure, a valuable descriptive History already exists, in that language, under the title of *Satan's Invisible World Displayed;* which, however, by search in all the Weissnichtwo Libraries, I have not yet succeeded in procuring (*vermöchte nicht aufzutreiben*).'   5

Thus does the good Homer not only nod, but snore. Thus does Teufelsdröckh, wandering in regions where he had little business, confound the old authentic Presbyterian Witchfinder with a new, spurious, imaginary Historian of the *Brittische Journalistik;* and so stumble on perhaps the most egregious blunder in Modern Literature!   10

CHAPTER VII.

HAPPIER is our Professor, and more purely scientific and historic, when he reaches the Middle Ages in Europe, and down to the end of the Seventeenth Century; the true era of extravagance in Costume. It is here that the Antiquary and Student of Modes comes upon his
5 richest harvest. Fantastic garbs, beggaring all fancy of a Teniers or a Callot, succeed each other, like monster devouring monster in a Dream. The whole too in brief authentic strokes, and touched not seldom with that breath of genius which makes even old raiment live. Indeed, so learned, precise, graphical, and every way interesting have we found
10 these Chapters, that it may be thrown out as a pertinent question for parties concerned, Whether or not a good English Translation thereof might henceforth be profitably incorporated with Mr. Merrick's valuable Work *On Ancient Armour?* Take, by way of example, the following sketch; as authority for which Paulinus's *Zeitkürzende Lust* (II.
15 678) is, with seeming confidence, referred to:

'Did we behold the German fashionable dress of the Fifteenth Century, we might smile; as perhaps those bygone Germans, were they to rise again, and see our haberdashery, would cross themselves, and invoke the Virgin. But happily no bygone German, or man, rises
20 again; thus the Present is not needlessly trammelled with the Past; and only grows out of it, like a Tree, whose roots are not intertangled with its branches, but lie peaceably under ground. Nay it is very

36

mournful, yet not useless, to see and know, how the Greatest and
Dearest, in a short while, would find his place quite filled up here,
and no room for him; the very Napoleon, the very Byron, in some
seven years, has become obsolete, and were now a foreigner to his
Europe. Thus is the Law of Progress secured; and in Clothes, as in   5
all other external things whatsoever, no fashion will continue.

'Of the military classes in those old times, whose buff-belts, complicated chains and gorgets, huge churn-boots, and other riding and
fighting gear have been bepainted in modern Romance, till the whole
has acquired somewhat of a signpost character,—I shall here say noth-   10
ing: the civil and pacific classes, less touched upon, are wonderful
enough for us.

'Rich men, I find, have *Teusinke*' (a perhaps untranslateable article); 'also a silver girdle, whereat hang little bells; so that when a
man walks it is with continual jingling. Some few, of musical turn,   15
have a whole chime of bells (*Glockenspiel*) fastened there; which,
especially in sudden whirls, and the other accidents of walking, has a
grateful effect. Observe too how fond they are of peaks, and Gothic-
arch intersections. The male world wears peaked caps, an ell long,
which hang bobbing over the side (*schief*): their shoes are peaked in   20
front, also to the length of an ell, and laced on the side with tags;
even the wooden shoes have their ell-long noses: some also clap bells
on the peak. Farther, according to my authority, the men have breeches
without seat (*ohne Gesäss*): these they fasten peakwise to their shirts;
and the long round doublet must overlap them.   25

'Rich maidens, again, flit abroad in gowns scolloped out behind
and before, so that back and breast are almost bare. Wives of quality,
on the other hand, have train-gowns four or five ells in length; which
trains there are boys to carry. Brave Cleopatras, sailing in their silk-
cloth Galley, with a Cupid for steersman! Consider their welts, a   30
handbreadth thick, which waver round them by way of hem; the long
flood of silver buttons, or rather silver shells, from throat to shoe,
wherewith these same welt-gowns are buttoned. The maidens have
bound silver snoods about their hair, with gold spangles, and pendent
flames (*Flammen*), that is, sparkling hair-drops: but of their mothers'   35
headgear who shall speak? Neither in love of grace is comfort forgotten. In winter weather you behold the whole fair creation (that can

afford it) in long mantles, with skirts wide below, and, for hem, not
one but two sufficient handbroad welts; all ending atop in a thick
well-starched Ruff, some twenty inches broad: these are their Ruff-
mantles (*Kragenmäntel*).

5   'As yet among the womankind hoop-petticoats are not; but the
men have doublets of fustian, under which lie multiple ruffs of cloth,
pasted together with batter (*mit Teig zusammengekleistert*), which
create protuberance enough. Thus do the two sexes vie with each
other in the art of Decoration; and as usual the stronger carries it.'

10   Our Professor, whether he have Humour himself or not, manifests
a certain feeling of the Ludicrous, a sly observance of it, which, could
emotion of any kind be confidently predicated of so still a man, we
might call a real love. None of those bell-girdles, bushel-breeches,
cornuted shoes, or other the like phenomena, of which the History

15   of Dress offers so many, escape him; more especially the mischances,
or striking adventures, incident to the wearers of such, are noticed
with due fidelity. Sir Walter Raleigh's fine mantle, which he spread in
the mud under Queen Elizabeth's feet, appears to provoke little
enthusiasm in him; he merely asks, Whether at that period the Maiden

20   Queen 'was red-painted on the nose, and white-painted on the cheeks,
as her tirewomen, when from spleen and wrinkles she would no longer
look in any glass, were wont to serve her?' We can answer that Sir
Walter knew well what he was doing, and had the Maiden Queen
been stuffed parchment dyed in verdigris, would have done the same.

25   Thus too, treating of those enormous habiliments, that were not
only slashed and galooned, but artificially swollen out on the broader
parts of the body, by introduction of Bran,—our Professor fails not
to comment on that luckless Courtier, who having seated himself on
a chair with some projecting nail on it, and therefrom rising, to pay

30   his *devoir* on the entrance of Majesty, instantaneously emitted several
pecks of dry wheat-dust; and stood there diminished to a spindle, his
galoons and slashes dangling sorrowful and flabby round him. Whereupon the Professor publishes this reflection:

'By what strange chances do we live in History! Erostratus by a

35   torch; Milo by a bullock; Henry Darnley, an unfledged booby and
bustard, by his limbs; most Kings and Queens by being born under
such and such a bed-tester; Boileau Despréaux (according to Helvetius)

by the peck of a turkey; and this ill-starred individual by a rent in his breeches,—for no Memoirist of Kaiser Otto's Court omits him. Vain was the prayer of Themistocles for a talent of Forgetting: my Friends, yield cheerfully to Destiny, and read since it is written.'—Has Teufelsdröckh to be put in mind that, nearly related to the impossible talent of Forgetting, stands that talent of Silence, which even travelling Englishmen manifest?

'The simplest costume,' observes our Professor, 'which I anywhere find alluded to in History, is that used as regimental, by Bolivar's Cavalry, in the late Columbian wars. A square Blanket, twelve feet in diagonal, is provided (some were wont to cut off the corners, and make it circular): in the centre a slit is effected, eighteen inches long; through this the mother-naked Trooper introduces his head and neck; and so rides shielded from all weather, and in battle from many strokes (for he rolls it about his left arm); and not only dressed, but harnessed and draperied.'

With which picture of a State of Nature, affecting by its singularity, and Old-Roman contempt of the superfluous, we shall quit this part of our subject.

CHAPTER VIII.

THE WORLD OUT OF CLOTHES.

IF in the Descriptive-Historical Portion of this Volume, Teufelsdröckh, discussing merely the *Werden* (Origin and successive Improvement) of Clothes, has astonished many a reader, much more will he in the Speculative-Philosophical Portion, which treats of their *Wirken*, or

5 Influences. It is here that the present Editor first feels the pressure of his task; for here properly the higher and new Philosophy of Clothes commences: an untried, almost inconceivable region, or chaos; in venturing upon which, how difficult, yet how unspeakably important is it to know what course, of survey and conquest, is the true one;

10 where the footing is firm substance and will bear us, where it is hollow, or mere cloud, and may engulf us! Teufelsdröckh undertakes no less than to expound the moral, political, even religious Influences of Clothes; he undertakes to make manifest, in its thousandfold bearings, this grand Proposition, that Man's earthly interests 'are all hooked

15 and buttoned together, and held up, by Clothes.' He says in so many words, 'Society is founded upon Cloth;' and again, 'Society sails through the Infinitude on Cloth, as on a Faust's Mantle, or rather like the Sheet of clean and unclean beasts in the Apostle's Dream; and without such Sheet or Mantle, would sink to endless depths, or mount

20 to inane limbos, and in either case be no more.'

By what chains, or indeed infinitely complected tissues, of Meditation this grand Theorem is here unfolded, and innumerable practical Corollaries are drawn therefrom, it were perhaps a mad ambition to attempt exhibiting. Our Professor's method is not, in any case, that of common school Logic, where the truths all stand in a row, each holding by the skirts of the other; but at best that of practical Reason, proceeding by large Intuition over whole systematic groups and kingdoms; whereby we might say, a noble complexity, almost like that of Nature, reigns in his Philosophy, or spiritual Picture of Nature: a mighty maze, yet, as faith whispers, not without a plan. Nay we complained above, that a certain ignoble complexity, what we must call mere confusion, was also discernible. Often, also, we have to exclaim: Would to Heaven those same Biographical Documents were come! For it seems as if the demonstration lay much in the Author's individuality; as if it were not Argument that had taught him, but Experience. At present it is only in local glimpses, and by significant fragments, picked often at wide enough intervals from the original Volume, and carefully collated, that we can hope to impart some outline or foreshadow of this Doctrine. Readers of any intelligence are once more invited to favour us with their most concentrated attention: let these, after intense consideration, and not till then, pronounce, Whether on the utmost verge of our actual horizon there is not a looming as of Land; a promise of new Fortunate Islands, perhaps whole undiscovered Americas, for such as have canvass to sail thither?—As exordium to the whole, stand here the following long citation:

'With men of a speculative turn,' writes Teufelsdröckh, 'there come seasons, meditative, sweet, yet awful hours, when in wonder and fear you ask yourself that unanswerable question: Who am I; the thing that can say "I" (*das Wesen das sich* ICH *nennt*)? The world, with its loud trafficking, retires into the distance; and, through the paper-hangings, and stone-walls, and thick-plied tissues of Commerce and Polity, and all the living and lifeless integuments (of Society and a Body), wherewith your Existence sits surrounded,—the sight reaches forth into the void Deep, and you are alone with the Universe, and silently commune with it, as one mysterious Presence with another.

'Who am I; what is this ME? A Voice, a Motion, an Appearance;— some embodied, visualised Idea in the Eternal Mind? *Cogito, ergo sum*. Alas, poor Cogitator, this takes us but a little way. Sure enough, I am; and lately was not: but Whence? How? Whereto? The answer lies around, written in all colours and motions, uttered in all tones of

jubilee and wail, in thousand-figured, thousand-voiced, harmonious Nature: but where is the cunning eye and ear to whom that God-written Apocalypse will yield articulate meaning? We sit as in a boundless Phantasmagoria and Dream-grotto; boundless, for the faintest star,
5   the remotest century, lies not even nearer the verge thereof: sounds and many-coloured visions flit round our sense; but Him, the Unslumbering, whose work both Dream and Dreamer are, we see not; except in rare half-waking moments, suspect not. Creation, says one, lies before us, like a glorious Rainbow; but the Sun that made
10 it lies behind us, hidden from us. Then, in that strange Dream, how we clutch at shadows as if they were substances; and sleep deepest while fancying ourselves most awake! Which of your Philosophical Systems is other than a dream-theorem; a net quotient, confidently given out, where divisor and dividend are both unknown? What are
15 all your national Wars, with their Moscow Retreats, and sanguinary hate-filled Revolutions, but the Somnambulism of uneasy Sleepers? This Dreaming, this Somnambulism is what we on Earth call Life; wherein the most indeed undoubtingly wander, as if they knew right hand from left; yet they only are wise who know that they know
20 nothing.

'Pity that all Metaphysics had hitherto proved so inexpressibly unproductive! The secret of Man's Being is still like the Sphinx's secret: a riddle that he cannot rede; and for ignorance of which he suffers death, the worst death, a spiritual. What are your Axioms, and
25 Categories, and Systems, and Aphorisms? Words, words. High Air-castles are cunningly built of Words, the Words well bedded also in good Logic-mortar; wherein, however, no Knowledge will come to lodge. *The whole is greater than the part:* how exceedingly true! *Nature abhors a vacuum:* how exceedingly false and calumnious! Again, *Nothing*
30 *can act but where it is:* with all my heart; only WHERE is it? Be not the slave of Words: is not the Distant, the Dead, while I love it, and long for it, and mourn for it, Here, in the genuine sense, as truly as the floor I stand on? But that same WHERE, with its brother WHEN, are from the first the master-colours of our Dream-grotto; say rather, the
35 Canvass (the warp and woof thereof) whereon all our Dreams and Life-visions are painted. Nevertheless, has not a deeper meditation taught certain of every climate and age, that the WHERE and WHEN, so mysteriously inseparable from all our thoughts, are but superficial

terrestrial adhesions to thought; that the Seer may discern them where they mount up out of the celestial EVERYWHERE and FOREVER: have not all nations conceived their God as Omnipresent and Eternal; as existing in a universal HERE, an ever-lasting NOW? Think well, thou too wilt find that Space is but a mode of our human Sense, so likewise Time; there *is* no Space and no Time: WE are—we know not what;— light-sparkles floating in the æther of Deity!

'So that this so solid-seeming World, after all, were but an air-image, our ME the only reality: and Nature, with its thousandfold production and destruction, but the reflex of our own inward Force, the "phantasy of our Dream;" or what the Earth-Spirit in *Faust* names it, *the living visible Garment of God:*

> "In Being's floods, in Action's storm,
> I walk and work, above, beneath,
> Work and weave in endless motion!
> Birth and Death,
> An infinite ocean;
> A seizing and giving
> The fire of Living:
> 'Tis thus at the roaring Loom of Time I ply,
> And weave for God the Garment thou seest Him by."

Of twenty millions that have read and spouted this thunder-speech of the *Erdgeist*, are there yet twenty units of us that have learned the meaning thereof?

'It was in some such mood, when wearied and foredone with these high speculations, that I first came upon the question of Clothes. Strange enough, it strikes me, is this same fact of there being Tailors and Tailored. The Horse I ride has his own whole fell: strip him of the girths and flaps and extraneous tags I have fastened round him, and the noble creature is his own sempster and weaver and spinner: nay his own bootmaker, jeweller, and man-milliner; he bounds free through the valleys, with a perennial rainproof court-suit on his body; wherein warmth and easiness of fit have reached perfection; nay, the graces also have been considered, and frills and fringes, with gay variety of colour, featly appended, and ever in the right place, are not wanting. While I—Good Heaven!—have thatched myself over with the dead fleeces of sheep, the bark of vegetables, the entrails of worms, the hides of oxen or seals, the felt of furred beasts; and walk abroad a moving Rag-screen, overheaped with shreds and tatters raked from the Charnel-house of Nature, where they would have rotted, to rot on me more slowly! Day after day, I must thatch myself anew; day after day, this despicable thatch must lose some film of its thickness; some film of it, frayed away by tear and wear, must be brushed off into the Ashpit, into the Laystall; till by degrees the whole has been brushed thither, and I, the dust-making, patent Rag-grinder, get new material to grind down. O subter-brutish! vile! most vile! For have not I too a compact all-enclosing Skin, whiter or dingier? Am I a botched mass of tailors' and cobblers' shreds, then; or a tightly-articulated, homogeneous little Figure, automatic, nay alive?

'Strange enough how creatures of the human-kind shut their eyes to plainest facts; and, by the mere inertia of Oblivion and Stupidity, live at ease in the midst of Wonders and Terrors. But indeed man is, and was always, a blockhead and dullard; much readier to feel and digest, than to think and consider. Prejudice, which he pretends to hate, is his absolute lawgiver; mere use-and-wont everywhere leads him by the nose: thus let but a Rising of the Sun, let but a Creation of the World happen *twice*, and it ceases to be marvellous, to be noteworthy, or noticeable. Perhaps not once in a lifetime does it occur to your ordinary biped, of any country or generation, be he gold-mantled Prince or russet-jerkined Peasant, that his Vestments and his Self are not one and indivisible; that *he* is naked, without vestments, till he buy or steal such, and by forethought sew and button them.

'For my own part, these considerations, of our Clothes-thatch, and how, reaching inwards even to our heart of hearts, it tailorises and demoralises us, fill me with a certain horror at myself and mankind; almost as one feels at those Dutch Cows, which, during the wet season, you see grazing deliberately with jackets and petticoats (of striped sacking), in the meadows of Gouda. Nevertheless there is something great in the moment when a man first strips himself of adventitious wrappages; and sees indeed that he is naked, and, as Swift has it, "a forked straddling animal with bandy legs;" yet also a Spirit, and unutterable Mystery of Mysteries.'

CHAPTER IX.

ADAMITISM.

LET no courteous reader take offence at the opinions broached in the conclusion of the last Chapter. The Editor himself, on first glancing over that singular passage, was inclined to exclaim: What, have we got not only a Sansculottist, but an enemy to Clothes in the abstract? A new Adamite, in this century, which flatters itself that it is the Nine- 5 teenth, and destructive both to Superstition and Enthusiasm?

Consider, thou foolish Teufelsdröckh, what benefits unspeakable all ages and sexes derive from Clothes. For example, when thou thyself, a watery, pulpy, slobbery freshman and new-comer in this Planet, sattest muling and puking in thy nurse's arms; sucking thy coral, and 10 looking forth into the world in the blankest manner, what hadst thou been, without thy blankets, and bibs, and other nameless hulls? A terror to thyself and mankind! Or hast thou forgotten the day when thou first receivedst breeches, and thy long clothes became short? The village where thou livedst was all apprised of the fact; and 15 neighbour after neighbour kissed thy pudding cheek, and gave thee, as handsel, silver or copper coins, on that the first gala-day of thy existence. Again, wert not thou, at one period of life, a Buck, or Blood, or Macaroni, or Incroyable, or Dandy, or by whatever name, according to year and place, such phenomenon is distinguished? In 20 that one word lie included mysterious volumes. Nay, now when the reign of folly is over, or altered, and thy clothes are not for triumph but for defence, hast thou always worn them perforce, and as a consequence

45

of Man's Fall; never rejoiced in them as in a warm moveable House, a Body round thy Body, wherein that strange THEE of thine sat snug, defying all variations of Climate? Girt with thick double-milled kerseys; half-buried under shawls and broadbrims, and overalls and mudboots, thy very fingers cased in doeskin and mittens, thou hast bestrode that 'Horse I ride;' and, though it were in wild winter, dashed through the world, glorying in it as if thou wert its lord. In vain did the sleet beat round thy temples; it lighted only on thy impenetrable, felted or woven, case of wool. In vain did the winds howl,—forests sounding and creaking, deep calling unto deep,—and the storms heap themselves together into one huge Arctic whirlpool: thou flewest through the middle thereof, striking fire from the highway; wild music hummed in thy ears, thou too wert as a 'sailor of the air;' the wreck of matter and the crash of worlds was thy element and propitiously wafting tide. Without Clothes, without bit or saddle, what hadst thou been; what had thy fleet quadruped been?—Nature is good, but she is not the best: here truly was the victory of Art over Nature. A thunderbolt indeed might have pierced thee; all short of this thou couldst defy.

Or, cries the courteous reader, has your Teufelsdröckh forgotten what he said lately about 'Aboriginal Savages,' and their 'condition miserable indeed?' Would he have all this unsaid; and us betake ourselves again to the 'matted cloak,' and go sheeted in a 'thick natural fell?'

Nowise, courteous reader! The Professor knows full well what he is saying; and both thou and we, in our haste, do him wrong. If Clothes, in these times, 'so tailorise and demoralise us,' have they no redeeming value; can they not be altered to serve better; must they of necessity be thrown to the dogs? The truth is, Teufelsdröckh, though a Sansculottist, is no Adamite: and much perhaps as he might wish to go forth before this degenerate age 'as a Sign,' would nowise wish to do it, as those old Adamites did, in a state of Nakedness. The utility of Clothes is altogether apparent to him: nay perhaps he has an insight into their more recondite, and almost mystic qualities, what we might call the omnipotent virtue of Clothes, such as was never before vouchsafed to any man. For example:

'You see two individuals,' he writes, 'one dressed in fine Red, the other in coarse threadbare Blue: Red says to Blue, "Be hanged and anatomised;" Blue hears with a shudder, and (O wonder of wonders!)

marches sorrowfully to the gallows; is there noosed up, vibrates his hour, and the surgeons dissect him, and fit his bones into a skeleton for medical purposes. How is this; or what make ye of your *Nothing can act but where it is?* Red has no physical hold of Blue, no *clutch* of him, is nowise in *contact* with him: neither are those ministering 5 Sheriffs and Lord-Lieutenants and Hangmen and Tipstaves so related to commanding Red, that he can tug them hither and thither; but each stands distinct within his own skin. Nevertheless, as it is spoken, so is it done: the articulated Word sets all hands in Action; and Rope and Improved-drop perform their work. 10

'Thinking reader, the reason seems to me twofold: First, that *Man is a Spirit*, and bound by invisible bonds to *All Men;* Secondly, that *he wears Clothes*, which are the visible emblems of that fact. Has not your Red hanging-individual a horsehair wig, squirrel skins, and a plush gown; whereby all mortals know that he is a JUDGE?—Society, 15 which the more I think of it astonishes me the more, is founded upon Cloth.

'Often in my atrabiliar moods, when I read of pompous ceremonials, Frankfort Coronations, Royal Drawing-rooms, Levees, Couchees; and how the ushers and macers and pursuivants are all in waiting; how 20 Duke this is presented by Archduke that, and Colonel A by General B, and innumerable Bishops, Admirals, and miscellaneous Functionaries, are advancing gallantly to the Anointed Presence; and I strive, in my remote privacy, to form a clear picture of that solemnity,—on a sudden, as by some enchanter's wand, the—shall I speak it?—the 25 Clothes fly off the whole dramatic corps; and Dukes, Grandees, Bishops, Generals, Anointed Presence itself, every mother's son of them, stand straddling there, not a shirt on them; and I know not whether to laugh or weep. This physical or psychical infirmity, in which perhaps I am not singular, I have, after hesitation, thought right to 30 publish, for the solace of those afflicted with the like.'

Would to Heaven, say we, thou hadst thought right to keep it secret! Who is there now that can read the five columns of Presentations in his Morning Newspaper without a shudder? Hypochondriac men, and all men are to a certain extent hypochondriac, should 35 be more gently treated. With what readiness our fancy, in this shattered state of the nerves, follows out the consequences which Teufelsdröckh, with a devilish coolness, goes on to draw:

'What would Majesty do, could such an accident befall in reality; should the buttons all simultaneously start, and the solid wool evaporate, in very Deed, as here in Dream? *Ach Gott!* How each skulks into the nearest hiding-place; their high State Tragedy (*Haupt- und Staats-*
5   *Action*) becomes a Pickleherring-Farce to weep at, which is the worst kind of Farce; *the tables* (according to Horace), and with them, the whole fabric of Government, Legislation, Property, Police, and Civilised Society, *are dissolved*, in wails and howls.'

Lives the man that can figure a naked Duke of Windlestraw ad-
10   dressing a naked House of Lords? Imagination, choked as in mephitic air, recoils on itself, and will not forward with the picture. The Woolsack, the Ministerial, the Opposition Benches—*infandum! infandum!* And yet why is the thing impossible? Was not every soul, or rather every body, of these Guardians of our Liberties, naked, or
15   nearly so, last night; 'a forked Radish with a head fantastically carved?' And why might he not, did our stern Fate so order it, walk out to St. Stephen's, as well as into bed, in that no-fashion; and there, with other similar Radishes, hold a Bed of Justice? 'Solace of those afflicted with the like!' Unhappy Teufelsdröckh, had man ever such a
20   'physical or psychical infirmity' before? And now how many, perhaps, may thy unparalleled confession (which we, even to the sounder British world, and goaded on by Critical and Biographical duty, grudge to re-impart) incurably infect therewith! Art thou the malignest of Sansculottists, or only the maddest?
25   'It will remain to be examined,' adds the inexorable Teufelsdröckh, 'in how far the SCARECROW, as a Clothed Person, is not also entitled to benefit of clergy, and English trial by jury: nay perhaps, considering his high function (for is not he too a Defender of Property, and Sovereign armed with the *terrors* of the Law?), to a certain royal Immunity and
30   Inviolability; which, however, misers and the meaner class of persons are not always voluntarily disposed to grant him.' * *
* * 'O my Friends, we are (in Yorick Sterne's words) but as "turkeys driven, with a stick and red clout, to the market:" or if some drivers, as they do in Norfolk, take a dried bladder and put peas in
35   it, the rattle thereof terrifies the boldest!'

CHAPTER X.

It must now be apparent enough that our Professor, as above hinted, is a speculative Radical, and of the very darkest tinge; acknowledging, for most part, in the solemnities and paraphernalia of civilised Life, which we make so much of, nothing but so many Cloth-rags, turkey-poles, and 'bladders with dried peas.' To linger among such specula- 5
tions, longer than mere Science requires, a discerning public can have no wish. For our purposes the simple fact that such a *Naked World* is possible, nay actually exists (under the Clothed one), will be suf-ficient. Much, therefore, we omit about 'Kings wrestling naked on the green with Carmen,' and the Kings being thrown: 'dissect them 10
with scalpels,' says Teufelsdröckh; 'the same viscera, tissues, livers, lights, and other Life-tackle are there: examine their spiritual mecha-nism; the same great Need, great Greed, and little Faculty; nay ten to one but the Carman, who understands draught-cattle, the rimming of wheels, something of the laws of unstable and stable equilibrium, 15
with other branches of waggon-science, and has actually put forth his hand and operated on Nature, is the more cunningly gifted of the two. Whence, then, their so unspeakable difference? From Clothes.' Much also we shall omit about confusion of Ranks, and Joan and My Lady, and how it would be every where 'Hail fellow well met,' and 20
Chaos were come again: all which to any one that has once fairly pictured out the grand mother-idea, *Society in a state of Nakedness,* will spontaneously suggest itself. Should some sceptical individual still

entertain doubts whether in a World without Clothes, the smallest
Politeness, Polity, or even Police, could exist, let him turn to the
original Volume, and view there the boundless Serbonian Bog of
Sansculottism, stretching sour and pestilential: over which we have
5 lightly flown; where not only whole armies but whole nations might
sink! If indeed the following argument, in its brief riveting emphasis,
be not of itself incontrovertible and final:

'Are we Opossums; have we natural Pouches, like the Kangaroo?
Or how, without Clothes, could we possess the master-organ, soul's-
10 seat, and true pineal gland of the Body Social: I mean, a PURSE?'

Nevertheless it is impossible to hate Professor Teufelsdröckh; at
worst, one knows not whether to hate or to love him. For though in
looking at the fair tapestry of human Life, with its royal and even
sacred figures, he dwells not on the obverse alone, but here chiefly on
15 the reverse; and indeed turns out the rough seams, tatters, and manifold thrums of that unsightly wrong-side, with an almost diabolic
patience and indifference, which must have sunk him in the estimation of most readers,—there is that within which unspeakably distinguishes him from all other past and present Sansculottists. The grand
20 unparalleled peculiarity of Teufelsdröckh is, that with all this
Descendentalism, he combines a Transcendentalism no less superla-
tive; whereby if on the one hand he degrade man below most animals,
except those jacketed Gouda Cows, he, on the other, exalts him
beyond the visible Heavens, almost to an equality with the gods.

25 'To the eye of vulgar Logic,' says he, 'what is man? An omnivorous Biped that wears Breeches. To the eye of Pure Reason what is
he? A Soul, a Spirit, and divine Apparition. Round his mysterious ME,
there lies, under all those wool-rags, a Garment of Flesh (or of Senses),
contextured in the Loom of Heaven; whereby he is revealed to his
30 like, and dwells with them in UNION and DIVISION; and sees and
fashions for himself a Universe, with azure Starry Spaces, and long
Thousands of Years. Deep-hidden is he under that strange Garment;
amid Sounds and Colours and Forms, as it were, swathed in, and
inextricably overshrouded: yet is it sky-woven, and worthy of a God.
35 Stands he not thereby in the centre of Immensities, in the conflux of
Eternities? He feels; power has been given him to Know, to Believe;
nay does not the spirit of Love, free in its celestial primeval brightness, even here, though but for moments, look through? Well said

Saint Chrysostom, with his lips of gold, "the true SHEKINAH is Man:" where else is the GOD'S-PRESENCE manifested not to our eyes only, but to our hearts, as in our fellow man?'

In such passages, unhappily too rare, the high Platonic Mysticism of our Author, which is perhaps the fundamental element of his na- 5 ture, bursts forth, as it were, in full flood: and, through all the vapour and tarnish of what is often so perverse, so mean in his exterior and environment, we seem to look into a whole inward Sea of Light and Love;—though, alas, the grim coppery clouds soon roll together again, and hide it from view. 10

Such tendency to Mysticism is everywhere traceable in this man; and indeed, to attentive readers, must have been long ago apparent. Nothing that he sees but has more than a common meaning, but has two meanings: thus, if in the highest Imperial Sceptre and Charlemagne-Mantle, as well as in the poorest Ox-goad and Gipsy-Blanket, he finds 15 Prose, Decay, Contemptibility; there is in each sort Poetry also, and a reverend Worth. For Matter, were it never so despicable, is Spirit, the manifestation of Spirit: were it never so honourable, can it be more? The thing Visible, nay the thing Imagined, the thing in any way conceived as Visible, what is it but a Garment, a Clothing of the 20 higher, celestial Invisible, 'unimaginable, formless, dark with excess of bright?' Under which point of view the following passage, so strange in purport, so strange in phrase, seems characteristic enough:

'The beginning of all Wisdom is to look fixedly on Clothes, or even with armed eyesight, till they become *transparent*. "The Phi- 25 losopher," says the wisest of this age, "must station himself in the middle:" how true! The Philosopher is he to whom the Highest has descended, and the Lowest has mounted up; who is the equal and kindly brother of all.

'Shall we tremble before cloth-webs and cobwebs, whether woven 30 in Arkwright looms, or by the silent Arachnes that weave unrestingly in our Imagination? Or, on the other hand, what is there that we cannot love; since all was created by God?

'Happy he who can look through the Clothes of a Man (the woollen, and fleshly, and official Bank-paper and State-paper Clothes), into the 35 Man himself; and discern, it may be, in this or the other Dread Potentate, a more or less incompetent Digestive-apparatus; yet also an inscrutable venerable Mystery, in the meanest Tinker that sees with eyes!'

For the rest, as is natural to a man of this kind, he deals much in the feeling of Wonder; insists on the necessity and high worth of universal Wonder, which he holds to be the only reasonable temper for the denizen of so singular a Planet as ours. 'Wonder,' says he, 'is the basis of Worship: the reign of Wonder is perennial, indestructible in Man; only at certain stages (as the present), it is, for some short season, a reign *in partibus infidelium.*' That progress of Science, which is to destroy Wonder, and in its stead substitute Mensuration and Numeration, finds small favour with Teufelsdröckh, much as he otherwise venerates these two latter processes.

'Shall your Science,' exclaims he, 'proceed in the small chink-lighted, or even oil-lighted, underground workshop of Logic alone; and man's mind become an Arithmetical Mill, whereof Memory is the Hopper, and mere Tables of Sines and Tangents, Codification, and Treatises of what you call Political Economy, are the Meal? And what is that Science, which the scientific Head alone, were it screwed off, and (like the Doctor's in the Arabian Tale) set in a basin, to keep it alive, could prosecute without shadow of a heart,—but one other of the mechanical and menial handicrafts, for which the Scientific Head (having a Soul in it) is too noble an organ? I mean that Thought without Reverence is barren, perhaps poisonous; at best, dies like Cookery with the day that called it forth; does not live, like sowing, in successive tilths and wider-spreading harvests, bringing food and plenteous increase to all Time.'

In such wise does Teufelsdröckh deal hits, harder or softer, according to ability; yet ever, as we would fain persuade ourselves, with charitable intent. Above all, that class of 'Logic-choppers, and treble-pipe Scoffers, and professed Enemies to Wonder; who, in these days, so numerously patrol as night-constables about the Mechanics' Institute of Science, and cackle, like true Old-Roman geese and goslings round their Capitol, on any alarm, or on none; nay who often, as illuminated Sceptics, walk abroad into peaceable society, in full daylight, with rattle and lantern, and insist on guiding you and guarding you therewith, though the Sun is shining, and the street populous with mere justice-loving men:' that whole class is inexpressibly wearisome to him. Hear with what uncommon animation he perorates:

'The man who cannot wonder, who does not habitually wonder (and worship), were he President of innumerable Royal Societies, and carried the whole *Mécanique Céleste* and *Hegel's Philosophy*, and the epitome of all Laboratories and Observatories with their results, in his single head,—is but a Pair of Spectacles behind which there is no Eye. Let those who have Eyes look through him, then he may be useful. 5

'Thou wilt have no Mystery and Mysticism; wilt walk through thy world by the sunshine of what thou callest Truth, or even by the Handlamp of what I call Attorney Logic; and "explain" all, "account" for all, or believe nothing of it? Nay, thou wilt attempt laughter; whoso recognises the unfathomable, all-pervading domain of Mys- 10 tery, which is everywhere under our feet and among our hands; to whom the Universe is an Oracle and Temple, as well as a Kitchen and Cattle-stall,—he shall be a delirious Mystic; to him thou, with sniffing charity, wilt protrusively proffer thy Handlamp, and shriek, as one injured, when he kicks his foot through it?—*Armer Teufel!* Doth not 15 thy Cow calve, doth not thy Bull gender? Thou thyself, wert thou not Born, wilt thou not Die? "Explain" me all this, or do one of two things: Retire into private places with thy foolish cackle; or, what were better, give it up, and weep, not that the reign of wonder is done, and God's world all disembellished and prosaic, but that thou 20 hitherto art a Dilettante and sandblind Pedant.'

CHAPTER XI.

PROSPECTIVE.

THE Philosophy of Clothes is now to all readers, as we predicted it would do, unfolding itself into new boundless expansions, of a cloudcapt, almost chimerical aspect, yet not without azure loomings in the far distance, and streaks as of an Elysian brightness; the highly
5 questionable purport and promise of which it is becoming more and more important for us to ascertain. Is that a real Elysian brightness, cries many a timid wayfarer, or the reflex of Pandemonian lava? Is it of a truth leading us into beatific Asphodel meadows, or the yellow-burning marl of a Hell-on-Earth?
10   Our Professor, like other Mystics, whether delirious or inspired, gives an Editor enough to do. Ever higher and dizzier are the heights he leads us to; more piercing, all-comprehending, all-confounding are his views and glances. For example, this of Nature being not an Aggregate but a Whole:
15   'Well sang the Hebrew Psalmist: "If I take the wings of the morning and dwell in the uttermost parts of the universe, God is there." Thou thyself, O cultivated reader, who too probably art no Psalmist, but a Prosaist, knowing GOD only by tradition, knowest thou any corner of the world where at least FORCE is not? The drop which thou
20 shakest from thy wet hand, rests not where it falls, but to-morrow thou findest it swept away; already, on the wings of the Northwind, it is nearing the Tropic of Cancer. How came it to evaporate, and not lie motionless? Thinkest thou there is aught motionless; without Force, and utterly dead?

54

'As I rode through the Schwarzwald, I said to myself: That little
fire which glows star-like across the dark-growing (*nachtende*) moor,
where the sooty smith bends over his anvil, and thou hopest to replace thy lost horse-shoe,—is it a detached, separated speck, cut off
from the whole universe; or indissolubly joined to the whole? Thou   5
fool, that smithy-fire was (primarily) kindled at the Sun; is fed by air
that circulates from before Noah's Deluge, from beyond the Dogstar;
therein, with Iron Force, and Coal Force, and the far stranger Force
of Man, are cunning affinities and battles and victories of Force brought
about: it is a little ganglion, or nervous centre, in the great vital   10
system of Immensity. Call it, if thou wilt, an unconscious Altar, kindled
on the bosom of the All; whose iron sacrifice, whose iron smoke and
influence reach quite through the All; whose Dingy Priest, not by
word, yet by brain and sinew, preaches forth the mystery of Force;
nay preaches forth (exoterically enough) one little textlet from the   15
Gospel of Freedom, the Gospel of Man's Force, commanding, and
one day to be all-commanding.

'Detached, separated! I say there is no such separation: nothing
hitherto was ever stranded, cast aside; but all, were it only a withered
leaf, works together with all; is borne forward on the bottomless,   20
shoreless flood of Action, and lives through perpetual metamorphoses. The withered leaf is not dead and lost, there are Forces in it and
around it, though working in inverse order; else how could it *rot*?
Despise not the rag from which man makes Paper, or the litter from
which the Earth makes Corn. Rightly viewed no meanest object is   25
insignificant; all objects are as windows, through which the philosophic eye looks into Infinitude itself.'

Again, leaving that wondrous Schwarzwald Smithy-Altar, what vacant, high-sailing air-ships are these, and whither will they sail with us?

'All visible things are Emblems; what thou seest is not there on its   30
own account; strictly taken, is not there at all: Matter exists only
spiritually, and to represent some Idea, and *body* it forth. Hence Clothes,
as despicable as we think them, are so unspeakably significant. Clothes,
from the King's-mantle downwards, are Emblematic, not of want
only, but of a manifold cunning Victory over Want. On the other   35
hand, all Emblematic things are properly Clothes, thought-woven or
hand-woven: must not the Imagination weave Garments, visible Bodies,
wherein the else invisible creations and inspirations of our Reason

are, like Spirits, revealed, and first become all-powerful;—the rather if, as we often see, the Hand too aid her, and (by wool Clothes or otherwise) reveal such even to the outward eye?

'Men are properly said to be clothed with Authority, clothed with
5   Beauty, with Curses, and the like. Nay, if you consider it, what is Man himself, and his whole terrestrial Life, but an Emblem; a Clothing or visible Garment for that divine ME of his, cast hither, like a light-particle, down from Heaven? Thus is he said also to be clothed with a Body.

10   'Language is called the Garment of Thought: however, it should rather be, Language is the Flesh-Garment, the Body, of Thought. I said that Imagination wove this Flesh-Garment; and does not she? Metaphors are her stuff: examine Language; what, if you except some few primitive elements (of natural sound), what is it all but Meta-
15   phors, recognised as such, or no longer recognised; still fluid and florid, or now solid-grown and colourless? If those same primitive elements are the osseous fixtures in the Flesh-garment, Language,— then are Metaphors its muscles and tissues and living integuments. An unmetaphorical style you shall in vain seek for: is not your very
20   *Attention* a *Stretching-to?* The difference lies here: some styles are lean, adust, wiry, the muscle itself seems osseous; some are even quite pallid, hunger-bitten, and dead-looking; while others again glow in the flush of health and vigorous self-growth, sometimes (as in my own case) not without an apoplectic tendency. Moreover, there are
25   sham Metaphors, which overhanging that same Thought's-Body (best naked), and deceptively bedizening, or bolstering it out, may be called its false stuffings, superfluous show-cloaks (*Putz-Mäntel*), and tawdry woollen rags: whereof he that runs and reads may gather whole hampers,—and burn them.'

30   Than which paragraph on Metaphors did the reader ever chance to see a more surprisingly metaphorical? However, that is not our chief grievance; the Professor continues:

'Why multiply instances? It is written the Heavens and the Earth shall fade away like a Vesture; which indeed they are: the Time-
35   vesture of the Eternal. Whatsoever sensibly exists, whatsoever represents Spirit to Spirit, is properly a Clothing, a suit of Raiment, put on for a season, and to be laid off. Thus in this one pregnant subject of CLOTHES, rightly understood, is included all that men have thought,

dreamed, done, and been: the whole external Universe and what it holds is but Clothing; and the essence of all Science lies in the PHILOSOPHY OF CLOTHES.'

Towards these dim infinitely-expanded regions, close-bordering on the impalpable Inane, it is not without apprehension, and per- 5 petual difficulties, that the Editor sees himself journeying and struggling. Till lately a cheerful daystar of hope hung before him, in the expected Aid of Hofrath Heuschrecke; which daystar, however, melts now, not into the red of morning, but into a vague, gray, half-light, uncertain whether dawn of day or dusk of utter darkness. For the last 10 week, these so-called Biographical Documents are in his hand. By the kindness of a Scottish Hamburgh Merchant, whose name, known to the whole mercantile world, he must not mention; but whose honourable courtesy, now and often before spontaneously manifested to him, a mere literary stranger, he cannot soon forget,—the bulky 15 Weissnichtwo Packet, with all its Customhouse seals, foreign hieroglyphs, and miscellaneous tokens of Travel, arrived here in perfect safety, and free of cost. The reader shall now fancy with what hot haste it was broken up, with what breathless expectation glanced over; and, alas, with what unquiet disappointment it has, since then, 20 been often thrown down, and again taken up.

Hofrath Heuschrecke, in a too long-winded Letter, full of compliments, Weissnichtwo politics, dinners, dining repartees, and other ephemeral trivialities, proceeds to remind us of what we knew well already: that however it may be with Metaphysics, and other abstract 25 Science originating in the Head (*Verstand*) alone, no Life-Philosophy (*Lebensphilosophie*), such as this of Clothes pretends to be, which originates equally in the Character (*Gemüth*), and equally speaks thereto, can attain its significance till the Character itself is known and seen; 'till the Author's View of the World (*Weltansicht*), and how 30 he actively and passively came by such view, are clear: in short, till a Biography of him has been philosophico-poetically written, and philosophico-poetically read.' 'Nay,' adds he, 'were the speculative scientific Truth even known, you still, in this inquiring age, ask yourself, Whence came it, and Why, and How?—and rest not, till, if no 35 better may be, Fancy have shaped out an answer; and, either in the authentic lineaments of Fact, or the forged ones of Fiction, a complete picture and Genetical History of the Man and his spiritual

Endeavour lies before you. But why,' says the Hofrath, and indeed say we, 'do I dilate on the uses of our Teufelsdröckh's Biography? The great Herr Minister von Goethe has penetratingly remarked that "Man is properly the *only* object that interests man:" thus I too have
5   noted, that in Weissnichtwo our whole conversation is little or nothing else but Biography or Autobiography; ever humano-anecdotical (*menschlich-anekdotisch*). Biography is by nature the most universally profitable, universally pleasant of all things: especially Biography of distinguished individuals.
10   'By this time, *mein Verehrtester* (my Most Esteemed),' continues he, with an eloquence which, unless the words be purloined from Teufelsdröckh, or some trick of his, as we suspect, is well nigh unaccountable, 'by this time, you are fairly plunged (*vertieft*) in that mighty forest of Clothes-Philosophy; and looking round, as all readers do,
15   with astonishment enough. Such portions and passages as you have already mastered, and brought to paper, could not but awaken a strange curiosity touching the mind they issued from; the perhaps unparalleled psychical mechanism, which manufactured such matter, and emitted it to the light of day. Had Teufelsdröckh also a father and
20   mother; did he, at one time, wear drivel-bibs, and live on spoon-meat? Did he ever, in rapture and tears, clasp a friend's bosom to his; looks he also wistfully into the long burial-aisle of the Past, where only winds, and their low harsh moan, give inarticulate answer? Has he fought duels;—good Heaven! how did he comport himself when
25   in Love? By what singular stair-steps, in short, and subterranean passages, and sloughs of Despair, and steep Pisgah hills, has he reached this wonderful prophetic Hebron (a true Old-Clothes Jewry) where he now dwells?
     'To all these natural questions the voice of public History is as yet
30   silent. Certain only that he has been, and is, a Pilgrim, and Traveller from a far Country; more or less footsore and travel-soiled; has parted with road-companions; fallen among thieves, been poisoned by bad cookery, blistered with bugbites; nevertheless, at every stage (for they have let him pass), has had the Bill to discharge. But the whole
35   particulars of his Route, his Weather-observations, the picturesque Sketches he took, though all regularly jotted down (in indelible sympathetic-ink by an invisible interior Penman), are these nowhere forthcoming? Perhaps quite lost: one other leaf of that mighty Volume

(of human Memory) left to fly abroad, unprinted, unpublished, unbound up, as waste paper; and to rot, the sport of rainy winds? 'No, *verehrtester Herr Herausgeber*, in no wise! I here, by the unexampled favour you stand in with our Sage, send not a Biography only, but an Autobiography: at least the materials for such; wherefrom, if I misreckon not, your perspicacity will draw fullest insight; and so the whole Philosophy and Philosopher of Clothes stand clear to the wondering eyes of England; nay thence, through America, through Hindostan, and the antipodal New Holland, finally conquer (*einnehmen*) great part of this terrestrial Planet!'

And now let the sympathising reader judge of our feeling when, in place of this same Autobiography with 'fullest insight,' we find— Six considerable PAPER-BAGS, carefully sealed, and marked successively, in gilt China-ink, with the symbols of the Six southern Zodiacal Signs, beginning at Libra; in the inside of which sealed Bags, lie miscellaneous masses of Sheets, and oftener Shreds and Snips, written in Professor Teufelsdröckh's scarce-legible *cursiv-schrift*; and treating of all imaginable things under the Zodiac and above it, but of his own personal history only at rare intervals, and then in the most enigmatic manner!

Whole fascicles there are, wherein the Professor, or, as he here speaking in the third person calls himself, 'the Wanderer,' is not once named. Then again, amidst what seems to be a Metaphysico-theological Disquisition, 'Detached Thoughts on the Steam-engine,' or 'The continued Possibility of Prophecy,' we shall meet with some quite private, not unimportant Biographical fact. On certain sheets stand Dreams, authentic or not, while the circumjacent waking Actions are omitted. Anecdotes, oftenest without date of place or time, fly loosely on separate slips, like Sibylline leaves. Interspersed also are long purely Autobiographical delineations; yet without connexion, without recognisable coherence; so unimportant, so superfluously minute, they almost remind us of 'P. P. Clerk of this Parish.' Thus does famine of intelligence alternate with waste. Selection, order appears to be unknown to the Professor. In all Bags the same imbroglio; only perhaps in the Bag *Capricorn*, and those near it, the confusion a little worse confounded. Close by a rather eloquent Oration 'On receiving the Doctor's-Hat,' lie washbills, marked *bezahlt* (settled). His Travels are indicated by the Street-Advertisements of the various cities he has

visited; of which Street-Advertisements, in most living tongues, here
is perhaps the completest collection extant.

So that if the Clothes-Volume itself was too like a Chaos, we have
now instead of the solar Luminary that should still it, the airy Limbo
which by intermixture will farther volatilise and discompose it! As we
shall perhaps see it our duty ultimately to deposit these Six Paper
Bags in the British Museum, farther description, and all vituperation
of them, may be spared. Biography or Autobiography of Teufelsdröckh
there is, clearly enough, none to be gleaned here: at most some
sketchy, shadowy, fugitive likeness of him may, by unheard-of efforts,
partly of intellect partly of imagination, on the side of Editor and of
Reader, rise up between them. Only as a gaseous-chaotic Appendix
to that aqueous-chaotic Volume can the contents of the Six Bags
hover round us, and portions thereof be incorporated with our
delineation of it.

Daily and nightly does the Editor sit (with green spectacles) de-
ciphering these unimaginable Documents from their perplexed *cursiv-
schrift;* collating them with the almost equally unimaginable Volume,
which stands in legible print. Over such a universal medley of high
and low, of hot, cold, moist and dry, is he here struggling (by union
of like with like, which is Method) to build a firm Bridge for British
travellers. Never perhaps since our first Bridge-builders, Sin and Death,
built that stupendous Arch from Hell-gate to the Earth, did any
Pontifex, or Pontiff, undertake such a task as the present Editor. For
in this Arch too, leading as we humbly presume, far otherwards than
that grand primeval one, the materials are to be fished up from the
weltering deep, and down from the simmering air, here one mass,
there another, and cunningly cemented, while the elements boil beneath: nor is there any supernatural force to do it with; but simply the
Diligence and feeble thinking Faculty of an English Editor,
endeavouring to evolve printed Creation out of a German printed
and written Chaos, wherein, as he shoots to and fro in it, gathering,
clutching, piecing the Why to the far-distant Wherefore, his whole
Faculty and Self are like to be swallowed up.

Patiently, under these incessant toils and agitations, does the Editor, dismissing all anger, see his otherwise robust health declining;
some fraction of his allotted natural sleep nightly leaving him, and
little but an inflamed nervous-system to be looked for. What is the

use of health, or of life, if not to do some work therewith? And what work nobler than transplanting foreign Thought into the barren domestic soil; except indeed planting Thought of your own, which the fewest are privileged to do? Wild as it looks, this Philosophy of Clothes, can we ever reach its real meaning, promises to reveal new- ⁵ coming Eras, the first dim rudiments and already-budding germs of a nobler Era, in Universal History. Is not such a prize worth some striving? Forward with us, courageous reader; be it towards failure, or towards success! The latter thou sharest with us, the former also is not all our own.   10

BOOK II.

CHAPTER I.

GENESIS.

IN a psychological point of view, it is perhaps questionable whether from birth and genealogy, how closely scrutinised soever, much insight is to be gained. Nevertheless, as in every phenomenon the Beginning remains always the most notable moment; so, with regard to any great man, we rest not till, for our scientific profit or not, the whole circumstances of his first appearance in this Planet, and what manner of Public Entry he made, are with utmost completeness rendered manifest. To the Genesis of our Clothes-Philosopher, then, be this First Chapter consecrated. Unhappily, indeed, he seems to be of quite obscure extraction; uncertain, we might almost say, whether of any: so that this Genesis of his can properly be nothing but an Exodus (or transit out of Invisibility into Visibility); whereof the preliminary portion is nowhere forthcoming.

'In the village of Entepfuhl,' thus writes he, in the Bag *Libra*, on various Papers, which we arrange with difficulty, 'dwelt Andreas Futteral and his wife; childless, in still seclusion, and cheerful though now verging towards old age. Andreas had been grenadier Sergeant, and even regimental Schoolmaster under Frederick the Great; but now, quitting the halbert and ferule for the spade and pruning-hook, cultivated a little Orchard, on the produce of which he, Cincinnatus-like, lived not without dignity. Fruits, the peach, the apple, the grape, with other varieties came in their season; all which Andreas knew how to sell: on evenings he smoked largely, or read (as beseemed a

regimental Schoolmaster), and talked to neighbours that would listen about the Victory of Rossbach; and how Fritz the Only (*der Einzige*) had once with his own royal lips spoken to him, had been pleased to say, when Andreas as camp-sentinel demanded the pass-word, "*Schweig*
5 *Hund* (Peace, hound)!" before any of his staff-adjutants could answer. "*Das nenn' ich mir einen König*, There is what I call a King," would Andreas exclaim: "but the smoke of Kunersdorf was still smarting his eyes."

'Gretchen, the housewife, won like Desdemona by the deeds rather
10 than the looks of her now veteran Othello, lived not in altogether military subordination; for, as Andreas said, "the womankind will not drill (*wer kann die Weiberchen dressiren*):" nevertheless she at heart loved him both for valour and wisdom; to her a Prussian grenadier Sergeant and Regiment's-Schoolmaster was little other than a Cicero
15 and Cid: what you see, yet cannot see over, is as good as infinite. Nay, was not Andreas in very deed a man of order, courage, downrightness (*Geradheit*); that understood Büsching's *Geography*, had been in the victory of Rossbach, and left for dead in the camisade of Hochkirch? The good Gretchen, for all her fretting, watched over him and hov-
20 ered round him, as only a true housemother can: assiduously she cooked and sewed and scoured for him; so that not only his old regimental sword and grenadier-cap, but the whole habitation and environment where, on pegs of honour, they hung, looked ever trim and gay: a roomy painted Cottage, embowered in fruit-trees and
25 forest-trees, evergreens and honeysuckles; rising many-coloured from amid shaven grass-plots, flowers struggling in through the very windows; under its long projecting eaves nothing but garden-tools in methodic piles (to screen them from rain), and seats, where, especially on summer nights, a King might have wished to sit and smoke
30 and call it his. Such a *Bauergut* (Copyhold) had Gretchen given her veteran; whose sinewy arms, and long-disused gardening talent, had made it what you saw.

'Into this umbrageous Man's-nest, one meek yellow evening or dusk, when the Sun, hidden indeed from terrestrial Entepfuhl, did
35 nevertheless journey visible and radiant along the celestial Balance (*Libra*), it was that a Stranger of reverend aspect entered; and, with grave salutation, stood before the two rather astonished housemates. He was close-muffled in a wide mantle; which without farther parley

unfolding, he deposited therefrom what seemed some Basket, overhung with green Persian silk; saying only: *Ihr lieben Leute, hier bringe
ein unschätzbares Verleihen; nehmt es in aller Acht, sorgfältigst benützt
es: mit hohem Lohn, oder wohl mit schweren Zinsen, wird's einst zurück-
gefordert,* "Good Christian people, here lies for you an invaluable 5
Loan; take all heed thereof, in all carefulness employ it: with high
recompense, or else with heavy penalty, will it one day be required
back." Uttering which singular words, in a clear, bell-like, forever
memorable tone, the Stranger gracefully withdrew; and before Andreas
or his wife, gazing in expectant wonder, had time to fashion either 10
question or answer, was clean gone. Neither out of doors could aught
of him be seen or heard; he had vanished in the thickets, in the dusk;
the Orchard-gate stood quietly closed: the Stranger was gone once
and always. So sudden had the whole transaction been, in the autumn
stillness and twilight, so gentle, noiseless, that the Futterals could 15
have fancied it all a trick of Imagination, or some visit from an authentic Spirit. Only that the green-silk Basket, such as neither Imagination nor authentic Spirits are wont to carry, still stood visible and
tangible on their little parlour-table. Towards this the astonished couple,
now with lit candle, hastily turned their attention. Lifting the green 20
veil, to see what invaluable it hid, they descried there, amid down and
rich white wrappages, no Pitt Diamond or Hapsburg Regalia, but in
the softest sleep, a little red-coloured Infant! Beside it, lay a roll of
gold Friedrichs, the exact amount of which was never publicly known;
also a *Taufschein* (baptismal certificate), wherein unfortunately noth- 25
ing but the Name was decipherable; other document or indication
none whatever.

'To wonder and conjecture was unavailing, then and always thenceforth. Nowhere in Entepfuhl, on the morrow or next day, did tidings
transpire of any such figure as the Stranger; nor could the Traveller, 30
who had passed through the neighbouring Town in coach-and-four,
be connected with this Apparition, except in the way of gratuitous
surmise. Meanwhile, for Andreas and his wife, the grand practical
problem was: What to do with this little sleeping red-coloured Infant?
Amid amazements and curiosities, which had to die away without 35
external satisfying, they resolved, as in such circumstances charitable
prudent people needs must, on nursing it, though with spoon-meat,
into whiteness, and if possible into manhood. The Heavens smiled on

their endeavour: thus has that same mysterious Individual ever since had a status for himself in this visible Universe, some modicum of victual and lodging and parade-ground; and now expanded in bulk, faculty, and knowledge of good and evil, he, as HERR DIOGENES
5   TEUFELSDRÖCKH, professes or is ready to profess, perhaps not altogether without effect, in the new University of Weissnichtwo, the new Science of Things in General.'

Our Philosopher declares here, as indeed we should think he well might, that these facts, first communicated, by the good Gretchen
10 Futteral, in his twelfth year, 'produced on the boyish heart and fancy a quite indelible impression. Who this reverend Personage,' he says, 'that glided into the Orchard Cottage when the Sun was in Libra, and then, as on spirit's wings, glided out again, might be? An inexpressible desire, full of love and of sadness, has often since struggled
15 within me to shape an answer. Ever, in my distresses and my loneliness, has Fantasy turned, full of longing (*sehnsuchtsvoll*), to that unknown Father, who perhaps far from me, perhaps near, either way invisible, might have taken me to his paternal bosom, there to lie screened from many a woe. Thou beloved Father, dost thou still, shut
20 out from me only by thin penetrable curtains of earthly Space, wend to and fro among the crowd of the living? Or art thou hidden by those far thicker curtains of the Everlasting Night, or rather of the Everlasting Day, through which my mortal eye and outstretched arms need not strive to reach? Alas! I know not, and in vain vex myself to
25 know. More than once, heart-deluded, have I taken for thee this and the other noble-looking Stranger; and approached him wistfully, with infinite regard: but he too had to repel me, he too was not thou.

'And yet, O Man born of Woman,' cries the Autobiographer, with one of his sudden whirls, 'wherein is my case peculiar? Hadst thou,
30 any more than I, a Father whom thou knowest? The Andreas and Gretchen, or the Adam and Eve,who led thee into Life, and for a time suckled and pap-fed thee there, whom thou namest Father and Mother; these were, like mine, but thy nursing-father and nursing-mother: thy true Beginning and Father is in Heaven, whom with the bodily eye
35 thou shalt never behold, but only with the spiritual.'

'The little green veil,' adds he, among much similar moralising, and embroiled discoursing, 'I yet keep; still more inseparably the Name, Diogenes Teufelsdröckh. From the veil can nothing be inferred:

a piece of now quite faded Persian silk, like thousands of others. On the Name I have many times meditated and conjectured; but neither in this lay there any clue. That it was my unknown Father's name I must hesitate to believe. To no purpose have I searched through all the Herald's Books, in and without the German Empire, and through all manner of Subscriber-Lists (*Pränumeranten*), Militia-Rolls, and other Name-catalogues; extraordinary names as we have in Germany, the name Teufelsdröckh, except as appended to my own person, nowhere occurs. Again, what may the unchristian rather than Christian "Diogenes" mean? Did that reverend Basket-bearer intend, by such designation, to shadow forth my future destiny, or his own present malign humour? Perhaps the latter, perhaps both. Thou ill-starred Parent, who like an Ostrich hadst to leave thy ill-starred offspring to be hatched into self-support by the mere sky-influences of Chance, can thy pilgrimage have been a smooth one? Beset by Misfortune thou doubtless hast been; or indeed by the worst figure of Misfortune, by Misconduct. Often have I fancied how, in thy hard life-battle, thou wert shot at and slung at, wounded, handfettered, hamstrung, browbeaten and bedevilled, by the Time-Spirit (*Zeitgeist*) in thyself and others, till the good soul first given thee was seared into grim rage; and thou hadst nothing for it but to leave in me an indignant appeal to the Future, and living speaking Protest against the Devil, as that same Spirit not of the Time only, but of Time itself, is well named! Which Appeal and Protest, may I now modestly add, was not perhaps quite lost in air.

'For indeed as Walter Shandy often insisted, there is much, nay almost all, in Names. The Name is the earliest Garment you wrap round the Earth-visiting ME; to which it thenceforth cleaves, more tenaciously (for there are Names that have lasted nigh thirty centuries) than the very skin. And now from without, what mystic influences does it not send inwards, even to the centre; especially in those plastic first-times, when the whole soul is yet infantine, soft, and the invisible seed-grain will grow to be an all over-shadowing tree! Names? Could I unfold the influence of Names, which are the most important of all Clothings, I were a second greater Trismegistus. Not only all common Speech, but Science, Poetry itself is no other, if thou consider it, than a right *Naming*. Adam's first task was giving names to natural Appearances: what is ours still but a continuation of the same;

be the Appearances exotic-vegetable, organic, mechanic, stars, or starry
movements (as in Science); or (as in Poetry) passions, virtues, calami-
ties, God-attributes, Gods?—In a very plain sense the Proverb says,
Call one a thief and he will steal; in an almost similar sense, may we
5 not perhaps say, *Call one Diogenes Teufelsdröckh and he will open the
Philosophy of Clothes.*

'Meanwhile the incipient Diogenes, like others, all ignorant of his
Why, his How or Whereabout, was opening his eyes to the kind
Light; sprawling out his ten fingers and toes; listening, tasting, feel-
10 ing; in a word, by all his Five Senses, still more by his Sixth Sense of
Hunger, and a whole infinitude of inward, spiritual, half awakened
Senses, endeavouring daily to acquire for himself some knowledge of
this strange Universe where he had arrived, be his task therein what
it might. Infinite was his progress; thus in some fifteen months, he
15 could perform the miracle of—Speech! To breed a fresh Soul, is it not
like brooding a fresh (celestial) Egg; wherein as yet all is formless,
powerless; yet by degrees organic elements and fibres shoot through
the watery albumen; and out of vague Sensation, grows Thought,
grows Fantasy and Force, and we have Philosophies, Dynasties, nay
20 Poetries and Religions!

'Young Diogenes, or rather young Gneschen, for by such diminutive had they in their fondness named him, travelled forward to those
high consummations, by quick yet easy stages. The Futterals, to avoid
vain talk, and moreover keep the roll of gold Friedrichs safe, gave out
25 that he was a grand-nephew; the orphan of some sister's daughter,
suddenly deceased, in Andreas's distant Prussian birth-land; of whom,
as of her indigent sorrowing widower, little enough was known at
Entepfuhl. Heedless of all which, the Nurseling took to his spoon-
meat, and throve. I have heard him noted as a still infant, that kept
30 his mind much to himself; above all, that seldom or never cried. He
already felt that Time was precious; that he had other work cut out
for him than whimpering.'

Such, after utmost painful search and collation among these
35 miscellaneous Paper-masses, is all the notice we can gather of Herr
Teufelsdröckh's genealogy. More imperfect, more enigmatic it can
seem to few readers than to us. The Professor, in whom truly we
more and more discern a certain satirical turn, and deep undercurrents

of roguish whim, for the present stands pledged in honour, so we will
not doubt him: but seems it not conceivable that, by the 'good
Gretchen Futteral,' or some other perhaps interested party, he has
himself been deceived? Should these Sheets, translated or not, ever
reach the Entepfuhl Circulating-Library, some cultivated native of   5
that district might feel called to afford explanation. Nay, since Books,
like invisible scouts, permeate the whole habitable globe, and
Timbuctoo itself is not safe from British Literature, may not some
Copy find out even the mysterious Basket-bearing Stranger, who in
a state of extreme senility perhaps still exists; and gently force even   10
him to disclose himself; to claim openly a son, in whom any father
may feel pride?

CHAPTER II.

IDYLLIC.

'HAPPY season of Childhood!' exclaims Teufelsdröckh: 'Kind Nature, that art to all a bountiful mother; that visitest the poor man's hut with auroral radiance; and for thy Nurseling hast provided a soft swathing of Love and infinite Hope, wherein he waxes and slumbers, danced-round (*umgaukelt*) by sweetest Dreams! If the paternal Cottage still shuts us in, its roof still screens us; with a Father we have as yet a prophet, priest and king, and an Obedience that makes us Free. The young spirit has awakened out of Eternity, and knows not what we mean by Time; as yet Time is no fast-hurrying stream, but a sportful sunlit ocean; years to the child are as ages: ah! the secret of Vicissitude, of that slower or quicker decay and ceaseless downrushing of the universal World-fabric, from the granite mountain to the man or day-moth, is yet unknown; and in a motionless Universe, we taste, what afterwards in this quick-whirling Universe is forever denied us, the balm of Rest. Sleep on, thou fair Child, for thy long rough journey is at hand! A little while, and thou too shalt sleep no more, but thy very dreams shall be mimic battles; thou too, with old Arnauld, wilt have to say in stern patience: "Rest? Rest? Shall I not have all Eternity to rest in?" Celestial Nepenthe! though a Pyrrhus conquer empires, and an Alexander sack the world, he finds thee not; and thou hast once fallen gently, of thy own accord, on the eyelids, on the heart of every mother's child. For as yet, sleep and waking are one: the fair Life-garden rustles infinite around, and everywhere is

70

dewy fragrance, and the budding of Hope; which budding, if in youth, too frostnipt, it grow to flowers, will in manhood yield no fruit, but a prickly, bitter-rinded stone-fruit, of which the fewest can find the kernel.'

In such rose-coloured light does our Professor, as Poets are wont, look back on his childhood; the historical details of which (to say nothing of much other vague oratorical matter) he accordingly dwells on, with an almost wearisome minuteness. We hear of Entepfuhl standing 'in trustful derangement' among the woody slopes; the paternal Orchard flanking it as extreme outpost from below; the little Kuhbach gushing kindly by, among beech-rows, through river after river, into the Donau, into the Black Sea, into the Atmosphere and Universe; and how 'the brave old Linden,' stretching like a parasol of twenty ells in radius, overtopping all other rows and clumps, towered up from the central *Agora* and *Campus Martius* of the Village, like its Sacred Tree; and how the old men sat talking under its shadow (Gneschen often greedily listening), and the wearied labourers reclined, and the unwearied children sported, and the young men and maidens often danced to flute-music. 'Glorious summer twilights,' cries Teufelsdröckh, 'when the Sun like a proud Conqueror and Imperial Taskmaster turned his back, with his gold-purple emblazonry, and all his fire-clad bodyguard (of Prismatic Colours); and the tired brickmakers of this clay Earth might steal a little frolic, and those few meek Stars would not tell of them!'

Then we have long details of the *Weinlesen* (Vintage), the Harvest-Home, Christmas, and so forth; with a whole cycle of the Entepfuhl Children's-games, differing apparently by mere superficial shades from those of other countries. Concerning all which, we shall here, for obvious reasons, say nothing. What cares the world for our as yet miniature Philosopher's achievements under that 'brave old Linden?' Or even where is the use of such practical reflections as the following? 'In all the sports of Children, were it only in their wanton breakages and defacements, you shall discern a creative instinct (*schaffenden Trieb*): the Mankin feels that he is a born Man, that his vocation is to Work. The choicest present you can make him is a Tool; be it knife or pengun, for construction or for destruction; either way it is for Work, for Change. In gregarious sports of skill or strength, the Boy trains himself to Cooperation, for war or peace, as governor or governed: the little Maid again, provident of her domestic destiny, takes with preference to Dolls.'

Perhaps, however, we may give this anecdote, considering who it is that relates it: 'My first short-clothes were of yellow serge; or 5 rather, I should say, my first short-cloth, for the vesture was one and indivisible, reaching from neck to ankle, a mere body with four limbs: of which fashion how little could I then divine the architectural, how much less the moral significance!'

More graceful is the following little picture: 'On fine evenings I 10 was wont to carry forth my supper (bread-crumb boiled in milk), and eat it out of doors. On the coping of the Orchard-wall, which I could reach by climbing, or still more easily if Father Andreas would set up the pruning-ladder, my porringer was placed: there, many a sunset, have I, looking at the distant western Mountains, consumed, not 15 without relish, my evening meal. Those hues of gold and azure, that hush of World's expectation as Day died, were still a Hebrew Speech for me; nevertheless I was looking at the fair illuminated Letters, and had an eye for their gilding.'

With 'the little one's friendship for cattle and poultry' we shall 20 not much intermeddle. It may be that hereby he acquired 'a certain deeper sympathy with animated Nature:' but when, we would ask, saw any man, in a collection of Biographical Documents, such a piece as this: 'Impressive enough (*bedeutungsvoll*) was it to hear, in early morning, the Swineherd's horn; and know that so many hungry, 25 happy quadrupeds, were on all sides starting in hot haste to join him, for breakfast on the Heath. Or to see them, at eventide, all marching in again, with short squeak, almost in military order; and each, topographically correct, trotting off in succession to the right or left, through its own lane, to its own dwelling; till old Kunz, at the Village- 30 head, now left alone, blew his last blast, and retired for the night. We are wont to love the Hog chiefly in the form of Ham: yet did not these bristly thick-skinned beings here manifest intelligence, perhaps humour of character; at any rate, a touching, trustful submissiveness to Man,—who were he but a Swineherd, in darned gabardine, and 35 leather breeches more resembling slate or discoloured tin breeches, is still the Hierarch of this lower world?'

It is maintained, by Helvetius and his set, that an infant of genius is quite the same as any other infant, only that certain surprisingly favourable influences accompany him through life, especially through childhood, and expand him, while others lie close-folded and continue dunces. Herein, say they, consists the whole difference between an inspired Prophet and a double-barrelled Game-preserver: the inner man of the one has been fostered into generous development; that of the other, crushed down perhaps by vigour of animal digestion, and the like, has exuded and evaporated, or at best sleeps now irresuscitably stagnant at the bottom of his stomach. 'With which opinion,' cries Teufelsdröckh, 'I should as soon agree as with this other, that an acorn might, by favourable or unfavourable influences of soil and climate, be nursed into a cabbage, or the cabbage-seed into an oak.

'Nevertheless,' continues he, 'I too acknowledge the all-but omnipotence of early culture and nurture: hereby we have either a doddered dwarf bush, or a high-towering, wide-shadowing tree; either a sick yellow cabbage, or an edible, luxuriant, green one. Of a truth, it is the duty of all men, especially of all philosophers, to note down with accuracy the characteristic circumstances of their Education, what furthered, what hindered, what in any way modified it: to which duty, now-a-days so pressing for many a German Autobiographer, I also zealously address myself.'—Thou rogue! Is it by short-clothes of yellow serge, and swineherd horns, that an infant of genius is educated? And yet, as usual, it ever remains doubtful whether he is laughing in his sleeve at these Autobiographical times of ours, or writing from the abundance of his own fond ineptitude. For he continues: 'If among the ever-streaming currents of Sights, Hearings, Feelings for Pain or Pleasure, whereby, as in a Magic Hall, young Gneschen went about environed, I might venture to select and specify, perhaps these following were also of the number:

'Doubtless, as childish sports call forth Intellect, Activity, so the young creature's Imagination was stirred up, and a Historical tendency given him by the narrative habits of Father Andreas; who, with his battle-reminiscences, and gray, austere, yet hearty patriarchal aspect, could not but appear another Ulysses and "Much-enduring Man." Eagerly I hung upon his tales, when listening neighbours enlivened the hearth: from these perils and these travels, wild and far almost as Hades itself, a dim world of Adventure expanded itself within me. Incalculable also was the knowledge I acquired in standing by the Old Men under the Linden-tree: the whole of Immensity was yet new

to me; and had not these reverend seniors, talkative enough, been
employed in partial surveys thereof for nigh fourscore years? With
amazement I began to discover that Entepfuhl stood in the middle of
a Country, of a World; that there was such a thing as History, as
Biography; to which I also, one day, by hand and tongue, might
contribute.

'In a like sense worked the *Postwagen* (Stage-Coach), which, slow-
rolling under its mountains of men and luggage, wended through our
Village: northwards, truly, in the dead of night; yet southwards visibly
at eventide. Not till my eighth year, did I reflect that this Postwagen
could be other than some terrestrial Moon, rising and setting by mere
Law of Nature, like the heavenly one; that it came on made highways,
from far cities towards far cities; weaving them like a monstrous shuttle
into closer and closer union. It was then that, independently of Schiller's
Wilhelm Tell, I made this not quite insignificant reflection (so true
also in spiritual things): *Any road, this simple Entepfuhl road, will lead
you to the end of the World!*

'Why mention our Swallows, which, out of far Africa as I learned,
threading their way over seas and mountains, corporate cities and
belligerent nations, yearly found themselves, with the month of May,
snug-lodged in our Cottage Lobby? The hospitable Father (for cleanliness' sake) had fixed a little bracket, plumb under their nest: there
they built, and caught flies, and twittered, and bred; and all, I chiefly,
from the heart loved them. Bright, nimble creatures, who taught *you*
the mason-craft; nay, stranger still, gave you a masonic incorporation,
almost social police? For if, by ill chance, and when time pressed,
your House fell, have I not seen five neighbourly Helpers appear next
day; and swashing to and fro, with animated, loud, long-drawn
chirpings, and activity almost super-hirundine, complete it again before nightfall?

'But undoubtedly the grand summary of Entepfuhl child's-culture,
where as in a funnel its manifold influences were concentrated and
simultaneously poured down on us, was the annual Cattle-fair. Here,
assembling from all the four winds, came the elements of an unspeakable hurly-burly. Nutbrown maids and nutbrown men, all clear-washed,
loud-laughing, bedizened and beribanded; who came for dancing, for
treating, and if possible, for happiness. Topbooted Graziers from the
North; Swiss Brokers, Italian Drovers, also topbooted, from the South;

these with their subalterns in leather jerkins, leather skullcaps, and
long oxgoads; shouting in half-articulate speech, amid the inarticulate
barking and bellowing. Apart stood Potters from far Saxony, with
their crockery in fair rows; Nürnberg Pedlars, in booths that to me
seemed richer than Ormuz bazaars; Showmen from the Lago Maggiore;   5
detachments of the *Wiener Schub* (Offscourings of Vienna) vocifer-
ously superintending games of chance. Ballad-singers brayed, Auc-
tioneers grew hoarse; cheap New Wine (*heuriger*) flowed like water,
still worse confounding the confusion; and high over all, vaulted, in
ground-and-lofty tumbling, a particoloured Merry Andrew; like the   10
genius of the place and of Life itself.

'Thus encircled by the mystery of Existence; under the deep heavenly Firmament; waited on by the four golden Seasons, with their
vicissitudes of contribution, for even grim Winter brought its skating-   15
matches and shooting-matches, its snow-storms and Christmas car-
ols,—did the Child sit and learn. These things were the Alphabet,
whereby in after-time he was to syllable and partly read the grand
Volume of the World: what matters it whether such Alphabet be in
large gilt letters or in small ungilt ones, so you have an eye to read   20
it? For Gneschen, eager to learn, the very act of looking thereon was
a blessedness that gilded all: his existence was a bright, soft element
of Joy; out of which, as in Prospero's Island, wonder after wonder
bodied itself forth, to teach by charming.
'Nevertheless I were but a vain dreamer to say, that even then my   25
felicity was perfect. I had, once for all, come down from Heaven into
the Earth. Among the rainbow colours that glowed on my horizon,
lay even in childhood a dark ring of Care, as yet no thicker than a
thread, and often quite overshone; yet always it reappeared, nay ever
waxing broader and broader; till in after-years it almost overshadowed   30
my whole canopy, and threatened to engulf me in final night. It was
the ring of Necessity, whereby we are all begirt: happy he for whom
a kind heavenly Sun brightens it into a ring of Duty, and plays round
it with beautiful prismatic diffractions; yet ever, as basis and as bourne
for our whole being, it is there.   35
'For the first few years of our terrestrial Apprenticeship, we have
not much work to do; but, boarded and lodged gratis, are set down
mostly to look about us over the workshop, and see others work, till

we have understood the tools a little, and can handle this and that.
If good Passivity alone, and not good Passivity and good Activity
together, were the thing wanted, then was my early position favourable
beyond the most. In all that respects openness of Sense, affectionate
Temper, ingenuous Curiosity, and the fostering of these, what more
could I have wished? On the other side, however, things went not so
well. My Active Power (*Thatkraft*) was unfavourably hemmed in; of
which misfortune how many traces yet abide with me! In an orderly
house, where the litter of children's sports is hateful enough, your
training is too stoical; rather to bear and forbear than to make and
do. I was forbid much: wishes in any measure bold I had to renounce;
everywhere a strait bond of Obedience inflexibly held me down. Thus
already Freewill often came in painful collision with Necessity; so that
my tears flowed, and at seasons the Child itself might taste that root
of bitterness, wherewith the whole fruitage of our life is mingled and
tempered.

'In which habituation to Obedience, truly, it was beyond measure
safer to err by excess than by defect. Obedience is our universal duty
and destiny; wherein whoso will not bend must break: too early and
too thoroughly we cannot be trained to know that Would, in this
world of ours, is as mere zero to Should, and for most part as the
smallest of fractions even to Shall. Hereby was laid for me the basis
of worldly Discretion, nay, of Morality itself. Let me not quarrel with
my upbringing! It was rigorous, too frugal, compressively secluded,
every way unscientific: yet in that very strictness and domestic solitude might there not lie the root of deeper Earnestness, of the stem
from which all noble fruit must grow? Above all, how unskilful soever,
it was loving, it was well-meant, honest; whereby every deficiency was
helped. My kind Mother, for as such I must ever love the good
Gretchen, did me one altogether invaluable service: she taught me,
less indeed by word than by act and daily reverent look and habitude,
her own simple version of the Christian Faith. Andreas too attended
Church; yet more like a parade-duty, for which he in the other world
expected pay with arrears,—as, I trust, he has received: but my Mother,
with a true woman's heart, and fine though uncultivated sense, was
in the strictest acceptation Religious. How indestructibly the Good
grows, and propagates itself, even among the weedy entanglements of
Evil! The highest whom I knew on Earth I here saw bowed down,

with awe unspeakable, before a Higher in Heaven: such things, especially in infancy, reach inwards to the very core of your being; mysteriously does a Holy of Holies build itself into visibility in the
mysterious deeps; and Reverence, the divinest in man, springs forth
undying from its mean envelopment of Fear. Wouldst thou rather be   5
a peasant's son that knew, were it never so rudely, there was a God
in Heaven and in Man; or a duke's son that only knew there were two
and thirty quarters on the family-coach?'

   To which last question we must answer: Beware, O Teufelsdröckh,
of spiritual pride!   10

CHAPTER III.

HITHERTO we see young Gneschen, in his indivisible case of yellow serge, borne forward mostly on the arms of kind Nature alone; seated, indeed, and much to his mind, in the terrestrial workshop; but (except his soft hazel eyes, which we doubt not already gleamed with a still intelligence) called upon for little voluntary movement there. Hitherto accordingly his aspect is rather generic, that of an incipient Philosopher and Poet in the abstract: perhaps it would puzzle Herr Heuschrecke himself to say wherein the special Doctrine of Clothes is as yet foreshadowed or betokened. For with Gneschen, as with others, the Man may indeed stand pictured in the Boy (at least, all the pigments are there); yet only some half of the Man stands in the Child, or young Boy, namely, his Passive endowment, not his Active. The more impatient are we to discover what figure he cuts in this latter capacity; how when, to use his own words, 'he understands the tools a little, and can handle this or that,' he will proceed to handle it.

Here, however, may be the place to state that, in much of our Philosopher's history, there is something of an almost Hindoo character: nay, perhaps in that so well-fostered and every-way-excellent 'Passivity' of his, which, with no free development of the antagonist Activity, distinguished his childhood, we may detect the rudiments of much that, in after-days, and still in these present days, astonishes the world. For the shallow-sighted, Teufelsdröckh is oftenest a man with-

out Activity of any kind, a No-man; for the deep-sighted, again, a man with Activity almost superabundant, yet so spiritual, close-hidden, enigmatic, that no mortal can foresee its explosions, or even when it has exploded, so much as ascertain its significance. A dangerous, difficult temper for the modern European; above all, disadvantageous in   5
the hero of a Biography! Now as heretofore it will behove the Editor of these pages, were it never so unsuccessfully, to do his endeavour.

Among the earliest tools of any complicacy which a man, especially a man of letters, gets to handle, are his Class-books. On this portion of   10
his History, Teufelsdröckh looks down professedly as indifferent. Reading he 'cannot remember ever to have learned;' so perhaps had it by nature. He says generally: 'Of the insignificant portion of my Education, which depended on Schools, there need almost no notice be taken. I learned what others learn; and kept it stored by in a corner of my head,   15
seeing as yet no manner of use in it. My Schoolmaster, a downbent, brokenhearted, underfoot martyr, as others of that guild are, did little for me, except discover that he could do little: he, good soul, pronounced me a genius, fit for the learned professions; and that I must be sent to the Gymnasium, and one day to the University. Meanwhile, what   20
printed thing soever I could meet with I read. My very copper pocket-money I laid out on stall-literature; which, as it accumulated, I with my own hands sewed into volumes. By this means was the young head furnished with a considerable miscellany of things and shadows of things: History in authentic fragments lay mingled with Fabulous chimeras,   25
wherein also was reality; and the whole not as dead stuff, but as living pabulum, tolerably nutritive for a mind as yet so peptic.'
    That the Entepfuhl Schoolmaster judged well we now know. Indeed, already in the youthful Gneschen, with all his outward stillness, there may have been manifest an inward vivacity that promised much;   30
symptoms of a spirit singularly open, thoughtful, almost poetical. Thus, to say nothing of his Suppers on the Orchard-wall, and other phenomena of that earlier period, have many readers of these pages stumbled, in their twelfth year, on such reflections as the following? 'It struck me much, as I sat by the Kuhbach, one silent noontide,   35
and watched it flowing, gurgling, to think how this same streamlet had flowed and gurgled, through all changes of weather and of fortune, from beyond the earliest date of History. Yes, probably on the

morning when Joshua forded Jordan; even as at the mid-day when
Cæsar, doubtless with difficulty, swam the Nile, yet kept his *Commentaries* dry,—this little Kuhbach, assiduous as Tiber, Eurotas, or
Siloa, was murmuring on across the wilderness, as yet unnamed, unseen:
5 here too, as in the Euphrates and the Ganges, is a Vein or Veinlet of
the grand World-circulation of Waters, which, with its atmospheric
Arteries, has lasted and lasts simply with the World. Thou fool! Nature alone is antique, and the oldest Art a mushroom; that idle crag
thou sittest on is six thousand years of age.' In which little thought,
10 as in a little fountain, may there not lie the beginning of those well-
nigh unutterable meditations on the grandeur and mystery of TIME,
and its relation to ETERNITY, which play such a part in this Philosophy
of Clothes?

Over his Gymnasic and Academic years the Professor by no means
15 lingers so lyrical and joyful as over his childhood. Green sunny tracts
there are still; but intersected by bitter rivulets of tears, here and
there stagnating into sour marshes of discontent. 'With my first view
of the Hinterschlag Gymnasium,' writes he, 'my evil days began. Well
do I still remember the red sunny Whitsuntide morning, when trot-
20 ting full of hope, by the side of Father Andreas, I entered the main
street of the place, and saw its steeple-clock (then striking Eight), and
Schuldthurm (Jail), and the aproned or disaproned Burghers moving
in to breakfast: a little dog, in mad terror, was rushing past; for some
human imps had tied a tin kettle to its tail; thus did the agonised
25 creature loud-jingling career through the whole length of the Borough, and become notable enough. Fit emblem of many a Conquering Hero, to whom Fate (wedding Fantasy to Sense, as it often
elsewhere does) has malignantly appended a tin kettle of Ambition,
to chase him on; which, the faster he runs, urges him the faster, the
30 more loudly and more foolishly! Fit emblem also of much that awaited
myself, in that mischievous Den; as in the World, whereof it was a
portion and epitome!

'Alas, the kind beech-rows of Entepfuhl were hidden in the distance: I was among strangers, harshly, at best indifferently, disposed
35 towards me; the young heart felt, for the first time, quite orphaned
and alone.' His schoolfellows, as is usual, persecuted him: 'They were
Boys,' he says, 'mostly rude Boys, and obeyed the impulse of rude
Nature, which bids the deerherd fall upon any stricken hart, the

duck-flock put to death any broken-winged brother or sister, and on all hands the strong tyrannise over the weak.' He admits that though 'perhaps in an unusual degree morally courageous,' he succeeded ill in battle, and would fain have avoided it; a result, as would appear, owing less to his small personal stature (for, in passionate seasons, he was 'incredibly nimble'), than to his 'virtuous principles:' 'if it was disgraceful to be beaten,' says he, 'it was only a shade less disgraceful to have so much as fought; thus was I drawn two ways at once, and in this important element of school-history, the war-element, had little but sorrow.' On the whole, that same excellent 'Passivity,' so notable in Teufelsdröckh's childhood, is here visibly enough again getting nourishment. 'He wept often; indeed to such a degree, that he was nicknamed *Der Weinende* (the Tearful), which epithet, till towards his thirteenth year, was indeed not quite unmerited. Only at rare intervals did the young soul burst forth into fire-eyed rage, and, with a Stormfulness (*Ungestüm*) under which the boldest quailed, assert that he too had Rights of Man, or at least of Mankin.' In all which, who does not discern a fine flower-tree and cinnamon-tree (of genius) nigh choked among pumpkins, reedgrass, and ignoble shrubs; and forced, if it would live, to struggle upwards only, and not out-wards; into a *height* quite sickly and disproportioned to its *breadth?*

We find, moreover, that his Greek and Latin were 'mechanically' taught; Hebrew scarce even mechanically; much else which they called History, Cosmography, Philosophy, and so forth, no better than not at all. So that, except inasmuch as Nature was still busy; and he himself 'went about, as was of old his wont, among the Craftsmen's workshops, there learning many things;' and farther lighted on some small store of curious reading, in Hans Wachtel the Cooper's house, where he lodged,—his time, it would appear, was utterly wasted. Which facts the Professor has not yet learned to look upon with any contentment. Indeed, throughout the whole of this Bag *Scorpio*, where we now are, and often in the following Bag, he shews himself unusually animated on the matter of Education, and not without some touch of what we might presume to be anger.

'My Teachers,' says he, 'were hide-bound Pedants, without knowl-edge of man's nature or of boy's; or of aught save their lexicons and quarterly account-books. Innumerable dead Vocables (no dead Lan-guage, for they themselves knew no Language) they crammed into us, and called it fostering the growth of mind. How can an inanimate, mechanical Gerund-grinder, the like of whom will, in a subsequent century, be manufactured at Nürnberg out of wood and leather, foster the growth of any thing; much more of Mind, which grows, not like a vegetable (by having its roots littered with etymological compost), but like a Spirit, by mysterious contact of Spirit; Thought kindling itself at the fire of living Thought? How shall *he* give kindling, in whose own inward man there is no live coal, but all is burnt out to a dead grammatical cinder? The Hinterschlag Professors knew Syntax enough; and of the human soul thus much: that it had a faculty called Memory, and could be acted on through the muscular integument by appliance of birch rods.

'Alas, so is it every where, so will it ever be; till the Hodman is discharged, or reduced to Hodbearing; and an Architect is hired, and on all hands fitly encouraged: till communities and individuals discover, not without surprise, that fashioning the souls of a generation by Knowledge can rank on a level with blowing their bodies to pieces by Gunpowder; that with Generals and Field-marshals for killing, there should be world-honoured Dignitaries, and were it possible, true God-ordained Priests, for teaching. But as yet, though the Soldier wears openly, and even parades, his butchering-tool, nowhere, far as I have travelled, did the Schoolmaster make show of his instructing-tool: nay, were he to walk abroad with birch girt on thigh, as if he therefrom expected honour, would there not, among the idler class, perhaps a certain levity be excited?'

In the third year of this Gymnasic period, Father Andreas seems to have died: the young Scholar, otherwise so maltreated, saw himself for the first time clad outwardly in sables, and inwardly in quite inexpressible melancholy. 'The dark bottomless Abyss, that lies under our feet, had yawned open; the pale kingdoms of Death, with all their innumerable silent nations and generations stood before him; the inexorable word, NEVER! now first showed its meaning. My Mother wept, and her sorrow got vent; but in my heart there lay a whole lake of tears, pent up in silent desolation. Nevertheless, the unworn Spirit is strong, Life is so healthful that it even finds nourishment in Death: these stern experiences, planted down by Memory in my Imagination, rose there to a whole cypress forest, sad but beautiful; waving, with not unmelodious sighs, in dark luxuriance, in the hottest sunshine, through long years of youth:—as in manhood also it does, and will do; for I have now pitched my tent under a Cypress tree; the Tomb is now my inexpugnable Fortress, ever close by the gate of which I look upon the hostile armaments, and pains and penalties, of tyrannous Life placidly enough, and listen to its loudest threatenings with a still smile. O ye loved ones, that already sleep in the noiseless Bed of Rest, whom in life I could only weep for and never help; and ye, who wide-scattered still toil lonely in the monster-bearing Desert, dyeing the flinty ground with your blood,—yet a little while, and we shall all meet THERE, and our Mother's bosom will screen us all; and Oppression's harness, and Sorrow's fire-whip, and all the Gehenna Bailiffs that patrol and inhabit ever-vexed Time, cannot thenceforth harm us any more!'

Close by which rather beautiful apostrophe, lies a laboured Character of the deceased Andreas Futteral; of his natural ability, his deserts in life (as Prussian Sergeant); with long historical inquiries into the genealogy of the Futteral Family, here traced back as far as Henry the Fowler: the whole of which we pass over, not without astonishment. It only concerns us to add, that now was the time when Mother Gretchen revealed to her foster-son that he was not at all of this kindred; or indeed of any kindred, having come into historical existence in the way already known to us. 'Thus was I doubly orphaned,' says he; 'bereft not only of Possession, but even of Remembrance. Sorrow and Wonder, here suddenly united, could not but produce abundant fruit. Such a disclosure, in such a season, struck its roots through my whole nature: ever till the years of mature manhood, it mingled with my whole thoughts, was as the stem whereon all my day-dreams and night-dreams grew. A certain poetic elevation, yet also a corresponding civic depression, it naturally imparted: *I was like no other;* in which fixed-idea, leading sometimes to highest, and oftener to frightfullest results, may there not lie the first spring of Tendencies, which in my Life have become remarkable enough? As in birth, so in action, speculation, and social position, my fellows are perhaps not numerous.'

In the Bag *Sagittarius,* as we at length discover, Teufelsdröckh has become a University man; though how, when, or of what quality, will nowhere disclose itself with the smallest certainty. Few things, in the

way of confusion and capricious indistinctness, can now surprise our
readers; not even the total want of dates, almost without parallel in
a Biographical work. So enigmatic, so chaotic we have always found,
and must always look to find, these scattered Leaves. In *Sagittarius*,
however, Teufelsdröckh begins to shew himself even more than usually Sibylline: fragments of all sorts; scraps of regular Memoir, College Exercises, Programs, Professional Testimoniums, Milkscores, torn
Billets, sometimes to appearance of an amatory cast; all blown together as if by merest chance, henceforth bewilder the sane Historian.
To combine any picture of these University, and the subsequent,
years; much more, to decipher therein any illustrative primordial elements of the Clothes-Philosophy, becomes such a problem as the
reader may imagine.

So much we can see; darkly, as through the foliage of some wavering thicket: a youth of no common endowment, who has passed
happily through Childhood, less happily yet still vigorously through
Boyhood, now at length perfect in 'dead vocables,' and set down, as
he hopes, by the living Fountain, there to superadd Ideas and Capabilities. From such Fountain he draws, diligently, thirstily, yet never
or seldom with his whole heart, for the water nowise suits his palate;
discouragements, entanglements, aberrations are discoverable or sup-
posable. Nor perhaps are even pecuniary distresses wanting; for 'the
good Gretchen, who in spite of advices from not disinterested relatives has sent him hither, must after a time withdraw her willing but
too feeble hand.' Nevertheless in an atmosphere of Poverty and
manifold Chagrin, the Humour of that young Soul, what character is
in him, first decisively reveals itself; and, like strong sunshine in weeping
skies, gives out variety of colours, some of which are prismatic. Thus
with the aid of Time, and of what Time brings, has the stripling
Diogenes Teufelsdröckh waxed into manly stature; and into so questionable an aspect, that we ask with new eagerness How he specially
came by it, and regret anew that there is no more explicit answer.
Certain of the intelligible and partially significant fragments, which
are few in number, shall be extracted from that Limbo of a Paperbag,
and presented with the usual preparation.

As if, in the Bag *Scorpio*, Teufelsdröckh had not already expecto-
rated his antipedagogic spleen; as if, from the name *Sagittarius*, he
had thought himself called upon to shoot arrows, we here again fall

in with such matter as this: 'The University where I was educated still stands vivid enough in my remembrance, and I know its name well; which name, however, I from tenderness to existing interests and persons, shall in no wise divulge. It is my painful duty to say that, out of England and Spain, ours was the worst of all hitherto discovered   5 Universities. This is indeed a time when right Education is, as nearly as may be, impossible: however, in degrees of wrongness there is no limit; nay, I can conceive a worse system than that of the Nameless itself; as poisoned victual may be worse than absolute hunger.

'It is written, When the blind lead the blind, both shall fall into   10 the ditch: wherefore, in such circumstances, may it not sometimes be safer, if both leader and led simply—sit still? Had you, any where in Crim Tartary, walled-in a square enclosure; furnished it with a small, ill-chosen Library; and then turned loose into it eleven hundred Christian striplings, to tumble about as they listed, from three to   15 seven years; certain persons, under the title of Professors, being stationed at the gates, to declare aloud that it was a University, and exact considerable admission-fees,—you had, not indeed in mechanical structure, yet in spirit and result, some imperfect resemblance of our High Seminary. I say, imperfect; for if our mechanical structure was quite   20 other, so neither was our result altogether the same: unhappily, we were not in Crim Tartary, but in a corrupt European city, full of smoke and sin; moreover, in the middle of a Public, which, without far costlier apparatus, than that of the Square Enclosure, and Declaration aloud, you could not be sure of gulling.   25

'Gullible, however, by fit apparatus, all Publics are; and gulled, with the most surprising profit. Towards any thing like a *Statistics of Imposture*, indeed, little as yet has been done: with a strange indifference, our Economists, nigh buried under Tables for minor Branches of Industry, have altogether overlooked the grand all-overtopping   30 Hypocrisy Branch; as if our whole arts of Puffery, of Quackery, Priestcraft, Kingcraft, and the innumerable other crafts and mysteries of that genus, had not ranked in Productive Industry at all! Can any one, for example, so much as say, What monies, in Literature and Shoeblacking, are realised by actual Instruction and actual jet Polish;   35 what by fictitious-persuasive Proclamation of such; specifying, in distinct items, the distributions, circulations, disbursements, incomings of said monies, with the smallest approach to accuracy? But to ask,

How far, in all the several infinitely complected departments of social business, in government, education, in manual, commercial, intellectual fabrication of every sort, man's Want is supplied by true Ware; how far by the mere Appearance of true Ware:—in other words, To what extent, by what methods, with what effects, in various times and countries, Deception takes the place and wages of Performance: here truly is an Inquiry big with results for the future time, but to which hitherto only the vaguest answer can be given. If for the present, in our Europe, we estimate the ratio of Ware to Appearance of Ware so high even as at One to a Hundred (which, considering the Wages of a Pope, Russian Autocrat, or English Game-Preserver, is probably not far from the mark),—what almost prodigious saving may there not be anticipated, as the *Statistics of Imposture* advances, and so the manufacturing of Shams (that of Realities rising into clearer and clearer distinction therefrom) gradually declines, and at length becomes all but wholly unnecessary!

'This for the coming golden ages. What I had to remark, for the present brazen one, is, that in several provinces, as in Education, Polity, Religion, where so much is wanted and indispensable, and so little can as yet be furnished, probably Imposture is of sanative, anodyne nature, and man's Gullibility not his worst blessing. Suppose your sinews of war quite broken; I mean your military chest insolvent, forage all but exhausted; and that the whole army is about to mutiny, disband, and cut your and each other's throat,—then were it not well could you, as if by miracle, pay them in any sort of fairy-money, feed them on coagulated water, or mere imagination of meat; whereby, till the real supply came up, they might be kept together, and quiet? Such perhaps was the aim of Nature, who does nothing without aim, in furnishing her favourite, Man, with this his so omnipotent or rather omnipatient Talent of being Gulled.

'How beautifully it works, with a little mechanism; nay, almost makes mechanism for itself! These Professors in the Nameless lived with ease, with safety, by a mere Reputation, constructed in past times, and then too with no great effort, by quite another class of persons. Which Reputation, like a strong, brisk-going, undershot-wheel, sunk into the general current, bade fair, with only a little annual repainting on their part, to hold long together, and of its own accord, assiduously grind for them. Happy that it was so, for the

Millers! They themselves needed not to work; their attempts at working, at what they called Educating, now when I look back on it, fill
me with a certain mute admiration.

'Besides all this, we boasted ourselves a Rational University; in the
highest degree, hostile to Mysticism: thus was the young vacant mind   5
furnished with much talk about Progress of the Species, Dark Ages,
Prejudice, and the like; so that all were quickly enough blown out
into a state of windy argumentativeness; whereby the better sort had
soon to end in sick, impotent Scepticism; the worser sort explode
(*crepiren*) in finished Self-conceit, and to all spiritual intents become   10
dead.—But this too is portion of mankind's lot. If our era is the Era
of Unbelief, why murmur under it; is there not a better coming, nay
come? As in longdrawn Systole and longdrawn Diastole, must the
period of Faith alternate with the period of Denial; must the vernal
growth, the summer luxuriance of all Opinions, Spiritual Representa-   15
tions and Creations, be followed by, and again follow, the autumnal
decay, the winter dissolution. For man lives in Time, has his whole
earthly being, endeavour, and destiny shaped for him by Time: only
in the transitory Time-Symbol is the ever-motionless Eternity we
stand on made manifest. And yet, in such winter-seasons of Denial,   20
it is for the nobler-minded perhaps a comparative misery to have been
born, and to be awake, and work; and for the duller a felicity, if like
hibernating animals, safe-lodged in some Salamanca University, or
Sybaris City, or other superstitious or voluptuous Castle of Indolence,
they can slumber through, in stupid dreams, and only awaken when   25
the loud-roaring hailstorms have all done their work, and to our
prayers and martyrdoms the new Spring has been vouchsafed.'

That in the environment, here mysteriously enough shadowed forth,
Teufelsdröckh must have felt ill at ease, cannot be doubtful. 'The
hungry young,' he says, 'looked up to their spiritual Nurses; and, for   30
food, were bidden eat the east wind. What vain jargon of controversial Metaphysic, Etymology, and mechanical Manipulation falsely
named Science, was current there, I indeed learned, better perhaps
than the most. Among eleven hundred Christian youths, there will
not be wanting some eleven eager to learn. By collision with such, a   35
certain warmth, a certain polish was communicated; by instinct and
happy accident, I took less to rioting (*renommiren*), than to thinking
and reading, which latter also I was free to do. Nay from the chaos

of that Library, I succeeded in fishing up more books perhaps than had been known to the very keepers thereof. The foundation of a Literary Life was hereby laid: I learned, on my own strength, to read fluently in almost all cultivated languages, on almost all subjects, and sciences; farther, as man is ever the prime object to man, already it was my favourite employment to read character in speculation, and from the Writing to construe the Writer. A certain groundplan of Human Nature and Life began to fashion itself in me; wondrous enough, now when I look back on it; for my whole Universe, physical and spiritual, was as yet a Machine! However, such a conscious, recognised groundplan, the truest I had, *was* beginning to be there, and by additional experiments, might be corrected and indefinitely extended.'

Thus from poverty does the strong educe nobler wealth; thus in the destitution of the wild desert, does our young Ishmael acquire for himself the highest of all possessions, that of Self-help. Nevertheless a desert this was, waste, and howling with savage monsters. Teufelsdröckh gives us long details of his 'fever-paroxysms of Doubt;' his Inquiries concerning Miracles, and the Evidences of religious Faith; and how 'in the silent night-watches, still darker in his heart than over sky and earth, he has cast himself before the All-seeing, and with audible prayers, cried vehemently for Light, for deliverance from Death and the Grave. Not till after long years, and unspeakable agonies, did the believing heart surrender; sink into spell-bound sleep, under the nightmare, Unbelief; and, in this hag-ridden dream, mistake God's fair living world for a pallid, vacant Hades and extinct Pandemonium. But through such Purgatory pain,' continues he, 'it is appointed us to pass: first must the dead Letter of Religion own itself dead, and drop piecemeal into dust, if the living Spirit of Religion, freed from this its charnel-house, is to arise on us, newborn of Heaven, and with new healing under its wings.'

To which Purgatory pains, seemingly severe enough, if we add a liberal measure of Earthly distresses, want of practical guidance, want of sympathy, want of money, want of hope; and all this in the fervid season of youth, so exaggerated in imagining, so boundless in desires, yet here so poor in means,—do we not see a strong incipient spirit oppressed and overloaded from without and from within; the fire of genius struggling up among fuel-wood of the greenest, and as yet with more of bitter vapour than of clear flame?

From various fragments of Letters and other documentary scraps, it is to be inferred that Teufelsdröckh, isolated, shy, retiring as he was, had not altogether escaped notice: certain established men are aware of his existence; and, if stretching out no helpful hand, have at least their eyes on him. He appears, though in dreary enough humour, to be addressing himself to the Profession of Law;—whereof, indeed, the world has since seen him a public graduate. But omitting these broken, unsatisfactory thrums of Economical relation, let us present rather the following small thread of Moral relation; and therewith, the reader for himself weaving it in at the right place, conclude our dim arras-picture of these University years.

'Here also it was that I formed acquaintance with Herr Towgood, or, as it is perhaps better written, Herr Toughgut; a young person of quality (*von Adel*), from the interior parts of England. He stood connected, by blood and hospitality, with the Counts von Zähdarm, in this quarter of Germany; to which noble Family I likewise was, by his means, with all friendliness, brought near. Towgood had a fair talent, unspeakably ill-cultivated; with considerable humour of char- acter: and, bating his total ignorance, for he knew nothing except Boxing and a little Grammar, shewed less of that aristocratic impas- sivity and silent fury than for most part belongs to Travellers of his nation. To him I owe my first practical knowledge of the English and their ways; perhaps also something of the partiality with which I have ever since regarded that singular people. Towgood was not without an eye, could he have come at any light. Invited doubtless by the presence of the Zähdarm Family, he had travelled hither, in the al- most frantic hope of perfecting his studies; he, whose studies had as yet been those of infancy, hither to a University where so much as the notion of perfection, not to say the effort after it, no longer existed! Often we would condole over the hard destiny of the Young in this era: how, after all our toil, we were to be turned out into the world, with beards on our chins, indeed, but with few other attributes of manhood; no existing thing that we were trained to Act on, nothing that we could so much as Believe. "How has our Head on the outside a polished Hat," would Towgood exclaim, "and in the inside Va- cancy, or a froth of Vocables and Attorney Logic! At a small cost men are educated to make leather into shoes; but, at a great cost, what am I educated to make? By Heaven, Brother! what I have already eaten and worn, as I came thus far, would endow a considerable Hospital

of Incurables." —"Man, indeed," I would answer, "has a Digestive faculty, which must be kept working, were it even partly by stealth. But as for our Miseducation, make not bad worse; waste not the time yet ours, in trampling on thistles because they have yielded us no figs.
5 *Frisch zu, Bruder!* Here are Books, and we have brains to read them; here is a whole Earth and a whole Heaven, and we have eyes to look on them: *Frisch zu!*"

'Often also our talk was gay; not without brilliancy, and even fire. We looked out on Life, with its strange scaffolding, where all at once
10 harlequins dance, and men are beheaded and quartered: motley, not unterrific was the aspect; but we looked on it like brave youths. For myself, these were perhaps my most genial hours. Towards this young warmhearted, strongheaded and wrongheaded Herr Towgood, I was even near experiencing the now obsolete sentiment of Friendship.
15 Yes, foolish Heathen that I was, I felt that, under certain conditions, I could have loved this man, and taken him to my bosom, and been his brother once and always. By degrees, however, I understood the new time, and its wants. If man's *Soul* is indeed, as in the Finnish Language, and Utilitarian Philosophy, a kind of *Stomach*, what else is
20 the true meaning of Spiritual Union but an Eating together? Thus we, instead of Friends, are Dinner-guests; and here as elsewhere have cast away chimeras.'

So ends, abruptly as is usual, and enigmatically, this little incipient romance. What henceforth becomes of the brave Herr Towgood, or
25 Toughgut? He has dived under, in the Autobiographical Chaos, and swims we see not where. Does any reader 'in the interior parts of England' know of such a man?

CHAPTER IV.

'THUS nevertheless,' writes our Autobiographer, apparently as quitting College, 'was there realised Somewhat; namely, I, Diogenes Teufelsdröckh: a visible Temporary Figure (*Zeitbild*), occupying some cubic feet of Space, and containing within it Forces both physical and spiritual; hopes, passions, thoughts; the whole wondrous furniture, in more or less perfection, belonging to that mystery, a Man. Capabilities there were in me to give battle, in some small degree, against the great Empire of Darkness: Does not the very Ditcher and Delver, with his spade, extinguish many a thistle and puddle; and so leave a little Order, where he found the opposite? Nay your very Daymoth has capabilities in this kind; and ever organises something (into its own Body, if no otherwise), which was before Inorganic; and of mute dead air makes living music, though only of the faintest, by humming.

'How much more, one whose capabilities are spiritual; who has learned or begun learning the grand thaumaturgic art of Thought! Thaumaturgic I name it; for hitherto all Miracles have been wrought thereby, and henceforth innumerable will be wrought; whereof we, even in these days, witness some. Of the Poet's and Prophet's inspired Message, and how it makes and unmakes whole worlds, I shall forbear mention: but cannot the dullest hear Steam-engines clanking around him? Has he not seen the Scottish Brassmith's IDEA (and this but a mechanical one) travelling on fire-wings round the Cape, and

across two Oceans; and stronger than any other Enchanter's Familiar, on all hands unweariedly fetching and carrying: at home, not only weaving Cloth; but rapidly enough overturning the whole old system of Society; and, for Feudalism and Preservation of the Game, prepar-
5 ing us, by indirect but sure methods, Industrialism and the Government of the Wisest. Truly a Thinking Man is the worst enemy the Prince of Darkness can have; every time such a one announces himself, I doubt not, there runs a shudder through the Nether Empire; and new Emissaries are trained, with new tactics, to, if possible, en-
10 trap him, and hoodwink and handcuff him.

'With such high vocation had I too, as denizen of the Universe, been called. Unhappy it is, however, that though born to the amplest Sovereignty, in this way, with no less than sovereign right of Peace and War against the Time-Prince (*Zeitfürst*), or Devil, and all his
15 Dominions, your coronation-ceremony costs such trouble, your sceptre is so difficult to get at, or even to get eye on!'

By which last wiredrawn similitude, does Teufelsdröckh mean no more than that young men find obstacles in what we call 'getting under way?' 'Not what I Have,' continues he, 'but what I Do is my
20 Kingdom. To each is given a certain inward Talent, a certain outward Environment of Fortune; to each, by wisest combination of these two, a certain maximum of Capability. But the hardest problem were ever this first: To find by study of yourself, and of the ground you stand on, what your combined inward and outward Capability spe-
25 cially is. For, alas, our young soul is all budding with Capabilities, and we see not yet which is the main and true one. Always too the new man is in a new time, under new conditions; his course can be the *fac-simile* of no prior one, but is by its nature original. And then how seldom will the outward Capability fit the inward: though talented
30 wonderfully enough, we are poor, unfriended, dyspeptical, bashful; nay what is worse than all, we are foolish. Thus, in a whole imbroglio of Capabilities, we go stupidly groping about, to grope which is ours, and often clutch the wrong one: in this mad work, must several years of our small term be spent, till the purblind Youth, by practice, ac-
35 quire notions of distance, and become a seeing Man. Nay, many so spend their whole term, and in ever-new expectation, ever-new disappointment, shift from enterprise to enterprise, and from side to

side; till at length, as exasperated striplings of threescore and ten, they shift into their last enterprise, that of getting buried.

'Such, since the most of us are too ophthalmic, would be the general fate; were it not that one thing saves us: our Hunger. For on this ground, as the prompt nature of Hunger is well known, must a prompt choice be made: hence have we, with wise foresight, Indentures and Apprenticeships for our irrational young; whereby, in due season, the vague universality of a Man shall find himself ready-moulded into a specific Craftsman; and so thenceforth work, with much or with little waste of Capability, as it may be; yet not with the worst waste, that of time. Nay even in matters spiritual, since the spiritual artist too is born blind, and does not, like certain other creatures, receive sight in nine days, but far later, sometimes never,—is it not well that there should be what we call Professions, or Bread-studies (*Brodzwecke*), preappointed us? Here, circling like the gin-horse, for whom partial or total blindness is no evil, the Bread-artist can travel contentedly round and round, still fancying that it is forward and forward, and realise much: for himself victual; for the world an additional horse's power in the grand corn-mill or hemp-mill of Economic Society. For me too had such a leading-string been provided; only that it proved a neck-halter, and had nigh throttled me, till I broke it off. Then, in the words of Ancient Pistol, did the World generally become mine oyster, which I, by strength or cunning, was to open, as I would and could. Almost had I deceased (*fast wär ich umgekommen*), so obstinately did it continue shut.'

We see here, significantly foreshadowed, the spirit of much that was to befall our Autobiographer; the historical embodiment of which, as it painfully takes shape in his Life, lies scattered, in dim disastrous details, through this Bag *Pisces*, and those that follow. A young man of high talent, and high though still temper, like a young mettled colt, 'breaks off his neck-halter,' and bounds forth, from his peculiar manger, into the wide world; which, alas, he finds all rigourously fenced in. Richest clover-fields tempt his eye; but to him they are forbidden pasture: either pining in progressive starvation, he must stand; or, in mad exasperation, must rush to and fro, leaping against sheer stone-walls, which he cannot leap over, which only lacerate and lame him; till at last, after thousand attempts and endurances, he, as

if by miracle, clears his way; not indeed into luxuriant and luxurious clover, yet into a certain bosky wilderness where existence is still possible, and Freedom though waited on by Scarcity is not without sweetness. In a word, Teufelsdröckh having thrown up his legal Pro-
5 fession, finds himself without landmark of outward guidance; whereby his previous want of decided Belief, or inward guidance, is frightfully aggravated. Necessity urges him on; Time will not stop, neither can he, a Son of Time; wild passions without solacement, wild faculties without employment, ever vex and agitate him. He too must enact
10 that stern Monodrama, *No Object and no Rest;* must front its successive destinies, work through to its catastrophe, and deduce therefrom what moral he can.

Yet let us be just to him, let us admit that his 'neck-halter' sat nowise easy on him; that he was in some degree forced to break it off.
15 If we look at the young man's civic position, in this Nameless Capital, as he emerges from its Nameless University, we can discern well that it was far from enviable. His first Law-Examination he has come through triumphantly; and can even boast that the *Examen Rigorosum* need not have frightened him: but though he is hereby 'an *Auscultator*
20 of respectability,' what avails it? There is next to no employment to be had. Neither, for a youth without connexions is the process of Expectation very hopeful in itself; nor for one of his disposition much cheered from without. 'My fellow Auscultators,' he says, 'were Auscultators: they dressed, and digested, and talked articulate words;
25 other vitality shewed they almost none. Small speculation in those eyes, that they did glare withal! Sense neither for the high nor for the deep, nor for aught human or divine, save only for the faintest scent of coming Preferment.' In which words, indicating a total estrangement on the part of Teufelsdröckh, may there not also lurk traces of
30 a bitterness as from wounded vanity? Doubtless these prosaic Auscultators may have sniffed at him, with his strange ways; and tried to hate, and, what was much more impossible, to despise him. Friendly communion, in any case, there could not be: already has the young Teufelsdröckh left the other young geese; and swims apart, though as
35 yet uncertain whether he himself is cygnet or gosling.

Perhaps too what little employment he had was performed ill, at best unpleasantly. 'Great practical method and expertness' he may brag of; but is there not also great practical pride, though

deep-hidden, only the deeper-seated? So shy a man can never have
been popular. We figure to ourselves, how in those days he may have
played strange freaks with his Independence, and so forth: do not his
own words betoken as much? 'Like a very young person, I imagined
it was with Work alone, and not also with Folly and Sin, in myself and   5
others, that I had been appointed to struggle.' Be this as it may, his
progress from the passive Auscultatorship, towards any active Assessorship, is evidently of the slowest. By degrees, those same established
men, once partially inclined to patronise him, seem to withdraw their
countenance, and give him up as 'a man of genius;' against which   10
procedure he, in these Papers loudly protests. 'As if,' says he, 'the
higher did not presuppose the lower; as if he who can fly into heaven,
could not also walk post if he resolved on it! But the world is an old
woman, and mistakes any gilt farthing for a gold coin; whereby being
often cheated she will thenceforth trust nothing but the common   15
copper.'

How our winged sky-messenger, unaccepted as a terrestrial runner,
contrived, in the meanwhile, to keep himself from flying skyward without return, is not too clear from these Documents. Good old Gretchen
seems to have vanished from the scene, perhaps from the Earth; other   20
Horn of Plenty, or even of Parsimony, nowhere flows for him; so that
'the prompt nature of Hunger being well known,' we are not without
our anxiety. From private Tuition, in never so many languages and
sciences, the aid derivable is small; neither, to use his own words, 'does
the young Adventurer hitherto suspect in himself any literary gift; but   25
at best earns bread-and-water wages, by his wide faculty of Translation.
Nevertheless,' continues he, 'that I subsisted is clear, for you find me
even now alive.' Which fact, however, except upon the principle of our
true-hearted, kind old Proverb, that 'there is always life for a living one,'
we must profess ourselves unable to explain.   30

Certain Landlords' Bills, and other economic Documents, bearing
the mark of Settlement, indicate that he was not without money; but,
like an independent Hearth-holder, if not House-holder, paid his
way. Here also occur, among many others, two little mutilated Notes,
which perhaps throw light on his condition. The first has now no   35
date, or writer's name, but a huge Blot; and runs to this effect: 'The
(*Inkblot*), tied down by previous promise, cannot, except by best
wishes, forward the Herr Teufelsdröckh's views on the Assessorship

in question; and sees himself under the cruel necessity of forbearing, for the present, what were otherwise his duty and joy, to assist in opening the career for a man of genius, on whom far higher triumphs are yet waiting.' The other is on gilt paper; and interests us like a sort
5 of epistolary mummy now dead, yet which once lived and beneficently worked. We give it in the original: *'Herr Teufelsdröckh wird von der Frau Gräfinn, auf Donnerstag, zum* ÆSTHETISCHEN THEE, *schönstens eingeladen.'*

Thus, in answer to a cry for solid pudding, whereof there is the most
10 urgent need, comes, epigrammatically enough, the invitation to a wash of quite fluid *Æsthetic Tea!* How Teufelsdröckh, now at actual handgrips with Destiny herself, may have comported himself among these Musical and Literary Dilettanti of both sexes, like a hungry lion invited to a feast of chickenweed, we can only conjecture. Perhaps in expressive
15 silence, and abstinence: otherwise if the lion, in such case, is to feast at all, it cannot be on the chickenweed, but only on the chickens. For the rest, as this Frau Gräfinn dates from the *Zähdarm House,* she can be no other than the Countess and mistress of the same; whose intellectual tendencies, and good will to Teufelsdröckh, whether on the
20 footing of Herr Towgood, or on his own footing, are hereby manifest. That some sort of relation, indeed, continued, for a time, to connect our Autobiographer, though perhaps feebly enough, with this noble House, we have elsewhere express evidence. Doubtless, if he expected patronage, it was in vain; enough for him if he here obtained occasional
25 glimpses of the great world, from which we at one time fancied him to have been always excluded. 'The Zähdarms,' says he, 'lived in the soft, sumptuous garniture of Aristocracy; whereto Literature and Art, attracted and attached from without, were to serve as the handsomest fringing. It was to the *Gnädigen Frau* (her Ladyship) that this latter
30 improvement was due: assiduously she gathered, dexterously she fitted on, what fringing was to be had; lace or cobweb, as the place yielded.' Was Teufelsdröckh also a fringe, of lace or cobweb; or promising to be such? 'With His *Excellenz* (the Count),' continues he, 'I have more than once had the honour to converse; chiefly on general affairs, and
35 the aspect of the world, which he, though now past middle life, viewed in no unfavourable light; finding indeed, except the Outrooting of Journalism (*die auszurottende Journalistik*), little to desiderate therein. On some points, as his *Excellenz* was not uncholeric, I found it more

pleasant to keep silence. Besides, his occupation being that of Owning Land, there might be faculties enough, which, as superfluous for such use, were little developed in him.'

That to Teufelsdröckh the aspect of the world was nowise so faultless, and many things, besides 'the Outrooting of Journalism,' might have seemed improvements, we can readily conjecture. With nothing but a barren Auscultatorship from without, and so many mutinous thoughts and wishes from within, his position was no easy one. 'The Universe,' he says, 'was as a mighty Sphinx-riddle, which I knew so little of, yet must rede, or be devoured. In red streaks of unspeakable grandeur, yet also in the blackness of darkness, was Life, to my too-unfurnished Thought, unfolding itself. A strange contradiction lay in me; and I as yet knew not the solution of it; knew not that spiritual music can spring only from discords set in harmony; that but for Evil there were no Good, as Victory is only possible by Battle.'

'I have heard affirmed (surely in jest),' observes he elsewhere, 'by not unphilanthropic persons, that it were a real increase of human happiness, could all young men from the age of nineteen be covered under barrels, or rendered otherwise invisible; and there left to follow their lawful studies and callings, till they emerged, sadder and wiser, at the age of twenty-five. With which suggestion, at least as considered in the light of a practical scheme, I need scarcely say that I nowise coincide. Nevertheless it is plausibly urged that, as young ladies (*Mädchen*) are, to mankind, precisely the most delightful in those years; so young gentlemen (*Bübchen*) do then attain their maximum of detestability. Such gawks (*Gecken*) are they, and foolish peacocks, and yet with such a vulturous hunger for self-indulgence; so obstinate, obstreperous, vainglorious; in all senses, so froward and so forward. No mortal's endeavour or attainment will, in the smallest, content the as yet unendeavouring, unattaining young gentleman; but he could make it all infinitely better, were it worthy of him. Life every where is the most manageable matter, simple as a question in the Rule of Three: multiply your second and third term together, divide the product by the first, and your quotient will be the answer, —which you are but an ass if you cannot come at. The booby has not yet found out, by any trial, that, do what one will, there is ever a cursed fraction, oftenest a decimal repeater, and no net integer quotient so much as to be thought of.'

In which passage does not there lie an implied confession that Teufelsdröckh himself, besides his outward obstructions, had an inward, still greater, to contend with; namely, a certain temporary, youthful, yet still afflictive derangement of head? Alas! on the former side alone, his case was hard enough. 'It continues ever true,' says he, 'that Saturn, or Chronos, or what we call TIME, devours all his Children: only by incessant Running, by incessant Working, may you (for some threescore and ten years) escape him; and you too he devours at last. Can any Sovereign, or Holy Alliance of Sovereigns, bid Time stand still; even in thought, shake themselves free of Time? Our whole terrestrial being is based on Time, and built of Time; it is wholly a Movement, a Time-impulse; Time is the author of it, the material of it. Hence also our Whole Duty, which is to move, to work,—in the right direction. Are not our Bodies and our Souls in continual movement, whether we will or not; in a continual Waste, requiring a continual Repair? Utmost satisfaction of our whole outward and inward Wants were but satisfaction for a space of Time; thus whatso we have done, is done, and for us annihilated, and ever must we go and do anew. O Time-Spirit, how hast thou environed and imprisoned us, and sunk us so deep in thy troublous dim Time-Element, that, only in lucid moments, can so much as glimpses of our upper Azure Home be revealed to us! Me, however, as a Son of Time, unhappier than some others, was Time threatening to eat quite prematurely; for, strive as I might, there was no good Running, so obstructed was the path, so gyved were the feet.' That is to say, we presume, speaking in the dialect of this lower world, that Teufelsdröckh's whole duty and necessity was, like other men's, 'to work,—in the right direction,' and that no work was to be had; whereby he became wretched enough. As was natural: with haggard Scarcity threatening him in the distance; and so vehement a soul languishing in restless inaction, and forced thereby, like Sir Hudibras's sword by rust,

> To eat into itself, for lack
> Of something else to hew and hack!

But on the whole, that same 'excellent Passivity,' as it has all along done, is here again vigorously flourishing; in which circumstance, may we not trace the beginnings of much that now characterises our Professor; and perhaps, in faint rudiments, the origin of the

Clothes-Philosophy itself? Already the attitude he has assumed towards the World is too defensive; not, as would have been desirable, a bold attitude of attack. 'So far hitherto,' he says, 'as I had mingled with mankind, I was notable, if for any thing, for a certain stillness of manner, which, as my friends often rebukingly declared, did but ill 5
express the keen ardour of my feelings. I, in truth, regarded men with an excess both of love and of fear. The mystery of a Person, indeed, is ever divine, to him that has a sense for the Godlike. Often, notwithstanding, was I blamed, and by half-strangers hated, for my so-called Hardness (*Härte*), my Indifferentism towards men; and the 10
seemingly ironic tone I had adopted, as my favourite dialect in conversation. Alas, the panoply of Sarcasm was but as a buckram-case, wherein I had striven to envelope myself; that so my own poor Person might live safe there, and in all friendliness, being no longer exasperated by wounds. Sarcasm I now see to be, in general, the language 15
of the Devil; for which reason I have, long since, as good as renounced it. But how many individuals did I, in those days, provoke into some degree of hostility thereby! An ironic man, with his sly stillness, and ambuscading ways, more especially an ironic young man, from whom it is least expected, may be viewed as a pest to society. 20
Have we not seen persons of weight and name, coming forward, with gentlest indifference, to tread such a one out of sight, as an insignificancy and worm, start ceiling-high (*balkenhoch*), and thence fall shattered and supine, to be borne home on shutters, not without indignation, when he proved electric and a torpedo!' 25
    Alas, how can a man with this devilishness of temper make way for himself in Life; where the first problem, as Teufelsdröckh too admits, is 'to unite yourself with some one and with somewhat (*sich anzuschliessen*)?' Division, not union, is written on most part of his procedure. Let us add too that, in no great length of time, the only 30
important connexion he had ever succeeded in forming, his connexion with the Zähdarm Family, seems to have been paralysed, for all practical uses, by the death of the 'not uncholeric' old Count. This fact stands recorded, quite incidentally, in a certain *Discourse on Epitaphs*, huddled into the present Bag, among so much else; of which Essay 35
the learning and curious penetration are more to be approved of than the spirit. His grand principle is, that lapidary inscriptions, of what sort soever, should be Historical rather than Lyrical. 'By request of

that worthy Nobleman's survivors,' says he, 'I undertook to compose his Epitaph; and not unmindful of my own rules, produced the following; which, however, for an alleged defect of Latinity, a defect never yet fully visible to myself, still remains unengraven;'—wherein, we may predict, there is more than the Latinity that will surprise an English reader:

HIC JACET

PHILIPPUS ZAEHDARM, COGNOMINE MAGNUS,

ZAEHDARMI COMES,

EX IMPERII CONCILIO,

VELLERIS AUREI, PERISCELIDIS, NECNON VULTURIS NIGRI

EQUES.

QUI DUM SUB LUNA AGEBAT,

QUINQUIES MILLE PERDRICES

PLUMBO CONFECIT:

VARII CIBI

CENTUMPONDIA MILLIES CENTENA MILLIA,

PER SE, PERQUE SERVOS QUADRUPEDES BIPEDESVE,

HAUD SINE TUMULTU DEVOLVENS,

IN STERCUS

PALAM CONVERTIT.

NUNC A LABORE REQUIESCENTEM

OPERA SEQUUNTUR.

SI MONUMENTUM QUÆRIS,

FIMETUM ADSPICE.

PRIMUM IN ORBE DEJECIT [*sub dato*]; POSTREMUM [*sub dato*].

CHAPTER V.

ROMANCE.

'FOR long years,' writes Teufelsdröckh, 'had the poor Hebrew, in this Egypt of an Auscultatorship, painfully toiled, baking bricks without stubble, before ever the question once struck him with entire force: For what?—*Beym Himmel!* For Food and Warmth! And are Food and Warmth nowhere else, in the whole wide Universe, discoverable?— 5 Come of it what might, I resolved to try.'

Thus then are we to see him in a new independent capacity, though perhaps far from an improved one. Teufelsdröckh is now a man without Profession. Quitting the common Fleet of herring-busses and whalers, where indeed his leeward, laggard condition was painful 10 enough, he desperately steers off, on a course of his own, by sextant and compass of his own. Unhappy Teufelsdröckh! Though neither Fleet, nor Traffic, nor Commodores pleased thee, still was it not *a Fleet*, sailing in prescribed track, for fixed objects; above all, in combination, wherein, by mutual guidance, by all manner of loans and 15 borrowings, each could manifoldly aid the other? How wilt thou sail in unknown seas; and for thyself find that shorter, Northwest Passage to thy fair Spice-country of a Nowhere?—A solitary rover, on such a voyage, with such nautical tactics, will meet with adventures. Nay, as we forthwith discover, a certain Calypso-Island detains him at the 20 very outset; and as it were falsifies and oversets his whole reckoning.

'If in youth,' writes he once, 'the Universe is majestically unveiling, and everywhere Heaven revealing itself on Earth, nowhere to the

101

Young Man does this Heaven on Earth so immediately reveal itself as in the Young Maiden. Strangely enough, in this strange life of ours, it has been so appointed. On the whole, as I have often said, a Person (*Persönlichkeit*) is ever holy to us; a certain orthodox Anthropomor-
5 phism connects my *Me* with all *Thees* in bonds of Love: but it is in this approximation of the Like and Unlike, that such heavenly attraction, as between Negative and Positive, first burns out into a flame. Is the pitifullest mortal Person, think you, indifferent to us? Is it not rather our heartfelt wish to be made one with him; to unite him to us, by
10 gratitude, by admiration, even by fear; or failing all these, unite ourselves to him? But how much more, in this case of the Like-Unlike! Here is conceded us the higher mystic possibility of such a union, the highest in our Earth; thus, in the conducting medium of Fantasy, flames forth that *fire*-development of the universal Spiritual Electric-
15 ity, which, as unfolded between man and woman, we first emphatically denominate LOVE.

'In every well-conditioned stripling, as I conjecture, there already blooms a certain prospective Paradise, cheered by some fairest Eve; nor, in the stately vistas, and flowerage and foliage of that Garden, is
20 a Tree of Knowledge, beautiful and awful in the midst thereof, wanting. Perhaps too the whole is but the lovelier, if Cherubim and a flaming sword divide it from all footsteps of men; and grant him, the imaginative stripling, only the view, not the entrance. Happy season of virtuous youth, when Shame is still an impassable celestial
25 barrier; and the sacred air-cities of Hope have not shrunk into the mean clay-hamlets of Reality; and man, by his nature, is yet infinite and free!

'As for our young Forlorn,' continues Teufelsdröckh, evidently meaning himself, 'in his secluded way of life, and with his glowing
30 Fantasy, the more fiery that it burnt under cover, as in a reverberating furnace, his feeling towards the Queens of this Earth was, and indeed is, altogether unspeakable. A visible Divinity dwelt in them; to our young Friend all women were holy, were heavenly. As yet he but saw them flitting past, in their many-coloured angel-plumage; or hovering
35 mute and inaccessible on the outskirts of *Æsthetic Tea:* all of air they were, all Soul and Form; so lovely, like mysterious priestesses, in whose hand was the invisible Jacob's-ladder, whereby man might mount into very Heaven. That he, our poor Friend, should ever win

for himself one of these Gracefuls (*Holden*)—*Ach Gott!* how could he hope it; should he not have died under it? There was a certain delirious vertigo in the thought.

'Thus was the young man, if all sceptical of Demons and Angels, such as the vulgar had once believed in, nevertheless not unvisited by hosts of true Skyborn, who visibly and audibly hovered round him whereso he went; and they had that religious worship in his thought, though as yet it was by their mere earthly and trivial name that he named them. But now, if on a soul so circumstanced, some actual Airmaiden, incorporated into tangibility and reality, should cast any electric glance of kind eyes, saying thereby, "Thou too mayest love and be loved;" and so kindle him,—good Heaven, what a volcanic, earthquake-bringing, all-consuming fire were probably kindled!'

Such a fire, it afterwards appears, did actually burst forth, with explosions more or less Vesuvian, in the inner man of Herr Diogenes; as indeed how could it fail? A nature, which, in his own figurative style, we might say, had now not a little carbonised tinder, of Irritability; with so much nitre of latent Passion, and sulphurous Humour enough; the whole lying in such hot neighbourhood, close by 'a reverberating furnace of Fantasy:' have we not here the components of driest Gunpowder, ready, on occasion of the smallest spark, to blaze up? Neither, in this our Life-element, are sparks anywhere wanting. Without doubt, some Angel, whereof so many hovered round, would one day, leaving 'the outskirts of *Æsthetic Tea*,' flit nigher; and, by electric Promethean glance, kindle no despicable firework. Happy, if it indeed proved a Firework, and flamed off rocket-wise, in successive beautiful bursts of splendour, each growing naturally from the other, through the several stages of a happy Youthful Love; till the whole were safely burnt out; and the young soul relieved, with little damage! Happy, if it did not rather prove a Conflagration and mad Explosion; painfully lacerating the heart itself; nay perhaps bursting the heart in pieces (which were Death); or at best, bursting the thin walls of your 'reverberating furnace,' so that it rage thenceforth all unchecked among the contiguous combustibles (which were Madness): till of the so fair and manifold internal world of our Diogenes, there remained Nothing, or only the 'Crater of an extinct volcano!'

From multifarious Documents in this Bag *Capricornus*, and in the adjacent ones on both sides thereof, it becomes manifest that our

Philosopher, as stoical and cynical as he now looks, was heartily and even franticly in Love: here therefore may our old doubts whether his heart were of stone or of flesh give way. He loved once; not wisely but too well. And once only: for as your Congreve needs a new case
5 or wrappage for every new rocket, so each human heart can properly exhibit but one Love, if even one; the 'First Love which is infinite' can be followed by no second like unto it. In more recent years, accordingly, the Editor of these Sheets was led to regard Teufelsdröckh as a man not only who would never wed, but who would never even
10 flirt; whom the grand-climacteric itself, and *St. Martin's Summer* of incipient Dotage, would crown with no new myrtle garland. To the Professor, women are henceforth Pieces of Art; of Celestial Art, indeed; which celestial pieces he glories to survey in galleries, but has lost thought of purchasing.
15   Psychological readers are not without curiosity to see how Teufelsdröckh, in this for him unexampled predicament, demeans himself; with what specialties of successive configuration, splendour and colour, his Firework blazes off. Small, as usual, is the satisfaction that such can meet with here. From amid these confused masses of
20 Eulogy and Elegy, with their mad Petrarchan and Werterean ware lying madly scattered among all sorts of quite extraneous matter, not so much as the fair one's name can be deciphered. For, without doubt, the title *Blumine*, whereby she is here designated, and which means simply Goddess of Flowers, must be fictitious. Was her real
25 name Flora, then? But what was her surname, or had she none? Of what station in Life was she; of what parentage, fortune, aspect? Specially, by what Pre-established Harmony of occurrences did the Lover and the Loved meet one another in so wide a world; how did they behave in such meeting? To all which questions, not unessential
30 in a Biographic work, mere Conjecture must for most part return answer. 'It was appointed,' says our Philosopher, 'that the high celestial orbit of Blumine should intersect the low sublunary one of our Forlorn; that he, looking in her empyrean eyes, should fancy the upper Sphere of Light was come down into this nether sphere of
35 Shadows; and finding himself mistaken, make noise enough.'
      We seem to gather that she was young, hazel-eyed, beautiful, and some one's Cousin; highborn, and of high spirit; but unhappily

dependent and insolvent; living, perhaps, on the not too gracious bounty of monied relatives. But how came 'the Wanderer' into her circle? Was it by the humid vehicle of *Æsthetic Tea*, or by the arid one of mere Business? Was it on the hand of Herr Towgood; or of the Gnädige Frau, who, as an ornamental Artist, might sometimes like to promote flirtation, especially for young cynical Nondescripts? To all appearance, it was chiefly by Accident, and the grace of Nature.

'Thou fair Waldschloss,' writes our Autobiographer, 'what stranger ever saw thee, were it even an absolved Auscultator, officially bearing in his pocket the last *Relatio ex Actis* he would ever write; but must have paused to wonder! Noble Mansion! There stoodest thou, in deep Mountain Amphitheatre, on umbrageous lawns, in thy serene solitude; stately, massive, all of granite; glittering in the western Sunbeams, like a palace of El Dorado, overlaid with precious metal. Beautiful rose up, in wavy curvature, the slope of thy guardian Hills: of the greenest was their sward, embossed with its dark-brown frets of crag, or spotted by some spreading solitary Tree and its shadow. To the unconscious Wayfarer thou wert also as an Ammon's Temple, in the Libyan Waste; where, for joy and woe, the tablet of his Destiny lay written. Well might he pause and gaze; in that glance of his were prophecy and nameless forebodings.'

But now let us conjecture that the so presentient Auscultator has handed in his *Relatio ex Actis;* been invited to a glass of Rhine-wine; and so, instead of returning dispirited and athirst to his dusty Town-home, is ushered into the Gardenhouse, where sit the choicest party of dames and cavaliers; if not engaged in Æsthetic Tea, yet in trustful evening conversation, and perhaps Musical Coffee, for we hear of 'harps and pure voices making the stillness live.' Scarcely, it would seem, is the Gardenhouse inferior in respectability to the noble Mansion itself. 'Embowered amid rich foliage, rose-clusters, and the hues and odours of thousand flowers, here sat that brave company; in front, from the wide-opened doors, fair outlook over blossom and bush, over grove and velvet green, stretching, undulating onwards to the remote Mountain peaks: so bright, so mild, and everywhere the melody of birds and happy creatures: it was all as if man had stolen a shelter from the Sun in the bosom-vesture of Summer herself. How came it that the Wanderer advanced thither with such forecasting heart (*ahndungsvoll*), by the side

of his gay host? Did he feel that to these soft influences his hard bosom
ought to be shut; that here, once more, Fate had it in view to try him;
to mock him, and see whether there were Humour in him?

'Next moment he finds himself presented to the party; and specially by name to—Blumine! Peculiar among all dames and damosels,
glanced Blumine, there in her modesty, like a star among earthly
lights. Noblest maiden! whom he bent to, in body and in soul; yet
scarcely dared look at, for the presence filled him with painful yet
sweetest embarrassment.

'Blumine's was a name well known to him; far and wide, was the
fair one heard of, for her gifts, her graces, her caprices: from all which
vague colourings of Rumour, from the censures no less than from the
praises, had our Friend painted for himself a certain imperious Queen
of Hearts, and blooming, warm Earth-angel, much more enchanting
than your mere white Heaven-angels of women, in whose placid veins
circulates too little naphtha-fire. Herself also he had seen in public
places; that light yet so stately form; those dark tresses, shading a face
where smiles and sunlight played over earnest deeps: but all this he
had seen only as a magic vision, for him inaccessible, almost without
reality. Her sphere was too far from his; how should she ever think
of him; O Heaven! how should they so much as once meet together?
And now that Rose-goddess sits in the same circle with him; the light
of *her* eyes has smiled on him, if he speak she will hear it! Nay, who
knows, since the heavenly Sun looks into lowest valleys, but Blumine
herself might have aforetime noted the so unnotable; perhaps, from
his very gainsayers, as he had from hers, gathered wonder, gathered
favour for him? Was the attraction, the agitation mutual, then; pole
and pole trembling towards contact, when once brought into
neighbourhood? Say rather, heart swelling in presence of the Queen
of Hearts; like the Sea swelling when once near its Moon! With the
Wanderer it was even so: as in heavenward gravitation, suddenly as at
the touch of a Seraph's wand, his whole soul is roused from its
deepest recesses; and all that was painful, and that was blissful there,
dim images, vague feelings of a whole Past and a whole Future are
heaving in unquiet eddies within him.

'Often, in far less agitating scenes, had our still Friend shrunk
forcibly together; and shrouded up his tremours and flutterings, of
what sort soever, in a safe cover of Silence, and perhaps of seeming

Stolidity. How was it, then, that here, when trembling to the core of his heart, he did not sink into swoons, but rose into strength, into fearlessness and clearness? It was his guiding Genius (*Dämon*) that inspired him; he must go forth and meet his Destiny. Shew thyself now, whispered it, or be forever hid. Thus sometimes it is even when   5 your anxiety becomes transcendental, that the soul first feels herself able to transcend it; that she rises above it, in fiery victory; and, borne on new-found wings of victory, moves so calmly, even because so rapidly, so irresistibly. Always must the Wanderer remember, with a certain satisfaction and surprise, how in this case he sat not silent, but   10 struck adroitly into the stream of conversation; which thenceforth, to speak with an apparent not a real vanity, he may say that he continued to lead. Surely, in those hours, a certain inspiration was imparted him, such inspiration as is still possible in our late era. The self-secluded unfolds himself in noble thoughts, in free, glowing words; his soul is   15 as one sea of light, the peculiar home of Truth and Intellect; wherein also Fantasy bodies forth form after form, radiant with all prismatic hues.'

It appears, in this otherwise so happy meeting, there talked one 'Philistine;' who even now, to the general weariness, was dominantly   20 pouring forth Philistinism (*Philistriositäten*); little witting what hero was here entering to demolish him! We omit the series of Socratic, or rather Diogenic utterances, not unhappy in their way, whereby the monster, 'persuaded into silence,' seems soon after to have withdrawn for the night. 'Of which dialectic marauder,' writes our hero, 'the   25 discomfiture was visibly felt as a benefit by most: but what were all applauses to the glad smile, threatening every moment to become a laugh, wherewith Blumine herself repaid the victor? He ventured to address her, she answered with attention: nay, what if there were a slight tremour in that silver voice; what if the red glow of evening   30 were hiding a transient blush!

'The conversation took a higher tone, one fine thought called forth another: it was one of those rare seasons, when the soul expands with full freedom, and man feels himself brought near to man. Gaily in light, graceful abandonment, the friendly talk played round that   35 circle: for the burden was rolled from every heart; the barriers of Ceremony, which are indeed the laws of polite living, had melted as into vapour; and the poor claims of *Me* and *Thee*, no longer parted by rigid fences, now flowed softly into one another; and Life lay all harmonious, many-tinted, like some fair royal champaign, the sovereign and owner of which were Love only. Such music springs from kind hearts, in a kind environment of place and time. And yet as the light grew more aërial on the mountain-tops, and the shadows fell longer over the valley, some faint tone of sadness may have breathed through the heart; and, in whispers more or less audible, reminded every one that as this bright day was drawing towards its close, so likewise must the Day of man's Existence decline into dust and darkness; and with all its sick toilings, and joyful and mournful noises, sink in the still Eternity.

'To our Friend the hours seemed moments; holy was he and happy: the words from those sweetest lips came over him like dew on thirsty grass; all better feelings in his soul seemed to whisper: It is good for us to be here. At parting, the Blumine's hand was in his: in the balmy twilight, with the kind stars above them, he spoke something of meeting again, which was not contradicted; he pressed gently those small soft fingers, and it seemed as if they were not hastily, not angrily withdrawn.'

Poor Teufelsdröckh! it is clear to demonstration thou art smit: the Queen of Hearts would see a 'man of genius' also sigh for her; and there, by art magic, in that preternatural hour, has she bound and spell-bound thee. 'Love is not altogether a Delirium,' says he elsewhere; 'yet has it many points in common therewith. I call it rather a discerning of the Infinite in the Finite, of the Idea made Real; which discerning again may be either true or false, either seraphic or demoniac, Inspiration or Insanity. But in the former case too, as in common Madness, it is Fantasy that superadds itself to Sight; on the so petty domain of the Actual plants its Archimedes'-lever, whereby to move at will the infinite Spiritual. Fantasy I might call the true Heaven-gate and Hell-gate of man: his sensuous life is but the small temporary stage (*Zeitbühne*), whereon thick-streaming influences from both these far yet near regions meet visibly, and act tragedy and melodrama. Sense can support herself handsomely, in most countries, for some eighteenpence a day; but for Fantasy planets and solar-systems will not suffice. Witness your Pyrrhus conquering the world, yet drinking no better red wine than he had before.' Alas, witness also your Diogenes, flame-clad, scaling the upper Heaven, and verging towards

Insanity, for prize of a 'highsouled Brunette,' as if the Earth held but
one, and not several of these!

He says that, in Town, they met again: 'day after day, like his
heart's sun, the blooming Blumine shone on him. Ah! a little while
ago, and he was yet all in darkness: him what Graceful (*Holde*) would   5
ever love? Disbelieving all things, the poor youth had never learned
to believe in himself. Withdrawn, in proud timidity, within his own
fastnesses; solitary from men, yet baited by night-spectres enough, he
saw himself, with a sad indignation, constrained to renounce the
fairest hopes of existence. And now, O now! "She looks on thee,"   10
cried he: "she the fairest, noblest; do not her dark eyes tell thee, thou
art not despised? The Heaven's-Messenger! All Heaven's blessings be
hers!" Thus did soft melodies flow through his heart; tones of an
infinite gratitude; sweetest intimations that he also was a man, that
for him also unutterable joys had been provided.   15

'In free speech, earnest or gay, amid lambent glances, laughter,
tears, and often with the inarticulate mystic speech of Music: such
was the element they now lived in; in such a many-tinted, radiant
Aurora, and by this fairest of Orient Light-bringers must our Friend
be blandished, and the new Apocalypse of Nature unrolled to him.   20
Fairest Blumine! And, even as a Star, all Fire and humid Softness, a
very Light-ray incarnate! Was there so much as a fault, a "caprice,"
he could have dispensed with? Was she not to him in very deed a
Morning-Star; did not her presence bring with it airs from Heaven?
As from Æolean Harps in the breath of dawn, as from the Memnon's   25
Statue struck by the rosy-finger of Aurora, unearthly music was around
him, and lapped him into untried balmy Rest. Pale Doubt fled away
to the distance; Life bloomed up with happiness and hope. The Past,
then, was all a haggard dream; he had been in the Garden of Eden,
then, and could not discern it! But lo now! the black walls of his   30
prison melt away; the captive is alive, is free. If he loved his Disenchantress? *Ach Gott!* His whole heart and soul and life were hers, but
never had he named it Love: existence was all a Feeling, not yet
shaped into a Thought.'

Nevertheless, into a Thought, nay into an Action, it must be shaped;   35
for neither Disenchanter nor Disenchantress, mere 'Children of Time,'
can abide by Feeling alone. The Professor knows not, to this day,

'how in her soft, fervid bosom, the Lovely found determination, even on hest of Necessity, to cut asunder these so blissful bonds.' He even appears surprised at the 'Duenna Cousin,' whoever she may have been, 'in whose meagre, hunger-bitten philosophy, the religion of young hearts was, from the first, faintly approved of.' We, even at such distance, can explain it without necromancy. Let the Philosopher answer this one question: What figure, at that period, was a Mrs. Teufelsdröckh likely to make in polished society? Could she have driven so much as a brass-bound Gig, or even a simple iron-spring one? Thou foolish 'absolved Auscultator,' before whom lies no prospect of capital, will any yet known 'religion of young hearts' keep the human kitchen warm? Pshaw! thy divine Blumine, when she 'resigned herself to wed some richer,' shews more philosophy, though but 'a woman of genius,' than thou, a pretended man.

Our readers have witnessed the origin of this Love-mania, and with what royal splendour it waxes, and rises. Let no one ask us to unfold the glories of its dominant state; much less the horrors of its almost instantaneous dissolution. How from such inorganic masses, henceforth madder than ever, as lie in these Bags, can even fragments of a living delineation be organised? Besides, of what profit were it? We view, with a lively pleasure, the gay silk Montgolfier start from the ground, and shoot upwards, cleaving the liquid deeps, till it dwindle to a luminous star: but what is there to look longer on, when once, by natural elasticity, or accident of fire, it has exploded? A hapless air-navigator, plunging, amid torn parachutes, sand-bags, and confused wreck, fast enough into the jaws of the Devil! Suffice it to know that Teufelsdröckh rose into the highest regions of the Empyrean, by a natural parabolic track, and returned thence in a quick perpendicular one. For the rest, let any feeling reader who has been unhappy enough to do the like, paint it out for himself; considering only that if he, for his perhaps comparatively insignificant mistress, underwent such agonies and frenzies, what must Teufelsdröckh's have been, with a fire-heart, and for a nonpareil Blumine! We glance merely at the final scene:

'One morning, he found his Morning-star all dimmed and dusky-red; the fair creature was silent, absent, she seemed to have been weeping. Alas, no longer a Morning-star, but a troublous skyey Portent, announcing that the Doomsday had dawned! She said, in a tremulous voice, they were to meet no more.' The thunderstruck Air-sailor is not wanting to himself in this dread hour: but what avails it? We omit the passionate expostulations, entreaties, indignations, since all was vain, and not even an explanation was conceded him; and hasten to the catastrophe. '"Farewell, then, Madam!" said he, not 5 without sternness, for his stung pride helped him. She put her hand in his, she looked in his face, tears started to her eyes: in wild audacity he clasped her to his bosom; their lips were joined, their two souls, like two dew-drops, rushed into one,—for the first time, and for the last!' Thus was Teufelsdröckh made immortal by a kiss. And then? 10 Why, then—'thick curtains of Night rushed over his soul, as rose the immeasurable Crash of Doom; and through the ruins as of a shivered Universe was he falling, falling, towards the Abyss.'

CHAPTER VI.

SORROWS OF ΓEUFELSDRÖCKH.

WE have long felt that, with a man like our Professor, matters must often be expected to take a course of their own; that, in so multiplex, intricate a nature, there might be channels, both for admitting and emitting, such as the Psychologist had seldom noted; in short, that on no grand occasion and convulsion, neither in the joy-storm nor in the woe-storm, could you predict his demeanour.

To our less philosophical readers, for example, it is now clear that the so passionate Teufelsdröckh, precipitated through 'a shivered Universe' in this extraordinary way, has only one of three things which he can next do: Establish himself in Bedlam; begin writing Satanic Poetry; or blow out his brains. In the progress towards any of which consummations, do not such readers anticipate extravagance enough; breast-beating, brow-beating (against walls), lion-bellowings of blasphemy and the like, stampings, smitings, breakages of furniture, if not arson itself?

Nowise so does Teufelsdröckh deport him. He quietly lifts his *Pilgerstab* (Pilgrim-staff), 'old business being soon wound up;' and begins a perambulation and circumambulation of the terraqueous Globe! Curious it is, indeed, how with such vivacity of conception, such intensity of feeling; above all, with these unconscionable habits of Exaggeration in speech, he combines that wonderful stillness of his, that stoicism in external procedure. Thus if his sudden bereavement, in this matter of the Flower-goddess, is talked of as a real

112

Doomsday and Dissolution of Nature, in which light doubtless it partly appeared to himself, his own nature is nowise dissolved thereby; but rather is compressed closer. For once, as we might say, a Blumine by magic appliances has unlocked that shut heart of his, and its hidden things rush out tumultuous, boundless, like genii enfranchised 5 from their glass phial: but no sooner are your magic appliances withdrawn, than the strange casket of a heart springs-to again; and perhaps there is now no key extant that will open it; for a Teufelsdröckh, as we remarked, will not love a second time. Singular Diogenes! No sooner has that heart-rending occurrence fairly taken place, than he 10 affects to regard it as a thing natural, of which there is nothing more to be said. 'One highest Hope, seemingly legible in the eyes of an Angel, had recalled him as out of Death-shadows into celestial Life: but a gleam of Tophet passed over the face of his Angel; he was rapt away in whirlwinds, and heard the laughter of Demons. It was a 15 Calenture,' adds he, 'whereby the Youth saw green Paradise-groves in the waste Ocean-waters: a lying vision, yet not wholly a lie, for *he* saw it.' But what things soever passed in him, when he ceased to see it; what ragings and despairings soever Teufelsdröckh's soul was the scene of, he has the goodness to conceal under a quite opaque cover 20 of Silence. We know it well; the first mad paroxysm past, our brave Gneschen collected his dismembered philosophies, and buttoned himself together; he was meek, silent, or spoke of the weather, and the Journals: only by a transient knitting of those shaggy brows, by some deep flash of those eyes, glancing one knew not whether with tear- 25 dew or with fierce fire,—might you have guessed what a Gehenna was within; that a whole Satanic School were spouting, though inaudibly, there. To consume your own choler, as some chimneys consume their own smoke; to keep a whole Satanic School spouting, if it must spout, inaudibly, is a negative yet no slight virtue, nor one of the 30 commonest in these times.

Nevertheless, we will not take upon us to say, that in the strange measure he fell upon, there was not a touch of latent Insanity; whereof indeed the actual condition of these Documents in *Capricornus* and *Aquarius* is no bad emblem. His so unlimited Wanderings, toilsome 35 enough, are without assigned or perhaps assignable aim; internal Unrest seems his sole guidance; he wanders, wanders, as if that curse of the Prophet had fallen on him, and he were 'made like unto a wheel.'

Doubtless, too, the chaotic nature of these Paperbags aggravates our obscurity. Quite without note of preparation, for example, we come upon the following slip: 'A peculiar feeling it is that will rise in the Traveller, when turning some hill-range in his desert road, he descries lying far below, embosomed among its groves and green natural bulwarks, and all diminished to a toybox, the fair Town, where so many souls, as it were seen and yet unseen, are driving their multifarious traffic. Its white steeple is then truly a starward-pointing finger; the canopy of blue smoke seems like a sort of Life-breath: for always, of its own unity, the soul gives unity to whatso it looks on with love: thus does the little Dwellingplace of men, in itself a congeries of houses and huts, become for us an individual, almost a person. But what thousand other thoughts unite thereto, if the place has to ourselves been the arena of joyous or mournful experiences; if perhaps the cradle we were rocked in still stands there, if our Loving ones still dwell there, if our Buried ones there slumber!' Does Teufelsdröckh, as the wounded eagle is said to make for its own eyrie, and indeed military deserters, and all hunted outcast creatures, turn as if by instinct in the direction of their birthland,—fly first, in this extremity, towards his native Entepfuhl; but reflecting that there no help awaits him, take only one wistful look from the distance, and then wend elsewhither?

Little happier seems to be his next flight: into the wilds of Nature; as if in her mother-bosom he would seek healing. So at least we incline to interpret the following Notice, separated from the former by some considerable space, wherein, however, is nothing noteworthy:

'Mountains were not new to him; but rarely are Mountains seen in such combined majesty and grace as here. The rocks are of that sort called Primitive by the mineralogists, which always arrange themselves in masses of a rugged, gigantic character; which ruggedness, however, is here tempered by a singular airiness of form, and softness of environment: in a climate favourable to vegetation, the gray cliff, itself covered with lichens, shoots up through a garment of foliage or verdure; and white, bright cottages, tree-shaded, cluster round the everlasting granite. In fine vicissitude, Beauty alternates with Grandeur: you ride through stony hollows, along strait passes, traversed by torrents, overhung by high walls of rock; now winding amid broken shaggy chasms, and huge fragments; now suddenly emerging into some emerald valley, where the streamlet collects itself into a Lake, and man has again found a fair dwelling, and it seems as if Peace had established herself in the bosom of Strength.

'To Peace, however, in this vortex of existence, can the Son of Time not pretend: still less if some Spectre haunt him from the Past; and the Future is wholly a Stygian Darkness, spectre-bearing. Reasonably might the Wanderer exclaim to himself: Are not the gates of this world's Happiness inexorably shut against thee; hast thou a hope that is not mad? Nevertheless, one may still murmur audibly, or in the original Greek if that suit thee better: "Whoso can look on Death will start at no shadows."

'From such meditations is the Wanderer's attention called outwards: for now the Valley closes in abruptly, intersected by a huge mountain mass, the stony water-worn ascent of which is not to be accomplished on horseback. Arrived aloft, he finds himself again lifted into the evening sunset light; and cannot but pause, and gaze round him, some moments there. An upland irregular expanse of wold, where valleys in complex branchings are suddenly or slowly arranging their descent towards every quarter of the sky. The mountain-ranges are beneath your feet, and folded together; only the loftier summits look down here and there as on a second plain; lakes also lie clear and earnest in their solitude. No trace of man now visible; unless indeed it were he who fashioned that little visible link of Highway, here, as would seem, scaling the inaccessible to unite Province with Province. But sunwards, lo you! how it towers sheer up, a world of Mountains, the diadem and centre of the mountain region! A hundred and a hundred savage peaks, in the last light of Day; all glowing, of gold and amethyst, like giant spirits of the wilderness; there in their silence, in their solitude, even as on the night when Noah's deluge first dried! Beautiful, nay solemn, was the sudden aspect to our Wanderer. He gazed over those stupendous masses with wonder, almost with longing desire; never till this hour had he known Nature, that she was One, that she was his Mother and divine. And as the ruddy glow was fading into clearness in the sky, and the Sun had now departed, a murmur of Eternity and Immensity, of Death and of Life, stole through his soul; and he felt as if Death and Life were

one, as if the Earth were not dead, as if the Spirit of the Earth had
its throne in that splendour, and his own spirit were therewith holding
communion.

'The spell was broken by a sound of carriage-wheels. Emerging
5   from the hidden Northward, to sink soon into the hidden Southward,
came a gay barouche-and-four: it was open; servants and postilions
wore wedding-favours: that happy pair, then, had found each other,
it was their marriage-evening! Few moments brought them near: *Du
Himmel!* It was Herr Towgood and — — Blumine! With slight, unre-
10   cognising salutation they passed me; plunged down amid the neighbouring thickets, onwards, to Heaven, and to England; and I, in my
friend Richter's words, *I remained alone, behind them, with the Night.*'

Were it not cruel in these circumstances, here might be the place
to insert an observation, gleaned long ago from the great *Clothes-*
15   *Volume*, where it stands with quite other intent: 'Some time before
Small-pox was extirpated,' says the Professor, 'there came a new malady
of the spiritual sort on Europe: I mean the epidemic, now endemical,
of View-hunting. Poets of old date, being privileged with Senses, had
also enjoyed external Nature; but chiefly as we enjoy the crystal cup
20   which holds good or bad liquor for us; that is to say, in silence, or
with slight incidental commentary: never, as I compute, till after the
Sorrows of Werter, was there man found who would say: Come let us
make a Description! Having drunk the liquor, come let us eat the
glass! Of which endemic the Jenner is unhappily still to seek.' Too
25   true!

We reckon it more important to remark that the Professor's Wanderings, so far as his stoical and cynical envelopment admits us to
clear insight, here first take their permanent character, fatuous or not.
That basilisk-glance of the Barouche-and-four seems to have withered
30   up what little remnant of a purpose may have still lurked in him: Life
has become wholly a dark labyrinth; wherein, through long years, our
Friend, flying from spectres, has to stumble about at random, and
naturally with more haste than progress.

Foolish were it in us to attempt following him, even from afar, in
35   this extraordinary world-pilgrimage of his; the simplest record of which,
were clear record possible, would fill volumes. Hopeless is the obscurity, unspeakable the confusion. He glides from country to country,
from condition to condition; vanishing and re-appearing, no man can

calculate how or where. Through all quarters of the world he wanders, and apparently through all circles of society. If in any scene, perhaps difficult to fix geographically, he settles for a time, and forms connexions, be sure he will snap them abruptly asunder. Let him sink out of sight as Private Scholar (*Privatisirender*), living by the grace of God, in some European capital, you may next find him as Hadjee in the neighbourhood of Mecca. It is an inexplicable Phantasmagoria, capricious, quick-changing; as if our Traveller, instead of limbs and highways, had transported himself by some wishing-carpet, or Fortunatus' Hat. The whole, too, imparted emblematically, in dim multifarious tokens (as that collection of Street-Advertisements); with only some touch of direct historical notice sparingly interspersed: little light-islets in the world of haze! So that from this point, the Professor is more of an enigma than ever. In figurative language, we might say he becomes, not indeed a spirit, yet spiritualised, vaporised. Fact unparalleled in Biography! The river of his History, which we have traced from its tiniest fountains, and hoped to see flow onward, with increasing current, into the ocean, here dashes itself over that terrific Lover's Leap; and, as a mad-foaming cataract, flies wholly into tumultuous clouds of spray! Low down it indeed collects again into pools and plashes; yet only at a great distance, and with difficulty, if at all, into a general stream. To cast a glance into certain of those pools and plashes, and trace whither they run, must, for a chapter or two, form the limit of our endeavour.

For which end doubtless those direct historical Notices, where they can be met with, are the best. Nevertheless, of this sort too there occurs much, which, with our present light, it were questionable to emit. Teufelsdröckh, vibrating everywhere between the highest and the lowest levels, comes into contact with Public History itself. For example, those conversations and relations with illustrious Persons, as Sultan Mahmoud, the Emperor Napoleon, and others, are they not as yet rather of a diplomatic character, than of a biographic? The Editor, appreciating the sacredness of crowned heads, nay perhaps suspecting the possible trickeries of a Clothes-Philosopher, will eschew this province for the present: a new time may bring new insight and a different duty.

If we ask now, not indeed with what ulterior Purpose, for there was none, yet with what immediate outlooks; at all events, in what

mood of mind, the Professor undertook and prose cuted this world-
pilgrimage,—the answer is more distinct than favourable. 'A nameless
Unrest,' says he, 'urged me forward; to which the outward motion
was some momentary lying solace. Whither should I go? My Loadstars
5 were blotted out; in that canopy of grim fire shone no star. Yet
forward must I; the ground burnt under me; there was no rest for the
sole of my foot. I was alone! alone! Ever too the strong inward
longing shaped Fantasms for itself: towards these, one after the other,
must I fruitlessly wander. A feeling I had that, for my fever-thirst,
10 there was and must be somewhere a healing Fountain. To many
fondly imagined Fountains, the Saints' Wells of these days, did I
pilgrim; to great Men, to great Cities, to great Events: but found
there no healing. In strange countries, as in the well-known; in savage
deserts as in the press of corrupt civilisation, it was ever the same:
15 how could your Wanderer escape from—*his own Shadow?* Nevertheless still Forward! I felt as if in great haste; to do I saw not what.
From the depths of my own heart, it called to me, Forwards! The
winds and the streams, and all Nature sounded to me, Forwards! *Ach
Gott!* I was even, once for all, a Son of Time.'
20   From which is it not clear that the internal Satanic School was still
active enough? He says elsewhere: 'The *Enchiridion of Epictetus* I had
ever with me, often as my sole rational companion; and regret to
mention that the nourishment it yielded was trifling.' Thou foolish
Teufelsdröckh! How could it else? Hadst thou not Greek enough to
25 understand thus much: *The end of Man is an Action, and not a Thought,*
though it were the noblest?
     'How I lived?' writes he once: 'Friend, hast thou considered the
"rugged all-nourishing Earth," as Sophocles well names her; how she
feeds the sparrow on the housetop, much more her darling, man?
30 While thou stirrest and livest, thou hast a probability of victual. My
breakfast of tea has been cooked by a Tartar woman, with water of
the Amur, who wiped her earthen-kettle with a horse-tail. I have
roasted wild eggs in the sand of Sahara; I have awakened in Paris
Estrapades and Vienna *Malzleins*, with no prospect of breakfast be-
35 yond elemental liquid. That I had my Living to seek saved me from
Dying,—by suicide. In our busy Europe, is there not an everlasting
demand for Intellect, in the chemical, mechanical, political, religious,
educational, commercial departments? In Pagan countries, cannot one

write Fetishes? Living! Little knowest thou what alchemy is in an inventive Soul; how, as with its little finger, it can create provision enough for the body (of a Philosopher); and then, as with both hands, create quite other than provision; namely, spectres to torment itself withal.'

Poor Teufelsdröckh! Flying with Hunger always parallel to him; and a whole Infernal Chase in his rear; so that the countenance of Hunger is comparatively a friend's! Thus must he, in the temper of ancient Cain, or of the modern Wandering Jew, save only that he feels himself not guilty and but suffering the pains of guilt,—wend to and fro with aimless speed. Thus must he, over the whole surface of the Earth (by foot-prints), write his *Sorrows of Teufelsdröckh;* even as the great Goethe, in passionate words, had to write his *Sorrows of Werter*, before the spirit freed herself, and he could become a Man. Vain truly is the hope of your swiftest Runner to escape 'from his own Shadow!' Nevertheless, in these sick days, when the Born of Heaven first descries himself (about the age of twenty) in a world such as ours, richer than usual in two things: in Truths grown obsolete, and Trades grown obsolete,—what can the fool think but that it is all a Den of Lies, wherein whoso will not speak Lies and act Lies, must stand Idle, and despair? Whereby it happens that, for your nobler minds, the publishing of some such Work of Art, in one or the other dialect, becomes almost a necessity. For what is it properly but an Altercation with the Devil, before you begin honestly Fighting him? Your Byron publishes his *Sorrows of Lord George*, in verse and in prose, and copiously otherwise: your Bonaparte represents his *Sorrows of Napoleon* Opera, in an all-too stupendous style; with music of cannon-volleys, and murder-shrieks of a world; his stage-lights are the fires of Conflagration; his rhyme and recitative are the tramp of embattled Hosts and the sound of falling Cities.—Happier is he who, like our Clothes-Philosopher, can write such matter, since it must be written, on the insensible Earth, with his shoe-soles only; and also survive the writing thereof!

CHAPTER VII.

THE EVERLASTING NO.

UNDER the strange nebulous envelopment, wherein our Professor has now shrouded himself, no doubt but his spiritual nature is nevertheless progressive, and growing: for how can the 'Son of Time,' in any case, stand still? We behold him, through those dim years, in a state of crisis, of transition: his mad Pilgrimings, and general solution into aimless Discontinuity, what is all this but a mad Fermentation; wherefrom, the fiercer it is, the clearer product will one day evolve itself?

Such transitions are ever full of pain: thus the Eagle, when he moults, is sickly; and, to attain his new beak, must harshly dash off the old one upon rocks. What Stoicism soever our Wanderer, in his individual acts and motions may affect, it is clear that there is a hot fever of anarchy and misery raging within; coruscations of which flash out: as, indeed, how could there be other? Have we not seen him disappointed, bemocked of Destiny, through long years? All that the young heart might desire and pray for has been denied; nay, as in the last worst instance, offered and then snatched away. Ever an 'excellent Passivity;' but of useful, reasonable Activity, essential to the former as Food to Hunger, nothing granted: till at length, in this wild Pilgrimage, he must forcibly seize for himself an Activity, though useless, unreasonable. Alas! his cup of bitterness, which had been filling drop by drop, ever since that first 'ruddy morning' in the Hinterschlag Gymnasium, was at the very lip; and then with that poison-drop, of

120

the Towgood-and-Blumine business, it runs over, and even hisses over in a deluge of foam.

He himself says once, with more justness than originality: 'Man is, properly speaking, based upon Hope, he has no other possession but Hope; this world of his is emphatically the Place of Hope.' What then was our Professor's possession? We see him, for the present, quite shut out from Hope; looking not into the golden orient, but vaguely all round into a dim copper firmament, pregnant with earthquake and tornado.

Alas, shut out from Hope, in a deeper sense than we yet dream of! For as he wanders wearisomely through this world, he has now lost all tidings of another and higher. Full of religion, or at least of religiosity, as our Friend has since exhibited himself, he hides not that, in those days, he was wholly irreligious: 'Doubt had darkened into Unbelief,' says he; 'shade after shade goes grimly over your soul, till you have the fixed, starless, Tartarean black.' To such readers as have reflected, what can be called reflecting, on man's life, and happily discovered, in contradiction to much Profit-and-Loss Philosophy, speculative and practical, that Soul is *not* synonymous with Stomach; who understand, therefore, in our Friend's words, 'that, for man's well-being, Faith is properly the one thing needful; how, with it, Martyrs, otherwise weak, can cheerfully endure the shame and the cross; and, without it, Worldlings puke up their sick existence, by suicide, in the midst of luxury:' to such it will be clear that, for a pure moral nature, the loss of his religious Belief was the loss of every thing. Unhappy young man! All wounds, the crush of long-continued Destitution, the stab of false Friendship, and of false Love, all wounds in thy so genial heart would have healed again, had not its life-warmth been withdrawn. Well might he exclaim, in his wild way: 'Is there no God, then; but at best an absentee God, sitting idle, ever since the first Sabbath, at the outside of his Universe, and *see*ing it go? Has the word Duty no meaning; is what we call Duty no divine Messenger and Guide, but a false earthly Fantasm, made up of Desire and Fear, of emanations from the Gallows and from Doctor Graham's Celestial-Bed? Happiness of an approving Conscience! Did not Paul of Tarsus, whom admiring men have since named Saint, feel that *he* was "the chief of sinners;" and Nero of Rome, jocund in spirit (*wohlgemuth*), spend much of his time in fiddling? Foolish Word-monger, and Motive-grinder, that in

thy Logic-mill hast an earthly mechanism for the Godlike itself, and
wouldst fain grind me out Virtue from the husks of Pleasure,—I tell
thee, Nay! To the unregenerate Prometheus Vinctus of a man, it is
ever the bitterest aggravation of his wretchedness that he is conscious
5   of Virtue, that he feels himself the victim not of suffering only, but
of injustice. What then? Is the heroic inspiration we name Virtue but
some Passion; some bubble of the blood, bubbling in the direction
others *profit* by? I know not: only this I know, If what thou namest
Happiness be our true aim, then are we all astray. With Stupidity and
10   sound Digestion man may front much. But what, in these dull
unimaginative days, are the terrors of Conscience to the diseases of
the Liver! Not on Morality, but on Cookery let us build our stronghold:
there brandishing our fryingpan, as censer, let us offer sweet incense
to the Devil, and live at ease on the fat things *he* has provided for his
15   Elect!'
    Thus has the bewildered Wanderer to stand, as so many have
done, shouting question after question into the Sibyl-cave of Destiny,
and receive no Answer but an Echo. It is all a grim Desert, this once
fair world of his; wherein is heard only the howling of wild beasts, or
20   the shrieks of despairing, hate-filled men; and no Pillar of Cloud by
day, and no Pillar of Fire by night, any longer guides the Pilgrim. To
such length has the spirit of Inquiry carried him. 'But what boots it
(*was thut's*)?' cries he: 'it is but the common lot in this era. Not
having come to spiritual majority prior to the *Siècle de Louis Quinze*,
25   and not being born purely a Loghead (*Dummkopf*), thou hadst no
other outlook. The whole world is, like thee, sold to Unbelief: their
old Temples of the Godhead, which for long have not been rainproof,
crumble down; and men ask now: Where is the Godhead; our eyes
never saw him!'
30   Pitiful enough were it, for all these wild utterances, to call our
Diogenes wicked. Unprofitable Servants as we all are, perhaps at no
era of his life was he more decisively the Servant of Goodness, the
Servant of God, than even now when doubting God's existence. 'One
circumstance I note,' says he: 'after all the nameless woe that Inquiry,
35   which for me, what it is not always, was genuine Love of Truth, had
wrought me, I nevertheless still loved Truth, and would bate no jot
of my allegiance to her. "Truth!" I cried, "though the Heavens crush
me for following her: no Falsehood! though a whole celestial

Lubberland were the price of Apostacy." In conduct it was the same. Had a divine Messenger from the clouds, or miraculous Handwriting on the wall, convincingly proclaimed to me, *This shalt thou do*, with what passionate readiness, as I often thought, would I have done it, had it been leaping into the infernal Fire! Thus, in spite of all Motive- 5
grinders, and Mechanical Profit-and-Loss Philosophies, with the sick ophthalmia and hallucination they had brought on, was the Infinite nature of Duty still dimly present to me: living without God in the world, of God's light I was not utterly bereft; if my as yet sealed eyes, with their unspeakable longing, could nowhere see Him, nevertheless 10
in my heart He was present, and His Heaven-written Law still stood legible and sacred there.'

Meanwhile, under all these tribulations, and temporal and spiritual destitutions, what must the Wanderer, in his silent soul, have endured! 'The painfullest feeling,' writes he, 'is that of your own Feeble- 15
ness (*Unkraft*); ever, as the English Milton says, to be weak is the true misery. And yet of your Strength there is and can be no clear feeling, save by what you have prospered in, by what you have done. Between vague wavering Capability and fixed indubitable Performance, what a difference! A certain inarticulate Self-consciousness dwells dimly 20
in us; which only our Works can render articulate and decisively dis- cernible. Our Works are the mirror wherein the spirit first sees its natural lineaments. Hence, too, the folly of that impossible Precept, *Know thyself;* till it be translated into this partially possible one, *Know what thou canst work at.* 25

'But for me, so strangely unprosperous had I been, the net result of my Workings amounted as yet simply to—Nothing. How then could I believe in my Strength, when there was as yet no mirror to see it in? Ever did this agitating, yet, as I now perceive, quite frivo- lous question, remain to me insoluble: Hast thou a certain Faculty, 30
a certain Worth, such even as the most have not; or art thou the completest Dullard of these modern times? Alas! the fearful Unbelief is unbelief in yourself; and how could I believe? Had not my first, last Faith in myself, when even to me the Heavens seemed laid open, and I dared to love, been all-too cruelly belied? The speculative 35
Mystery of Life grew ever more mysterious to me: neither in the practical Mystery had I made the slightest progress, but been every- where buffeted, foiled, and contemptuously cast out. A feeble unit

in the middle of a threatening Infinitude, I seemed to have nothing given me but eyes, whereby to discern my own wretchedness. Invisible yet impenetrable walls, as of Enchantment, divided me from all living: was there, in the wide world, any true bosom I could press
5 trustfully to mine? O Heaven, No, there was none! I kept a lock upon my lips: why should I speak much with that shifting variety of so-called Friends, in whose withered, vain, and too-hungry souls, Friendship was but an incredible tradition? In such cases, your resource is to talk little, and that little mostly from the Newspapers.
10 Now when I look back, it was a strange isolation I then lived in. The men and women round me, even speaking with me, were but Figures; I had, practically, forgotten that they were alive, that they were not merely automatic. In midst of their crowded streets, and assemblages, I walked solitary; and (except as it was my own heart, not
15 another's, that I kept devouring) savage also, as the tiger in his jungle. Some comfort it would have been, could I, like a Faust, have fancied myself tempted and tormented of the Devil; for a Hell, as I imagine, without Life, though only diabolic Life, were more frightful: but in our age of Downpulling and Disbelief, the very Devil has
20 been pulled down, you cannot so much as believe in a Devil. To me the Universe was all void of Life, of Purpose, of Volition, even of Hostility: it was one huge, dead, immeasurable Steam-engine, rolling on, in its dead indifference, to grind me limb from limb. O the vast, gloomy, solitary Golgotha, and Mill of Death! Why was the Living
25 banished thither companionless, conscious? Why if there is no Devil; nay, unless the Devil is your God?'

A prey incessantly to such corrosions, might not, moreover, as the worst aggravation to them, the iron constitution even of a Teufelsdröckh threaten to fail? We conjecture that he has known
30 sickness; and, in spite of his locomotive habits, perhaps sickness of the chronic sort. Hear this, for example: 'How beautiful to die of broken-heart, on Paper! Quite another thing in Practice; every window of your Feeling, even of your Intellect, as it were, begrimed and mud-bespattered, so that no pure ray can enter; a whole Drugshop in your
35 inwards; the foredone soul drowning slowly in quagmires of Disgust!'

Putting all which external and internal miseries together, may we not find in the following sentences, quite in our Professor's still vein, significance enough? 'From Suicide a certain after-shine (*Nachschein*) of Christianity withheld me: perhaps also a certain indolence of character; for, was not that a remedy I had at any time within reach? Often, however, was there a question present to me: Should some one now, at the turning of that corner, blow thee suddenly out of Space, into the other World, or other No-world, by pistol-shot,— 5 how were it? On which ground, too, I have often, in sea-storms and sieged cities and other death-scenes, exhibited an imperturbability, which passed, falsely enough, for courage.'

'So had it lasted,' concludes the Wanderer, 'so had it lasted, as in bitter protracted Death-agony, through long years. The heart within 10 me, unvisited by any heavenly dew-drop, was smouldering in sulphurous, slow-consuming fire. Almost since earliest memory I had shed no tear; or once only when I, murmuring half-audibly, recited Faust's Deathsong, that wild *Selig der den er im Siegesglanze findet* (Happy whom *he* finds in Battle's splendour), and thought that of this last 15 Friend even I was not forsaken, that Destiny itself could not doom me not to die. Having no Hope, neither had I any definite Fear, were it of Man or of Devil: nay, I often felt as if it might be solacing, could the Arch-Devil himself, though in Tartarean terrors, but rise to me, that I might tell him a little of my mind. And yet, strangely enough, 20 I lived in a continual, indefinite, pining Fear; tremulous, pusillanimous, apprehensive of I knew not what: it seemed as if all things in the Heavens above and the Earth beneath would hurt me; as if the Heavens and the Earth were but boundless jaws of a devouring monster, wherein I, palpitating, waited to be devoured. 25

'Full of such humour, and perhaps the miserablest man in the whole French Capital or Suburbs, was I, one sultry Dogday, after much perambulation, toiling along the dirty little *Rue Saint-Thomas de l'Enfer*, among civic rubbish enough, in a close atmosphere, and over pavements hot as Nebuchadnezzar's Furnace; whereby doubtless 30 my spirits were little cheered; when, all at once, there rose a Thought in me, and I asked myself: "What *art* thou afraid of? Wherefore, like a coward, dost thou forever pip and whimper, and go cowering and trembling? Despicable biped! what is the sum-total of the worst that lies before thee? Death? Well, Death; and say the pangs of Tophet 35 too, and all that the Devil and Man may, will, or can do against thee! Hast thou not a heart; canst thou not suffer whatso it be; and, as a Child of Freedom, though outcast, trample Tophet itself under thy

feet, while it consumes thee? Let it come, then; I will meet it and defy
it!" And as I so thought, there rushed like a stream of fire over my
whole soul; and I shook base Fear away from me forever. I was
strong, of unknown strength; a spirit, almost a god. Ever from that
5 time, the temper of my misery was changed: not Fear or whining
Sorrow was it, but Indignation and grim fire-eyed Defiance.

'Thus had the EVERLASTING NO (*das ewige Nein*) pealed authorita-
tively through all the recesses of my Being, of my ME; and then was
it that my whole ME stood up, in native God-created majesty, and
10 with emphasis recorded its Protest. Such a Protest, the most important transaction in Life, may that same Indignation and Defiance, in
a psychological point of view, be fitly called. The Everlasting No had
said: "Behold, thou art fatherless, outcast, and the Universe is mine
(the Devil's);" to which my whole Me now made answer: "*I* am not
15 thine, but Free, and forever hate thee!"

'It is from this hour that I incline to date my Spiritual New-birth,
or Baphometic Fire-baptism; perhaps I directly thereupon began to
be a Man.'

CHAPTER VIII.

THOUGH, after this 'Baphometic Fire-baptism' of his, our Wanderer signifies that his Unrest was but increased; as, indeed, 'Indignation and Defiance,' especially against things in general, are not the most peaceable inmates; yet can the Psychologist surmise that it was no longer a quite hopeless Unrest; that henceforth it had at least a fixed 5 centre to revolve round. For the fire-baptised soul, long so scathed and thunder-riven, here feels its own Freedom, which feeling is its Baphometic Baptism: the citadel of its whole kingdom it has thus gained by assault, and will keep inexpugnable; outwards from which the remaining dominions, not indeed without hard battling, will 10 doubtless by degrees be conquered and pacificated. Under another figure, we might say, if in that great moment, in the *Rue Saint-Thomas de l'Enfer*, the old inward Satanic School was not yet thrown out of doors, it received peremptory judicial notice to quit;—whereby, for the rest, its howl-chauntings, Ernulphus-cursings, and rebellious 15 gnashings of teeth, might, in the meanwhile, become only the more tumultuous, and difficult to keep secret.

Accordingly, if we scrutinize these Pilgrimings well, there is perhaps discernible henceforth a certain incipient method in their madness. Not wholly as a Spectre does Teufelsdröckh now storm through 20 the world; at worst as a spectre-fighting Man, nay who will one day be a Spectre-queller. If pilgriming restlessly to so many 'Saints' Wells,' and ever without quenching of his thirst, he nevertheless finds little

127

secular wells, whereby from time to time some alleviation is minis-
tered. In a word, he is now, if not ceasing, yet intermitting to 'eat his
own heart;' and clutches round him outwardly on the NOT-ME for
wholesomer food. Does not the following glimpse exhibit him in a
5   much more natural state?

'Towns also and Cities, especially the ancient, I failed not to look
upon with interest. How beautiful to see thereby, as through a long
vista, into the remote Time; to have, as it were, an actual section of
almost the earliest Past brought safe into the Present, and set before
10   your eyes! There, in that old City, was a live ember of Culinary Fire
put down, say only two thousand years ago; and there, burning more
or less triumphantly, with such fuel as the region yielded, it has burnt,
and still burns, and thou thyself seest the very smoke thereof. Ah! and
the far more mysterious live ember of Vital Fire was then also put
15   down there; and still miraculously burns and spreads; and the smoke
and ashes thereof (in these Judgment-Halls and Churchyards), and its
bellows-engines (in these Churches), thou still seest; and its flame,
looking out from every kind countenance, and every hateful one, still
warms thee or scorches thee.

20   'Of Man's Activity and Attainment the chief results are aeriform,
mystic, and preserved in Tradition only: such are his Forms of Government, with the Authority they rest on; his Customs, or Fashions
both of Cloth-habits and of Soul-habits; much more his collective
stock of Handicrafts, the whole Faculty he has acquired of manipu-
25   lating Nature: all these things, as indispensable and priceless as they
are, cannot in any way be fixed under lock and key, but must flit,
spirit-like, on impalpable vehicles, from Father to Son; if you demand sight of them, they are nowhere to be met with. Visible
Ploughmen and Hammermen there have been, ever from Cain and
30   Tubalcain downwards: but where does your accumulated Agricultural, Metallurgic, and other Manufacturing SKILL lie warehoused? It
transmits itself on the atmospheric air, on the sun's rays (by Hearing
and by Vision); it is a thing aeriform, impalpable, of quite spiritual
sort. In like manner, ask me not, Where are the LAWS; where is the
35   GOVERNMENT? In vain wilt thou go to Schönbrunn, to Downing Street,
to the Palais Bourbon: thou findest nothing there, but brick or stone
houses, and some bundles of Papers tied with tape. Where then is
that same cunningly-devised almighty GOVERNMENT of theirs to be

laid hands on? Everywhere, yet nowhere: seen only in its works, this too is a thing aeriform, invisible; or if you will, mystic and miraculous. So spiritual (*geistig*) is our whole daily Life: all that we do springs out of Mystery, Spirit, invisible Force; only like a little Cloud-image, or Armida's Palace, air-built, does the Actual body itself forth   5
from the great mystic Deep.

'Visible and tangible products of the Past, again, I reckon up to the extent of three: Cities, with their Cabinets and Arsenals; then tilled Fields, to either or to both of which divisions Roads with their Bridges may belong; and thirdly——Books. In which third truly, the   10
last-invented, lies a worth far surpassing that of the two others. Wondrous indeed is the virtue of a true Book. Not like a dead City of stones, yearly crumbling, yearly needing repair; more like a tilled field, but then a spiritual field: like a spiritual tree, let me rather say, it stands from year to year, and from age to age (we have Books that   15
already number some hundred-and-fifty human ages); and yearly comes its new produce of leaves (Commentaries, Deductions, Philosophical, Political Systems; or were it only Sermons, Pamphlets, Journalistic Essays), every one of which is talismanic and thaumaturgic, for it can persuade men. O thou who art able to write a Book, which once in   20
the two centuries or oftener there is a man gifted to do, envy not him whom they name City-builder, and inexpressibly pity him whom they name Conqueror or City-burner! Thou too art a Conqueror and Victor; but of the true sort, namely over the Devil: thou too hast built what will outlast all marble and metal, and be a wonder-bringing   25
City of the Mind, a Temple and Seminary and Prophetic Mount, whereto all kindreds of the Earth will pilgrim.—Fool! why journeyest thou wearisomely, in thy antiquarian fervour, to gaze on the stone Pyramids of Geeza, or the clay ones of Sacchara? These stand there, as I can tell thee, idle and inert, looking over the Desart, foolishly   30
enough, for the last three thousand years: but canst thou not open thy Hebrew BIBLE, then, or even Luther's Version thereof?'

No less satisfactory is his sudden appearance not in Battle, yet on some Battle-field; which, we soon gather, must be that of Wagram; so that here, for once, is a certain approximation to distinctness of date.   35
Omitting much, let us impart what follows:

'Horrible enough! A whole Marchfeld strewed with shell-splinters, cannon-shot, ruined tumbrils, and dead men and horses; stragglers still remaining not so much as buried. And those red mould heaps: ay, there lie the Shells of Men, out of which all the Life and Virtue has been blown; and now are they swept together, and crammed down out of sight, like blown Egg-shells!—Did Nature, when she bade the Donau bring down his mould-cargos fom the Carinthian and Carpathian Heights, and spread them out here into the softest, richest level,—intend thee, O Marchfeld, for a corn-bearing Nursery, whereon her children might be nursed; or for a Cockpit, wherein they might the more commodiously be throttled and tattered? Were thy three broad Highways, meeting here from the ends of Europe, made for Ammunition-waggons, then? Were thy Wagrams and Stillfrieds but so many ready-built Casemates, wherein the house of Hapsburg might batter with artillery, and with artillery be battered? König Ottokar, amid yonder hillocks, dies under Rodolf's truncheon; here Kaiser Franz falls a-swoon under Napoleon's: within which five centuries, to omit the others, how has thy breast, fair Plain, been defaced and defiled! The greensward is torn up and trampled down; man's fond care of it, his fruit-trees, hedgerows, and pleasant dwellings, blown away with gunpowder; and the kind seedfield lies a desolate, hideous Place-of-Sculls.—Nevertheless, Nature is at work; neither shall these Powder-Devilkins with their utmost devilry gainsay her: but all that gore and carnage will be shrouded in, absorbed into manure; and next year the Marchfeld will be green, nay greener. Thrifty unwearied Nature, ever out of our great waste educing some little profit of thy own,—how dost thou, from the very carcass of the Killer, bring Life for the Living!

'What, speaking in quite unofficial language, is the net purport and upshot of War? To my own knowledge, for example, there dwell and toil, in the British village of Dumdrudge, usually some five hundred souls. From these, by certain "Natural Enemies" of the French, there are successively selected, during the French war, say thirty ablebodied men: Dumdrudge, at her own expense, has suckled and nursed them; she has, not without difficulty and sorrow, fed them up to manhood, and even trained them to crafts, so that one can weave, another build, another hammer, and the weakest can stand under thirty stone avoirdupois. Nevertheless, amid much weeping and swearing, they are selected; all dressed in red; and shipped away, at the public charges, some two thousand miles, or say only to the south of

Spain; and fed there till wanted. And now, to that same spot in the south of Spain, are thirty similar French artisans, from a French Dumdrudge, in like manner wending: till at length, after infinite effort, the two parties come into actual juxta-position; and Thirty stands fronting Thirty, each with a gun in his hand. Straightway the word "Fire!" is given; and they blow the souls out of one another; and in place of sixty brisk useful craftsmen, the world has sixty dead carcasses, which it must bury, and anew shed tears for. Had these men any quarrel? Busy as the Devil is, not the smallest! They lived far enough apart; were the entirest strangers; nay, in so wide a Universe, there was even, unconsciously, by Commerce, some mutual helpfulness between them. How then? Simpleton! their Governors had fallen out; and, instead of shooting one another, had the cunning to make these poor blockheads shoot.—Alas, so is it in Deutschland, and hitherto in all other lands; still as of old, "what devilry soever Kings do, the Greeks must pay the piper!"—In that fiction of the English Smollett, it is true, the final Cessation of War is perhaps prophetically shadowed forth; where the two Natural Enemies, in person, take each a Tobacco-pipe, filled with Brimstone; light the same, and smoke in one another's faces, till the weaker gives in: but from such predicted Peace-Era, what blood-filled trenches, and contentious centuries, may still divide us!'

Thus can the Professor, at least in lucid intervals, look away from his own sorrows, over the many-coloured world, and pertinently enough note what is passing there. We may remark, indeed, that for the matter of spiritual culture, if for nothing else, perhaps few periods of his life were richer than this. Internally, there is the most momentous instructive Course of Practical Philosophy, with Experiments, going on; towards the right comprehension of which his Peripatetic habits, favourable to Meditation, might help him rather than hinder. Externally, again, as he wanders to and fro, there are, if for the longing heart little substance, yet for the seeing eye Sights enough: in these so boundless Travels of his, granting that the Satanic School was even partially kept down, what an incredible Knowledge of our Planet, and its Inhabitants and their Works, that is to say, of all knowable things, might not Teufelsdröckh acquire!

'I have read in most Public Libraries,' says he, 'including those of Constantinople and Samarcand: in most Colleges, except the Chinese

Mandarin ones, I have studied, or seen that there was no studying. Unknown Languages have I oftenest gathered from their natural repertory, the Air, by my organ of Hearing; Statistics, Geographics, Topographics came, through the Eye, almost of their own accord.
5 The ways of Man, how he seeks food, and warmth, and protection for himself, in most regions, are ocularly known to me. Like the great Hadrian, I meted out much of the terraqueous Globe with a pair of Compasses that belonged to myself only.

'Of great Scenes, why speak? Three summer days, I lingered re-
10 flecting, and even composing (*dichtete*), by the Pine-chasms of Vaucluse; and in that clear Lakelet moistened my bread. I have sat under the palm-trees of Tadmor; smoked a pipe among the ruins of Babylon. The great Wall of China I have seen; and can testify that it is of grey brick, coped and covered with granite, and shows only second-rate
15 masonry.—Great Events, also, have not I witnessed? Kings sweated down (*ausgemergelt*) into Berlin-and-Milan Customhouse-officers; the World well won, and the World well lost; oftener than once a hundred thousand individuals shot (by each other) in one day. All kindreds and peoples and nations dashed together, and shifted and shovelled
20 into heaps, that they might ferment there, and in time unite. The birth-pangs of Democracy, wherewith convulsed Europe was groaning in cries that reached Heaven, could not escape me.

'For great Men I have ever had the warmest predilection; and can perhaps boast that few such in this era have wholly escaped me. Great
25 Men are the inspired (speaking and acting) Texts of that divine BOOK OF REVELATIONS, whereof a Chapter is completed from epoch to epoch, and by some named HISTORY; to which inspired Texts your numerous talented men, and your innumerable untalented men, are the better or worse exegetic Commentaries, and waggon-load of too-
30 stupid, heretical or orthodox, weekly Sermons. For my study, the inspired Texts themselves! Thus, did not I, in very early days, having disguised me as tavern-waiter, stand behind the field-chairs, under that shady Tree at Treisnitz by the Jena Highway; waiting upon the great Schiller and greater Goethe; and hearing what I have not for-
35 gotten. For——'

——But at this point the Editor recalls his principle of caution, some time ago laid down, and must suppress much. Let not the sacredness of Laurelled, still more, of Crowned Heads, be tampered with. Should we, at a future day, find circumstances altered, and the time come for Publication, then may these glimpses into the privacy of the Illustrious be conceded; which for the present were little better than treacherous, perhaps traitorous Eavesdroppings. Of Lord Byron, therefore, of Pope Pius, Emperor Tarakwang, and the 'White Water-roses' (Chinese Carbonari) with their mysteries, no notice here! Of Napoleon himself we shall only, glancing from afar, remark that Teufelsdröckh's relation to him seems to have been of very varied character. At first we find our poor Professor on the point of being shot as a spy; then taken into private conversation, even pinched on the ear, yet presented with no money; at last indignantly dismissed, almost thrown out of doors, as an 'Ideologist.' 'He himself,' says the Professor, 'was among the completest Ideologists, at least Ideopraxists: in the Idea (*in der Idee*) he lived, moved, and fought. The man was a divine Missionary, though unconscious of it; and preached, through the cannon's throat, that great doctrine, *La carrière ouverte aux talens* (The Tools to him that can handle them), which is our ultimate Political Evangile, wherein alone can Liberty lie. Madly enough he preached, it is true, as Enthusiasts and first Missionaries are wont, with imperfect utterance, amid much frothy rant; yet as articulately perhaps as the case admitted. Or call him, if you will, an American Backwoods-man, who had to fell unpenetrated forests, and battle with innumerable wolves, and did not entirely forbear strong liquor, rioting, and even theft; whom, notwithstanding, the peaceful Sower will follow, and, as he cuts the boundless harvest, bless.'

More legitimate and decisively authentic is Teufelsdröckh's appearance and emergence (we know not well whence) in the solitude of the North Cape, on that June Midnight. He has a 'light-blue Spanish cloak' hanging round him, as his 'most commodious, principal, indeed sole upper-garment;' and stands there, on the World-promontory, looking over the infinite Brine, like a little blue Belfry (as we figure), now motionless indeed, yet ready, if stirred, to ring quaintest changes.

'Silence as of death,' writes he; 'for Midnight, even in the Arctic latitudes, has its character: nothing but the granite cliffs ruddy-tinged, the peaceable gurgle of that slow-heaving Polar Ocean, over which

in the utmost North the great Sun hangs low and lazy, as if he too were slumbering. Yet is his cloud-couch wrought of crimson and cloth-of-gold; yet does his light stream over the mirror of waters, like a tremulous fire-pillar, shooting downwards to the abyss, and hide
5   itself under my feet. In such moments, Solitude also is invaluable; for who would speak, or be looked on, when behind him lies all Europe and Africa, fast asleep, except the watchmen; and before him the silent Immensity, and Palace of the Eternal, whereof our Sun is but a porch-lamp.
10   'Nevertheless, in this solemn moment, comes a man, or monster, scrambling from among the rock-hollows; and, shaggy, huge as the Hyperborean Bear, hails me in Russian speech: most probably, therefore, a Russian Smuggler. With courteous brevity, I signify my indifference to contraband trade, my humane intentions, yet strong wish
15   to be private. In vain: the monster, counting doubtless on his superior stature, and minded to make sport for himself, or perhaps profit, were it with murder, continues to advance; ever assailing me with his importunate train-oil breath; and now has advanced, till we stand both on the verge of the rock, the deep Sea rippling greedily down
20   below. What argument will avail? On the thick Hyperborean, cherubic reasoning, seraphic eloquence were lost. Prepared for such extremity, I, deftly enough, whisk aside one step; draw out, from my interior reservoirs, a sufficient Birmingham Horse-pistol, and say: "Be so obliging as retire, Friend (*Er ziehe sich zurück, Freund*), and
25   with promptitude!" This logic even the Hyperborean understands: fast enough, with apologetic, petitionary growl, he sidles off; and, except for suicidal, as well as homicidal purposes, need not return.
        'Such I hold to be the genuine use of Gunpowder: that it makes all men alike tall. Nay, if thou be cooler, cleverer than I, if thou have
30   more *Mind*, though all but no *Body* whatever, then canst thou kill me first, and art the taller. Hereby, at last, is the Goliath powerless, and the David resistless; savage Animalism is nothing, inventive Spiritualism is all.
        'With respect to Duels, indeed, I have my own ideas. Few things,
35   in this so surprising world, strike me with more surprise. Two little visual Spectra of men, hovering with insecure enough cohesion in the midst of the UNFATHOMABLE, and to dissolve therein, at any rate, very soon,—make pause at the distance of twelve paces asunder;

whirl round; and, simultaneously by the cunningest mechanism, explode one another into Dissolution; and off-hand become Air, and Non-extant! Deuce on it (*verdammt*)! The little spitfires!—Nay, I think with old Hugo von Trimberg: "God must needs laugh outright, could such a thing be, to see his wondrous Manikins here below."'   5

But amid these specialities, let us not forget the great generality, which is our chief quest here: How prospered the inner man of Teu-felsdröckh under so much outward shifting? Does Legion still lurk in him, though repressed; or has he exorcised that Devil's Brood? We   10
can answer that the symptoms continue promising. Experience is the grand spiritual Doctor; and with him Teufelsdröckh has now been long a patient, swallowing many a bitter bolus. Unless our poor Friend belong to the numerous class of Incurables, which seems not likely, some cure will doubtless be effected. We should rather say that Le-   15
gion, or the Satanic School, was now pretty well extirpated and cast out, but next to nothing introduced in its room; whereby the heart remains, for the while, in a quiet but no comfortable state.

'At length, after so much roasting,' thus writes our Autobiogra-pher, 'I was what you might name calcined. Pray only that it be not   20
rather, as is the more frequent issue, reduced to a *caput-mortuum!* But in any case, by mere dint of practice, I had grown familiar with many things. Wretchedness was still wretched; but I could now partly see through it, and despise it. Which highest mortal, in this inane Existence, had I not found a Shadow-hunter, or Shadow-hunted;   25
and, when I looked through his brave garnitures, miserable enough? Thy wishes have all been sniffed aside, thought I: but what, had they even been all granted! Did not the Boy Alexander weep because he had not two Planets to conquer; or a whole Solar System; or after that, a whole Universe? *Ach Gott!* when I gazed into these Stars, have   30
they not looked down on me as if with pity, from their serene spaces; like Eyes glistening with heavenly tears over the little lot of man! Thousands of human generations, all as noisy as our own, have been swallowed up of Time, and there remains no wreck of them any more; and Arcturus and Orion and Sirius and the Pleiades are still   35
shining in their courses, clear and young, as when the Shepherd first noted them in the plain of Shinar. Pshaw! what is this paltry little Dog-cage of an Earth; what art thou that sittest whining there? Thou

art still Nothing, Nobody: true; but who then is Something, Somebody? For thee the Family of Man has no use; it rejects thee; thou art wholly as a dissevered limb: so be it; perhaps it is better so!'

Too heavy-laden Teufelsdröckh! Yet surely his bands are loosening; one day he will hurl the burden far from him, and bound forth free, and with a second youth.

'This,' says our Professor, 'was the CENTRE OF INDIFFERENCE I had now reached; through which whoso travels from the Negative Pole to the Positive must necessarily pass.'

CHAPTER IX.

THE EVERLASTING YEA.

'TEMPTATIONS in the Wilderness!' exclaims Teufelsdröckh: 'Have we not all to be tried with such? Not so easily can the old Adam, lodged in us by birth, be dispossessed. Our Life is compassed round with Necessity; yet is the meaning of Life itself no other than Freedom, than Voluntary Force: thus have we a warfare; in the beginning, 5 especially, a hard-fought Battle. For the God-given mandate, *Work thou in Welldoing,* lies mysteriously written, in Promethean, Prophetic Characters, in our hearts; and leaves us no rest, night or day, till it be deciphered and obeyed; till it burn forth, in our conduct, a visible, acted Gospel of Freedom. And as the clay-given mandate, *Eat thou* 10 *and be filled,* at the same time, persuasively proclaims itself through every nerve,—must not there be a confusion, a contest, before the better Influence can become the upper?

'To me nothing seems more natural than that the Son of Man, when such God-given mandate first prophetically stirs within him, 15 and the Clay must now be vanquished or vanquish,—should be carried of the spirit into grim Solitudes, and there fronting the Tempter do grimmest battle with him; defiantly setting him at nought, till he yield and fly. Name it as we choose; with or without visible Devil, whether in the natural Desart of rocks and sands, or in the popu- 20 lous, moral Desart of selfishness and baseness,—to such Temptation are we all called. Unhappy if we are not! Unhappy if we are but Half-men, in whom that divine hand-writing has never blazed forth,

137

all-subduing, in true sun-splendour; but quivers dubiously amid
meaner lights; or smoulders, in dull pain, in darkness, under earthly
vapours!—Our Wilderness is the wide World in an Atheistic Century;
our Forty Days are long years of suffering and fasting: nevertheless,
5 to these also comes an end. Yes, to me also was given, if not Victory,
yet the consciousness of Battle, and the resolve to persevere therein
while life or faculty is left. To me also, entangled in the enchanted
forests, demon-peopled, doleful of sight and of sound, it was given,
after weariest wanderings, to work out my way into the higher sunlit
10 slopes—of that Mountain which has no summit, or whose summit
is in Heaven only!'

He says elsewhere, under a less ambitious figure; as figures are,
once for all, natural to him: 'Has not thy Life been that of most
sufficient men (*tüchtigen Männer*) thou hast known in this genera-
15 tion? An outflush of foolish young Enthusiasm, like the first fallow-
crop, wherein are as many weeds as valuable herbs: this all parched
away, under the Droughts of practical and spiritual Unbelief; as Disappointment, in thought and act, often-repeated gave rise to Doubt,
and Doubt gradually settled into Denial! If I have had a second-crop,
20 and now see the perennial greensward, and sit under umbrageous
cedars, which defy all Drought (and Doubt): herein too, be the Heavens
praised, I am not without examples, and even exemplars.'

So that, for Teufelsdröckh also, there has been a 'glorious revolution:' these mad shadow-hunting and shadow-hunted Pilgrimings of
25 his were but some purifying 'Temptation in the Wilderness,' before
his apostolic work (such as it was) could begin; which Temptation is
now happily over, and the Devil once more worsted! Was 'that high
moment in the *Rue de l'Enfer*,' then, properly the turning point of
the battle; when the Fiend said, *Worship me, or be torn in shreds*, and
30 was answered valiantly with an *Apage, Satana?*—Singular Teufelsdröckh, would thou hadst told thy singular story in plain words! But
it is fruitless to look there, in those Paperbags, for such. Nothing but
innuendoes, figurative crotchets: a typical Shadow, fitfully wavering,
prophetico-satiric; no clear logical Picture. 'How paint to the sensual
35 eye,' asks he once, 'what passes in the Holy-of-Holies of Man's Soul;
in what words, known to these profane times, speak even afar off of
the Unspeakable?' We ask in turn: Why perplex these times, profane
as they are, with needless obscurity, by omission and by commission?

Not mystical only is our Professor, but whimsical; and involves himself, now more than ever, in eye-bewildering *chiaroscuro*. Successive glimpses, here faithfully imparted, our more gifted readers must endeavour to combine for their own behoof.

He says: 'The hot Harmattan-wind had raged itself out; its howl 5
went silent within me; and the long-deafened soul could now hear. I paused in my wild wanderings; and sat me down to wait, and consider; for it was as if the hour of change drew nigh. I seemed to surrender, to renounce utterly, and say: Fly, then, false shadows of Hope; I will chase you no more, I will believe you no more. And ye 10
too, haggard spectres of Fear, I care nut for you; ye too are all shadows and a lie. Let me rest here; for I am way-weary and life-weary; I will rest here, were it but to die: to die or to live is alike to me; alike insignificant.'—And again: 'Here, then, as I lay in that CENTRE OF INDIFFERENCE; cast, doubtless, by benignant upper Influ- 15
ence, into a healing sleep, the heavy dreams rolled gradually away, and I awoke to a new Heaven and a new Earth. The first preliminary moral Act, Annihilation of Self (*Selbst-tödtung*), had been happily accomplished; and my mind's eyes were now unsealed, and its hands ungyved.' 20

Might we not also conjecture that the following passage refers to his Locality, during this same 'healing sleep;' that his Pilgrim-staff lies cast aside here, on 'the high table-land;' and indeed that the repose is already taking wholesome effect on him? If it were not that the tone, in some parts, has more of riancy, even of levity, than we could 25
have expected. However, in Teufelsdröckh, there is always the strangest Dualism: light dancing, with guitar-music, will be going on in the fore-court, while by fits from within comes the faint whimpering of woe and wail. We transcribe the piece entire:

'Beautiful it was to sit there, as in my skyey Tent, musing and 30
meditating; on the high table-land, in front of the Mountains; over me, as roof, the azure Dome; and around me, for walls, four azure flowing curtains,—namely, of the Four azure Winds, on whose bottom-fringes also I have seen gilding. And then to fancy the fair Castles that stood sheltered in these Mountain hollows; with their 35
green flower-lawns, and white dames and damosels, lovely enough: or better still, the straw-roofed Cottages, wherein stood many a Mother baking bread, with her children round her:—all hidden and

protectingly folded up in the valley-folds; yet there and alive, as sure as if I beheld them. Or to see, as well as fancy, the nine Towns and Villages, that lay round my mountain-seat, which, in still weather, were wont to speak to me (by their steeple-bells) with metal tongue; and, in almost all weather, proclaimed their vitality by repeated Smoke-clouds; whereon, as on a culinary horologe, I might read the hour of the day. For it was the smoke of cookery, as kind housewives, at morning, midday, eventide, were boiling their husbands' kettles; and ever a blue pillar rose up into the air, successively or simultaneously, from each of the nine, saying, as plainly as smoke could say: Such and such a meal is getting ready here. Not uninteresting! For you have the whole Borough, with all its love-makings and scandal-mongeries, contentions and contentments, as in miniature, and could cover it all with your hat.—If, in my wide Wayfarings, I had learned to look into the business of the World in its details, here perhaps was the place for combining it into general propositions, and deducing inferences therefrom.

'Often also could I see the black Tempest marching in anger through the Distance: round some Schreckhorn, as yet grim-blue, would the eddying vapour gather, and there tumultuously eddy, and flow down like a mad witch's hair; till, after a space, it vanished, and, in the clear sunbeam, your Schreckhorn stood smiling grim-white, for the vapour had held snow. How thou fermentest and elaboratest, in thy great fermenting-vat and laboratory of an Atmosphere, of a World, O Nature!—Or what is Nature? Ha! why do I not name thee GOD? Art not thou the "Living Garment of God?" O Heavens, is it, in very deed, HE, then, that ever speaks through thee; that lives and loves in thee, that lives and loves in me?

'Fore-shadows, call them rather fore-splendours, of that Truth, and Beginning of Truths, fell mysteriously over my soul. Sweeter than Dayspring to the Shipwrecked in Nova Zembla; ah! like the mother's voice to her little child that strays bewildered, weeping, in unknown tumults; like soft streamings of celestial music to my too exasperated heart, came that Evangile. The Universe is not dead and demoniacal, a charnel-house with spectres; but godlike, and my Father's!

'With other eyes, too, could I now look upon my fellow man; with an infinite Love, an infinite Pity. Poor, wandering, wayward man! Art thou not tried, and beaten with stripes, even as I am? Ever, whether thou bear the royal mantle or the beggar's gabardine, art thou not so weary, so heavy-laden; and thy Bed of Rest is but a Grave. O my Brother, my Brother, why cannot I shelter thee in my bosom, and wipe away all tears from thy eyes!—Truly, the din of many-voiced Life, which, in this solitude, with the mind's organ, I could hear, was no longer a maddening discord, but a melting one: like inarticulate cries, and sobbings of a dumb creature, which in the ear of Heaven are prayers. The poor Earth, with her poor joys, was now my needy Mother, not my cruel Stepdame; Man, with his so mad Wants and so mean Endeavours, had become the dearer to me; and even for his sufferings and his sins, I now first named him Brother. Thus was I standing in the porch of that *"Sanctuary of Sorrow;"* by strange, steep ways, had I too been guided thither; and ere long its sacred gates would open, and the *"Divine Depth of Sorrow"* lie disclosed to me.'

The Professor says, he here first got eye on the Knot that had been strangling him, and straightway could unfasten it, and was free. 'A vain interminable controversy,' writes he, 'touching what is at present called Origin of Evil, or some such thing, arises in every soul, since the beginning of the world; and in every soul, that would pass from idle Suffering into actual Endeavouring, must first be put an end to. The most, in our time, have to go content with a simple, incomplete enough Suppression of this controversy; to a few some Solution of it is indispensable. In every new era, too, such Solution comes out in different terms; and ever the Solution of the last era has become obsolete, and is found unserviceable. For it is man's nature to change his Dialect from century to century; he cannot help it though he would. The authentic *Church-Catechism* of our present century has not yet fallen into my hands: meanwhile, for my own private behoof, I attempt to elucidate the matter so. Man's Unhappiness, as I construe, comes of his Greatness; it is because there is an Infinite in him, which with all his cunning he cannot quite bury under the Finite. Will the whole Finance Ministers and Upholsterers and Confectioners of modern Europe undertake, in joint-stock company, to make one Shoeblack HAPPY? They cannot accomplish it, above an hour or two; for the Shoeblack also has a Soul quite other than his Stomach; and would require, if you consider it, for his permanent satisfaction and saturation, simply this allotment, no more, and no less: *God's infinite*

Universe altogether to himself, therein to enjoy infinitely, and fill every wish as fast as it rose. Oceans of Hochheimer, a Throat like that of Ophiuchus! speak not of them; to the infinite Shoeblack they are as nothing. No sooner is your ocean filled, than he grumbles that it
5 might have been of better vintage. Try him with half of a Universe, of an Omnipotence, he sets to quarrelling with the proprietor of the other half, and declares himself the most maltreated of men.—Always there is a black spot in our sunshine: it is even, as I said, the *Shadow of Ourselves.*
10   'But the whim we have of Happiness is somewhat thus. By certain valuations, and averages, of our own striking, we come upon some sort of average terrestrial lot; this we fancy belongs to us by nature, and of indefeasible right. It is simple payment of our wages, of our deserts; requires neither thanks nor complaint: only such *overplus* as
15 there may be do we account Happiness; any *deficit* again is Misery. Now consider that we have the valuation of our own deserts ourselves, and what a fund of Self-conceit there is in each of us,—do you wonder that the balance should so often dip the wrong way, and many a Blockhead cry: See there, what a payment; was ever worthy
20 gentleman so used!—I tell thee, Blockhead, it all comes of thy Vanity; of what thou *fanciest* those same deserts of thine to be. Fancy that thou deservest to be hanged (as is most likely), thou wilt feel it happiness to be only shot: fancy that thou deservest to be hanged in a hair-halter, it will be a luxury to die in hemp.
25   'So true is it, what I then said, that *the Fraction of Life can be increased in value not so much by increasing your Numerator, as by lessening your Denominator.* Nay, unless my Algebra deceive me, *Unity* itself divided by *Zero* will give *Infinity.* Make thy claim of wages a zero, then; thou hast the world under thy feet. Well did the Wisest
30 of our time write: "It is only with Renunciation (*Entsagen*) that Life, properly speaking, can be said to begin."
       'I asked myself: What is this that, ever since earliest years, thou hast been fretting and fuming, and lamenting and self-tormenting, on account of? Say it in a word: is it not because thou art not HAPPY?
35 Because the THOU (sweet gentleman) is not sufficiently honoured, nourished, soft-bedded, and lovingly cared for? Foolish soul! What Act of Legislature was there that *thou* shouldst be Happy? A little while ago thou hadst no right to *be* at all. What if thou wert born and

predestined not to be Happy, but to be Unhappy! Art thou nothing other than a Vulture, then, that fliest through the Universe seeking after somewhat to *eat;* and shrieking dolefully because carrion enough is not given thee? Close thy *Byron;* open thy *Goethe.*'

'*Es leuchtet mir ein,* I see a glimpse of it!' cries he elsewhere: 'there is in man a HIGHER than Love of Happiness: he can do without Happiness, and instead thereof find Blessedness! Was it not to preach forth this same HIGHER that sages and martyrs, the Poet and the Priest, in all times, have spoken and suffered; bearing testimony, through life and through death, of the Godlike that is in Man, and how in the Godlike only has he Strength and Freedom? Which God-inspired Doctrine art thou also honoured to be taught; O Heavens! and broken with manifold merciful Afflictions, even till thou become contrite, and learn it! O thank thy Destiny for these; thankfully bear what yet remain: thou hadst need of them; the Self in thee needed to be annihilated. By benignant fever-paroxysms is Life rooting out the deep-seated chronic Disease, and triumphs over Death. On the roaring billows of Time, thou art not engulphed, but borne aloft into the azure of Eternity. Love not Pleasure; love God. This is the EVERLASTING YEA, wherein all contradiction is solved; wherein whoso walks and works, it is well with him.'

And again: 'Small is it that thou canst trample the Earth with its injuries under thy feet, as old Greek Zeno trained thee: thou canst love the Earth while it injures thee, and even because it injures thee; for this a Greater than Zeno was needed, and he too was sent. Knowest thou that "*Worship of Sorrow?*" The Temple thereof, founded some eighteen centuries ago, now lies in ruins, overgrown with jungle, the habitation of doleful creatures: nevertheless, venture forward; in a low crypt, arched out of falling fragments, thou findest the Altar still there, and its sacred Lamp perennially burning.'

Without pretending to comment on which strange utterances, the Editor will only remark, that there lies beside them much of a still more questionable character; unsuited to the general apprehension; nay wherein he himself does not see his way. Nebulous disquisitions on Religion, yet not without bursts of splendour; on the 'perennial continuance of Inspiration;' on Prophecy; that there are 'true Priests, as well as Baal-Priests, in our own day:' with more of the like sort. We select some fractions, by way of finish to this farrago.

'Cease, my much-respected Herr von Voltaire,' thus apostrophises the Professor: 'shut thy sweet voice; for the task appointed thee seems finished. Sufficiently hast thou demonstrated this proposition, considerable or otherwise: That the Mythus of the Christian Religion looks
5 not in the eighteenth century as it did in the eighth. Alas, were thy six-and-thirty quartos, and the six-and-thirty thousand other quartos and folios, and flying sheets or reams, printed before and since on the same subject, all needed to convince us of so little! But what next? Wilt thou help us to embody the divine Spirit of that Religion in a
10 new Mythus, in a new vehicle and vesture, that our Souls, otherwise too like perishing, may live? What! thou hast no faculty in that kind? Only a torch for burning, no hammer for building? Take our thanks, then, and——thyself away.

'Meanwhile what are antiquated Mythuses to me? Or is the God
15 present, felt in my own heart, a thing which Herr von Voltaire will dispute out of me; or dispute into me? To the *"Worship of Sorrow"* ascribe what origin and genesis thou pleasest, *has* not that Worship originated, and been generated; is it not *here*? Feel it in thy heart, and then say whether it is of God! This is Belief; all else is Opinion,—for
20 which latter whoso will, let him worry and be worried.'

'Neither,' observes he elsewhere, 'shall ye tear out one another's eyes, struggling over "Plenary Inspiration," and such like: try rather to get a little even Partial Inspiration, each of you for himself. One BIBLE I know, of whose Plenary Inspiration doubt is not so much as
25 possible; nay with my own eyes I saw the God's-Hand writing it: thereof all other Bibles are but Leaves,—say, in Picture-Writing to assist the weaker faculty.'

Or to give the wearied reader relief, and bring it to an end, let him take the following perhaps more intelligible passage:
30 'To me, in this our Life,' says the Professor, 'which is an internecine warfare with the Time-spirit, other warfare seems questionable. Hast thou in any way a Contention with thy brother, I advise thee, think well what the meaning thereof is. If thou gauge it to the bottom, it is simply this: "Fellow, see! thou art taking more than thy share of
35 Happiness in the world, something from *my* share: which, by the Heavens, thou shalt not; nay I will fight thee rather."—Alas! and the whole lot to be divided is such a beggarly matter, truly a "feast of shells," for the substance has been spilled out: not enough to quench

one Appetite; and the collective human species clutching at them!—
Can we not, in all such cases, rather say: "Take it, thou too-ravenous
individual; take that pitiful additional fraction of a share, which I
reckoned mine, but which thou so wantest; take it with a blessing:
would to Heaven I had enough for thee!"—If Fichte's *Wissenschaftslehre*   5
be, "to a certain extent, Applied Christianity," surely to a still greater
extent, so is this. We have here not a Whole Duty of Man, yet a Half
Duty, namely the Passive half: could we but do it, as we can demonstrate it!

'But indeed Conviction, were it never so excellent, is worthless till   10
it convert itself into Conduct. Nay properly Conviction is not possible till then; inasmuch as all Speculation is by nature endless, formless, a vortex amid vortices: only by a felt indubitable certainty of
Experience does it find any centre to revolve round, and so fashion
itself into a system. Most true is it, as a wise man teaches us, that   15
"Doubt of any sort cannot be removed except by Action." On which
ground too let him who gropes painfully in darkness or uncertain
light, and prays vehemently that the dawn may ripen into day, lay this
other precept well to heart, which to me was of invaluable service:
"*Do the Duty which lies nearest thee*," which thou knowest to be a   20
Duty! Thy second Duty will already have become clearer.

'May we not say, however, that the hour of Spiritual Enfranchise-
ment is even this: When your Ideal World, wherein the whole man
has been dimly struggling and inexpressibly languishing to work,
becomes revealed, and thrown open; and you discover, with amaze-   25
ment enough, like the Lothario in *Wilhelm Meister*, that your "America
is here or nowhere?" The Situation that has not its Duty, its Ideal,
was never yet occupied by man. Yes here, in this poor, miserable,
hampered, despicable Actual, wherein thou even now standest, here
or nowhere is thy Ideal: work it out therefrom; and working, believe,   30
live, be free. Fool! the Ideal is in thyself, the Impediment too is in
thyself: thy Condition is but the stuff thou art to shape that same
Ideal out of: what matters whether such stuff be of this sort or of
that, so the Form thou give it be heroic, be poetic? O thou that
pinest in the imprisonment of the Actual, and criest bitterly to the   35
gods for a kingdom wherein to rule and create, know this of a truth:
the thing thou seekest is already with thee, "here or nowhere," couldst
thou only see!

'But it is with man's Soul as it was with Nature: the beginning of
Creation is—Light. Till the eye have vision, the whole members are
in bonds. Divine moment, when over the tempest-tost Soul, as once
over the wild-weltering Chaos, it is spoken: Let there be Light! Ever
5 to the greatest that has felt such moment, is it not miraculous and
God-announcing; even, as under simpler figures, to the simplest and
least? The mad primeval Discord is hushed; the rudely-jumbled con-
flicting elements bind themselves into separate Firmaments: deep silent rock-foundations are built beneath; and the skyey vault with its
10 everlasting Luminaries above: instead of a dark wasteful Chaos, we
have a blooming, fertile, Heaven-encompassed World.

'I too could now say to myself: Be no longer a Chaos, but a
World, or even Worldkin. Produce! Produce! Were it but the pitifullest
infinitesimal fraction of a Product, produce it in God's name! 'Tis the
15 utmost thou hast in thee; out with it then. Up, up! Whatsoever thy
hand findeth to do, do it with thy whole might. Work while it is
called Today, for the Night cometh wherein no man can work.'

CHAPTER X.

THUS have we, as closely and perhaps satisfactorily as, in such circumstances, might be, followed Teufelsdröckh through the various
successive states and stages of Growth, Entanglement, Unbelief, and
almost Reprobation, into a certain clearer state of what he himself
seems to consider as Conversion. 'Blame not the word,' says he;   5
'rejoice rather that such a word, signifying such a thing, has come to
light in our Modern Era, though hidden from the wisest Ancients.
The Old World knew nothing of Conversion: instead of an *Ecce
Homo*, they had only some *Choice of Hercules*. It was a new-attained
progress in the Moral Development of man: hereby has the Highest   10
come home to the bosoms of the most Limited; what to Plato was
but a hallucination, and to Socrates a chimera, is now clear and
certain to your Zinzendorfs, your Wesleys, and the poorest of their
Pietists and Methodists.'

It is here then that the spiritual majority of Teufelsdröckh com-   15
mences: we are henceforth to see him 'Work in Welldoing,' with the
spirit and clear aims of a Man. He has discovered that the Ideal Workshop he so panted for, is even this same Actual ill-furnished Workshop
he has so long been stumbling in. He can say to himself: 'Tools?
Thou hast no Tools? Why, there is not a Man, or a Thing, now alive   20
but has tools. The basest of created animalcules, the Spider itself, has
a spinning-jenny, and warping-mill, and power-loom, within its head;
the stupidest of Oysters has a Papin's-Digester, with stone-and-lime
house to hold it in: every being that can live can do something; this

let him *do.*—Tools? Hast thou not a Brain, furnished, furnishable
with some glimmerings of Light; and three fingers to hold a Pen
withal? Never since Aaron's Rod went out of practice, or even before
it, was there such a wonder-working Tool: greater than all recorded
miracles have been performed by Pens. For strangely in this so solid-
seeming World, which nevertheless is in continual restless flux, it is
appointed that *Sound*, to appearance the most fleeting, should be the
most continuing of all things. The WORD is well said to be omnipotent
in this world; man, thereby divine, can create as by a *Fiat.* Awake,
arise! Speak forth what is in thee; what God has given thee, what the
Devil shall not take away. Higher task than that of Priesthood was
allotted to no man: wert thou but the meanest in that sacred Hierarchy,
is it not honour enough therein to spend and be spent?

'By this Art, which whoso will may sacrilegiously degrade into a
handicraft,' adds Teufelsdröckh, 'have I thenceforth abidden. Writings of mine, not indeed known as mine (for what am *I*?), have fallen,
perhaps not altogether void, into the mighty seedfield of Opinion;
fruits of my unseen sowing gratifyingly meet me here and there. I
thank the Heavens that I have now found my Calling; wherein, with
or without perceptible result, I am minded diligently to persevere.

'Nay how knowest thou,' cries he, 'but this and the other pregnant
Device, now grown to be a world-renowned far-working Institution;
like a grain of right mustard-seed once cast into the right soil, and
now stretching out strong boughs to the four winds, for the birds of
the air to lodge in,—may have been properly my doing? Some one's
doing it without doubt was; from some Idea in some single Head it
did first of all take beginning: why not from some Idea in mine?' Does
Teufelsdröckh here glance at that 'SOCIETY FOR THE CONSERVATION OF
PROPERTY (*Eigenthums-conservirende Gesellschaft*),' of which so many
ambiguous notices glide spectre-like through these inexpressible
Paperbags? 'An Institution,' hints he, 'not unsuitable to the wants of
the time; as indeed such sudden extension proves: for already can the
Society number, among its office-bearers or corresponding members,
the highest Names, if not the highest Persons, in Germany, England,
France; and contributions, both of money and of meditation, pour in
from all quarters; to, if possible, enlist the remaining Integrity of the
world, and, defensively and with forethought, marshal it round this
Palladium.' Does Teufelsdröckh mean, then, to give himself out as the

originator of that so notable *Eigenthums-conservirende* ('Owndom-conserving') *Gesellschaft;* and, if so, what, in the Devil's name, is it? He again hints: 'At a time when the divine Commandment, *Thou shalt not steal,* wherein truly, if well understood, is comprised the whole Hebrew Decalogue, with Solon's and Lycurgus's Constitutions, Justinian's   5
Pandects, the Code Napoléon, and all Codes, Catechisms, Divinities, Moralities whatsoever, that man has hitherto devised (and enforced with Altar-fire and Gallows-ropes) for his social guidance: at a time, I say, when this divine Commandment has all but faded away from the general remembrance; and, with little disguise, a new opposite Commandment,   10
Thou shalt steal, is every where promulgated,—it perhaps behoved, in this universal dotage and deliration, the sound portion of mankind to bestir themselves and rally. When the widest and wildest violations of that divine right of Property, the only divine right now extant or con-ceivable, are sanctioned and recommended by a vicious Press, and the   15
world has lived to hear it asserted that *we have no Property in our very Bodies, but only an accidental Possession, and Life-rent,* what is the issue to be looked for? Hangmen and Catchpoles may, by their noose-gins and baited fall-traps, keep down the smaller sort of vermin: but what, except perhaps some such Universal Association, can protect us against whole   20
meat-devouring and man-devouring hosts of Boa-constrictors? If, there-fore, the more sequestered Thinker have wondered, in his privacy, from what hand that perhaps not ill-written *Program* in the Public Journals, with its high *Prize-Questions* and so liberal *Prizes,* could have proceeded,— let him now cease such wonder; and, with undivided faculty, betake   25
himself to the *Concurrenz* (Competition).'

We ask: Has this same 'perhaps not ill-written *Program*,' or any other authentic Transaction of that Property-conserving Society, fallen under the eye of the British Reader, in any Journal, foreign or domes-tic? If so, what are those *Prize-Questions;* what are the terms of   30
Competition, and when, and where? No printed Newspaper leaf, no farther light of any sort, to be met with in these Paperbags! Or is the whole business one other of those whimsicalities, and perverse inex-plicabilities, whereby Herr Teufelsdröckh, meaning much or nothing, is pleased so often to play fast and loose with us?   35

Here, indeed, at length, must the Editor give utterance to a pain-ful suspicion which, through late Chapters, has begun to haunt him;

paralysing any little enthusiasm, that might still have rendered his
thorny Biographical task a labour of love. It is a suspicion grounded
perhaps on trifles, yet confirmed almost into certainty by the more
and more discernible humoristico-satirical tendency of Teufelsdröckh,
5   in whom underground humours, and intricate sardonic rogueries,
wheel within wheel, defy all reckoning: a suspicion, in one word, that
these Autobiographical Documents are partly a Mystification! What if
many a so-called Fact were little better than a Fiction; if here we had
no direct Camera-obscura Picture of the Professor's History; but only
10   some more or less fantastic Adumbration, symbolically, perhaps significantly enough, shadowing forth the same! Our theory begins to
be that, in receiving as literally authentic what was but hieroglyphi-
cally so, Hofrath Heuschrecke, whom in that case we scruple not to
name Hofrath Nose-of-Wax, was made a fool of, and set adrift to
15   make fools of others. Could it be expected, indeed, that a man so
known for impenetrable reticence as Teufelsdröckh, would all at once
frankly unlock his private citadel to an English Editor and a German
Hofrath; and not rather deceptively *in*lock both Editor and Hofrath,
in the labyrinthic tortuosities and covered ways of said citadel (having
20   enticed them thither), to see, in his half-devilish way, how the fools
would look?

Of one fool, however, the Herr Professor will perhaps find himself
short. On a small slip, formerly thrown aside as blank, the ink being
all but invisible, we lately notice, and with effort decipher, the fol-
25   lowing: 'What are your historical Facts; still more your biographical?
Wilt thou know a Man, above all, a Mankind, by stringing together
beadrolls of what thou namest Facts? The Man is the spirit he worked
in; not what he did, but what he became. Facts are engraved
Hierograms, for which the fewest have the key. And then how your
30   Blockhead (*Dummkopf*) studies not their Meaning; but simply whether
they are well or ill cut, what he calls Moral or Immoral! Still worse
is it with your Bungler (*Pfuscher*): such I have seen reading some
Rousseau, with pretences of interpretation; and mistaking the ill-cut
Serpent-of-Eternity for a common poisonous Reptile.' Was the Pro-
35   fessor apprehensive lest an Editor, selected as the present boasts himself, might mistake the Teufelsdröckh Serpent-of-Eternity in like
manner? For which reason it was to be altered, not without underhand satire, into a plainer Symbol? Or is this merely one of his

half-sophisms, half-truisms, which if he can but set on the back of a
Figure, he cares not whither it gallop? We say not with certainty; and
indeed, so strange is the Professor, can never say. If our Suspicion be
wholly unfounded, let his own questionable ways, not our necessary
circumspectness, bear the blame.   5

But be this as it will, the somewhat exasperated and indeed exhausted
Editor determines here to shut these Paperbags, for the present. Let
it suffice that we know of Teufelsdröckh, so far, if 'not what he did,
yet what he became:' the rather, as his character has now taken its
ultimate bent, and no new revolution, of importance, is to be looked   10
for. The imprisoned Chrysalis is now a winged Psyche; and such, wheresoever be its flight, it will continue. To trace by what complex gyra-
tions (flights or involuntary waftings) through the mere external
Life-element, Teufelsdröckh reaches his University Professorship, and
the Psyche clothes herself in civic Titles, without altering her now fixed 15
nature,—would be comparatively an unproductive task; were we even
unsuspicious of its being, for us at least, a false and impossible one.
His outward Biography, therefore, which, at the Blumine Lover's-Leap,
we saw churned utterly into spray-vapour, may hover in that condition, for aught that concerns us here. Enough that by survey of cer-   20
tain 'pools and plashes,' we have ascertained its general direction: do
we not already know that, by one way and other, it *has* long since
rained down again into a stream; and even now, at Weissnichtwo, flows
deep and still, fraught with the *Philosophy of Clothes*, and visible to whoso
will cast eye thereon? Over much invaluable matter that lies scattered,   25
like jewels among quarry-rubbish, in those Paper-catacombs, we may
have occasion to glance back, and somewhat will demand insertion at
the right place: meanwhile be our toilsome diggings therein suspended.

If now, before reopening the great *Clothes-Volume*, we ask what
our degree of progress, during these Ten Chapters, has been, towards   30
right understanding of the *Clothes-Philosophy*, let not our discourage-
ment become total. To speak in that old figure of the Hell-gate
Bridge over Chaos, a few flying pontoons have perhaps been added,
though as yet they drift straggling on the Flood; how far they will
reach, when once the chains are straightened and fastened, can, at   35
present, only be matter of conjecture.

So much we already calculate. Through many a little loophole, we
have had glimpses into the internal world of Teufelsdröckh: his strange

mystic, almost magic Diagram of the Universe, and how it was gradually drawn, is not henceforth altogether dark to us. Those mysterious ideas on TIME, which merit consideration, and are not wholly unintelligible with such, may by and by prove significant. Still more may his somewhat peculiar view of Nature; the decisive Oneness he ascribes to Nature. How all Nature and Life are but one *Garment*, a 'Living Garment,' woven and ever a-weaving in the 'Loom of Time:' is not here, indeed, the outline of a whole *Clothes-Philosophy;* at least the arena it is to work in? Remark too that the Character of the man, nowise without meaning in such a matter, becomes less enigmatic: amid so much tumultuous obscurity, almost like diluted madness, do not a certain indomitable Defiance and yet a boundless Reverence seem to loom forth, as the two mountain-summits, on whose rock-strata all the rest were based and built?

Nay farther, may we not say that Teufelsdröckh's Biography, allowing it even, as suspected, only a hieroglyphical truth, exhibits a man, as it were preappointed for Clothes-Philosophy? To look through the Shows of things into Things themselves he is led and compelled. The 'Passivity' given him by birth is fostered by all turns of his fortune. Everywhere cast out, like oil out of water, from mingling in any Employment, in any public Communion, he has no portion but Solitude, and a life of Meditation. The whole energy of his existence is directed, through long years, on one task: that of enduring pain, if he cannot cure it. Thus everywhere do the Shows of things oppress him, withstand him, threaten him with fearfullest destruction: only by victoriously penetrating into Things themselves, can he find peace and a stronghold. But is not this same looking through the Shows, or Vestures, into the Things, even the first preliminary to a *Philosophy of Clothes?* Do we not, in all this, discern some beckonings towards the true higher purport of such a Philosophy; and what shape it must assume with such a man, in such an era?

Perhaps in entering on Book Third, the courteous Reader is not utterly without guess whither he is bound: nor, let us hope, for all the fantastic Dream-Grottoes through which, as is our lot with Teufelsdröckh, he must wander, will there be wanting between whiles some twinkling of a steady Polar Star.

BOOK III.

CHAPTER I.

INCIDENT IN MODERN HISTORY.

As a wonder-loving and wonder-seeking man, Teufelsdröckh, from an early part of this Clothes-Volume, has more and more exhibited himself. Striking it was, amid all his perverse cloudiness, with what force of vision and of heart he pierced into the mystery of the World; recognising in the highest sensible phenomena, so far as Sense went,   5 only fresh or faded Raiment; yet ever, under this, a celestial Essence thereby rendered visible: and while, on the one hand, he trod the old rags of Matter, with their tinsels, into the mire, he on the other every where exalted Spirit above all earthly principalities and powers, and worshipped it, though under the meanest shapes, with a true Platonic   10 Mysticism. What the man ultimately purposed by thus casting his Greek-fire into the general Wardrobe of the Universe; what such more or less complete rending and burning of Garments throughout the whole compass of Civilised Life and Speculation, should lead to; the rather as he was no Adamite, in any sense, and could not, like   15 Rousseau, recommend either bodily or intellectual Nudity, and a return to the savage state: all this our readers are now bent to discover; this is, in fact, properly the gist and purport of Professor Teufelsdröckh's Philosophy of Clothes.

Be it remembered, however, that such purport is here not so much   20 evolved as detected to lie ready for evolving. We are to guide our British Friends into the new Gold-country, and shew them the mines; nowise to dig out and exhaust its wealth, which indeed remains for

153

all time inexhaustible. Once there, let each dig for his own behoof, and enrich himself.

Neither, in so capricious inexpressible a Work as this of the Professor's, can our course now more than formerly be straightforward, step by step, but at best leap by leap. Significant Indications stand out here and there; which for the critical eye, that looks both widely and narrowly, shape themselves into some ground-scheme of a Whole: to select these with judgement, so that a leap from one to the other be possible; and (in our old figure) by chaining them together, a passable Bridge be effected: this, as heretofore, continues our only method. Among such light-spots, the following, floating in much wild matter about *Perfectibility*, has seemed worth clutching at:

'Perhaps the most remarkable incident in Modern History,' says Teufelsdröckh, 'is not the Diet of Worms, still less the Battle of Austerlitz, Waterloo, Peterloo, or any other Battle; but an incident passed carelessly over by most Historians, and treated with some degree of ridicule by others; namely, George Fox's making to himself a Suit of Leather. This man, the first of the Quakers, and by trade a Shoemaker, was one of those, to whom, under ruder or purer form, the Divine Idea of the Universe is pleased to manifest itself; and, across all the hulls of Ignorance and earthly Degradation, shine through, in unspeakable Awfulness, unspeakable Beauty, on their souls: who therefore are rightly accounted Prophets, God-possessed; or even Gods, as in some periods it has chanced. Sitting in his stall; working on tanned hides, amid pincers, paste-horns, rosin, swine-bristles, and a nameless flood of rubbish, this youth had nevertheless a Living Spirit belonging to him; also an antique Inspired Volume, through which, as through a window, it could look upwards, and discern its celestial Home. The task of a daily pair of shoes, coupled even with some prospect of victuals, and an honourable Mastership in Cordwainery, and perhaps the post of Thirdborough in his Hundred, as the crown of long faithful sewing,—was nowise satisfaction enough to such a mind: but ever amid the boring and hammering, came tones from that far country, came Splendours and Terrors; for this poor Cordwainer, as we said, was a Man; and the Temple of Immensity, wherein as Man he had been sent to minister, was full of holy mystery to him.

'The Clergy of the neighbourhood, the ordained Watchers and Interpreters of that same holy mystery, listened with unaffected tedium to his consultations, and advised him, as the solution of such doubts, to "drink beer, and dance with the girls." Blind leaders of the blind! For what end were their tithes levied and eaten; for what were their shovel-hats scooped out, and their surplices and cassock-aprons girt on; and such a church-repairing, and chaffering, and organing, and other racketing, held over that spot of God's Earth,—if Man were but a Patent Digester, and the Belly with its adjuncts the grand Reality? Fox turned from them, with tears and a sacred scorn, back to his Leather-parings and his Bible. Mountains of encumbrance, higher than Ætna, had been heaped over that Spirit: but it was a Spirit, and would not lie buried there. Through long days and nights of silent agony, it struggled and wrestled, with a man's force, to be free: how its prison-mountains heaved and swayed tumultuously, as the giant spirit shook them to this hand and that, and emerged into the light of Heaven! That Leicester shoe-shop, had men known it, was a holier place than any Vatican or Loretto-shrine.—"So bandaged, and hampered, and hemmed in," groaned he, "with thousand requisitions, obligations, straps, tatters, and tagrags, I can neither see nor move: not my own am I, but the World's; and Time flies fast, and Heaven is high, and Hell is deep: Man! bethink thee, if thou hast power of Thought! Why not; what binds me here? Want, want!—Ha, of what? Will all the shoe-wages under the Moon ferry me across into that far Land of Light? Only Meditation can, and devout Prayer to God. I will to the woods: the hollow of a tree will lodge me, wild berries feed me; and for Clothes, cannot I stitch myself one perennial Suit of Leather!"

'Historical Oil-painting,' continues Teufelsdröckh, 'is one of the Arts I never practised; therefore shall I not decide whether this sub-ject were easy of execution on the canvass. Yet often has it seemed to me as if such first outflashing of man's Freewill, to lighten, more and more into Day, the Chaotic Night that threatened to engulph him in its hindrances and its horrors, were properly the only grandeur there is in History. Let some living Angelo or Rosa, with seeing eye and understanding heart, picture George Fox on that morning, when he spreads out his cutting-board for the last time, and cuts cow-hides by unwonted patterns, and stitches them together into one continuous all-including Case, the farewell service of his awl! Stitch away, thou noble Fox: every prick of that little instrument is pricking into the heart of Slavery, and World-worship, and the Mammon-god. Thy elbows jerk, as in strong swimmer-strokes, and every stroke is bearing thee across the Prison-ditch, within which Vanity holds her Work-house and Ragfair, into lands of true Liberty; were the work done, there is in broad Europe one Free Man, and thou art he!

'Thus from the lowest depth there is a path to the loftiest height; and for the Poor also a Gospel has been published. Surely, if, as D'Alembert asserts, my illustrious namesake, Diogenes, was the greatest man of Antiquity, only that he wanted Decency, then by stronger reason is George Fox the greatest of the Moderns; and greater than Diogenes himself: for he too stands on the adamantine basis of his Manhood, casting aside all props and shoars; yet not, in half-savage Pride, undervaluing the Earth; valuing it rather, as a place to yield him warmth and food, he looks Heavenward from his Earth, and dwells in an element of Mercy and Worship, with a still Strength, such as the Cynic's Tub did nowise witness. Great, truly, was that Tub; a temple from which man's dignity and divinity was scornfully preached abroad: but greater is the Leather Hull, for the same sermon was preached there, and not in Scorn but in Love.'

George Fox's 'perennial suit,' with all that it held, has been worn quite into ashes for nigh two centuries: why, in a discussion on the *Perfectibility of Society*, reproduce it now? Not out of blind sectarian partisanship: Teufelsdröckh himself is no Quaker; with all his pacific tendencies, did not we see him, in that scene at the North Cape, with the Archangel Smuggler, exhibit fire-arms?

For us, aware of his deep Sansculottism, there is more meant in this passage than meets the ear. At the same time, who can avoid smiling at the earnestness and Bœotian simplicity (if indeed there be not an underhand satire in it), with which that 'Incident' is here brought forward; and, in the Professor's ambiguous way, as clearly perhaps as he durst in Weissnichtwo, recommended to imitation! Does Teufelsdröckh anticipate that, in this age of refinement, any considerable class of the community, by way of testifying against the 'Mammon-god,' and escaping from what he calls 'Vanity's Workhouse and Ragfair,' where doubtless some of them are toiled and whipped and hoodwinked sufficiently,—will sheathe themselves in close-fitting cases of Leather? The idea is ridiculous in the extreme. Will Majesty lay aside its robes of state, and Beauty its frills, and train-gowns, for a second-skin of tanned hide? By which change Huddersfield and Manchester, and Coventry and Paisley, and the Fancy-Bazaar, were reduced to hungry solitudes; and only Day and Martin could profit. For neither would Teufelsdröckh's mad daydream, here as we presume covertly intended, of levelling Society (*levelling* it indeed with a vengeance, into one huge drowned marsh!), and so attaining the political effects of Nudity without its frigorific or other consequences,—be thereby realized. Would not the rich man purchase a waterproof suit of Russia Leather; and the highborn Belle step forth in red or azure morocco, lined with shamoy: the black cowhide being left to the Drudges and Gibeonites of the world; and so all the old Distinctions be re-established?

Or has the Professor his own deeper intention; and laughs in his sleeve at our strictures and glosses, which indeed are but a part thereof?

CHAPTER II.

CHURCH-CLOTHES.

NOT less questionable is his Chapter on *Church-Clothes*, which has the farther distinction of being the shortest in the Volume. We here translate it entire:

'By Church-Clothes, it need not be premised, that I mean infinitely
5 more than Cassocks and Surplices; and do not at all mean the mere haberdasher Sunday Clothes that men go to Church in. Far from it! Church-Clothes are, in our vocabulary, the Forms, the *Vestures*, under which men have at various periods embodied and represented for themselves the Religious Principle; that is to say, invested the Divine
10 Idea of the World with a sensible and practically active Body, so that it might dwell among them as a living and life-giving WORD.

'These are unspeakably the most important of all the vestures and garnitures of Human Existence. They are first spun and woven, I may say, by that wonder of wonders, SOCIETY; for it is still only when "two
15 or three are gathered together" that Religion, spiritually existent, and indeed indestructible however latent, in each, first outwardly manifests itself (as with "cloven tongues of fire"), and seeks to be embodied in a visible Communion and Church Militant. Mystical, more than magical, is that Communing of Soul with Soul, both
20 looking heavenward: here properly Soul first speaks with Soul; for only in looking heavenward, take it in what sense you may, not in looking earthward, does what we can call Union, mutual Love, Society, begin to be possible. How true is that of Novalis: "It is certain,

my Belief gains quite *infinitely* the moment I can convince another mind thereof!" Gaze thou in the face of thy Brother, in those eyes where plays the lambent fire of Kindness, or in those where rages the lurid conflagration of Anger; feel how thy own so quiet Soul is straight-way involuntarily kindled with the like, and ye blaze and reverberate on each other, till it is all one limitless confluent flame (of embracing Love, or of deadly-grappling Hate); and then say what miraculous virtue goes out of man into man. But if so, through all the thick-plied hulls of our Earthly Life; how much more when it is of the Divine Life we speak, and inmost ME is, as it were, brought into contact with inmost ME!

'Thus was it that I said, the Church-Clothes are first spun and woven by Society; outward Religion originates by Society, Society becomes possible by Religion. Nay, perhaps every conceivable Society, past and present, may well be figured as properly and wholly a Church, in one or other of these three predicaments: an audibly preaching and prophesying Church, which is the best; second, a Church that struggles to preach and prophesy, but cannot as yet, till its Pentecost come; and third and worst, a Church gone dumb with old age, or which only mumbles delirium prior to dissolution. Whoso fancies that by Church is here meant Chapterhouses and Cathedrals, or by preaching and prophesying, mere speech and chaunting, let him,' says the oracular Professor, 'read on light of heart (*getrosten Muthes*).

'But with regard to your Church proper, and the Church-Clothes specially recognised as Church-Clothes, I remark, fearlessly enough, that without such Vestures and sacred Tissues Society has not existed, and will not exist. For if Government is, so to speak, the outward SKIN of the Body Politic, holding the whole together and protecting it; and all your Craft-Guilds, and Associations for Industry, of hand or of head, are the Fleshly Clothes, the muscular and osseous Tissues (lying *under* such SKIN), whereby Society stands and works;—then is Religion the inmost Pericardial and Nervous Tissue, which ministers Life and warm Circulation to the whole. Without which Pericardial Tissue the Bones and Muscles (of Industry) were inert, or animated only by a Galvanic vitality; the SKIN would become a shrivelled pelt, or fast-rotting raw-hide; and Society itself a dead carcass,—deserving to be buried. Men were no longer Social, but Gregarious; which latter state also could not continue, but must gradually issue in universal selfish discord, hatred, savage isolation, and dispersion;—whereby, as we might continue to say, the very dust and dead body of Society would have evaporated and become abolished. Such, and so all-important, all-sustaining, are the Church-Clothes, to civilised or even to rational man.

'Meanwhile, in our era of the World, those same Church-Clothes have gone sorrowfully out at elbows: nay, far worse, many of them have become mere hollow Shapes, or Masks, under which no living Figure or Spirit any longer dwells; but only spiders and unclean beetles, in horrid accumulation, drive their trade; and the Mask still glares on you with its glass-eyes, in ghastly affectation of Life,—some generation and half after Religion has quite withdrawn from it, and in unnoticed nooks is weaving for herself new Vestures, wherewith to reappear, and bless us, or our sons or grandsons. As a Priest, or Interpreter of the Holy, is the noblest and highest of all men, so is a Sham-priest (*Scheinpriester*) the falsest and basest: neither is it doubtful that his Canonicals, were they Popes' Tiaras, will one day be torn from him, to make bandages for the wounds of mankind; or even to burn into tinder, for general scientific or culinary purposes.

'All which, as out of place here, falls to be handled in my Second Volume, *On the Palingenesia, or Newbirth of Society;* which volume, as treating practically of the Wear, Destruction, and Re-texture of Spiritual Tissues, or Garments, forms, properly speaking, the Transcendental or ultimate Portion of this my Work *on Clothes*, and is already in a state of forwardness.'

And herewith, no farther exposition, note, or commentary being added, does Teufelsdröckh, and must his Editor now, terminate the Singular Chapter on Church-Clothes!

CHAPTER III.

PROBABLY it will elucidate the drift of these foregoing obscure utterances, if we here insert somewhat of our Professor's speculations on *Symbols*. To state his whole doctrine, indeed, were beyond our compass: nowhere is he more mysterious, impalpable, than in this of 'Fantasy being the organ of the Godlike;' and how 'Man thereby, 5 though based, to all seeming, on the small Visible, does nevertheless extend down into the infinite deeps of the Invisible, of which Invisible, indeed, his Life is properly the bodying forth.' Let us, omitting these high transcendental aspects of the matter, study to glean (whether from the Paperbags or the Printed Volume) what little seems logical 10 and practical, and cunningly arrange it into such degree of coherence as it will assume. By way of proem, take the following not injudicious remarks:

'The benignant efficacies of Concealment,' cries our Professor, 'who shall speak or sing? SILENCE and SECRECY! Altars might still be 15 raised to them (were this an altar-building time) for universal worship. Silence is the element in which great things fashion themselves together; that at length they may emerge, full-formed and majestic, into the daylight of Life, which they are thenceforth to rule. Not William the Silent only, but all the considerable men I have known, 20 and the most undiplomatic and unstrategic of these, forbore to babble of what they were creating and projecting. Nay, in thy own mean perplexities, do thou thyself but *hold thy tongue for one day:* on the

161

morrow, how much clearer are thy purposes, and duties; what wreck and rubbish have those mute workmen within thee swept away, when intrusive noises were shut out! Speech is too often not, as the Frenchman defined it, the art of concealing Thought; but of quite stifling and suspending Thought, so that there is none to conceal. Speech too is great, but not the greatest. As the Swiss Inscription says: *Sprechen ist silbern, Schweigen ist golden* (Speech is silvern, Silence is golden); or as I might rather express it: Speech is of Time, Silence is of Eternity.

'Bees will not work except in darkness; Thought will not work except in Silence: neither will Virtue work except in Secrecy. Let not thy right hand know what thy left hand doeth! Neither shalt thou prate even to thy own heart of "those secrets known to all." Is not Shame (*Schaam*) the soil of all Virtue, of all good manners, and good morals? Like other plants, Virtue will not grow unless its root be hidden, buried from the eye of the sun. Let the Sun shine on it, nay, do but look at it privily thyself, the root withers, and no flower will glad thee. O my Friends, when we view the fair clustering flowers that over-wreathe, for example, the Marriage-bower, and encircle man's life with the fragrance and hues of Heaven, what hand will not smite the foul plunderer that grubs them up by the roots, and, with grinning, grunting satisfaction, shews us the dung they flourish in! Men speak much of the Printing Press with its Newspapers: *du Himmel!* what are these to Clothes and the Tailor's Goose?'

'Of kin to the so incalculable influences of Concealment, and connected with still greater things, is the wondrous agency of *Symbols*. In a Symbol there is concealment and yet revelation: here, therefore, by Silence and by Speech acting together, comes a doubled significance. And if both the Speech be itself high, and the Silence fit and noble, how expressive will their union be! Thus in many a painted Device, or simple Seal-emblem, the commonest Truth stands out to us proclaimed with quite new emphasis.

'For it is here that Fantasy with her mystic wonderland plays into the small prose domain of Sense, and becomes incorporated therewith. In the Symbol proper, what we can call a Symbol, there is ever, more or less distinctly and directly, some embodiment and revelation of the Infinite; the Infinite is made to blend itself with the Finite, to stand visible, and as it were attainable, there. By Symbols, accordingly, is man guided and commanded, made happy, made wretched. He everywhere finds himself encompassed with Symbols, recognised

as such or not recognised: the Universe is but one vast Symbol of
God; nay, if thou wilt have it, what is man himself but a Symbol of
God; is not all that he does symbolical; a revelation to Sense of the
mystic god-given Force that is in him; a "Gospel of Freedom," which
he, the "Messias of Nature," preaches, as he can, by act and word?   5
Not a Hut he builds but is the visible embodiment of a Thought; but
bears visible record of invisible things; but is, in the transcendental
sense, symbolical as well as real.'

'Man,' says the Professor elsewhere, in quite antipodal contrast
with these high-soaring delineations, which we have here cut short on   10
the verge of the inane, 'man is by birth somewhat of an owl. Perhaps
too of all the owleries that ever possessed him, the most owlish, if we
consider it, is that of your actually existing Motive-Millwrights. Fantastic tricks enough has man played, in his time; has fancied himself
to be most things, down even to an animated heap of Glass: but to   15
fancy himself a dead Iron-Balance for weighing Pains and Pleasures
on, was reserved for this his latter era. There stands he, his Universe
one huge Manger, filled with hay and thistles to be weighed against
each other; and looks long-eared enough. Alas, poor devil! spectres
are appointed to haunt him: one age, he is hagridden, bewitched; the   20
next, priestridden, befooled; in all ages, bedevilled. And now the
Genius of Mechanism smothers him worse than any Nightmare did;
till the Soul is nigh choked out of him, and only a kind of Digestive,
Mechanic life remains. In Earth and in Heaven he can see nothing
but Mechanism; has fear for nothing else, hope in nothing else: the   25
world would indeed grind him to pieces; but cannot he fathom the
Doctrine of Motives, and cunningly compute these and mechanise
them to grind the other way?

'Were he not, as has been said, purblinded by enchantment, you
had but to bid him open his eyes and look. In which country, in which   30
time, was it hitherto that man's history, or the history of any man,
went on by calculated or calculable "Motives?" What make ye of your
Christianities, and Chivalries, and Reformations, and Marseillese Hymns,
and Reigns of Terror? Nay, has not perhaps the Motive-grinder himself been in Love? Did he never stand so much as a contested Election?   35
Leave him to Time, and the medicating virtue of Nature.'

'Yes, Friends,' elsewhere observes the Professor, 'not our Logical,
Mensurative faculty, but our Imaginative one is King over us; I might
say, Priest and Prophet to lead us heavenward; or Magician and Wizard

to lead us hellward. Nay, even for the basest Sensualist, what is Sense but the implement of Fantasy; the vessel it drinks out of? Ever in the dullest existence, there is a sheen either of Inspiration or of Madness (thou partly hast it in thy choice, which of the two) that gleams in from the circumambient Eternity, and colours with its own hues our little islet of Time. The Understanding is indeed thy window, too clear thou canst not make it; but Fantasy is thy eye, with its colour-giving retina, healthy or diseased. Have not I myself known five hundred living soldiers sabred into crows' meat, for a piece of glazed cotton, which they called their Flag; which, had you sold it at any market-cross, would not have brought above three groschen? Did not the whole Hungarian Nation rise, like some tumultuous moon-stirred Atlantic, when Kaiser Joseph pocketed their Iron Crown; an implement, as was sagaciously observed, in size and commercial value, little differing from a horse-shoe? It is in and through *Symbols* that man, consciously or unconsciously, lives, works, and has his being: those ages, moreover, are accounted the noblest which can the best recognise symbolical worth, and prize it the highest. For is not a Symbol ever, to him who has eyes for it, some dimmer or clearer revelation of the Godlike?

'Of Symbols, however, I remark farther, that they have both an extrinsic and intrinsic value; oftenest the former only. What, for instance, was in that clouted Shoe which the Peasants bore aloft with them as ensign in their *Bauernkrieg* (Peasants' War)? Or in the Wallet-and-staff round which the Netherland *Gueux*, glorying in that nickname of Beggars, heroically rallied and prevailed, though against King Philip himself? Intrinsic significance these had none: only extrinsic; as the accidental Standards of multitudes more or less sacredly uniting together; in which union itself, as above noted, there is ever something mystical and borrowing of the Godlike. Under a like category too, stand, or stood, the stupidest heraldic coats-of-arms; military Banners everywhere; and generally all national or other sectarian Costumes and Customs: they have no intrinsic, necessary divineness, or even worth; but have acquired an extrinsic one. Nevertheless through all these there glimmers something of a Divine Idea; as through military Banners themselves, the Divine Idea of Duty, of heroic Daring; in some instances of Freedom, of Right. Nay, the highest ensign that men ever met and embraced under, the Cross itself, had no meaning save an accidental extrinsic one.

'Another matter it is, however, when your Symbol has intrinsic meaning, and is of itself *fit* that men should unite round it. Let but the Godlike manifest itself to Sense; let but Eternity look, more or less visibly, through the Time-Figure (*Zeitbild*)! Then is it fit that men unite there; and worship together before such Symbol; and so from day to day, and from age to age, superadd to it new divineness.

'Of this latter sort are all true Works of Art: in them (if thou know a Work of Art from a Daub of Artifice) wilt thou discern Eternity looking through Time; the Godlike rendered visible. Here too may an extrinsic value gradually superadd itself: thus certain *Iliads*, and the like, have, in three thousand years, attained quite new significance. But nobler than all in this kind are the Lives of heroic, god-inspired Men; for what other Work of Art is so divine? In Death too, in the Death of the Just, as the last perfection of a Work of Art, may we not discern symbolic meaning? In that divinely transfigured Sleep, as of Victory, resting over the beloved face which now knows thee no more, read (if thou canst for tears) the confluence of Time with Eternity, and some gleam of the latter peering through.

'Highest of all Symbols are those wherein the Artist or Poet has risen into Prophet, and all men can recognise a present God, and worship the same: I mean religious Symbols. Various enough have been such religious Symbols, what we call *Religions;* as men stood in this stage of culture or the other, and could worse or better body forth the Godlike: some Symbols with a transient intrinsic worth; many with only an extrinsic. If thou ask to what height man has carried it in this matter, look on our divinest Symbol: on Jesus of Nazareth, and his Life, and his Biography, and what followed therefrom. Higher has the human Thought not yet reached: this is Christianity and Christendom; a Symbol of quite perennial, infinite character; whose significance will ever demand to be anew inquired into, and anew made manifest.

'But, on the whole, as Time adds much to the sacredness of Symbols, so likewise in his progress he at length defaces, or even desecrates them; and Symbols, like all terrestrial Garments, wax old. Homer's Epos has not ceased to be true; yet it is no longer *our* Epos, but shines in the distance, if clearer and clearer, yet also smaller and smaller, like a receding Star. It needs a scientific telescope, it needs to be reinterpreted and artificially brought near us, before we can so much as know that it *was* a Sun. So likewise a day comes when the

Runic Thor, with his Eddas, must withdraw into dimness; and many an African Mumbo-Jumbo, and Indian Pawaw be utterly abolished. For all things, even Celestial Luminaries, much more atmospheric meteors, have their rise, their culmination, their decline.'

'Small is this which thou tellest me, that the Royal Sceptre is but a piece of gilt wood; that the Pyx has become a most foolish box, and truly, as Ancient Pistol thought, "of little price." A right Conjuror might I name thee, couldst thou conjure back into these wooden tools the divine virtue they once held.'

'Of this thing, however, be certain: wouldst thou plant for Eternity, then plant into the deep infinite faculties of man, his Fantasy and Heart; wouldst thou plant for Year and Day, then plant into his shallow superficial faculties, his Self-love and Arithmetical Understanding, what will grow there. A Hierarch, therefore, and Pontiff of the World will we call him, the Poet and inspired Maker; who, Prometheus-like, can shape new Symbols, and bring new Fire from Heaven to fix it there. Such too will not always be wanting; neither perhaps now are. Meanwhile, as the average of matters goes, we account him Legislator and wise who can so much as tell when a Symbol has grown old, and gently remove it.

'When, as the last English Coronation* was preparing,' concludes this wonderful Professor, 'I read in their Newspapers that the "Champion of England," he who has to offer battle to the Universe for his new King, had brought it so far that he could now "mount his horse with little assistance," I said to myself: Here also have we a Symbol well nigh superannuated. Alas, move whithersoever you may, are not the tatters and rags of superannuated worn-out Symbols (in this Ragfair of a World) dropping off everywhere, to hoodwink, to halter, to tether you; nay, if you shake them not aside, threatening to accumulate, and perhaps produce suffocation!'

---

* That of George IV.—ED.

CHAPTER IV.

HELOTAGE.

AT this point we determine on adverting shortly, or rather reverting, to a certain Tract of Hofrath Heuschrecke's, entitled *Institute for the Repression of Population;* which lies, dishonourably enough (with torn leaves, and a perceptible smell of aloetic drugs), stuffed into the Bag *Pisces*. Not indeed for sake of the Tract itself, which we admire little; but of the marginal Notes, evidently in Teufelsdröckh's hand, which rather copiously fringe it. A few of these may be in their right place here.

Into the Hofrath's *Institute*, with its extraordinary schemes, and machinery of Corresponding Boards and the like, we shall not so much as glance. Enough for us to understand that Heuschrecke is a disciple of Malthus; and so zealous for the doctrine, that his zeal almost literally eats him up. A deadly fear of Population possesses the Hofrath; something like a fixed-idea; undoubtedly akin to the more diluted forms of Madness. Nowhere, in that quarter of his intellectual world, is there light; nothing but a grim shadow of Hunger; open mouths opening wider and wider; a world to terminate by the frightfullest consummation: by its too dense inhabitants, famished into delirium, universally eating one another. To make air for himself in which strangulation, choking enough to a benevolent heart, the Hofrath founds, or proposes to found, this *Institute* of his, as the best he can do. It is only with our Professor's comments thereon that we concern ourselves.

First, then, remark that Teufelsdröckh, as a speculative Radical, has his own notions about human dignity; that the Zähdarm palaces and courtesies have not made him forgetful of the Futteral cottages. On the blank cover of Heuschrecke's Tract, we find the following, indistinctly engrossed:

'Two men I honour, and no third. First, the toilworn Craftsman that with earth-made Implement laboriously conquers the Earth, and makes her man's. Venerable to me is the hard Hand; crooked, coarse; wherein notwithstanding lies a cunning virtue, indefeasibly royal, as of the Sceptre of this Planet. Venerable too is the rugged face, all weather-tanned, besoiled, with its rude intelligence; for it is the face of a Man living manlike. Oh, but the more venerable for thy rudeness, and even because we must pity as well as love thee! Hardly-entreated Brother! For us was thy back so bent, for us were thy straight limbs and fingers so deformed: thou wert our Conscript, on whom the lot fell, and fighting our battles wert so marred. For in thee too lay a god-created Form, but it was not to be unfolded; encrusted must it stand with the thick adhesions and defacements of Labour; and thy body, like thy soul, was not to know freedom. Yet toil on, toil on: *thou* art in thy duty, be out of it who may; thou toilest for the altogether indispensable, for daily bread.

'A second man I honour, and still more highly: Him who is seen toiling for the spiritually indispensable; not daily bread, but the Bread of Life. Is not he too in his duty; endeavouring towards inward Harmony; revealing this, by act or by word, through all his outward endeavours, be they high or low? Highest of all, when his outward and his inward endeavour are one: when we can name him Artist; not earthly Craftsman only, but inspired Thinker, who with heaven-made Implement conquers Heaven for us! If the poor and humble toil that we have Food, must not the high and glorious toil for him in return that he have Light, have Guidance, Freedom, Immortality?—These two, in all their degrees, I honour: all else is chaff and dust, which let the wind blow whither it listeth.

'Unspeakably touching is it, however, when I find both dignities united; and he that must toil outwardly for the lowest of man's wants, is also toiling inwardly for the highest. Sublimer in this world know I nothing than a Peasant Saint, could such now any where be met with. Such a one will take thee back to Nazareth itself; thou wilt see the splendour of Heaven spring forth from the humblest depths of Earth, like a light shining in great darkness.'

And again: 'It is not because of his toils that I lament for the poor: we must all toil, or steal (howsoever we name our stealing) which is worse; no faithful workman finds his task a pastime. The poor is hungry and athirst; but for him also there is food and drink: he is heavy-laden and weary; but for him also the Heavens send Sleep, and of the deepest; in his smoky cribs, a clear dewy heaven of Rest envelopes him, and fitful glitterings of cloud-skirted Dreams. But what I do mourn over is, that the lamp of his soul should go out; that no ray of heavenly, or even of earthly knowledge, should visit him; but only, in the haggard darkness, like two spectres, Fear and Indignation bear him company. Alas, while the Body stands so broad and brawny, must the Soul lie blinded, dwarfed, stupified, almost annihilated! Alas, was this too a Breath of God; bestowed in Heaven, but on Earth never to be unfolded!—That there should one Man die Ignorant who had capacity for Knowledge, this I call a tragedy, were it to happen more than twenty times in the minute, as by some computations it does. The miserable fraction of Science which our united Mankind, in a wide Universe of Nescience, has acquired, why is not this, with all diligence, imparted to all?'

Quite in an opposite strain is the following: 'The old Spartans had a wiser method; and went out and hunted down their Helots, and speared and spitted them, when they grew too numerous. With our improved fashions of hunting, Herr Hofrath, now after the invention of fire-arms, and standing armies, how much easier were such a hunt! Perhaps in the most thickly-peopled country, some three days annually might suffice to shoot all the able-bodied Paupers that had accumulated within the year. Let Governments think of this. The expense were trifling: nay, the very carcasses would pay it. Have them salted and barrelled; could not you victual therewith, if not Army and Navy, yet richly such infirm Paupers, in workhouses and elsewhere, as enlightened Charity, dreading no evil of them, might see good to keep alive?'

'And yet,' writes he farther on, 'there must be something wrong. A full-formed Horse will, in any market, bring from twenty to as high as two hundred Friedrichs d'or: such is his worth to the world. A full-formed Man is not only worth nothing to the world, but the

world could afford him a round sum would he simply engage to go and hang himself. Nevertheless, which of the two was the more cunningly-devised article, even as an Engine? Good Heavens! A white European Man, standing on his two Legs, with his two five-fingered
5 Hands at his shackle-bones, and miraculous Head on his shoulders, is worth, I should say, from fifty to a hundred Horses!'

'True, thou Gold-Hofrath!' cries the Professor elsewhere: 'Too crowded indeed. Meanwhile, what portion of this inconsiderable terraqueous Globe have ye actually tilled and delved, till it will grow
10 no more? How thick stands your Population in the Pampas and Savannas of America; round ancient Carthage, and in the interior of Africa; on both slopes of the Altaic chain, in the central Platform of Asia; in Spain, Greece, Turkey, Crim Tartary, the Curragh of Kildare? One man, in one year, as I have understood it, if you lend him Earth,
15 will feed himself and nine others. Alas, where now are the Hengsts and Alarics of our still glowing, still expanding Europe; who, when their home is grown too narrow, will enlist and, like Fire-pillars, guide onwards those superfluous masses of indomitable living Valour; equipped, not now with the battle-axe and war-chariot, but with the
20 steam-engine and ploughshare? Where are they?—Preserving their Game!'

CHAPTER V.

THE PHŒNIX.

PUTTING which four singular Chapters together, and alongside of them numerous hints, and even direct utterances, scattered over these Writings of his, we come upon the startling yet not quite unlooked-for conclusion, that Teufelsdröckh is one of those who consider Society, properly so called, to be as good as extinct; and that only the Gregarious feelings, and old inherited habitudes, at this juncture, hold us from Dispersion, and universal national, civil, domestic and personal war! He says expressly: 'For the last three centuries, above all, for the last three quarters of a century, that same Pericardial Nervous Tissue (as we named it) of Religion, where lies the Life-essence of Society, has been smote at and perforated, needfully and needlessly; till now it is quite rent into shreds; and Society, long pining, diabetic, consumptive, can be regarded as defunct; for those spasmodic, galvanic sprawlings are not life, neither indeed will they endure, galvanise as you may, beyond two days.'

'Call ye that a Society,' cries he again, 'where there is no longer any Social Idea extant; not so much as the Idea of a common Home, but only of a common, over-crowded Lodging-house? Where each, isolated, regardless of his neighbour, turned against his neighbour, clutches what he can get, and cries "Mine!" and calls it Peace, because, in the cut-purse and cut-throat Scramble, no steel knives, but only a far cunninger sort, can be employed? Where Friendship, Communion, has become an incredible tradition; and your holiest Sacramental

171

Supper is a smoking Tavern Dinner, with Cook for Evangelist? Where your Priest has no tongue but for plate-licking: and your high Guides and Governors cannot guide; but on all hands hear it passionately proclaimed: *Laissez faire*; Leave us alone of *your* guidance, such light
5 is darker than darkness; eat you your wages, and sleep!

'Thus, too,' continues he, 'does an observant eye discern everywhere that saddest spectacle: The Poor perishing, like neglected, foundered Draught-Cattle, of Hunger and Overwork; the Rich, still more wretchedly, of Idleness, Satiety, and Overgrowth. The Highest
10 in rank, at length, without honour from the Lowest; scarcely, with a little mouth-honour, as from tavern-waiters who expect to put it in the bill. Once sacred Symbols fluttering as empty Pageants, whereof men grudge even the expense; a World becoming dismantled: in one word, the CHURCH fallen speechless, from obesity and apoplexy; the
15 STATE shrunken into a Police-Office, straitened to get its pay!'

We might ask, are there many 'observant eyes,' belonging to Practical men, in England or elsewhere, which have descried these phenomena; or is it only from the mystic elevation of a German *Wahngasse* that such wonders are visible? Teufelsdröckh contends that the aspect
20 of a 'deceased or expiring Society' fronts us everywhere, so that whoso runs may read. 'What, for example,' says he, 'is the universally-arrogated Virtue, almost the sole remaining Catholic Virtue, of these days? For some half century, it has been the thing you name "Independence." Suspicion of "Servility," of reverence for Superiors, the
25 very dogleech is anxious to disavow. Fools! Were your Superiors worthy to govern, and you worthy to obey, reverence for them were even your only possible freedom. Independence, in all kinds, is rebellion; if unjust rebellion, why parade it, and everywhere prescribe it?'

But what then? Are we returning, as Rousseau prayed, to the state
30 of Nature? 'The Soul Politic having departed,' says Teufelsdröckh, 'what can follow but that the Body Politic be decently interred, to avoid putrescence? Liberals, Economists, Utilitarians enough I see marching with its bier, and chaunting loud pæans, towards the funeral-pile, where, amid wailings from some, and saturnalian revel-
35 ries from the most, the venerable Corpse is to be burnt. Or, in plain words, that these men, Liberals, Utilitarians, or whatsoever they are called, will ultimately carry their point, and dissever and destroy most existing Institutions of Society, seems a thing which has some time ago ceased to be doubtful.

'Do we not see a little subdivision of the grand Utilitarian Armament come to light even in insulated England? A living nucleus, that will attract and grow, does at length appear there also; and under curious phasis; properly as the inconsiderable fag-end, and so far in rear of the others as to fancy itself the van. Our European Mechanisers are a Sect of boundless diffusion, activity, and co-operative spirit: has not Utilitarianism flourished in high places of Thought, here among ourselves, and in every European country, at some time or other, within the last fifty years? If now in all countries, except perhaps England, it has ceased to flourish, or indeed to exist, among Thinkers, and sunk to Journalists and the popular mass,—who sees not that, as hereby it no longer preaches, so the reason is, it now needs no Preaching, but is in full universal Action, the doctrine everywhere known, and enthusiastically laid to heart? The fit pabulum, in these times, for a certain rugged workshop-intellect and heart, nowise without their corresponding workshop-strength and ferocity, it requires but to be stated in such scenes to make proselytes enough.— Admirably calculated for destroying, only not for rebuilding! It spreads like a sort of Dog-madness; till the whole World-kennel will be rabid: then woe to the Huntsmen, with or without their whips! They should have given the quadrupeds water,' adds he; 'the water, namely, of Knowledge and of Life, while it was yet time.'

Thus, if Professor Teufelsdröckh can be relied on, we are at this hour in a most critical condition; beleaguered by that boundless 'Armament of Mechanisers' and Unbelievers, threatening to strip us bare! 'The World,' says he, 'as it needs must, is under a process of devastation and waste, which, whether by silent assiduous corrosion, or open quicker combustion, as the case chances, will effectually enough annihilate the past Forms of Society; replace them with what it may. For the present, it is contemplated that when man's whole Spiritual Interests are once *divested*, these innumerable stript-off Garments shall mostly be burnt; but the sounder Rags among them be quilted together into one huge Irish watch-coat for the defence of the Body only!' —This, we think, is but Job's news to the humane reader.

'Nevertheless,' cries Teufelsdröckh, 'who can hinder it; who is there that can clutch into the wheel-spokes of Destiny, and say to the Spirit of the Time: Turn back, I command thee?—Wiser were it that we yielded to the Inevitable and Inexorable, and accounted even this the best.'

Nay, might not an attentive Editor, drawing his own inferences from what stands written, conjecture that Teufelsdröckh individually had yielded to this same 'Inevitable and Inexorable' heartily enough; and now sat waiting the issue, with his natural diabolico-angelical Indifference, if not even Placidity? Did we not hear him complain that the World was a 'huge Ragfair,' and the 'rags and tatters of old Symbols' were raining down everywhere, like to drift him in, and suffocate him? What with those 'unhunted Helots' of his; and the uneven *sic-vos-non-vobis* pressure, and hard-crashing collision he is pleased to discern in existing things; what with the so hateful 'empty Masks,' full of beetles and spiders, yet glaring out on him, from their glass-eyes, 'with a ghastly affectation of life,'—we feel entitled to conclude him even willing that much should be thrown to the Devil, so it were but done gently! Safe himself in that 'Pinnacle of Weissnichtwo,' he would consent, with a tragic solemnity, that the monster UTILITARIA, held back, indeed, and moderated by nose-rings, halters, foot-shackles, and every conceivable modification of rope, should go forth to do her work;—to tread down old ruinous Palaces and Temples, with her broad hoof, till the whole were trodden down, that new and better might be built! Remarkable in this point of view are the following sentences.

'Society,' says he, 'is not dead: that Carcass, which you call dead Society, is but her mortal coil which she has shuffled off, to assume a nobler; she herself, through perpetual metamorphoses, in fairer and fairer developement, has to live till Time also merge in Eternity. Wheresoever two or three Living Men are gathered together, there is Society; or there it will be, with its cunning mechanisms and stupendous structures, overspreading this little Globe, and reaching upwards to Heaven and downwards to Gehenna: for always, under one or the other figure, has it two authentic Revelations, of a God and of a Devil; the Pulpit, namely, and the Gallows.'

Indeed, we already heard him speak of 'Religion, in unnoticed nooks, weaving for herself new Vestures;'—Teufelsdröckh himself being one of the loom-treaddles? Elsewhere he quotes without censure that strange aphorism of Saint-Simon's, concerning which and whom so much were to be said: '*L'âge d'or, qu'une aveugle tradition a placé jusqu' ici dans le passé, est devant nous;* The golden age, which a blind tradition has hitherto placed in the Past, is Before us.'—But listen again:

'When the Phœnix is fanning her funeral pyre, will there not be sparks flying? Alas, some millions of men, and among them such as a Napoleon, have already been licked into that high-eddying Flame, and like moths consumed there. Still also have we to fear that incautious beards will get singed.

'For the rest, in what year of grace such Phœnix-cremation will be completed, you need not ask. The law of Perseverance is among the deepest in man: by nature he hates change; seldom will he quit his old house till it has actually fallen about his ears. Thus have I seen Solemnities linger as Ceremonies, sacred Symbols as idle Pageants, to the extent of three hundred years and more after all life and sacredness had evaporated out of them. And then, finally, what time the Phœnix Death-Birth itself will require depends on unseen contingencies.—Meanwhile, would Destiny offer Mankind that after, say two centuries of convulsion and conflagration, more or less vivid, the fire-creation should be accomplished, and we to find ourselves again in a Living Society, and no longer fighting but working,—were it not perhaps prudent in Mankind to strike the bargain?'

Thus is Teufelsdröckh content that old sick Society should be deliberately burnt (alas! with quite other fuel than spice-wood); in the faith that she is a Phœnix; and that a new heavenborn young one will rise out of her ashes! We ourselves, restricted to the duty of Indicator, shall forbear commentary. Meanwhile, will not the judicious reader shake his head, and reproachfully, yet more in sorrow than in anger, say or think: From a *Doctor utriusque Juris,* titular Professor in a University, and man to whom hitherto, for his services, Society, bad as she is, has given not only food and raiment (of a kind), but books, tobacco and gukguk, we expected more gratitude to his benefactress; and less of a blind trust in the future, which resembles that rather of a philosophical Fatalist and Enthusiast, than of a solid householder paying scot and lot in a Christian country.

CHAPTER VI.

OLD CLOTHES.

As mentioned above, Teufelsdröckh, though a Sansculottist, is in practice probably the politest man extant: his whole heart and life are penetrated and informed with the spirit of Politeness; a noble natural Courtesy shines through him, beautifying his vagaries; like sunlight,
5 making a rosy-fingered, rainbow-dyed Aurora out of mere aqueous clouds; nay, brightening London-smoke itself into gold vapour, as from the crucible of an alchemist. Hear in what earnest though fantastic wise he expresses himself on this head:

'Shall Courtesy be done only to the rich, and only by the rich? In
10 Good-breeding, which differs, if at all, from High-breeding, only as it gracefully remembers the rights of others, rather than gracefully insists on its own rights, I discern no special connexion with wealth or birth: but rather that it lies in human nature itself, and is due from all men towards all men. Of a truth, were your Schoolmaster at his
15 post, and worth any thing when there, this, with so much else, would be reformed. Nay, each man were then also his neighbour's schoolmaster; till at length a rude-visaged, unmannered Peasant, could no more be met with than a Peasant unacquainted with botanical Physiology, or who felt not that the clod he broke was created in Heaven.
20 'For whether thou bear a sceptre or a sledge-hammer, art not thou ALIVE; is not this thy brother ALIVE? "There is but one Temple in the world," says Novalis, "and that Temple is the Body of Man. Nothing is holier than this high Form. Bending before men is a reverence

176

done to this Revelation in the Flesh. We touch Heaven, when we lay our hands on a human Body."

'On which ground, I would fain carry it farther than most do; and whereas the English Johnson only bowed to every Clergyman, or man with a shovel-hat, I would bow to every Man with any sort of hat, or with no hat whatever. Is not he a Temple, then; the visible Manifestation and Impersonation of the Divinity? And yet, alas, such indiscriminate bowing serves not. For there is a Devil dwells in man, as well as a Divinity; and too often the bow is but pocketed by the *former*. It would go to the pocket of Vanity (which is your clearest phasis of the Devil, in these times); therefore must we withhold it.

'The gladder am I, on the other hand, to do reverence to those Shells and outer Husks of the Body, wherein no devilish passion any longer lodges, but only the pure emblem and effigies of Man: I mean, to Empty, or even to Cast Clothes. Nay, is it not to Clothes that most men do reverence; to the fine frogged broad-cloth, nowise to the "straddling animal with bandy legs" which it holds, and makes a Dignitary of? Who ever saw any Lord my-lorded in tattered blanket, fastened with wooden skewer? Nevertheless, I say, there is in such worship a shade of hypocrisy, a practical deception: for how often does the Body appropriate what was meant for the Cloth only! Whoso would avoid Falsehood, which is the essence of all Sin, will perhaps see good to take a different course. That reverence which cannot act without obstruction and perversion when the Clothes are full, may have free course when they are empty. Even as, for Hindoo Worshippers, the Pagoda is not less sacred than the God; so do I too worship the hollow cloth Garment with equal fervour, as when it contained the Man: nay, with more, for I now fear no deception, of myself or of others.

'Did not King *Toomtabard*, or, in other words, John Balliol, reign long over Scotland; the man John Balliol being quite gone, and only the "Toom Tabard" (Empty Gown) remaining? What still dignity dwells in a suit of Cast Clothes! How meekly it bears its honours! No haughty looks, no scornful gesture; silent and serene, it fronts the world; neither demanding worship, nor afraid to miss it. The Hat still carries the physiognomy of its Head: but the vanity and the stupidity, and goose-speech which was the sign of these two, are gone. The Coat-arm is stretched out, but not to strike; the Breeches, in modest

simplicity, depend at ease, and now at last have a graceful flow; the
Waistcoat hides no evil passion, no riotous desire; hunger or thirst
now dwells not in it. Thus all is purged from the grossness of Sense,
from the carking Cares and foul Vices of the World; and rides there,
5   on its Clothes-horse; as, on a Pegasus, might some skyey Messenger,
or purified Apparition, visiting our low Earth.

'Often, while I sojourned in that monstrous Tuberosity of Civilised
Life, the Capital of England; and meditated, and questioned Destiny,
under that ink-sea of vapour, black, thick, and multifarious as Spartan
10   broth; and was one lone Soul amid those grinding millions;—often
have I turned into their Old-Clothes Market to worship. With awestruck heart I walk through that Monmouth Street, with its empty
Suits, as through a Sanhedrim of stainless Ghosts. Silent are they, but
expressive in their silence: the past witnesses and instruments of Woe
15   and Joy, of Passions, Virtues, Crimes, and all the fathomless tumult
of Good and Evil in "the Prison men call Life." Friends! trust not the
heart of that man for whom Old Clothes are not venerable. Watch
too, with reverence, that bearded Jewish Highpriest, who with hoarse
voice, like some Angel of Doom, summons them from the four winds!
20   On his head, like the Pope, he has three Hats,—a real triple tiara; on
either hand, are the similitude of Wings, whereon the summoned
Garments come to alight; and ever, as he slowly cleaves the air, sounds
forth his deep fateful note, as if through a trumpet he were proclaiming: "Ghosts of Life, come to Judgment!" Reck not, ye fluttering
25   Ghosts: he will purify you in his Purgatory, with fire and with water;
and, one day, new-created ye shall reappear. Oh! let him in whom the
flame of Devotion is ready to go out, who has never worshipped, and
knows not what to worship, pace and repace, with austerest thought,
the pavement of Monmouth Street, and say whether his heart and his
30   eyes still continue dry. If Field Lane, with its long fluttering rows of
yellow handkerchiefs, be a Dionysius' Ear, where, in stifled jarring
hubbub, we hear the Indictment which Poverty and Vice bring against
lazy Wealth, that it has left them there cast out and trodden under
foot of Want, Darkness, and the Devil,—then is Monmouth Street a
35   Mirza's Hill, where, in motley vision, the whole Pageant of Existence
passes awfully before us; with its wail and jubilee, mad loves and
mad hatreds, church-bells and gallows-ropes, farce-tragedy, beast-
godhood,—the Bedlam of Creation!'

To most men, as it does to ourselves, all this will seem over-charged. We too have walked through Monmouth Street; but with little feeling of 'Devotion:' probably in part because the contemplative process is so fatally broken in upon by the brood of money-changers, who nestle in that Church, and importune the worshipper with merely secular proposals. Whereas Teufelsdröckh might be in that happy middle-state, which leaves to the Clothes-broker no hope either of sale or of purchase, and so be allowed to linger there without molestation.—Something we would have given to see the little philosophical Figure, with its steeple-hat and loose-flowing skirts, and eyes in a fine frenzy, 'pacing and repacing in austerest thought' that foolish Street; which to him was a true Delphic avenue, and supernatural Whispering-gallery, where the 'Ghosts of Life' rounded strange secrets in his ear. O thou philosophic Teufelsdröckh, that listenest while others only gabble, and with thy quick tympanum hearest the grass grow!

At the same time, is it not strange that, in Paperbag Documents, destined for an English Work, there exists nothing like an authentic diary of this his sojourn in London; and of his Meditations among the Clothes-shops only the obscurest emblematic shadows? Neither, in conversation (for, indeed, he was not a man to pester you with his Travels), have we heard him more than allude to the subject.

For the rest, however, it cannot be uninteresting that we here find how early the significance of Clothes had dawned on the now so distinguished Clothes-Professor. Might we but fancy it to have been even in Monmouth Street, at the bottom of our own English 'ink-sea,' that this remarkable Volume first took being, and shot forth its salient point in his soul,—as in Chaos did the Egg of Eros, one day to be hatched into a Universe!

CHAPTER VII.

ORGANIC FILAMENTS.

FOR us, who happen to live while the World-Phœnix is burning herself, and burning so slowly that, as Teufelsdröckh calculates, it were a handsome bargain would she engage to have done 'within two centuries,' there seems to lie but an ashy prospect. Not altogether so,
5   however, does the Professor figure it. 'In the living subject,' says he, 'change is wont to be gradual: thus, while the serpent sheds its old skin, the new is already formed beneath. Little knowest thou of the burning of a World-Phœnix, who fanciest that she must first burn out, and lie as a dead cinereous heap; and therefrom the young one
10   start up by miracle, and fly heavenward. Far otherwise! In that Fire-whirlwind, Creation and Destruction proceed together; ever as the ashes of the Old are blown about, do organic filaments of the New mysteriously spin themselves; and amid the rushing and the waving of the Whirlwind-Element, come tones of a melodious Deathsong, which
15   end not but in tones of a more melodious Birthsong. Nay, look into the Fire-whirlwind with thy own eyes, and thou wilt see.' Let us actually look, then: to poor individuals, who cannot expect to live two centuries, those same organic filaments, mysteriously spinning themselves, will be the best part of the spectacle. First, therefore, this
20   of Mankind in general:

'In vain thou deniest it,' says the Professor; 'thou *art* my Brother. Thy very Hatred, thy very Envy, those foolish Lies thou tellest of me

in thy splenetic humour: what is all this but an inverted Sympathy?
Were I a Steam-engine, wouldst thou take the trouble to tell Lies of
me? Not thou! I should grind all unheeded, whether badly or well.

'Wondrous truly are the bonds that unite us one and all; whether
by the soft binding of Love, or the iron chaining of Necessity, as we   5
like to choose it. More than once, have I said to myself, of some
perhaps whimsically strutting Figure, such as provokes whimsical
thoughts: "Wert thou, my little Brotherkin, sudddenly covered up
with even the largest imaginable Glass-bell,—what a thing it were,
not for thyself only, but for the world! Post Letters, more or fewer,   10
from all the four winds, impinge against thy Glass walls, but have to
drop unread: neither from within comes there question or response
into any Postbag; thy Thoughts fall into no friendly ear or heart, thy
Manufacture into no purchasing hand; thou art no longer a circulat-
ing venous-arterial Heart, that, taking and giving, circulatest through   15
all Space and all Time: there has a Hole fallen out in the immeasurable, universal World-tissue, which must be darned up again!"

'Such venous-arterial circulation, of Letters, verbal Messages, paper and other Packages, going out from him and coming in, are a
blood-circulation, visible to the eye: but the finer nervous circulation,   20
by which all things, the minutest that he does, minutely influence all
men, and the very look of his face blesses or curses whomso it lights
on, and so generates ever new blessing or new cursing: all this you
cannot see, but only imagine. I say, there is not a red Indian, hunting
by Lake Winnipic, can quarrel with his squaw, but the whole world   25
must smart for it: will not the price of beaver rise? It is a mathematical
fact that the casting of this pebble from my hand alters the centre-
of-gravity of the Universe.

'If now an existing generation of men stand so woven together,
not less indissolubly does generation with generation. Hast thou ever   30
meditated on that word, Tradition: how we inherit not Life only, but
all the garniture and form of Life; and work, and speak, and even
think and feel, as our Fathers, and primeval grandfathers, from the
beginning, have given it us?—Who printed thee, for example, this
unpretending Volume on the Philosophy of Clothes? Not the Herren   35
Stillschweigen and Company: but Cadmus of Thebes, Faust of Mentz,
and innumerable others whom thou knowest not. Had there been no

Mœsogothic Ulfila, there had been no English Shakspeare, or a different one. Simpleton! it was Tubalcain that made thy very Tailor's needle, and sewed that court suit of thine.

'Yes, truly, if Nature is one, and a living indivisible whole, much more is Mankind, the Image that reflects and creates Nature, without which Nature were not. As palpable life-streams in that wondrous Individual, Mankind, among so many life-streams that are not palpable, flow-on those main-currents of what we call Opinion; as preserved in Institutions, Polities, Churches, above all in Books. Beautiful it is to understand and know that a Thought did never yet die; that as thou, the originator thereof, hast gathered it and created it from the whole Past, so thou wilt transmit it to the whole Future. It is thus that the heroic Heart, the seeing Eye of the first times, still feels and sees in us of the latest; that the Wise Man stands ever encompassed, and spiritually embraced, by a cloud of witnesses and brothers; and there is a living, literal *Communion of Saints*, wide as the World itself, and as the History of the World.

'Noteworthy also, and serviceable for the progress of this same Individual, wilt thou find his subdivision into Generations. Generations are as the Days of toilsome Mankind; Death and Birth are the vesper and the matin bells, that summon Mankind to sleep, and to rise refreshed for new advancement. What the Father has made, the Son can make and enjoy; but has also work of his own appointed him. Thus all things wax, and roll onwards; Arts, Establishments, Opinions, nothing is completed, but ever completing. Newton has learned to see what Kepler saw; but there is also a fresh heaven-derived force in Newton; he must mount to still higher points of vision. So too the Hebrew Lawgiver is, in due time, followed by an Apostle of the Gentiles. In the business of Destruction, as this also is from time to time a necessary work, thou findest a like sequence and perseverance: for Luther it was as yet hot enough to stand by that burning of the Pope's Bull; Voltaire could not warm himself at the glimmering ashes, but required quite other fuel. Thus likewise, I note, the English Whig has, in the second generation, become an English Radical; who, in the third again, it is to be hoped, will become an English Rebuilder. Find Mankind where thou wilt, thou findest it in living movement, in progress faster or slower: the Phœnix soars aloft, hovers with outstretched wings, filling Earth with her music; or, as now, she sinks, and with spheral swan-song immolates herself in flame, that she may soar the higher and sing the clearer.'

Let the friends of social order, in such a disastrous period, lay this to heart, and derive from it any little comfort they can. We subjoin another passage, concerning Titles: 5

'Remark, not without surprise,' says Teufelsdröckh, 'how all high Titles of Honour come hitherto from Fighting. Your *Herzog* (Duke, *Dux*) is Leader of Armies; your Earl (*Jarl*) is Strong Man; your Marshall cavalry Horse-shoer. A Millennium, or reign of Peace and Wisdom, having from of old been prophesied, and becoming now daily more 10 and more indubitable, may it not be apprehended that such Fighting-titles will cease to be palatable, and new and higher need to be devised?

'The only Title wherein I, with confidence, trace eternity, is that of King. *König* (King), anciently *Könning*, means Ken-ning (Cunning), or which is the same thing, Can-ning. Ever must the Sovereign 15 of Mankind be fitly entitled King.'

'Well, also,' says he elsewhere, 'was it written by Theologians: a King rules by divine right. He carries in him an authority from God, or man will never give it him. Can I choose my own King? I can choose my own King Popinjay, and play what farce or tragedy I may 20 with him: but he who is to be my Ruler, whose will is to be higher than my will, was chosen for me in Heaven. Neither except in such Obedience to the Heaven-chosen is Freedom so much as conceivable.'

The Editor will here admit that, among all the wondrous provinces 25 of Teufelsdröckh's spiritual world, there is none he walks in with such astonishment, hesitation, and even pain, as in the Political. How, with our English love of Ministry and Opposition, and that generous conflict of Parties, mind warming itself against mind in their mutual wrestle for the Public Good, by which wrestle, indeed, is our invaluable 30 Constitution kept warm and alive; how shall we domesticate ourselves in this spectral Necropolis, or rather City both of the Dead and of the Unborn, where the Present seems little other than an inconsiderable Film dividing the Past and the Future? In those dim longdrawn expanses, all is so immeasurable; much so disastrous, ghastly; your very radiances, 35 and straggling light-beams, have a supernatural character. And then with such an Indifference, such a prophetic peacefulness (accounting the inevitably-coming as already here, to him all one whether it be

distant by centuries or only by days), does he sit;—and live, you would say, rather in any other age than in his own! It is our painful duty to announce, or repeat, that, looking into this man, we discern a deep, silent, slow-burning, inextinguishable Radicalism, such as fills us with
5   shuddering admiration.

Thus, for example, he appears to make little even of the Elective Franchise; at least so we interpret the following: 'Satisfy yourselves,' he says, 'by universal, indubitable experiment, even as ye are now doing or will do, whether FREEDOM, heavenborn and leading heaven-
10 ward, and so vitally essential for us all, cannot peradventure be mechanically hatched and brought to light in that same Ballot-Box of yours; or at worst, in some other discoverable or devisable Box, Edifice, or Steam-mechanism. It were a mighty convenience; and beyond all feats of manufacture witnessed hitherto.' Is Teufelsdröckh acquainted
15 with the British Constitution, even slightly?—He says, under another figure: 'But after all, were the problem, as indeed it now everywhere is, To rebuild your old House from the top downwards (since you must live in it the while), what better, what other, than the Representative Machine will serve your turn? Meanwhile, however, mock
20 me not with the name of Free, "when you have but knit up my chains into ornamental festoons."'—Or what will any member of the Peace Society make of such an assertion as this: 'The lower people everywhere desire War. Not so unwisely; there is then a demand for lower people—to be shot!'
25 Gladly, therefore, do we emerge from those soul-confusing labyrinths of speculative Radicalism, into somewhat clearer regions. Here, looking round, as was our hest, for 'organic filaments,' we ask, may not this, touching 'Hero-worship,' be of the number? It seems of a cheerful character; yet so quaint, so mystical, one knows not what, or
30 how little, may lie under it. Our readers shall look with their own eyes:

'True is it that, in these days, man can do almost all things, only not obey. True likewise that whoso cannot obey cannot be free, still less bear rule; he that is the inferior of nothing, can be the superior of nothing, the equal of nothing. Nevertheless, believe not that man
35 has lost his faculty of Reverence; that if it slumber in him, it has gone dead. Painful for man is that same rebellious Independence, when it has become inevitable; only in loving companionship with his fellows does he feel safe; only in reverently bowing down before the Higher does he feel himself exalted.

'Or what if the character of our so troublous Era lay even in this: that man had forever cast away Fear, which is the lower; but not yet risen into perennial Reverence, which is the higher and highest? 'Meanwhile, observe with joy, so cunningly has Nature ordered it, that whatsoever man ought to obey he cannot but obey. Before no   5 faintest revelation of the Godlike did he ever stand irreverent; least of all, when the Godlike shewed itself revealed in his fellow-man. Thus is there a true religious Loyalty forever rooted in his heart; nay, in all ages, even in ours, it manifests itself as a more or less orthodox *Hero-worship*. In which fact, that Hero-worship exists, has existed, and will   10 forever exist, universally among Mankind, mayst thou discern the corner-stone of living rock, whereon all Polities for the remotest time may stand secure.'

Do our readers discern any such corner-stone, or even so much as what Teufelsdröckh is looking at? He exclaims: 'Or hast thou forgot-   15 ten Paris and Voltaire? How the aged, withered man, though but a Sceptic, Mocker, and millinery Court-poet, yet because even he seemed the Wisest, Best, could drag mankind at his chariot-wheels, so that princes coveted a smile from him, and the loveliest of France would have laid their hair beneath his feet! All Paris was one vast Temple of   20 Hero-Worship; though their Divinity, moreover, was of feature too apish.

'But if such things,' continues he, 'were done in the dry tree, what will be done in the green? If, in the most parched season of man's History, in the most parched spot of Europe, when Parisian life was   25 at best but a scientific *Hortus Siccus*, bedizened with some Italian Gumflowers, such virtue could come out of it: what is to be looked for when Life again waves leafy and bloomy, and your Hero-Divinity shall have nothing apelike, but be wholly human? Know that there is in man a quite indestructible Reverence for whatsoever holds of Heaven,   30 or even plausibly counterfeits such holding. Shew the dullest clodpole, shew the haughtiest featherhead, that a soul Higher than himself is actually here; were his knees stiffened into brass, he must down and worship.'

35

Organic filaments, of a more authentic sort, mysteriously spinning themselves, some will perhaps discover in the following passage: 'There is no Church, sayest thou? The voice of Prophecy has gone dumb? This is even what I dispute: but, in any case, hast thou not still

Preaching enough? A Preaching Friar settles himself in every village; and builds a pulpit, which he calls Newspaper. Therefrom he preaches what most momentous doctrine is in him, for man's salvation; and dost not thou listen, and believe? Look well, thou seest every where
5 a new Clergy of the Mendicant Orders, some bare-footed, some almost bare-backed, fashion itself into shape, and teach and preach, zealously enough, for copper alms and the love of God. These break in pieces the ancient idols; and, though themselves too often reprobate, as idol-breakers are wont to be, mark out the sites of new
10 Churches, where the true God-ordained, that are to follow, may find audience, and minister. Said I not, Before the old skin was shed, the new had formed itself beneath it?'

Perhaps, also, in the following; wherewith we now hasten to knit up this ravelled sleeve:
15 'But there is no Religion?' reiterates the Professor. 'Fool! I tell thee, there is. Hast thou well considered all that lies in this immeasurable froth-ocean we name LITERATURE? Fragments of a genuine Church-*Homiletic* lie scattered there, which Time will assort: nay, fractions even of a *Liturgy* could I point out. And knowest thou no Prophet,
20 even in the vesture, environment, and dialect of this age? None to whom the Godlike had revealed itself, through all meanest and highest forms of the Common; and by him been again prophetically revealed: in whose inspired melody, even in these rag-gathering and rag-burning days, Man's Life again begins, were it but afar off, to be
25 divine? Knowest thou none such? I know him, and name him—Goethe.

'But thou as yet standest in no Temple; joinest in no Psalm-worship; feelest well that, where there is no ministering Priest, the people perish? Be of comfort! Thou art not alone, if thou have Faith. Spake we not of a Communion of Saints, unseen, yet not unreal,
30 accompanying and brother-like embracing thee, so thou be worthy? Their heroic Sufferings rise up melodiously together to Heaven, out of all lands, and out of all times, as a sacred *Miserere;* their heroic Actions also, as a boundless, everlasting Psalm of Triumph. Neither say that thou hast now no Symbol of the Godlike. Is not God's
35 Universe a Symbol of the Godlike; is not Immensity a Temple; is not Man's History, and Men's History, a perpetual Evangile? Listen, and for organ-music thou wilt ever, as of old, hear the Morning Stars sing together.'

CHAPTER VIII.

NATURAL SUPERNATURALISM.

IT is in his stupendous Section, headed *Natural Supernaturalism*, that the Professor first becomes a Seer; and, after long effort, such as we have witnessed, finally subdues under his feet this refractory Clothes-Philosophy, and takes victorious possession thereof. Phantasms enough he has had to struggle with; 'Cloth-webs and Cobwebs,' of Imperial   5
Mantles, Superannuated Symbols, and what not: yet still did he courageously pierce through. Nay, worst of all, two quite mysterious, world-embracing Phantasms, TIME and SPACE, have ever hovered round him, perplexing and bewildering: but with these also he now resolutely grapples, these also he victoriously rends asunder. In a word, he   10
has looked fixedly on Existence, till one after the other, its earthly hulls and garnitures, have all melted away; and now to his rapt vision the interior, celestial Holy of Holies, lies disclosed.

Here therefore properly it is that the Philosophy of Clothes attains to Transcendentalism; this last leap, can we but clear it, takes us safe   15
into the promised land, where *Palingenesia*, in all senses, may be considered as beginning. 'Courage, then!' may our Diogenes exclaim, with better right than Diogenes the First once did. This stupendous Section we, after long, painful meditation, have found not to be unintelligible; but on the contrary to grow clear, nay radiant, and all-   20
illuminating. Let the reader, turning on it what utmost force of speculative intellect is in him, do his part; as we, by judicious selection and adjustment, shall study to do ours:

187

'Deep has been, and is, the significance of Miracles,' thus quietly begins the Professor; 'far deeper perhaps than we imagine. Meanwhile, the question of questions were: What specially is a Miracle? To that Dutch King of Siam, an icicle had been a miracle; whoso had carried with him an air-pump, and phial of vitriolic ether, might have worked a miracle. To my Horse again, who unhappily is still more unscientific, do not I work a miracle, and magical *"open sesame!"* every time I please to pay twopence, and open for him an impassable *Schlagbaum*, or shut Turnpike?

'"But is not a real Miracle simply a violation of the Laws of Nature?" ask several. Whom I answer by this new question: What are the Laws of Nature? To me perhaps the rising of one from the dead were no violation of these Laws, but a confirmation; were some far deeper Law, now first penetrated into, and by Spiritual Force, even as the rest have all been, brought to bear on us with its Material Force.

'Here too may some inquire, not without astonishment: On what ground shall one, that can make Iron swim, come and declare that therefore he can teach Religion? To us, truly, of the Nineteenth Century, such declaration were inept enough; which nevertheless to our fathers, of the First Century, was full of meaning.

'"But is it not the deepest Law of Nature that she be constant?" cries an illuminated class: "Is not the Machine of the Universe fixed to move by unalterable rules?" Probable enough, good friends: nay, I too must believe that the God, whom ancient inspired men assert to be "without variableness or shadow of turning," does indeed never change; that Nature, that the Universe, which no one whom it so pleases can be prevented from calling a Machine, does move by the most unalterable rules. And now of you too I make the old inquiry: What those same unalterable rules, forming the complete Statute-Book of Nature, may possibly be?

'They stand written in our Works of Science, say you; in the accumulated records of man's Experience?—Was man with his Experience present at the Creation, then, to see how it all went on? Have any deepest scientific individuals yet dived down to the foundations of the Universe, and gauged every thing there? Did the Maker take them into His counsel; that they read His ground-plan of the incomprehensible All; and can say, This stands marked therein, and no more than this? Alas, not in anywise! These scientific individuals have been nowhere but where we also are; have seen some handbreadths deeper than we see into the Deep that is infinite, without bottom as without shore.

'Laplace's Book on the Stars, wherein he exhibits that certain Planets, with their Satellites, gyrate round our worthy Sun, at a rate and in a course, which, by greatest good fortune, he and the like of him have succeeded in detecting,—is to me as precious as to another. But is this what thou namest "Mechanism of the Heavens," and "System of the World;" this, wherein Sirius and the Pleiades, and all Herschel's Fifteen thousand Suns per minute, being left out, some paltry handful of Moons, and inert Balls, had been—looked at, nicknamed, and marked in the Zodiacal Waybill; so that we can now prate of their Whereabout; their How, their Why, their What, being hid from us as in the signless Inane?

'System of Nature! To the wisest man, wide as is his vision, Nature remains of quite *infinite* depth, of quite infinite expansion; and all Experience thereof limits itself to some few computed centuries, and measured square-miles. The course of Nature's phases, on this our little fraction of a Planet, is partially known to us; but who knows what deeper courses these depend on; what infinitely larger Cycle (of causes) our little Epicycle revolves on? To the Minnow every cranny and pebble, and quality and accident, of its little native Creek may have become familiar: but does the Minnow understand the Ocean Tides and periodic Currents, the Trade-winds, and Monsoons, and Moon's Eclipses; by all which the condition of its little Creek is regulated, and may, from time to time (*un*miraculously enough), be quite overset and reversed? Such a minnow is man; his Creek this Planet Earth; his Ocean the immeasurable All; his Monsoons and periodic Currents the mysterious Course of Providence through Æons of Æons.

'We speak of the Volume of Nature: and truly a Volume it is,—whose Author and Writer is God. To read it! Dost thou, does man, so much as well know the Alphabet thereof? With its Words, Sentences, and grand descriptive Pages, poetical and philosophical, spread out through Solar Systems, and Thousands of Years, we shall not try thee. It is a Volume written in celestial hieroglyphs, in the true Sacred-writing; of which even Prophets are happy that they can read here a line and there a line. As for your Institutes, and

Academies of Science, they strive bravely; and, from amid the thick-crowded, inextricably intertwisted hieroglyphic writing, pick out, by dextrous combination, some Letters in the vulgar Character, and therefrom put together this and the other economic Recipe, of high
5 avail in Practice. That Nature is more than some boundless Volume of such Recipes, or huge, well-nigh inexhaustible Domestic-Cookery Book, of which the whole secret will in this manner one day evolve itself, the fewest dream.

10   'Custom,' continues the Professor, 'doth make dotards of us all. Consider well, thou wilt find that Custom is the greatest of Weavers; and weaves air-raiment for all the Spirits of the Universe; whereby indeed these dwell with us visibly, as ministering servants, in our houses and workshops; but their spiritual nature becomes, to the
15 most, forever hidden. Philosophy complains that Custom has hood-winked us, from the first; that we do every thing by Custom, even Believe by it; that our very Axioms, let us boast of Free-thinking as we may, are oftenest simply such Beliefs as we have never heard questioned. Nay, what is Philosophy throughout but a continual battle
20 against Custom; an ever-renewed effort to *transcend* the sphere of blind Custom, and so become Transcendental?
       'Innumerable are the illusions and legerdemain tricks of Custom: but of all these perhaps the cleverest is her knack of persuading us that the Miraculous, by simple repetition, ceases to be Miraculous.
25 True, it is by this means we live; for man must work as well as wonder: and herein is Custom so far a kind nurse, guiding him to his true benefit. But she is a fond foolish nurse, or rather we are false foolish nurselings, when, in our resting and reflecting hours, we pro-long the same deception. Am I to view the Stupendous with stupid
30 indifference, because I have seen it twice, or two hundred, or two million times? There is no reason in Nature or in Art why I should: unless, indeed, I am a mere Work-Machine, for whom the divine gift of Thought were no other than the terrestrial gift of Steam is to the Steam-engine; a power whereby Cotton might be spun, and money
35 and money's worth realised.
       'Notable enough too, here as elsewhere, wilt thou find the po-tency of Names; which indeed are but one kind of such Custom-woven, wonder-hiding garments. Witchcraft, and all manner of

Spectre-work, and Demonology, we have now named Madness, and Diseases of the Nerves. Seldom reflecting that still the new question comes upon us: What is Madness, what are Nerves? Ever, as before, does Madness remain a mysterious-terrific, altogether *infernal* boiling up of the Nether Chaotic Deep, through this fair-painted Vision of Creation, which swims thereon, which we name the Real. Was Luther's Picture of the Devil less a Reality, whether it were formed within the bodily eye, or without it? In every the wisest Soul lies a whole world of internal Madness, an authentic Demon-Empire; out of which, indeed, his world of Wisdom has been creatively built together, and now rests there, as on its dark foundations does a habitable flowery Earth-rind.

'But deepest of all illusory Appearances, for hiding Wonder, as for many other ends, are your two grand fundamental world-enveloping Appearances, SPACE and TIME. These, as spun and woven for us from before Birth itself, to clothe our celestial ME for dwelling here, and yet to blind it,—lie all-embracing, as the universal canvass, or warp and woof, whereby all minor Illusions, in this Phantasm Existence, weave and paint themselves. In vain, while here on Earth, shall you endeavour to strip them off; you can, at best, but rend them asunder for moments, and look through.

'Fortunatus had a wishing Hat, which when he put on, and wished himself Anywhere, behold he was There. By this means had Fortunatus triumphed over Space, he had annihilated Space; for him there was no Where, but all was Here. Were a Hatter to establish himself, in the Wahngasse of Weissnichtwo, and make felts of this sort for all mankind, what a world we should have of it! Still stranger, should, on the opposite side of the street, another Hatter establish himself; and, as his fellow-craftsman made Space-annihilating Hats, make Time-annihilating! Of both would I purchase, were it with my last groschen; but chiefly of this latter. To clap on your felt, and, simply by wishing that you were Any*where*, straightway to be *There!* Next to clap on your other felt, and, simply by wishing that you were Any*when*, straightway to be *Then!* This were indeed the grander: shooting at will from the Fire-Creation of the World to its Fire-Consummation; here historically present in the First Century, conversing face to face with Paul and Seneca; there prophetically in the Thirty-first, conversing

also face to face with other Pauls and Senecas, who as yet stand
hidden in the depth of that late Time!

'Or thinkest thou, it were impossible, unimaginable? Is the Past
annihilated, then, or only past; is the Future non-extant, or only
5   future? Those mystic faculties of thine, Memory and Hope, already
answer: already through those mystic avenues, thou the Earth-blinded
summonest both Past and Future, and communest with them, though
as yet darkly, and with mute beckonings. The curtains of Yesterday
drop down, the curtains of To-morrow roll up; but Yesterday and To-
10 morrow both *are*. Pierce through the Time-Element, glance into the
Eternal. Believe what thou findest written in the sanctuaries of Man's
Soul, even as all Thinkers, in all ages, have devoutly read it there: that
Time and Space are not God, but creations of God; that with God as
it is a universal HERE, so is it an everlasting Now.

15 'And seest thou therein any glimpse of IMMORTALITY?—O Heaven!
Is the white Tomb of our Loved One, who died from our arms, and
had to be left behind us there, which rises in the distance, like a pale,
mournfully receding Milestone, to tell how many toilsome uncheered
miles we have journeyed on alone,—but a pale spectral Illusion! Is the
20 lost Friend still mysteriously Here, even as we are Here mysteriously,
with God!—Know of a truth that only the Time-shadows have per-
ished, or are perishable; that the real Being of whatever was, and
whatever is, and whatever will be, *is* even now and forever. This,
should it unhappily seem new, thou mayst ponder at thy leisure; for
25 the next twenty years, or the next twenty centuries: believe it thou
must; understand it thou canst not.

'That the Thought-forms, Space and Time, wherein, once for all,
we are sent into this Earth to live, should condition and determine
our whole Practical reasonings, conceptions, and imagings or imag-
30 inings,—seems altogether fit, just, and unavoidable. But that they
should, furthermore, usurp such sway over pure spiritual Meditation,
and blind us to the wonder everywhere lying close on us, seems
nowise so. Admit Space and Time to their due rank as Forms of
Thought; nay, even, if thou wilt, to their quite undue rank of Reali-
35 ties: and consider, then, with thyself how their thin disguises hide
from us the brightest God-effulgences! Thus, were it not miraculous,
could I stretch forth my hand, and clutch the Sun? Yet thou seest me
daily stretch forth my hand, and therewith clutch many a thing,

and swing it hither and thither. Art thou a grown baby, then, to fancy that the Miracle lies in miles of distance, or in pounds avoirdupois of weight; and not to see that the true inexplicable God-revealing Miracle lies in this, that I can stretch forth my hand at all; that I have free Force to clutch aught therewith? Innumerable other of this sort   5
are the deceptions, and wonder-hiding stupefactions, which Space practises on us.

'Still worse is it with regard to Time. Your grand anti-magician, and universal wonder-hider, is this same lying Time. Had we but the Time-annihilating Hat, to put on for once only, we should see our-   10
selves in a World of Miracles, wherein all fabled or authentic Thaumaturgy, and feats of Magic, were outdone. But unhappily we have not such a Hat; and man, poor fool that he is, can seldom and scantily help himself without one.

'Were it not wonderful, for instance, had Orpheus, or Amphion,   15
built the walls of Thebes by the mere sound of his Lyre? Yet tell me, who built these walls of Weissnichtwo; summoning out all the sandstone rocks, to dance along from the *Steinbruch* (now a huge Troglodyte Chasm, with frightful green-mantled pools); and shape themselves into Doric and Ionic pillars, squared ashlar houses, and   20
noble streets? Was it not the still higher Orpheus, or Orpheuses, who, in past centuries, by the divine Music of Wisdom, succeeded in civilising Man? Our highest Orpheus walked in Judea, eighteen hundred years ago: his sphere-melody, flowing in wild native tones, took captive the ravished souls of men; and, being of a truth sphere-melody, still flows   25
and sounds, though now with thousandfold Accompaniments, and rich symphonies, through all our hearts; and modulates, and divinely leads them. Is that a wonder, which happens in two hours; and does it cease to be wonderful if happening in two million? Not only was Thebes built by the Music of an Orpheus; but without the music of   30
some inspired Orpheus was no city ever built, no work that man glories in ever done.

'Sweep away the Illusion of Time: glance, if thou have eyes, from the near moving-cause to its far distant Mover: The stroke that came transmitted through a whole galaxy of elastic balls, was it less a stroke   35
than if the last ball only had been struck, and sent flying? Oh, could I (with the Time-annihilating Hat) transport thee direct from the Beginnings to the Endings, how were thy eyesight unsealed, and thy

heart set flaming in the Light-sea of celestial wonder! Then sawest thou that this fair Universe, were it in the meanest province thereof, is in very deed the star-domed City of God; that through every star, through every grass-blade, and most through every Living Soul, the glory of a present God still beams. But Nature, which is the Time-vesture of God, and reveals Him to the wise, hides Him from the foolish.

'Again, could any thing be more miraculous than an actual authentic Ghost? The English Johnson longed, all his life, to see one; but could not, though he went to Cock Lane, and thence to the church-vaults, and tapped on coffins. Foolish Doctor! Did he never, with the mind's eye as well as with the body's, look round him into that full tide of human Life he so loved; did he never so much as look into Himself? The good Doctor was a Ghost, as actual and authentic as heart could wish; well nigh a million of Ghosts were travelling the streets by his side. Once more I say, sweep away the illusion of Time; compress the three-score years into three minutes: what else was he, what else are we? Are we not Spirits, that are shaped into a body, into an Appearance; and that fade away again into air, and Invisibility? This is no metaphor, it is a simple scientific *fact:* we start out of Nothingness, take figure, and are Apparitions; round us, as round the veriest spectre, is Eternity; and to Eternity minutes are as years and æons. Come there not tones of Love and Faith, as from celestial harp-strings, like the Song of beatified Souls? And again, do not we squeak and gibber (in our discordant, screech-owlish debatings and recrim-inatings); and glide bodeful, and feeble, and fearful; or uproar (*poltern*), and revel in our mad Dance of the Dead,—till the scent of the morning-air summons us to our still Home; and dreamy Night becomes awake and Day? Where now is Alexander of Macedon: does the steel Host, that yelled in fierce battle-shouts at Issus and Arbela, remain behind him; or have they all vanished utterly, even as per-turbed Goblins must? Napoleon too, and his Moscow Retreats and Austerlitz Campaigns! Was it all other than the veriest Spectre-hunt; which has now, with its howling tumult that made Night hideous, flitted away?—Ghosts! There are nigh a thousand million walking the Earth openly at noontide; some half-hundred have vanished from it, some half-hundred have arisen in it, ere thy watch ticks once.

'O Heaven, it is mysterious, it is awful to consider that we not only carry each a future Ghost within him; but are, in very deed, Ghosts! These Limbs, whence had we them; this stormy Force; this life-blood with its burning Passion? They are dust and shadow; a Shadow-system gathered round our ME; wherein, through some moments or years, the Divine Essence is to be revealed in the Flesh. That warrior on his strong war-horse, fire flashes through his eyes; Force dwells in his arm and heart: but warrior and war-horse are a vision; a revealed Force, nothing more. Stately they tread the Earth, as if it were a firm substance: fool! the Earth is but a film; it cracks in twain, and warrior and war-horse sink beyond plummet's sounding. Plummet's? Fantasy herself will not follow them. A little while ago they were not; a little while and they are not, their very ashes are not.

'So has it been from the beginning, so will it be to the end. Generation after generation takes to itself the Form of a Body; and forth-issuing from Cimmerian Night, on Heaven's mission, APPEARS. What Force and Fire is in each he expends: one grinding in the mill of Industry; one hunter-like climbing the giddy Alpine heights of Science; one madly dashed in pieces on the rocks of Strife, in war with his fellow:—and then the Heaven-sent is recalled; his earthly Vesture falls away, and soon even to Sense becomes a vanished Shadow. Thus, like some wild-flaming, wild-thundering train of Heaven's Artillery, does this mysterious MANKIND thunder and flame, in long-drawn, quick-succeeding grandeur, through the unknown Deep. Thus, like a God-created, fire-breathing Spirit-host, we emerge from the Inane; haste stormfully across the astonished Earth; then plunge again into the Inane. Earth's mountains are levelled, and her seas filled up, in our passage: can the Earth, which is but dead and a vision, resist Spirits which have reality and are alive? On the hardest adamant some foot-print of us is stamped in; the last Rear of the host will read traces of the earliest Van. But whence?—O Heaven, whither? Sense knows not; Faith knows not; only that it is through Mystery to Mystery, from God and to God.

> "We *are such stuff*
> As Dreams are made of, and our little Life
> Is rounded with a sleep!"'

CHAPTER IX.

HERE then arises the so momentous question: Have many British
Readers actually arrived with us at the new promised country; is the
Philosophy of Clothes now at last opening around them? Long and
adventurous has the journey been: from those outmost vulgar, pal-
5   pable Woollen-Hulls of Man; through his wondrous Flesh-Garments,
and his wondrous Social Garnitures; inwards to the Garments of his
very Soul's Soul, to Time and Space themselves! And now does the
spiritual, eternal Essence of Man, and of Mankind, bared of such
wrappages, begin in any measure to reveal itself? Can many readers
10   discern, as through a glass darkly, in huge wavering outlines, some
primeval rudiments of Man's Being, what is changeable divided from
what is unchangeable? Does that Earth-Spirit's speech in *Faust*,—

'   ' 'Tis thus at the roaring Loom of Time I ply,
        And weave for God the Garment thou see'est him by;'

15   or that other thousand-times-repeated speech of the Magician,
Shakspeare,—

'And like the baseless fabric of this vision,
        The cloudcapt Towers, the gorgeous Palaces,
        The solemn Temples, the great Globe itself,
20   And all which it inherit, shall dissolve;
        And like this unsubstantial pageant faded,
        Leave not a wrack behind;'

begin to have some meaning for us? In a word, do we at length stand safe in the far region of Poetic Creation and Palingenesia, where that Phœnix Death-Birth of Human Society, and of all Human things, appears possible, is seen to be inevitable?

Along this most insufficient, unheard-of Bridge, which the Editor, by Heaven's blessing, has now seen himself enabled to conclude if not complete, it cannot be his sober calculation, but only his fond hope, that many have travelled without accident. No firm arch, overspanning the Impassable with paved highway, could the Editor construct; only, as was said, some zigzag series of rafts floating tumultuously thereon. Alas, and the leaps from raft to raft were too often of a breakneck character; the darkness, the nature of the element, all was against us!

Nevertheless, may not here and there one of a thousand, provided with a discursiveness of intellect rare in our day, have cleared the passage, in spite of all? Happy few! little band of Friends! be welcome, be of courage. By degrees, the eye grows accustomed to its new Whereabout; the hand can stretch itself forth to work there: it is in this grand and indeed highest work of Palingenesia that ye shall labour, each according to ability. New labourers will arrive; new Bridges will be built: nay, may not our own poor rope-and-raft Bridge, in your passings and repassings, be mended in many a point, till it grow quite firm, passable even for the halt?

Meanwhile, of the innumerable multitude that started with us, joyous and full of hope, where now is the innumerable remainder, whom we see no longer by our side? The most have recoiled, and stand gazing afar off, in unsympathetic astonishment, at our career: not a few, pressing forward with more courage, have missed footing, or leaped short; and now swim weltering in the Chaos-flood, some towards this shore, some towards that. To these also a helping hand should be held out; at least some word of encouragement be said.

Or, to speak without metaphor, with which mode of utterance Teufelsdröckh unhappily has somewhat infected us,—can it be hidden from the Editor that many a British Reader sits reading quite bewildered in head, and afflicted rather than instructed by the present Work? Yes, long ago has many a British Reader been, as now, demanding with something like a snarl: Whereto does all this lead; or what use is in it?

In the way of replenishing thy purse, or otherwise aiding thy digestive faculty, O British Reader, it leads to nothing, and there is no use in it; but rather the reverse, for it costs thee somewhat. Nevertheless, if through this unpromising Horn-gate, Teufelsdröckh, and we by means of him, have led thee into the true Land of Dreams; and through the Clothes-Screen, as through a magical *Pierre-Pertuis*, thou lookest, even for moments, into the region of the Wonderful, and seest and feelest that thy daily life is girt with Wonder, and based on Wonder, and thy very blankets and breeches are Miracles,—then art thou profited beyond money's worth, and hast a thankfulness towards our Professor; nay, perhaps in many a literary Tea-circle, wilt open thy kind lips, and audibly express that same.

Nay, farther art not thou too perhaps by this time made aware that all Symbols are properly Clothes; that all Forms whereby Spirit manifests itself to Sense, whether outwardly or in the imagination, are Clothes; and thus not only the parchment Magna Charta, which a Tailor was nigh cutting into measures, but the Pomp and Authority of Law, the sacredness of Majesty, and all inferior Worships (Worthships) are properly a Vesture and Raiment; and the Thirty-nine Articles themselves are articles of wearing apparel (for the Religious Idea)? In which case, must it not also be admitted that this Science of Clothes is a high one, and may with infinitely deeper study on thy part yield richer fruit: that it takes scientific rank beside Codification, and Political Economy, and the Theory of the British Constitution; nay, rather, from its prophetic height looks down on all these, as on so many weaving-shops and spinning-mills, where the Vestures which *it* has to fashion, and consecrate, and distribute, are, too often by haggard hungry operatives who see no farther than their nose, mechanically woven and spun?

But omitting all this, much more all that concerns Natural Supernaturalism, and indeed whatever has reference to the Ulterior or Transcendental Portion of the Science, or bears never so remotely on that promised Volume of the *Palingenesie der menschlichen Gesellschaft* (Newbirth of Society),—we humbly suggest that no province of Clothes-Philosophy, even the lowest, is without its direct value, but that innumerable inferences of a practical nature may be drawn therefrom. To say nothing of those pregnant considerations, ethical, political, symbolical, which crowd on the Clothes-Philosopher from the

very threshold of his Science; nothing even of those 'architectural
ideas' which, as we have seen, lurk at the bottom of all Modes, and
will one day, better unfolding themselves, lead to important revolutions,—let us glance, for a moment, and with the faintest light of
Clothes-Philosophy, on what may be called the Habilatory Class of   5
our fellow-men. Here too overlooking, where so much were to be
looked on, the million spinners, weavers, fullers, dyers, washers, and
wringers, that puddle and muddle in their dark recesses, to make us
Clothes, and die that we may live,—let us but turn the reader's attention upon two small divisions of mankind, who, like moths, may   10
be regarded as Cloth-animals, creatures that live, move, and have
their being in Cloth: we mean, Dandies and Tailors.

  In regard to both which small divisions it may be asserted without
scruple that the public feeling, unenlightened by Philosophy, is at
fault; and even that the dictates of humanity are violated. As will   15
perhaps abundantly appear to readers of the two following Chapters.

CHAPTER X.

FIRST, touching Dandies, let us consider, with some scientific strictness, what a Dandy specially is. A Dandy is a Clothes-wearing Man, a Man whose trade, office, and existence consists in the wearing of Clothes. Every faculty of his soul, spirit, purse, and person is hero-
5 ically consecrated to this one object, the wearing of Clothes wisely and well: so that as others dress to live, he lives to dress. The all-importance of Clothes, which a German Professor, of unequalled learning and acumen, writes his enormous Volume to demonstrate, has sprung up in the intellect of the Dandy, without effort, like an
10 instinct of genius: he is inspired with Cloth, a Poet of Cloth. What Teufelsdröckh would call a 'Divine Idea of Cloth' is born with him; and this, like other such Ideas, will express itself outwardly, or wring his heart asunder with unutterable throes.

But, like a generous, creative enthusiast, he fearlessly makes his
15 Idea an Action; shows himself, in peculiar guise, to mankind; walks forth, a witness and living Martyr to the eternal Worth of Clothes. We called him a Poet: is not his body the (stuffed) parchment-skin whereon he writes, with cunning Huddersfield dyes, a Sonnet to his mistress' eyebrow? Say, rather, an Epos, and *Clotha Virumque cano*, to the
20 whole world, in Macaronic verses, which he that runs may read. Nay, if you grant, what seems to be admissible, that the Dandy has a Thinking-principle in him, and some notions of Time and Space, is there not in this Life-devotedness to Cloth, in this so willing sacrifice

of the Immortal to the Perishable, something (though in reverse order) of that blending and identification of Eternity with Time, which, as we have seen, constitutes the Prophetic character?

And now, for all this perennial Martyrdom, and Poesy, and even Prophecy, what is it that the Dandy asks in return? Solely, we may say, that you would recognise his existence; would admit him to be a living object; or even failing this, a visual object, or thing that will reflect rays of light. Your silver or your gold (beyond what the nig-gardly Law has already secured him) he solicits not; simply the glance of your eyes. Understand his mystic significance, or altogether miss and misinterpret it; do but look at him, and he is contented. May we not well cry shame on an ungrateful world, which refuses even this poor boon; which will waste its optic faculty on dried Crocodiles, and Siamese Twins; and over the domestic wonderful wonder of wonders, a live Dandy, glance with hasty indifference, and a scarcely concealed contempt! Him no Zoologist classes among the Mammalia, no Anato-mist dissects with care: when did we see any injected Preparation of the Dandy, in our Museums; any specimen of him preserved in spir-its? Lord Herringbone may dress himself in a snuff-brown suit, with snuff-brown shirt and shoes: it skills not; the undeerning public, occupied with grosser wants, passes by regardless on the other side.

The age of Curiosity, like that of Chivalry, is indeed, properly speak-ing, gone. Yet perhaps only gone to sleep: for here arises the Clothes-Philosophy to resuscitate, strangely enough, both the one and the other! Should sound views of this Science come to prevail, the essential na-ture of the British Dandy, and the mystic significance that lies in him, cannot always remain hidden under laughable and lamentable hallu-cination. The following long Extract from Professor Teufelsdröckh may set the matter, if not in its true light, yet in the way towards such. It is to be regretted however that here, as so often elsewhere, the Professor's keen philosophic perspicacity is somewhat marred by a certain mixture of almost owlish purblindness, or else of some per-verse, ineffectual, ironic tendency; our readers shall judge which:

'In these distracted times,' writes he, 'when the Religious Prin-ciple, driven out of most Churches, either lies unseen in the hearts of good men, looking and longing and silently working there towards some new Revelation; or else wanders homeless over the world, like

a disembodied soul seeking its terrestrial organisation,—into how many strange shapes, of Superstition and Fanaticism, does it not tentatively and errantly cast itself! The higher Enthusiasm of man's nature is for the while without Exponent; yet does it continue in-
5 destructible, unweariedly active, and work blindly in the great chaotic deep: thus Sect after Sect, and Church after Church, bodies itself forth, and melts again into new metamorphosis.

'Chiefly is this observable in England, which, as the wealthiest and worst-instructed of European nations, offers precisely the elements
10 (of Heat, namely, and of Darkness), in which such moon-calves and monstrosities are best generated. Among the newer Sects of that country, one of the most notable, and closely connected with our present subject, is that of the *Dandies;* concerning which, what little information I have been able to procure may fitly stand here.

15 'It is true, certain of the English Journalists, men generally without sense for the Religious Principle, or judgment for its manifestations, speak, in their brief enigmatic notices, as if this were perhaps rather a Secular Sect, and not a Religious one: nevertheless, to the psychologic eye its devotional and even sacrificial character plainly
20 enough reveals itself. Whether it belongs to the class of Fetish-worships, or of Hero-worships or Polytheisms, or to what other class, may in the present state of our intelligence remain undecided (*schweben*). A certain touch of Manicheism, not indeed in the Gnostic shape, is discernible enough: also (for human Error walks in a cycle,
25 and reappears at intervals) a not inconsiderable resemblance to that Superstition of the Athos Monks, who by fasting from all nourishment, and looking intensely for a length of time into their own navels, came to discern therein the true Apocalypse of Nature, and Heaven Unveiled. To my own surmise, it appears as if this Dandiacal
30 Sect were but a new modification, adapted to the new time, of that primeval Superstition, *Self-Worship;* which Zerdusht, Quangfoutchee, Mohamed, and others, strove rather to subordinate and restrain than to eradicate; and which only in the purer forms of Religion has been altogether rejected. Wherefore, if any one chooses to name it revived
35 Ahrimanism, or a new figure of Demon-Worship, I have, so far as is yet visible, no objection.

'For the rest, these people, animated with the zeal of a new Sect, display courage and perseverance, and what force there is in man's

nature, though never so enslaved. They affect great purity and sepa-
ratism; distinguish themselves by a particular costume (whereof some
notices were given in the earlier part of this Volume); likewise, so far
as possible, by a particular speech (apparently some broken *Lingua-
franca*, or English-French); and, on the whole, strive to maintain a
true Nazarene deportment, and keep themselves unspotted from the
world.

'They have their Temples, whereof the chief, as the Jewish Temple
did, stands in their metropolis; and is named *Almack's*, a word of
uncertain etymology. They worship principally by night; and have
their Highpriests and Highpriestesses, who, however, do not continue for life. The rites, by some supposed to be of the Menadic sort,
or perhaps with an Eleusinian or Cabiric character, are held strictly
secret. Nor are Sacred Books wanting to the Sect; these they call
Fashionable Novels: however, the Canon is not completed, and some
are canonical and others not.

'Of such Sacred Books I, not without expense, procured myself
some samples; and in hope of true insight, and with the zeal which
beseems an Inquirer into Clothes, set to interpret and study them.
But wholly to no purpose: that tough faculty of reading, for which the
world will not refuse me credit, was here for the first time foiled and
set at nought. In vain that I summoned my whole energies (*mich
weidlich anstrengte*), and did my very utmost: at the end of some
short space, I was uniformly seized with not so much what I can call
a drumming in my ears, as a kind of infinite, unsufferable Jew's-
harping and scrannel-piping there; to which the frightfullest species of
Magnetic Sleep soon supervened. And if I strove to shake this away,
and absolutely would not yield, there came a hitherto unfelt sensation, as of *Delirium Tremens*, and a melting into total deliquium:—
till at last, by order of the Doctor, dreading ruin to my whole
intellectual and bodily faculties, and a general breaking-up of the
constitution, I reluctantly but determinedly forbore. Was there some
miracle at work here; like those Fire-balls, and supernal and infernal
prodigies, which, in the case of the Jewish Mysteries, have also more
than once scared back the Alien? Be this as it may, such failure on my
part, after best efforts, must excuse the imperfection of this sketch;
altogether incomplete, yet the completest I could give of a Sect too
singular to be omitted.

'Loving my own life and senses as I do, no power shall induce me, as a private individual, to open another *Fashionable Novel.* But luckily, in this dilemma, comes a hand from the clouds; whereby if not victory, deliverance is held out to me. Round one of those Book-
5 packages, which the *Stillschweigen'sche Buchhandlung* is in the habit of importing from England, come, as is usual, various waste printed-sheets (*Maculatur-blätter*), by way of interior wrappage: into these the Clothes-Philosopher, with a certain Mohamedan reverence even for waste paper, where curious knowledge will sometimes hover, dis-
10 dains not to cast his eye. Readers may judge of his astonishment when on such a defaced stray sheet, probably the outcast fraction of some English Periodical, such as they name *Magazine*, appears something like a Dissertation on this very subject of *Fashionable Novels!* It sets out, indeed, chiefly from the Secular point of view; directing
15 itself, not without asperity, against some to me unknown individual, named *Pelham*, who seems to be a Mystagogue, and leading Teacher and Preacher of the Sect; so that, what indeed otherwise was not to be expected in such a fugitive fragmentary sheet, the true secret, the Religious physiognomy and physiology of the Dandiacal Body, is
20 nowise laid fully open there. Nevertheless, scattered lights do from time to time sparkle out, whereby I have endeavoured to profit. Nay, in one passage selected from the Prophecies, or Mythic Theogonies, or whatever they are (for the style seems very mixed), of this Mystagogue, I find what appears to be a Confession of Faith, or
25 Whole Duty of Man, according to the tenets of that Sect. Which Confession, or Whole Duty, therefore, as proceeding from a source so authentic, I shall here arrange under Seven distinct Articles, and in very abridged shape lay before the German world; therewith taking leave of this matter. Observe, also, that to avoid possibility of
30 error, I, as far as may be, quote literally from the Original:

'ARTICLES OF FAITH.

"1. Coats should have nothing of the triangle about them; at the
    same time, wrinkles behind should be carefully avoided.
"2. The collar is a very important point: it should be low behind,
35   and slightly rolled.
"3. No license of fashion can allow a man of delicate taste to
    adopt the posterial luxuriance of a Hottentot.

"4. There is safety in a swallow-tail.

"5. The good sense of a gentleman is nowhere more finely developed than in his rings.

"6. It is permitted to mankind, under certain restrictions, to wear white waistcoats.

"7. The trowsers must be exceedingly tight across the hips."

'All which Propositions, I, for the present, content myself with modestly but peremptorily and irrevocably denying.

'In strange contrast with this Dandiacal Body stands another British Sect, originally, as I understand, of Ireland, where its chief seat still is; but known also in the main Island, and indeed every where rapidly spreading. As this Sect has hitherto emitted no Canonical Books, it remains to me in the same state of obscurity as the Dandiacal, which has published Books that the unassisted human faculties are inadequate to read. The members appear to be designated by a considerable diversity of names, according to their various places of establishment: in England they are generally called the *Drudge* Sect; also, unphilosophically enough, the *White-Negroes;* and, chiefly in scorn by those of other communions, the *Ragged-Beggar* Sect. In Scotland, again, I find them entitled *Hallan-shakers,* or the *Stook-of-Duds* Sect; any individual communicant is named *Stook-of-Duds* (that is, Shock of Rags), in allusion, doubtless, to their professional Costume. While in Ireland, which, as mentioned, is their grand parent hive, they go by a perplexing multiplicity of designations, such as *Bogtrotters, Redshanks, Ribbonmen, Cottiers, Peep-of-day Boys, Babes of the Wood, Rockites, Poor-Slaves;* which last, however, seems to be the primary and generic name; whereto, probably enough, the others are only subsidiary species, or slight varieties; or, at most, propagated offsets from the parent stem, whose minute subdivisions, and shades of difference, it were here loss of time to dwell on. Enough for us to understand, what seems indubitable, that the original Sect is that of the *Poor-Slaves;* whose doctrines, practices, and fundamental characteristics, pervade and animate the whole Body, howsoever denominated or outwardly diversified.

'The precise speculative tenets of this Brotherhood: how the Universe, and Man, and Man's Life, picture themselves to the mind of an Irish Poor-Slave; with what feelings and opinions he looks forward on the Future, round on the Present, back on the Past, it were extremely difficult to specify. Something Monastic there appears to be in their Constitution: we find them bound by the two Monastic Vows, of Poverty and Obedience; which Vows, especially the former, it is said, they observe with great strictness; nay, as I have understood it, they are pledged, and be it by any solemn Nazarene ordination or not, irrevocably consecrated thereto, even *before* birth. That the third Monastic Vow, of Chastity, is rigidly enforced among them, I find no ground to conjecture.

'Furthermore, they appear to imitate the Dandiacal Sect in their grand principle of wearing a peculiar Costume. Of which Irish Poor-Slave Costume no description will indeed be found in the present Volume; for this reason, that by the imperfect organ of Language it did not seem describable. Their raiment consists of innumerable skirts, lappets, and irregular wings, of all cloths and of all colours; through the labyrinthic intricacies of which their bodies are introduced by some unknown process. It is fastened together by a multiplex combination of buttons, thrums, and skewers; to which frequently is added a girdle of leather, of hempen or even of straw rope, round the loins. To straw rope, indeed, they seem partial, and often wear it by way of sandals. In head-dress they affect a certain freedom: hats with partial brim, without crown, or with only a loose, hinged, or valve crown; in the former case, they sometimes invert the hat, and wear it brim uppermost, like a University-cap, with what view is unknown.

'The name, Poor-Slaves, seems to indicate a Slavonic, Polish, or Russian origin: not so, however, the interior essence and spirit of their Superstition, which rather displays a Teutonic or Druidical character. One might fancy them worshippers of Hertha, or the Earth: for they dig and affectionately work continually in her bosom; or else, shut up in private Oratories, meditate and manipulate the substances derived from her; seldom looking up towards the Heavenly Luminaries, and then with comparative indifference. Like the Druids, on the other hand, they live in dark dwellings; often even breaking their glass-windows, where they find such, and stuffing them up with pieces of raiment, or other opaque substances, till the fit obscurity is restored. Again, like all followers of Nature-Worship, they are liable to outbreakings of an enthusiasm rising to ferocity; and burn men, if not in wicker idols, yet in sod cottages.

'In respect of diet, they have also their observances. All Poor-Slaves are Rhizophagous (or Root-eaters); a few are Ichthyophagous, and use Salted Herrings: other animal food they abstain from; except indeed, with perhaps some strange inverted fragment of a Brahminical feeling, such animals as die a natural death. Their universal sustenance is the root named Potato, cooked by fire alone; and generally without condiment or relish of any kind, save an unknown condiment named *Point*, into the meaning of which I have vainly inquired; the victual *Potatoes-and-Point* not appearing, at least not with specific accuracy of description, in any European Cookery-Book whatever. For drink they use, with an almost epigrammatic counterpoise of taste, Milk, which is the mildest of liquors, and *Potheen*, which is the fiercest. This latter I have tasted, as well as the English *Blue-Ruin*, and the Scotch *Whisky*, analogous fluids used by the Sect in those countries: it evidently contains some form of alcohol, in the highest state of concentration, though disguised with acrid oils; and is, on the whole, the most pungent substance known to me,—indeed, a perfect liquid fire. In all their Religious Solemnities, Potheen is said to be an indispensable requisite, and largely consumed.

'An Irish Traveller, of perhaps common veracity, who presents himself under the to me unmeaning title of *The late John Bernard*, offers the following sketch of a domestic establishment, the inmates whereof, though such is not stated expressly, appear to have been of that Faith. Thereby shall my German readers now behold an Irish Poor-Slave, as it were with their own eyes; and even see him at meat. Moreover, in the so precious waste-paper sheet, above mentioned, I have found some corresponding picture of a Dandiacal Household, painted by that same Dandiacal Mystagogue, or Theogonist: this also, by way of counterpart and contrast, the world shall look into.

'First, therefore, of the Poor-Slave, who appears likewise to have been a species of Innkeeper. I quote from the original:

Poor-Slave Household.

'"The furniture of this Caravansera consisted of a large iron Pot, two oaken Tables, two Benches, two Chairs, and a Potheen Noggin. There was a Loft above (attainable by a ladder), upon which the inmates slept; and the space below was divided by a hurdle into two Apartments; the one for their cow and pig, the other for themselves and guests. On entering the house we discovered the family, eleven

in number, at dinner: the father sitting at the top, the mother at
bottom, the children on each side of a large oaken Board which was
scooped out in the middle, like a Trough, to receive the contents of
their Pot of Potatoes. Little holes were cut at equal distances to
5 contain Salt; and a bowl of Milk stood on the table: all the luxuries
of meat and beer, bread, knives, and dishes were dispensed with."
The Poor-Slave himself our Traveller found, as he says, broad-backed,
black-browed, of great personal strength, and mouth from ear to ear.
His Wife was a sun-browned but well-featured woman; and his young
10 ones, bare and chubby, had the appetite of ravens. Of their Philosophical, or Religious tenets or observances, no notice or hint.

'But now, secondly, of the Dandiacal Household; in which, truly,
that often-mentioned Mystagogue and inspired Penman himself has
his abode:
15   *Dandiacal Household.*
'"A Dressing-room splendidly furnished: violet-coloured curtains,
chairs and ottomans of the same hue. Two full-length Mirrors are
placed, one on each side of a table, which supports the luxuries of the
Toilet. Several Bottles of Perfumes, arranged in a peculiar fashion,
20 stand upon a smaller table of mother-of-pearl: opposite to these are
placed the appurtenances of Lavation richly wrought in frosted silver.
A Wardrobe of Buhl is on the left; the doors of which being partly
open discover a profusion of Clothes; Shoes of a singularly small size
monopolise the lower shelves. Fronting the wardrobe a door ajar
25 gives some slight glimpse of a Bath-room. Folding-doors in the back-
ground.—Enter the Author," our Theogonist in person, "obsequiously preceded by a French Valet, in white silk Jacket and cambric
Apron."

30   'Such are the two Sects which, at this moment, divide the more
unsettled portion of the British People; and agitate that ever-vexed
country. To the eye of the political Seer, their mutual relation, pregnant with the elements of discord and hostility, is far from consoling.
These two principles of Dandiacal Self-worship or Demon-worship,
35 and Poor-Slavish or Drudgical Earth-worship, or whatever that same
Drudgism may be, do as yet indeed manifest themselves under distant
and nowise considerable shapes: nevertheless, in their roots and subterranean ramifications, they extend through the entire structure of

Society, and work unweariedly in the secret depths of English national Existence; striving to separate and isolate it into two contradic-
tory, uncommunicating masses.

'In numbers, and even individual strength, the Poor-Slaves or
Drudges, it would seem, are hourly increasing. The Dandiacal, again,   5
is by nature no proselytising Sect; but it boasts of great hereditary
resources, and is strong by union: whereas the Drudges, split into
parties, have as yet no rallying-point; or at best, only co-operate by
means of partial secret affiliations. If, indeed, there were to arise a
Communion of Drudges, as there is already a Communion of Saints,   10
what strangest effects would follow therefrom! Dandyism as yet affects to look down on Drudgism: but perhaps the hour of trial, when
it will be practically seen which ought to look down, and which up,
is not so distant.

'To me it seems probable that the two Sects will one day part   15
England between them; each recruiting itself from the intermediate
ranks, till there be none left to enlist on either side. Those Dandiacal
Manicheans, with the host of Dandyising Christians, will form one
body: the Drudges, gathering round them whosoever is Drudgical,
be he Christian or Infidel Pagan; sweeping up likewise all manner   20
of Utilitarians, Radicals, refractory Potwalloppers, and so forth, into
their general mass, will form another. I could liken Dandyism and
Drudgism to two bottomless boiling Whirlpools that had broken out
on opposite quarters of the firm land: as yet they appear only disqui-
eted, foolishly bubbling wells, which man's art might cover in; yet   25
mark them, their diameter is daily widening; they are hollow Cones
that boil up from the infinite Deep, over which your firm land is but
a thin crust or rind! Thus daily is the intermediate land crumbling in,
daily the empire of the two Buchan-Bullers extending; till now there
is but a foot-plank, a mere film of Land between them; this too is   30
washed away; and then—we have the true Hell of Waters, and Noah's
Deluge is outdeluged!

'Or better, I might call them two boundless, and indeed unexampled Electric Machines (turned by the "Machinery of Society"),
with batteries of opposite quality; Drudgism the Negative, Dandyism   35
the Positive: one attracts hourly towards it and appropriates all the
Positive Electricity of the nation (namely, the Money thereof); the
other is equally busy with the Negative (that is to say the Hunger),

which is equally potent. Hitherto you see only partial transient sparkles and sputters: but wait a little, till the entire nation is in an electric state; till your whole vital Electricity, no longer healthfully Neutral, is cut into two isolated portions of Positive and Negative (of Money and of Hunger); and stands there bottled up in two World-Batteries! The stirring of a child's finger brings the two together; and then— What then? The Earth is but shivered into impalpable smoke by that Doom's-thunder-peal; the Sun misses one of his Planets in Space, and thenceforth there are no eclipses of the Moon.—Or better still, I might liken'——

Oh! enough, enough of likenings and similitudes; in excess of which, truly, it is hard to say whether Teufelsdröckh or ourselves sin the more.

We have often blamed him for a habit of wire-drawing and over-refining; from of old we have been familiar with his tendency to Mysticism and Religiosity, whereby in every thing he was still scenting out Religion: but never perhaps did these amaurosis-suffusions so cloud and distort his otherwise most piercing vision, as in this of the *Dandiacal Body!* Or was there something of intended satire; is the Professor and Seer not quite the blinkard he affects to be? Of an ordinary mortal we should have decisively answered in the affirmative; but with a Teufelsdröckh there ever hovers some shade of doubt. In the meanwhile, if satire were actually intended, the case is little better. There are not wanting men who will answer: Does your Professor take us for simpletons? His irony has overshot itself; we see through it, and perhaps through him.

CHAPTER XI.

TAILORS.

THUS, however, has our first Practical Inference from the Clothes-Philosophy, that which respects Dandies, been sufficiently drawn; and we come now to the second, concerning Tailors. On this latter our opinion happily quite coincides with that of Teufelsdröckh himself, as expressed in the concluding page of his Volume; to whom there- 5 fore we willingly give place. Let him speak his own last words, in his own way:

'Upwards of a century,' says he, 'must elapse, and still the bleeding fight of Freedom be fought, whoso is noblest perishing in the van, 10 and thrones be hurled on altars like Pelion on Ossa, and the Moloch of Iniquity have his victims, and the Michael of Justice his Martyrs, before Tailors can be admitted to their true prerogatives of manhood, and this last wound of suffering Humanity be closed.

'If aught in the history of the world's blindness could surprise us, 15 here might we indeed pause and wonder. An idea has gone abroad, and fixed itself down into a wide-spreading rooted Error, that Tailors are a distinct species in Physiology, not Men, but fractional Parts of a Man. Call any one a *Schneider* (Cutter, Tailor), is it not, in our dislocated, hoodwinked, and indeed delirious condition of So- 20 ciety, equivalent to defying his perpetual fellest enmity? The epithet *Schneidermässig* (Tailorlike) betokens an otherwise unapproachable degree of pusillanimity: we introduce a *Tailor's-Melancholy*, more

211

opprobrious than any Leprosy, into our Books of Medicine; and fable
I know not what of his generating it by living on Cabbage. Why
should I speak of Hans Sachs (himself a Shoemaker, or kind of Leather-
Tailor), with his *Schneider mit dem Panier*? Why of Shakspeare, in his
5   *Taming of the Shrew*, and elsewhere? Does it not stand on record that
the English Queen Elizabeth, receiving a deputation of Eighteen
Tailors, addressed them with a: Good morning, gentlemen both! Did
not the same virago boast that she had a Cavalry Regiment, whereof
neither horse nor man could be injured: her Regiment, namely, of
10   Tailors on Mares? Thus everywhere is the falsehood taken for granted,
and acted on as an indisputable fact.

'Nevertheless, need I put the question to any Physiologist, Whether
it is disputable or not? Seems it not at least presumable, that, under
his Clothes, the Tailor has bones, and viscera, and other muscles than
15   the sartorius? Which function of manhood is the Tailor not conjectured to perform? Can he not arrest for Debt? Is he not in most
countries a tax-paying animal?

'To no reader of this Volume can it be doubtful which conviction
is mine. Nay, if the fruit of these long vigils, and almost preternatural
20   Inquiries is not to perish utterly, the world will have approximated
towards a higher Truth; and the doctrine, which Swift, with the keen
forecast of genius, dimly anticipated, will stand revealed in clear light:
that the Tailor is not only a Man, but something of a Creator or
Divinity. Of Franklin it was said, that "he snatched the Thunder from
25   Heaven and the Sceptre from Kings:" but which is greater, I would
ask, he that lends, or he that snatches? For, looking away from individual cases, and how a Man is by the Tailor new-created into a
Nobleman, and clothed not only with Wool but with Dignity and a
Mystic Dominion,—is not the fair fabric of Society itself, with all its
30   royal mantles and pontifical stoles, whereby, from nakedness and dis-
memberment, we are organised into Polities, into Nations, and a
whole co-operating Mankind, the creation, as has here been often
irrefragably evinced, of the Tailor alone?—What too are all Poets, and
moral Teachers, but a species of Metaphorical Tailors? Touching which
35   high Guild the greatest living Guild-Brother has triumphantly asked
us: "Nay, if thou wilt have it, who but the Poet first made Gods for
men; brought them down to us; and raised us up to them?"

'And this is he, whom sitting downcast, on the hard basis of his Shop-board, the world treats with contumely, as the ninth part of a man! Look up, thou much injured one, look up with the kindling eye of hope, and prophetic bodings of a noble better time. Too long hast thou sat there, on crossed legs, wearing thy ancle-joints to horn; like some sacred Anchorite, or Catholic Fakir, doing penance, drawing down Heaven's richest blessings, for a world that scoffed at thee. Be of hope! Already streaks of blue peer through our clouds; the thick gloom of Ignorance is rolling asunder, and it will be Day. Mankind will repay with interest their long-accumulated debt: the Anchorite that was scoffed at will be worshipped; the Fraction will become not an Integer only, but a Square and Cube. With astonishment the world will recognise that the Tailor is its Hierophant, and Hierarch, or even its God.

'As I stood in the Mosque of St. Sophia, and looked upon these Four-and-Twenty Tailors, sewing and embroidering that rich Cloth, which the Sultan sends yearly for the Caaba of Mecca, I thought within myself: How many other Unholies has your covering Art made holy, besides this Arabian Whinstone!

'Still more touching was it when, turning the corner of a lane, in the Scottish Town of Edinburgh, I came upon a Signpost, whereon stood written that such and such a one was "Breeches-Maker to his Majesty;" and stood painted the Effigies of a Pair of Leather Breeches, and between the knees these memorable words, SIC ITUR AD ASTRA. Was not this the martyr prison-speech of a Tailor sighing indeed in bonds, yet sighing towards deliverance; and prophetically appealing to a better day? A day of justice, when the worth of Breeches would be revealed to man, and the Scissors become forever venerable.

'Neither, perhaps, may I now say, has his appeal been altogether in vain. It was in this high moment, when the soul, rent, as it were, and shed asunder, is open to inspiring influence, that I first conceived this Work on Clothes; the greatest I can ever hope to do; which has already, after long retardations, occupied, and will yet occupy, so large a section of my Life; and of which the Primary and simpler Portion may here find its conclusion.'

CHAPTER XII.

So have we endeavoured, from the enormous, amorphous Plumpudding, more like a Scottish Haggis, which Herr Teufelsdröckh had kneaded for his fellow mortals, to pick out the choicest Plums, and present them separately on a cover of our own. A laborious, perhaps
5 a thankless enterprise; in which, however, something of hope has occasionally cheered us, and of which we can now wash our hands not altogether without satisfaction. If hereby, though in barbaric wise, some morsel of spiritual nourishment have been added to the scanty ration of our beloved British world, what nobler recompense could
10 the Editor desire? If it prove otherwise, why should he murmur? Was not this a Task which Destiny, in any case, had appointed him; which having now done with, he sees his general Day's-work so much the lighter, so much the shorter?

15   Of Professor Teufelsdröckh it seems impossible to take leave without a mingled feeling of astonishment, gratitude and disapproval. Who will not regret that talents, which might have profited in the higher walks of Philosophy, or in Art itself, have been so much devoted to a rummaging among lumber-rooms; nay, too often to a
20 scraping in kennels, where lost rings and diamond-necklaces are nowise the sole conquests? Regret is unavoidable; yet Censure were loss of time. To cure him of his mad humours British Criticism would essay in vain: enough for her if she can, by vigilance, prevent the spreading

214

of such among ourselves. What a result, should this piebald, entangled, hyper-metaphorical style of writing, not to say of thinking,
become general among our Literary men! as it might so easily do.
Thus has not the Editor himself, working over Teufelsdröckh's German, lost much of his own English purity? Even as the smaller whirl-   5
pool is sucked into the larger, and made to whirl along with it, so has
the lesser mind, in this instance, been forced to become portion of
the greater, and, like it, see all things figuratively: which habit time,
and assiduous effort, will be needed to eradicate.

Nevertheless, wayward as our Professor shows himself, is there any   10
reader that can part with him in declared enmity? Let us confess,
there is that in the wild, much-suffering, much-inflicting man, which
almost attaches us. His attitude, we will hope and believe, is that of
a man who had said to Cant, Begone; and to Dilettantism, Here thou
canst not be; and to Truth, Be thou in place of all to me: a man who   15
had manfully defied the 'Time-Prince,' or Devil, to his face; nay,
perhaps, Hannibal-like, was mysteriously consecrated from birth to
that warfare, and now stood minded to wage the same, by all weapons, in all places, at all times. In such a cause, any soldier, were he
but a Polack Scythe-man, shall be welcome.   20

Still the question returns on us: How could a man occasionally of
keen insight, not without keen sense of propriety, who had real
Thoughts to communicate, resolve to emit them in a shape bordering
so closely on the absurd? Which question he were wiser than the
present Editor who should satisfactorily answer. Our conjecture has   25
sometimes been, that perhaps Necessity as well as Choice was concerned in it. Seems it not conceivable that, in a Life like our Professor's,
where so much bountifully given by Nature had in Practice failed and
misgone, Literature also would never rightly prosper: that striving
with his characteristic vehemence to paint this and the other Picture,   30
and ever without success, he at last desperately dashes his sponge, full
of all colours, against the canvass, to try whether it will paint Foam?
With all his stillness, there were perhaps in Teufelsdröckh desperation
enough for this.

A second conjecture we hazard with even less warranty. It is that   35
Teufelsdröckh is not without some touch of the universal feeling, a
wish to proselytise. How often already have we paused, uncertain
whether the basis of this so enigmatic nature were really Stoicism and

Despair, or Love and Hope only seared into the figure of these! Remarkable, moreover, is this saying of his: 'How were Friendship possible? In mutual devotedness to the Good and True: otherwise impossible; except as Armed Neutrality, or hollow Commercial League. A man, be the Heavens ever praised, is sufficient for himself; yet were ten men, united in Love, capable of being and of doing what ten thousand singly would fail in. Infinite is the help man can yield to man.' And now in conjunction therewith consider this other: 'It is the Night of the World, and still long till it be Day: we wander amid the glimmer of smoking ruins, and the Sun and the Stars of Heaven are as if blotted out for a season; and two immeasurable Fantoms, HYPOCRISY and ATHEISM, with the Gowle, SENSUALITY, stalk abroad over the Earth, and call it theirs: well at ease are the Sleepers for whom Existence is a shallow Dream.'

But what of the awestruck Wakeful who find it a Reality? Should not these unite; since even an authentic Spectre is not visible to Two?—In which case were this enormous Clothes-Volume properly an enormous Pitchpan, which our Teufelsdröckh in his lone watchtower had kindled, that it might flame far and wide through the Night, and many a disconsolately wandering spirit be guided thither to a Brother's bosom!—We say as before, with all his malign Indifference, who knows what mad Hopes this man may harbour?

Meanwhile there is one fact to be stated here, which harmonises ill with such conjecture; and, indeed, were Teufelsdröckh made like other men, might as good as altogether subvert it. Namely, that while the Beaconfire blazed its brightest, the Watchman had quitted it; that no pilgrim could now ask him: Watchman, what of the Night? Professor Teufelsdröckh, be it known, is no longer visibly present at Weissnichtwo, but again to all appearance lost in Space! Some time ago the Hofrath Heuschrecke was pleased to favour us with another copious Epistle; wherein much is said about the 'Population-Institute;' much repeated in praise of the Paperbag Documents, the hieroglyphic nature of which our Hofrath still seems not to have surmised; and, lastly, the strangest occurrence communicated, to us for the first time, in the following paragraph:

'*Ew. Wohlgeboren* will have seen, from the public Prints, with what affectionate and hitherto fruitless solicitude Weissnichtwo regards the disappearance of her Sage. Might but the united voice of Germany prevail on him to return; nay, could we but so much as elucidate for ourselves by what mystery he went away! But, alas, old Lieschen experiences or affects the profoundest deafness, the profoundest ignorance: in the Wahngasse all lies swept, silent, sealed up; the Privy Council itself can hitherto elicit no answer.

'It had been remarked that while the agitating news of those Parisian Three Days flew from mouth to mouth, and dinned every ear in Weissnichtwo, Herr Teufelsdröckh was not known, at the *Gans* or elsewhere, to have spoken, for a whole week, any syllable except once these three: *Es geht an* (It is beginning). Shortly after, as *Ew. Wohlgeboren* knows, was the public tranquillity here, as in Berlin, threatened by a Sedition of the Tailors. Nor did there want Evil-wishers, or perhaps mere desperate Alarmists, who asserted that the closing Chapter of the Clothes-Volume was to blame. In this appalling crisis, the serenity of our Philosopher was indescribable: nay, perhaps, through one humble individual, something thereof might pass into the *Rath* (Council) itself, and so contribute to the country's deliverance. The Tailors are now entirely pacificated.—To neither of these two incidents can I attribute our loss: yet still comes there the shadow of a suspicion out of Paris and its Politics. For example, when the *Saint-Simonian Society* transmitted its Propositions hither, and the whole *Gans* was one vast cackle of laughter, lamentation, and astonishment, our Sage sat mute; and at the end of the third evening, said merely: "Here also are men who have discovered, not without amazement, that Man is still Man; of which high, long-forgotten Truth you already see them make a false application." Since then, as has been ascertained by examination of the Post Director, there passed at least one Letter with its Answer between the Messieurs Bazard-Enfantin and our Professor himself; of what tenor can now only be conjectured. On the fifth night following, he was seen for the last time!

'Has this invaluable man, so obnoxious to most of the hostile Sects that convulse our Era, been spirited away by certain of their emissaries; or did he go forth voluntarily to their head-quarters to confer with them, and confront them? Reason we have, at least of a negative sort, to believe the Lost still living: our widowed heart also whispers that ere long he will himself give a sign. Otherwise, indeed, must his archives, one day, be opened by Authority; where much, perhaps the *Palingenesie* itself, is thought to be reposited.'

Thus far the Hofrath; who vanishes, as is his wont, too like an Ignis Fatuus, leaving the dark still darker.

So that Teufelsdröckh's public History were not done, then, or reduced to an even, unromantic tenor; nay, perhaps, the better part thereof were only beginning? We stand in a region of conjectures, where substance has melted into shadow, and one cannot be distinguished from the other. May Time, which solves or suppresses all problems, throw glad light on this also. Our own private conjecture, now amounting almost to certainty, is that, safe-moored in some stillest obscurity, not to lie always still, Teufelsdröckh is actually in London!

Here, however, can the present Editor, with an ambrosial joy as of over-weariness falling into sleep, lay down his pen. Well does he know, if human testimony be worth aught, that to innumerable British readers likewise, this is a satisfying consummation; that innumerable British readers consider him, during these current months, but as an uneasy interruption to their ways of thought and digestion; and indicate so much, not without a certain irritancy and even spoken invective. For which, as for other mercies, ought not he to thank the Upper Powers? To one and all of you, O irritated readers, he, with outstretched arms and open heart, will wave a kind farewell. Thou too, miraculous Entity, who namest thyself YORKE and OLIVER, and with thy vivacities and genialities, with thy all-too Irish mirth and madness, and odour of palled punch, makest such strange work, farewell; long as thou canst, fare-*well!* Have we not, in the course of eternity, travelled some months of our Life-journey in partial sight of one another; have we not existed together, though in a state of quarrel?

THE END.

APPENDIX A:
TESTIMONIES OF AUTHORS

The following appendix, including Carlyle's "Author's Note," first appeared as such in the 1869 Library Edition and was also attached to the 1871 People's Edition, in both cases preceded by a half-title page reading "APPENDIX: TESTIMONIES OF AUTHORS." The "Testimonies" had appeared as a preface in the editions of 1838, 1841, and 1849, but had been omitted from the 1858 Uniform Edition (see Introduction, pp. lxxxvi–xciv, and Note on the Text, pp. ciii–civ). The text of the introductory paragraphs is that of their first appearance in 1869; the text of the "Testimonies" themselves follows that of their first appearance in 1838.

THIS questionable little Book was undoubtedly written among the mountain solitudes, in 1831; but, owing to impediments natural and accidental, could not, for seven years more, appear as a Volume in England;—and had at last to clip itself in pieces, and be content to struggle out, bit by bit, in some courageous *Magazine* that offered. Whereby now, to certain idly curious readers, and even to myself till I make study, the insignificant but at last irritating question, What its real history and chronology are, is, if not insoluble, considerably involved in haze.

To the first English Edition, 1838, which an American, or two American had now opened the way for, there was slightingly prefixed, under the title *'Testimonies of Authors,'* some straggle of real documents, which, now that I find it again, sets the matter into clear light and sequence;—and shall here, for removal of idle stumbling-blocks and nugatory guessings from the path of every reader, be reprinted as it stood. (*Author's Note, of* 1868.)

TESTIMONIES OF AUTHORS.

I. HIGHEST CLASS, BOOKSELLER'S TASTER.

Taster to Bookseller.—"The Author of *Teufelsdröckh* is a person of talent; his work displays here and there some felicity of thought and expression, considerable fancy and knowledge: but whether or not it would take with the public seems doubtful. For a *jeu d'esprit* of that kind it is too long; it would have suited better as an essay or article than as a volume. The Author has no great tact: his wit is frequently heavy; and reminds one of the German Baron who took to leaping on tables, and answered that he was learning to be lively. *Is* the work a translation?"

Bookseller to Editor.—"Allow me to say that such a writer requires only a little more tact to produce a popular as well as an able work. Directly on receiving your permission, I sent your *MS.* to a gentleman in the highest class of men of letters, and an accomplished German scholar; I now inclose you his opinion, which, you may rely upon it, is a just one; and I have too high an opinion of your good sense to" &c. &c.—*MS. (penes nos), London, 17th September,* 1831.

II. CRITIC OF THE SUN.

"Fraser's Magazine exhibits the usual brilliancy, and also the" &c. "*Sartor Resartus* is what old Dennis used to call 'a heap of clotted nonsense,' mixed however, here and there, with passages marked by thought and striking poetic vigour. But what does the writer mean by 'Baphometic fire-baptism?' Why cannot he lay aside his pedantry, and write so as to make himself generally intelligible? We quote by way of curiosity a sentence from the *Sartor Resartus;* which may be read either backwards or forwards, for it is equally intelligible either way. Indeed, by beginning at the tail, and so working up to the head, we think the reader will stand the fairest chance of getting at its meaning: 'The fire-baptized soul, long so scathed and thunder-riven, here feels its own freedom; which feeling is its Baphometic baptism: the citadel of its whole kingdom it has thus gained by assault, and will keep inexpugnable; outwards from which the remaining dominions, not indeed without hard battering, will doubtless by degrees be conquered and pacificated.' Here is a"— .... —*Sun Newspaper, 1st April,* 1834.

III. NORTH AMERICAN REVIEWER.

.... "After a careful survey of the whole ground, our belief is that no such persons as Professor Teufelsdröckh or Counsellor Heuschrecke ever existed; that the six Paper-bags, with their China-ink inscriptions and multifarious contents, are a mere figment of the brain; that the 'present Editor' is the only person who has ever written upon the Philosophy of Clothes; and that the *Sartor Resartus* is the only treatise that has yet appeared upon that subject;—in short, that the whole account of the origin of the work before us, which the supposed Editor relates with so much gravity, and of which we have given a brief abstract, is, in plain English, a *hum.*

"Without troubling our readers at any great length with our reasons for entertaining these suspicions, we may remark, that the absence of all other information on the subject, except what is contained in the work, is itself a fact of a most significant character. The whole German press, as well as the particular one where the work purports to have been printed, seems to be under the control of *Stillschweigen and Co.*,—Silence and Company. If the Clothes-Philosophy and its author are making so great a sensation throughout Germany as is pretended, how happens it that the only notice we have of the fact is contained in a few numbers of a monthly Magazine published at London? How happens it that no intelligence about the matter has come out directly to this country? We pique ourselves here in New England upon knowing at least as much of what is going on in the literary way in the old Dutch Mother-land as our brethren of the fast-anchored Isle; but thus far we have no tidings whatever of the 'extensive close-printed close-meditated volume,' which forms the subject of this pretended commentary. Again, we would respectfully inquire of the 'present Editor' upon what part of the map of Germany we are to look for the city of *Weissnichtwo,*— 'Know-not-where,' at which place the work is supposed to have been printed and the Author to have resided. It has been our fortune to visit several portions of the German territory, and to examine pretty carefully, at different times and for various purposes, maps of the whole, but we have no recollection of any such place. We suspect that the city of *Know-not-where* might be called, with at least as much propriety, *Nobody-knows-where*, and is to be found in the kingdom of *Nowhere*. Again, the village of *Entepfuhl,*—'Duck-pond,' where the supposed Author of the work is said to have passed his youth, and that of *Hinterschlag*, where he had his education, are equally foreign to our geography. Duck-ponds enough there undoubtedly are in almost every village in Germany, as the traveller in that country knows too well to his cost, but any particular village denominated Duck-pond is to us altogether *terra incognita*. The names of the personages are not less singular than those of the places. Who can refrain from a smile at the yoking together of such a pair of appellatives as Diogenes Teufelsdröckh? The supposed bearer of this strange title is represented as admitting, in his pretended autobiography, that 'he had searched to no purpose through all the

Heralds' books in and without the German empire, and through all manner of Subscribers'-lists, Militia-rolls, and other Name-catalogues,' but had nowhere been able to find 'the name Teufelsdröckh, except as appended to his own person.' We can readily believe this, and we doubt very much whether any Christian parent would think of condemning a son to carry through life the burden of so unpleasant a title. That of Counsellor Heuschrecke,—Grasshopper, though not offensive, looks much more like a piece of fancy work than a 'fair business transaction.' The same may be said of *Blumine*,—Flower-Goddess, the heroine of the fable, and so of the rest.

"In short, our private opinion is, as we have remarked, that the whole story of a correspondence with Germany, a university of Nobody-knows-where, a Professor of Things in General, a Counsellor Grasshopper, a Flower-Goddess Blumine, and so forth, has about as much foundation in truth, as the late entertaining account of Sir John Herschel's discoveries in the moon. Fictions of this kind are, however, not uncommon, and ought not, perhaps, to be condemned with too much severity; but we are not sure that we can exercise the same indulgence in regard to the attempt, which seems to be made to mislead the public as to the substance of the work before us, and its pretended German original. Both purport, as we have seen, to be upon the subject of Clothes, or dress. *Clothes, their Origin and Influence*, is the title of the supposed German treatise of Professor Teufelsdröckh, and the rather odd name of *Sartor Resartus*—the Tailor Patched,—which the present Editor has affixed to his pretended commentary, seems to look the same way. But though there is a good deal of remark throughout the work in a half-serious, half-comic style upon dress, it seems to be in reality a treatise upon the great science of Things in General, which Teufelsdröckh is supposed to have professed at the university of Nobody-knows-where. Now, without intending to adopt a too rigid standard of morals, we own that we doubt a little the propriety of offering to the public a treatise on Things in General, under the name and in the form of an Essay on Dress. For ourselves, advanced as we unfortunately are in the journey of life, far beyond the period when dress is practically a matter of interest, we have no hesitation in saying, that the real subject of the work, is to us more attractive than the ostensible one. But this is probably not the case with the mass of readers. To the younger portion of the community which constitutes every where the very great majority, the subject of dress is one of intense and paramount importance. An author who treats it appeals, like the poet, to the young men and maidens—*virginibus puerisque,*—and calls upon them by all the motives which habitually operate most strongly upon their feelings, to buy his book. When, after opening their purses for this purpose, they have carried home the work in triumph, expecting to find in it some particular instruction in regard to the tying of their neckcloths, or the cut of their corsets, and meet with nothing better than a dissertation on Things in General, they will,—to use the mildest term—not be in very good humour. If the last improvements in legislation, which we have made in this country, should have found their way to England, the author we think would stand some chance of being *Lynched.* Whether his object in this piece of *supercherie* be merely pecuniary profit or whether he takes a malicious pleasure in quizzing the Dandies, we shall not undertake to say. In the latter part of the work, he devotes a separate chapter to this class of persons, from the tenour of which we should be disposed to conclude, that he would consider any mode of divesting them of their property very much in the nature of a spoiling of the Egyptians.

"The only thing about the work, tending to prove that it is what it purports to be, a commentary on a real German treatise, is the style, which is a sort of Babylonish dialect, not destitute, it is true, of richness, vigour, and at times a sort of singular felicity of expression, but very strongly tinged throughout with the peculiar idiom of the German language. This quality in the style, however, may be a mere result of a great familiarity with German literature, and we cannot, therefore, look upon it as in itself decisive, still less as outweighing so much evidence of an opposite character."—*North American Review, No. 89, October,* 1835.

IV. NEW-ENGLAND EDITORS.

"The Editors have been induced, by the expressed desire of many persons, to collect the following sheets out of the ephemeral pamphlets[*] in which they first appeared, under the conviction that they contain in themselves the assurance of a longer date.

[*] "Fraser's (London) Magazine, 1833–4."

"The Editors have no expectation that this little Work will have a sudden and general popularity. They will not undertake, as there is no need, to justify the gay costume in which the Author delights to dress his thoughts, or the German idioms with which he has sportively sprinkled his pages. It is his humour to advance the gravest speculations upon the gravest topics in a quaint and burlesque style. If his masquerade offend any of his audience, to that degree that they will not hear what he has to say, it may chance to draw others to listen to his wisdom; and what work of imagination can hope to please all? But we will venture to remark that the distaste excited by these peculiarities in some readers is greatest at first, and is soon forgotten; and that the foreign dress and aspect of the Work are quite superficial, and cover a genuine Saxon heart. We believe, no book has been published for many years, written in a more sincere style of idiomatic English, or which discovers an equal mastery over all the riches of the language. The Author makes ample amends for the occasional eccentricity of his genius, not only by frequent bursts of pure splendour, but by the wit and sense which never fail him.

"But what will chiefly commend the Book to the discerning reader is the manifest design of the work, which is, a Criticism upon the Spirit of the Age,—we had almost said, of the hour, in which we live; exhibiting in the most just and novel light the present aspects of Religion, Politics, Literature, Arts, and Social Life. Under all his gaiety the Writer has an earnest meaning, and discovers an insight into the manifold wants and tendencies of human nature, which is very rare among our popular authors. The philanthropy and the purity of moral sentiment, which inspire the work, will find their way to the heart of every lover of virtue."—*Preface to Sartor Resartus: Boston*, 1836, 1837.

SUNT, FUERUNT VEL FUERE.

London, 30th June, 1838.

APPENDIX B:
1858 SUMMARY

A Summary and an Index of Sartor Resartus *were prepared under Carlyle's supervision for the 1858 Uniform Edition (see Note on the Text, pp. cxx–cxxi) and were included in the two subsequent lifetime editions. The Summary is presented here, its text as it appeared in the 1858 edition, its page references, which are merely the first pages of each chapter, renumbered to correspond to the present edition. The headings of the 1858 Index have been incorporated into the Index of the present volume (pp. 607–646), where they are distinguished by being printed in boldface.*

APPENDIX B
1855 SUMMARY

SUMMARY OF SARTOR RESARTUS.

BOOK I.

Chap. I. *Preliminary.*

No Philosophy of Clothes yet, notwithstanding all our Science. Strangely forgotten that Man is by nature a *naked* animal. The English mind all too practically absorbed for any such inquiry. Not so deep-thinking Germany. Advantage of Speculation having free course. Editor receives from Professor Teufelsdröckh his new Work on Clothes. (p. 3).

Chap. II. *Editorial Difficulties.*

How to make known Teufelsdröckh and his Book to English readers; especially *such* a book? Editor receives from the Hofrath Heuschrecke a letter promising Biographic Documents. Negotiations with Oliver Yorke. *Sartor Resartus* conceived. Editor's assurances and advice to his British reader. (p. 8).

Chap. III. *Reminiscences.*

Teufelsdröckh at Weissnichtwo. Professor of Things in General at the University there: Outward aspect and character; memorable coffee-house utterances; domicile and watch-tower: Sights thence of City-Life by day and by night; with reflections thereon. Old 'Liza and her ways. Character of Hofrath Heuschrecke, and his relation to Teufelsdröckh. (p. 12).

229

Chap. IV. *Characteristics.*

Teufelsdröckh and his Work on Clothes: Strange freedom of speech; transcendentalism; force of insight and expression; multifarious learning: Style poetic, uncouth: Comprehensiveness of his humour and moral feeling. How the Editor once saw him laugh. Different kinds of Laughter and their significance. (p. 22).

Chap. V. *The World in Clothes.*

Futile cause-and-effect Philosophies. Teufelsdröckh's Orbis Vestitus. Clothes first invented for the sake of Ornament. Picture of our progenitor, the Aboriginal Savage. Wonders of growth and progress in mankind's history. Man defined as a Tool-using Animal. (p. 27).

Chap. VI. *Aprons.*

Divers Aprons in the world with divers uses. The Military and Police Establishment Society's working Apron. The Episcopal Apron with its corner tucked-in. The Laystall. Journalists now our only Kings and Clergy. (p. 33).

Chap. VII. *Miscellaneous-Historical.*

How Men and Fashions come and go. German Costume in the fifteenth century. By what strange chances do we live in History! The costume of Bolivar's Cavalry. (p. 36).

Chap. VIII. *The World out of Clothes.*

Teufelsdröckh's Theorem, "Society founded upon Cloth;" his Method, Intuition quickened by Experience.—The mysterious question, Who am I? Philosophic systems all at fault: A deeper meditation has always taught, here and there an individual, that all visible things are appearances only; but also emblems and revelations of God. Teufelsdröckh first comes upon the question of Clothes: Baseness to which Clothing may bring us. (p. 40).

Chap. IX. *Adamitism.*

The universal utility of Clothes, and their higher mystic virtue, illustrated. Conception of Mankind stripped naked; and immediate consequent dissolution of civilised Society. (p. 45).

Chap. X. *Pure Reason.*

A Naked World possible, nay actually exists, under the clothed one. Man in the eye of Pure Reason, a visible God's-Presence. The beginning of all wisdom, to look fixedly on Clothes till they become transparent. Wonder, the basis of Worship: Perennial in man. Modern Sciolists who cannot wonder: Teufelsdröckh's contempt for, and advice to them. (p. 49).

Chap. XI. *Prospective.*

Nature not an Aggregate, but a Whole. All visible things are emblems, Clothes; and exist for a time only. The grand scope of the Philosophy of Clothes.—Biographic Documents arrive. Letter from Heuschrecke on the importance of Biography. Heterogeneous character of the documents: Editor sorely perplexed; but desperately grapples with his work. (p. 54).

BOOK II.

Chap. I. *Genesis.*

Old Andreas Futteral and Gretchen his wife: Their quiet home. Advent of a mysterious stranger, who deposits with them a young infant, the future Herr Diogenes Teufelsdröckh. After-yearnings of the youth for his unknown Father. Sovereign power of Names and Naming. Diogenes a flourishing Infant. (p 63).

Chap. II. *Idyllic.*

Happy Childhood! Entepfuhl: Sights, hearings and experiences of the boy Teufelsdröckh; their manifold teaching. Education; what it can do, what cannot. Obedience our universal duty and destiny. Gneschen sees the good Gretchen pray. (p. 70).

Chap. III. *Pedagogy.*

Teufelsdröckh's School. Education. How the ever-flowing Kuhbach speaks of Time and Eternity. The Hinterschlag Gymnasium: Rude Boys; and pedant Professors. The need of true Teachers, and their due recognition. Father Andreas dies; and Teufelsdröckh learns the secret of his birth: His reflections thereon. The Nameless University. Statistics of Imposture much wanted. Bitter fruits of Rationalism: Teufelsdröckh's religious difficulties. The young Englishman Herr Towgood. Modern Friendship. (p. 78).

Chap. IV. *Getting under Way.*

The grand thaumaturgic art of Thought. Difficulty in fitting Capability to Opportunity, or of getting under way. The advantage of Hunger and Bread-Studies. Teufelsdröckh has to enact the stern monodrama of *No object and no rest.* Sufferings as Auscultator. Given up as a man of genius. Zähdarm House. Intolerable presumption of young men. Irony and its consequences. Teufelsdröckh's Epitaph on Count Zähdarm. (p. 91).

Chap. V. *Romance.*

Teufelsdröckh gives up his Profession. The heavenly mystery of Love. Teufelsdröckh's feeling of worship towards women. First and only love. Blumine. Happy hearts and free tongues. The infinite nature of Fantasy. Love's joyful progress; sudden dissolution; and final catastrophe. (p. 101).

Chap. VI. *Sorrows of Teufelsdröckh.*

Teufelsdröckh's demeanour thereupon. Turns pilgrim. A last wistful look on native Entepfuhl: Sunset amongst primitive Mountains. Basilisk-glance of the Barouche-and-four. Thoughts on Viewhunting. Wanderings and Sorrowings. (p. 112).

Chap. VII. *The Everlasting No.*

Loss of Hope, and of Belief. Profit-and-Loss Philosophy. Teufelsdröckh in his darkness and despair still clings to Truth and follows Duty. Inexpressible pains and fears of Unbelief. Fever-crisis: Protest against the Everlasting No: Baphometic Fire-baptism. (p. 120).

CHAP. VIII. *Centre of Indifference.*

Teufelsdröckh turns now outwardly to the *Not-me;* and finds wholesomer food. Ancient Cities: Mystery of their origin and growth: Invisible inheritances and possessions. Power and virtue of a true Book. Wagram Battlefield: War. Great Scenes beheld by the Pilgrim: Great Events, and Great Men. Napoleon, a divine missionary, preaching, *La carrière ouverte aux talens.* Teufelsdröckh at the North Cape: Modern means of self-defence. Gunpowder and Duelling. The Pilgrim, despising his miseries, reaches the Centre of Indifference. (p. 127).

CHAP. IX. *The Everlasting Yea.*

Temptations in the Wilderness: Victory over the Tempter. Annihilation of Self. Belief in God, and love to man. The Origin of Evil, a problem ever requiring to be solved anew: Teufelsdröckh's solution. Love of Happiness a vain whim: A Higher in man than Love of Happiness. The Everlasting Yea. Worship of Sorrow. Voltaire: his task now finished. Conviction worthless, impossible, without Conduct. The true Ideal, the Actual: Up and work! (p. 137).

CHAP. X. *Pause.*

Conversion; a spiritual attainment peculiar to the modern Era. Teufelsdröckh accepts Authorship as his divine calling. The scope of the command *Thou shalt not steal.*—Editor begins to suspect the authenticity of the Biographical documents; and abandons them for the great Clothes volume. Result of the preceding ten Chapters: Insight into the character of Teufelsdröckh: His fundamental beliefs, and how he was forced to seek and find them. (p. 147).

BOOK III.

CHAP. I. *Incident in Modern History.*

Story of George Fox the Quaker; and his perennial suit of Leather. A man God-possessed, witnessing for spiritual freedom and manhood. (p. 153).

CHAP. II. *Church-Clothes.*

Church-Clothes defined; the Forms under which the Religious Principle is temporarily embodied. Outward Religion originates by Society: Society becomes possible by Religion. The condition of Church-Clothes in our time. (p. 158).

CHAP. III. *Symbols.*

The benignant efficacies of Silence and Secrecy. Symbols; revelations of the Infinite in the Finite: Man everywhere encompassed by them; lives and works by them. Theory of Motive-millwrights, a false account of human nature. Symbols of an extrinsic value; as Banners, Standards: Of intrinsic value; as Works of Art, Lives and Deaths of Heroic men. Religious Symbols; Christianity. Symbols hallowed by Time; but finally defaced and desecrated. Many superannuated Symbols in our time, needing removal. (p. 161).

CHAP. IV. *Helotage.*

Heuschrecke's Malthusian Tract, and Teufelsdröckh's marginal notes thereon. The true workman, for daily bread, or spiritual bread, to be honoured; and no other. The real privation of the Poor not poverty or toil, but ignorance. Over-population: With a world like ours and wide as ours, can there be too many men? Emigration. (p. 167).

CHAP. V. *The Phœnix.*

Teufelsdröckh considers Society as *dead;* its soul (Religion) gone, its body (existing Institutions) going. Utilitarianism, needing little farther preaching, is now in full activity of destruction.—Teufelsdröckh would yield to the Inevitable, accounting that the best: Assurance of a fairer Living Society, arising, Phœnix-like, out of the ruins of the old dead one. Before that Phœnix death-birth is accomplished, long time, struggle, and suffering must intervene. (p. 171).

CHAP. VI. *Old Clothes.*

Courtesy due from all men to all men: The Body of Man, a Revelation in the Flesh. Teufelsdröckh's respect for Old Clothes, as the "Ghosts of Life." Walk in Monmouth Street, and meditations there. (p. 176).

CHAP. VII. *Organic Filaments.*

Destruction and Creation ever proceed together; and organic filaments of the Future are even now spinning. Wonderful connection of each man with all men; and of each generation with all generations, before and after: Mankind is one. Sequence and progress of all human work, whether of creation or destruction, from age to age.— Titles, hitherto derived from Fighting, must give way to others. Kings will remain and their title. Political Freedom, not to be attained by any mechanical contrivance. Hero-worship, perennial amongst men; the cornerstone of polities in the Future. Organic filaments of the New Religion: Newspapers and Literature. Let the faithful soul take courage! (p. 180).

CHAP. VIII. *Natural Supernaturalism.*

Deep significance of Miracles. Littleness of human Science: Divine incomprehensibility of Nature. Custom blinds us to the miraculousness of daily-recurring miracles; so do Names. Space and Time, appearances only; forms of human Thought: A glimpse of Immortality. How Space hides from us the wondrousness of our commonest powers; and Time, the divinely miraculous course of human history. (p. 187).

CHAP. IX. *Circumspective.*

Recapitulation. Editor congratulates the few British readers who have accompanied Teufelsdröckh through all his speculations. The true use of the *Sartor Resartus*, to exhibit the Wonder of daily life and common things; and to show that all Forms are but Clothes, and temporary. Practical inferences enough will follow. (p. 196).

CHAP. X. *The Dandiacal Body.*

The Dandy defined. The Dandiacal Sect a new modification of the primeval superstition Self-worship: How to be distinguished. Their Sacred Books (Fashionable Novels) unreadable. Dandyism's Articles of Faith.—Brotherhood of Poor-Slaves; vowed to perpetual Poverty; worshipers of Earth; distinguished by peculiar costume and diet. Picture of a Poor-Slave Household; and of a Dandiacal. Teufelsdröckh fears these two Sects may spread, till they part all England between them, and then frightfully collide. (p. 200).

CHAP. XI. *Tailors.*

Injustice done to Tailors, actual and metaphorical. Their rights and great services will one day be duly recognised. (p. 211).

CHAP. XII. *Farewell.*

Teufelsdröckh's strange manner of speech, but resolute, truthful character: His purpose seemingly to proselytise, to unite the wakeful earnest in these dark times. Letter from Hofrath Heuschrecke announcing that Teufelsdröckh has disappeared from Weissnichtwo. Editor guesses he will appear again. Friendly Farewell. (p. 214).

NOTES

BOOK I

NOTES TO CHAPTER I. PRELIMINARY

3.1–2. Torch of Science: The "motto" for the lectures of William Hamilton, the most famous of which was the "Philosophy of the Unconditioned" (1829), a critique of the *Cours de philosophie* (*Course of Philosophy*, 1815–29) by Victor Cousin. Hamilton argued that to give definition to the Infinite, as Cousin attempted, was a logical impossibility. As a Professor of Logic and Metaphysics at the University of Edinburgh, Hamilton did a great deal to rekindle the Kantian notion of the Infinite and in consequence helped to rescue the then waning Scottish School of Metaphysics. Carlyle was influenced by Hamilton while writing *Sartor Resartus*, as he later acknowledged in his *Memoir of Sir William Hamilton*, 120–28.

3.5. Rush-lights and Sulphur-matches: Rush-lights were candles with the pith of a rush as the wick, which gave a feeble, glimmering flame. The friction match using sulphur was devised in England in 1827 by John Walker; in 1831, the phosphorous match, an improvement on the sulphur, was invented in France by Charles Sauria.

3.10. Clothes: The controlling metaphor of *Sartor Resartus*. The dialectic of the Body ("The World in Clothes") and the Spirit ("The World out of Clothes") provides the argument for Carlyle's transcendent message. The metaphor itself predates Christianity, and was of course a popular trope in medieval literature that dealt with biblical themes. Although the possible sources of the clothes metaphor are legion, it seems likely that Carlyle's immediate source was *A Tale of a Tub* (1704) by Jonathan Swift.

3.11. Theory of Gravitation: While at the University of Edinburgh, Carlyle read widely in mathematics, and was a student of John Leslie (1766–1832) who edited *Elements of Geometry and Plane Trigonometry* (1817), to which Carlyle contributed a solution on the division of a straight line. Between December 1819 and January 1820, Carlyle wrote for Francis Jeffrey (1773–1850), editor of the *Edinburgh Review*, a speculative article, never published and now lost, on what he referred to as Pictet's *Theory of Gravitation*. In fact, he was writing a review of Alfred Gautier, *Essai historique sur le problème des trois corps* (*Historical Essay on the Three-Body Problem*, 1817), which was reviewed in *Bibliothèque Universelle* 5:253–75, edited by, among others, Marc Auguste Pictet. See Tarr, *Bibliography*, 515.

3.11. **Lagrange**: Joseph Louis, Comte Lagrange (1736–1813) was a critic of Isaac Newton and author of *Mécanique analytique* (*Analytical Mechanics*, 1788), a treatise on mechanics founded upon algebra and calculus.

3.13. **Laplace**: Pierre Simon, Marquis de Laplace (1749–1827), astronomer and mathematician, proved Newton's hypothesis of gravitation and published his theories in *Mécanique céleste* (*Celestial Mechanics*, 1799–1825). Carlyle saw Laplace at the *Institut* in Paris in 1824 (*Reminiscences* 2:163), and refers to him in "Signs of the Times" (1829), *Essays* 2:64: "Without undervaluing the wonderful results which a Lagrange or Laplace educes by means of [mathematics], we may remark, that their calculus, differential and integral, is little else than a more cunningly-constructed arithmetical mill. . . ." Carlyle's interest in mathematics continued throughout the 1820s; his most significant work in the field was a translation of Adrien Marie Legendre, *Éléments de géométrie* (1794), entitled *Elements of Geometry and Trigonometry* (1824), to which he appended an original essay on proportion. For an overview of Carlyle as mathematician, see Moore, "Carlyle, Mathematics and 'Mathesis.'"

3.16. **Geognosy**: In his *Principles of Geology* (1830–33), Charles Lyell ascribes the word *geognosy*, "the natural position of minerals in particular rocks, together with the grouping of those rocks, their geographical distribution, and various relations," to Werner (see following note), who was the first to classify minerals systematically. Lyell also helped to gain acceptance for Hutton's theory of Uniformitarianism, the theory that geological phenomena may be explained as the result of existing forces having operated uniformly since creation.

3.17. **Werners and Huttons**: Abraham Gottlob Werner (1750–1817), German geologist, accounted for geological formation by the action of water, the "Neptunian" theory. James Hutton (1729–1797), Werner's Scottish rival, argued the "Plutonic" theory, which explained formations based upon the fire in the core of the earth.

3.19. Royal Society: The Royal Society is the oldest scientific orga-
nization in Britain, founded in 1660 to promote "Improving Natural
Knowledge" through the physical sciences.

3.21–22. *How the apples were got in*: This is an allusion to a satirical
verse on George III entitled "The Apple Dumplings and a King" by
Peter Pindar (pseudonym of John Wolcot, 1738–1819). After looking in vain for sewn seams in the dumplings, the King exclaims,
"How, how the devil got the Apple in?" (Pindar, *Poems*, 32).

3.23. Social Contract: In *Du contrat social* (1762), Jean Jacques
Rousseau argues that human freedom is based upon the individual's
obedience to the general will, or what rational people would call the
common good.

3.23. Standard of Taste: An allusion to David Hume's essay "Of the
Standard of Taste" in *Four Dissertations* (1757), and to the equally
famous *Essays on the Nature and Principles of Taste* (1790) by Archibald
Alison. The second edition of Alison's work was reviewed by Francis
Jeffrey in the *Edinburgh Review* in 1811 (18:1–46). Both arguments
are founded upon the principles of Associationism, the theory, developed by David Hartley, that all consciousness is the result of the
combination of simple elements derived from sensory experience. In
a *Journal* entry for December 7, 1826, Carlyle writes of the
Associationists, "*Can* you believe that the Beautiful and Good have
no deeper root in us than 'Association,' 'Sympathy,' 'Calculation?'
Then if so, whence in Heaven's name, comes this sympathy, the *pleasure* of this Association, the *obbligante pleasure* of this Utility?" (*Two
Note Books*, 84). In "Signs of the Times" (1829), *Essays* 2:76, he
dismisses "'Theories of Taste'" that attempt to explain and to make
"mechanically visible" through "'Association'" the "Love of Wisdom
and Beauty."

3.23–4.1. Migrations of the Herring: The naturalists Thomas Pennant and Thomas Gilpin each published essays arguing that the herring annually return to their place of origin under the polar caps.
Pennant's appeared in *British Zoology* (1776), Gilpin's in the *Transactions of the American Philosophical Society* (1786).

4.1. Doctrine of Rent: An allusion to John Locke, *Two Treatises of Government* (1690), which argues that as long as the rent is paid per agreement the tenant has protection from seizure by the landlord, a theory later used by Adam Smith, Thomas R. Malthus, and David Ricardo to arrive at their definition of political economy.

4.1–2. Theory of Value: The concept espoused by Adam Smith, and expanded by Ricardo, that the value of anything is directly related to the labor needed to produce it.

4.2–3. Philosophies of Language, of History, of Pottery, of Apparitions, of Intoxicating Liquors: The Germans, especially Friedrich von Schlegel (1772–1829), Johann Gottlieb Fichte (1762–1814), Friedrich von Schelling (1775–1854), Johann Gottlieb von Herder (1744–1803), Johann Wolfgang von Goethe (1749–1832), and Friedrich von Schiller (1759–1805), wrote extensively on etymology and the history of language. Carlyle was familiar with Schlegel's *Philosophie der Geschichte* (*Philosophy of History*, 1829) and his *Philosophie der Sprache und des Wortes* (*Philosophy of Language and Words*, 1830). Articles on "The Philosophy of Pottery" and "The Philosophy of Apparitions" had recently appeared in *Fraser's Magazine* (April 1830, 287–91 and August 1830, 33–41). The philosophy of "Intoxicating Liquors" refers to Robert Macnish, *The Anatomy of Drunkenness* (1827), and to his *The Philosophy of Sleep* (1830). Carlyle was also probably aware of Macnish's article "The Philosophy of Burking" in *Fraser's Magazine* for February 1832, 5:52–65 ("burking" is murder by suffocation).

4.7–8. Stewarts, Cousins, Royer-Collards: Dugald Stewart (1753–1828) was Professor of Moral Philosophy at the University of Edinburgh from 1795–1820, and was referred to as the "Plato of the Scotch School." Victor Cousin (1792–1867), a French philosopher, was an advocate of the Infinite, a doctrine criticized by William Hamilton in his 1829 essay (see note at 3.1–2 above). Pierre Paul Royer-Collard (1793–1845), a student of Cousin, also an opponent of materialism, taught philosophy at the Sorbonne.

4.8–9. Lawrences, Majendies, Bichâts: William Lawrence (1783–1867), François Magendie (1783–1855), and Maria François Xavier Bichât (1771–1802) were famous physicians and physiologists, whose empirical research Carlyle contrasts with the metaphysical inquiries of Stewart, Cousin, and Royer-Collard.

4.10. How, then, comes it: A direct translation of the German phrase, "*Wie kommt es dann.*"

4.15–16. his whole Self lives, moves, and has its being: Acts 17:28: "For in him [God] we live, and move, and have our being."

4.18–19. property, not an accident: Philosophical terms, deriving from Aristotle and the Scholastics, used to distinguish the essential qualities of a thing (properties) from the variable (accidents).

4.21. *Clothed Animal* . . . *Naked Animal*: An anticipation of the chapters "The World in Clothes" and "The World Out of Clothes" later in Book I.

4.23–24. Shakespeare says, we are creatures that look before and after: *Hamlet* 4.4.36–39: "Sure He that made us with such large discourse, / Looking before and after, gave us not / That capability and godlike reason / To fust in us unus'd."

4.29. abstract Thought: In "Signs of the Times" (1829), *Essays* 2:65, Carlyle satirically observes, "One of their [continental] philosophers has lately discovered, that 'as the liver secretes bile, so does the brain secrete thought'; which astonishing discovery Dr. Cabanis . . . has pushed into its minutest developments. . . ."

4.30. Catholic Emancipations: Until the passage of the Emancipation Bill in 1829, Catholics were generally excluded from public office in Britain and Ireland. However, the so-called Act of Settlement continued to exclude Catholics from the throne and the office of Lord Chancellor.

4.30. Rotten Boroughs: Because of demographic shifts caused by the Industrial Revolution, depopulated electoral districts were able to send a disproportionate number of members to Parliament. The Reform Bill of 1832 did much to correct this practice by suppressing fifty-six such boroughs, especially those with less than 2,000 voters.

4.31. **Revolts of Paris**: On July 27–29, 1830, the "second French Revolution" took place in Paris, and Charles X was dethroned.

4.34–35. *Höret ihr Herren und lasset's Euch sagen*: "Listen, gentlemen, and let it be told to you"; the first line of the song sung by the watchman each hour during his nightly rounds to tell the time. Compare "Dumb Love," *German Romance* 1:59. In his German translation of *Sartor Resartus* (Leipzig, 1882), Thomas Fischer corrected part of the line to read: "*lazt euch sagen*."

5.3. **slaughter of fat oxen whereby a man himself grows fat**: Carlyle alters slightly Samuel Johnson's famous line: "Who drives fat oxen should himself be fat," which is Johnson's *reductio ad absurdum* of a line from *The Earl of Essex* by Henry Brooke (1703?–1783): "Who rules o'er freeman should himself be free." See Boswell, *Life of Johnson* (ed. Mowbray Morris), 646.

5.7–8. '**By geometric scale / Doth take the size of pots of ale**': Samuel Butler, *Hudibras* 1.1.121–22: "For he by *Geometrick* scale / Could take the size of *Pots of Ale*."

5.17–18. '**Many shall run to and fro, and knowledge shall be increased**': Daniel 12:4.

5.20. **all men make up mankind**: Compare *Wilhelm Meister* (1824) 2:131: "'It is all men that make up mankind; all powers taken together that make up the world.'"

5.28. **Nothingness and Night**: An echo of Milton's *Paradise Lost* 1.543: "Reign of *Chaos* and old Night"; 2.959–63: "Throne of / *Chaos* . . . Sable-vested Night"; and 2.970: "*Chaos* and *ancient Night*."

5.29. **Speculation should have free course**: Compare 2 Thessalonians 3:1: "[P]ray for us, that the word of the Lord may have *free* course."

5.30–31. **whithersoever and howsoever it listed**: Compare John 3:8: "The wind bloweth where it listeth"; and James 3:4, where the ships are turned "whithersoever the governor listeth."

6.15. **Professor Teufelsdröckh of Weissnichtwo**: Diogenes Teufelsdröckh: literally "God-born Devil's-Dung." The first name embraces the traits of Diogenes the Cynic (born c. 400 B.C.), who taught that happiness is only attainable by the satisfaction of one's basic needs at the least possible cost and who is often pictured carrying a lantern in search of truth; and those of Diogenes Laërtius (early third century), the Greek biographer, whose *Lives of Eminent Philosophers* is a model for the fragmentary chronicle presented by Carlyle as a "life" of the philosopher Teufelsdröckh. In Goethe's *Wilhelm Meisters Lahrjahre* (1796), translated by Carlyle in 1824, Jarno addresses Wilhelm as "thou second Diogenes" (*Wilhelm Meister* 2:223); and in Jean Paul Friedrich Richter's "Quintus Fixlein" (1796), translated by Carlyle in 1827, the "Academical burgher[s]" are described as "humourists and Diogeneses" (*German Romance* 2:206).

Teufelsdreck (Teufelsdröckh) is the German name for asafoetida, an herb used as a powerful emetic. In a letter to his brother John, July 12, 1831, Carlyle refers to his "Dreck" manuscript as "(medicinal) *Devil's Dung*" (*Letters* 5:303). The Scottish expression for asafoetida is "Devil's Dirt." The name may also have been suggested by Richter's *Titan* (1805) in which Richter speaks of "*Teufelsdreck, den sie aus Persien holen*" (Teufelsdreck, who [in a ship] came from Persia). The infant Teufelsdröckh's basket was "overhung with green Persian silk" (at 65.1–2 below), and Persia was the land of the emetic asafoetida. *Teufelsdreck* may also mean "Devil's Dust," and thus may be an allusion to the process of reducing old cloth to fragments in a machine called a devil for the purpose of making paper (see note at 44.8 below). See G. B. Tennyson, *"Sartor" Called "Resartus"* (146, 152, 200–201, 220–22), who discusses the meaning of the name and the change from Teufelsdreck to the subtler Teufelsdröckh; and Stowell, "Teufelsdröckh as Devil's Dust," 31–33.

Weissnichtwo, or "Know-not-where," may have been suggested by Kennaquhair in Scott's *The Monastery* (1820).

6.21–23. *Die Kleider ihr Werden und Wirken* (Clothes, their Origin and Influence): *von Diog. Teufelsdröckh, J.U.D. etc. Stillschweigen, und Co^gnie*. Weissnichtwo, 1831: Literally: "Clothes, their origin and influence by Diogenes Teufelsdröckh, *Juris Utriusque Doctor.* etc. Silence and Company. Know-not-where, 1831." The title may have been suggested to Carlyle by Ludwig Wachler's *Über Werden und Wirken der Literatur* (1829), sent to him by Goethe in June 1830. The conventional abbreviation "*D.u.J.*" (for *Doctor utriusque Juris*, literally "Doctor of both Laws," i.e., of both civil and canon law) is here altered to "*J.U.D.*," perhaps to suggest *Jud(e)* or Jew, which in turn anticipates the Wandering Jew figure (see note at 14.18–19 below), an archetype especially popular in Romantic literature.

6.24. *Weissnichtwo'sche Anzeiger*: "Know-not-where Advertiser."

6.34. opposition in high places: Compare Ephesians 6:12: "For we wrestle . . . against spiritual wickedness in high *places*."

6.35. exalt the almost new name: Compare Psalms 34:3: "O magnify the Lord with me, and let us exalt his name together"; and Isaiah 25:1: "O Lord, thou *art* my God; I will exalt thee, I will praise thy name."

7.4–5. *Möchte es . . . auch im Brittischen Boden gedeihen!*: "May it . . . thrive also on British soil."

NOTES TO CHAPTER II. EDITORIAL DIFFICULTIES

8.1–2. 'whose seedfield . . . is Time': See the motto on the title page, from Goethe's *Wilhelm Meisters Wanderjahre* (1821). Carlyle's translations of these lines vary: the most widely used is in "Characteristics" (1831), *Essays* 3:43: "My inheritance how wide and fair! / Time is my fair seed-field, of Time I'm heir." In "Jean Paul Friedrich Richter" (1830), *Essays* 2:133, the last line is translated: "TIME is my estate, to TIME I'm heir."

8.3–4. marked with chalk: Compare Horace, *Odes* 1.36.10: "Cressa ne careat pulcha dies nota" ("Chalk up the day in white").

8.4. 'extensive Volume': Referring back to the "well nigh enthusiastic Reviewer" for the "*Weissnichtwo'sche Anzeiger*," quoted above at 6.24–36.

8.8. true orients: I.e., pearls. Compare *Paradise Lost* 5.1–2: "Now Morn her rosie steps in th' Eastern Clime / Advancing, sow'd the Earth with Orient Pearle."

8.10. new Branch of Philosophy: The Philosophy of Clothes.

8.12–13. new human Individuality: Carlyle's invitation to look forward to Book II, where he concentrates upon the trials of individuality, a subject anticipated in his unfinished novel *Wotton Reinfred* (1827).

8.20–21. business and bosoms: Compare Francis Bacon, *Essays* (1625), xxvii: "I doe now publish my *Essayes*" for "they come home, to Mens Businesse, and Bosomes."

9.2. Article after Article . . . Critical Journals: A reference to the initial difficulties in finding a publisher for *Sartor Resartus*, and to its subsequent serialization in *Fraser's Magazine* and the anticipated problems with the readership. See the Introduction.

9.8. Whig, Tory, and Radical: Whigs were identified with liberal causes and reform, and took responsibility for the passage of the Reform Bill in 1832. Tories were identified with conservative policies, and the Tory movement itself was nearly destroyed by the passage of the Whig-sponsored Reform Bill. Radicals embraced speculative philosophy and rejected the tenets of both the Whigs and the Tories. Teufelsdröckh is a radical, and *Fraser's Magazine* was the vehicle for radical thought.

9.13. Waterloo-Crackers: Large fireworks made to celebrate Napoleon's defeat at Waterloo in 1815. Here, Carlyle means facile publications of no consequence. The irony is pervasive, since Carlyle often published in *Fraser's Magazine*.

9.31–33. Herr Hofrath Heuschrecke . . . in Weissnichtwo: "Mister Privy-Councillor Locust (Grasshopper) from Know-not-where." Compare Richter, *Fruit, Flower, and Thorn Pieces; the Wedded Life, Death, and Marriage of Firmian Stanislaus Siebenkäs* (1796–97), 4.22.527–28, where Hof is described as a country of gardens; also Carlyle's translation of Richter's "Life of Quintus Fixlein," where *Hofrath* is rendered as "Councillor" (*German Romance* 2:229); and Hoffmann's "The Golden Pot," in which Carlyle translates *Hofrath* as "Privy Councillor" (*German Romance* 2:53). Heuschrecke might be Francis Jeffrey, the editor of the *Edinburgh Review*, whom Carlyle referred to as a grasshopper; or Dr. Alexander Fyffe, a physician from Haddington, whom Carlyle referred to as a cricket. See Tennyson, *"Sartor" Called "Resartus,"* 190–91, and *Letters* 2:363.

10.2. distant West: New England.

10.3–4. *Family . . . National . . . Libraries*: Custodians of encyclopedic knowledge. In 1825, Henry Peter, Lord Brougham founded the Society for the Diffusion of Useful Knowledge, and under its auspices William Knight, who had previously planned a National Library, edited the *Library of Entertaining Knowledge* and the *Library of Useful Knowledge*. Concurrently, John Murray was publishing the *Family Library* (1829–42). See Carlyle's complaint about these publications in a letter to Johann P. Eckermann, March 20, 1830, *Letters* 5:84–85.

10.8. requisite Documents: An allusion to a common German legal term that was often used as a joke: "*alle nothige Documente.*"

10.17. twopenny post: An area within central London where letters were collected and delivered several times a day. See *Letters* 5:336.

10.18. OLIVER YORKE: Pseudonym of William Maginn (1794–1842), the editor of *Fraser's Magazine*. See text at 218.25 below.

10.26–27. *Sartor Resartus . . .* 'Life and Opinions of Herr Teufelsdröckh': The title may have been taken from a lost Scottish ballad, *The Tailor Patched*, and suggests its patch-work (that is, serial) appearance in *Fraser's Magazine*. The "Life and Opinions" may have been suggested by Sterne's *The Life and Opinions of Tristram Shandy, Gentleman* (1760–67), which like *Sartor Resartus* is, among other things, a parody of the novel.

10.34. Cant: A term popularized by Samuel Johnson, found throughout Carlyle's writings. In "Boswell's Life of Johnson" (1832), *Essays* 3:125–26, Carlyle writes: "Quite spotless . . . is Johnson's love of Truth. . . . 'Clear your mind of Cant'; *clear* it, throw Cant utterly away: such was his emphatic, repeated precept." See also *On Heroes* 156.32–33 and note.

11.1. Voice publishing tidings of the Philosophy of Clothes: An adaptation of Luke 2:10, where the angel announces the birth of Jesus: "I bring you good tidings of great joy."

11.2. whoso hath ears let him hear: Compare Matthew 11:15, 13:9, and 13:43: "He that hath ears to hear, let him hear." Also Mark 4:9, 4:23, 7:16; Luke 8:8, 14:35.

11.10. **the Logical wear**: Perhaps a pun on weir, a milldam. Also "pile . . . wear" may be a pun on textiles and clothes. But the clearest pun is between "wear," *OED* sense I.3: "What one wears or should wear; the thing or things worn or proper to be worn at a particular time or in certain circumstances," taking "the Logical wear" to mean "the Logical fashion," and sense II.5: "The process or condition of being worn or gradually reduced in bulk or impaired in quality by continued use, friction, attrition," as the "Institutions of our Ancestors" are being worn down by "the current of Innovation" (another pun: current as in flow versus current as in contemporary).

11.16–17. **those nights and suppers of the gods**: Horace, *Satires* 2.6.65: "O noctes cenaeque deum."

11.19. **feast of reason**: From Pope's *Imitation of Horace*, Satire 1 of Book 2: "There *St. John* mingles with my friendly Bowl / The Feast of Reason and the Flow of Soul" (*Poems of Pope* 4:127–28).

11.20. *Amicus Plato, magis amica veritas*: "Plato is my friend, but truth is more my friend." The origin of this saying can be traced to Plato, *Phaedo* 91c ("And I would ask you to be thinking of the truth and not of Socrates") and Aristotle, *Nichomachean Ethics* 1.4.1 ("Both Plato and truth are dear to us, yet 'tis our duty to prefer the truth"). The Latin version is found in Cervantes' *Don Quixote*, Part 2, Chapter 51, but it is likely that Carlyle's proximate source is Sterne's *Tristram Shandy* 1.21.77.

11.24. **Prince of Lies and Darkness**: Satan. Compare *King Lear* 3.4.143–44: "The prince of darkness is a gentleman. Modo he's call'd, and Mahu."

11.25. **Puffery**: Corrupt or undue praise in advertising, more commonly called puffing. Carlyle equated puffing with popularity and believed that the problems he was encountering in finding a publisher for *Sartor Resartus* were linked to puffery. In a letter to his brother John, July 31, 1832, he laments that he might have to publish the manuscript on his own because "*Bookselling*, slain by Puffery, is dead, and will not come alive again, tho worms for some time may live on the carcase" (*Letters* 6:195).

11.27–28. **Chinese Shopkeepers . . .** *No cheating here*: A reference to the widely held belief, found in the periodical literature of the time, that Chinese merchants were notorious for cheating their customers even though the signs that hung in their shops proclaimed otherwise.

NOTES TO CHAPTER III. REMINISCENCES

12.7. **Hegel and Bardili**: Georg W. Hegel (1770–1831), German absolute idealist and opponent of the philosophic compromise argued by Immanuel Kant (1724–1804). His most famous work, *Die Phänomenologie des Geistes* (*The Phenomenology of the Mind*, 1807), led to the development of the Hegelian dialectic: one concept (thesis) inevitably generates its opposite (antithesis), and the interchange of these leads to a new concept (synthesis), and this synthesis in turn creates a new dialectic. Christoph G. Bardili (1761–1808), German rational realist, who in *Grundriss der ersten Logik* (*Outline of Primary Logic*, 1800) argued against the theoretical boundaries of Kant.

12.9. **descend . . . into the . . . Forum**: Cicero: "*In forum descendere.*"

12.12. **Transcendentalism**: An elusive term that holds that certain truths cannot be proved through empirical reasoning. Hence, it rejects the constraints of empiricism and rationalism, and instead embraces a philosophic system that abjures "sensuous logic" and accepts "non-sensuous intuition." The sources of transcendentalism are as old as history itself, but its prominence in the nineteenth century can be traced to Kant who in *Kritik der reinen Vernunft* (*Critique of Pure Reason*, 1781) addressed the philosophic contradictions raised by the materialism of Thomas Hobbes (1588–1679), the subjective idealism of George Berkeley (1685–1753), the monism of Baruch Spinoza (1632–1677), the empiricism of John Locke (1632–1704), and the skepticism of David Hume (1711–1776). Kant's terms were the phenomena ("beings of the senses") and noumena ("beings of the understanding"). The former was the home of that which could be proved; the latter was the home of that which existed *a priori*, but was beyond proof. Implicit in this dialectic is a hierarchical value; that is, the realm of noumenon (concept) is an extension of, but also a higher order of knowing than, the realm of phenomenon (object). In effect, that which transcends the arena of phenomenon is Transcendental. *Sartor Resartus* can be seen as a refinement of the *Critique of*

Pure Reason, but it also owes a considerable debt to *Biographia Literaria* (1817), in which Coleridge reforms Kant's noumenon into the "Primary Imagination," which is "a repetition in the finite mind of the eternal act of creation in the infinite I am" (1:304). In "Novalis" (1829), *Essays* 2:24–26, the appeal of Transcendentalism to Carlyle is clear as he sets it against the backdrop of "Common-sense Philosophers, men who brag chiefly of their irrefragable logic, and keep watch and ward . . . against 'Mysticism' and 'Visionary Theories.'" Carlyle then adds, "The Idealist . . . boasts that his Philosophy is Transcendental, that is, 'ascending *beyond* the senses'; which, he asserts, *all* Philosophy, properly so called, by its nature is and must be. . . . To a Transcendentalist, Matter has an existence, but only as a Phenomenon: were *we* not there, neither would it be there. . . . Nay, to the Transcendentalist . . . the whole question of the origin and existence of Nature must be greatly simplified[;] the old hostility of Matter [Time and Space] is at an end, for Matter is itself annihilated; and the black Spectre, Atheism, . . . melts into nothingness forever."

12.16. **Herr Oken of Jena**: Lorenz Oken or Ockenfuss (1779–1851), Professor of Physiology at the University of Munich, known for his theory that nature is unified. Oken edited the controversial encyclopedic journal *Isis* from 1818 to 1848. In a letter to Carlyle, February 6–7, 1828, Carlyle's brother John, who was in Germany from November 1827 through February 1829, writes of Oken's lectures on *Entwickelungs-Geschichte der Natur* (History of the Development of Nature) which John describes as "a sort of air-philosophy, an intellectual '*fantasy*ing' with the philosophy of Nature." See John Clubbe, "John Carlyle in Germany," 279–80, who feels that Teufelsdröckh's character and appearance are modelled upon Oken's.

12.23. *Gukguk*: Compare Richter's "Life of Quintus Fixlein," *German Romance* 2:205.

13.1. **coffeehouse**: Carlyle's description of the *Grüne Gans* as a coffeehouse is curious, since a German coffeehouse would not have served beer. No doubt he was thinking of a pub (*Schenke*) or tavern (*Gasthaus*).

13.2. *Zur Grünen Gans*: "At the Green Goose." The scene may have been suggested in part by Carlyle's brother John, who visited a similar tavern in Munich known as the "Schelling Club." John also seems responsible in part for the description of the lodging and watchtower in Wahngasse. John's later claim that the "framework of *Sartor*" was built upon his "experiences in Germany" is of course a considerable exaggeration. See Clubbe, "John Carlyle in Germany," 278. Carlyle's name for the tavern could have several explanations: A "green goose" may mean either an undercooked or a rotting goose, in either case a humorously unappetizing name for a tavern. Alternatively, "green goose" was a slang term for a harlot or prostitute in the sixteenth and seventeenth centuries (compare *Love's Labour's Lost* 4.3.73). In the 1858 Uniform Edition and thereafter, the gender of the goose was changed throughout the text, from "*Ganse*" (female goose) to "*Gans*" (gander), a change which was evidently deliberate, but inexplicable.

13.6–7. *Die Sache der Armen in Gottes und Teufels Namen* (The Cause of the Poor in Heaven's name and ——'s): The blank, of course, stands for "the Devil." The sentiment of this toast seems closer to the ideals of the Saint-Simonians than to the ethereal frivolity that took place at the *Grünen Gans*. See 174.35 below.

13.8. breaking the leaden silence . . . returned him loud acclaim: Compare *Paradise Lost* 1.82–83: "Satan, with bold words / Breaking the horrid silence thus began"; and 2.519–20: ". . . and all the host of Hell / With deafning shout, return'd them loud acclaim."

13.13–14. *Bleibt doch ein echter Spass- und Galgen-vogel*: "He is a real joker and gallows-bird."

13.15. *Wo steckt doch der Schalk?*: "Where is the scoundrel hiding, then?"

13.28. 'think and smoke tobacco': From a famous drinking song attributed to George Wither (1588–1667), as it appears in Thomas D'Urfey's *Wit and Mirth: or, Pills to Purge Melancholy* (1719–20; 1876 reprint, 3:292):

Tobacco is but an *Indian* Weed;
Grows green in the Morn, cut
  down at Eve,
    It shows our decay,
    We are but clay,
Think of this and take Tobacco.

The Ashes that are left behind
Does serve to put us all in mind;
    That into Dust,
    Return we must,
Think of this, &c.

The Pipe that is so Lilly-white,
Where so many take delight;
   Is broke with a touch,
   Man's life is such,
Think of this, &c.

The Pipe that is so foul within,
Shews how Man's Soul is
   stain'd with Sin;
   It does require,
   To be purg'd with fire,
Think of this, &c.

The Smoak that does so high
   ascend,
Shews you Man's Life must
   have an end;
   The Vapour's gone,
   Man's Life is done,
Think of this and take Tobacco.

See also Thomas Jenner, *The Soules Solace* (1626), Emblem 31, where tobacco ash is compared to bodily ash, and the refrain reads: "Thus thinke, then drinke *tobacco*."

13.31. *in petto*: "Within the breast," in reserve or in secret. A phrase used by the College of Cardinals.

13.33. **Sansculottism**: The radicalism associated with the Jacobins of the French Revolution, from the *Sanscoulottes* (literally, "without knee breeches"), the lower class who wore long trousers rather than the knee breeches worn by the upper class.

14.15. **Melchizedek**: Canaanite priest-king of Salem, in Genesis 14:18–20, who blesses Abraham after the "slaughter of the kings" and in turn is given one-tenth of Abraham's booty. In Hebrews 7:1–3, Melchizedek is described as "Without father, without mother, without descent, having neither beginning of days, nor end of life; but like unto the Son of God; abideth a priest continually."

14.18–19. *Ewige Jude*: "Wandering Jew." Teufelsdröckh becomes identified here with the expansive tradition of the Wandering Jew, a legend set down in the thirteenth century by Roger of Wendover who from earlier oral tradition conveyed the story of the man who refused sustenance to Christ on the way to the crucifixion and thus was condemned to wander forever. The motif in various forms was especially popular among the Romantics: Goethe used it in *Wilhelm Meister*, William Wordsworth in *The Excursion* (1814), Coleridge in "The Ancient Mariner" (1798), and Shelley in "Queen Mab" (1813).

14.23. *Allgemeine Zeitung*: "Universal Newspaper," a publication founded in Stuttgart in 1798, and transferred to Augsburg in 1810.

14.35–37. *Professor der Allerley-Wissenschaft . . .* 'Professor of Things in General': Literally, "Professor of the Science of All Sorts of Things." Carlyle might be recalling his unsuccessful applications for professorships: In 1827, he applied for a yet unnamed Chair at University College, London; and for the Chair of Moral Philosophy at St. Andrews University. For the latter his letters of recommendation were from, among others, Goethe, Francis Jeffrey, and Edward Irving, the "highest Names" referred to at 15.11 below.

15.2. New University: Perhaps the new University College, Gower Street, London. In the *Encyclopedia of Philosophy* 3:307, Lewis White Beck writes, "The role of the universities in the history and shaping of German philosophy cannot be overemphasized. Whereas the strictly philosophical importance of Oxford, Cambridge, and even Paris has been comparatively small during much of their histories, German philosophy has been intimately related to German university life. The founding of new universities (such as Leipzig in 1409, Halle in 1694, Berlin in 1809) has often symbolized important changes in the philosophical climate. The variety of competing German philosophies is, no doubt, partly attributable to the large number of universities (large compared to that of England, France, or Italy), in each of which the *professor ordinarius* was expected (even in Wolffian and Hegelian times) to produce his own multivolume system and to start his own school."

15.3. Program: An outline or abstract of courses in a German university, often accompanied by a thesis or an address.

15.6. bodying somewhat forth: Compare *Midsummer Night's Dream* 5.1.14–17: "And as imagination bodies forth / The forms of things unknown, the poet's pen / Turns them to shapes, and gives to aery nothing / A local habitation and a name."

15.16–17. Denial and Destruction . . . Affirmation and Re-construction: The philosophical dialectic implied here is central to the argument of *Sartor Resartus*, and it anticipates the famous injunction in Book II, Chapter IX, "Close thy *Byron*; open thy *Goethe*." Carlyle viewed Voltaire (and Byron) as proponents of skepticism, and Goethe as the father of the 'New Belief.'

15.24. **nine days**: Proverbial; for example, *3 Henry VI* 3.2.113–14: "That would be ten days' wonder at the least. / That's a day longer than a wonder lasts"; and *As You Like It* 3.2.174–75: "I was seven of the nine days out of the wonder before you came."

16.14. **Wahngasse**: "Illusion (or Delusion) Lane."

16.15. **pinnacle of Weissnichtwo**: Compare Matthew 4:5 and Luke 4:9, where Satan sets Jesus on a "pinnacle of the temple," and dares him to jump off.

16.18. *Airts*: Scots for Ortes, the cardinal points on a compass.

16.21–22. **speculum**: An error: *speculum* is a mirror; *specula* is a watch-tower.

16.28. **choking by sulphur**: The antiquated method of collecting honey by killing the swarm with sulphur smoke.

16.29. **Serene Highness**: In German, *Durchlaucht*, a prince of a lesser state.

16.32. **Schlosskirche**: "Castle-chapel."

16.32. **biped**: Perhaps an anticipation of the featherless biped referred to at 18.9–10, 31.11, 44.22, 50.26, 100.18, and 125.34 below. See note at 18.9–10.

16.33. **Couriers arrive . . . bearing Joy and Sorrow**: Compare William Cowper's description of the arrival of the post in *The Task* 4.5–15 ([1785] *Poems* 2:187):

> He comes, the herald of a noisy world,
> With spatter'd boots, strapp'd waist, and frozen locks;
> News from all nations lumb'ring at his back.
> . . . messenger of grief
> Perhaps to thousands, and of joy to some;
> To him indiff'rent whether grief or joy.

16.34–35. **topladen . . . household**: A use by Carlyle of his own translation of *Wilhelm Meister* 2:410: "But observe also, on beaten

highways, how dust on dust, in long cloudy trains, mounts up, beto-
kening the track of commodious top-laden carriages, in which the
rich, the noble, and so many others, are whirled along."

16.37. wains: Wagons or carts.

17.3. whence it is coming, whither it is going: John 3:8: "The
wind bloweth where it listeth, and thou hearest the sound thereof,
but canst not tell whence it cometh, and whither it goeth."

17.3–4. *Aus der Ewigkeit, zu der Ewigkeit hin*: Compare Richter,
"Life of Quintus Fixlein": "In truth, a man must never have reflected
on the Creation-moment, when the Universe first rose from the bosom
of an Eternity, if he does not view with philosophic reverence a woman,
whose thread of life a secret all-wondrous Hand is spinning to a
second thread, and who veils within her the transition from Nothingness to Existence, from Eternity to Time" (*German Romance* 2:299–
300).

17.4–5. These are Apparitions: Carlyle expands on this idea in
"Natural Supernaturalism," Book III, Chapter VIII (especially at
194.20–23 and following paragraphs).

17.6. melting into air: *The Tempest* 4.1.148–50: "These our actors
/ (As I foretold you) were all spirits, and / Are melted into air, into
thin air."

17.7. Picture of the Sense: An allusion to the subjective idealism of
George Berkeley, who in *A Treatise Concerning the Principles of Human
Knowledge* (1710) argues that our experience is limited to what is
given by our senses, and that the actual nature of things is therefore
hidden from us.

17.9. Clothes-screen: Perhaps a soldier. A "screen" in this sense is "a
contrivance . . . for affording an upright surface for the display of
objects for exhibition" (*OED*, s.v. "screen," sense 1d). Compare 31.6,
44.2, 198.6 below.

17.11. Hengst and Horsa: Two brothers, possibly mythical, who in
the fifth century are said to have led a Jutish invasion and settlement

of Kent. See Venerable Bede's *Ecclesiastical History of the English Nation*, Chapter 25.

17.13–14. watch well . . . seen no more: Compare Matthew 24:42: "Watch therefore: for ye know not what hour your Lord doth come"; Matthew 25:13; and Mark 13:35; 13:37.

17.15. *Ach, mein Lieber!*: "Oh, my dear fellow!"

17.19. reign of Night: Compare *Paradise Lost* 2.961–63: "[W]ith him [Chaos] Enthron'd / Sat Sable-vested Night, eldest of things, / The consort of his Reign"; also Spenser's *Faerie Queene* (1589) 1.5.20.

17.19–20. Boötes: Constellation in the northern hemisphere, a herdsman with a staff in one hand and two leashed dogs (*Canes Venatici*) in the other, who is known as the Keeper of the Great Bear (*Ursa Major*).

17.27–28. Fermenting-vat: In German *Gärbottich*, a favorite metaphor of Richter's.

17.33. truckle-beds: A trundle bed, a small bed designed to fit under a larger one.

17.34. *Rouge-et-Noir*: A gambling card game played at a table marked with two red and two black diamond-shaped spots, on which bets are placed.

17.37–18.1. Lover . . . over the borders: Carlyle might be alluding here to Gretna Green, ten miles south of his birthplace Ecclefechan, a favorite haunt for lovers who eloped there to escape the stricter English marriage laws.

18.8. *Rabenstein*: "Raven-stone," gallows. Compare Goethe's *Faust* 1.24.4399.

18.9–10. two-legged animals without feathers: In Plato's *Statesman* (266e), the Eleatic Stranger tells the young Socrates that we ought to divide "walking animals immediately into biped and quadruped, then seeing that the human race falls into the same division with the feathered creatures and no others, we must again divide the biped class into featherless and feathered." According to Diogenes

Laërtius, in his life of Diogenes the Cynic (see note at 6.15), "Plato had defined Man as an animal, biped and featherless, and was applauded. Diogenes plucked a fowl and brought it into the lecture-room with the words, 'Here is Plato's man.' In consequence of which there was added to the definition, 'having broad nails'" (*Lives of Eminent Philosophers* 6.40). Compare John Dryden, *Absalom and Achitophel* (1682) 1.170: "To that unfeather'd two-legg'd thing, a son."

18.19. *mein Werther*: "My good friend." From Goethe's *Die Leiden des Jungen Werthers* (*The Sorrows of Young Werther*, 1774).

18.19–20. **I am alone with the Stars**: Compare Byron's *Manfred* (1817), where Manfred, who is among the stars, says, "I'll die as I have lived—alone" (3.4.90).

18.22. **Night-thoughts**: Possibly a reference to the famous poem by Edward Young, *The Complaint; or, Night Thoughts on Life, Death, and Immortality* (1742–46).

18.32. **'united in a common element of dust'**: From Carlyle's translation of Goethe's description of Mariana's housekeeping in *Wilhelm Meister* 1:88: "[N]o article despised the neighbourhood of another; all were united by a common element, powder and dust."

18.36. **Blücher Boots**: A heavy half boot named after Gebhard L. von Blücher (1742–1819), the Prussian field marshall who helped in Napoleon's defeat at Waterloo.

18.36. **Old Lieschen (Lisekin, 'Liza)**: Perhaps a description of the Carlyles' servant Betty, who was with them at Craigenputtoch in the winter of 1830–31.

19.4. **jail-delivery**: Compare "Historic Survey of German Poetry" (1831), *Essays* 2:349–50, where Carlyle uses the term to deride worthless literature.

19.6. **pestilence**: A reference to the cholera epidemic that ravaged Europe in 1831.

19.20. **coif with its lappets**: According to the *OED*, coif is "a close-fitting cap covering the top, back, and sides of the head." A lappet is "an appendage or pendant to head-gear of any kind, esp. one of the streamers attacked to a lady's head-dress," here the ties that held the coif in place.

19.28–29. **'they never appear without their umbrella'**: Perhaps a satirical comment on the widely held belief during the Regency that it was socially improper to appear without an umbrella.

19.29. **with what 'little-wisdom' the world is governed**: "*Nescis, mi fili, quantilla sapientia regitur mundus*" (Learn, my son, with how little wisdom the world is governed), an often-quoted remark of Pope Julius III (1487–1555) in a letter to a monk who had pitied him for the burdens of sovereignty, possibly recalling a phrase of Sallust, "*Satis eloquentiae sapientiae parum*" (Plenty of eloquence, but little wisdom; *Catilina* 5). Also attributed to Count Axel von Oxenstierna (1583–1654), Chancellor of Sweden, in a letter to his son, who hesitated to accept appointment to the Peace Conference of Westphalia in 1648 because he thought he was too young.

19.30–31. **ninety and nine Public Men**: Compare Matthew 18:12: "How think ye? if a man have an hundred sheep, and one of them be gone astray, doth he not leave the ninety and nine, and goeth into the mountains, and seeketh that which is gone astray?"; also Luke 15:4.

19.38. **confusion worse confounded**: *Paradise Lost* 2.993–96: "I saw and heard, for such a numerous host / Fled not in silence through the frighted deep / With ruin upon ruin, rout on rout, / Confusion worse confounded." Compare also *Two Note Books*, 191, and 59.35–36 below.

20.5. **burin**: A pointed cutting-tool used by engravers or sculptors.

20.6–9. **hat wenigstens gehabt . . . at least has had such**: For Carlyle's translation to be faithful to the original, the emendation, "*hat solches wenigstens gehabt*," would have to be made.

20.29. *Das glaub' ich*: "I believe it" or "I agree."

20.31. Dalai-Lama: "Grand priest," the chief priest of Tibetan Buddhism. See *On Heroes* 6.25–28 and note.

20.33. Talapoin: "A Buddhist monk or priest, properly of Pegu; extended by Europeans to those of Siam, Burmah, and other Buddhist countries" (*OED*, s.v. "Talapoin"), as here by Carlyle to those of Tibet.

20.38. outwatching the Bear: Milton, *Il Penseroso* (1645), lines 86–88: "Or let my Lamp at midnight hour, / Be seen in som high lonely Towr, / Where I may oft out-watch the *Bear*." In the northern latitudes, the Great Bear (*Ursa Major*) never sets; hence Teufelsdröckh sits up until dawn.

21.1. Dulness and Darkness: Compare Alexander Pope, *The Dunciad* (1728–29), *passim*.

21.14–15. Pedro Garcia's . . . Bag of Doubloons: A tale told in the "Preface to the Reader" of the picaresque novel *Gil Blas* (1715–35) by Alain René Le Sage. Two travelling scholars happen upon a stone with the faint inscription: "The soul of the licentiate *Pedro Garcias* is here enclosed." The younger scholar scoffs at the "foolish Epitaph" for implying that a soul can be enclosed. "His Companion who had more Judgment, said to himself, There must be some Mystery in it; I'll stay and see whether I can find it out. Accordingly, he let the other Scholar go before him, and when he was gone, he pull'd out his Knife, and dug up the Earth about the Stone, which at last he remov'd, and found under it a Leather Purse which he open'd. There were a Hundred Ducats in it, with a Card, wherein was written in *Latin* to this Effect. *Be thou my Heir, Thou who hast Wit enough to find out the Meaning of this Inscription, and make a better use of my Money than I did*" (1716 London translation).

NOTES TO CHAPTER IV. CHARACTERISTICS

23.6. pier-glasses, and or-molu: Pier-glass: a tall mirror set in the "pier," or wall section, between windows. Ormolu: furniture gilded with gold leaf or with a gold-colored alloy of copper, zinc, and tin.

23.10. Malines laces: Malines or Mechelen, a town in Belgium, once famous for lace-making.

23.10–11. **star of a Lord**: An insignia in the shape of a star worn by the nobility.

23.12. **spelter**: Crude zinc from the smelter.

23.21–22. **Transcendental Philosophies . . . Matter and Material things as Spirit**: These subjects are amplified in Book I, Chapter X (49–53) and Book III, Chapter VIII (187–95).

23.28. **weasand**: Gullet, esophagus.

23.31–32. **Baptist living on locusts and wild honey**: John the Baptist lived on "locusts and wild honey" (Matthew 3:4, Mark 1:6).

24.8. *Sanchoniathon*: Or Sanchuniatho, an alleged seer from Phoenicia, said to have lived before the Trojan War, whose writings were supposedly used by Philon Bybllos (64–141), author of a Phoenician history. Compare Sterne's *Tristram Shandy* 5.28.462, where it is pointed out that Sanchuniatho "circumcised his whole army one morning," but "not without a court martial."

24.8. *Dr. Lingard*: John Lingard (1771–1851), Roman Catholic historian and author of *Antiquities of the Anglo-Saxon Church* (1806) and a *History of England* (1819–30).

24.9. *Shasters,* **and** *Talmuds,* **and** *Korans*: Shaster ["Book"], the religious and legal book of the Hindus; Talmud ["Learn"], the code book of Jewish civil and canonical law; Koran or Qur'an ["Read"], the sacred book of the Moslems.

24.9–10. **Cassini's** *Siamese Tables*: Gian Domenico Cassini (1625–1712), an Italian astronomer, later French citizen, the founder and first director of the Royal Observatory in Paris. He examined and explained the "*Règles de l'Astronomie Siamoise pour calculer les mouvements du Soleil et de la Lune,*" which Simon de la Loubère (1642–1729), French Ambassador to Siam, had translated from the Siamese.

24.10. **Laplace's** *Mécanique Céleste*: See above at 3.13 and note.

24.10. Robinson Crusoe: *The Life and Strange Surprising Adventures of Robinson Crusoe, of York, Mariner* (1719), a novel by Daniel Defoe (1660?–1731).

24.11. Belfast Town and Country Almanack: As a young man, Carlyle worked out mathematical puzzles and consulted the astrological tables in this almanac, which was published from 1786 to 1849. See *Letters* 1:82, 88; 2:252.

24.20–21. Minervas . . . from Jove's head: Minerva, the Roman goddess of crafts and later war, is often identified with the Greek goddess of wisdom, Athena, who sprang, fully armed, from the forehead of Zeus (identified with the Roman Jove or Jupiter).

25.8. ethereal Love . . . infinite Pity: See below at 140.37.

25.9. clasp the whole Universe into his bosom: Compare Richter's *Siebenkäs* 3.9.311–12, where Siebenkäs confronts the universe of sorrow.

25.15. Mephistopheles: The tempter and mocker in Faustian legend, more specifically the Devil in Goethe's *Faust*. In "Goethe's Helena" (1828), *Essays* 1:157, Carlyle calls him the "Devil, not of Superstition, but of Knowledge . . . a genuine Son of Night."

25.17. Whirligig: A spinning toy.

25.21. Chancery: Originally formed to control access to the royal court, the High Court of Chancery, presided over by the Lord Chancellor, evolved into a judiciary which decided cases in "equity," a special jurisdiction, collateral to the common law, which dealt with wills and trusts, and could give relief not otherwise provided by the law courts. Rife with corruption and delay, the courts of chancery were reorganized in 1873 by the Judicature Act, which amalgamated the jurisdictions of law and equity.

25.31. Seven Sleepers: In Syrian legend, the Seven Sleepers of Ephesus were Christian youths who fled to a cave to escape the persecutions of Decius (c.250), not to awaken until the fifth century; they became martyrs to those who were determined never to waver in their faith.

25.31. **Jean Paul's:** Jean Paul Friedrich Richter (1763–1825), German humorist and moralist, about whom Carlyle wrote two articles, in the *Edinburgh Review* (46 [June 1827]:176–95; reprinted in *Essays* 1:1–25) and the *Foreign Review* (5 [January 1830]:1–52; reprinted in *Essays* 2:96–159). Carlyle also translated some of Richter's fiction, most notably the "Life of Quintus Fixlein," *German Romance* 2:197–332. Unlike the Editor/narrator persona of *Sartor Resartus*, Carlyle never met Richter.

25.32. **world-Mahlstrom:** The Maelstrom (German *Mahlstrom*) is a whirlpool near the Loffoden Isles, off the west coast of Norway. Carlyle might be punning here on the German word *mahlen*, which means to grind or to mill.

25.32–33. **heaven-kissing:** *Hamlet* 3.4.58–59: "A station like the herald Mercury / New lighted on a heaven-kissing hill."

25.37. **'Extra-harangues':** Digressions and interpolations, like the *Extra-blatt* (extra chapter) that Richter sometimes inserts into his tales.

26.2–3. **radiant ever-young Apollo . . . like the neighing of all Tattersall's:** A description of the laugh of Walter Welsh, Jane Carlyle's maternal grandfather. In *Reminiscences*, 123, Carlyle writes, "[I]n Walter's [laugh] there was audible something as of infinite flutes and harps. . . . I remember one such laugh . . . and how the old face looked suddenly so beautiful and *young* again. 'Radiant ever-young Apollo' etc. of Teufelsdröckh's laugh is a reminiscence of that." Tattersall's: a famous horse-market and stable in London.

26.20–21. **who cannot laugh . . . fit for treasons, stratagems, and spoils:** *Merchant of Venice* 5.1.82–85: "The man that hath no music in himself, / Nor is not moved with concord of sweet sounds, / Is fit for treasons, stratagems, and spoils." In "Jean Paul Friedrich Richter" (1827), *Essays* 1:17, Carlyle says, "True humour springs not more from the head than from the heart; it is not contempt, its essence is love; it issues not in laughter, but in still smiles, which lie far deeper."

NOTES TO CHAPTER V. THE WORLD IN CLOTHES

27.1. Montesquieu: Charles Louis de Secondat, Baron de la Brede et de Montesquieu (1689–1755), French political author and philosopher. Carlyle discusses Montesquieu's *L'Esprit des lois* (*The Spirit of Laws*, 1748), a comparative study of republican, monarchic, and despotic governments, in his article "Montesquieu" (1820) in the *Edinburgh Encyclopædia*. Carlyle is punning in his suggested titles *Esprit de Coutumes* and *Esprit de Costumes: coutume* (custom, law) and *costume* (clothes) are from the same etymological root.

27.11. ruffs: High, frilled or pleated collars of starched muslin or lace, worn in the sixteenth and seventeenth centuries.

27.13. Agglomeration: A jumbled mass or heap, which within the context of *Sartor Resartus* is the problem facing the Editor, who must edit Teufelsdröckh's manuscript.

27.14–15. Later-Gothic: The so-called Gothic Revival which took place in the late eighteenth and nineteenth centuries and which was characterized by a return to various styles of medieval architecture. The revival was to be given authority by figures such as A. W. N. Pugin (*Contrasts*, 1836) and John Ruskin (*The Stones of Venice*, 1851–53), both of whom argued for a return to the clarity of design and moral purpose represented by Gothic architecture. The revival complemented Carlyle's argument that the Body Politic must be re-tailored, a thesis he continued in *Past and Present* (1843).

27.15. Anglo-Dandiacal: An allusion to Dandyism, a style of elaborate dress and radical behavior popular during the Regency Period, epitomized by individuals like Beau Brummel (1778–1840) and Count D'Orsay (1801–1852). See Book III, Chapter X, "The Dandiacal Body."

27.16–17. drab to . . . scarlet: As from the drab gray of Quakers to the scarlet of the British army.

28.1. Cause-and-effect Philosophy: An allusion to empirical philosophers, such as John Locke and David Hume, who took the expression from Aristotle and expanded it to include a discussion of the interrelationship of cause and effect, known as causality. Hume's argument that the causal relation cannot be an object of experience and must be inferred from mere "constant conjunction" called into question Newtonian physics which held that every deviation from law-governed motion has a cause.

28.5–6. Letters from a hieroglyphical prophetic Book: A reference to the commonly held belief among German Romantics, such as Schiller, Novalis, and Schelling, that Nature, hence Man, is a hieroglyphic manifestation of God.

28.21–22. Compilers of some *Library* of General, Entertaining, Useful, or even Useless Knowledge: See 10.3–5 above and note.

28.27. First Chapter . . . Paradise and Fig-leaves: An allusion to Genesis, the first book of the Bible. See Genesis 2:8–3:24.

28.29. cabalistico-sartorial: A coinage of Carlyle's, alluding to the Cabala or cabbala, an esoteric system of interpreting the scriptures, with its origins in medieval Jewish mysticism, founded upon the belief that each word, letter, and number contains mysteries that can be deciphered only by initiates. Cabalistic signs and symbols are used as amulets and in occult practices.

28.31. Lilis: Or Lilith, Adam's first wife according to a Talmudic tradition. A Babylonian demon in Hebrew folklore, Lilith came to be associated with infanticide and sexual lust. She appears in the "*Walpurgisnacht*" section of Goethe's *Faust*. In a *Journal* entry, December 7, 1826, Carlyle wrote, "Adam is fabled by the Talmudists to have had a wife before Eve: she was called Lilis (see *Faust — Goldne Hochzeit*); and their progeny was all manner of terrestrial, aquatic and aërial—Devils!" (*Two Note Books*, 81–82).

28.35. *Adam-Kadmon*: Or Adam-Cadmon, the first man, according to Hebraic tradition; the ideal man of the Cabalists.

28.36. *Nifl* and *Muspel* (Darkness and Light): In Scandinavian myth, *Niflheimr* ("mist-home") is the northern region of night and cold, and *Múspellheimr* ("bright-home") is the southern region of light and warmth. Between them is *Ginnungagap*, the central chaos. See *On Heroes* 15.29–30 and note.

29.4. Tower of Babel . . . dispersion of Mankind: Genesis 11:1–9: At Babel, "the Lord did there confound the language of all the earth: and from thence did the Lord scatter them abroad upon the face of all the earth."

29.5. habilable globe: *Habilable* is apparently a Carlylean coinage, punning on *habitable* and meaning "able to be clothed."

29.5. Pelasgic: The culture and especially the architecture of pre-Hellenic Greece.

29.6. Otaheitean: Of Tahiti, one of the Society Islands in the South Pacific.

29.8. *Orbis Pictus* . . . *Orbis Vestitus*: *Orbis Pictus* (*The World in Pictures*), an illustrated schoolbook compiled by Amos Comenius (1592–1670), a Moravian scholar and educational reformer, was published in Nürnberg in 1658. Goethe read the book as a child, and Richter mentions it in "Quintus Fixlein" (*German Romance* 2:322), where it is referred to as "*orbis pictus* or *fictus*." *Orbis Vestitus* (*The World in Clothes*) is the title given to this chapter.

29.12. King Nibelung: The hero of the Middle High German epic, *Nibelungenlied* (early 13th century). Carlyle wrote a review-essay on the work for the *Westminster Review*, 15 (July 1831):1–45 (reprinted in *Essays* 2:216–73). He is quoting here from memory: the "twelve wagons in twelve days" should read "in four days" (*Essays* 2:232).

29.14. wampum belts: Belts of beads made of shells, used by the North American Indians for barter. Also mentioned in "On History" (1830), *Essays* 2:83.

29.14. phylacteries: (Hebrew: *tefillin*) Two small leather cases, holding passages of scripture; one is attached by leather thongs to the forehead and one to the left arm. Worn by orthodox Jews during morning prayer on weekdays. See Exodus 13:16 and Deuteronomy 6:8 and 11:18.

29.14. stoles, albs: Ecclesiastical vestments.

29.15. chlamydes: The plural of *chlamys*, a short mantle, clasped at the shoulder, worn by men in ancient Greece.

29.15. trunk hose: Breeches coming to just above the knees, popular in the sixteenth and seventeenth centuries.

29.16. Celtic philibegs: Kilts.

29.16–17. *Gallia Braccata*: "Breeches-clad Gaul," the land and people north of the Alps, as opposed to toga-wearing Rome.

29.17. Hussar cloaks: The Hussars were originally a body of light cavalry organized in Hungary in the fifteenth century, subsequently imitated in most European armies including the British. "The dress of the Hungarian force set the type for that of the hussars of other nations, these being distinguished by uniforms of brilliant colours and elaborate ornament" (*OED*, s.v. "Hussar").

29.17–18. Vandyke tippets: Long, hanging parts of a hood, cape, or sleeve, as seen in the paintings of the Flemish artist Anthony Van Dyck (1599–1641).

29.18. fardingales: Farthingale, a hoop, openwork frame, or circular pad worn around the hips by women in the sixteenth and seventeenth centuries.

29.19. Kilmarnock nightcap: A knitted woolen cap, or cowl, made in Kilmarnock, Scotland.

29.37. *Putz*: German for "finery." *Putzen* means "to polish, clean" and *sich putzen* means "to dress up."

30.12. Anthropophagus: A cannibal. Compare *Othello* 1.3.143–45: "And of the Cannibals that each other eat, / The Anthropophagi, and men whose heads / Do grow beneath their shoulders."

30.12–13. Out of the eater . . . cometh forth sweetness: Samson's riddle, Judges 14:14.

30.17–18. seed-grain . . . Banyan-grove: Compare Matthew 13:31–32: "The kingdom of heaven is like to a grain of mustard seed, which a man took, and sowed in his field: Which indeed is the least of all seeds: but when it is grown, it is the greatest among herbs, and becometh a tree." Carlyle often interchanges the banyan and Igdrasil, the ash tree which, in Scandinavian myth, binds together heaven, earth, and hell.

30.19. Hemlock-forest: Carlyle here conflates the evergreen hemlock tree (genus *Tsuga*) and poison hemlock (*Conium maculatum*), an herb of the carrot family; an extract of the latter was used to execute Socrates.

30.20–21. *Movable Types*: An invention attributed to Johann Gutenberg (c.1397–1468), who in 1436–37? was the first European to print with movable type cast in molds. Gutenberg was financed by Johann Fust, or Faust (d. 1466?), a Mainz goldsmith who seems to have contributed to the development of the invention. In "Voltaire" (1829), Carlyle says that the "'movable types' of Johannes Faust . . . wrought a benefit, which is yet immeasurably expanding itself, and will continue to expand itself through all countries and through all times" (*Essays* 1:399–400).

30.22–23. Democratic . . . Art of Printing: In *On Heroes*, Carlyle again links printing and democracy: "Printing, which comes necessarily out of Writing, I say often, is equivalent to Democracy: invent Writing, Democracy is inevitable" (141.30–32).

30.24. Monk Schwartz's pestle: "The invention of gun-powder is ascribed by Polydore Virgil to a chemist, who having accidentally put some of the ingredients in this composition in a mortar, and covered it over with a stone, it happened to take fire, and blew up the stone. Thevet says, the person here spoken of was a monk of Friburg, named Constantine Anelzen; but Belleforet and others hold it to be Bartholdus Schwartz, or the black" (*Encyclopædia Britannica* 1st ed., 1771, s.v. "Gun-powder").

30.29–30. Ox (or *Pecus*) . . . *Pecunia*, Money: The etymological linking of *pecus* ("cattle") and *pecunia* ("wealth") has its source in Varro, *De Lingua Latina* 5.95: "Quod in pecore pecunia tum pastoribus consistebat (Because the herdsmen's *pecunia* 'wealth' then lay in their *pecus* 'flocks')."

30.32. Rothschilds: The English branch of the German financial house of Rothschild was founded by Nathan Meyer Rothschild (1777–1836), who underwrote the forces opposing Napoleon, and who in consequence saved the London stock exchange from collapse.

30.33. English National Debts: There is an instructive and amusing narration of the origin and growth of the national debt in Chapter XIX of Macaulay's *History of England* (1848–61).

31.7–8. Man is a Tool-using Animal (*Handthierendes Thier*): In a *Journal* entry, January 1832, Carlyle writes, "[Benjamin] Franklin, I find twice or thrice in Boswell, defines man as 'a Tool-making Animal.' Teufelsdreck therefore has so far been anticipated. *Vivant qui ante nos nostra dixerunt!*" (*Two Note Books*, 245) "Long live those who said our [things] before us." See Boswell's *Life of Johnson*, April 7, 1778: "Boswell: 'I think Dr. Franklin's definition of a *Man* a good one—'a tool-making animal.' Johnson: 'But many a man never made a tool: and suppose a man without arms, he could not make a tool'" (449).

31.11. quintals: A quintal, or kintal, is a unit of weight that can variously refer to 100 pounds, or one "hundredweight" (112 pounds), or, in the metric system, 100 kilograms (220 pounds).

31.21. Laughing Animal: William Whitehead, *On Ridicule* (1743): "T'was said of old, deny it who can, / The only laughing animal is man." Compare also Whitehead's *An Essay on Ridicule* (London, 1753), Part 2, pp. 67–82; and Hazlitt, "Man is the only animal that laughs and weeps; for he is the only animal that is struck with the difference between what things are, and what they ought to be" (*Lectures on the English Comic Writers*, 1).

31.24–25. Cooking Animal: In a footnote to *The Journal of a Tour to the Hebrides* (1785) (in *Life of Johnson*, ed. George B. Hill, rev. L. F. Powell [Oxford, 1950], 5:33n, August 15, 1773), Boswell writes: "My definition of *Man* is, 'a Cooking animal.' The beasts have memory, judgment, and all the faculties and passions of our mind, in a certain degree; but no beast is a cook."

31.26. Tartar . . . readies his steak: The reference is to Butler's *Hudibras* 1.2.275–80: "And though his Country-men, the *Huns*, /

Did use to stew between their Bums / And their warm Horses backs, their meat / And every man his Saddle eat: / He was not half so nice as they, / But eat it raw, when't came in's way."

31.29. Monsieur Ude: Louis Eustache Ude, the famous cook and author of *The French Cook; or the Art of Cookery*, which was in its tenth printing in 1829. Ude appears as portrait number twenty-five in *Fraser's Magazine*.

31.30. Humboldt: Alexander von Humboldt (1769–1859), German naturalist and explorer, who sought to determine the courses of the Orinoco and Amazon rivers, and who later attempted to explain the unity between the ideals of philosophy and the exact requirements of science. Carlyle's authority here is Humboldt's *Tableaux de la Nature* (*Pictures of Nature*, 1828), 188–99, which discusses the Orinoco Indians' dependence on "clay-earth." See Carlyle's letter to his brother John, January 21, 1831 (*Letters* 5:214).

32.1. Dibble: A pointed stick used to make holes in the soil for planting seeds or seedlings.

32.2. Liverpool Steam-carriages: George Stephenson built the steam locomotive "Rocket," which in 1829 won an invitational race held near Liverpool at a top speed of 35 miles per hour. On September 15, 1830, the first commercial railroad was opened between Liverpool and Manchester. Carlyle saw the steam coaches for the first time on August 6, 1831, on his way to London with the manuscript of *Sartor Resartus*; see *Two Note Books*, 192.

32.6–7. six hundred and fifty-eight miscellaneous individuals: I.e., the members of Parliament.

NOTES TO CHAPTER VI. APRONS

33.2. Gao: Variously known as Gaváh, Káwa, Kaweh, or Kawah, from the mythic verse-epic "Shah-nama" (King-book) by Ferdowi (d. 1020?), which tells the story of Gaváh, a blacksmith, whose sons have been slain by the tyrannical King Dahhák (Devil) to feed the two-headed serpent that grows from his shoulders. Dahhák agrees to spare the last of Gaváh's eighteen sons if he will in turn sign a loyalty oath. On the principle of justice Gaváh refuses and instead leads a rebellion after placing his leather apron on top of a spearhead which in subsequent legend became a symbol of freedom for the oppressed Persians. Known as "The Kaviani Banner," it was decorated with precious jewels by each new king until the conquest of Persia by the Mohammedan Omar (Umar), who had the leather burned and the jewels distributed among the poor. Carlyle alludes to the story in his article "Persia" (1820), the *Edinburgh Encyclopædia*.

33.5. John Knox's Daughter: Elizabeth Knox, the third and youngest daughter of John Knox (1505–1572), married John Welsh, the Scot reformer, in 1595. When Welsh was banished from Scotland, Elizabeth petitioned James I for his return, and the king consented if Welsh would acknowledge the authority of the Church by Bishops. Legend has it that Elizabeth held out her apron and said that she would rather have her husband's head in her lap. Jane Carlyle's father, John Welsh, claimed descent from John and Elizabeth Welsh and thus from John Knox. Carlyle was dubious about the claim. See *Reminiscences*, 108–09.

33.8. Landgravine Elizabeth: St. Elizabeth of Hungary (1207–1231), daughter of King Andrew II of Hungary and wife of Landgrave Louis II of Thuringia. Against her husband's wishes, Elizabeth often took food to the poor. Upon being surprised one day by her husband, she hid a basket of food under her apron and said that she was gathering roses. When Louis looked under her apron, the food had miraculously turned to roses. See Carlyle's translation of Johann August Musæus, "Melechsala," *German Romance* 1:139–42, where the story is told in full.

33.15. Nürnberg Workboxes and Toyboxes: Nürnberg was famous in the nineteenth century for its woodwork, especially clocks and toys. See also 82.2–4 below.

33.19. half-naked Vulcans: Vulcan, in Roman myth the god of fire and metal. The language here is similar to that used by Carlyle to record his impressions of Birmingham in 1824. In a letter to his brother Alexander, August 11, he describes how the "blast-furnaces were roaring like the voice of many whirlwinds all around; the fiery metal was hissing thro' its moulds, or sparkling and spitting under hammers of a monstrous size," where "thro' the whole, half-naked demons pouring with sweat and besmeared with soot were hurrying to and fro in their red nightcaps and sheet-iron breeches" (*Letters* 3:125).

33.19. Smelt-furnace: Where ore is smelted, refined to purity.

34.3. Devil's-smithy (*Teufels-schmiede*): Teufelsdröckh is also associated with the Devil; compare 177.8–11 below.

34.4. Episcopal, or Cassock: Often called a Bishop's apron, an allusion to the Protestant cassock which, rather than buttoned down the front in the traditional manner, was folded over, "tucked in," and held by the cincture. Compare 155.6 below.

34.10. Paper Aprons . . . Parisian Cooks: Compare Carlyle's translation of Richter's "Life of Quintus Fixlein," where Fixlein's collection of waste-paper literature discarded by grocers is recounted: "It was also this respect for all waste-paper that inspired him with such esteem for the aprons of French cooks, which it is well known consist of printed paper; and he often wished some German would translate these aprons: indeed I am willing to believe that a good version of more than one of such paper aprons might contribute to elevate our literature . . . and serve her in place of drivel-bib" (*German Romance* 2:223).

34.13. celebrated London Firm: Since *Sartor Resartus* is in part a translation of waste-paper fragments, it is possible that Carlyle is referring here to the notoriety of *Fraser's*, or perhaps to his earlier translation *German Romance*, published by Charles Tait, which itself is made up of fragments.

34.24. Laystall: A place where refuse or dung is kept, from *leystall*, which is part of a church chapel (*OED*). The laystall is also where the rotted vestures of man are claimed, at 44.7 below.

34.27. Rags or Clothes-rubbish: Fine stationery was made from rag pulp or the cotton cuttings from weaving mills. The demand for such materials quickly outstripped the supply, making rag-gathering a profitable business. Compare 55.24 and 186.23–24 below.

34.27–28. Electric Battery . . . Fountain-of-Motion: Carlyle was no doubt aware of Georg S. Ohm, the German physicist whose *The*

Galvanic Current Investigated Mathematically (1829) contributed in part to Ohm's Law of electrical resistance. In 1831, Michael Faraday, an English scientist, was credited with the discovery of electro-magnetic induction, a dynamo or copper disk that rotated between the poles of a permanent magnet, a precursor of the electric motor. See the following note.

34.29. vitreous and resinous Electricities: A reference to static electricity, made by rubbing either silk on glass (vitreous or positive) or amber (Greek, *elektron*) on fur (resinous or negative). Compare the attraction between "Negative and Positive" at 102.7, the "Spiritual Electricity" at 102.14–15, "pole and pole trembling towards contact" at 106.27–28, and the travelling from "Negative Pole to the Positive" at 136.8–9.

34.33–34. Journalists . . . Kings and Clergy: In "Signs of the Times" (1829), Carlyle says, "The true Church of England, at this moment, lies in the Editors of its Newspapers" (*Essays* 2:77). In *On Heroes*, he similarly concludes, "I many a time say, the writers of Newspapers, Pamphlets, Poems, Books, these *are* the real working effective Church of a modern country" (*On Heroes* 140.22–24). This general theme is repeated in Book III, Chapter VII, "Organic Filaments."

34.35. Bourbon Dynasties, and Tudors and Hapsburgs: The French Bourbon monarchy survived from 1272–1883 (with interruptions), the English Tudor from 1485–1603, and the Austrian Hapsburg from 1282–1918.

34.36. Stamped Broad-sheet Dynasties: That is, newspapers. In 1712 Parliament passed the Stamp Act, which required a stamp surcharge to be affixed to all newspapers.

35.3–4. *Satan's Invisible World Displayed*: An allusion to George Sinclair, *Satan's Invisible World Discovered* (1685), which argues that devils, witches, spirits, and apparitions exist; and perhaps also to Cotton Mather, *The Wonders of the Invisible World* (1693), which extends Sinclair's argument to include witch hunts and witch trials. In "Goethe's Helena" (1828), Carlyle warns that Goethe's *Faust* is not "a new 'Satan's Invisible World displayed'" (*Essays* 1:156), and in "Signs of the Times" (1829), he describes the "New-England Puritan [who] burns witches, wrestles for months with the horrors of Satan's invisible world, and all ghastly phantasms, the daily and hourly precursors of the Last Day" (*Essays* 2:57). Compare Teufelsdröckh's separation from the "Satanic School" at 127.13–14, and later rejection of Satan, "*Apage, Satana*" at 138.30.

35.6. Homer . . . nod: Horace, *Ars Poetica*: "*et idem / indignor quandoque bonus dormitat Homerus*" (and likewise, I am offended when good Homer nods; lines 358–59). In *An Essay on Criticism* (1711; Part I, lines 179–80), Pope says, in calling for prudence among critics: "Those oft are stratagems which error seem, / Nor is it Homer nods, but we that dream."

35.8. Presbyterian Witchfinder: Compare Carlyle's equating "Demonology" with "Madness" at 191.1 below.

35.9. *Brittische Journalistik*: British journalism.

NOTES TO CHAPTER VII. MISCELLANEOUS-HISTORICAL

36.3. Costume: Compare 27.3 above.

36.5–6. Teniers . . . Callot: Perhaps David Teniers the elder (1582–1649), a Flemish painter; but more likely David Teniers (1610–1690), his son and pupil, a genre painter and protégé of Rubens, known for his quiet scenes from peasant life. Jacques Callot (c.1592–1635), French etcher and engraver, known for his grotesques, caricatures, and studies of the horrors of war. Carlyle knew Callot through his translation of E. T. W. Hoffmann's *Der Goldne Topf* ("The Golden Pot," *German Romance* 2:23–114), which is part of the larger *Fantasiestücke in Callots Manier* (*Fantasy-Pieces in Callot's Style*, 1814–1815), a collection of gothic, supernatural, and often grotesque stories. In his biographic sketch of Hoffmann, Carlyle describes Callot as a "Lorraine painter of the seventeenth century; a wild genius, whose *Temptations of St. Anthony* is said to exceed in chaotic incoherence that of Teniers himself," and later concludes that Teniers and Callot were "models" for Hoffmann's work (*German Romance* 2:12–13, 20).

36.12–13. Merrick's . . . *On Ancient Armour*: Samuel R. Meyrick (1783–1848), *A Critical Inquiry into Antient Armour* (1824) and *Engraved Illustrations of Antient Arms and Armour* (1830).

36.14. Paulinus's . . . *Zeitkürtzende Lust*: Christian Franz Paullini (1643–1711), compiler of *Das Zeitkurtzende lust- und spiel-hauss* (*The Entertaining Pleasure and Gambling House,* n.d.), Chapter 123 of which Carlyle loosely paraphrases.

36.18. rise again: Later, in "Natural Supernaturalism" (at 188.12–13), Carlyle turns this ironic allusion to Lazarus (John 11:38–44) into a metaphor for the "confirmation" of miracles.

36.21. Tree: Carlyle is contrasting here the tree whose roots flourish underground to the Banyan tree, mentioned at 30.18 above, whose roots grow downward from its branches.

37.3. Napoleon: Napoleon I (1769–1821), whom Teufelsdröckh later describes as a "divine Missionary" (133.16).

37.3. Byron: George Gordon, Lord Byron, whose misanthropic personality Carlyle admired in his youth. However, by the time of the writing of *Sartor Resartus,* he had come to reject what he saw as the Byronic worship of sorrow and sought to replace it with the Goethean doctrine of hope; compare "Close thy *Byron*; open thy *Goethe*" at 143.4 below.

37.5. Law of Progress: The finite Law of Progress here becomes the contrast for the infinite Laws of Nature defined in "Natural Supernaturalism," Book III, Chapter VIII below.

37.7–8. buff-belts . . . gorgets . . . churn-boots: Buff-belts: belts of buff leather (a thick leather of buffalo- or ox-hide). Gorgets: pieces of armor to protect the throat. Churn-boots: large boots shaped like butter churns.

37.13. *Teusinke*: From Paullini, as cited by Carlyle at 36.14 above (see note): "*Die reichen Leute hatten Teusincke um, was ein silberner Gürtel*" (Rich men have Teusincke [a bell-shaped girdle] near, also a silver girdle).

37.22. ell-long: A cloth measurement, originally the distance from elbow to finger-tips. The English ell equalled 45 inches, the Scottish 37.2 inches.

37.24. *ohne Gesäss*: Again from Paullini: "*Auch hatten die Männer Hosen ohne Gesäss, bunden solche an die Hembder.*"

37.29. **Cleopatras**: Compare Shakespeare's *Antony and Cleopatra* 2.2.201–3, 208–10: "On each side her / Stood pretty dimpled boys, like smiling Cupids, / With divers-color'd fans," and "At the helm / A seeming mermaid steers; the silken tackle / Swell with the touches of those flower-soft hands." Compare also Dryden's *All for Love* (1677) 3.1.160–87.

37.30. **welts**: "A narrow strip of material put on the edge of a garment, etc., as a border, binding, or hem; a frill, fringe, or trimming" (*OED*, s.v. "Welt").

37.34. **snoods**: Ties or ribbons in the hair, formerly worn by unmarried women in Scotland.

38.6. **fustian**: Thick cotton cloth, like corduroy or velveteen.

38.14. **cornuted shoes**: Horn-shaped shoes.

38.17. **Raleigh's fine mantle**: Sir Walter Raleigh (1554?–1618), English soldier, explorer, courtier, and man of letters, who according to tradition placed his coat in the mud in order that Elizabeth I would not soil her shoes.

38.20–22. **red-painted . . . glass**: In *Notes of Conversations with Ben Jonson Made by William Drummond of Hawthornden* (1619), 15, it is reported: "Queen Elizabeth never saw her self after she became old in a true Glass. [T]hey painted her & sometymes would vermilion her nose."

38.24. **verdigris**: A greenish-blue pigment, prepared by treating copper with acetic acid.

38.26. **slashed**: Slits made in a garment to show an underlying fabric.

38.26. **galooned**: Trimmed with galloon, a decorative ribbon or braid made of gold, silver, or silk thread.

38.28. **luckless** **Courtier:** Compare John Bulwer, *Anthropometamorphosis: Man Transformed; or, the Artificial Change-ling . . . Monstrosities That Have Appeared to Disfigure the Humane Fabrick* (1650).

38.34. Erostratus: Also Herostratus, an Ephesian who set fire to the Temple of Artemis on the night that Alexander the Great was born, 356 B.C., in order to immortalize himself.

38.35. Milo: Greek athlete from Crotona (sixth century B.C.) who myth says carried a heifer on his shoulders through the Olympic stadium, killed it with one blow, and then ate it all in one day.

38.35. Henry Darnley: Henry Stewart, Lord Darnley (1545–1567), cousin and second husband of Mary Queen of Scots, whom Carlyle elsewhere calls a "foolish tall booby" (Carlyle's *The Guises* (1855), ed. Rodger L. Tarr in *Victorian Studies*, 25 [Autumn, 1981], 32). Mary allegedly fell in love with him because of his long limbs.

38.37. bed-tester: The canopy over a bed.

38.37. Boileau Despréaux: Nicolas Boileau-Despréaux (1636–1711), French critic and poet, whose work, according to Helvétius in *De l'esprit* (1758), *Discours* 3, was supposedly lacking in feeling because as a child he was frightened by a turkey-cock. On Helvétius, see note at 72.37 below.

39.2. Kaiser Otto's Court: Otto I (1815–1867), first King of the Hellenes, was chosen to rule independent Greece by a conference of European powers in London in 1832. The second son of Louis I of Bavaria, Otto proved to be unpopular, led a weak government, and sought to attack Turkey after the outbreak of the Crimean War in 1854.

39.3. Themistocles: Athenian political leader and naval commander (525?–460? B.C.), whose "prayer . . . for a talent of Forgetting" Cicero made famous in *De Oratore* 2.74.299: "It is said that a certain learned . . . person . . . offered to impart to him the science of mnemonics, which . . . the professor asserted . . . would enable him to remember everything; and Themistocles replied that he would be doing him a greater kindness if he taught him to forget what he wanted than if he taught him to remember."

39.9–10. **Bolivar's Cavalry**: Simón Bolívar (1783–1830), South American revolutionary whom Carlyle called "the Washington of Columbia," a modern-day Ulysses whose military ventures were "analogous to Hannibal's." In "Dr. Francia" ([1843], *Essays* 4:262), Carlyle describes in detail the ponchos depicted here.

NOTES TO CHAPTER VIII. THE WORLD OUT OF CLOTHES

40.6. **new Philosophy**: Transcendentalism, variously referred to as new views, newness, new school, intuitional philosophy, and the Movement, is summarized, using Carlylean metaphor, by Ralph Waldo Emerson in his essay "Transcendentalism" (1842). Both Carlyle and Emerson equate transcendentalism with German idealism. In "State of German Literature" (1827), Carlyle refers to it as the "*New School*" which caused "such stir and strife in the intellect of Germany" (*Essays* 1:54). See 12.12 above and note.

40.17. **Faust's Mantle**: The cloak used by Mephistopheles and Faust to explore the world. Compare *Faust* 1.4.2065–66: "*Wir breiten nur den Mantel aus, / Der soll uns durch die Lüfte tragen*" (We will lay my cloak out flat; / It will carry us through the air).

40.18. **Sheet . . . Apostle's Dream**: A reference to the apparition in Simon Peter's trance during which God instructs him on the difference between clean and unclean food. See Acts 10:11–12: "And [he] saw heaven opened, and a certain vessel descending unto him, as it had been a great sheet knit at the four corners, and let down to the earth: Wherein were all manner of four-footed beasts of the earth, and wild beasts, and creeping things, and fowls of the air."

40.20. **inane limbos**: Compare Dante's *Inferno*, Canto 4, where Limbo is described as the First Circle just inside the Gate of Hell, the place where the Virtuous Pagans live without hope. See also *Paradise Lost* 3.489–91, where Limbo is described in sartorial imagery: "[T]hen might ye see / Cowles, Hoods and Habits with their wearers tost / And fluttered in Raggs . . . / Into a *Limbo* large and broad, since calld / The Paradise of Fools."

41.2–4. **Logic** . . . **Reason** . . . **Intuition**: Terms found in Kant's *Critique of Pure Reason*, in which he argues against the empiricism of Locke, who asserted that the mind was a *tabula rasa* (blank tablet), and argues for a tripartite division of the mind into Sensibility (that which intuits time and space into concrete images), Understanding (that which transforms these concrete perceptions into abstract theorems) and Reason (that which attempts to synthesize these abstractions into ontological or metaphysical truths). Pure Reason was to Kant speculative or theoretical reason, which can only suggest patterns of thought but which can never objectify experience. In the "State of German Literature" (1827), Carlyle interprets the difference between the schools of Lockean logic and Kantian intuition: Kant's philosophy "commences from within, and proceeds outwards; instead of commencing from without, and . . . endeavouring to proceed inwards." Reason, Carlyle continues, "is of a higher nature than Understanding; . . . for Reason discerns Truth itself, the absolutely and primitively *True*; while Understanding discerns only *relations*, and cannot decide without *it*." Reason "is to be cultivated as the highest faculty in man" (*Essays* 1:79, 82–83). Later Carlyle elaborates upon the difference between "vulgar Logic" and "Pure Reason" (50.25 below), and then concludes that the Imagination weaves a visible manifestation from the otherwise invisible Reason (at 55.37ff); hence the Imagination is the corporeal garment of God. See Harrold, *Carlyle and German Thought*, 135–47, who argues that there is less of Kant and more of Jacobi and Coleridge in Carlyle's perception that "Reason is little else than a mystical penetration to spiritual truth."

41.7. **mighty maze** . . . **not without a plan**: Pope, *An Essay on Man* (1734) 1.5–6: "Expatiate free o'er all this scene of Man; / A mighty maze! but not without a plan."

41.20–21. **Fortunate Islands**: *Fortunatae Insulae*, those islands in Greek myth off the west coast of Africa where the souls of heroes passed after death. See Homer's *Odyssey*, Book 4.

41.26. **Who am I**: In "Jean Paul Friedrich Richter" (1830), Carlyle translates the epiphanic experience from *Wahrheit aus Jean Pauls Leben* (*The Truth of Jean Paul's Life*, 1826–28), in which Richter describes the "inward occurrence . . . the birth of my Self-consciousness . . . the internal vision, 'I am a ME (*ich bin ein Ich*),' came like a flash from heaven before me, and in gleaming light ever afterwards continued: then had my Me, for the first time, seen itself, and forever" (*Essays* 2:111). Richter also describes the experience in *Siebenkäs*, 429, as a "lightning flash," when we ask, "'What is it that thou art, *now*, my *me*!'" At 123.20ff below, the idea of self-consciousness as a metaphor is used to describe the articulation of speculative reason into imaginative form. Through such questioning both Richter and Carlyle can be placed in the existential tradition that in the nineteenth century finds its development in the writings of Sören Kierkegaard (1813–1855).

41.30. integuments: Outer covering or coat.

41.35–36. *Cogito, ergo sum*: "I think, therefore I am," from René Descartes (1596–1650) who in *Discours de la méthodè* (1637) argued against scholastic authoritarianism and for the universality of doubt. The one thing that cannot be doubted is doubt itself. Thus, intuitive self-consciousness is the beginning of all thought and experience. In *Siebenkäs* (471), Richter extends Descartes, "'I both *think* and *am thought*.'"

42.4. Phantasmagoria: A word invented by M. Philipstal as the title of his magic-lantern show, which involved optical illusions and dancing shadow figures, in London in 1802. By 1803, the word had already begun to acquire its more general sense of "a shifting . . . succession of phantasms or imaginary figures" (*OED*). In his Preface to Goethe's "The Tale" (1832), Carlyle draws a distinction between Allegory and Phantasmagoria: In the former "you have only once for all to find the key of, and so go on unlocking" while the latter "would require not one key to unlock it, but . . . a dozen successive keys" (*Essays* 2:449).

42.4. Dream-grotto: Perhaps an allusion to Plato's cave (*Republic*, Book 7), where the chained inhabitants can see only shadows of reality on the cave wall, cast by the fire which is behind them.

42.6–8. but Him . . . we see not: This argument is presented in Friedrich Schiller's *Don Carlos* (1785), in a passage translated by Carlyle in *The Life of Friedrich Schiller* (1825), 74: "Him the maker we behold not; calm / He veils himself in everlasting laws."

42.8–9. Creation . . . Rainbow: In "Jean Paul Friedrich Richter" (1830), Carlyle translates from *Siebenkäs* a passage on Christ's denial of God, as viewed by a dreamer lost in the "half-shadows of reality": "I descended as far as Being casts its shadow, and looked down into the Abyss and cried, Father, where art thou? But I heard only the everlasting storm which no one guides, and the gleaming Rainbow of Creation hung without a Sun" (*Essays* 2:157).

42.11–12. sleep deepest . . . most awake: Compare Novalis, *Fragmente*: "Sleep is for the inhabitants of Planets only. In another time, Man will sleep and wake continually at once. The greater part of our Body, of our Humanity itself, yet sleeps a deep sleep" (Carlyle's translation in "Novalis" [1829], *Essays* 2:39).

42.15–16. Moscow Retreats . . . hate-filled Revolutions: In June of 1812, Napoleon's *Grande Armée* entered Moscow, but by the middle of October he was in full retreat toward Paris and by the end of November the retreat became a rout. The Retreat from Moscow is mentioned again at 194.32 below. The revolutions referred to are probably the first French Revolution (1789) and the second French Revolution (1830).

42.18–19. right hand from left: Compare Jonah 4:11, where the citizens of Nineveh "cannot discern between their right hand and their left hand."

42.19–20. they only are wise who know that they know nothing: In Plato's *Apology of Socrates* (21a–23b), Socrates reports that when the Delphic Oracle said no one was wiser than he, he interpreted this to mean that the wisest are those who confess their ignorance.

42.21–22. Metaphysics . . . unproductive: In *Les rêveries du promeneur solitaire* (*The Reveries of a Solitary Walker*, 1776), 27, Rousseau argues that metaphysics is hair-splitting logic-chopping. Carlyle might very well be echoing Rousseau here, especially since the *Rêveries* begins with the question, "What am I?"

42.22–23. Sphinx's secret: The Sphinx was a monster who lived near Thebes and put any passerby to death who could not answer her riddle: "What creature moves on four feet in the morning, two at mid-day, and three toward night?" Oedipus correctly answered, "Man, who creeps on hands and feet as an infant, walks upright in adulthood, and leans upon a cane in old age." The Sphinx then either committed suicide or was slain by Oedipus.

42.23. rede: Reckon or understand. "The same word as *Read*, *v*., the common ME spelling being usually retained to distinguish the archaic from the current senses of the word" (*OED*).

42.24–25. What are your Axioms ... Words, words: Compare *Hamlet* 2.2.191–92: "*Polonius*. What do you read, my lord? / *Hamlet*. Words, words, words."

42.28. The *whole is greater than the part*: An axiom attributed to Euclid.

42.28–29. *Nature abhors a vacuum*: Suggested by Aristotle and refuted by Galileo and his pupil Evangelista Torricelli, the former using water and the latter mercury to achieve a near perfect vacuum. The experiment was repeated successfully by Blaise Pascal, and is alluded to by Carlyle in his article "Pascal" (1823) in the *Edinburgh Encyclopædia*. Compare François Rabelais, *Gargantua and Pantagruel* (1532) 1.5.21: "*Natura abhorret vacuum*—Nature abhors emptiness."

42.29–30. *Nothing can act but where it is*: Refuted by Isaac Newton in his *Principia* (1687), which demonstrates that the force of gravity acts at a distance.

43.5–6. Space ... Time: Kant, in the "Transcendental Aesthetic" section of the *Critique of Pure Reason*, calls Space and Time "the pure forms of sensible intuition" (A39, B56). Space "does not represent any property of things in themselves, nor does it represent them in their relation to one another. . . . Space is nothing but the form of all appearances of outer sense. It is the subjective condition of sensibility, under which alone outer intuition is possible" (A26, B42), and "Time is the formal *a priori* condition of all appearances whatsoever [i.e., of both outer and inner intuitions]" (A34, B50). In "Novalis" (1829), Carlyle emphasizes the mystical implications of these ideas: "Time and Space themselves are not external but internal entities: they have no outward existence, there is no Time and no Space *out* of the mind; they are mere *forms* of man's spiritual being. . . . If Time and Space have no absolute existence, no existence out of our minds, it removes a stumbling-block from the very threshold of our Theology. For on this ground, when we say that the Diety is omnipresent and eternal, that with Him it is a universal Here and Now, we say nothing wonderful; nothing but that He also created Time and Space, that Time and Space are not laws of His being, but only of ours" (*Essays* 2:25–26).

43.11. **"phantasy of our Dream"**: In "Novalis" (1829), Carlyle translates from *Lehrlinge zu Sais* (*Pupils at Sais*, 1826): "Can they not recognise in Nature the true impress of their own Selves? . . . They know not that this so-called Nature of theirs is a Sport of the Mind, a waste Fantasy of their Dream" (*Essays* 2:35).

43.23. *Erdgeist*: "Earth-Spirit." The verses are quoted from Goethe's *Faust*, Part 1, 2.502–10.

43.29. **Horse . . . fell**: Compare Swift's description of the Houyhnhnms in *Gulliver's Travels*, Part 4, Chapter 1. *Fell* is the skin or hide.

44.3. **Charnel-house**: A vault where the bones or bodies of the dead are placed. In "Jean Paul Friedrich Richter" (1830), Carlyle translates from *Siebenkäs* the vision of the dead Christ, which is preceded by a dream of the churchyard where "All the Graves were open, and the iron doors of the charnel-house were swinging to and fro by invisible hands" (*Essays* 2:156). The charnel-house metaphor is extended to include the rebirth of religion and the universe; compare 88.30 and 140.35 below.

44.8. **Rag-grinder**: A drum, known as a devil, with teeth that ground rags down to small pieces for the pulp used to manufacture paper.

44.23. **russet-jerkined**: Russet is a course reddish-brown cloth. A jerkin is a sleeveless waistcoat or vest.

44.24. **one and indivisible**: The motto of the first French Republic.

44.30. **Dutch Cows**: A reference to the Dutch custom of providing protective garments for cows during inclement weather. Gouda is a town in southern Holland known for its cloth and cheese.

44.35. "a forked straddling animal with bandy legs": Carlyle is quoting the *Memoirs of Martinus Scriblerus* by John Arbuthnot, Alexander Pope, and Jonathan Swift (1741), Chapter 9, 136, where it is suggested that a vain man should "survey himself naked, divested of artificial charms, and he will find himself a forked stradling Animal, with bandy legs, a short neck, a dun hide, and a pot-belly." Carlyle attributes this observation to Swift, but in fact this chapter was written by Pope. Compare *King Lear* 3.4.106–8: "[U]naccommodated man is no more but such a poor, bare, fork'd animal as thou art." Then Lear tears off his clothes, which parallels here man's first stripping himself. Also see note at 48.14–15 below.

Notes to Chapter IX. Adamitism

45.5. Adamite: "In *Eccl. Hist.* the name of sects, ancient and modern, who affected to imitate Adam," especially in respect of his nakedness (*OED*).

45.10. muling and puking: *As You Like It* 2.7.142–44: "[O]ne man in his time plays many parts, / His acts being seven ages. At first the infant, / Mewling and puking in the nurse's arms." Mewling: whimpering or crying weakly.

45.10 coral: Polished coral or bone used for teething.

45.12. hulls: Coverings, such as clothes or other garments.

45.17. handsel: A gift to express good wishes at the New Year or other important event.

45.18–19. a Buck, or Blood, or Macaroni, or Incroyable, or Dandy: Each a type of elegant dresser, affecting foppish or rakish attitudes in manner and in style: Buck, a high-spirited young man; blood, a dashing young man; macaroni, a fashionable fop; incroyable, a French dandy. On dandies, see note at 27.15 above and Book III, Chapter X below.

46.1. Man's Fall: After Adam and Eve fell from grace, they covered their nakedness with clothes as emblems of their loss of innocence. See Genesis 3:7: "And the eyes of them both were opened, and they knew that they *were* naked; and they sewed fig leafs together, and made themselves aprons"; and Genesis 3:21: "Unto Adam also and to his wife did the Lord God make coats of skins, and clothed them." Also *Paradise Lost* 9.1113–15, where they gathered fig leaves "To gird thir waste, vain Covering if to hide / Thir guilt and dreaded shame; O how unlike / To that first naked Glorie." Compare also 28.27 above.

46.3. kerseys: A twilled woolen fabric used for coats and trousers.

46.6 'Horse I ride': A reference to Teufelsdröckh's dictum at 43.29 above.

46.10. deep calling unto deep: Psalms 42:7: "Deep calleth unto deep at the noise of thy waterspouts."

46.13. 'sailor of the air': A cloud. The phrase, "*Segler der Lüfte*" (literally, "sailing ship of the air"), from Schiller's *Maria Stuart* (1800), Carlyle translates as "sailors of the air" in *The Life of Friedrich Schiller* (1825), 153.

46.13–14. wreck of matter . . . crash of worlds: Compare Joseph Addison, *Cato* (1713), 5.1.31: "The wrecks of matter, and the crush of worlds."

46.30. 'as a Sign': Compare Isaiah 20:3: "And the Lord said, Like as my servant Isaiah hath walked naked and barefoot three years *for* a sign."

46.36–47.10. 'You see two individuals . . . : In a *Journal* entry, August 1830, Carlyle writes, "You see two men fronting each other; one sits dressed in red cloth, the other stands dressed in threadbare blue; the first says to the other: Be hanged and anatomised!—and it is forthwith put in execution, and the matter rests not till Number Two is a skeleton! Whence comes it? These men have no *physical hold* of each other, they are not in *contact*; each of the Bailiffs &c. is included within his own *skin*, and not hooked to any other" (*Two Note Books*, 160–61).

47.6. Tipstaves: Constables or bailiffs who carry staves (*i.e.*, staffs) with a metal tip as a sign of office.

47.11-17. 'Man is a Spirit . . . : In a *Journal* entry, August 1830, Carlyle writes, "*Man is a spirit*; invisible influences run thro' *Society*, and make it a mysterious whole, full of Life and inscrutable activities and capabilities. Our individual existence is mystery; our social still more" (*Two Note Books*, 161).

47.15-17. Society . . . **is founded upon Cloth**: Compare Swift, *A Tale of a Tub*, Section 2, which differentiates between clothes worn for physical comfort and those worn for spiritual truth.

47.19. Frankfort Coronations . . . **Levees, Couchees**: Frankfort Coronations: German emperors were elected and crowned at Frankfort cathedral. Levees: royal receptions held in the morning. Couchees: royal receptions held before retiring at night.

47.20. macers and pursuivants: Respectively, bearers of ceremonial staffs (maces) and officers ("attendants") ranking below heralds in the Colleges of Heralds.

47.33-34. Presentations: The reporting of who has been "presented" at Court.

48.3. *Ach Gott!*: "Oh God," a favorite exclamation of Carlyle's.

48.4-5. *Haupt- und Staats-Action*: Compare Goethe's *Faust* 1:583: "*Haupt- und Staatsaktion*," a stock-drama in Germany in the seventeenth century employing strolling characters.

48.5. Pickleherring-Farce: "*Picklehäringsspiele*," a type of German comedy that employs clowns. Compare Addison, *The Spectator*, no. 47 (April 24, 1711), 180, where it is pointed out that Pickled Herrings in Holland are "merry Drolls . . . circumforaneous Wits . . . merry Wags."

48.6. *the tables* . . . *are dissolved*: Horace, *Satires* 2.1.86: "Solventur risu tabulae, tu missus abibis" (the case [lit., the tables, or written indictment] will be dismissed [lit., dissolved] with a laugh, and you will be free to go). In Satire 2.1, Horace is defending his art of satire, which he defines as "to strip off the skin with which each strutted all bedecked before the eyes of men, though foul within" (2.1.64-65), and punningly argues at lines 80-86 that if the poem is *bona* ("good") then it will not be judged to be *mala*, meaning "bad" but specifically "criminally libellous" under the law of the Twelve Tables prohibiting "libellous verses" (*mala carmina*).

48.8. wails and howls: See Micah 1:8, where the Lord says, "Therefore I will wail and howl, I will go stripped and naked."

48.9. Duke of Windlestraw: A windlestraw is a withered stalk of grass. Perhaps an allusion to Arthur Wellesley, Duke of Wellington, who as prime minister opposed parliamentary reform in 1830, and in consequence lost the support of the Tory party.

48.12. Woolsack: The official seat of the Lord Chancellor in the House of Lords.

48.12–13. *infandum! infandum!*: "Unspeakable! unspeakable!"

48.14–15. naked . . . forked Radish: From *2 Henry VI* 3.2.310–12, where Falstaff says, "When 'a was naked, he was for all the world like a fork'd redish, with a head fantastically carv'd upon it with a knife"; compare *King Lear* 3.4.106–11: "[U]naccommodated man is no more but such a poor, bare, fork'd animal as thou art." See also *On Heroes*, 157.37–158.2.

48.16–17. St. Stephen's: St. Stephen's Hall, part of the House of Commons.

48.18. Bed of Justice: *Lit de Justice*, the King's Throne in the Bed Chamber, where the King through granted authority could overrule parliament. In *German Romance* (2:178), Carlyle quotes Richter's reference in "Army-Captain Schmelzle's Journey to Flætz" to the "passive *lit de justice*." Compare Sterne, *Tristram Shandy*, vol. 6, chs. 16–17, where Shandy's father called for "*beds of justice*" on the first Saturday and Sunday nights of the month to talk over with his wife matters of momentous importance, at this juncture whether Shandy would be permitted to wear breeches.

48.27. benefit of clergy: A practice begun in the twelfth century that exempted clerics from criminal prosecution in a civil court for any felony. Instead they could appeal to be heard in an ecclesiastical court where the sentences were always lighter and where death sentences were forbidden. The privilege was restricted in 1489, abolished as regards murderers and other serious offenders in 1512, and the test of reading was eliminated in 1706. The practice was abolished by law in 1827.

48.32. Yorick Sterne's words: Sterne, *Tristram Shandy*, Volume 5, Chapter 7 (1:433): "Ye, lastly, who drive——and why not, Ye also who are driven, like turkeys to market, with a stick and a red clout—meditate—meditate, I beseech you, upon *Trim's* hat."]

48.33. clout: A blow, but also a patch of material.

48.34–35. dried bladder . . . peas in it: Compare Swift, *Gulliver's Travels*, 3.2.132–33, where the inhabitants of Laputa, who are devoted to science and mathematics rather than ethics, are observed to communicate with bladders: "In each Bladder was a small Quantity of dried Pease."

NOTES TO CHAPTER X. PURE REASON

49.15. laws of unstable and stable equilibrium: The stability of a body is the measure of its ability to return to a position of equilibrium, balance, after being moved or disturbed.

49.19–20. Joan and My Lady: Joan, a servant, as in the expression, "Joan's as good as my lady." Compare *King John* 1.1.184: "Well, now can I make any Joan a lady"; and *Love's Labour's Lost* 3.1.205: "Some men must love my lady and some Joan."

49.20. 'Hail fellow well met': From Swift's "My Lady's Lamentation" (1765), lines 165–68: "Hail fellow, well met, / All dirty and wet: / Find out, if you can, / Who's master, who's man."

49.21. Chaos were come again: *Othello* 3:3:92: "Chaos is come again."

50.3. Serbonian Bog . . . where . . . whole armies . . . might sink: A marshy swamp, Lake Serbonis, in the Nile delta in ancient Egypt. See *Paradise Lost* 9.592–94: "A gulf profound as that *Serbonian* Bog . . . Where Armies whole have sunk."

50.10. **pineal gland**: Or pineal body, located above the cerebellum in the brain, became a favorite object of satire in the eighteenth century. Earlier Descartes, in *Passiones Animae* (1649), argued that it was the seat of the soul. The source here is probably Sterne's *Tristram Shandy* 2.19.173, where this belief is disputed by Shandy's father: "[H]e was satisfied it [the soul] could not be where *Des Cartes* had fixed it, upon the top of the *pineal* gland of the brain; which, as he philosophised, formed a cushion for her about the size of a marrow pea." Compare also Pope's *Martinus Scriblerus*, Chapter 12, which ridicules those, particularly the Free-Thinkers, who hold such a belief.

50.16. **thrums**: The fringes of the weaver's warp threads which are trimmed from the finished weaving.

50.21. **Descendentalism**: Coined by Carlyle, that branch of science which depends upon empirical data (Logic), the opposite of transcendentalism which embraces speculative thought (Reason).

50.23. **Gouda Cows**: See above at 44.30 and note.

50.25–26. **To the eye of vulgar Logic . . .** : In a *Journal* entry, August 1830, Carlyle writes, "What is a man if you look at him with the mere Logical sense, with the Understanding? A pitiful hungry biped that wears breeches" (*Two Note Books*, 162–63).

50.26. **Pure Reason**: The title for this chapter is taken from Kant's *Critique of Pure Reason*. However, the blending of Reason with Intuition is not Kantian, but rather closer to the philosophy of Friedrich H. Jacobi, who in *Brief über die Lehre des Spinzoza* (*Letter on the Doctrine of Spinoza*, 1785) and *David Hume über den Glauben; oder, Idealismus und Realismus* (*David Hume on Faith; or, Idealism and Realism*, 1787) argues that Reason is a faculty of Intuition, a demonstration of Faith; and to that of Coleridge in *The Friend* (1812) and *Aids to Reflection* (1825), who views Reason as pre-eminently spiritual and the highest form of self-affirmation. Distinguished from Logic or Understanding, according to Coleridge Pure Reason is theoretical or speculative thought which seeks to inform but never to explain experience. Pure Reason cannot offer proof, but can bring a sense of order to the highest form of abstract thinking and spiritual truth. See *Aids to Reflection*, 223–26, 406–7. In a *Journal* entry, December 1826, Carlyle writes, "Yes, it is true! the decisions of Reason

(Vernunft) are superior to those of Understanding (Verstand): the latter vary in every age . . . , while the former last forever." In another *Journal* entry, late 1827, he concludes that "the *mistico* [is] much the same as *Vernunft.*" In an entry on August 5, 1829, he writes, "Understanding is to Reason as the talent of a Beaver (which can build houses, and uses its tail for a trowel) to the genius of a Prophet and Poet. Reason is all but extinct in this age: it can never be altogether extinguished." (*Two Note Books*, 83–84, 124, 142)

50.27–36. A Soul, a Spirit, and divine Apparition . . . conflux of Eternities: This whole passage echoes in language and in metaphor Richter's description of his transformation in *Siebenkäs*, 429: "There come to us moments of twilight in which it seems as though day and night were in the act of dividing—as if we were in the very process of being created or annihilated; the stage of life and the spectators fly back out of view, our part is played out, we stand far off, in darkness and alone, but we have still got on our theatre dress, and we look at ourselves in it, and ask, 'What is it that thou art, *now*, my *me*!' When we thus ask ourselves this, there is, beyond ourselves, nothing of great or of firm—everything has turned to an endless cloud of night (with rare and feeble gleams within it), which keeps falling lower and lower, and heavier with drops. Only high up above the cloud shines a resplendence—and that is God; and far beneath it a minute speck of light—and that is a human 'Me'!" Compare also "Signs of the Times" (1829), "The poorest Day that passes over us is the conflux of two Eternities; it is made up of currents that issue from the remotest Past, and flow onwards into the remotest Future" (*Essays* 2:59). In a *Journal* entry, August 1830, Carlyle writes, "*Man is a spirit. . . .* Our individual existence is mystery; our social still more. . . . we are— we know not what; light-sparkles floating in the Aether of the Divinity!—So that this solid world, after all, is but an air-image; our *Me* is the only reality, 'and all is Godlike or God'" (*Two Note Books*, 161).

51.1. Saint Chrysostom: St. John Chrysostom (Greek, "Golden Mouth"; 347?–407), most famous of the Greek theologians, known for his homilies and his literal and historical reading of the Bible.

51.1. true Shekinah is Man: *Shekinah*, from Rabbinical lore, literally means the dwelling place or Presence of the Holy Spirit. Carlyle almost certainly took the term from Sterne's *Tristram Shandy* 5.1.408: "Who made Man— . . . the Shekinah of the divine presence, as

Chrysostom" called him. For discussions on the source of this un-usual expression, see G. B. Tennyson, "The true Shekinah is man," *American Notes and Queries*, 3(1964):58; and Michael K. Goldberg, "The True Shekinah is Man," *American Notes and Queries*, 24(1985):42–44.

51.8–9. Sea of Light and Love: The brief moment of epiphany described here, soon to be covered by "grim coppery clouds," paral-lels Carlyle's impression of the mystical experience as described in "Novalis" (1829), *Essays* 2:22: "How shall we understand it, and in any measure shadow it forth? How may that spiritual condition, which by its own account is like pure Light, colourless, formless, infinite, be represented by mere Logic-Painters, mere Engravers we might say, who, except copper and burin, producing the most finite black-on-white, have no means of representing anything?" Compare also Wordsworth's *The Excursion*, Book 1, lines 198–200, 203–5, where the Youth's transcendent experience is described: "What soul was his, when, from the naked top / Of some bold headland, he beheld the sun / Rise up, and bathe the world in light! / . . . / Far and wide the clouds were touched, / And in their silent faces could he read / Unutterable love." The complement suggested here between the sun which illumines Nature and the eyes which illumine Truth is from Plato's *Republic*, Book 4.

51.11. Such tendency to Mysticism: The suggestion here that Teufelsdröckh has a "tendency" toward mysticism need not be mis-leading, for Transcendentalism is in part an outgrowth of the mystical tradition. Each shares common ground, but especially the tripartite archetype: Mysticism is formed upon the contemplative progression from the Purgative Way (Purification), through the Illuminative Way (Understanding), to the Unitive Way (Faith), which anticipates the conversion pattern of Carlyle's Transcendentalism from "The Ever-lasting No" through the "Centre of Indifference" to "The Everlast-ing Yea." By placing Teufelsdröckh in the mystical/transcendental tradition, Carlyle is then able to adapt rather than reject the other-wise unyielding principles of Christianity; or, as G. B. Tennyson puts it: "It is . . . Carlyle's mysticism that keeps him from gnosticism, from the pursuit of knowledge rather than wisdom, *gnosis* rather than *sophia*" (*"Sartor" Called "Resartus*," 313). The more specific allusion here is to Novalis, who Carlyle felt was a "Mystic, or had an affinity with Mysticism, in the primary and true meaning of that word," which "means only a man whom we do not understand" ("Novalis" [1829], *Essays* 2:22). Carlyle may also have in mind the distinction made by Coleridge between "Fanatic" and "Enthusiastic" mystics in *Aids to Reflection*, 383–88. The former is a "dangerous Member of Society" because he is allowed "to persecute the fresh competitor." The latter is divided into two types: The first is an interpreter whose recorded perceptions are considered mad by society, and the second and higher order is a quietist whose unspoken dreams are illustrative of spiritual truths. Curiously, Teufelsdröckh's life encompasses both types of Coleridge's enthusiastic mystic.

51.14–15. Charlemagne-Mantle: The robe of Charlemagne (742?–814), King of the Franks (768–814), who was crowned Emperor of Rome in 800.

51.21–22. dark with excess of bright: An echo of *Paradise Lost* 3.376–80, where the seraphim cannot look directly at God's "glorious brightness," even though a cloud intervenes: "Dark with excessive bright thy skirts appeer."

51.24. The beginning of all Wisdom: An adaptation of Psalms 111:10 and Proverbs 9:10: "The fear of the Lord *is* the beginning of wisdom."

51.25–27. "The Philosopher," says the wisest of this age, "must station himself in the middle": The "wisest of this age" is Goethe, who wrote in *Wilhelm Meister* (2:267) that the second of the three religions (first: Ethnic; third: Christian) is called the "Philosophical; for the philosopher stations himself in the middle, and must draw down to him all that is higher, and up to him all that is lower, and only in this medium condition does he merit the title of Wise. . . . he alone, in a cosmic sense, lives in Truth."

51.31. Arkwright looms: Sir Richard Arkwright (1732–1792) patented the water frame for spinning cotton in 1769, a machine which helped to usher in the factory system and hence the Industrial Revolution.

51.31. Arachnes: In Greek mythology, Arachne of Lydia challenged the goddess Athena to a weaving contest. When Athena destroyed

Arachne's work, Arachne hanged herself, and Athena then turned her into a spider.

52.4–7. 'Wonder . . . in *partibus infidelium*': Carlyle takes this passage almost verbatim from his *Journal*, August 1830 (*Two Note Books*, 162). Carlyle might be alluding to Novalis: "*Aller Glaube ist wunderbar und wundertätig*" (All faith is wonderful and wonderworking; *Fragmente I, Werke* 3:183). In *On Heroes*, at 10.15–17, Carlyle says, "Worship is transcendent wonder; wonder for which there is no limit or measure; that is worship." Compare Plato, "Wonder is the only beginning of philosophy" (*Theaetetus* 155d). In *partibus infidelium* (lit., "in infidel regions") is an expression used in the Roman Catholic Church to characterize a bishop's seat of authority in a country which has ceased to be Roman Catholic.

52.13–15. Arithmetical Mill . . . Political Economy: A pun, which Carlyle often used (see, e.g., *On Heroes* 149.2, and perhaps below at 163.13), on the name of James Mill (1773–1836), father of John Stuart Mill, who together with Jeremy Bentham became one of the leading exponents of utilitarianism, and who was particularly known for his mathematical calculations of human behavior. Mill's *Elements of Political Economy* (1821) was a utilitarian tract. Also pun on mill, or factory. In a *Journal* entry, September 9, 1830, Carlyle writes, "What is Jeremy Bentham's significance? Altogether intellectual, logical. I name him as the representative of a class, important only for their numbers; intrinsically wearisome, almost pitiable and pitiful. Logic is their sole foundation, no other even recognized as possible: wherefore their system is a *Machine*, and cannot *grow* or endure; but after thrashing for a little . . . must thrash itself to pieces, and be made fuel.—Alas poor England, stupid, purblind, pudding-eating England! Bentham with his *Mills* grinding thee out Morality" (*Two Note Books*, 171–72). Also, Carlyle may have been aware of the work of Charles Babbage, who was just beginning the construction of his "analytical engine," a mechanical computer with punchcards and memory, in the early 1830s, with the assistance of Byron's daughter Ada.

52.17. Arabian Tale: "The Tale of the Wazir and the Sage Duban" in *The Book of the Thousand Nights and a Night*, trans. Sir Richard Burton, 1:45–49, in which the king is cured of leprosy by Duban, who then is beheaded on the advice of a jealous vizier. After being beheaded, Duban's head speaks and advises the king to turn the leaves of a magic book, which the king does with moistened fingers that activate the invisible poison put there by Duban. The revenge is complete and the ungrateful king dies, as does the head of Duban but not before it warns that God will punish the injustices of tyrants.

52.27. Logic-choppers: Compare *Romeo and Juliet* 3.5.149, where Capulet, who is confused by Juliet's quibbling, exclaims: "How how, how how, chopp'd logic! What is this?"

52.27–28. treble-pipe Scoffers: The treble pipe is the high-pitched "chanter" pipe on Scottish bagpipes, the pipe with finger-holes on which the melody is played. Compare Dryden, *Mac Flecknoe, or a satyr upon the true-blew-protestant poet, T[homas] S[hadwell]* (1682), 46: "At thy well-sharpened thumb, . . . The treble squeaks for fear, the basses roar."

52.29–30. Mechanics' Institute of Science: George Birkbeck (1776–1841) established a course of lectures on science for the workingmen of Glasgow which led to the founding of the Glasgow Mechanics Institute in 1823. In 1824, Birkbeck became president of the London Mechanics Institute, and in 1827 he founded University College of the University of London to further scientific study.

52.30. Old-Roman geese: In 390 B.C., the geese in Juno's temple warned the Romans of the impending assault of the Gauls.

53.1. *Mécanique Céleste*: See 3.13 and 24.10 above, and note at 3.13.

53.1. *Hegel's Philosophy*: See 12.7 above and note.

53.6. Mystery and Mysticism: In "State of German Literature" (1827), Carlyle defines and defends German mysticism and links it directly to transcendentalism: "The chief mystics in Germany . . . are the Transcendental philosophers, Kant, Fichte, and Schelling!" (*Essays* 1:73–74). Compare also "Novalis" (1829), *Essays* 2:21–23. The genesis of this paragraph was a *Journal* entry in August 1830 (*Two Note Books*, 161–62).

53.8. Attorney Logic: In "Novalis" (1829), Carlyle says, in defense of Coleridge, "[T]he creative intellect of a Philosopher is destitute of that mere faculty of logic which belongs to 'all Attorneys, and men educated in Edinburgh'" (*Essays* 2:3).

53.15. *Armer Teufel!*: "Poor devil," a favorite expression of Carlyle's. See *Two Note Books*, 161, 219.

53.16. Cow calve . . . Bull gender: Compare Job 21:10: "Their bull gendereth, and faileth not; their cow calveth, and casteth not her calf." In a *Journal* entry, August 1830, *Two Note Books*, 161–62, Carlyle writes, "Doth not thy Cow calve, doth not thy Bull gender? Nay (peradventure) dost not thyself gender? *Explain* me that; or do one of two things: Retire into private places with thy foolish cackle; or, what were better, give it up, and weep, not that the world is mean and disenchanted and prosaic, but that thou art vain and blind."

53.21. Dilettante: An amateur, a dabbler in the arts. In a *Journal* entry of September 1830: "The Sin of this age is Dilettantism; the Whigs, and all 'moderate Tories,' are the grand Dilettanti. . . . There is more hope of an Atheist Utilitarian, of a Superstitious Ultra, than of such a lukewarm, withered mongrel" (*Two Note Books*, 172–73). Compare Teufelsdröckh's clash with the "Literary Dilettanti" at 96.13 below, and the comparison of "Dilettantism" to Cant at 215.14.

NOTES TO CHAPTER XI. PROSPECTIVE

54.7. Pandemonian: Compare *Paradise Lost* 1.756–57: "*Pandæmonium*, the high Capital / Of Satan and his peers"; 10.424–25: "Citie and proud seate / Of *Lucifer*."

54.8. Asphodel meadows: A flower, thought to be like the narcissus, that covered the Elysian Fields. Compare Shelley's "Arethusa" (1824), line 84, where the waters flow through "meadows of asphodel."

54.8–9. yellow-burning marl: Marl is a rich, clayey soil. Compare *Paradise Lost* 1.296, where the fires of Hell are described as "burning Marle."

54.13–14. Nature being not an Aggregate but a Whole: An allusion to the Romantic concept of organicism, or the superiority of the whole to its parts, where form is considered innate rather than mechanical. In his lecture on "Shakespeare" (1812), Coleridge defends the language of organic form and argues in effect that the whole is greater than the sum of its parts. This concept of organic unity is the philosophic framework upon which Carlyle builds his transcendent argument. Compare 91.11–12 and 182.4 below.

54.15–16. **"If I take the wings . . . God is there"**: Psalms 139:9–10: "*If* I take the wings of morning, *and* dwell in the uttermost parts of the sea; Even there shall thy hand lead me, and thy right hand shall hold me."

54.19. FORCE: An inner presence. The idea of the inexorableness of the universe complements the concept of organicism, and can be found in Richter's *Siebenkäs*, 470–71: "'Wandering skeleton! with strings of nerves clasped in thy bony hand, thou playest not on thyself. The breath of endless life is breathing on the Æolian harp, which answers back in music, and thou are played *upon*. . . . The life of the body depends as intimately on the life of the soul, as that of the latter on that of the former. Life and force are at work, with power, everywhere.'" Compare also Coleridge's "Eolian Harp" (1796; *Poetical Works*, lines 26–29, 44–48), where force is described as the rhythm of the universe: "O! the one Life within us and abroad, / Which meets all motion and becomes its soul, / A light in sound, a sound-like power in light, / Rhythm in all thought. . . . And what if all of animated nature / Be but organic Harps diversely fram'd, / That tremble into thought, as o'er them sweeps / Plastic and vast, one intellectual breeze, / At once the Soul of each, and God of all." In *On Heroes* (at 9.18–24), Carlyle says, "This Universe, ah me!—what could the wild man know of it; what can we yet know? That it is a Force, and thousandfold Complexity of Forces; a Force which is *not we*. That is all; it is not we, it is altogether different from *us*. Force, Force, everywhere Force; we ourselves a mysterious Force in the centre of that. 'There is not a leaf rotting on the highway but has Force in it: how else could it rot?'"

54.22. **Tropic of Cancer**: The parallel of latitude 23° 27' north of the equator, the farthest point north at which the sun can be seen directly overhead, or the northernmost limits of the tropics.

55.1. **Schwarzwald**: The "Black Forest" in southwest Germany.

55.4. **horse-shoe**: In 1830, Carlyle with his father James invented a threaded stob that could be inserted into the horseshoe to prevent slipping on ice. The benefit of this stob was that it could be easily screwed into the shoe and then removed when not needed. The invention was used widely afterwards, even though the Carlyles received little or no credit for it.

55.7. Dogstar: Sirius, the brightest star in the sky, located in the constellation Canis Major.

55.11–12. Altar, kindled on the bosom of the All: The erection of an altar here echoes Swift's *A Tale of a Tub*, 76, where an altar to tailors is erected. Further, the concept of All seems to echo Richter's vision of the Universe of God, The All, from *Siebenkäs*, Book 2, Chapter 8, in which the fiction of the dead Christ denying God prepares the way for the persona to experience a conversion of faith. Carlyle quotes extensively from this chapter in "Jean Paul Friedrich Richter" (1830) *Essays* 2:155–58, where Christ questions God: "'How is each so solitary in this wide grave of the All! I am alone with myself! O Father, O Father! where is thy infinite bosom, that I might rest on it?'" After witnessing Christ's agony, the persona relates, "And as I fell down, and looked into the sparkling Universe, I saw the upborne Rings of the Giant-Serpent, the Serpent of Eternity, which had coiled itself round the All of Worlds,—and the Rings sank down, and encircled the All doubly."

55.19–20. all . . . works together with all: A restatement of the philosophy of organicism. Compare 1 Corinthians 15:28: "And when all things shall be subdued unto him . . . that God may be all in all." Compare also Swift's *A Tale of a Tub*, 80: The body and the soul "are *All in All, and All in every Part*"; Goethe's *Wilhelm Meister* 2:131: "'It is all men that make up mankind; all powers taken together that make up the world. These are frequently at variance: and as they endeavour to destroy each other, Nature holds them together, and again produces them.'" Compare also Shelley's "Ode to the West Wind" (1820), lines 63–64, where the West Wind is invoked: "Drive my dead thoughts over the universe / Like withered leaves to quicken a new birth."

55.21. flood of Action: Compare the words of the Earth Spirit in Goethe's *Faust*, as quoted above at 43.13.

55.21–22. perpetual metamorphoses: The idea that perception is in a constant state of transition, an accumulation of ever-changing

metaphors, is primary to the aesthetic fabric of *Sartor Resartus,* and
is a precept that Carlyle got from the German Romantics, but especially from Herder. In a *Journal* entry, March 1822 (*Two Note Books,*
4), he writes, "Nine tenths of our reasonings are *artificial* processes,
depending not on the real nature of things but on our peculiar mode
of viewing things, and therefore varying with all the variations both
in the kind and extent of our perceptions. How is this? Truth *immer*
WIRD *nie* IST?" (Is truth always relative, never absolute?). The sense
that life is spontaneous and infinite rather than patterned and finite
comes from Herder's *Ideen zur Philosophie der Geschichte der Menschheit*
(*Outlines of the Philosophy of Man,* 1784–91), which informs Carlyle's
belief in perpetual *Entwicklung* (development) and infinite *Bildung*
(shaping). For discussions on this point, see Hill Shine, "Carlyle's
Early Writings and Herder's *Ideen,*" 3–33; and Ruth apRoberts, *The
Ancient Dialect,* 16–26. Compare 174.24 and 202.7 below.

55.22–23. **Forces . . .** *rot*: Compare Goethe's *Wilhelm Meister* 1:106,
where the "forces" work on the body "till all is disunited and inert,
till we see the whole mouldered down into indifferent dust."

55.26–27. **philosophic eye**: Compare Wordsworth's "Ode: Intimations of Immortality" (1807), lines 186–90, where the infinity of
perception is found in the "philosophic mind."

55.30. **All visible things are Emblems**: The concept of emblem, or
symbol, is integral to the clothes philosophy. Compare 33.14, where
aprons are described as emblems; 60.6, where clothes become the
"visible emblems of fact"; and Book III, Chapter III, "Symbols," the
pivotal chapter on the symbol as manifestation of the transcendental
movement from visible (finite) to invisible (infinite).

55.31–32. **Matter . . . Idea**: The belief that matter exists only as a
revelation of an idea is basic to German idealistic philosophy, and can
be found throughout the works of Goethe, Novalis, Fichte, and
Schelling.

56.4. **Men are . . . clothed with Authority**: *Measure for Measure*
2.2.117–18: "[B]ut man, proud man, / Dress'd in a little brief authority."

56.4–5. **clothed with Beauty, with Curses**: Compare Job 40:10:
"Deck thyself *with* majesty and excellency; and array thyself with

glory and beauty"; and Psalms 109:18: "As he clothed himself with cursing like as with his garment."

56.5–6. what is Man himself . . . but an Emblem: Compare Swift's *A Tale of a Tub*, 78: "[W]at is Man himself but a *Micro-Coat*, or rather a compleat Suit of Cloaths with all its Trimmings?"

56.8–9. clothed with a Body: Compare Job 10:11: "Thou hast clothed me with skin and flesh, and hast fenced me with bones and sinews."

56.10. Language is called the Garment of Thought: Compare Samuel Wesley, "Style is the dress of thought," *An Epistle to a Friend Concerning Poetry* (1700); and Samuel Johnson, "Cowley," *Lives of the Poets* (1779–81), 1:58: "Language is the dress of thought."

56.13–15. Language . . . what is it all but Metaphors: In a *Journal* entry, August 5, 1829, Carlyle writes: "All language but that concerning *sensual* objects is or has been figurative. Prodigious influence of metaphors! Never saw into it till lately. A truly useful and philosophical work would be a good *Essay on Metaphors*. Some day I will write one!" (*Two Note Books*, 141–42). This passage is the impetus, if not the genesis, for *Sartor Resartus*.

56.20. *Attention a Stretching-to*: Latin: *ad* ("toward") + *tendere* ("to stretch").

56.33–34. Heavens and the Earth shall fade away like a Vesture: Compare Psalms 102:25–26: "[T]he heavens *are* the work of thy hands. They shall perish, but thou shalt endure: yea, all of them shall wax like a garment; as a vesture shalt thou change them, and they shall be changed"; Hebrews 1:10–12: "[T]he heavens are the works of thine hands: They shall perish; but thou remainest; and they all shall wax old as doth a garment; And as a vesture shalt thou fold them up, and they shall be changed."

57.1–2. External Universe . . . is but Clothing: Compare Swift's *A Tale of a Tub*, 77–78: "They [Worshippers of Cloth] held the Universe to be a large *Suit of Cloaths*, which *invests* every Thing. . . . Look at this Globe of Earth, you will find it to be a very compleat and fashionable *Dress*."

57.12. Scottish Hamburgh Merchant: Perhaps Messrs. Parish, through whom Carlyle and Goethe exchanged packages; compare a letter to Goethe, September 25, 1828, *Letters* 4:404. See Discussion of Editorial Decisions, p. 513 below.

57.32–33. Biography . . . written . . . read: Carlyle here both anticipates the style of the biographical Book II and suggests how it should be read. Thus he controls his audience much as the Editor controls Teufelsdröckh's.

58.3–4. Goethe . . . "Man is properly the *only* object that interests man": In Goethe's *Wilhelm Meister* 1:131: "[M]an is ever the most interesting object to man, and perhaps should be the only one that interests." Compare also Pope's *Essay on Man*, Epistle 2, lines 1–2: "Know then thyself, presume not God to scan; / The proper study of Mankind is Man."

58.6. Biography or Autobiography: The aesthetic link of biography to conversation and art is found in "Biography" (1832), *Essays* 3:44–45, where the Goethean idea above is restated: "It is written, 'The proper study of mankind is man. . . . Man is perennially interesting to man; nay, if we look strictly to it, there is nothing else interesting.'" This idea is connected to Biography: "Not only in the common Speech of men; but in all Art too, . . . Biography is almost the one thing needful. . . . Even in the highest works of Art, our interest . . . is too apt to be strongly or even mainly of a Biographic sort. In the Art we can nowise forget the Artist." In a *Journal* entry, January 1832, Carlyle writes, "Biography is the only History" (*Two Note Books*, 238).

58.24. duels: Compare 134.34ff below. Carlyle returned to the subject of duelling (with the suggestive subtitle) in "Two Hundred and Fifty Years Ago [*From a Waste-Paper Bag of T. Carlyle*]," *Leigh Hunt's London Journal*, Part 1, nos. 1, 3 (December 7 and 21, 1850), 6–7, 37–38 (reprinted in *Essays* 4:384–96), where he describes it as "one of the sincerities of Human Life" (*Essays* 4:384).

58.26. sloughs of Despair: Compare the "Slough of Dispond" in John Bunyan, *Pilgrim's Progress* (1678), where the "scum and filth that attends conviction for sin doth continually run" (15).

58.26. Pisgah hills: Pisgah, a mountain east of the northern end of the Dead Sea, where Moses was taken to see the Promised Land (Deuteronomy 3:27; 34:1).

58.27. Hebron: A town south of Jerusalem, in the land of Canaan, where Abraham and Isaac sojourned, the home of King David and burial ground of the patriarchs, a land of peace originally given by God to Abraham who had rejected the wickedness of Sodom.

58.27. Old-Clothes 'ewry: Jewry is the name of a district in London in Cheapside, inhabited primarily by Jews, where tailoring (and retailoring) were principal occupations. Through the fusion of metaphors here Teufelsdröckh has shed his old (worldly) clothes for his new (spiritual) clothes.

58.32. fallen among thieves: Compare Luke 10:30, where a man who "fell among thieves, which stripped him of his raiment" was saved by the Good Samaritan.

58.35–36. picturesque Sketches: Although Carlyle read widely in travel literature of all kinds, this seems to be an allusion to Washington Irving's *The Sketch Book* (1820), which he mentions in a letter to his mother, September 28, 1830 (*Letters* 5:166–67). Carlyle had long been an admirer of Irving's sketches, of both real and imaginary travels, the most famous of which are "The Legend of Sleepy Hollow" and "Rip Van Winkle."

58.37. sympathetic-ink: "Invisible ink," invisible until treated with a chemical, heat, or special light. In the *Reminiscences*, 250, Carlyle recalls that Dr. Thomas Chalmers told him that Christianity is "'all written in us already, . . . as in *sympathetic ink*; Bible awakens it, and you can read!'"

58.38–59.2. leaf . . . sport of rainy winds: An image from Virgil, *Aeneid* 6.105–7, where Aeneas pleads with the Sibyl of Cumae, whose words were written on leaves that blew about in the wind, "Only do not entrust / your verses to the leaves, lest they fly off / in disarray, the play of rapid winds." Compare also Shelley's "Ode to the West Wind," lines 2–8, where "[T]he leaves dead / Are driven . . . to their dark wintry bed . . . where they lie cold and low, / Each like a corpse within its grave."

59.3. *verehrtester Herr Herausgeber*: "Venerable Mr. Editor."

59.9. **Hindostan . . . New Holland**: India, Australia.

59.14. **China-ink**: Also called India ink, usually made from lampblack.

59.14–15. **Six southern Zodiacal Signs**: The six signs through which the sun passes on the arc of its ecliptic south of the equator are Libra (Balance), Scorpio (Scorpion), Sagittarius (Archer), Capricorn (Goat), Aquarius (Water-bearer), and Pisces (Fish).

59.17. *cursiv-schrift*: "Cursive handwriting."

59.21. **fascicles**: Separately bound sections of a book published in serial parts or installments.

59.22. **Wanderer**: See note at 14.18–19 above. Teufelsdröckh is repeatedly referred to as the Wanderer; for example, 105.2, 106.31, 107.9, 115.13, 115.32, 120.11, 122.16, 123.14, 125.9, and 127.2.

59.32. **P. P. Clerk of this Parish**: A reference to *Memoirs of P. P. Clerk of This Parish* (1727), by Pope and John Gay, which is a burlesque of the inflated, fatuous memoirs of the period.

59.35–36. **confusion a little worse confounded**: See note at 19.38 above.

59.38–60.2. **Street-Advertisements . . . completest collection extant**: Compare Richter's "Life of Quintus Fixlein": "Much also did the Quintus *collect*: he had a fine *Almanac Collection*, a *Catechism* and *Pamphlet Collection*; also a *Collection of Advertisements*, which he began, is not so incomplete as you most frequently see such things" (*German Romance* 2:216).

60.4. **solar Luminary . . . airy Limbo**: Compare *Paradise Lost* 3.576, where the sun is referred to as the "great Luminarie," and 3:440, where the Limbo of Vanity is called a "windie Sea of Land."

60.7. **British Museum**: That is, the library in the British Museum, now the British Library.

60.22. first Bridge-builders: *Paradise Lost* 2.1024–30: "Sin and Death amain / Following his [Satan's] track, . . . / Pav'd after him a broad and beat'n way / Over the dark Abyss, whose boiling Gulf / Tamely endur'd a Bridge of wondrous length / From Hell continu'd reaching th' utmost Orbe / Of this frail World."

60.24. Pontifex: Latin: literally, "bridge-maker" (but the original significance is obscure), the title of various priests in Roman religion, especially the High Priest, *pontifex maximus*. Later adopted as a title by the Bishop of Rome, i.e., the Pope, hence Pontiff.

60.34. swallowed up: Perhaps an allusion to the story of Jonah and the whale; Jonah 1:17: "Now the Lord had prepared a great fish to swallow up Jonah."

61.2. transplanting foreign Thought: Carlyle is no doubt alluding to his own efforts, particularly his translation of *Wilhelm Meister* (1824); his *The Life of Friedrich Schiller* (1825); his translations of short fiction, *German Romance* (1827); and his numerous review-essays on German language and literature.

Book II

Notes to Chapter I. Genesis

63.4–11. Beginning . . . Genesis . . . Exodus: The allusion to the Bible here provides the basis for the structural movement of Book II, from Genesis (Beginning, Innocence, Infinite) to Exodus (Going-Out, Experience, Finite), a movement which is reiterated in "Invisibility into Visibility" on line 12. Compare Richter's "Life of Quintus Fixlein," *German Romance* 2:299–300, where the movement from "Nothingness to Existence, from Eternity to Time" is anticipated.

63.14. Entepfuhl: German for "duck-pond"; namely, Ecclefechan, a small village in Dumfriesshire in southwest Scotland, where Carlyle was born in the Arched House on December 4, 1795. This and many of the other biographical allusions in this chapter and in Book II enrich the larger fabric of *Sartor Resartus* whose thread may be personal but whose cloth is universal.

63.14. Bag *Libra*: The first of the six bags which contain the autobiographical documents of Teufelsdröckh's life. Compare 59.11–20. The Sun transits Libra (Balance) from September 22 to October 23.

63.15–16. Andreas Futteral and his wife: Andreas: (from the Greek) "Man"; Futteral: (German) "Case or Cover." His wife's name, Gretchen, is a German diminutive of Margaret. Andreas and Gretchen are modelled in part after Carlyle's parents: James Carlyle (1758–1832) and Margaret Aitken Carlyle (1771–1853). In "Goethe's Works" (1832), *Essays* 2:416, Carlyle defines "Gretchen (Margarete, Marg'ret'-kin)," and says, "The name of Gretchen . . . has been made world-famous in the Play of *Faust*."

63.18. Frederick the Great: Friedrich II (1712–1786), King of Prussia (1740–86), whom Carlyle later lionized in his six-volume biography (1858–65).

63.19. halbert and ferule: Halbert, or halberd, an ax-like weapon, employed when Andreas was a soldier; ferule, a cane or stick used to punish children, employed when Andreas was a teacher.

63.20. cultivated a little Orchard: Compare the conclusion reached by Voltaire's Candide: "*Il faut cultiver notre jardin*" (We must cultivate our garden; *Candide* [1759], 77). No doubt Carlyle was aware that Voltaire once resided in the court of Friedrich II, which might account for the interplay here.

63.20–21. Cincinnatus-like: Lucius Quinctius Cincinnatus (fifth century B.C.), Roman patriot, consul, and dictator who in legend left farming to defeat Rome's enemies and then returned to it. George Washington, who also returned to farming after his military victories, was often compared to Cincinnatus.

64.2. Victory of Rossbach: The celebrated defeat of the French by Friedrich II on November 5, 1757, at Rossbach, a village in Saxony in southern Germany.

64.2. Fritz the Only: Fritz was Carlyle's nickname for Friedrich II. Compare *Letters* 5:102.

64.7. Kunersdorf: A village in Brandenburg, where the Austro-Russian armies routed Friedrich's forces on August 12, 1759.

64.9–10. Desdemona ... Othello: Compare *Othello* 1.3.167–68: "She lov'd me for the dangers I had pass'd, / And I lov'd her that she did pity them."

64.14–15. Cicero and Cid: Marcus Tullius Cicero (106–43 B.C.), Roman politician, philosopher, and orator, renowned for his wisdom. Rodrigo Díaz de Vivar (1040?–1099), called El Cid, or Cid Campeador, "Lord Conqueror," soldier and national hero, immortalized in Spanish literature.

64.17. Büsching's *Geography*: Anton Friedrich Büsching (1724–1793), German geographer and educator who introduced the collection of data and statistics in his *Neue Erdbeschreibung* (*A New Description of the World*, 10 vols., 1754–1792), the first six volumes of which, dealing with the geography of Europe, were translated into English with the title *A New System of Geography* (1762).

64.18. camisade of Hochkirch: Camisade, or camisado, a surprise attack at night, from the Spanish *camisada* (shirted) because the soldiers wore white shirts over their armor for identification. Hochkirch, a village in Saxony where the Austrians defeated Friedrich on October 14, 1758.

64.19. good Gretchen: The account of the domestic life of the Futterals to the end of the paragraph is reminiscent in language and in metaphor of Wordsworth's description of the industrious but ill-fated Margaret in *The Excursion*, Book 1, especially lines 511–916, where Margaret is praised for her "steady mind" and her husband for his "busy spade," and where finally the "honeysuckle crowd around the porch" of the cottage.

65.1. Basket: An echo of the story of Moses in Exodus 2:1–10. While a baby, Moses was put into an ark made of bulrushes by his Hebrew mother and was subsequently found and raised by Pharaoh's daughter. Moses provides the link between Genesis and Exodus, as does the infant Teufelsdröckh here. The basket as maternal symbol is found throughout Greek myth and in the European myth of the stork bringing a newborn child to its parents.

65.20–21. Lifting the green veil: A possible allusion to Shelley's "Lift Not the Painted Veil" (1824), which concerns in part the distortion of expectation.

65.22. Pitt Diamond: The so-called Regent Diamond, brought from India by Thomas Pitt, Governor of Madras, in 1702. It was sold to the Duc d'Orléans in 1717, stolen during the French Revolution in 1792, later recovered, and is now in the Louvre. Carlyle discusses the diamond in his article "William Pitt, Earl of Chatham" (1823) in the *Edinburgh Encyclopædia*.

65.24. gold Friedrichs: *Friedrichs d'or*, Prussian coins.

66.22. thicker curtains: Compare *The Life of Friedrich Schiller*, 50–51, where Carlyle quotes from *Der Geisterseher* (*The Visionary*) on the "dark condition" of man: "'What went before and what will follow me, I regard as two black impenetrable curtains, which hang down at the two extremities of human life, and which no living man has yet drawn aside. Many hundreds of generations have already stood before them with their torches, guessing anxiously what lies behind. On the curtain of Futurity, many see their own shadows. . . . To the other side of this curtain we are all bound.'"

66.28. O Man born of Woman: Compare Job 14:1: "Man *that is* born of a woman *is* of a few days, and full of trouble." Also Job 15:14, 25:4; Matthew 11:11; and Luke 7:28.

66.33. nursing-father and nursing-mother: The idea that Andreas and Gretchen play the role of foster parents to Teufelsdröckh whose father is God is reminiscent of the assertion of Wordsworth in "Ode: Intimations of Immortality" (1807), lines 81–84: "The homely Nurse doth all she can / To make her Foster-child, her Inmate Man, / Forget the glories he hath known, / And that imperial palace whence he came."

66.33–34. thy true Beginning and Father is in Heaven: An allusion to the expression and the belief found throughout the Gospels: "Father, which is in heaven." For example, Matthew 5:16; Mark 11:26; and Luke 11:2.

67.5. Herald's Books: Books of heraldry. Carlyle had a life-long interest in genealogy, reflected in the concern for the meaning of names in this chapter.

67.13. Ostrich: Compare Job 39:13–15: "*Gavest thou . . .* wings and feathers unto the ostrich? Which leaveth her eggs in the earth, and warmeth them in the dust, And forgetteth that the foot may crush them, or that the wild beast may break them."

67.19. Time-Spirit (*Zeitgeist*): Following the German idealist tradition, Carlyle saw Time as a paradoxical interruption in the flow of eternity. He wrote in his *Journal* (November 1831), "But on the whole, our conception of Immortality (as Dreck [*Sartor Resartus*] too has it) depends on that of *Time*. . . . Believe that there properly *is* no Space and no Time, how many contradictions become reconciled!" (*Two Note Books*, 221–22). The paradox of Time (and Space) is also discussed in "Characteristics" (1831), *Essays* 3:34, where it is presented as the manifestation of both phenomenon and noumenon;

and in "Boswell's Life of Johnson" (1832), *Essays* 3:79, where Time is referred to as the "outer veil of Eternity."

67.22. Devil: In "Wotton Reinfred," Carlyle through his character Maurice describes the devil: "Your arch fault-finder is the devil; it is no one's trade but his to dwell on negations, to impugn the darkness and overlook the light; and out of the glorious All itself to educe not beauty but deformity" (*Last Words*, 92).

67.26. Walter Shandy: Father of Tristram Shandy, who believed passionately in the influence of names. In Sterne's *Tristram Shandy* 1.19.57, Tristram reports his father's conviction that with respect to "the choice and imposition of Christian names . . . he thought a great deal more depended than what superficial minds were capable of conceiving." Compare also Richter's "The Life of Quintus Fixlein," where clothes and names are linked: "It might be that, as, according to Tristram Shandy, clothes; according to Walter Shandy and Lavater, proper names exert an influence on men, appellatives would do so still more; since, on us . . . *the foam so often hardens into shell*" (*German Romance* 2:230).

67.33. invisible seed-grain . . . over-shadowing tree: Compare 30.17–18.

67.35. Trismegistus: Hermes Trismegistus (Thrice-Great), who was credited with the authorship of the so-called Hermetic Books. Trismegistus was claimed to have been an Egyptian seer-priest who lived just after the time of Moses, or perhaps the Egyptian god Thoth himself, whom the Greeks identified with Hermes. The *Corpus Hermetica*, actually written in the first centuries of the Christian era, is a collection of writings on astrology, alchemy, and other occult matters, as well as metaphysical works dealing with the unity of all things. Mentioned in *Tristram Shandy*, Volume 1, Chapter 19.

67.37. Adam's first task was giving names: Genesis 2:19: "[A]nd whatsoever Adam called every living creature, that *was* the name thereof."

68.7–20. Meanwhile the incipient Diogenes . . . Poetries and Religions: This paragraph shows the influence on Carlyle of British empiricist theories of knowledge, in contrast to the German idealist epistemology found throughout *Sartor*. Carlyle's description of the infant Teufelsdröckh's first efforts "to acquire . . . some knowledge of this strange Universe" (lines 12–13) is reminiscent of Locke's image of the infant as a blank slate (*tabula rasa*) and of Locke's and Hume's accounts of knowledge as wholly derived from initial "vague Sensation" (line 18).

68.21. Gneschen: A nickname of doubtful etymology, perhaps from *Gneiste*, or spark, hence "Little Spark"; perhaps derived from *Gnadenbild*, wonder-working, hence "Little Wonder-Worker"; or perhaps a diminutive of *Genese*, genesis, hence "Little Beginning."

69.8. Timbuctoo: Timbuktu, a city in the western Sudan, near the Niger River, once a cultural center. The adventures of René Caillié, the French explorer who was the first European to visit and to return from Timbuktu in 1828, were widely discussed. Alfred Tennyson, while at Trinity College, Cambridge, won the Chancellor's Medal for his poem "Timbuctoo" (1829).

NOTES TO CHAPTER II. IDYLLIC

70.1. HAPPY season of Childhood: The language and philosophy of this paragraph are remarkably similar to Wordsworth's "Ode: Intimations of Immortality." The beliefs that the child is ignorant of time, that his parents are foster parents for God, that his dreams are prophecies of things to come, that he should not hasten into adulthood, repeat Wordsworthian dicta, especially from stanzas 5–8. The child as prophet who resides outside of nature only to be consumed by it as an adult is also found in Shelley's "Ode to the West Wind," lines 47–52: "If even / I were as in my boyhood, and could be, / The comrade of thy wanderings over Heaven, / As then, when to outstrip thy skiey speed / Scarce seemed a vision; I would ne'er have striven / As thus with thee in prayer in my sore need." Compare also Richter, *Siebenkäs*, 261, and "Jean Paul Friedrich Richter" (1830), *Essays* 2:156.

70.13. day-moth: Carlyle reverses the subject of his first poem, "Tragedy of the Night-Moth," written circa 1818–19, but not published until 1830. See *The Collected Poems of Thomas and Jane Welsh Carlyle*, 1–3. The *OED* glosses "day-moth" in this sentence as meaning "existing by day, diurnal"; there is also the implication of "lasting for only one day" as in "day-fly," "day-fever," and "day-lily." "Daymoth" is mentioned again at 91.11.

70.18. **Arnauld**: Antoine Arnauld (1612–1694), French philosopher and Jansenist, who created controversy by speaking against Jesuits, and later against Calvinists and Freethinkers. Because of his contro-versial views on mysticism and holiness, he was expelled from the Sorbonne. When Pierre Nicole, a fellow Jansenist, complained about his life of controversy, Arnauld allegedly responded with the quoted remark on rest and eternity. Carlyle alludes to this anecdote in his article "Pascal" in the *Edinburgh Encyclopædia*. Pascal, himself a Jansenist, wrote the celebrated *Lettres provincial* (*Provincial Letters*, 1656) in defense of Arnauld. Jansenism, following the principles of the Dutch Roman Catholic theologian Cornelis Janssen, emphasized predestination, denied free will, and maintained that human nature is incapable of good.

70.19. **Nepenthe**: A drug used to relieve sorrow and pain by causing forgetfulness and sleep. See Homer's *Odyssey*, Book 4, lines 294–96, where Helen employs a "medicine to their wine, / That (drowning Cares and Angers) did decline / All thought of ill." Also Milton's *Comus* (1634), line 674.

70.19. **Pyrrhus**: (318?–272 B.C.), King of Epirus, who was at con-stant war with the Romans. After one of his many bloody victories, he is said to have declared, "One more such victory and I am lost," whence the expression "Pyrrhic victory." Compare 108.35.

70.20. **Alexander**: Alexander the Great (356–323 B.C.), King of Macedon, extraordinary leader and warrior who conquered most of ancient Asia, and who effected the spread of Hellenism.

71.11. **Kuhbach**: "Cow-brook," the burn that flowed through the center of Ecclefechan.

71.12. **Donau**: The Danube, perhaps also an allegorical reference to Scotland's river Annan, which flows into the Solway Firth, the "Black Sea."

71.13. **Linden:** The German lime tree, used here as an archetype for the beginning, the sustaining, and the renewal of life. In his use of the tree, Carlyle fuses a number of traditions: classical and Norse myth portrays the tree as the center of the universe, with its branches reaching upwards in union with the gods and its roots downwards in union with the nether world; and in Christian iconography it is usually portrayed as the Tree of Knowledge or the Tree of Life. In Romantic literature the shade of the tree became synonymous with the acquisition of knowledge, an association which Carlyle uses repeatedly both as a structural and as a thematic device. Compare 30.17–19 and 36.21, where the present grows out of the past "like a Tree, whose roots are not intertangled with its branches, but lie peaceably under ground"; in 67.33 it is referred to as the "all over-shadowing tree"; 73.14 and called the "high-towering, wide-shadowing tree"; in 83.2 Gneschen pitches his "tent under a Cypress tree"; in 102.20 it becomes the sustaining "Tree of Knowledge"; in 105.17 the hills are "spotted by some spreading solitary Tree and its shadow"; in 114.34 the cottages are "tree-shaded"; in 129.14 a book is described as a "spiritual tree"; in 132.30–34 the "inspired" of Schiller and Goethe are found under a "shady Tree"; in 155.26 Teufelsdröckh lodges in a "hollow of a tree"; and 185.23–24 where from the "dry tree" of skepticism comes the "green" tree of hope. Compare also an undated manuscript fragment by Carlyle: "Igdrasil. From the Norse." *Igdrasil* 1 (February, 1890): 41–42, the content of which follows the spirit of *Sartor Resartus:* "O Tree of Igdrasil, deep-rooted down in Hela's death-realms. Whose boughs fill all Immensity and reach to Heaven. Tree of Existence, ever-growing, ever-dying; mounting out of deep Death-Kingdoms, and deciduous returning thither; old, oldest, yet ever new; another, yet the same." Compare also *Past and Present* (1843), 38, 129, and 250.

71.15. *Agora:* A marketplace in ancient Greece, a place of assembly.

71.15. *Campus Martius:* The "Field of Mars" outside the walls of Rome where armies mustered and exercised and where the *comitia centuriata*, legislative and electoral assemblies, were held.

71.23. **tired brickmakers:** Compare Exodus 5:5–23, where Pharaoh commands the "idle" Israelites to make more bricks.

71.25–26. Harvest-Home: A festival to celebrate the bringing home of the fall harvest.

71.36. pengun: "A toy air-gun made from a quill; a pop-gun" (*OED*).

72.16. Hebrew Speech: Here an unknown language in which the philosophic truths of life are concealed, truths which at present are only suggested in the hieroglyphs of the child. Compare Wordsworth's "Ode: Intimations of Immortality," lines 90–91.

72.21. animated Nature: Compare Coleridge's "The Eolian Harp," lines 44–45: "And what if all of animated nature / Be but organic Harps diversely framed."

72.26–27. see them, at eventide, all marching in again: Compare *Korân*, Chapter 16, 257: "When ye drive *them* home *in the evening*"; and *On Heroes* 59.18–19.

72.37. Helvetius: Claude Adrien Helvétius (1715–1771), French encyclopedist and philosopher, who in *De l'esprit* (*Essays on the Mind*, 1758) embraced Locke's view that man is born with a blank mind and that distinctions of intellect are the result of environment. Helvétius argued that self-interest was the sole motivation for action. His posthumously published *De l'homme* (*A Treatise on Man*, 1772) expands this thesis. In "Diderot" (1833), Carlyle describes Helvétius as "the well-fed Farmer-general, enlivening his sybaritic life with metaphysic paradoxes . . . the greater is our astonishment to find him here so ardent a Preserver of the Game." Carlyle then quotes Diderot on how Helvétius tyrannized the poor for poaching and vandalizing his estate: "Alas! are not Helvetius's preserves, at this hour, all broken up, and lying desecrated? Neither can the others, in what latitude and longitude soever, remain eternally impregnable. But if a Rome were once saved by geese, need we wonder that an England is lost by partridges?" (*Essays* 3:210–11). See following note.

73.4. Game-preserver: A favorite epithet of Carlyle's which appears in various forms throughout his writings expressive of his contempt for what he called the "do-nothing Aristocracy." In a *Journal* entry, June 30, 1830, he sounds the warning: "[W]hat do those highly beneficed individuals [the aristocracy] *do* to society for their wages? *Kill Partridges.* Can this last? No, by the soul that is in man, it cannot and will not and shall not!—" (*Two Note Books*, 159–60). Compare 86.11 and the epitaph of Count Zähdarm at 100.7–26.

73.13–14. doddered: Lacking the top branches because of age or decay.

73.17–19. Education . . . German Autobiographer: Carlyle is thinking of Goethe, *Wilhelm Meisters Wanderjahre* (*Wilhelm Meister's Travels*; in Carlyle's translation *Wilhelm Meister* (1824) 2:269–278), where Wilhelm is taught the importance of recording his education.

73.26. Magic Hall: In a magic show, a room with concave and convex mirrors.

73.33. "Much-enduring Man": Compare Homer's *Odyssey*, Book 6, lines 1–2, where Ulysses is described as "The much-sustaining, patient, heavenly Man, / Whom Toile and Sleepe had worne so weake and wan."

74.7. *Postwagen* (Stage-Coach): Ecclefechan was a stagecoach stop for the Glasgow–London coaches.

74.14–15. Schiller's *Wilhelm Tell*: Schiller's play *Wilhelm Tell* (1804) is a dramatization of the medieval legend of a father who was forced to shoot, with bow and arrow, an apple off his young son's head. The reference in the text is to *Wilhelm Tell* 4.3.2619: "*Denn jede Strasse führt ans End' der Welt*," which Carlyle had translated in *The Life of Friedrich Schiller* (1825), 179: "For every road / Will lead one to the end o' th' World."

74.18–23. Swallows . . . twittered: Compare Carlyle's poem on the same subject, "To a Swallow Building Under Our Eaves," *Collected Poems*, 56–57, which may have been composed at Craigenputtoch, where *Sartor Resartus* was written. Also Keats, "To Autumn" (1820), line 33: "And gathering swallows twitter in the skies."

74.25. mason-craft . . . masonic incorporation: An allusion to the Fraternal Brotherhood of Freemasonry, a secret society, originally open only to stonemasons, whose symbolic rites employ the instruments of the trade, such as plumbs, squares, levels, and compasses. Goethe was a mason and his poem, "*Symbolum*," translated by Carlyle as "Mason-Lodge" (1842–43; *Collected Poems*, 94–95), has become the official poem of the society. The poem ends with the famous injunction, "Work, and despair not," which forms the philosophic progression of Book II, Chapter IX of *Sartor Resartus*.

74.29. **super-hirundine**: Hirundine: characteristic of a swallow.

74.29. **complete it again**: The emphasis here on reconstruction complements in general the theme of rebirth in *Sartor Resartus*, but also prepares for the specific introduction of George Fox and the Quakers (in Book III, Chapter I), who were known especially for their industry and the sharing of labor.

74.33. **Cattle-fair**: During Carlyle's childhood Ecclefechan was the site of an annual cattle-fair.

74.35. **Nutbrown maids and nutbrown men**: From the old Scots ballad "The Not-Browne Mayd" (*c.* 1100), a moral poem which argues that women are as worthy as men. Compare also the search for the "Nut-brown Maid" in *Wilhelm Meister* 2:258.

74.37. **Topbooted Graziers**: Top-boot, a high boot with a fancy top often in contrasting color or texture; a grazier is one who raises grazing cattle.

75.1. **subalterns**: subordinates.

75.5. **Ormuz bazaars**: Ormuz, or Hormuz, an island in the Stait of Hormuz between the Persian Gulf and the Gulf of Oman, once a wealthy trading link between India and Europe. Compare *Paradise Lost* 2.2, where Satan's throne "Outshon the wealth of *Ormus* and of *Ind*."

75.5. **Lago Maggiore**: Lake Maggiore or Verbano, the second largest lake in Italy, lies partly in Switzerland.

75.9. **confounding the confusion**: See note at 19.38.

75.10. **Merry Andrew**: A prankster, jester, or clown. The general theme here that life is a stage of confusions is anticipated in the remarks of the Player in *Faust*, The Prelude, lines 170–71, where the play (life) is described as "Lively scenes that aren't too lucid— / much confusion, a glimmer of truth."

75.18. **to syllable**: To sound out by syllables, as one who is first learning to read phonetically.

75.23. **Prospero's Island**: A place of charm and enchantment in *The Tempest* 4.1.154–58, quoted at 195.35–37 below. See also Carlyle's *Wilhelm Meister's Travels* (1824) 1:32, where he compares Goethe's *Wanderjahre* to the "pageants of Prospero in his enchanted Island"; and "Goethe" (1828), *Essays* 1:233.

76.14–15. **root of bitterness**: From Hebrews 12:15, where the advice is to look to the "grace of God; lest any root of bitterness springing up trouble *you*."

76.24. **my upbringing**: The description that follows seems especially autobiographical. Carlyle is no doubt reflecting here upon his stern yet compassionate father James, who in part at least provided the symbol for "man's Free-will." Compare "James Carlyle," *Reminiscences*, 3–39.

76.36–38. **Good grows . . . Evil**: Compare the parable of the seeds in Matthew 13:3–8 and Luke 8:5–15, where the good seed grows and the evil turns to waste.

77.3. **Holy of Holies**: An allusion to the ark, the "most holy," in the tabernacle, the "holy *place*." See Exodus 26:33–34.

77.4. **Reverence**: Compare *Wilhelm Meister* 2:265–67: "threefold Reverence": that which is above us, around us, and below us, which becomes the three Religions: Ethnic (above), Philosophic (around), and Christian (below).

77.7–8. **two and thirty quarters**: In heraldry "quarters" are the divisions on a shield or coat of arms, which can be multiplied by the incorporation of the arms of heiresses to whom the family has allied by marriage, resulting in a shield subdivided into more, smaller "quarterings."

NOTES TO CHAPTER III. PEDAGOGY

78.10. **Man . . . Boy**: The idea that what is innate in the boy finally manifests itself in the man echoes Wordsworth's dictum that the child is the father of the man; see especially "Ode: Intimations of Immortality" (1807), stanzas 5–7. Compare also Milton's *Paradise Regained* (1671), 4.220–21: "[T]he childhood shews the man, / As morning shews the day." At yet another level the passive–active (innocence–experience) progression of contraries is much like that employed by William Blake, especially as found in "The Marriage of Heaven and Hell" (1790), where the movement is defined through the assimilation of knowledge, the subject of this chapter. See "The Last of the Supernaturalists," *Fraser's Magazine* 1 (March, 1830): 217–35, an essay on Blake which has been attributed—perhaps erroneously—to Carlyle (Tarr, *Bibliography*, 466). The title and the subject matter of the essay anticipate, in part, Carlyle's chapter "Natural Supernaturalism" (Book III, Chapter VIII).

78.18. Hindoo character: A reference to the alleged Hindu passivity acquired through contemplation.

79.9. earliest tools: An echo perhaps of *Tristram Shandy*, Book 5, Chapter 42, where knowledge is measured by the sharpness of the tools of learning.

79.10–11. this portion of his History: The history of Teufelsdröckh's education is in large measure the history of Carlyle's. The autobiographical element often gives way to the fictive, but in the end the account given here articulates Carlyle's own struggle from the village school at Ecclefechan, to Annan Academy (1806–1809), and finally to Edinburgh University (1809–1814). In his marginalia to Friedrich Althaus's biographical account, Carlyle corrects the impression that *Sartor Resartus* is an exact description of his own experiences: "*Sartor* is quite unsafe for details! Fiction *founded* perhaps on fact—a long way off"; "*Sartor* here [on Annan Academy], in good part; not to be trusted in details"; and "Mythically *true* is what Sartor says of his Schoolfellows, and not half of the truth" (*Two Reminiscences*, 28, 31–32). Yet there are portions of the chronicle in *Sartor Resartus* that are accurate in detail, such as the account of Carlyle being taken to Annan by his father: "He took me down to Annan Academy on the Whitsunday morning, 1806; I trotting at his side in the way alluded to in *Teufelsdrockh* [sic]" (*Reminiscences*, 34); see 80.17–20 below.

79.11–13. Reading . . . by nature: Compare *Much Ado About Nothing* 3.3.15–16: "[T]o write and read comes by nature."

79.16. **Schoolmaster**: Carlyle was taught basic reading and writing by his mother, and mathematical tables by his father. His first schoolmaster was Tom Donaldson at Ecclefechan, and then Sandy Beattie at Hoddam Hill, who pronounced him "complete in English" at the age of seven but who was unable to teach him much Latin. Carlyle's first serious lessons in Latin were from the Rev. John Johnstone and his son (*Two Reminiscences*, 29–30). In 1806, he was sent to Annan Academy, represented here by the Gymnasium.

79.22. **stall-literature**: Cheap copies of serials, periodicals, broadsides, and the like sold in booksellers' stalls.

79.25. **chimeras**: See Homer's *Iliad*, 6.183–85.

80.1. **Joshua forded Jordan**: In Joshua 3:14–17, the Israelites under Joshua walked across the Jordan River on dry ground with the Ark of the Covenant after the waters were cut off by God. Compare also Carlyle's poem, "Drumwhirn Bridge" (written in 1832), where the waters of the River Orr are viewed within the context of the crossing of the Jordan (*Collected Poems*, 48).

80.2–3. **Cæsar . . . kept his *Commentaries* dry**: After the battle of Pharos (47 B.C.) Caesar, "[h]aving several valuable papers, which he was not willing either to lose or to wet, . . . held them above water with one hand, and swam with the other" while escaping the Egyptians (Plutarch, *Lives*, 512).

80.3–5. **Tiber, Eurotas, or Siloa . . . Euphrates and the Ganges**: Tiber, the river in central Italy that flows through Rome; Eurotas, a river in Laconia in ancient Greece where Sparta stood; Siloa (Siloah or Siloam), a pool near Jerusalem; Euphrates, a river in southwestern Asia flowing through ancient Babylon; Ganges, the river in northern India which is sacred to the Hindus.

80.5–7. **Vein . . . Arteries**: See Wordsworth's "Tintern Abbey" (1798), stanzas 1–2, where the flow of the River Wye is compared to a flow of blood, where veins and arteries are used in a different metaphor. See 181.15–20 below.

80.9. **six thousand years of age**: Bishop Ussher, in his *Annales Veteris et Novi Testamenti* (1650–54), dated the creation of the world according to biblical chronology to 4004 B.C., a matter being debated in the pages of *Fraser's Magazine* in the 1830s as Carlyle was writing.

80.18. Hinterschlag: "Swipe on the backside." Vulgar: "kick in the ass."

80.19. Whitsuntide: The week beginning with Whitsunday or Pentecost, the seventh Sunday after Easter, but especially the first three days of this week.

81.13. the Tearful: Autobiography again intrudes into fiction as Carlyle describes his treatment by his schoolmates and his education at Annan Academy. Compare Carlyle's unfinished novel "Wotton Reinfred" (1826), *Last Words*, 23: "They flouted him, they beat him, they jeered and tweaked and tortured him . . . ; and so shy and soft withal, that he generally passed for cowardly, and his tormentors had named him 'weeping Wotton,' and marked him down as a proper enough bookworm, but one without a particle of spirit. However, in this latter point they sometimes overshot themselves, and the boldest and tallest of the house have quailed before the 'weeping Wotton,' when thoroughly provoked, for his fury while it lasted was boundless." Also see *Two Reminiscences*, 32: "Unspeakable is the damage & defilement I got out of those coarse unguided tyrannous cubs,—especially till I revolted against them, and gave stroke for stroke. . . . One way and another I had never been so wretched as here in that School, and the first 2 years of my time in it still count among the miserable of my life. 'Academies,' 'High Schools,' 'Instructors of Youth'—Oh ye unspeakable!—" Compare also Carlyle's fragment on education entitled "Scavenger Age" (c.1844–50) in Michael Timko, "Carlyle, Sterling, and the Scavenger Age," 11–33. "The Tearful" is perhaps also a reference to Heraclitus (540?–480? B.C.) who argued that permanence is an illusion and who was known as the "Weeping Philosopher." See Heraclitus, *Cosmic Fragments*; and *Two Reminiscences*, 31n.

81.17. Rights of Man: An allusion to the Declaration of the Rights of Man and Citizen, passed by the Constituent Assembly on August 4, 1789, which formally abolished the feudal structure of France. Compare *French Revolution* 1:219: "[W]e get the *Rights of Man* . . . true paper basis of all paper Constitutions. Neglecting, cry the opponents, to declare the Duties of Man! Forgetting, answer we, to ascertain the *Mights* of Man;—one of the fatalest omissions!" Compare also Thomas Paine, *The Rights of Man* (1791–92).

81.22–24. Greek and Latin . . . and so forth: In the marginalia to Althaus, Carlyle corrects this account of his experience at Annan Academy: "'Greek,' for example, consisted of the *Alphabet* mainly; 'Hebrew' is quite a *German* entity. . . . I did get to read Latin & French with fluency . . . ; some geometry, algebra (*arithmetic* thoroughly well), vague outlines of geography &c I did learn" (*Two Reminiscences*, 31).

81.26–27. Craftsmen's workshops: Compare "Goethe's Works" (1832), *Essays* 2:415, where Goethe's boyhood education is characterized by the observation of and the participation in the work of craftsmen.

81.28 Hans Wachtel: "John Quail."

81.31. Bag *Scorpio*: The second of the six bags. See "Bag *Libra*" at 63.14.

82.2–3. Gerund-grinder . . . at Nürnberg: Compare *Tristram Shandy*, Book 5, Chapter 32, where myopic education is satirized: "Here is the glass of pedagogues, preceptors, tutors, governours, gerund-grinders and bear-leaders to view themselves in, in their true dimensions.—"; Pope's *Martinus Scriblerus*, 141, where a "great Virtuoso at Nuremberg" creates an artificial man to illustrate the possibility of creating mechanical thinking; and Carlyle's introduction to Richter in *German Romance* 2:124, where Richter's characters are described as "Engines, with no more life than the Freethinkers' model in *Martinus Scriblerus*, the Nuremberg Man, who operated by a combination of pipes and levers, and though he could breathe and digest perfectly, and even reason as well as most country parsons, was made of wood and leather."

82.13–14. Hodman . . . Architect: Compare Fichte's *Über das Wesen des Gelehrten* (*On the Nature of Literary Men*, 1805), where it is argued that the literary hodman (one who possesses practical but not creative wisdom) is apprentice to the literary architect (one who deals in the metaphysics of the Divine Idea). Compare also "State of German Literature" (1827), *Essays* 1:59; *Letters* 4:271–72; 5:152–53; and *On Heroes* 136.3.

82.26–27. Andreas . . . died: Here Carlyle departs from the generally autobiographical flavor of this part of Teufelsdröckh's narrative. Carlyle's father actually died on January 22, 1832, while Carlyle was working on the manuscript of *Sartor Resartus*: "[N]ews came suddenly of my Father's Death: a plunge for me into deepest gloom; say rather, [s]addest grief, retrospect*n*, & feeling of bereave*t* and eternity" (*Letters* 6:105).

82.29. dark bottomless Abyss: Compare *Paradise Lost* 2.405, where Chaos is described as "The dark unbottom'd infinite Abyss."

82.30. pale kingdoms of Death: Compare *Aeneid* 6.358–65, the "phantom kingdom" of Dis (Pluto), where "Grief and goading Cares" and "pale Diseases dwell"; and Revelation 6:8: "And I looked, and behold a pale horse: and his name that sat on him was Death."

83.11. Gehenna: The Valley of Hinnom (Hebrew: *Gê' Hinnom*), outside ancient Jerusalem, also known as the Valley of Slaughter, where the Israelites made sacrifices and where refuse was dumped into perpetual fire; later became identified as a place of suffering and torment, Hell. See Jeremiah 7:30–34, 19:2–6.

83.14–15. apostrophe . . . Character: Perhaps a reference to his own reminiscence of his father which Carlyle began on January 25, and completed on January 29, 1832. See "James Carlyle," *Reminiscences*, 3–39.

83.17–18. Henry the Fowler: Henry I (876?–936), German king (919–936) and first of the Saxon house, credited with restoring monarchical authority that had been usurped by the dukes. Reflected here is the belief held by members of the Carlyle family that they were descended from the nobility, namely Sir John Carlyle, Lord Carlyle of Torthorwald, who came to Scotland with David Bruce (1329–1371), King of Scotland.

83.36. Bag *Sagittarius*: The third of the six bags.

84.7. Milkscores: "A tally or other account of the purchase and sale of milk" (*OED*).

84.18. **living Fountain**: An adaptation of Revelation 7:16–17: "They shall hunger no more, neither thirst any more; . . . For the Lamb . . . shall lead them unto living fountains of waters."

84.30–31. **so questionable an aspect**: Compare *Hamlet* 1.4.43, where the Ghost appears to Hamlet "in such a questionable shape."

85.1. **University**: Like many Romantics, Carlyle claims that he found little of value at university: "Except [John] Leslie in Mathematics no Professor did me almost any good" (*Two Reminiscences*, 34). Such comments should be considered in light of others more temperate: "[W]hat I have found the University did for me, is, That it taught me to read, in various languages, in various sciences; so that I could go into the books which treated of these things, and gradually penetrate into any department I wanted to make myself master of" ("Inaugural Address" [1866], *Essays* 4:454–55). Also see 88.3–5 and note at 15.2.

85.10–11. **When the blind lead the blind . . . ditch**: Matthew 15:14, Luke 6:39. Compare 155.4.

85.13. **Crim Tartary**: The Crimea, *Krim* in Russian, was occupied by the Tartars from the thirteenth through the fifteenth centuries.

86.17. **golden ages**: Compare 174.36, where the *"L'âge d'or"* is satirized through the language of the Saint-Simonians.

86.17–18. **golden ages . . . brazen one**: Possible sources for this allusion are myriad. See, for example, Daniel 2:32–33: "This image's head *was* of fine gold, his breast and arms of silver, his belly and his thighs of brass, His legs of iron, his feet part of iron and part of clay"; and Thomas Love Peacock (1785–1866), *Four Ages of Poetry* (1820), who describes the history of poetry through the metaphors of iron, gold, silver, and brass.

86.30. **Talent of being Gulled**: The subject of Butler's *Hudibras* 2.3.152, where "Doubtless, The pleasure is as great, / Of being *cheated*, as to *cheat*" (lines 1–2). Compare also Carlyle's letter to Robert Mitchell, March 1817, *Letters* 1:97: "Si populus vult decipi, decipiatur" (If a people wishes to be deceived, let it be).

86.35–36. undershot-wheel: A water wheel, as in a grinding mill, that is driven by water passing below.

87.6. Progress of the Species . . . and the like: The language of contempt here and in the following passage more accurately reflects Carlyle's attitude in the late 1820s than that of his university days. Compare, for example, "Signs of the Times" (1829), *Essays* 2:59–61, where Carlyle laments that the past "Moral Age" has become the present "Mechanical Age": "Thus we have machines for Education. . . . Instruction, that mysterious communing of Wisdom with Ignorance, is no longer an indefinable tentative process, . . . but a secure, universal, straightforward business, to be conducted in the gross, by proper mechanism, with such intellect as comes to hand."

87.10. (*crepiren*): Modern German spelling *krepieren:* to die or to burst.

87.13. Systole . . . Diastole: Contraction and dilation of the heart. Compare Butler's *Hudibras* 2.3.307–08: "If *Systole* or *Diastole* move / Quickest, when hee's in wrath, or love."

87.14. Faith . . . Denial: Compare 15.15–17. Carlyle saw the history of humankind as a pattern of opposites, where "UNBELIEF and BELIEF" were the paradoxical requisites of progress. Hence, as much as he deplored the mechanism of inaction, it in itself was part of the larger fabric of spiritual action necessary for the health of society. Ages of Unbelief create Ages of Apocalypse. This dialectic of Inaction followed by Action, Renunciation by Reformation, is indicative of the alternate but orderly progress of the universe. See also "Diderot" (1833), *Essays* 3:248; and "The Phoenix," Book III, Chapter V (171–75) below.

87.17–19. Time . . . Eternity: See note at 67.19 above. Time is of course a contradiction of Eternity, but it too inevitably contributes to the progress of the soul. This progress can be seen in the Time-Symbol, here cloth, which is the visible manifestation of invisible Eternity. Carlyle is following the dictum of Goethe: "*Die Zeit ist mein Vermächtniss, mein Acker ist die Zeit*" (Time is my Legacy, my Field is Time), the motto on the title page of *Sartor Resartus*.

87.23. Salamanca University: Celebrated Spanish university founded in 1218, once noted as a center of Arabic philosophy and letters.

87.24. Sybaris City: Greek town in southern Italy, founded in 720 B.C. and destroyed in 510 B.C., whose inhabitants were known for their luxurious lifestyle.

87.24. Castle of Indolence: A reference to James Thomson's *Castle of Indolence* (1748), a poem in imitation of Spenser and from the so-called Graveyard School of poetry.

87.30–31. hungry young . . . bidden eat the east wind: Compare Milton's attack on the corrupt clergy in *Lycidas* (1638), lines 125–27: "The hungry Sheep look up, and are not fed, / But swoln with wind, and the rank mist they draw, / Rot inwardly, and foul contagion spread"; and Job 15:2: "Should a wise man utter vain knowledge, and fill his belly with the east wind?"

87.37. (*renommiren*): Modern German *renommieren*: to brag, to flaunt.

88.1. Library . . . books: Compare *On Heroes*, 140.12–13, "The true University of these days is a Collection of Books." See Finlayson, "Thomas Carlyle's Borrowings from Edinburgh University Library"; Campbell, "Carlyle's Borrowings from the Theological Library of Edinburgh University"; and Tarr, "Thomas Carlyle's Libraries at Chelsea and Ecclefechan."

88.15. Ishmael: In Genesis 16:1–16; 21:9–20, the son of Abraham and Hagar, the Egyptian handmaiden, who because of the jealousy of Sarah was cast out, "dwelt in the wilderness, and became an archer." Muslim tradition holds that the Arabs, as wanderers, were the descendants of Ishmael.

88.18. fever-paroxysms of Doubt: Compare Schiller, *Philosophische Briefe* (*Philosophical Letters*, 1786), *Schillers Werke* 20:108: "*Scepticismus und Freidenkerei sind die Fieberparoxysmen des menschlichen Geistes*" (Skepticism and Free-thinking are but the fever-paroxysms of the human spirit).

88.26–27. Pandemonium . . . Purgatory: Pandæmonium: the center of Hell in Milton's *Paradise Lost* where the sinner is condemned forever, see 1.756 and 10.424; Purgatory: the temporary place of expiation before the soul passes into Heaven, the subject of the second book of Dante's *Divine Comedy*.

88.27–28. it is appointed us to pass: An allusion to Hebrews 9:27: "And as it is appointed unto men once to die, but after this the judgment."

88.30–31. arise . . . with new healing under its wings: Malachi 4:2: "But unto you that fear my name shall the Sun of righteousness arise with healing in his wings."

89.3. established men: After leaving the University of Edinburgh in 1814, Carlyle went through a number of years of uncertainty about what career to pursue. In 1815, he met Edward Irving with whom he taught in Kirkcaldy in 1816, and who later introduced him to Jane Welsh. In 1817, he gave up any thoughts of the ministry and gained the attention of Professor John Leslie, who used Carlyle's solution to a mathematic problem in his *Elements of Geometry* (1817). He gave up the studies of natural history and of law at the University in 1818 and 1819 respectively; and in 1820 began to translate scientific papers and to write biographies and articles for the Edinburgh publisher David Brewster. In 1822, he became a tutor to the Charles Buller family, and he completed a translation for Brewster of A. M. Legendre's *Elements of Geometry* (1822). It was in August of 1822 that Carlyle probably experienced the famous conversion described in "The Everlasting No," Book III, Chapter VII. In *Two Reminiscences*, 41, Carlyle describes this period as "4 such years of solitary darkness . . . as centuries would not make me forget."

89.8. thrums: See note at 50.16 above.

89.12. Herr Towgood: Tow is Scots for rope or halter. Perhaps Charles Buller (1806–1848) whom Carlyle tutored, together with his younger brother Arthur, from January 1822 to July 1824. Educated at Harrow and Cambridge, Buller was a liberal Member of Parliament from 1830, and later distinguished himself as President of the Poor-Law Board. See Carlyle's obituary of Buller in the *Examiner* (December 2, 1848), 777–78; and *Reminiscences*, 270–71.

89.14. (*von Adel*): Of noble blood.

89.15. **Zähdarm**: Literally "tough-gut," as in tenacious or stubborn.

90.4. **thistles . . . figs**: Matthew 7:16: "Do men gather grapes of thorns, or figs of thistles?" Also Luke 6:44.

90.5. *Frisch zu, Bruder!*: "Fresh to work, brother"; in the sense of the proverb "Never put off until tomorrow what you can do today."

90.18–19. *Soul . . . Stomach*: Compare "Schiller" (1831), *Essays* 2:189, where a similar association is made: "Does not [man's] Soul,—which, as in some Slavonic dialects, means his Stomach,—sit forever at its ease, enwrapped in warm condiments, amid spicy odours; enjoying the past, the present and the future; and only awakening from its soft trance to the sober certainty of a still higher bliss each meal-time,— three, or even four visions of Heaven in the space of one solar day!" Carlyle's claim that soul and stomach are equivalent in the Finnish language has not been confirmed.

90.19. **Utilitarian Philosophy**: A philosophy developed by Jeremy Bentham that grew out of, in varying degrees, the socio-economic theories of Adam Smith and David Ricardo, and popularized by James Mill and later by his son John Stuart Mill. Utilitarianism measures the rightness or wrongness of an action by the goodness or badness of its consequences—hence, the end justifies the means. As a democratic philosophy it defines utility as the greatest pleasure for the greatest number, although John Stuart Mill later argued that quality as well as quantity should be a governing principle. In a *Journal* entry, August 5, 1829, Carlyle's contempt for such a philosophy is demonstrated: "The Utilitarians are the 'crowning mercy' of this age: the summit (now first appearing to view) of a mass of tendencies which stretch downwards and spread sidewards over the whole intellect and moral of the time. By and by, the clouds will disperse, and we shall see it all, in dead nakedness and brutishness; and Utilitaria will pass away with a great noise. You think not? — Can the Reason of man be trodden under foot forever by his sense; can the Brute in us prevail forever over the angel!" (*Two Note Books*, 145). Compare *Past and Present*, passim, but especially Book I. Compare also "Signs of the Times" (1829), *Essays* 2:58. Compare 4.1, 52.13–15, and 53.21, above.

NOTES TO CHAPTER IV. GETTING UNDER WAY

91.16. thaumaturgic: Miracle- or wonder-working. The thesis on the primacy of miracles is expanded in "Natural Supernaturalism," Book III, Chapter VIII.

91.22. Scottish Brassmith's IDEA: The steam engine, perfected by the Scottish inventor James Watt while an instrument maker at the University of Glasgow, which in turn led to steam-powered vessels. The first ocean crossing of the Atlantic, aided by sails, was in 1819. Carlyle would have been particularly familiar with Henry Bell's steamship, the Comet, which sailed around Scotland previous to any attempt to cross the ocean. The first ocean crossing fully under steam was not until 1838. In "Signs of the Times" (1829), *Essays* 2:59–60, Carlyle sees the steamship as a metaphor for the rise of mechanism: "The sailor furls his sail, and lays down his oar; and bids a strong, unwearied servant, on vaporous wings, bear him through the waters. Men have crossed oceans by steam; . . . and the genius of the Cape . . . has again been alarmed, and with far stranger thunders than Gamas [*sic*—the reference is to the Portuguese explorer Vasco da Gama]. There is no end to machinery." In the "Death of Goethe" (1832), *Essays* 2:377, he observes: "A poor, quite mechanical Magician speaks; and fire-winged ships cross the Ocean at his bidding."

92.19. 'Not what I Have': An echo of Luke 12:15–31.

92.34–35. purblind Youth . . . seeing Man: The movement here from the innocence of youth toward the mature philosophic mind is found in Wordsworth's "Ode: Intimations of Immortality." Compare also Richter's "Schmelzle's Journey to Flætz": "In youth, like a blind man just couched . . . , you take the Distant for the Near; . . . to the young man, the whole world is sitting on his very nose, till repeated bandaging and unbandaging have at last taught him, like the blind patient, to estimate *Distance* and *Appearance*" (*German Romance* 2:172).

92.35–93.2. many so spend . . . getting buried: Compare Young's *Night Thoughts*, (1854), ed. James Nichols (Hildesheim, 1968), 1:412–22, pp. 12–13: "All promise is poor dilatory man, / And that through every stage . . . / Resolves, and re-resolves; then dies the same."

93.1. threescore and ten: Psalms 90:10: "The days of our years *are* threescore years and ten." Compare 98.8 and 194.17 below.

93.14–16. Bread-studies . . . Bread-artist: Here associated with the mechanical, mundane application of servile talent; in literature the hack writer whose sole interest was in extrinsic recognition and reward rather than intrinsic aim and accomplishment. In the "State of German Literature" (1827), *Essays* 1:57, the literary Bread-artist is regarded by the German poets such as Schiller as "the fair tradesman, who offers his talent in open market, to do work of a harmless and acceptable sort for hire."

93.15. gin-horse: A horse that travels repetitively, often in a circle, supplying power for a gin, a machine to move heavy objects such as ore in a mine. Carlyle is playing here with the idea of horsepower, a word thought to have been coined by James Watt and applied by him to steam engines.

93.20–21. leading-string . . . neck-halter: An allusion to Carlyle's rejection of careers in the ministry (1817) and in Scots law (1819). In a letter to Robert Mitchell, March 31, 1817, he says of the patronage found in the former, "If we follow its members into the world, and observe their destination, we shall find it very pitiful" (*Letters* 1:98–99). In another letter to Robert Mitchell, March 18, 1820, he says of the latter: "Law, I fear, must be renounced: it is a shapeless mass of absurdity & chichane" (*Letters* 1:231).

93.21–22. Ancient Pistol: In *The Merry Wives of Windsor* 2.2.1–4, when Falstaff refuses to lend Pistol a penny, Pistol responds: "Why then the world's mine oyster, / Which I with sword will open."

93.29. Bag *Pisces*, and those that follow: Carlyle uses zodiacal signs to (mis)lead the reader through the symbolic and chronological progressions of an already obtuse if not deliberately confusing discourse on the nature of biographical fragment. Alexander Carlyle, ed., *Love Letters* 2:369, calls this labeling of the paper bags with the Southern Zodiacal Signs a "quaint device." G. B. Tennyson, *"Sartor" Called "Resartus,"* 219–20, elaborates: "The paper bags cover the winter months of the year. . . . Carlyle has taken the zodiac as another means of symbolizing events. [The signs] represent The winter of

Teufelsdröckh's discontent [and] a comment on the age." The six Southern Zodiacal Signs are: Libra (The Balance, September 23–October 23), Scorpio (The Scorpion, October 24–November 21), Sagittarius (The Archer, November 22–December 21), Capricornus (The Goat, December 22–January 19), Aquarius (The Water Bearer, January 20–February 18), and Pisces (The Fishes, February 19–March 20).

94.8. Son of Time: From Goethe's *Gott, Gemüth und Welt*: "*Ihr Söhne der Zeit.*"

94.10. *No Object and no Rest*: Goethe's *Faust*, line 3349: "*Der Unmensch ohne Zweck und Ruh*," inhuman creature without purpose or rest.

94.18. *Examen Rigorosum*: "Rigorous Examination," the third and final law examination in a German university.

94.19. *Auscultator*: Latin: "examiner" (literally "listener"); a lawyer who has passed his first law examinations and who is often employed as a law clerk. In his introduction to E. T. W. Hoffmann in *German Romance* 2:6–7, Carlyle writes how Hoffmann "passed his first professional trial, and was admitted Auscultator," and then how later he "passed his third and last trial, the *examen rigorosum*" and became an assessor, a professional.

94.25–26. Small speculation . . . glare withal: *Macbeth* 3.4.95–96: "Thou hast no speculation in those eyes / Which thou dost glare with!"

95.19. Gretchen: Carlyle's mother Margaret, on the other hand, did not die until 1853.

95.23. private Tuition: After giving up his post as teacher at Kirkcaldy in 1818, Carlyle turned to tutoring. In the spring of 1822, on the recommendation of his close friend, the Scottish preacher Edward Irving, he secured a position as tutor of Charles Buller, who later distinguished himself in Parliament, and of Arthur William Buller, who like his father became a judge in India. See *Letters* 2:4–5.

95.26. **Translation**: In 1819 Carlyle translated Jacob Berzelius' treatise on compounds, and in 1820 Professor Mohs's essay on crystallography and mineralogy for the *Edinburgh Philosophical Journal*; in 1822, with his brother John, Adrien M. Legendre's *Éléments de géométrie*; in 1824 Goethe's *Wilhelm Meisters Lehrjahre*; and in 1827 *German Romance*, a collection of German short fiction, and *Wilhelm Meisters Wanderjahre*.

95.29. **life for a living one**: Compare *Wilhelm Meister* 2:215: "Life belongs to the living; and he who lives must be prepared for vicissitudes."

96.6-8. **'Herr Teufelsdröckh ... eingeladen'**: "The Countess takes pleasure in inviting Herr Teufelsdröckh to Aesthetic Tea on Thursday." The source for the tea-party may have been Wilhelm Hauff, *Mitteilungenen aus den Memoiren des Satan* (*Notes on the Memoirs of Satan*, 1825-26), the central section of which is about Satan's encounter with a Wandering Jew whom he subsequently invites to an "*aesthetischen Tee*" (see Tennyson, "*Sartor*" *Called "Resartus*," 206).

96.9. **solid pudding**: Compare Pope's *The Dunciad* 1:52-54, "where on her scales Poetic Justice weighs solid pudding against empty praise."

96.17. **Zähdarm House**: Perhaps the home of the Bullers, Kinnaird House in Perthshire. See notes at 89.3, 89.12, and 89.15.

96.36-37. **Outrooting of Journalism**: Compare Fichte, *Grundzüge des gegenwärtigen Zeitalters* (*Characteristics of the Present Age*, 1804), *Fichte's Popular Works* 2:90. Carlyle owned Smith's translation; see Tarr, "Thomas Carlyle's Libraries at Chelsea and Ecclefechan," 254.

97.11. **blackness of darkness**: Compare Jude 13, where sinners are described as "wandering stars, to whom is reserved the blackness of darkness for ever."

97.15. **Victory ... Battle**: The idea here, that the capability to overcome hardship is attained through the "consciousness of Battle" (138.6), is one of the central points of Carlyle's message of spiritual reward through temporal labor. Action through work is "our Whole

Duty" (98.13). Compare "Characteristics" (1831), *Essays* 3:28: "Ever must Pain urge us to Labour; and only in free Effort can any blessedness be imagined for us." In a *Journal* entry, September 1831, Carlyle writes, "Up and be doing! Hast thou not the strangest grandest of all talents committed to thee; namely LIFE itself? . . . Up and be doing; and pray . . . to the Unseen Author of all thy Strength to guide thee and aid thee; to give thee if not Victory and Possession, unwearied Activity and *Entsagen*. . . . The quantity of Pain thou feelest is indication of the quantity of Life, of Talent, thou hast" (*Two Note Books*, 165–66, 169).

97.20. **sadder and wiser**: Compare Coleridge's "The Rime of the Ancient Mariner," lines 624–25: "A sadder and a wiser man, / He rose the morrow morn."

97.24–26. (*Mädchen*) . . . (*Bübchen*) . . . (*Gecken*): Respectively, "girl," "little boy," "fops or dandies."

97.33. **Rule of Three**: The formula for finding the fourth term of a proportion, i.e., first term is to second term as third term is to x (1:2::3:x or 1/2 = 3/x); so, following the Rule of Three, x = (2 x 3) ÷ 1 = 6. Compare *Wilhelm Meister* 1:306: The Children of Joy "were a set of clever, strong-headed, lively geniuses, who saw well enough that the sum of our existence, divided by reason, never gives an integer number, but that a surprising fraction is always left behind"; "Wotton Reinfred," *Last Words*, 88: "Rule of Three. Multiply the second and third terms together, and divide the product by the first, and the quotient will be the answer"; and 142.25–28.

98.6. **Saturn, or Chronos**: The Roman god Saturn came to be identified with the Greek Titan Cronus, the father of the Olympian gods, who devoured his children to keep them from overthrowing him. Here Cronus is confused with *chronos* (time).

98.9. **Holy Alliance of Sovereigns**: An agreement signed on September 26, 1815, by the rulers of Russia, Austria, and Prussia to settle European boundaries after the defeat of Napoleon.

98.13–14. **Whole Duty . . . right direction**: Compare Ecclesiastes 12:13: "Fear God, and keep his commandments: for this *is* the whole *duty* of man."

98.21. **Azure Home**: Compare the "azure sky" in Shelley's "Adonais" (1821), stanza 42.

98.31. **Hudibras's sword**: Butler's *Hudibras*, 1.1.356–60: "The trenchant blade, *Toledo* trusty, / For want of fighting was grown rusty, / And ate into itself, for lack / Of somebody to hew and hack."

99.12. **panoply of Sarcasm**: Compare *Reminiscences*, 216, where Carlyle describes his own posturing during his first meeting with Edward Irving: "Not sanguine and diffusive, he; but biliary and intense;—'far too sarcastic for a young man,' said several in the years now coming." In a similar tone Carlyle describes himself in "Wotton Reinfred," *Last Words*, 34: "Gloomy mockery was in his once kind and gentle heart; mockery of the world, of himself, of all things; yet bitterest sadness lay within it, and through his scowl there often glistened a tear."

99.12. **buckram-case**: Coarse cotton cloth, sized with glue, used for stiffening garments.

99.25. **torpedo**: A fish related to the electric ray.

99.28. **to unite . . . with somewhat**: Compare *Wilhelm Meister* 2:277, where a parable about clothes is told to demonstrate the "peculiar property of human nature, . . . the tendency to imitate, the inclination to unite with something."

99.34. *Discourse on Epitaphs*: An allusion to Wordsworth's essay "Upon Epitaphs" (1810) which distinguishes between the personal tone of the epitaph and the universal tone of the elegy.

100.7–26. HIC JACET . . . [*sub dato*]: "Here lies Philip Zaehdarm, called the Great, Count of Zaehdarm, member of the Imperial Council, Knight of the Golden Fleece, of the Garter, and of the Black Vulture. Who, while he lived on earth, shot five thousand partridges: a hundred million hundred-weights of various kinds of food he openly, by himself and by his servants, quadrupeds and bipeds, not without tumult in the course of it, converted into manure. Now resting from his labor, his works follow him. If you seek his monument, look at this pile. Commenced [on the date]; finished [on the date]" (translation of G. B. Tennyson). "Now resting . . . follow him": Compare

Revelation 14:13, where the dead "may rest from their labours; and their works do follow them." "If you seek his monument, look at this pile" is a parody of the inscription to Christopher Wren in St. Paul's Cathedral: *Si monumentum requiris, circumspice* (If you seek his monument, look about you).

NOTES TO CHAPTER V. ROMANCE

101.2–3. baking bricks without stubble: An allusion to Exodus 5:6–18, where Pharaoh commands the Israelites: "Go therefore now, *and* work; for there shall no straw be given you, yet shall ye deliver the tale of bricks." Compare 71.23 above.

101.4. *Beym Himmel!*: "By Heaven!"

101.9. herring-busses: From the Dutch *haring-buis*, fishing ships of approximately fifty tons.

101.17. Northwest Passage: Although the search for a northwest passage to the orient began as early as the sixteenth century, it is likely that Carlyle is referring to the more contemporary attempts. In 1818 and again in 1829, John Ross led expeditions. William Edward Parry, who sailed with Ross in 1818, also led unsuccessful expeditions in 1819, 1821, and 1824. Carlyle may also have in mind Sterne's *Tristram Shandy*, Book 5, Chapter 42, where Teufelsdröckh's journey is anticipated in the metaphorical words of Walter Shandy, "I am convinced . . . that there is a North west passage to the intellectual world; and that the soul of man has shorter ways of going to work, in furnishing itself with knowledge and instruction."

101.20. Calypso-Island: The island of Ogygia, where the nymph Calypso, daughter of Atlas, entertained Odysseus (Ulysses) for eight years. She offered him immortality to stay; Odysseus declined and by the command of Zeus she released him. See Homer's *Odyssey*, Book 1, especially lines 141–44.

102.6–7. Like and Unlike . . . Negative and Positive: Compare 34.27 above and 136.8–9 and 209.35–36 below.

102.18–20. Paradise . . . Garden . . . Tree: An allusion to the fall of man. Compare Genesis 2:8–25, and *Paradise Lost*, Book 9.

102.21–22. Cherubim . . . sword: Compare Genesis 3:24, where God "placed at the east of the garden of Eden Cherubims, and a flaming sword" to guard the tree of life.

102.25. sacred air-cities: See Tennyson's "Timbuctoo" (1829), lines 22–26, where such cities are identified as "Divinest Atalantis" and "Imperial Eldorado," where "Men clung with yearning hope which would not die."

102.30–31. reverberating furnace: A type of kiln where the flame is reflected from the roof on the material below being heated. Compare Richter's *Siebenkäs*, 54, where the "sand-bath and reverberating furnace of a noble anger made all their emotions warmer to-day, just as a hot climate gives strength to poisons and spices."

102.37. Jacob's-ladder: Compare Genesis 28:12, where Jacob "dreamed, and behold a ladder set up on the earth, and the top of it reached to heaven."

103.4. Demons and Angels: The language and the tone of this paragraph are reminiscent of Pope's "The Rape of the Lock," lines 73–74, where Belinda, who is also guarded by "Sylphs and Sylphids . . . Fays, Fairies, Genii, Elves, and Daemons," loses her innocence because she cannot resist temptation. In legend demons and angels would hover over a dead body, each hoping to seize the soul.

103.15. Vesuvian: Of Vesuvius, the volcano on the eastern shore of the Bay of Naples, most famous for the eruption, recorded by Pliny the Younger, which destroyed Pompeii and Herculaneum in A.D. 79. There were also notable eruptions in the eighteenth and nineteenth centuries.

103.25. Promethean: I.e., fire-bearing. Prometheus is a Greek divinity who in myth created man out of clay and water, and who defied the gods by stealing fire from them and giving it to man to make him self-sufficient. According to Hesiod, the gods punished man for this by causing Hephaestus to create woman.

103.36. Crater of an extinct volcano: The language of conflagration and the theme of unrequited love in this entire episode finds parallel in *Wilhelm Meister* 1:105–07, where Wilhelm loses Mariana and looks with "horror into the gloomy abyss of a barren misery, as one looks down into the hollow crater of an extinguished volcano."

104.3–4. He loved . . . not wisely but too well: *Othello* 5.2.344.

104.4. Congreve: William Congreve (1772–1828), the inventor of a rocket-like weapon which was enclosed in a metal casing.

104.6. 'First Love which is infinite': Compare Goethe's autobiographical *Dichtung und Wahrheit* (*Poetry and Truth*, 1811–1813), translated in part by Carlyle in "Goethe" (1828), *Essays* 1:221: "The first love . . . is the only one."

104.10. grand-climacteric: Thought to be a critical period in one's life, found by multiplying seven years times any odd number, the most critical being the age sixty-three.

104.10. *St. Martin's Summer:* November 11, a time of final warmth before the onset of winter.

104.11. myrtle garland: Myrtle, together with the rose and the apple, was sacred to Venus, the goddess of love.

104.20. Petrarchan and Werterean: Petrarchan: Francesco Petrarch (1304–1374), Italian poet who celebrated corporeal love in his sonnets to Laura. Werterean: Goethe's *Die Leiden des jungen Werthers* (*The Sorrows of Young Werther*, 1774), an autobiographical novel of unrequited love which became an emblem of the passionate man spurned.

104.23. *Blumine:* Flower or Blossom, perhaps a pun on *Blume*. Similar to Wordsworth's Lucy, Blumine is a fictional composite of Carlyle's past romances. She is a recreation, in part, of Margaret Gordon, who was introduced to Carlyle by Edward Irving in Kirkcaldy in 1818, a romance that ended in the spring of 1820; of Catherine Aurora Kirkpatrick, daughter of a Begum, an Indian Princess, who was introduced to Carlyle by the Edward Stracheys in the fall of 1824; and of Jane Welsh, who was introduced to Carlyle by Edward Irving in May of 1821 and whom Carlyle married in October 1826. Jane Montagu, the heroine of Carlyle's unfinished novel "Wotton Reinfred," is herself a prototype for Blumine. Although the outcome is different, the hyperbolic language of love in this passage is not unlike that in Richter's "Life of Quintus Fixlein," *German Romance* 2:286–89. See also Carlyle's full portrait of Jane Welsh in *Reminiscences*, 40–199, and his remembrances of Margaret Gordon and Kitty Kirkpatrick in *Reminiscences*, 239–40, 280, 283, 285, 305–06.

104.27. Pre-established Harmony: Gottfried Leibnitz argued in *Nouveaux essais sur l'entendement humain* (*New Essays on Human Understanding*, 1765) that there is one universal context, the result of a divine plan, and that all occurrences can be seen in relationship to each other. The interaction of these occurrences is called Pre-established Harmony.

104.32. low sublunary one: Compare John Donne, "A Valediction: forbidding mourning" (1633), lines 13–14: "Dull sublunary lovers love / (Whose soule is sense) cannot admit / Absence."

105.5. Gnädige Frau: "Her Ladyship," i.e., the Countess Zähdarm. Probably Mrs. Edward Strachey who promoted a relationship between Carlyle and Kitty Kirkpatrick. See *Reminiscences*, 284–85.

105.7. Accident: Chance, but chance within the larger framework of Necessity or Pre-established Harmony.

105.8. Waldschloss: "Forest-castle."

105.9. absolved: From the German *absolvieren*, "to complete," as to complete one's university studies.

105.10. *Relatio ex Actis*: Law reports, here official examinations.

105.14. El Dorado: A mythical kingdom or city in South America, a land of utopian dreams where everything is covered with gold.

105.18. Ammon's Temple: Ammon, the supreme Egyptian deity, often associated with Zeus or Jupiter, had an oracular shrine at Siwa in the Libyan desert. The oracle was consulted by Alexander the Great in 331 B.C.; the priests saluted him as "Son of Ammon," and may have privately assured him of his divine parentage and destiny.

105.37. *ahnungsvoll*: "Full of foreboding."

106.13–14. **Queen of Hearts**: Elizabeth (1596–1662), Queen of Bohemia, daughter of James I of England, known for her emotional warmth and agreeable manner.

106.30. **Sea . . . Moon**: Compare Richter's "Life of Quintus Fixlein," *German Romance* 2:331: "Man swelled under the everlasting Heaven, as the seas swell under the Sun and under the Moon." Carlyle's description of the idyllic circumstances of Teufelsdröckh's love for Blumine is adapted rather freely from Richter's last chapter, including most notably the metaphors of the Moon, the Aurora (e.g., at 109.19), and the Aeolian Harp (e.g., at 109.25).

107.20. **'Philistine'**: A myopic, vulgar, dull pedant; in literature one who places utility over creativity. Compare "State of German Literature" (1827), *Essays* 1:68, where Philistines are ridiculed as *Philistern*. *Philistriositäten* should be *Philistrositäten*. The allusion is to David's slaying of Goliath; see 1 Samuel 17:1–58.

107.22. **Socratic**: Socrates (469–399 B.C.) often used the ploy of ignorance to ask questions in order to get his opponents to contradict themselves in Plato's dialogues.

108.12–18. **To our Friend . . . not angrily withdrawn**: Taken nearly verbatim from "Wotton Reinfred," *Last Words*, 47.

108.13–14. **dew on thirsty grass**: Compare Proverbs 19:12: "The king's . . . favour *is* as dew upon the grass."

108.14–15. **It is good for us to be here**: Peter's words at the transfiguration of Jesus; see Matthew 17:4; Mark 9:5; Luke 9:33.

108.28. **Archimedes'-lever**: Archimedes (287–212 B.C.), Greek mathematician and philosopher, who to illustrate the principle of the lever told Hiero II, "Give me a place to stand, and I will move the world."

108.29. **Fantasy**: German Romantic term, found particularly in Richter and Novalis, to express the intuitive state which transcends the physical realm.

108.29–30. **Heaven-gate and Hell-gate**: Compare *Paradise Lost* 3.540–41, and 2.724–25, where Satan stands on the "lower stair /

That scal'd by steps of gold to Heav'n gate" and stares into the darkness of the world; and where Sin is described as the "Snakie Sorceress that sat / Fast by Hell Gate."

108.34. **eighteen pence a day**: Compare Boswell, *Life of Johnson*, 75, "He saw a man might live in a garret at eighteen-pence a week."

108.35. **Pyrrhus**: See 70.19 above and note.

109.6–7. **Disbelieving . . . in himself**: This sentence is taken verbatim from "Wotton Reinfred," *Last Words*, 48.

109.11–19. **dark eyes . . . Aurora . . . Orient**: The "dark eyes" are perhaps those of Jane Montagu in "Wotton Reinfred," *Last Words*, 49, although it seems certain that the person alluded to is Catherine Aurora Kirkpatrick, the daughter of a "Hindoo princess" (*Letters* 3:172) whose "soft brown eyes" Carlyle describes in the *Reminiscences*, 280.

109.24. **airs from Heaven**: *Hamlet* 1.4.41–44, where Hamlet addresses the Ghost: "Bring with thee airs from heaven, or blasts from hell, / . . . I will speak to thee."

109.25–26. **Memnon's Statue**: In Greek myth Memnon, King of Ethiopia, fought against the Greeks in the Trojan War and was killed by Achilles. The Egyptians raised a colossal statue to him, which was said to make an unusual sound at daybreak when Memnon greeted his mother, Eos (Aurora), Greek goddess of dawn. It was one of two colossal statues, both actually of Amenophis III, but near the Memnoneia, on the west bank of the Nile at Thebes. Damaged by an earthquake, it emitted a sound at dawn when warmed by the sun. Pausanias (1.42.3) is apparently the authority for, or the source of, the conceit that the sound was Memnon greeting his mother's light. It was a considerable tourist attraction in the ancient world, visited by Strabo (17.1.46) in 26/5 B.C., for example, and by the Emperor Hadrian in A.D. 130, until it was repaired, and thus silenced, by Septimius Severus (late 2nd c.). See A. Bataille, *Les Memnoneia* (1952) and A. and É. Bernand, *Les Inscriptions du Colosse de Memnon* (1960).

110.2. **cut asunder**: A biblical expression; for example, Psalms 129:4: "The Lord *is* righteous: he hath cut asunder the cords of the wicked."

110.3. Duenna Cousin: Perhaps the aunt of Margaret Gordon, one of the models for Blumine; compare *Reminiscences*, 239–40. It is the "ancient maiden aunt" in "Wotton Reinfred," *Last Words*, 50, who caused Jane Montagu to reject Wotton: she had high hopes for her niece and in "her meagre, hunger-bitten philosophy, Wotton's visits had from the first been but faintly approved of." Compare also "Life of Quintus Fixlein," *German Romance* 2:238–39, where Carlyle employs the unusual phrase "meagre hunger-bitten existence."

110.9. Gig: A carriage.

110.21. Montgolfier: Joseph Michael Montgolfier (1740–1810) and Jacques Etienne Montgolfier (1745–1799), French inventors and brothers, who flew the first hot-air balloon. It had a linen exterior and a paper interior, which in turn permits a play on the idea of the paper bags of manuscripts sent to the editor. Carlyle uses the same metaphor in *The French Revolution* 1:51.

110.35. One morning: This final paragraph follows closely both in language and tone that found in "Wotton Reinfred," *Last Words*, 50–52. It is also remarkably similar to the scene of Lotte's final rejection of Werther, in Goethe's *The Sorrows of Young Werther*, which led to Werther's suicide.

111.8–9. two souls . . . rushed into one: Compare "Life of Quintus Fixlein," *German Romance* 2:253, where the lovers' "two souls, like two tears, melted into one," and the "sky stood full of glittering dewdrops."

111.10. immortal by a kiss: Compare Christopher Marlowe, *Doctor Faustus* (1592?), 14.93–95, where Faust says, "Was this the face that launched a thousand ships, / And burnt the topless towers of Ilium? / Sweet Helen, make me immortal with a kiss."

111.11–13. Night . . . Abyss: The language of destitution is like that of Richter's vision of the dead Christ in *Siebenkäs*, 261–65, part of which was translated by Carlyle in "Jean Paul Friedrich Richter" (1827), *Essays* 2:155–58.

NOTES TO CHAPTER VI. SORROWS OF TEUFELSDRÖCKH

112.10. Bedlam: A corruption of Bethlem, or the Royal Hospital of St. Mary of Bethlehem in London, an asylum for the mentally ill.

112.11. Satanic Poetry: Emotive poetry written by poets such as Byron and Shelley. Compare Robert Southey, "Preface," *A Vision of Judgment* (1821), 793–94, who accused certain writers of the age, such as Byron, Shelley, and Hunt, as being "Men of diseased hearts and depraved imaginations" who "labour to make others as miserable as themselves by infecting them with a moral virus that eats into the soul! The school which they have set up may properly be called the Satanic School ... characterized by a Satanic spirit of pride and audacious impiety, which still betrays the wretched feeling of hopelessness wherewith it is allied." Byron answered with his famous rejoinder *The Vision of Judgment* (1822).

112.11. blow out his brains: An allusion to Werther's suicide in Goethe's *Sorrows of Young Werther*.

112.13. brow-beating (against walls): An allusion perhaps to the Wailing Wall in Jerusalem, revered by Jews as a place of pilgrimage and lamentation for the destruction of the Temple and national independence.

113.4. magic appliances has unlocked: An allusion to the shears with which the Baron cut Belinda's lock in Pope's "The Rape of the Lock," Canto 3.

113.5. genii: Compare "The History of the Fisherman" in *The Book of the Thousand Nights and a Night* 9:93–94, where a Genii who rebelled against the sovereignty of God escapes from a vase of yellow copper only to be returned there by the fisherman who outwits him. "Necessity is the spur to invention" is the moral of the tale.

113.14. Tophet: From Hebrew *topheth*, or altar; a valley in Hinnom often associated with Gehenna, or Hell. Compare Jeremiah 19:2–6 and Isaiah 30:33.

113.16. **Calenture**: Tropical fever.

113.38. **made like unto a wheel**: Compare Psalms 83:13, where God is enjoined to punish the Israelites: "O my God, make them like a wheel; as the stubble before the wind." Compare also Sterne's *Tristram Shandy*, Volume 7, Chapter 13, "'*Make them like unto a wheel*,' is a bitter sarcasm."

114.4–6. **Traveler . . . Town**: The spirit of this passage echoes Richter, "Life of Quintus Fixlein," *German Romance* 2:193–94.

115.1. **chasms . . . huge fragments**: Compare Coleridge's "Kubla Khan" (1816), lines 12, 21.

115.7. **Stygian Darkness**: Styx, in Greek myth, the river of darkness in the lower world that the souls of the dead had to cross.

115.11–12. **Whoso . . . no shadows**: A fragment from an unknown poet, quoted in Plutarch's "*Consolatio ad Apollonium*" ("A Letter of Condolence to Apollonius," *c.* A.D. 100), *Moralia* 106(d): "'.Aidhn d' '.ecwn bohqo`n ou' tre´ mw skia´ V" (With Hades' help shadows I do not fear). Compare also "Jean Paul Friedrich Richter" (1827), *Essays* 2:121: "'The man who fears not death,' says the Greek Poet, 'will start at no shadows.'"

115.33–34. **Nature . . . One**: The transcendent moment when one recognizes the organic unity of the universe, a point which is amplified in Book III, Chapter VII, "Organic Filaments" (180–86 below).

116.3. **communion**: The archetypal journey of the Wanderer (Teufelsdröckh) through Nature, as described in the preceding paragraphs, is part of the lore of Romanticism, manifested dramatically in the Wandering Jew motif (see note at 14.18–19 above). The choice of language and the drama of movement are vividly anticipated in Wordsworth's *The Excursion*, especially in Book 2 where the Narrator experiences the transcendent world of the Wanderer as they journey through the veil of life toward Peace. Compare also "Wotton Reinfred," *Last Words*, Chapter IV, where the scene and the language are similar.

116.6. barouche-and-four: A four-wheeled carriage with a collapsible top, with two seats inside facing each other, and a seat for the driver outside at the front, drawn by four horses.

116.8–9 *Du Himmel!*: "Good Heavens!"

116.12. *I remained alone . . . with the Night*: From Richter's "Life of Quintus Fixlein" (*German Romance* 2:331): "I remained alone behind him with the Night." Compare Rousseau's *Reveries of a Solitary Walker*, First Walk, 27: "So now I am alone in the world, with no brother, neighbour or friend, nor any company left me but my own."

116.17. endemical: "Of diseases: Habitually prevalent in a certain country, and due to permanent local causes" (*OED*).

116.18. View-hunting: A criticism of certain types of Romantic literature and art that describe scenery for its own sake without understanding its larger role in organic unity, as parodied by Carlyle in the preceding long 'quotation' from Teufelsdröckh (114.27–116.12). Compare "Characteristics" (1831), *Essays* 3:24: "Consider . . . this peculiarity of Modern Literature, the sin that has been named View-hunting . . . , when every puny whipster plucks out his pencil, and insists on painting you a scene." Carlyle saw Goethe's *Sorrows of Young Werther* as the symbol of such self-conscious literature. In "Goethe" (1828), *Essays* 1:218, "For *Werter . . .* gave birth to a race of Sentimentalists, who have raged and wailed in every part of the world. . . . Byron was our English Sentimentalist and Power-man; the strongest of his kind in Europe; the wildest, the gloomiest, and it may be hoped the last."

116.24. Jenner: Edward Jenner (1749–1843), an English physician, who discovered in 1796 that vaccination with cowpox could provide immunity from smallpox.

116.29. basilisk-glance: A mythical reptile; "ancient authors stated that . . . its breath, and even its look, was fatal" (*OED*).

117.6. **Hadjee**: Or *hadji*, a Moslem who has made the pilgrimage to Mecca. Probably a reference to John Lewis (Johann Ludwig) Burckhardt (1784–1817), also known as Ibrahim ibn 'Abd Allah, who was a Swiss traveler who explored all over the Ottoman world disguised as an Arab, sponsored by an English society for promoting African discovery. He visited Syria in 1809, in 1812 he discovered Petra as well as Abu Simbel, and in 1815 he made it into Mecca with the Hadj. Several reports of his travels were published posthumously beginning in 1819, apparently written in English and published first in London. These include: *Travels of M. Burckhardt in Egypt and Nubia*; *New voyages and travels* v. 2, no. 5; *Travels in Syria and the Holy Land*; *Travels in Arabia, comprehending an account of those territories in Hadjaz which the Mohammedans regard as sacred. By the late John Lewis Burckhardt*; and *Notes on the Bedouins and Wahabys, collected during his travels in the East, by the late John Lewis Burckhardt.*

117.9. **wishing-carpet**: Compare "Prince Ahmed and the Fairy Peri-Banu" in *The Book of the Thousand Nights and a Night* 16:419–87, where Prince Houssain purchases a flying carpet.

117.10. **Fortunatus' Hat**: A sixteenth-century tale of German origin with a number of adaptations which has Fortunatus receiving from the Sultan a wishing cap that will transport him anywhere. Carlyle connects this story to the Wandering Jew figure in "On History Again" (1833), *Essays* 3:168.

117.11. **that collection of Street-Advertisements**: Referred to above at 59.38. See note at 59.38–60.2.

117.31. **Sultan Mahmoud**: Mahmud II (1785–1839), Sultan of Turkey (1808–1839), who attempted to subdue Greece with the aid of an Egyptian fleet which was destroyed by the combined forces of the British, French, and Russians. The Russo-Turkish War in 1828–1829 led to the independence of Greece. In 1876, in opposition to British intervention, Carlyle spoke out against the "unspeakable Turk" and in favor of the Russians as the crisis renewed itself, saying "for 50 years back my close belief about the Russians has been that they are a good and even noble element in Europe." See "Mr. Carlyle on the Eastern Question," *Times*, November 2, 1876, p. 6.

118.4. **Loadstars**: Or lodestars, stars that are used for guidance, especially Polaris, the North Star.

118.6–7. **no rest for the sole of my foot**: Compare Genesis 8:9: "But the dove found no rest for the sole of her foot"; and Deuteronomy 28:65: "And among these nations shalt thou find no ease, neither shall the sole of thy foot have rest."

118.9–10. **fever-thirst . . . healing Fountain**: An allusion the story of the Samaritan woman and Jesus at Jacob's well; see John 4:13–14: "Whosoever drinketh of this water shall thirst again: But whosoever drinketh of the water that I shall give him shall never thirst." Compare also Revelation 21:6: "I will give unto him that is athirst of the fountain of the water of life freely."

118.11. **Saints' Wells**: Springs of water thought to have curative properties.

118.15. *his own Shadow*: Compare Goethe's epigram: "*Was lehr' ich dich von allen Dingen?— / Könntest mich lehren von meiner Schatte zu springen!*" (What shall I teach thee, the foremost thing? / Couldst teach me off my own shadow to spring!) Compare also *The Life of John Sterling* (1851), 130.

118.21. *Enchiridion of Epictetus*: Epictetus (c.50–c.138), a former Phrygian slave and influential Stoic philosopher in Rome, who in his *Encheiridion*, a "Manual" of maxims collected by his student Arrian, emphasized that true good is within one's self and cannot be found externally.

118.25. *The end . . . Thought*: Central to the message of *Sartor Resartus*, this quotation is loosely adapted from Aristotle, *Nicomachean Ethics*, 1.3.6: "[T]he end of this science [of ethics] is not knowledge but action." This became one of Carlyle's favorite quotations: compare *Wilhelm Meister* 1:386: "[D]oubt of any kind can be removed by nothing but activity"; "Wotton Reinfred," *Last Words*, 13: "'*The end of man is an action, not a thought,*' says Aristotle; the wisest thing he ever said"; and "Characteristics" (1831), *Essays* 3:25: "Man is sent hither not to question, but to work: 'the end of man,' it was long ago written, 'is an Action, not a Thought.' In a perfect state, all Thought were but the picture and inspiring symbol of Action."

118.28. Sophocles: Sophocles (496?–406 B.C.), Greek tragedian, who wrote in *Philoctetes* (409), 12, where the sailors pray to "the bountiful earth" for the return of Achilles' armor. Compare "Wotton Reinfred," *Last Words*, 169, "'[T]hou rugged all-supporting earth!'"

118.29. sparrow on the housetop: Compare Psalms 102:7: "I watch, and am as a sparrow alone upon the house top."

118.29. darling, man: Compare *Wilhelm Meister* 1:106, where "nature, not inclined to let her darling [Wilhelm] perish utterly, visited him with sickness, to make an outlet for him on the other side."

118.32. Amur: A river on the border between China and Russia.

118.33–34. Paris *Estrapades*: Paris riding schools, or the *Place de l'Estrapade* near the *Panthéon* in Paris.

118.34. Vienna *Malzleins*: Vienna "malthouses," or perhaps Matzlein, a poor district of Vienna. Compare Richter's "Schmelzle's Journey to Flætz," *German Romance* 2:142.

118.35. elemental liquid: I.e., water.

118.36. suicide: In a *Journal* entry, December 23, 1823, *Two Note Books*, 55–60, Carlyle records that he has been suffering "the pangs of Tophet almost daily, grown sicker and sicker, alienated by my misery certain of my friends, and worn out from my own mind a certain few remaining capabilities of enjoyment, reduced my world a *little* nearer the condition of a bare haggard desart, where peace and rest for me is [*sic*] none." He then discusses the possibility of suicide, but concludes there will be plenty of time to consider that when "I have *lost* the game, which I am as yet but losing. You observe Sir I have still a glimmering of hope. . . . I do not design to be a *suicide*: God in Heaven forbid!" It was during this period that Carlyle was suffering from recurring bouts of dyspepsia, a condition usually treated with laudanum (tincture of opium), which in turn could cause mood fluctuations.

119.7. **Infernal Chase**: An allusion to Actæon, a young hunter who inadvertently observed Artemis bathing. As punishment Actæon was turned into a stag and he was torn apart by his own hounds (Ovid, *Metamorphoses* 3.138ff). Compare Shelley, "Adonais," Stanza 31. Compare also Carlyle's reference to Boötes at 17.19 above.

119.9. **Cain**: In Genesis 4:12, God curses Cain: "A fugitive and a vagabond shalt thou be in the earth."

119.9. **Wandering Jew**: See note at 14.18-19 above.

119.18-20. **Truths** . . . **Lies**: Compare Rousseau's *Reveries of the Solitary Walker*, Fourth Walk, a chapter devoted to the subject of truth and lies.

119.25. *Sorrows of Lord George*: As in "Sorrows of George Gordon, Lord Byron." Compare *Manfred* 3.4.90, where Byron's hero retreats into his misanthropic Romanticism: "I'll die as I have lived—alone." In a *Journal* entry, December 23, 1831, Carlyle writes: "Byron we call 'a Dandy of Sorrows, and acquainted with grief.' That is a brief definition of him" (*Two Note Books*, 230).

NOTES TO CHAPTER VII. THE EVERLASTING NO

[title]. THE EVERLASTING NO: There is a difference between the philosophical nature of "The Everlasting No" and the transitory period that Teufelsdröckh actually experiences in "The Everlasting No." The former is a state of moral and ethical negation where the philosophy of opposites is denied, where life is defined in terms of negative absolutes, and where contradiction precludes confirmation. In "Goethe's Helena" (1828), *Essays* 1:157–58, Carlyle defines this state as the arena of Satan, the "genuine Son of Night. . . . The shrewd, all-informed intellect he has, is an attorney intellect; it can contradict, but it cannot affirm. . . . Thus does he go along, qualifying, confuting, despising; . . . so universal a denier, both in heart and head,—is undoubtedly a child of Darkness, an emissary of the primeval Nothing." On the other hand, it is clear from the language at the outset of this chapter that Teufelsdröckh is only a visitor in this arena of negation and that he will overcome it through Activity (intellectual defiance) and Hope (spiritual renewal). For a full discussion of the structural movement, hence philosophic meaning, begun in "The

Everlasting No" and realized in "The Everlasting Yea," see Tennyson's
"Sartor" Called "Resartus," 294–98. It is Tennyson's view that "The
Everlasting No" (negation) represents the "turning point" in
Teufelsdröckh's spiritual development, and it is at this point that
Teufelsdröckh enters into "Centre of Indifference" (defiance), which
is followed by the "climax" in "The Everlasting Yea" (realization).
Such a dramatic schema helps to explain the linear movement(s) of
Sartor Resartus, but it tends to contradict the book's cyclical pattern(s).
It is more likely that the triad is interdependent and constantly in
flux; that is, "Centre of Indifference" occurs toward the end of "The
Everlasting No" and continues into the beginning of "The Everlasting Yea," making it the center and the link of the triadic structure
rather than merely the second of three movements in a linear progression. These three interlinked stages in Teufelsdröckh's moral and
spiritual development closely parallel the three stages of Dante's spiritual journey in the *Divine Comedy: Inferno, Purgatorio,* and *Paradiso.*
Carlyle, in his lecture on Dante in *On Heroes,* states that "the Three
compartments [of the *Divine Comedy*] mutually support one another,
are indispensible to one another" (*On Heroes,* 82.21–22). This structural relationship, constructed of intersecting cycles, allows Carlyle to
make the point that "No" (negation) and "Yea" (realization) have no
meaning without "Centre" (defiance). Put in Hegelian terms, the
"thesis" and the "synthesis" have definition only within the framework of the "antithesis," a theoretic (and aesthetic) dependence that
is in constant regeneration. Put in magnetic terms, the negative and
the positive poles achieve interdependent harmony through the tension created by the ever-adjusting center between the two opposing
poles, a principle which Carlyle thought had cosmic application.
Compare, for example, "Remarks on Professor Hansteen's 'Inquiries
concerning the Magnetism of the Earth,'" *Edinburgh Philosophical
Journal* 3 (July 1820–January 1821): 124–38, 114–24. Such cyclical
interdependence also serves to complement the larger structure of the
work (Book I = Vesture; Book II = Body; Book III = Spirit), which
Tennyson sees and represents as three interlocking circles (*"Sartor"
Called "Resartus,"* 168–70).

120.9. **Eagle:** Compare Psalms 103:5, where God sustains humankind "*so that* thy youth is renewed like the eagle's."

120.11. **What Stoicism soever:** Like that of Epictetus; see note at
118.21 above.

121.5. **Place of Hope**: The notion, founded upon Romantic idealism, that the world is imbued with Hope is the cornerstone of Teufelsdröckh's emerging positive philosophy and one that became to Carlyle a virtual credo. Without Hope the other operatives of Carlylean philosophy, such as Duty and Work, are stripped of meaning. Hope is a primal sympathy, ordained by God and realized by man. It is intuitive, theological, and is what permits Carlyle to distance himself from the objectivist philosophy of Utilitarianism. In a *Journal* entry, May 4, 1832, Carlyle writes: "Let us be content; let us hope. *Der Mensch ist eigenlich auf Hoffnung gestellt* [Man is properly made up of hope]. This is the 'Place of Hope'" (*Two Note Books*, 270).

121.7. **golden orient**: I.e., sunrise.

121.16. **Tartarean black**: Of Tartarus, the inner-most darkness of Hell. In Greek myth it was the region where the Titans were confined and where punishment was inflicted upon the shades of the guilty.

121.18. **Profit-and-Loss Philosophy**: A part of Utilitarianism, what Carlyle came to call the "dismal science" of economics, which held among other things that man's behavior was finally reducible to his need for sustenance.

121.20–21. **Faith is properly the one thing needful**: Compare Luke 10:42, "But one thing is needful." In a *Journal* entry, January 16, 1827, Carlyle notes the inevitable contradiction between Faith and Empiricism and then writes, "To prove the existence of God as Paley has attempted to do (a Kantean would say) is like lighting a lantern to seek for the Sun: if you look *hard* by your lantern, you may even miss your search" (*Two Note Books*, 103). See also *On Heroes*, 28.12.

121.22. **endure the shame and the cross**: Compare Hebrews 12:2, "Jesus the author and finisher of *our* faith; who for the joy that was set before him endured the cross, despising the shame, and is set down at the right hand of the throne of God."

121.30–31. **absentee God**: Carlyle is repeating here his distrust of the thesis that God created the universe and then withdrew to let it run its course. This belief was widespread among deists who further argued that the course of nature was sufficient proof of the existence of God. These rationalists, often referred to as freethinkers, found formal religion superfluous and scorned the idea of supernatural revelation, namely miracles. Carlyle may be alluding to the English theologian William Paley, whose *Natural Theology; or, Evidences of the Existence and Attributes of the Deity* (1802) gained wide popularity and whose complete works—largely in rational defense of God's existence—were published in 1825. In "Diderot" (1833), *Essays* 3:233, Carlyle in speaking of Diderot's rationalist atheism repeats Goethe's contempt for such "Metaphysical hurly-burly," the "current hypothesis of the Universe being 'a Machine,' and then of an Architect, who constructed it, sitting as it were apart, and guiding it, and *seeing* it go,—may turn out an inanity and nonentity; not much longer tenable. . . . Time, ought at length to compose itself: that seeking for a God *there*, and not *here*; everywhere outwardly in physical Nature, and not inwardly in our own Soul, where alone He is to be found by us,—begins to get wearisome."

121.30. **first Sabbath**: The seventh day of creation, when God "rested from all his work"; see Genesis 2:2–3.

121.31. **Duty**: Like Hope, Duty gained popular expression during the Romantic period, and was founded upon the fusion of corporeal and spiritual responsibility. Carlyle sees Duty as an act of theological commitment rather than materialistic acquisition. Duty is innate and everlasting. It is the point of Action in the triad of Hope-Duty-Work. In "Boswell's Life of Johnson" (1832), *Essays* 3:110–11, Carlyle calls Duty the "highest Gospel, which forms the basis and worth of all other Gospels whatsoever. . . . Such knowledge of the *transcendental*, immeasurable character of Duty we call the basis of all Gospels, the essence of all Religion." In *On Heroes* (64.38–65.2), he speaks of "that grand spiritual Fact, and Beginning of Facts, . . . the Infinite Nature of Duty." Compare 145.19–20 below.

121.34. **Doctor Graham's Celestial-Bed**: James Graham (1745–1794), a quack doctor, gained a wide reputation for his medicinal bed which, when a patient lay on it, allegedly cured sterility. Sarcastically referred to in Johann August Musæus, "Melechsala," *German Romance* 1:200, where for "fifty guineas" one might have "the costly pleasure of resting a night in Doctor Graham's *Celestial Bed* at London."

121.35–36. **Paul of Tarsus . . . chief of sinners**: Saul of Tarsus, Saint Paul (d. A.D. 64–67?), who was converted to Christianity on the road to Damascus (Acts 9:3–6). See I Timothy 1:15, where Paul says that "Christ Jesus came into the world to save sinners; of whom I am chief."

121.37–38. **Nero of Rome . . . fiddling**: Nero Claudius Caesar (A.D. 37–68), emperor of Rome (54–68), who allegedly let Rome burn in A.D. 64 while he recited poetry accompanying himself on the lyre. Nero accused the Christians of starting the fire and began to persecute them.

122.1. **Logic-mill**: A variation of logic-chopper, although it is likely that Carlyle also had in mind James Mill, father of John Stuart Mill. The elder Mill, a disciple of Jeremy Bentham, was one of the leading exponents of Utilitarianism during the 1820s. Compare 52.13–15 above.

122.2. **Virtue . . . Pleasure**: An allusion to the Utilitarian Jeremy Bentham, who in his *Introduction to the Principles of Morals and Legislation* (1789) argued that the first moral principle of man is the greatest happiness for the greatest number. He identified happiness with pleasure, and developed a mathematical system to judge the value of pleasure and pain.

122.3. **Prometheus Vinctus**: A reference to Aeschylus, *Prometheus Bound* (c. 470 B.C.), where Prometheus is chained to a rock by the command of Zeus for stealing fire from the gods and giving it to humankind, or variously for teaching humans the useful arts and sciences. In spite of the torture, which includes a vulture eating daily the regenerating liver of Prometheus, the conflict between Prometheus (Pride) and Zeus (Power) continues until Zeus in a fit of anger condemns Prometheus to an abysmal dungeon within the earth. Compare also Goethe's poem "Prometheus" (1785) and Shelley's drama *Prometheus Unbound* (1820).

122.5–6. **victim not of suffering only, but of injustice**: An allusion to the trials and tribulations of Job. The subject of social injustice is expanded in *Past and Present*, Book I.

122.13. **sweet incense**: An expression used throughout the Old Testament; for example, Exodus 25:6: "Oil for the light, spices for anointing oil, and for sweet incense."

122.17–18. **Sibyl-cave . . . Echo**: An allusion to the legend of the Sibyl who let her leaves be blown in the wind; compare 58.38–59.2 above and note. Compare Virgil's *Aeneid* 6.98–100: "In such words the Cumean Sibyl chants from the shrine her dread enigmas and echoes from the cavern, wrapping truth in darkness."

122.20–21. **Pillar of Cloud . . . Pillar of Fire**: From Exodus 13:21–22: "And the Lord went before them by day in a pillar of a cloud, to lead them the way; and by night in a pillar of fire, to give them light; to go by day and night: He took not away the pillar of the cloud by day, nor the pillar of fire by night, *from* before the people." Compare also Exodus 14:24; Nehemiah 9:19; and 170.17 below.

122.24. *Siècle de Louis Quinze*: "Century of Louis XV" (1710–1774), King of France (1715–1774) during the so-called Age of Reason, of Rationalism, of Science, of the Enclyclopaedists. Compare Voltaire's *Histoire du siècle de Louis XV* (1770). In "Voltaire" (1829), *Essays* 1:465, Carlyle says that the age of Louis XV was "an age without nobleness, without high virtue or high manifestations of talent; an age of shallow clearness, of polish, self-conceit, scepticism and all forms of *Persiflage*"; in "Diderot" (1833), *Essays* 3:180, he sees it as a "torch-and-crowbar period, of quick rushing-down and conflagration, . . . the Social System having all fallen into rottenness, rain-holes and noisome decay." Yet from this social chaos "traces of new foundation, of new building-up, may now also, to the eye of Hope, disclose themselves."

122.31. **Unprofitable Servants**: Matthew 25:30: "And cast ye the unprofitable servant into outer darkness"; and Luke 17:10, where Jesus recounts the parable of "unprofitable servants" who seek reward for obedience rather than seeing it as "the duty to do."

122.33. **Servant of God**: Compare 1 Chronicles 6:49; 2 Chronicles 24:9; Nehemiah 10:29; Daniel 6:20; 9:11; Titus 1:1; James 1:1; 1 Peter 2:16; Revelation 7:3; 15:3. Most commonly an epithet of Moses, which strengthens Teufelsdröckh's association with the legend of Moses implicit throughout *Sartor Resartus*.

122.35. Love of Truth: Compare "Wotton Reinfred," *Last Words*, 43, where Wotton "abandoned law and hurried into the country, not to possess his soul in peace as he hoped, but in truth . . . to eat his own heart. His love of truth, he often passionately said, had ruined him; yet he would not relinquish the search to whatever abysses it might lead," which in turn caused him to wander in the "endless labyrinths of doubt" and in the "void darkness of denial."

122.36. bate no jot: Compare "*To Mr.* Cyriack Skinner *upon his Blindness*" (1655), a sonnet in which Milton says of his blindness, "Yet I argue not / Against heaven's hand or will, nor bate a jot / Of heart or hope; but still bear up and steer / Right onward."

122.37-38. Truth! . . . though the Heavens crush me: A version of the widely attributed Latin saying, *Fiat justicia et ruant coeli*, e.g., William Watson, *A Decacondon of Ten Quodliticall Questions Concerning Religion and State* (1602).

123.2-3. Handwriting on the wall: A reference to the story told in Daniel 5, where at King Belshazzar's feast "came forth fingers of a man's hand, and wrote over against the candlestick upon the plaster of the wall of the king's palace" (5:5). Daniel then interprets the message on the wall as a judgment on the king for failing to humble his heart or to glorify God. Compare 137.23 and 144.25 below.

123.8-9. without God in the world: Ephesians 2:12, where the Gentiles are "without Christ, being aliens . . . , having no hope, and without God in the world."

123.11. in my heart He was present: Compare Proverbs 7:3, where the son is reminded to keep the commandments: "Bind them upon thy fingers, write them upon the table of thine heart."

123.16-17. to be weak is the true misery: From *Paradise Lost*, 1.157-58, where Satan says, "Fall'n Cherube, to be weak is miserable."

123.19. wavering Capability . . . indubitable Performance: A restatement of one of the central themes of *Sartor Resartus*, the necessity to turn potential activity (Capability) into demonstrable work (Performance).

123.20–21. **inarticulate Self-consciousness dwells dimly in us**: An echo here of the Neo-Platonic belief that individuals carry with them a certain innate goodness, a divinity of soul, which Carlyle translates into his divine-labor precept. Compare, for example, Wordsworth, who in "Ode: Intimations of Immortality" asserts that we come "Not in entire forgetfulness, / And not in utter nakedness, / But trailing clouds of glory do we come / From God" (lines 62–65). The "inarticulate Self-consciousness" here finds parallel in Wordsworth's "primal sympathy" (line 185).

123.24. *Know thyself*: *Gnw'qi seauto'n*, inscribed over the portico of the temple at Delphi, a proverb variously attributed to Chilon (c. 6th century B.C.), one of the Seven Wise Men of Greece; and to Solon (639?–559? B.C.), an Athenian statesman and poet. Compare Rousseau's *Reveries of the Solitary Walker*, Fourth Walk, who uses the precept to examine the differences between Truth and Falsehood. Carlyle rejected the Romantic self-indulgence implied in this proverb. In "Characteristics" (1831), *Essays* 3:40–43, he deplores the rational metaphysics of the English and French and turns instead to the enlightened metaphysics of the Germans: "'Whatever thy hand findeth to do, do it with all thy might.'"

123.34. **Heavens seemed laid open**: Compare Ezekiel 1:1: "Now it came to pass . . . *that* the heavens were opened, and I saw visions of God"; Matthew 3:16: "And Jesus, when he was baptized, . . . the heavens were opened unto him, and he saw the Spirit of God"; and Mark 1:10.

124.24. **Golgotha**: See Matthew 27:33, where Jesus was taken to "a place called Golgotha, that is to say, a place of a skull" to be crucified; also Mark 15:22.

124.24. **Mill of Death**: An allusion to Novalis's "Die Natur," *Die Lehrlinge zu Sais* (*The Pupils at Sais*, 1802), in *Werke* 4:246: "*Auch bleibe die Natur, so weit man käme, immer eine fruchtbare Mühle des Todes*," which Carlyle translates in "Novalis" (1829), *Essays* 2:33: "For Nature too remains, so far as we have yet come, ever a frightful Machine of Death." In *Die Christenheit oder Europa* (*Christendom or Europe*, 1802), *Werke* 4:291: Novalis argues that a world without religion, logic without intuition, is "*einer ungeheuren Mühle*" (a colossal mill).

124.38. **Suicide**: See note at 118.36 above.

125.12-13. **shed no tear**: Compare 76.14 above.

125.13-14. **Faust's Deathsong**: Goethe's *Faust*, 1.1572-78:
Mephistopheles: And yet Death never is a wholly welcome guest.
Faust: Happy the victor on whose brow
Death binds the blood-flecked wreath of laurel!
And happy he who, after the mad dance,
is found by Death in love's embrace!
What ecstasy to feel that lofty spirit's might—
if only, then, my soul had left this body.
Compare also Carlyle's translation of Faust's response (lines 1583-
1606) to Mephistopheles' teasing jibe that Faust could not bring
himself to suicide, entitled "Faust's Curse" (1822), *Collected Poems*,
80. Faust defiantly curses the world's vanities, and concludes: "A
curse on hoping, on believing! / And patience more than all be
curs'd." In *Sartor Resartus* it is this defiance that keeps Teufelsdröckh
from suicide.

125.16-17. **Destiny . . . die . . . no Hope**: Compare Dante, *Inferno*,
Canto 3, lines 40-45, where The Opportunists (Know Thyself) are
condemned to wander forever:
"Master, what gnaws at them so hideously
their lamentation stuns the very air?"
"They have no hope of death," he answered me,
"and in their blind and unattaining state
their miserable lives have sunk so low
that they must envy every other fate."
Compare also *Paradise Lost*, 10.769-70, where Adam confronts his
fate: "Be it so, for I submit, his doom is fair, / That dust I am, and
shall to dust returne." See *On Heroes* 81.26-27 and 81.29-30.

125.17-18. **Fear . . . of Man or of Devil**: Compare *Faust*, line 369,
where Faust boasts that he "fear[s] neither hell nor its devils."

125.23. **Heavens above and the Earth beneath**: Exodus 20:4: "Thou
shalt not make unto thee any graven image . . . *of any thing* that *is* in
heaven above, or that *is* in the earth beneath."

125.28–29. *Rue Saint-Thomas de l'Enfer*: "The Street of St. Thomas of Hell," appropriately named after St. Thomas, the doubting disciple. The "Rue" is Leith Walk; the "French Capital," Edinburgh. In December of 1821, Carlyle moved to 3 Moray Street (now Spey Street), which he says is a "within a cat-spring" of Leith Walk (*Letters* 1:417). It is therefore unlikely, as James A. Froude claims, that the conversion described here took place in June of 1821 (*First Forty Years* 1:81). Indeed, since the reference to a "sultry Dogday" suggests late July or early August, it is unlikely that it took place in 1821 at all. More probably it was in the late summer of 1822, when Carlyle seemed particularly depressed, a date originally set by Alexander Carlyle, *Love Letters* 2:381. At the beginning of August of 1822, Carlyle wrote to Jane Welsh: "I am not happy at present; and for the best of all reasons, I stand very low in my own esteem. Something must be done, if I would not sink into a mere driveller. For the last three years I have lived as under an accursed spell—how wretched, how vainly so, I need not say" (*Letters* 2:155). Whatever the date, it is improbable that Carlyle meant to suggest a single date, a single moment, in which he passed from "The Everlasting No" through the "Centre of Indifference" to "The Everlasting Yea"—that is, an instant conversion similar to that of St. Paul. In fact, it is likely that Carlyle's own conversion was spread out over a number of years, and did not include a single mythic, transcendental moment as implied in *Sartor Resartus*. However, in his notes to Friedrich Althaus's biography, Carlyle does recall, albeit forty years later, the moment at Leith Walk: "Nothing in '*Sartor*' thereabouts is *fact* (symbolical *myth* all) except that of the '*incident* in the Rue St. Thomas de l'Enfer,'—which occurred quite literally to myself in Lieth [Leith] Walk, during those 3 weeks of total sleeplessness, in which almost my one solace was that of a daily bathe on the sands between Lieth and Portobello. Incident was as I went *down* (coming *up* I generally felt a little refreshed for the hour); I remember it well, & could go yet to about the place." A paragraph later Carlyle describes his "fight with the dismallest Lernean Hydra of problems, spiritual, temporal, eternal;—'eat my own heart'; but authentically take the Devil by the nose withal (see 'incident in Rue St Thomas'), and fling *him* behind me, 1820, '21, '22 " (*Two Reminiscences*, 49–51). Carlyle's memory of forty years is slightly imperfect, for there is ample evidence to suggest that the first of a series of crises began for him as early as 1817, when he renounced his intention to enter the ministry, started to abate during the Hoddam Hill period of 1825–26, and ended at Craigenputtoch about 1830, when he commenced the writing of *Sartor Resartus*.

125.30. Nebuchadnezzar's Furnace: A reference to Daniel 3, in which King Nebuchadnezzar orders Shadrach, Meschach, and Abednego cast into the "burning fiery furnace" for refusing to worship his golden image.

125.38–126.2. Child of Freedom . . . meet it and defy it: It seems certain that Carlyle has in mind Schiller's *Die Raüber* (*The Robbers*, 1781), where the Moor rejects suicide as an alternative to wretchedness. See Carlyle's translation in "Schiller" (1831), *Essays* 2:205–6: "[*Gazing on the pistol*] TIME and ETERNITY . . . *whither,—whither* wilt thou lead me? . . . Be what thou wilt, so I take *myself* along with me—!—Outward things are but the colouring of the man—I am my Heaven and my Hell. . . . Thou canst make me Nothing;—but *this* freedom canst Thou not take from me. [*He loads the Pistol. Suddenly he stops.*] And shall I for terror of a miserable lie—die?—Shall I give wretchedness the victory over me?—No, I will endure it [*he throws the Pistol away*]. Let misery blunt itself on my pride! I will go through with it." Compare also Byron's *Manfred* 3.4.120–21, 138–40, where near death Manfred defies the Spirits who claim his wretchedness: "I do defy—deny— / Spurn back, and scorn ye! . . . I have not been thy dupe, nor am thy prey— / But was my own destroyer, and will be / My own hereafter.—Back, ye baffled fiends!—" Compare also Satan's defiance in *Paradise Lost*, 1.249–64.

125.38–126.2. Tophet . . . like a stream of fire: Compare Isaiah 30:33: "For Tophet is ordained of old; yea, for the king it is prepared; he hath made *it* deep *and* large: the pile thereof *is* fire and much wood; the breath of the Lord, like a stream of brimstone, doth kindle it."

126.17. Baphometric Fire-baptism: The etymology of the word is very uncertain. Baphomet is a form of the name Mahomet used by medieval writers. It is also the name of an idol which the Knights Templars, a religious-chivalric order founded in Jerusalem by the Crusaders in the early twelfth century, were accused of worshipping. Here the word seems to be used to describe a sudden vision or an enlightened state characterized by palingenesis. Carlyle's immediate source was Zacharias Werner, *Die Söhne des Thals* (*The Sons of the Valley*, 1803–1804), a tragedy based in part on Werner's life of dissipation and conversion. See "Life and Writings of Werner" (1828), *Essays* 1:99–101, where Carlyle translates the allegorical Story of the Fallen Master, Baffometus, who sold the stones of the Lord's Temple for gold and silver, and who as a result was transformed by the Lord into a "colossal Devil's-head" whose "eyeballs rolled like fire-flames."

NOTES TO CHAPTER VIII. CENTRE OF INDIFFERENCE

[title]. CENTRE OF INDIFFERENCE: The "Centre of Indifference" is that nebulous state between denial ("The Everlasting No") and affirmation ("The Everlasting Yea"). Teufelsdröckh is now in a state of waiting; he has defied negation though Hope, but he has yet to discover the final path to spiritual Freedom through corporeal Work. He is now looking outward toward a state of action rather than within toward introspection. He observes but does not react. The "Centre of Indifference" is for him a type of socio-moral-political purgatory; he knows what he must do, but he does not know how to do it. The phrase is from Johann August Musæus, "Dumb Love" (*German Romance* 1:80), where Mother Brigitta, who had once tried to control Fate but who now has learned to live with it, is little solace to her daughter Meta who anxiously awaits the unstated intentions of her love Franz. Brigitta "had so simplified the plan of her life, that Fate could not perplex it any more." However, "Meta was still far from this philosophical centre of indifference; and hence this doctrine, consolation and encouragement affected her quite otherwise."

127.5–6. **fixed centre**: An allusion to the dispute between the Ptolemaic and Copernican theories as to whether the earth or the sun was the motionless center of the universe around which all celestial bodies revolve.

127.7. **thunder-riven**: I.e., thunder-split. Compare *Paradise Lost*, 1.599–604, where Satan, whose "face / Deep scars of Thunder had intrencht," observes his host after the fall. Two of Carlyle earliest publications are on the properties of thunder; see "On the Phenomenon of Thunder" and "On Thunder," *Dumfries and Galloway Courier* June 6, 1815, p. 3; June 20, 1815, p. 3, which provide elucidations to Benjamin Franklin's observations. Compare also 212.24 below.

127.13. **Satanic School**: Compare 112.11 and note above.

127.15. **Ernulphus-cursings**: Ernulf (1040–1124) was the Bishop of Rochester (1114–24), whose ecclesiastic curse is recorded in *Tristram Shandy*, Book 3, Chapters 10–12. In a letter to his brother John, dated July 12, 1831, Carlyle says within the context of *Sartor Resartus*: "I have a deep, irrevocable all-comprehending Ernulphus Curse to read upon—GIGMANITY [Respectability]; that is the Baal worship of this time" (*Letters* 5:303).

127.16. **gnashings of teeth**: For example, Matthew 8:12: "But the children of the kingdom shall be cast out into outer darkness: there shall be weeping and gnashing of teeth"; also Matthew 13:42, 50; 22:13; 24:51; 25:30; and Luke 13:28.

127.19–20. **method in their madness**: *Hamlet* 2.2.205–06: "Though this be madness, yet there is method in't."

127.20–22. **Spectre . . . spectre-fighting Man . . . Spectre-queller**: A parallel to Teufelsdröckh's movement: "The Everlasting No" . . . "Centre of Indifference" . . . "The Everlasting Yea." Also see Samuel T. Coleridge, "The Rime of the Ancient Mariner" (1798), lines 143–202, where the Ancient Mariner, whose thirst has driven him nearly mad, spots the "spectre-bark" which bears Death and Life-in-Death, the latter of whom through chance wins the life of the Ancient Mariner and condemns him to wander.

127.22. **Saints' Wells**: See 118.11 above and note.

128.3. **NOT-ME**: From Johann G. Fichte, *Die Bestimmung des Menschen* (*The Vocation of Man*, 1800), who rejected the noumenal realm of Kant for a dialectical view of the universe founded upon the indivisible ego of the *Ich* (I) and the *Nicht-Ich* (Not-I), each of which is united into knowing by the absolute ego, the moral will or God. In "Novalis" (1829), *Essays* 2:25, Carlyle interprets Fichte by asking whether a tree exists or not: "There is, in fact, says Fichte, no Tree there; but only a Manifestation of Power from something which is *not I*. The same is true of material Nature at large, of the whole visible Universe . . . ; all are Impressions produced on *me* by something *different from me*. This . . . may be the foundation of what Fichte means by his far-famed *Ich* and *Nicht-Ich* (I and Not-I)." Hence the corporeal (phenomenon) and the ethereal (noumenon) were no longer to be considered as separate entities, but rather were linked in impression and in progression to the Divine-Me. Carlyle may, in part, be interpreting Fichte through Novalis, *Philosophische Fragmente* (*Philosophical Fragments*), *Werke* 3:90, who says, "*Das Nicht-Ich ist das Symbol des Ich, und dient nur zum Selbstverständnis des Ich. So versteht man das Nicht-Ich umgefehrt nur, insofern es vom Ich repräsentiert wird, und dieses sien Symbol wird*" (The Not-I is the symbol of the I, and serves only for the self-understanding of the I. Thus one understands the Not-I only insofar as it is representative of the I and becomes a symbol of it).

128.17. **bellows-engines**: As in a bellows to intensify the fire; perhaps also windbags. Compare the scatological humor in Swift, *A Tale of a Tub*, 153, where the Priests formed a "circular Chain, with every Man a Pair of Bellows applied to his Neighbour's Breech, by which they blew up each other to the Shape and Size of a *Tun* . . . and disembogue for the Public Good, a plentiful Share of their Acquirements into their Disciples Chaps."

128.20. **aeriform**: I.e., gaseous, insubstantial.

128.29–30. **Cain and Tubalcain**: Cain, first born of Adam and Eve, "a tiller of the ground"; Tubalcain, son of Lamech and Zillah, who was "an instructor of every artificer in brass and iron" (Genesis 4:1, 22).

128.35. **Schönbrunn**: The royal palace in Vienna, built during the reigns of Charles VI and Maria Theresa. In 1809, Napoleon oversaw the so-called Peace of Schönbrunn, which temporarily divided parts of Austria.

128.35. **Downing Street**: In Westminster, London, since the eighteenth century the home of the Prime Minister.

128.36. **Palais Bourbon**: In Paris, the Chambers of the Deputies, the home of the French parliament.

129.2–3. mystic and miraculous: The language and the focus here anticipate the argument for transcendentalism presented in "Natural Supernaturalism" (187–95 below).

129.5. Armida's Palace: The home of the enchantress in Tasso's *Jerusalem Delivered* (1575), Canto 16.

129.12. true Book: A favorite expression of Carlyle's. In "The Hero as Man of Letters," *On Heroes* (1841), he says, "In Books lies the *soul* of the whole Past Time. . . . They are the chosen possession of men" (138.9–20); "The true University of these days is a Collection of Books" (140.12–13); ". . . is it not verily, at bottom, the highest act of man's faculty that produces a Book? It is the *Thought* of man; the true thaumaturgic virtue; by which man works all things whatsoever" (142.13–16). Carlyle repeats these sentiments in "Inaugural Address" (1866), *Essays* 4:453–54.

129.19. talismanic and thaumaturgic: Magical and miraculous. Carlyle might be drawing here from Novalis whose belief in the magical nature of man is the foundation of his mysticism. Compare "*Die magische Wissenschaft*" ("Magical Knowledge"), *Fragmente* I, passim.

129.25. outlast all marble and metal: Compare Horace, *Odes* 3.30.1: "This, my monument, stands, destined to outlast bronze." Also Shakespeare, Sonnet 55: "Not marble, nor the gilded monuments / Of princes, shall outlive this powerful rhyme."

129.29. Geeza . . . Sacchara: Or Ghizeh and Sakkara, burial places of the pharaohs.

129.32. Hebrew BIBLE . . . Luther's Version: The "Hebrew Bible" is the Old Testament. Luther translated the New Testament into German in 1521, and by 1531 had completed his translation of the entire Bible, which was published in 1534.

129.34. Wagram: A village on the Marchfeld near Vienna where Napoleon's "grand battery" of artillery destroyed the Austrians on July 5–6, 1809, which led to their surrender a week later. The Emperor of Austria was Francis I.

129.37. **Marchfeld**: A plain between the Danube (*Ger.*, Donau, as at 130.5 below) and Morava (*Ger.*, March) rivers, a strategic approach to Vienna, where in 1278 Ottokar II of Bohemia was defeated by Rudolf I of the House of Hapsburg at the Battle of Marchfeld (Stielfried; see 130.11–14 below), and where in 1809 Napoleon was defeated by Archduke Charles at Aspern, which in turn led to the battle at Wagram. Compare "Early German Literature" (1831), *Essays* 2:277–78n.

130.6. **Carinthian and Carpathian Heights**: Carinthia is a province in southern Austria; the Carpathian Mountains are a range in eastern Europe.

130.8. **Cockpit**: An enclosure for cockfighting.

130.12. **Casemates**: On a rampart, an armored compartment for artillery. "*Fortif.* A vaulted chamber built in the thickness of the ramparts of a fortress, with embrasures [cannon ports] for the defence of the place" (*OED*).

130.20. **Place-of-Sculls**: Golgotha; see 124.24 above and note.

130.25–26. **Life for the Living**: An echo of the concept of cyclical mutability, a complement to organicism, that Nature recovers from the abuses of man. Compare Shelley, "Ozymandias" (1818) and "Ode to the West Wind" (1820). Compare also Judges 14:8–9, where Samson eats honey from the "carcase of the lion" that he has killed. See 95.29 above and note.

130.29. **Dumdrudge**: A fictional village.

130.30. **Natural Enemies**: The French and English, a theme pursued in *The French Revolution* 3:187, where the French refer to the English as "*ennemis du genre humain*" (enemies of humankind).

130.36. **thirty stone avoirdupois**: Four hundred and twenty pounds; the satiric thrust here of grooming men to have them killed in battle is hauntingly similar to Swift's fattening of children to have them eaten in "A Modest Proposal" (1729).

130.38–131.1. south of Spain: A reference to the Peninsular War (1808–14), fought against Napoleon by the British under the command of Arthur Wellesley, later Duke of Wellington.

131.15–16. Kings . . . Greeks . . . pay the piper: A loose adaptation of Horace, *Epistles* 1.2, where the "passions of foolish kings and peoples" led to the Trojan War and thus, "Whatever folly the kings commit, the Achaeans pay the penalty" (lines 8, 14).

131.16–17. English Smollett: Referring to Tobias Smollett (1721–1771), *The Adventures of Ferdinand Count Fathom* (1753), 2:41.23–24, where it is proposed that the combatants "retire into a corner, and funk one another with brimstone, till one of us should give out. Accordingly we crammed half a dozen tobacco pipes with sulphur, and, setting foot to foot, began to smoke, and kept up a constant fire, until Macmorris dropped down; then I threw away my pipe. . . ."

131.29. Peripatetic: Walking from place to place, as an itinerant; also the traditional name for the philosophy of Aristotle who conducted discussions while walking around the Lyceum in Athens.

131.38. Constantinople: Once the capitol of the Byzantine and Ottoman Empires, the site of the library of Hagia Sophia.

131.38. Samarcand: Or Samarkand, one of the oldest cities in the world and the oldest in central Asia, which when conquered by Alexander the Great (329 B.C.) was the meeting point of Chinese and Western culture. In the fourteenth century under Tamerlane it reached its full splendor.

131.38–132.1. Chinese Mandarin: Those colleges in or near Beijing, where the official Mandarin dialect is spoken.

132.7. Hadrian: Hadrian (76–138), Roman emperor (117–138), who traveled extensively, including to Britain where he ordered Hadrian's Wall built (122). Compare *Wilhelm Meister* 2:414: "Think first, with blessings and reverence, of the imperial wanderer Hadrian, who on foot, at the head of his army, paced out the circle of the world which was subject to him"; and a letter to Leigh Hunt, dated April 18,

1834, where Carlyle writes that walking is to him as it was to Hadrian, "to mete out my world with steps of my own, and so take possession of it" (*Letters* 7:131).

132.7–8. **pair of Compasses**: I.e., his legs; compare Alexander Pope, *Memoirs of Martinus Scriblerus*, 1.2.101, where Cornelius declares that his son shall "perambulate this terraqueous Globe . . . ; the son of Cornelius shall make his own legs his Compasses; with those he shall measure Continents, Islands, Capes, Bays, Straights [*sic*] and Isthmus's."

132.10. **Vaucluse**: A city (also a province) in southeast France near Avignon, once the home of Petrarch.

132.12. **Tadmor**: Palmyra, a city in Syria, built by Solomon and destroyed by the Romans in A.D. 273. It is called Tadmor in II Chronicles 8:4, and Tamar in Ezekiel 47:19.

132.12. **Babylon**: A city in ancient Mesopotamia, destroyed c. 689 B.C. by the Assyrians. It was rebuilt and became legendary for its gardens and sensual living a century later under Nebuchadnezzar, who held the Hebrews in their Babylonian captivity.

132.13. **great Wall of China**: A wall that winds nearly 1,500 miles across northern China, built to protect against invasion from the north, it was begun during the Ch'in Dynasty (third century B.C.), and took its present form during the Ming Dynasty (1368–1688).

132.16. *ausgemergelt*: "Emaciated."

132.16. **Customhouse-officers**: In 1806, in an attempt to destroy British commerce, Napoleon issued the Berlin and Milan Decrees which ordered the seizure of all goods and vessels that touched ports in Great Britain.

132.17. **World well won . . . World well lost**: Compare Dryden's *All for Love; or, The World Well Lost* (1677), a retelling of the Antony and Cleopatra story.

132.18. **All kindreds**: Compare Revelation 13:7, where the beast is given power "over all kindreds, and tongues, and nations."

132.21. **birth-pangs of Democracy**: An allusion to the American and French Revolutions, or more immediately to the so-called Three Days War, July 27–29, 1830, a riot in Paris which led to the over-throw of the plutocratic Charles X and to the seating of the libertine Louis Philippe, whose fall in 1848 occasioned a biting attack by Carlyle on the excesses of "Sham-King" Philippe in the *Examiner* (March 4, 1848), 145–46. The rioting and unrest in France during the late 1820s was mirrored in England. Agricultural protests in the South and industrial agitation in the North reached their zenith during 1830–1831 and led to the passage of the Reform Bill of 1832.

132.23. **great Men**: Carlyle is formulating here his theory of heroes. Compare *On Heroes, Hero-Worship, and the Heroic in History* (1841), where he develops the German Romantic belief, particularly that of Novalis and Fichte, that all great men are heroes, ordained to rise and to lead in all vocations of life from government to the arts.

132.33. **Tree at Treisnitz**: Treisnitz, a village near Jena, where, as Carlyle reports in *The Life of Friedrich Schiller* (1825), 124, Goethe and Schiller often met "beneath the shade of a spreading tree."

132.36–37. **principle of caution, some time ago laid down**: See 117.32–36 above.

133.6. **Pope Pius**: Pius VII (1740–1823), pope (1800–1823) who worked to bring stability to the church during Napoleon's reign.

133.6. **Emperor Tarakwang**: Tao-kuang (1782–1850), emperor of China (1821–1850), sixth of the Ch'ing dynasty.

133.6–7. **White Water-roses**: The White Lotus Society, founded for philanthropic purposes, became a secret revolutionary sect. Their revolt in 1774 was not fully suppressed until 1804.

133.7. **Carbonari**: Literally "charcoal burners," in the early nine-teenth century a secret revolutionary society in Italy, France, and Spain, possibly with origins in Freemasonry, which advocated political freedom.

133.14–15. **Ideologists ... Ideopraxists ... *Idee***: Napoleon re-ferred to those who remained faithful to the principles of the French Revolution as ideologists. Ideopraxists are those who put theories into practice. "*Idee*" is possibly from Goethe's *Maximen and Reflexionen* (*Maxims and Reflections* [1870]), nos. 240–41: "Napoleon lived wholly in a great idea, but was unable to take conscious hold of it. . . . He considered the idea as a thing of the mind, that had . . . no reality, but still, on passing away, left a residuum—a *caput mortuum*—to which some reality could not be altogether refused."

133.17. *La carrière ouverte aux talens*: Literally, "Careers open to those with talent" ("*talens*" should properly be *talents*), the idiomatic sense is as given in the text. In *On Heroes*, 205.26, Carlyle attributes the expression to Napoleon and says of it: "[T]his actually is the truth, and even the whole truth; it includes whatever the French Revolution or any Revolution could mean." Compare also "Mirabeau" (1837), *Essays* 3:409–10; and "Sir Walter Scott" (1838), *Essays* 4:37. See Barry O'Meara, *Napoleon in Exile* 1:249, *On Heroes*, note 205.26n.

133.20. **Enthusiasts**: Compare Carlyle's *Journal*, March 1830: "Religion . . . *is* a social thing. Without a Church there can be little or no Religion. . . . The derivation of *Schwärmerey* indicates some notion of this in the Germans. To *schwärmen* (to be enthusiastic) means . . . to *swarm*, to crowd together, and excite one another," as religious zealots do (*Two Note Books*, 149).

133.29. **North Cape**: The cape on Mageröy Island off the north coast of Norway, the northernmost point in Europe.

134.12. **Hyperborean Bear**: Hyperboreans, in Greek myth people from the extreme North, hence anything from the far North: from *hyper*, "beyond," and *Boreas*, the north wind. Compare *Macbeth* 3.4.99, "Approach thou like the rugged Russian bear."

134.18. **train-oil**: Oil obtained from whale blubber. In the *Reminiscences*, 224, Carlyle recalls the "Russian sailors" who "returning from their sprees in Edinburgh at late hours, . . . used to climb the lampposts in Leith Walk, and drink out the train-oil."

134.23. **Horse-pistol**: A large pistol carried by the cavalry.

134.31–32. **Goliath . . . David**: See I Samuel 17:4–51. The allusion enables Carlyle to extend his metaphor that it is not the Body (savage

Animalism) but the Mind (inventive Spiritualism) that identifies the true hero.

134.34. Duels: Carlyle found duels fascinating; compare, for example, his "Two Hundred and Fifty Years Ago," *Leigh Hunt's Journal*, nos. 1, 3 (December, 7–21, 1850), 6–7, 37–38.

135.4. Hugo von Trimberg: German minnesinger, moralist, and bibliophile (1260–1309), discussed by Carlyle in "Early German Literature" (1831), *Essays* 2:287–95.

135.9. Legion: From Mark 5:9, where the "unclean spirit" possessing the Gadarene man answered Jesus' demand for his name, "My name is Legion: for we are many"; compare Luke 8:30, where the demon is called Legion "because many devils were entered into him."

135.21. *caput-mortuum*: Literally, "dead head" or skull; in alchemy the worthless residue left after distillation or sublimation.

135.28. Boy Alexander: Compare Samuel Butler, *Hudibras*, 1.3.89: "The whole world was not half so wide / To *Alexander*, when he cri'd / Because he had but one to subdue, / As was a paultrie narrow tub to / *Diogenes* . . . / Because h' had ne're another *Tub*."

135.30. when I gazed into these Stars: Compare "Wotton Reinfred," *Last Words*, 9: "He stood gazing out upon the starry night. . . . 'Do they not look down on us as if with pity from their serene spaces . . . like eyes glistening with heavenly tears over the poor perplexities of man?' . . . Thousands of human generations all as noisy as our own have been engulphed in the abyss of time, and there is no wreck of them seen any more; and Arcturus and Orion and the Pleiades are still shining in their courses, clear and young as when the shepherd first noted them on the plain of Shinar."

135.34. wreck: In the sense of remnants, wrack.

135.35. Arcturus and Orion and Sirius and the Pleiades: Arcturus: the brightest star in the constellation of Boötes, often referred to as the "Guardian of the Bear"; Orion: constellation in the Celestial Equator, in Greek myth the giant hunter, the pursuer of the Pleiades and lover of Eos; Sirius: star in the constellation Canis Major, the brightest star in the sky, also known as the "Dog-Star" because it rises and sets with the sun during the hot months of July–September; the Pleiades: an open star cluster in the constellation of Taurus, in Greek myth the seven daughters of Atlas. Compare Job 9:9, where God's strength "maketh Arcturus, Orion, and Pleiades, and the chambers of the south."

135.37. **Shinar**: A country on the lower courses of the Tigris and Euphrates Rivers. The reference is to Genesis 11:1–9, where the Tower of Babel was built on "a plain in the land of Shinar."

135.38. **Dog-cage**: "A wheel-like cage in which a dog was placed to turn the jack of a turnspit, and so roast the meat. The term here suggests the aimless and mechanical nature of the world when seen without the eyes of faith" (Harrold ed., *Sartor Resartus*, 182n).

136.3. **dissevered limb**: During the Hoddam Hill period Carlyle writes of his "Centre of Indifference" in his *Journal*, September 21, 1825, "At present I am but an *abgerissenes Glied*, a limb torn off from the family of Man, excluded from activity, with Pain for my companion, and Hope that comes to all rarely visiting me, and what is stranger rarely desired with vehemence!"; in March of 1830, he repeats, "I am a 'dismembered limb'; and feel it again too deeply. Was I ever other? Stand to it tightly, man; and do thy utmost. Thou hast little or no hold on the world; . . . but hast thou not still a hold on Thyself?" (*Two Note Books*, 65, 149). Compare *On Heroes* 94.18. The source of the expression is Horace, *Satires* 1.4.62: "*Invenias etiam disiecti membra poetae*" (even when he is dismembered you would find the limbs of a poet).

136.5. **hurl the burden**: Possibly an allusion to John Bunyan, *Pilgrim's Progress*, 38, where when the allegorical sinner Christian came before the Cross, "his burden loosed from his Shoulders, and fell from off his back."

136.7. CENTRE OF INDIFFERENCE: In magnetism, the "point of indifference" is that point midway between the Negative and Positive Poles of a magnet when there is neither attraction nor repulsion, also called the magnetic equator. However, Teufelsdröckh has never been in such a fixed state, but rather has always been on the move travelling between the poles of "The Everlasting No" and "The Everlasting Yea."

NOTES TO CHAPTER IX. THE EVERLASTING YEA

137.1. TEMPTATIONS in the Wilderness: Compare Matthew 4:1: "Then was Jesus led up of the spirit into the wilderness to be tempted of the devil"; also Mark 1:12–13 and Luke 4:1–2.

137.2. old Adam: See I Corinthians 15:21–22: "For since by man *came* death, by man *came* also the resurrection of the dead. For as in Adam all die, even so in Christ shall all be made alive"; also Ephesians 4:22 and Colossians 3:9.

137.3–5. Life . . . Necessity . . . Freedom . . . Force: Compare 75.31–76.16 above.

137.6–7. *Work thou in Welldoing:* See II Thessalonians 3:13, where the good workers are exhorted to "be not weary in well doing." Compare also Romans 2:7; Galatians 6:9; I Peter 2:15, 3:17, 4:19.

137.7. Promethean: See 103.25 and 122.3 and notes above.

137.8. leaves us no rest: Compare *Wilhelm Meister* 1:444, where Necessity (Life without) is the fountain from which Freedom (Creativity within) springs: "Life lies before us, as a huge quarry lies before an architect. . . . All things without us, nay, I may add, all things on us, are mere elements: but deep within us lies the creative force, which out of these can produce what they were meant to be; and which leaves us neither sleep nor rest, till in one way or another, without us or on us, that same have been produced."

137.17. carried of the spirit: Matthew 4:1: "Then was Jesus led up of the spirit into the wilderness to be tempted by the devil" for forty days and forty nights; also Luke 4:1–2.

137.23. divine hand-writing: Compare 123.2–3 and note above, also 144.25 below.

138.6. if not Victory, yet the consciousness of Battle: See 97.15 and note above.

138.8. enchanted forests: Compare Torquato Tasso, *Jerusalem Delivered* (1575), Cantos 13, 18.

138.10. Mountain: An allusion perhaps to Dante's *Purgatorio*. In *On Heroes* (1841), 81.39–82.16, Carlyle says, "It is a noble thing that *Purgatorio*, 'Mountain of Purification;'" where to those seeking repentance "Hope has now dawned; never-dying Hope, if in company still with heavy sorrow. The obscure sojourn of dæmons and reprobate is under foot" until "they shall have reached the top, which is Heaven's gate. . . ."

138.24. shadow-hunting and shadow-hunted: Compare 135.25 above.

138.30. *Apage, Satana*: From the Vulgate (Latin) translation of Matthew 4:8–10, where Jesus rejects Satan's offer of "all the kingdoms of the world, and the glory of them" with the remonstrance: "Get thee hence, Satan." Compare also Matthew 16:23; Mark 8:33; and Luke 4:8.

138.35. Holy-of-Holies: See 77.3 and note above; compare Book III, Chapter III, 161–66 below, where Carlyle develops this theory of silence. Also see *Wilhelm Meister* 2:76, "Words are good, but they are not the best. The best is not to be explained by words. The spirit in which we act is the highest matter." The same point is made in Keats's "Ode on a Grecian Urn" (1820), lines 10–14: "Heard melodies are sweet, but those unheard / Are sweeter; therefore, ye soft pipes, play on; / Not to the sensual ear, but, more endear'd, / Pipe to the spirit ditties of no tone."

138.38. omission . . . commission: An allusion to the Catholic doctrine of sins of omission (venial sins) and commission (cardinal sins).

139.5. Harmattan-wind: A dry, dusty wind that blows a red dust cloud from the Sahara onto the western coast of Africa. In "Goethe" (1828), *Essays* 1:216, Carlyle sees Voltaire as the source for the widespread loss of faith in Europe: "Whatever belonged to the finer nature of man had withered under the Harmattan breath of Doubt."

139.13-14. to die or to live is alike to me: A saying attributed to Thales (636?-546? B.C.), one of the Seven Wise Men of Greece, by Diogenes Laërtius (3rd century B.C.), *Lives of Eminent Philosophers*, 1.35-36: Thales "held there was no difference between life and death. 'Why then,' said one, 'do you not die?' 'Because,' said he, 'there is no difference.'"

139.17. a new Heaven and a new Earth: Isaiah 65:17: "For, behold, I create new heavens and a new earth"; also Isaiah 66:22 and Revelation 21:1: "And I saw a new heaven and a new earth: for the first heaven and the first earth were passed away."

139.18. Annihilation of Self: The concept that one finds fulfillment through the sacrifice of one's being. It is a part of pre-Christian myth and is integral to Christian doctrine. Compare Matthew 16:24-25: "Then said Jesus unto his disciples, If any *man* will come after me, let him deny himself. . . . For whosoever will save his life shall lose it"; Mark 8:34-35; Luke 9:23-24; and John 12:24-26. It was also a favorite concept of the English and German Romantics, but particularly William Blake, whose language is like Carlyle's. For example, in *Jerusalem* (1804-20), Blake asserts, "O Saviour pour upon me thy Spirit of meekness & love! / Annihilate the Selfhood in me" (623, lines 21-22), or the people "Be lost for ever & ever; then they shall rise from Self / By Self Annihilation into Jerusalem's Courts" (680, lines 45-46). It is also found in Novalis's *Fragmente*, translated by Carlyle in "Novalis" (1829), *Essays* 2:39: "'The true philosophical Act is annihilation of self (*Selbsttödtung*); this is the true real beginning of all Philosophy. . . . This Act alone corresponds to all the conditions and characteristics of transcendental conduct.'" Carlyle made little distinction between *Selbsttödtung* and *Entsagen*; to Carlyle, each meant the denial of self to pave the way for spiritual (and social) renewal. However, to Goethe, *Entsagen* meant the subordination of self to attain harmony, which in *Wilhelm Meister* 2:274-75, is inextricably linked to the sacrifice of Christ on the Cross.

140.3. mountain-seat: In the *Reminiscences*, 133-34, Carlyle recalls a similar experience: "Once I remember mounting early. . . . I rode by the shoulder of the Black Craig (Dunscore Hill), might see Dumfries with its cap of early kitchen-smoke, all shrunk to the size of one's hat, though there were 11,000 souls in it, far away to the right; descended then by Cairn, by the Clone of Maxwellton . . . looked down into the pellucid glassy pool rushing through its rock chasms, . . . one of the finest mornings, one of the pleasantest rides." This whole passage is also reminiscent of Wordsworth's epiphanic experiences as described in Book II of *The Excursion* and Book VI of *The Prelude* (1850) upon crossing the Alps.

140.19. **Schreckhorn**: Literally "Terror-Peak"; one of two peaks so named in the Bernese Alps in south-central Switzerland.

140.21. **mad witch's hair**: Compare Byron's *Manfred* 2.2.13–14, where the scene also is on a mountain top, and where the Witch of the Alps is described as a "Beautiful Spirit! with thy hair of light, / And dazzling eyes of glory."

140.24. **fermenting-vat**: See 17.27–28 above and note.

140.26. **Living Garment of God**: Compare 43.12 above.

140.31. **Nova Zembla**: Willem Barents, or Barentz (died 1597), a Dutch navigator, made three voyages in an attempt to find the Northeast Passage to Asia, and on the third attempt was caught in the winter ice near the north point of Novaya Zemlya, an archipelago in the Arctic Ocean off the northeast coast of Russia. He died on the way home in the spring. In Richter's "Life of Quintus Fixlein," *German Romance* 2:295, Fixlein, at "dusk, this fair *chiaroscuro* of the day," read the "winter history of four Russian sailors on Nova Zembla." Compare *Letters* 2:283; and a letter to his brother John, August 6, 1830, *Letters* 5:128–29, where Carlyle writes that "Literature is thickly strowed with cold Russian Nova Zemblas, where you shiver and despair in loneliness. . . ."

140.37. **an infinite Love, an infinite Pity**: Compare Coleridge's "The Rime of the Ancient Mariner," lines 284–85, where the mariner experiences a similar transformation while viewing the water-snakes: "A spring of love gushed from my heart, / And I blessed them unaware: / Sure my kind saint took pity on me, / And I blessed them unaware."

141.2–3. thy Bed of Rest is but a Grave: Compare Thomas Gray, "Elegy Written in a Country Church-Yard," line 36: "The paths of glory lead but to the grave."

141.4. wipe away all tears from thy eyes: Isaiah 25:8: "God will wipe away tears from off all faces"; and Revelation 7:17, 21:4: "God shall wipe away all tears from their eyes."

141.12. *Sanctuary of Sorrow*: See *Wilhelm Meister* 2:275, where the sanctuary is described as that place where one in full humility, after renunciation, can discover the full scope of the sacrifice of Christ, the "divine depth of Sorrow"; and "The Diamond Necklace" (1837), *Essays* 3:363: "[T]hink of HIM whom thou worshippest, the Crucified,—who also treading the wine-press *alone*, fronted sorrow still deeper; and triumphed over it, and made it holy; and built of it a 'Sanctuary of Sorrow,' for thee and all the wretched!" In a letter to his brother John, February 16, 1832, Carlyle urges, "First I would have you know this: '*Doubt* of any sort can only be removed by *Action*.' . . . in the words of Goethe: '*Do* the Duty which liest nearest'; DO it (not merely *pretend* to have done it); the next Duty will already have become clear to thee. There is great truth here; in fact it is my opinion that he who . . . has once seen into the *infinite* nature of Duty, has seen all that costs difficulty: the universe has then become a Temple for him, and the Divinity and all the divine things thereof will infallibly become revealed. To the same purpose is this saying: *die hohe Bedeutung des Entsagens* [the sublime meaning of renunciation]. Once understand *Entsagen* [renunciation], then life *eigentlich beginnt* [actually begins]. You may also meditate on these words: 'the divine depth of *Sorrow*'; 'the Sanctuary of Sorrow': to me they have been full of significance" (*Letters* 6:122–23).

141.30–31. Man's Unhappiness . . . comes of his Greatness: Compare *Reveries of a Solitary Walker*, Ninth Walk, 137, where Rousseau argues, in much the same way, that temporal happiness is beyond the grasp of man: "Happiness is a lasting state which does not seem to be made for man in this world." Compare also Richard Hooker, *Of the Laws of Ecclesiastical Polity* (1593), 1.11.202–03, who concludes that happiness is "the highest degree of all our perfection. Of such perfection capable we are not in this life."

142.2. **Hochheimer**: A Rhine wine from Hochheim near Mainz.

142.3. **Ophiuchus**: A large constellation in the equatorial region near Hercules and Scorpius. Compare *Paradise Lost* 2.709–10, where Satan is "like a Comet burn'd, / That fires the length of *Ophiucus* huge."

142.8–9. *Shadow of Ourselves*: See 118.15 above and note.

142.10. **whim we have of Happiness**: Compare "Wotton Reinfred," *Last Words*, 93, where Williams asks, "'What claim have I to be in raptures? None in the world, except that I have taken such a whim into my own wise head.'" To which Maurice responds, "'It is our vanity, . . . our boundless self-conceit.'"

142.25–27. *the Fraction of Life . . . lessening your Denominator*: In a *Journal* entry, March 1827, Carlyle notes, "The fraction of life will increase equally by *diminishing* the denominator as by *augmenting* the numerator" (*Two Note Books*, 105). Compare 97.33–35 above.

142.30. **Renunciation (***Entsagen***)**: Compare *Wilhelm Meister* 2:334, where Goethe calls attention to the "high meaning of Renunciation, by which alone the first real entrance into life is conceivable." Compare also "Novalis" (1829), *Essays* 2:15, where Carlyle points out that Novalis teaches the "great doctrine of *Entsagen*, of 'Renunciation,' by which alone, as a wise man well known [Goethe] . . . has observed, 'can the real entrance on Life be properly said to begin.'" In a *Journal* entry of September 1830, Carlyle writes about the complementary roles of "Activity and *Entsagen*"; in another entry, November 1831, he writes of "The *hohe Bedeutung des Entsagen* [deep significance of renunciation]" (*Two Note Books*, 166, 221). Carlyle used the word "Entsagen" on his wax seal. Compare also 142.30.

143.4. **Close thy *Byron;* open thy *Goethe***: A challenge to move from despair ("The Everlasting No") to hope ("The Everlasting Yea"), that is: "Close thy Pessimism; open thy Optimism." Such a linear reading would depend upon the dialectic of *Sartor Resartus*, and at the same time reflect Carlyle's personal disenchantment with Byron's misanthropic message, an extension he thought of the Age of Unbelief, the Age of Voltaire. However, such a reading implies closure which is contrary to the spirit of *Sartor Resartus*. It suggests a goal, a utilitarian end that one can reach through linear movement rather than cyclical regeneration. Such certitude compromises partially, if not wholly, Carlyle's vision that corporeal life is in constant tension between the magnetic negative and the magnetic positive; and that finally life is but a grain of sand in the wind of eternity. Thus it is much more likely that this famous expression is an urging rather than a mandate, that one should seek a direction that leads away from despair (Byron), but with the understanding that one must always engage despair in order to find hope (Goethe). It is therefore a matter of emphasis not of exclusion. That each state is mutually dependent upon the other, that the emblematic Goethe would have no meaning without the emblematic Byron, brings Carlyle much closer to the elasticity of Fichte whose own view of *Entsagen* was relative to the inextricable link between *Nicht-Ich* and *Ich*, a link that Novalis sees when he says, "One understands the *Ich* only in so far as it is represented by the *Nicht-Ich*." Carlyle then is able here to ameliorate his Calvinist heritage (denial) within the framework of his transcendental philosophy (affirmation). Thus, *Entsagen*, here a denial of Byron to affirm Goethe, should be seen as a continual philosophic bathing not a single apocalyptic baptism.

143.5. *Es leuchtet mir ein*: Compare *Wilhelm Meister* 2:265, where of the "threefold Reverence" Wilhelm exclaims, "'I see a glimpse of it!'"

143.6–7. HIGHER **than Love of Happiness**: An amplification of Kant's point that one does not seek personal happiness at the expense of moral duty. Compare Kant's *Critique of Practical Reason*, 357: "[I]t is not to be happy, but to maintain the integrity of my morality, that is my end and also my duty." In "Schiller" (1831), *Essays* 2:190–91, Carlyle addresses the "foolish controversy on this subject of Happiness" and concludes, "Strictly considered, this truth, that man has in him something higher than a Love of Pleasure, take Pleasure in what sense you will, has been the text of all true Teachers and Preachers, since the beginning of the world; and in one or another dialect, we may hope, will continue to be preached and taught till the world end." Compare William Hazlitt, who repudiates the Pleasure Principle of Utility advanced by Jeremy Bentham, saying that it has "reduced the theory and practice of human life to a *caput mortuum* of reason, and dull, plodding, technical calculation" (*The Spirit of the Age*, 1825, 174–75). It was Bentham's system of "mechanical morality," the reducing of life to an equation of pleasure, that Carlyle found abhorrent.

143.13. broken with manifold merciful Afflictions . . . become contrite: Compare Psalms 34:18–19: "The Lord *is* nigh unto them that are of a broken heart; and saveth such as be of a contrite spirit. Many *are* the afflictions of the righteous: but the Lord delivereth him out of them all"; and 51:17: "The sacrifices of God *are* a broken spirit: a broken and a contrite heart."

143.19. Love not Pleasure; love God: An adaptation of II Timothy 3:4, where the sinners are described as "lovers of pleasures more than lovers of God."

143.23. Zeno: Most likely Zeno of Citium (334?–262? B.C.), Greek philosopher and founder of Stoicism which focuses on transcending external reality, especially painful reality. Zeno argued that philosophy is divided into three units, logic, physics, and ethics, and that the first two serve only to complement the last. But also possibly a reference to Zeno of Elea (490?–430? B.C.), the Greek philosopher who argued that motion was an illusion, which was a challenge to the then popular notions of finite Time and Space.

143.25. a Greater than Zeno: I.e., Jesus.

143.26. *Worship of Sorrow*: Another reference to Goethe's belief that after one reaches aesthetic understanding one can approach the "Sanctuary of Sorrow." Here Carlyle argues that one can only experience Joy (Elation) by submitting to Sorrow (Abjection). Once again Carlyle is accommodating his Calvinist instincts to his transcendental beliefs. It is the message of *Sartor Resartus* that one begins to appreciate both religious and philosophic fulfillment (Joy) while one is experiencing "The Everlasting No" (Sorrow). This idea of sacrifice for attainment provides the framework for Carlyle's prophetic vision of Christian doctrine. See 141.12 above and note.

143.28. doleful creatures: See Isaiah 13:21, where the glory of Babylon is condemned to "wild beasts" and "doleful creatures."

143.37. **Baal-Priests**: Canaanite priests of Baal. See I Kings 18:18–29.

144.1. **Voltaire**: Pen name of François-Marie Arouet (1694–1778), French philosopher, historian, intellectual, and littérateur, who disputed the science of intuition and who helped formulate the science of reason. Carlyle's attitudes toward him are ambiguous. In his lengthy essay "Voltaire" (1829), *Essays* 1:396–468, Carlyle confesses that Voltaire produced a "greater difference in the existing figure of things" than any other thinker of the eighteenth century. Indeed, except for Luther, there is "no other man of a merely intellectual character, whose influence and reputation have become so entirely European as that of Voltaire" (400–01). Yet he "is no great Man, but only a great *Persifleur* [banterer]; a man for whom life, and all that pertains to it, has, at best, but a despicable meaning" (426). Carlyle viewed Voltaire's rationalist philosophy of skepticism as the primary cause of the Age of Unbelief. However, there is little doubt that Carlyle secretly admired Voltaire, and as he grudgingly admits at the end of his essay, "Voltaire and his disciples . . . 'worked together for good'" (467). Yet as a symbol for the New Age, Carlyle saw Goethe as superior. In his introduction to *Wilhelm Meister* 1:28, Carlyle asserts, "Goethe is all, or the best of all, that Voltaire was, and he is much that Voltaire did not dream of. . . . He is not a questioner and a despiser, but a teacher and a reverencer; not a destroyer, but a builder-up; not a wit only, but a wise man." In "Goethe" (1828), *Essays* 1:249–50, Carlyle distinguishes between the "popular man," Voltaire, who "shows us a truth which we can see without shifting our present intellectual position," and the "original man," Goethe, who "stands above us" and "wrench[es] us from our old fixtures, and elevate[s] us to a higher and clearer level. . . ."

144.19. **whether it is of God**: Compare John 7:17: "If any man will do his will, he shall know of the doctrine, whether it be of God, or *whether* I [Jesus] speak of myself."

144.22. **Plenary Inspiration**: Full Inspiration, a term used by theologians who argue that the authority of the Bible comes from the inspiration of God. In "Voltaire" (1829), *Essays* 1:457, Carlyle points to Voltaire's rejection of this doctrine and concludes thereby that Voltaire mistakenly rejects the essence of Christianity, the "'Worship of Sorrow.'"

144.33. gauge it to the bottom: To gauge is to measure the capacity or contents of a barrel with a gauging rod.

144.37–38. feast of shells: Compare Ossian (third century), "Finegal," spurious trans. James MacPherson, 2.311–12: "where is fallen Crugal? He lies forgot on earth; the hall of shells is silent. Sad is [Degrena] the spouse of Crugal. . . . Pale, empty, is thy Crugal now!"; also "Biography" (1832), *Essays* 3:47. In a *Journal* entry, March 1830, Carlyle in similar language despairs at the human struggle to secure Pleasure: "Alas! and the whole lot to be divided is such a beggarly account of empty boxes; truly a 'feast of shells,' not eggs, for the yokes have all been blown out of them! Not enough to fill half a stomach, and the whole human species famishing to be at them! Better we would say to our Brother: Take it, poor fellow, take that larger share, which I reckon mine, and which thou so wantest: take it with a blessing: would to Heaven I had but enough for thee!" (*Two Note Books*, 150).

145.5. Fichte's *Wissenschaftslehre*: "*Science of Knowledge*," published in 1805. Compare "Novalis" (1829), *Essays* 2:42, where Carlyle quotes Novalis on Fichte: "'The Catholic Religion is to a certain extent applied Christianity. Fichte's Philosophy too is perhaps applied Christianity.'"

145.7. Whole Duty of Man: Ecclesiastes 12:13: "Fear God, and keep his commandments: for this *is* the whole *duty* of man." Compare also Richard Allestree, *The Whole Duty of Man* (1659), a primer on the "Christian graces."

145.10–11. Conviction . . . is worthless till it convert itself into Conduct: Compare James 2:20: "But wilt thou know, O vain man, that faith without works is dead?"

145.14. centre to revolve round: Compare 127.5–6 above.

145.16. Doubt . . . Action: Compare *Wilhelm Meister* 1:386, where the clergyman says, "[D]oubt of any kind can be removed by nothing but activity." See 118.25 above and note.

145.17. gropes painfully in darkness: Compare Job 12:24–25, where God causes the "people of the earth" to "grope in the dark without light."

145.19–20. *Do the Duty which lies nearest thee*: Compare *Wilhelm Meister* 2:2, where Wilhelm concludes, "'[W]e should think of what is nearest.'" Compare also 121.31–32 above. Also, "Whatsoever thy hand findeth to do, do *it*," Ecclesiastes 9:10. See note at 146.15–16.

145.26. **Lothario in *Wilhelm Meister***: In *Wilhelm Meister* 2:11, Lothario says of his misplaced loyalties, "'In America, I fancied I might accomplish something. . . . How differently do matters now appear! How precious, how important seems the duty which is nearest me, whatever it may be!' To which Jarno responds, 'I recollect the letter which you sent me from the Western world, . . . it contained the words: I will return, and in my house, amid my fields, among my people, I will say: *Here or nowhere is America!*'"

145.31–32. **Impediment too is in thyself**: Compare *Wilhelm Meister* 1:83, where Wilhelm says, "'Unhappy Melina! not in thy condition, but in thyself lies the mean impediment over which thou canst not gain mastery.'"

146.2. **Creation . . . Light**: Compare Genesis 1:3: "And God said, Let there be light; and there was light." The remainder of this paragraph makes many references to the account of creation in Genesis 1:6–17.

146.2. **Till the eye have vision**: Compare Matthew 6:22–23: "The light of the body is the eye: if therefore thine eye be single, thy whole body shall be full of light. But if thine eye be evil, thy whole body shall be full of darkness."

146.5–6. **miraculous and God-announcing**: Compare "Novalis" (1829), *Essays* 2:42, where Carlyle translates from Novalis' *Die Christenheit oder Europa* (*Christendom or Europe*, 1826): "'Can Miracles work Conviction? Or is it not real Conviction, this highest function of our soul and personality, the only true God-announcing Miracle?'"

146.15–16. **Whatsoever thy hand findeth . . . thy whole might**: Ecclesiastes 9:10.

146.16–17. **Work . . . for the Night cometh**: John 9:4: "I must work the works of him that sent me, while it is day: the night cometh, when no man can work." Compare also *Two Note Books*, 189. Samuel

Johnson had the Greek for "the night cometh" engraved on his watch-dial for a time until he laid it aside as "ostentatious." See note to *On Heroes* 155.38.

NOTES TO CHAPTER X. PAUSE

147.5. **Conversion**: Compare 125.26–126.6 above. For Carlyle, the climax of this conversion took place at Hoddam Hill in 1825, which he describes in the *Reminiscences*, 320–21: "This year I found that I had conquered all my scepticisms, agonising doubtings, fearful wrestlings . . . ; and was emerging, free in spirit, into the eternal blue of ether,—where, blessed be Heaven, I have, for the spiritual part, ever since lived. . . . I understood well what the old Christian people meant by their 'Conversion,' by God's Infinite Mercy to them:—I had, in effect, gained an immense victory. . . . I then felt, and still feel, endlessly indebted to *Goethe* in the business; he, in his fashion, I perceived, had travelled the steep rocky road before me,—the first of the moderns."

147.8. *Ecce Homo*: "Behold the man!" in the Vulgate translation of John 19:5.

147.9. *Choice of Hercules*: When a young man, Hercules met two women, allegorical representations of Virtue and Vice, and chose Virtue. See Xenophon, *Memorabilia* 1:27–33, pp. 45–49, where the story is told in full; and Cicero, *De Officiis* 1:32, p. 121, where Xenophon's account is repeated briefly. Compare also "Wotton Reinfred," *Last Words*, 100–01, where the story is attributed to Prodicus, the sophist and contemporary of Socrates: "O Prodicus! Was thy 'Choice of Hercules' written to shame us . . . ?"

147.11–12. **Plato . . . chimera**: The reference is to Plato's myth of the cave in the *Republic*. See note at 42.4 above.

147.12. **Zinzendorfs**: Followers of Nikolaus Ludwig, Count von Zinzendorf (1700–1760), German clergyman from the Pietist tradition who reformed and reorganized the ancient Moravian Church which emphasized religious insight through emotive experience.

147.13. **Wesleys**: Followers of John Wesley (1703–1791), English evangelical preacher who founded Methodism and who was greatly influenced by the Moravian tradition. In 1738, while listening to a sermon on Luther, Wesley experienced a religious conversion which in turn led to his thesis that one can experience salvation through Christ alone.

147.13. **Pietists**: A movement from within the Lutheran church that gained prominence under Philipp Jakob Spener (1635–1705) who argued that the spirit of Christian living, the so-called religion of the heart, should be put above mere adherence to Christian doctrine and intellectual dogma.

147.15. **Work in Welldoing**: Compare 137.6–7 above and note.

147.18. **Tools?**: Compare 31.7–8 and note above. In the "State of German Literature" (1827), *Essays* 1:58, Carlyle attributes this idea that the pen is the tool of salvation to Fichte: "Literary Men are the appointed interpreters of this Divine Idea; a perpetual priesthood . . . standing forth . . . as the dispensers and living types of God's everlasting wisdom. . . ."

147.20. **Spider**: Compare Butler's *Hudibras* 3.1.1461–62: "Those Spider Saints, that hang by Threads / Spun out of th'Entrails of their Heads."

147.21. **spinning-jenny**: An early form of the spinning machine which had several spindles.

147.21. **warping-mill**: A machine that arranges thread or yarn to form a warp, the threads that run lengthwise in a fabric, as opposed to the woof, the threads running crosswise. Warp and woof together forming the underlying structure or foundation of a thing is a favorite metaphor of Carlyle's (for example, at 42.35 above).

147.21. **power-loom**: A loom powered by a water wheel or steam.

147.22. **Papin's-Digester**: Denis Papin (1647–1712?), French physicist and inventor, who in 1679 invented the steam digester, a vessel in which the boiling point of water is raised by an increase in steam pressure, a forerunner of the pressure cooker. Papin was also a pioneer in the development of the steam engine.

148.3. **Aaron's rod**: See Exodus 7:9–17, where Aaron turns his rod into a serpent before Pharaoh, and then uses the rod to turn the river into blood; 8:5–7, 16–17, where Aaron employs the rod to cause a plague of frogs and lice throughout Egypt; and Numbers 17:1–13, where the rod is caused to blossom and bear almonds.

148.8. **The WORD**: Compare John 1:1: "In the beginning was the Word, and the Word was with God, and the Word was God."

148.9. *Fiat*: Latin: "Let it be done!"

148.9–10. **Awake, arise**: Compare *Paradise Lost* 1.330, where Satan counsels the Fallen Angels: "Awake, arise, or be forever fall'n." Compare also Judges 5:12: "Awake, awake, Deborah: awake, awake, utter a song: arise."

148.13. **spend and be spent**: A phrase from II Corinthians 12:15: "And I will very gladly spend and be spent for you; though the more abundantly I love you, the less I be loved."

148.15–17. **Writings of mine . . . not altogether void . . . seedfield of Opinion**: Compare Isaiah 55:10–11, where the rain comes "that it may give seed to the sower, and bread to the eater: So shall my word be that goeth forth out of my mouth: it shall not return unto me void." Compare also 8.1–8 and note at 8.1–2 above.

148.16. **what am *I?***: Compare 41.34 above. Compare also *Reveries of a Solitary Walker*, 27, where Rousseau says: "So now I am alone in the world. . . . But I, detached . . . from the whole world, what am I?"

148.23. **grain of right mustard-seed**: Compare 30.17 above; also Matthew 13:31–32; Mark 4:30–32; and Luke 13:18–19.

148.28–29. **SOCIETY FOR THE CONSERVATION OF PROPERTY**: Compare Locke's *Two Treatises of Government* 2.9.368–69, where it is argued that man gives up the total freedom enjoyed in Nature and submits to the partial freedom found in Government to protect his Property: "The great and *chief end* therefore, of Men's uniting into Commonwealths, and putting themselves under Government, *is the Preservation of their Property*." Compare also "Signs of the Times" (1829),

Essays 2:66–67, where Carlyle points out that "Civil government . . . includes much also that is not mechanical, and cannot be treated mechanically," that "Good government is a good balancing" of the "Body-politic" (Mechanical) and the "Soul-politic" (Spiritual). Compare "Chartism" (1839), *Essays* 4:163, where Carlyle argues that "'for protecting *property*' one need only turn to the Eighth Commandment: 'I know no better definition of the rights of man. *Thou shalt not steal, thou shalt not be stolen from.*' And further that property is defined as 'a god-given *capability* to be and do. . . .'"

149.3–4. *Thou shalt not steal*: Exodus 20:15, the Eighth Commandment.

149.5. **Solon's and Lycurgus's Constitutions**: Solon (639?–559? B.C.), Athenian statesman and reformer, who oversaw important constitutional changes, among them the opening of the governmental assembly to all free people, canceling all mortgages and debts, introducing land reforms, and abolishing serfdom (debt-slavery) in Attica. Lycurgus (seventh century B.C.?), the traditional founder of the Spartan constitution.

149.6. **Justinian's Pan-dects**: Justinian I (483–565), ruler of the Byzantine Empire (527–565), was responsible for the codification of Roman law into fifty books, the Pandects, which gave unity to the judicial system.

149.6. **Code Napoléon**: A modification of Roman law and a codification of French law instituted by Napoleon in 1804, which divided civil law into personal status (e.g., marriage), property (e.g., easements), and acquisition of property (e.g., wills), clarifying property rights.

149.8. **Altar-fire**: Contrast 143.29 above.

149.8. **Gallows-ropes**: Compare 121.34 and 142.23–24 above.

149.16–17. *no Property in our very Bodies . . . Life-rent*: Compare a *Journal* entry, October 28, 1830: "I have no *Property* in anything whatsoever; except perhaps . . . in my own Free-will: of my Body I have only a life-rent; of all that is without my Skin only an accidental Possession—so long as I can keep it" (*Two Note Books*, 179).

149.18. Catchpoles: Sheriff's officers, especially those who arrest debtors.

150.2. labour of love: Compare Hebrews 6:10: "For God *is* not unrighteous to forget your work and labour of love."

150.6. wheel within wheel: Compare Ezekiel 1:16: "their appearance and their work *was* as it were a wheel in the middle of a wheel"; and 10:10: "they four had one likeness, as if a wheel had been in the midst of a wheel."

150.7. Mystification: Carlyle's statement here that much in the documents about Teufelsdröckh's life and philosophy may in fact be myth, myth which is recreated and compounded by editing, is intended perhaps to draw a parallel to the documents about Christ's life and philosophy. Just as Carlyle could not take literally the words of the editors of the New Testament, the reader is not expected to take literally the words of the editor(s) of *Sartor Resartus*. Words lead to emblems, emblems to myth, and myth to the "New Mythus"—transcendentalism. To Carlyle, the Bible was a book of inspiration whose value was in its metaphors, not in its dogma. He came increasingly to distrust literalists who claimed special privilege, and in consequence he came to distrust his own Calvinist heritage. His own trauma is mirrored in the theological crisis of Edward Irving, the celebrated Scottish divine and at one time Carlyle's best friend. Early in his career Irving was content to interpret the Bible symbolically, but as he became more famous as a preacher he came to read it as a literal revelation of God's word to him. In the end Irving was discredited and died in ruin. Carlyle could not forgive Irving for succumbing to what he called "Fashion." (See "Death of Edward Irving" [1835], *Essays* 3:319–23). *Sartor Resartus* is Carlyle's key to the values *and* the mythologies of Christianity. It reflects in large measure the break between the literalist Irving and the symbolist Carlyle. One can believe, insists Carlyle, without blindly accepting *all*, a point not lost on the young evangelicals like Ralph Waldo Emerson and George Eliot who used Carlyle's "new mythus" as the foundation for their own.

150.14. Nose-of-Wax: That is, pliable. Compare Philip Massinger, *The Unnatural Combat* (1624–25?), 5.2.133–35, p. 266, where vows, like religion, are a "nose of wax / To be turn'd every way"; and Robert Burton, *The Anatomy of Melancholy* (1621), "Democritus to the Reader," 62–63: "Laws altered, misconstrued, interpreted pro and con, as the judge is made by friends, bribed, or otherwise affected as a nose of wax."

150.27–28. Man is the spirit he worked in: Compare *Wilhelm Meister* 2:76: "The best is not to be explained by words. The spirit in which we act is the highest matter. Action can be understood and again represented by the spirit alone."

150.28–29. Facts are engraved Hierograms: Compare 28.5–6 above; also Schelling's *Die Methode des akademischen Studiums* (*The Method of Academic Studies*, 1803), 40: "Nature is like some very ancient author whose message is written in hieroglyphics on colossal pages."

150.32. Bungler (*Pfuscher*): In the "State of German Literature" (1827), *Essays* 1:59–60, Carlyle translates from Fichte's *Über das Wesen des Gelehrten* (*On the Nature of the Literary Man*, 1805): "Bungler (*Stümper*)" is a literary man who has "not arrived at knowledge of the Divine Idea."

150.33–34. Rousseau . . . Serpent-of-Eternity: Rousseau felt that natural inclination superseded divine will. In *Reveries of a Solitary Walker*, 96–97, he says, "As soon as my duty came into conflict with the promptings of my heart, the victory rarely went to the former. . . . I always found it impossible to take any positive action against my natural leanings. Whether the command comes from other people, duty or even necessity, when my heart is silent, my will remains deaf and I cannot obey. . . . I soon find it impossible to do anything that I cannot do with pleasure." The divinity of Carlyle's Serpent-of-Eternity (Infinite Duty) contradicts the temporal manifestation of Rousseau's Noble Savage (Passionate Instinct). The Serpent-of-Eternity is variously represented as a serpent with its tail in its mouth. Such representations in western culture are at least as old as the Gnostic tradition, where as a symbol of eternity in the Naasene sect (*naas* = snake) it was called the Ouroboros and was pictured as a serpent biting its own tail. Carlyle's more immediate sources might well have been Samuel Richardson, *Clarrisa* (1747–48), 450: "The principal device, neatly etched on a plate of white metal, is a crowned serpent, with its tail in its mouth, forming a ring, the emblem of eternity"; or Richter's *Siebenkäs* from which Carlyle translates a passage in "Jean Paul Friedrich Richter" (1827), *Essays* 2:158: "And as

I [Christ] fell down, and looked into the sparkling Universe, I saw upborne Rings of the Giant-Serpent, the Serpent of Eternity, which had coiled itself round the All of Worlds"; or Richter's "Life of Quintus Fixlein," *German Romance* 2:317: "So does the Serpent of Eternity wind round us and our joys, and crush, like the royal-snake, what it does not poison." In a letter to his brother John, May 18, 1831, Carlyle writes of the seal he is having made as a tribute for Goethe: "Instead of a plain *Ring* round the *Star*, we will have a *Serpent-of-Eternity* (its tail in its mouth, universally understood as the emblem of Eternity) . . ." (*Letters* 5:273).

151.11. **winged Psyche**: In the Latin novel *The Golden Ass* by Lucius Apuleius (second century), Books 4–6, *yuch'* (*psyche*, "breath, soul") is personified as a mortal princess in the allegorical romance of Cupid and Psyche. After many adventures, Cupid and Psyche are married by Jupiter, who confers immortality on Psyche. She is represented in art with the wings of her lover.

151.18–23. **Blumine Lover's-Leap . . . flows deep and still**: Compare 117.16–22 above.

151.32–33. **Hell-gate Bridge**: Compare 60.22 and 108.29–30 and notes above.

152.5. **Nature . . . Oneness**: Compare 115.33–34 and note above.

152.7. **Living Garment**: Compare 43.12 and 140.26 above.

152.7. **Loom of Time**: Compare 43.20 above.

152.12. **Defiance . . . Reverence**: In effect, "The Everlasting No" (Defiance) and "The Everlasting Yea" (Reverence).

152.13. **two mountain-summits**: Compare 139.20–140.28 above.

152.13–14. **rock-strata . . . built**: Compare Matthew 7:24–25: "I will liken him unto a wise man, which built his house upon a rock: . . . and it fell not; for it was founded upon a rock."

152.17–18. **To look through the Shows of things into Things themselves**: Echoes Kant's concept of the noumenon, or "*Ding an* *sich*" (thing in itself). Compare *On Heroes* 48.6, 69.31, 73.8, 105.32–36, 110.17, and 100.20–22, where the "Hero as Priest" is called a "believer in the divine truth of things; a *seer*, seeing through the shows of things; a worshipper . . . of the divine truth of things."

152.19. **Passivity**: Compare 76.2 above.

152.34. **Dream-Grottoes**: Compare 42.4 and note above.

Book III

Notes to Chapter I. Incident in Modern History

153.1. wonder-loving and wonder-seeking man: In general a mystic, more specifically a transcendentalist, variously described by Carlyle as "wonder-bringing," "wonder-hider," "wonder-hiding," and "wonder-working." Compare 129.25, 148.4, 190.38.

153.9. all earthly principalities: Compare Ephesians 6:12, where the people are exhorted to transcend the corporeal and to assume the Spirit of God: "For we wrestle not against flesh and blood, but against principalities, against powers, against the rulers of the darkness of this world, against spiritual wickedness in high *places.*"

153.10–11. Platonic Mysticism: The belief that the value of the Soul is found in the realm of the Idea. Compare 51.4.

153.12. Greek-fire: Sometimes called liquid fire, a flammable composition discovered in antiquity. The compound was adapted and used by the Byzantines against the Saracen fleets in the seventh and eighth centuries. Gibbon (*Decline and Fall* 6:94) describes the "terrible effect" of the Greek fire and concludes, "To these liquid combustibles the city and empire of Constantinople owed their deliverance."

153.15. Adamite: Compare 45.5.

153.16. Rousseau . . . Nudity: An allusion to Rousseau's theory of the Natural Man, or Noble Savage, who is innately good and therefore can be redeemed from the corruption assumed in his social state by adopting a more natural one. This theory of "*la nudité*" is basic to Rousseau's philosophic system and can be found throughout his works, but principally in his *Discours sur l'origine de l'inégalité parmi les hommes* (*Discourse on the Origin of the Inequality among Men,* 1754). Compare *On Heroes,* 160.4–9, where Carlyle admires Rousseau's "celebrations of Nature, even of savage life in Nature," and sees him as a "Prophet to his Time. . . . [T]here is in the inmost heart of poor Rousseau a spark of real heavenly fire."

153.22. Gold-country: Germany, or German intellectual philosophy. The travel metaphor here is also suggestive of the opening line and subsequent import of Keats's "On First Looking into Chapman's Homer" (1817): "Much have I travell'd in the realms of gold." Compare the "mine-shafts" metaphor at 22.17.

154.5. step by step . . . leap by leap: A reiteration of Carlyle's rejection of the Newtonian mathematical model of phenomena forming the whole (step by step) and the articulation of the Kantian science of wonder formed by the inexplicable convergence (leap by leap) of noumena. Carlyle may also be satirizing the rationalism of Leibniz whose system of logic led him to the conclusion in *Nouveaux essais sur l'entendement humain* (*New Essays on Human Understanding*, 1704), 50, that "nature makes no leaps."

154.9. old figure: The Hell-gate Bridge from *Paradise Lost*; compare 151.32–33.

154.12. *Perfectibility*: A doctrine of the Enlightenment; compare Rousseau, and 156.26.

154.14. Diet of Worms: The assembly (diet) at Worms, the city in south central West Germany where, on April 16, 1521, Martin Luther was summoned by Charles V to recant the heresies of the Reformation. After a day of meditation, Luther refused and the Reformation was assured. Carlyle recalls Luther's defiance of papal authority in "Luther's Psalm" (1831), *Essays* 2:161–62: Luther "who, alone in that assemblage, before all emperors and principalities and powers, spoke forth these final and forever memorable words: 'It is neither safe nor prudent to do aught against conscience. Here stand I, I cannot otherwise.'" Compare also *On Heroes*, 115.12–13, where Carlyle calls the assembly "the greatest scene in Modern European History."

154.15. Austerlitz: A town in Moravia where Napoleon won a decisive victory over the armies of Czar Alexander I of Russia and Emperor Francis II of Austria on December 2, 1805.

154.15. Waterloo: As Austerlitz represents the zenith of Napoleon's martial fortunes, Waterloo, in central Belgium, represents the nadir.

Napoleon was routed by the British under Wellington and the Prussians on June 18, 1815.

154.15. Peterloo: Named after Waterloo, a confrontation between a group of Lancashire workers and the governmental yeomanry at St. Peter's Field, Manchester, on August 16, 1819. Eleven laborers were killed and some 500 injured. The event became a symbol of the repressive practices of the government. In 1819, Shelley popularized what he called the "Massacre at Manchester" in his three poems "The Mask of Anarchy," "Song to the Men of England," and "England 1819." Carlyle drew ominous parallels between it and the French Revolution in *Past and Present*, Chapter III.

154.17–18. George Fox's . . . Suit of Leather: George Fox (1624–1691), a leathersmith by trade, underwent a mystical experience in 1646, which led him to the belief that Christianity was an inward religion where one experienced divine illumination though direct inspiration. Branded a heretic and continually persecuted, Fox travelled throughout Europe and Colonial America advancing his convictions. According to tradition, supported in his *Journal* (1694), 83, Fox travelled in "leathern breeches." In 1668, he founded the Society of Friends, often referred to as Quakers because of Fox's command that they quake or shake before God. Much of the philosophy of the Quakers can be found in this chapter, including the belief in the "indwelling spirit" which held that God was in every person and that any communion between the Soul and God took place without the benefit of clergy or rite. Carlyle no doubt had read Robert Barclay, *An Apology for the True Christian Divinity* (1676), an outline and a defense of the philosophies of the Society of Friends.

154.20. Divine Idea of the Universe: Compare "State of German Literature" (1827), *Essays* 1:58–59, where Carlyle attributes the idea to Fichte's *Über die Aesthetische Erziehung des Menschen* (*On the Aesthetic Education of Man*, 1800): "According to Fichte, there is a 'Divine Idea' pervading the visible Universe; which visible Universe is indeed but its symbol and sensible manifestation, having in itself no meaning, or even true existence independent of it." Fichte's dialectic idealism rejected the noumena of Kant in an attempt to unify what he saw as an indivisible universe overseen by the moral will or the absolute ego of God. Carlyle saw "Literary Men" as the "appointed interpreters of this Divine Idea," as the "dispensers and living types of God's everlasting wisdom." Compare also *On Heroes*, 135.4–10: "Fichte, in conformity with the Transcendental Philosophy, of which he was a distinguished teacher, declares first, That all things which we see or work with in this Earth . . . are as a kind of vesture or sensuous Appearance: that under all there lies, as the essence of them, what he calls the 'Divine Idea of the World;' this is the Reality which 'lies at the bottom of all Appearance.'"

154.30–31. **Cordwainery**: A place where leather is fashioned; from the Spanish *cordován* or *cordobín*, a type of fine leather from Córdoba.

154.31. **Thirdborough in his Hundred**: In medieval law, a constable, or judicial official, in a district that contains a hundred families or manors.

154.35. **Temple of Immensity**: The universe. Carlyle may be recalling the "boundless temple" of the universe described in the episode of the Dead Christ in Richter's *Siebenkäs*, 2.8.265. Compare Carlyle's translation of *Blumenstück* (Flower-Piece), the first chapter, in "Jean Paul Friedrich Richter" (1827), *Essays* 2:158.

155.1–2. **Watchers . . . holy mystery**: An allusion to Daniel's interpretation of Nebuchadnezzar's dream; see Daniel 4, especially 4:17: "This matter *is* by the decree of the watchers, and the demand by the word of the holy ones."

155.4. **Blind leaders of the blind**: Compare Matthew 15:14, where the Pharisees are so described.

155.6. **shovel-hats**: Hats worn by certain English clergy, turned up at the sides, which made the broad brim appear like a scoop. To Carlyle, shovel-hats were a symbol of religious hypocrisy.

155.9. **Patent Digester**: Compare Papin's-Digester, 147.22.

155.12. **Ætna**: Mount Etna, in eastern Sicily, is the highest active volcano in Europe.

155.18. **Vatican or Loretto-shrine**: Vatican, the official residence of the Pope in Rome and the seat of Roman Catholicism; Loretto, or Loreto, a town in central Italy to which, as legend recounts, the Holy

House of the Virgin Mary in Nazareth was transported by angels in 1294. Swift treats the legend sarcastically in *A Tale of a Tub*, 120–21.

155.21–22. Heaven is high, and Hell is deep: Compare Job 11:8: "*It is* as high as heaven; . . . deeper than hell."

155.35. Angelo: Michelangelo Buonarroti (1475–1564), renowned Italian painter, sculptor, architect, and poet, especially known for his painting in the Sistine Chapel and for his sculptures the *Pietà* in St. Peter's and *David* at Florence.

155.35. Rosa: Salvator Rosa (1615–1673), Italian baroque painter, etcher, and poet, especially known for his landscapes and his battle-pieces.

156.4. Mammon-god: Compare Matthew 6:24 and Luke 16:13: "Ye cannot serve God and mammon."

156.6–7. Vanity . . . Workhouse . . . Ragfair: Compare John Bunyan's *Pilgrim's Progress*, 88–92, where the pilgrims are beaten and shackled by the inhabitants of Vanity for causing a Hubbub at Vanity-Fair, partly because of their dress and partly because they only wished to "*buy the Truth*." Ragfair was an old-clothes market in London.

156.10. Poor . . . Gospel: Compare Matthew 11:5, where the miracles performed by Jesus are confirmed, and "the poor have the gospel preached to them."

156.11. D'Alembert: Jean Le Rond d'Alembert (1717–1783), French mathematician, philosopher, and co-editor for a time with Denis Diderot of the *Encyclopédie*. In "Diderot" (1833), *Essays* 3:206–07, Carlyle describes d'Alembert as a person "who in speech and conduct agrees best with our English notions: an independent, patient, prudent man; of great faculty, . . . famous in Mathematics; no less so . . . in the intellectual provinces of Literature."

156.11. Diogenes: See note at 6.15 above.

156.19. Cynic's Tub: Diogenes the Cynic is said to have lived in a tub which he carried about on his head.

156.30. **Sansculottism**: Compare 13.33 above and see note.

156.32. **Bœotian simplicity**: The inhabitants of Boeotia, a district in Ancient Greece, were said to be dull-witted because of the gases emitted from nearby marshes. From this belief came the expression, *Boeoticum ingenium* (Boeotian nature); compare Horace, *Epistles* 2.1.244, and Pope's *Dunciad* 3.50.

157.6–7. **Huddersfield . . . Paisley**: Huddersfield, a city in Yorkshire; Manchester, a city in Lancaster; Coventry, a city in Warwickshire; and Paisley, a city in Renfrewshire, Scotland—each famous for its textile industries.

157.7. **Fancy-Bazaar**: A bazaar in London.

157.8. **Day and Martin**: A London firm well known for its manufacture of boot blacking.

157.10–11. **Society . . . drowned marsh**: A possible allusion to the story of Noah and the Flood from Genesis 6–9. As Noah through obedience was the savior of the World, Teufelsdröckh through the New Mythus will be the savior of Society.

157.16. **Gibeonites**: The inhabitants of Gibeon who were condemned by Joshua to serve as manual laborers. See Joshua 9.

NOTES TO CHAPTER II. CHURCH-CLOTHES

158.1. *Church-Clothes*: The association of the church with clothes and clothes with the garment of God can be found throughout the New Testament. However, a more immediate source is Swift's *A Tale of a Tub*, 77–80, where the Universe is held to be a "large *Suit of Cloaths*, which *invests* every Thing," where the "Globe of Earth . . . [is] a very compleat and fashionable *Dress*," and where "Religion [is] a *Cloak*." Humankind, Swift continues, is "an Animal compounded of two *Dresses*, the *Natural* and the *Celestial Suit*, which were the Body and the Soul: That the Soul was the outward, and the Body the inward Cloathing, . . . separate these two, and you will find the Body to be only a senseless unsavory Carcass. By all which it is manifest, that the outward Dress must needs be the Soul." Compare *All's Well that Ends Well* 2.5.43–44: "[T]he soul of this man is his clothes."

158.5. Cassocks and Surplices: Cassock, see note at 34.4 above; surplice, a loose-fitting, broad-sleeved white vestment worn over the cassock.

158.9–10. Divine Idea of the World: Compare 154.20.

158.10–11. Body . . . WORD: The practical nature of the argument for transcendence is that it can be realized through physical manifestation (Work) and hence be translated into spiritual language (Word). The Body Politic and the Celestial Word meet in the church, where Matter becomes the Idea (compare 55.31–32). The church is the embodiment of the Divine Idea.

158.14. SOCIETY: In its ideal as well as its practical sense, Society is a gathering of churches, a type of congregation that is invested with the moral will of God. Society is the visible emblem of God, the revelation of the divinity of God. In "Characteristics" (1831), *Essays* 3:12–14, "Society is the standing wonder of our existence; a true region of the Supernatural. . . . Every Society, every Polity, has a spiritual principle; is the embodiment . . . of an Idea. . . ."

158.14–15. "two or three are gathered together": Matthew 18:20, where Jesus says, "For where two or three are gathered together in my name, there am I in the midst of them." Compare 174.26.

158.17. "cloven tongues of fire": Acts 2:3, where the Apostles, inspired by the Holy Ghost, are caused to speak in a diversity of tongues: "And there appeared unto them cloven tongues like as of fire, and it sat upon each of them." This event, known as Pentecost (in Britain, Whitsunday), is celebrated on the seventh Sunday after Easter. Carlyle was no doubt also thinking of Edward Irving's congregation in London which beginning in April of 1831 gained notoriety for the alleged "Gift of (Speaking in) Tongues." See *Letters* 5:299.

158.18. Church Militant: That is, the church on earth struggling against evil.

158.23. **Novalis**: Pseudonym of Friedrich von Hardenberg (1772–1801), German philosopher and poet who exerted a major influence upon the mystical vein of German Romanticism and thus upon English Romantics like Coleridge, and finally Carlyle, who saw Novalis as the embodiment of Mysticism, variously referred to as Idealism and Transcendentalism. In "Novalis" (1829), *Essays* 2:22, 27, Carlyle laments that contemplating the mysticism of Novalis is like "looking into darkness visible." Yet it is this very brand of mysticism, which emphasizes harmony, unity, and oneness, that makes Novalis so much a part of the fabric of *Sartor Resartus*. He is, says Carlyle, as if foreshadowing Teufelsdröckh, "the most ideal of all Idealists. For him the material Creation is but an Appearance, a typical shadow in which the Deity manifests himself to man." In a *Journal* entry, July 1829, Carlyle writes, "Novalis is an Anti-Mechanist; a deep man; the most perfect of modern spirit-seers" (*Two Note Books*, 140). In an entry for March 1830, he writes, "Religion, as Novalis hints, *is* a social thing. Without a Church there can be little or no Religion. The action of mind on mind is mystical, infinite; Religion, worship can hardly (perhaps not at all) support itself without this aid. The derivation of *Schwärmerey* indicates some notion of this in the Germans. To *schwärmen* (to be enthusiastic) means, says Coleridge, to *swarm*, to crowd together, and excite one another" (*Two Note Books*, 149). In "Characteristics" (1831), *Essays* 3:10–11, Carlyle uses the quotation from Novalis to present his argument for the "communion of soul with soul" which manifests itself in the "spiritual activities" of Society.

159.8. **virtue goes out of man into man**: Compare Mark 5:30, where the sick woman touches Jesus's clothes and is healed: Jesus knew immediately that "virtue had gone out of him"; also Luke 6:19: "And the whole multitude sought to touch him: for there went virtue out of him, and healed *them* all." Compare also 185.27.

159.21. **Chapterhouses**: A building in which the chapter of a cathedral or monastery assembles.

159.23. *getrosten Muthes*: "[Be] of good courage."

159.25–26. **Church-Clothes . . . Tissues Society**: Compare Francis Bacon, "Of Unity in Religion," *The Essays*, 19, "Religion [is] the chief band of human society."

160.11. **ghastly affectation of Life**: Compare *The French Revolution* 1:37, where the expression is applied to the social malaise preceding the insurrection.

160.21. **On the Palingenesia, or Newbirth of Society**: The subject of Book III, Chapter V.

NOTES TO CHAPTER III. SYMBOLS

161.3. **Symbols**: Compare 198.14: "[A]ll Symbols are properly Clothes." In "Goethe's Works" (1832), *Essays* 2:392–93, Carlyle through the voice of Teufelsdröckh anticipates the infinite nature of symbols: "Man is never . . . altogether a clothes-horse: under the clothes there is always a body and a soul" which has not been "created wholly by the Tailor." There is a "difference between God-creation and Tailor-creation. Great is the Tailor, but not the greatest." All of which relates to the title: *Sartor* (Tailor, body) *Resartus* (Retailored, soul).

161.5. **Fantasy being the organ of the Godlike**: Compare Schlegel's *Ideen* (1800), 242: "*Ganz recht, die Phantasie ist das Organ des Menschen für die Gottheit*" (That is right, fantasy is the organ of man to perceive the Godhead). Schlegel is quoting from Friedrich Schleiermacher, *Reden über die Religion* (*Talks on Religion*, 1799): "*Der Verstand . . . weiss nur vom Universum; die Phantasie herrsche, so habt ihr einen Gott*" (The mind can only know the universe; let fantasy take over, and you will have a god). Schleiermacher, a Pietist, argued for a monotheistic God, reached through intuition rather than dogma.

161.5–8. **Man . . . bodying forth**: Compare Schlegel, *Ideen*, 242: "*Frei ist der Mensch, wenn er Gott hervorbringt oder sichtbar macht, und dadurch wird er unsterblich*" (Man frees himself by bringing forth God or making him visible, and this is how he becomes immortal). This is also a restatement of the paradigm of Eternity found in Novalis. Compare 41.34–43.7.

161.10. **Paperbags . . . Printed Volume**: Compare 59.13.

161.15. SILENCE **and** SECRECY: An adaptation of the Romantic philosophy of the supremacy of silence popularized by Keats in "Ode on a Grecian Urn": "Heard melodies are sweet, but those unheard / Are sweeter" (lines 11–12); and by Goethe in *Wilhelm Meister* 2:76: "Words are good, but they are not the best. The best is not explained by words. The spirit in which we act is the highest matter. . . . Whoever works with symbols only, is a pedant, a hypocrite, or a bungler. . . . Their babbling detains the scholar. . . . The true scholar learns from the known to unfold the unknown." In "Characteristics" (1831), *Essays* 3:16, Carlyle translates Speech and Silence into a theory of Consciousness and Unconsciousness: "Unconsciousness is the sign of creation; Consciousness, at best, that of manufacture. So deep . . . is the significance of Mystery. Well might the Ancients make Silence a god; for it is the element of all godhood, infinitude, or transcendental greatness; at once the source and the ocean wherein all such begins and ends." See Carlyle's discussion of the concept of silence in *Letters* 12:106.

161.20. **William the Silent**: William I, Prince of Orange (1533–1584), whose discretion in diplomacy earned him the surname Silent.

162.3–4. **Speech is . . . the art of concealing Thought**: An apothegm that has been attributed to Talleyrand: "*La parole a été donnée à l'homme pour déguiser sa pensée*"; to Voltaire, *Le Chapon et la Poularde* (*The Castrated Rooster and the Spayed Hen*, 1763), *Oeuvres* 36:100: "*N'emploient les paroles que pour déguiser leurs pensées*"; to Oliver Goldsmith, *The Bee* (1759), *Miscellaneous Works*, 368: "[T]he true use of speech is not so much to express our wants, as to conceal them"; and to Edward Young, "Love of Fame," *Satire* 2 (1725–1728), *Poetical Works* 2:75: "Where nature's end of language is declin'd / And men talk only to conceal the mind."

162.7. **Speech is silvern, Silence is golden**: An expression often found in the carved woodwork at the entrance of Swiss houses. This passage is the first appearance of the proverb in English.

162.9–10. **Thought . . . Silence . . . Virtue . . . Secrecy**: In "Characteristics" (1831), *Essays* 3:4–8, Carlyle enlarges this argument: "Under [Nature's] works, chiefly her noblest work, Life, lies a basis of Darkness, which she benignantly conceals; in Life too, the roots and inward circulations which stretch down fearfully to the regions of Death and Night, shall not hint of their existence, and only the fair stem with its leaves and flowers, shone on by the fair sun, shall disclose itself, and joyfully grow"; he concludes, "[H]e who talks about Virtue in the abstract, begins to be suspect; . . . Virtue, when it can be philosophised of . . . is sickly and beginning to decline." The articulation of this belief in Silence can be found in a *Journal* entry of October 1830: "[T]here is a deep significance in SILENCE. Were a man forced for a length of time but to *hold his peace*, it were in most cases an incalculable benefit to his insight. Thought works in Silence; so does Virtue. . . . Speech is human, Silence is divine: yet also brutish and dead; therefore we must learn *both* arts, they are both difficult. Flower-roots *hidden* under soil; Bees working in Darkness, &c. The soul too in Silence.—Let not thy left hand know what thy right hand doeth. Indeed, Secrecy is the element of all Goodness; every Virtue, every Beauty is *mysterious*" (*Two Note Books*, 176–77).

162.10–11. **Let not thy right hand know what thy left hand doeth**: Compare Matthew 6:3–4: "But when thou doest alms, let not thy left hand know what thy right hand doeth: That thine alms may be in secret."

162.12. **those secrets known to all**: Compare *Wilhelm Meister* 2:260: "'Certain secrets, even if known to everyone, men find that they must still reverence by concealment and silence, for this works on modesty and good morals.'"

162.12–13. **Is not Shame . . . the soil of all Virtue**: Compare Aristotle's *Nicomachean Ethics*, 4.9.1: Shame (*aidos*) "cannot properly be described as a virtue, for it seems to be a feeling rather than a disposition"; and Milton's *The Reason of Church Government* (1641–42), 533: "It was thought of old in philosophy, that shame . . . was the greatest incitement to virtuous deeds, and the greatest dissuasion from unworthy attempts that might be."

162.14–16. **Virtue . . . Sun shine . . . root withers**: Compare Matthew 13:6: "And when the sun was up, they [seeds] were scorched; and because they had no root, they withered away"; also Mark 4:6.

162.23. **Tailor's Goose**: A pressing iron, so named from the shape of its handle.

162.32. **Fantasy:** Compare 108.29, and "Characteristics" (1831), *Essays* 3:4, where Nature (Fantasy) "'bod[ies] forth the Finite from the Infinite'" and "guide[s] man safe on his wondrous path. . . . "

163.5. **Messias of Nature:** *Messias* is the Greek form of the Hebrew *mashiah*, or Messiah, "the anointed one" (Greek *christos* = "anointed"). Here, however, *messias* refers to mankind, Carlyle following Novalis's belief that as Christ redeemed humanity, humanity would redeem nature. In "Novalis" (1829), *Essays* 2:39–40, Carlyle translates from Novalis's *Fragmente*: "'There is but one Temple in the World; and that is the Body of Man. . . . [H]e is the Messiah of Nature.'" In "Boswell's Life of Johnson" (1832), *Essays* 3:90, Carlyle asserts mankind's divinity, "'Man is heaven-born; not the thrall of Circumstances, of Necessity, but the victorious subduer thereof: behold how he can become the 'Announcer of himself and of his Freedom'; and is ever what the Thinker [Novalis] has named him, 'the Messias of Nature.'" In "Count Cagliostro" (1833), *Essays* 3:249, Carlyle speaks through his narrator Sauerteig, "[Man] too issued from Above; is mystical and supernatural (as thou namest it): this know thou of a truth."

163.13. **Motive-Millwrights:** Utilitarians. Compare 90.19, 121.18.

163.13-14. **Fantastic tricks:** Compare *Measure for Measure* 2.2.117–22: "[B]ut man, proud man, / Dress'd in a little brief authority, / Most ignorant of what he's most assur'd, / His glassy essence, like an angry ape / Plays such fantastic tricks before high heaven / As makes the angels weep."

163.15. **heap of Glass:** Compare Burton's *Anatomy of Melancholy*, 403, 410, and 421 where humanity is compared to "glass, a pitcher," to "glass, pitcher, feathers," and to "pots, glasses."

163.18-19. **Manger . . . long-eared enough:** An allusion to the story of Buridan's Ass, attributed to the French scholastic philosopher Jean Buridan (1300–1358), who as a nominalist believed that choice is determined by the greater good. According to the story, an ass is placed between two identical bales of hay, and starves because it cannot choose which bale to eat. Legend has it that Buridan, an advocate of free will, believed that the ass would have chosen one bale over the other for its own good. For a slightly altered version, compare Goethe's *Faust* 1:1830–33.

163.22. **Mechanism**: Carlyle's catchall for the evils of Utilitarianism for which he coined the philosophical term Descendentalism. "Signs of the Times" (1829), *Essays* 2:56–82, contains his most famous assault on the "Age of Mechanism," which in *Chartism* (1839), *Essays* 4:141, he calls the "huge demon." Carlyle is arguing here against Utilitarian motive (measurement) and for Transcendental emotion (mystery), what Novalis called the Mechanic (Consciousness) and the Dynamic (Unconsciousness). More specifically, Carlyle is responding to Utilitarian philosophers like Bentham who argued that morals and conduct depend on choosing what best pleases, and that it is a mere arithmetic question. Bentham especially delighted in the fact that moral questions, in his estimation, could be determined by measurement, reason, calculation. Such arguments were anathema to Carlyle.

163.33. **Marseillese Hymns**: The French national anthem was written by Claude Joseph Rouget de Lisle on April 24, 1792, and was originally called *Chant de guerre pour l'armée du Rhin*. It is now called *La Marseillaise* because it was sung by the battalion which marched from Marseilles to Paris in July of 1792. In *The French Revolution* 2:273–74, Carlyle calls it the "luckiest musical-composition ever promulgated. The sound of which will make the blood tingle in men's veins; and whole Armies and Assemblages will sing it, with eyes weeping and burning, with hearts defiant of Death, Despot, and Devil."

163.34. **Reigns of Terror**: The Reign of Terror (March 1793–July 1794), a phase of the French Revolution during which the Committee of Public Safety, led by Robespierre, was established to eliminate any counter-revolutionary movements; it did so by exacting strict and often fatal measures of punishment.

164.6–7. **Understanding is indeed thy window . . . Fantasy is thy eye**: Carlyle seems to be fusing here Kantian Understanding (*Verstand*) with Reason (*Vernunft*), for it is unlikely that he means for Understanding here to assume the negative associations of logic and mechanism. In "Characteristics" (1831), *Essays* 3:5–6, he addresses the positive aim of Understanding: "The healthy Understanding . . . is not the Logical, argumentative, but the Intuitive; for the end of Understanding is not to prove and find reasons, but to know and believe. Of logic, . . . there were much to be said and examined; one fact . . . has long been familiar: that the man of logic and the man of insight; the Reasoner and the Discoverer, or even the Knower, are quite separable, . . . quite separate characters." Fantasy (Imagination) is the emotive tool necessary for the intuitive processes to operate.

164.11. **groschen**: An Austrian coin, literally meaning "thick penny."

164.13. **Kaiser Joseph**: Joseph II (1741–1790), Emperor of the Holy Roman Empire (1765–1790) and of Germany (1780–1790), whose social reforms were never fully appreciated because upon assuming the throne he demanded that German be the language of the empire and refused to wear the Iron Crown of Hungary, causing internal dissension.

164.16. **lives, works, and has his being**: Compare Acts 17:28: "For in him we live, and move, and have our being." Compare also 4.15–16, 133.15, and 199.11–12.

164.23-24. **clouted Shoe . . . Peasants' War**: The clouted (patched) shoe was the symbol of the periodic revolts of the German peasants against the repression of the princes, all of which came to a climax in 1524–1526. A move to improve the social conditions and to effect religious reform, the Peasants' War finally ended in defeat for the German poor because they failed to gain the support of Luther who condemned the uprisings.

164.25. **Netherland *Gueux***: "*Ces gueux,*" or beggars; a term given to those who, in 1566, protested against the atrocities of the Spanish Inquisition under Philip II, and who adopted as symbols of protest the leather wallet and the wooden bowl.

164.35. **Divine Idea**: Compare 154.20.

165.26-27. **divinest Symbol . . . Jesus of Nazareth**: Carlyle is verging here on the contemporary heresy that Christ should be viewed as a symbol of God rather than God. For such heretical suggestions Edward Irving was excluded from the Church of Scotland. The issue of the divinity of Christ is treated ambiguously by Carlyle, but it seems clear that he was becoming increasingly heterodox, especially in his unwillingness, manifested by his silence, to accept the current dogma that all the events of the gospels were historically true.

165.34. wax old: Compare Psalms 102:26: "They shall perish, but thou shalt endure: yea, all of them shall wax old like a garment."

166.1. Runic Thor . . . Eddas: Runes, symbolic alphabet from the Old Norse; Thor, Norse god of thunder; Eddas, Old Norse poems and prose written in the eleventh and twelfth centuries. For a larger view of Norse poetry and prose, see "The Hero as Divinity," *On Heroes*, 3–36, and *The Early Kings of Norway* (1875).

166.2. Mumbo-Jumbo: According to the accounts of their explorations in Africa published by Francis Moore (*Travels into the inland parts of Africa*, 1738) and Mungo Park (*Travels in the interior districts of Africa*, 1799), Mumbo-Jumbo was an idol among the Mandingo people of the Niger region. Both authors describe it as a "bugbear" used by the men to keep their wives "in awe."

166.2. Pawaw: Or powwow, from the Narraganset *powwaw*: a shaman or medicine man, or the ritual or social gathering conducted by him.

166.5. Royal Sceptre: A staff held by the British monarch on ceremonial occasions as a symbol of authority.

166.6. Pyx: The vessel in which the host, or consecrated bread, for the Eucharist is reserved.

166.7. Ancient Pistol: A character referred to as "Aunchient Pistol" in *Henry V* 3.6.18ff. (*aunchient* or *ancient* being a corruption of *ensign*, i.e., the rank of ensign-bearer). In the same scene Bardolph is to be hanged for having "stol'n a pax," a plate stamped with the image of Christ, perhaps a mistake for "pyx," as Holinshed's *Chronicles* (1577) contains a report of an English soldier in Henry's army having stolen a pyx and been "strangled" in punishment. Ancient Pistol is also mentioned at 93.21–22.

166.13. Self-love: An allusion to Rousseau's *Reveries of a Solitary Walker*, 129–30, in which the distinction between *amour de soi* (love of self), a natural instinct, and *amour-propre* (self-love), a materialistic instinct, is made: "Whatever our situation, it is only self-love that can make us constantly unhappy."

166.14. Pontiff: Compare 60.24.

166.15–19. Poet . . . Legislator: The promethean language of renewal in this passage is distinctly like that of Shelley, whose purpose in *Prometheus Unbound* was to establish a modern emblem for poetry, and whose conclusion in *A Defence of Poetry* (1840) was that "Poets are the hierophants of an unapprehended inspiration. . . . Poets are the unacknowledged legislators of the world." Compare Tennyson, "The Poet" (1830) for similar language and meaning.

166.16. Prometheus-like: Compare 103.25.

166.21. English Coronation: The 1833 *Fraser's Magazine* serialization had a footnote here reading "*Now* last but one—ED." In the 1838 edition and thereafter, the note was changed to "That of George IV.—ED." (see Textual Apparatus). George IV (1762–1830) became king in 1820; the coronation was in July 1821. The actual "last" coronation before the writing of *Sartor Resartus* was that of William IV in 1830. There had been another coronation prior to the 1838 publication, that of Victoria in June 1837.

166.22–23. Champion of England: A tradition that dates from the reign of William the Conqueror in which a knight, suited in armor, is appointed to challenge anyone who disputes the monarch's right of succession. The Champion of George IV was Henry Dymoke (1801–1865). In *Past and Present*, 140–41, Carlyle describes the world of this tradition as a "huge Imposture, and bottomless Inanity, thatched over with bright cloth and other ingenious tissues."

166.27–28. Ragfair of a World: See 156.7, 174.6.

166.28–29. to halter, to tether: A possible echo of Coleridge's poem "To a Young Ass" (1794), line 4, in which an oppressed foal has, among other things, a "ragged coat."

NOTES TO CHAPTER IV. HELOTAGE

167.2–3. *Institute for the Repression of Population*: The title is a parody of Malthus's *An Essay on the Principle of Population*, a document which Carlyle associated, somewhat inaccurately, with Utilitarian dogma. See below at 167.12.

167.4–5. **Bag** *Pisces*: Compare 93.29.

167.12. **Malthus**: Thomas Robert Malthus (1766–1834), whose theory that the population was growing geometrically while the means of subsistence were growing arithmetically caused a sensation. In the 1798 edition of *An Essay on the Principle of Population*, Malthus argued that the population was being held relatively in check by war, famine, and disease; however, in the 1803 revised edition he admitted the need for "moral restraint." In fact, Malthus's argument had been anticipated by Adam Smith, who in *The Wealth of Nations* (1776), 81, says: "Every species of animals naturally multiplies in proportion to the means of their subsistence, and no species can ever multiply beyond it"; and by Swift whose satiric language on the causes and the cures for over-population in *A Modest Proposal* (1729) finds its way into the fabric of this chapter.

167.12–13. **zeal . . . eats him up**: Compare Psalms 69.9 and John 2:17: "For the zeal of thine house hath eaten me up."

167.15. **diluted forms of Madness**: Compare 152.11, and *Reminiscences*, 84, where Carlyle, writing in 1832, describes Charles Lamb as suffering from "'diluted insanity' (as I defined it)."

168.2. **Zähdarm palaces**: Compare 96.26–31.

168.3. **Futteral cottages**: Compare 64.24–30.

168.14. **Brother**: A possible reference to the Saint-Simon Brotherhood. Compare 174.35.

168.20–21. **toilest for . . . daily bread**: Compare Genesis 3:19: "In the sweat of thy brow shalt thou eat bread."

168.23–24. Bread of Life: Compare John 6:35: "And Jesus said unto them, I am the bread of life: he that cometh to me shall never hunger."

168.28–31. Thinker . . . Immortality: In "Novalis" (1829), *Essays* 2:39, Carlyle translates from Novalis's *Fragmente*: "'Philosophy can bake no bread; but she can procure for us God, Freedom, and Immortality.'"

168.32. chaff and dust: Compare Psalms 1:4: "The ungodly *are* . . . like the chaff which the wind driveth away."

168.33. wind blow whither it listeth: Compare John 3:8: "The wind bloweth where it listeth, and thou hearest the sound thereof, but canst not tell whence it cometh, and whither it goeth."

168.37. Peasant Saint: Carlyle may have in mind here his father, James, who died January 24, 1832. Compare *Reminiscences*, 6, 10–11: "I call a man remarkable, who becomes a true Workman in this vineyard of the Highest. . . . I have a sacred pride in my Peasant Father, and would not exchange him even now for any King known to me." In a *Journal* entry, early in 1829 (*Two Note Books*, 138), Carlyle admires Luther's declaration, "Ich bin eines Bauern Sohn" (I am a peasant's son). The implication that Jesus also was a "peasant saint" is further evidence of Carlyle's apparent rejection of the divinity of Christ.

169.2. light shining in great darkness: Compare John 1:5: "And the light shineth in darkness."

169.7. heavy-laden and weary . . . Heavens send Sleep: Compare Matthew 11:28: "Come unto me, all *ye* that labour and are heavy-laden, and I will give you rest."

169.8. smoky cribs: Compare *II Henry IV* 3.1.5–12: "O gentle sleep! / Nature's soft nurse, how have I frighted thee, / That thou no more wilt weigh my eyelids down, / And steep my senses in forgetfulness? / Why rather, sleep, liest thou in smoky cribs, / . . . / Than in the perfum'd chambers of the great . . . ?"

169.10. lamp of his soul should go out: Compare I Samuel 3:3: "And ere the lamp of God went out in the temple of the Lord."

169.13–14. Body . . . Soul . . . annihilated: Compare 139.18.

169.15. Breath of God: Compare Genesis 2:7: "And the Lord God formed man *of* the dust of the ground, and breathed into his nostrils the breath of life."

169.20. Universe of Nescience: Ignorance, associated with the Science of Computation and opposite of the Science of Wonder. Compare 52.11–24.

169.22–23. Spartans . . . Helots: The Spartans enslaved the Helots and forced them to work in the fields. For an account of the Spartans' indiscriminate cruelty, including hunting the Helots like animals, see Plutarch's *Lives*, "Lycurgus," Section 28.

169.28. able-bodied Paupers: Carlyle is reflecting here the debate current in Parliament on how best to abate pauperism. There was widespread belief that pauperism was, in part at least, the result of a generous home-relief system that in turn created sloth. The so-called New Poor-Law of 1834 was to address this issue by mandating that any assistance must be below that which could be earned by an "able-bodied" laborer. Carlyle's sarcastic solution here to eat the poor instead of maltreating them in workhouses is of course founded upon Swift's similar solution (control the population by harvesting and eating babies) in *A Modest Proposal*. Carlyle is also under the influence of Saint-Simon, especially *Le Nouveau Christianisme* (The New Christianity) which he translated in December of 1830. The doctrine of Saint-Simon was particularly attractive, arguing that society should adopt the ethics of Christianity and make the condition of the poor a priority. See note at 174.35 below.

169.37. Friedrichs d'or: Compare 65.24.

170.7–21. True, thou Gold-Hofrath . . . : This last paragraph is quoted nearly verbatim in the last paragraph of *Chartism* (1839), *Essays* 4:204.

170.10–11. Pampas and Savannas: Nearly treeless grasslands or plains, the former largely in Argentina and Uruguay, the latter in tropical and subtropical Africa.

170.11. Carthage: An ancient city-state on the northern coast of Africa, near modern Tunis, which controlled the western Mediterranean until defeated by Rome in the second century B.C.

170.12. Altaic chain: The Altai mountains form the border between southwestern Mongolia and northeastern Sinkiang province of China.

170.13. Crim Tartary: Compare 85.13.

170.13. Curragh of Kildare: The Curragh is a plain in central County Kildare, Ireland, famous for its racecourse.

170.15. Hengsts: Compare 17.11.

170.16. Alarics: Alaric (370?–410), king of the Visigoths, who sacked Rome in 410.

170.17. Fire-pillars: See note at 122.20–21 above. Carlyle is here advocating emigration as a possible solution to social stagnation. In "Characteristics" (1831), *Essays* 3:39, he argues, "Must the indomitable millions . . . lie cooped-up in this Western Nook, choking one another, as in a Blackhole of Calcutta, while a whole fertile untenanted Earth, desolate for want of a ploughshare, cries: Come and till me, come and reap me?" At the writing of *Sartor Resartus* Carlyle was considering emigration himself, finding New Zealand particularly attractive. See K. J. Fielding, "Carlyle Among the Cannibals," who quotes from Carlyle's unpublished review of August Earle's *Narrative of a Residence in New Zealand* (London, 1832).

170.18. superfluous masses . . . living Valour: Compare Byron, *Childe Harold's Pilgrimage* (1816), Canto 3, Stanza 27, where the soldiers at the Battle of Waterloo are addressed as "this fiery mass / Of living valour."

170.20–21. Preserving their Game: Compare 73.4 and see note.

NOTES TO CHAPTER V. THE PHŒNIX

title. THE PHŒNIX: A symbol of regeneration. In Indo-European myth the phoenix is a fabulous bird that every five hundred years (some legends say one thousand years) flies from paradise to a desert where it lights a fire with its wings, self-immolates, and then is reborn from its own ashes, only to begin again the ritual cycle of Life, Death, and Resurrection. The story, in various forms, can be found throughout western philosophy and literature, and is especially adaptable to resurrection themes in religious iconography.

171.4–5. **Society**: Carlyle viewed Society, the Body Politic, and the Soul Politic, as being in a phoenix-like state of historical evolution in which the social ashes of despair are forever reborn upon the religious wings of hope. In "Signs of the Times" (1829), *Essays* 2:75, he rejects the utilitarian view of a democratic Society formed on mechanism and argues instead for organic Society led by spiritual heroes: "We figure Society as a 'Machine,' and that mind is opposed to mind, as is body to body; whereby two . . . little minds must be stronger than one great mind. Noble absurdity! For the plain truth, very plain, we think is, that minds are opposed to minds in quite a different way; and one man that has a higher Wisdom, a hitherto unknown spiritual Truth in him, is stronger, not than ten men that have it not, or than ten thousand, but than *all* men that have it not. . . ." In "Characteristics" (1831), *Essays* 3:11, he transforms the interaction of individual, spiritual man with individual, spiritual man into an apocalyptic vision of ideal social union: "Man has joined himself with man; soul acts and reacts on soul. . . . The lightning-spark of Thought, generated, or say rather heaven-kindled, in the solitary mind, awakens to its express likeness in another mind, in a thousand other minds, and all blaze-up together in combined fire; reverberated from mind to mind, fed also with fresh fuel in each, it acquires incalculable new light as Thought, incalculable new heat as converted into Action." This chapter addresses the above vision of Society.

171.9–14. **Pericardial Nervous Tissue . . . galvanic**: Compare 159.35. Galvanic: an allusion to Luigi Galvani (1737–1798), Italian physician who discovered that by using an electrical arc contractions could be induced in animal tissue. Compare also, Mary Shelley, *Frankenstein* (1818), Chapter 2.

171.20. **calls it Peace**: Possibly taken from Tacitus, *Agricola*, 30, where it is said of the Romans: "To plunder, butcher, steal, these things they misname empire; they make a desolation and they call it peace." In a *Journal* entry, September 21, 1825, Carlyle says of the aimlessness that follows depression: "My mood of mind is changed: is it improved? *Weiss nicht* [I know not]. This stagnation is not peace, or it is the peace of Galgacus' Romans: *ubi solitudinem faciunt pacem appellant*" (*Two Note Books*, 64–65). Compare Jeremiah 6:13–14, where "from the prophet even unto the priest every one dealeth falsely. They have healed also the hurt *of the daughter* of my people slightly, saying, Peace, peace; when *there is* no peace."

172.4. *Laissez faire*: Literally, "allow to do." Laissez-faire became the political philosophy of the early classical economists led by Adam Smith, who in *The Wealth of Nations* argued that the welfare of the individual was paramount and thus advocated free trade without governmental restrictions. Subsequent economists, such as David Ricardo, *The Principles of Political Economy* (1817) and James Mill, *Elements of Political Economy* (1821), refined Smith's belief that industrial mercantilism and state paternalism hindered economic vitality and that an economy functioned best on competition rather than by control. Carlyle came increasingly to blame the non-interference philosophy of laissez-faire for England's stagnant economy and spiritual crises. In *Chartism* (1839), *Essays* 4:155, he asserts, "[A] government of the under classes by the upper on a principle of *Let-alone* is no longer possible in England in these days. . . . The Working Classes cannot any longer go on without government; without being *actually* guided and governed; England cannot subsist in peace till . . . some guidance and government for them is found." In *Past and Present*, 184, laissez-faire becomes the "Gospel of Despair."

172.4–5. **such light is darker than darkness**: Compare 169.2.

172.18. **German *Wahngasse***: Compare 16.14.

172.21. **whoso runs may read**: Compare Habakkuk 2:2, where the prophet stands at his watchtower: "And the Lord answered me, and said, Write the vision, and make *it* plain upon tables, that he may run that readeth it." Compare 200.20.

172.23–24. **Independence**: Founded upon revolution in the name of Democracy, an allusion to the American Revolution of 1776, the French Revolution of 1789, and perhaps the lesser revolution in France in 1830. Carlyle throughout his life saw Democracy (Independence, Freedom, and Laissez-faire) as a utilitarian-driven social evil that had dire implications. In The *French Revolution* 1:46, he holds "inexpugnable, immeasurable" Democracy as responsible for the revolution; in "The Diamond Necklace" (1837), *Essays* 3:337, "the shoreless fire-lava of DEMOCRACY is at [the] back" of French bankruptcy; in *Past and Present*, 215, he says in the persona of Teufelsdröckh, "'Democracy . . . is of a kin to *Atheism'*"; in the *Latter-Day Pamphlets* (1850), 21, he asserts that a system founded upon social and/or economic equality "is forever impossible"; and in "Shooting Niagara: and After?" (1867), *Essays* 5:3, he laments that England seems destined to take the "Niagara leap of completed Democracy."

172.29. **Rousseau**: Compare 150.33.

172.32. **Utilitarians**: Compare 90.19.

173.4. **fag-end**: A frayed end of cloth, or an inferior remnant.

173.6. **Mechanisers**: Compare 163.22.

173.21–22. **the water . . . of Knowledge and of Life**: Compare Genesis 2:9–10, where "a river went out of Eden to water the garden" wherein was the Tree of Life and the Tree of Knowledge. Compare also 102.20.

173.31. *divested*: Literally, undressed; and in the legal sense (de-vest) to strip one of property.

173.33. **Irish watch-coat**: A patched coat worn in inclement weather. Compare Sterne's *The History of a Good Warm Watch-Coat*, a satire about the machinations of Trim who pleaded to have a parish watch-coat cut into a petticoat for his wife and a pair of breeches for his son.

173.34. **Job's news**: Compare Job 1:13–19, where Job repeatedly receives disastrous news as a test by God of his faith. Carlyle uses this phrase in his translation of the German *Hiobspost*, "bad news," in Musæus's "Dumb Love," *German Romance* 1:81.

173.36. **wheel-spokes of Destiny**: Compare *The Life of Friedrich Schiller*, 73, where Carlyle translates from Schiller's *Don Carlos* (1785): "*You* [the King] purpose, single / In all Europe, alone, to fling yourself / Against the wheel of Destiny that rolls / For ever its appointed course; to clutch / Its spokes with mortal arm?"

174.6. **Ragfair**: Compare 157.2.

174.8. **Helots**: Compare 169.22-23.

174.9. *sic-vos-non-vobis*: "Thus do ye, but not for yourselves," i.e., you do the work but another takes the credit. Attributed to Virgil.

174.15. **Weissnichtwo**: Compare 6.15.

174.23. **mortal coil . . . shuffled off**: Compare *Hamlet* 3:1:63–67: "To die, to sleep— / To sleep, perchance to dream—ay, there's the rub, / For in that sleep of death what dreams may come, / When we have shuffled off this mortal coil, / Must give us pause."

174.26. **two or three . . . gathered together**: Compare 158.14–15.

174.29. **Gehenna**: Compare 83.11.

174.35. **aphorism of Saint-Simon's**: Claude Henri de Rouvroy, Comte de Saint-Simon (1760–1825), French social philosopher who in his *Le Nouveau Christianisme* (*The New Christianity*, 1825) asserted the inequality of man and argued therefore for the necessity for a reorganization of labor on a scientific basis whereby the state would distribute reward based upon merit and capacity. The Saint-Simonian Brotherhood, which became quasi-religious in nature, flourished in the revolutionary period between 1828 and 1832, and Carlyle became one of its admirers. In a letter to Gustave d'Eichthal, August 9, 1830, *Letters* 5:134–39, he acknowledges receipt of a volume of materials (now in the National Library of Scotland) relating to Saint-Simonianism, upon which he later wrote on the fly-leaf in 1834: "'The little Truth that lay among their crudities has not disappeared, or even properly *appeared*. . . . As a constituted sect these men are not without significance; not undeserving some slight remembrance.'" Carlyle's qualified praise might be, in part, the result of Goethe's warning to him in a letter, October 17, 1830, *Letters* 5:156: "Von der

Société St. Simonienne bitte Sich fern zu halten" (From the St. Simonian Society pray hold yourself aloof). The fact is, however, that rather than heed Goethe's warning, Carlyle turned closer to Saint-Simonianism as he was writing *Sartor Resartus*. After having read "Signs of the Times," members of the Society visited Carlyle at Craigenputtock in an effort to persuade him to join them. Their influence upon Carlyle's social vision is pervasive, and for this period has been carefully documented by K. J. Fielding, "Carlyle and the Saint-Simonians (1830–1832): New Considerations," *Carlyle and His Contemporaries*, 35–59. Carlyle's translation of *Le Nouveau Christianisme* in December of 1830 was acknowledgment of the influence. This translation, now lost, was forwarded to d'Eichthal in 1832. See Tarr, *Thomas Carlyle: A Descriptive Bibliography*, 516.

175.3. **Napoleon**: Compare 37.3.

175.3–4. **Flame . . . moths**: Compare "Tragedy of the Night-Moth" (written 1818?, published 1830), *Collected Poems*, 1–3.

175.4–5. **incautious beards**: Compare Rousseau's *Discours si le rétablissment des sciences et des arts a contribué a épurer le moeurs* (*A Dissertation on the Effects of Cultivating the Arts and Sciences*, 1750), *Miscellaneous Works* 1:22n: "A certain satyr . . . , the first time he saw fire, was going to kiss and embrace it; but Prometheus cried out to him to forbear, or otherwise his beard would rue it. It burns . . . everything that it touches."

175.24–25. **more in sorrow than in anger**: Compare *Hamlet* 1.2.231–32, where Horatio says of the ghost of Hamlet's father, "A countenance more / In sorrow than in anger."

175.25. ***Doctor utriusque Juris***: A doctor of both civil and canonical law. See note at 6.21–23 above.

175.28. **gukguk**: Compare 12.22.

175.31. **scot and lot**: Parish tax originally levied according to the ability to pay.

NOTES TO CHAPTER VI. OLD CLOTHES

176.1. Sansculottist: Compare 13.33.

176.5. rosy-fingered . . . Aurora: Roman goddess of Dawn, identified with the Greek goddess Eos. Compare Homer's *Odyssey* 2.1–3, "Now when with rosie fingers, th'early borne / And throwne through all the aire, appear'd the morne, / Ulysses' lov'd son from his bed appeard."

176.16–17. each man . . . his neighbour's schoolmaster: A loose rewriting of Genesis 4:9: "And the Lord said unto Cain, Where *is* Abel thy brother? And he said, I know not: *Am* I my brother's keeper?"

176.21. ALIVE: In a *Journal* entry, September 1830 (*Two Note Books*, 166), Carlyle writes, "Why should Politeness be the peculiar characteristic of the Rich and Well-born? Is not every man *alive*; is not every man infinitely venerable to every other?"; and then repeats verbatim the quotation from Novalis below.

176.21–177.2. There is but one Temple . . . a human Body: Compare "Novalis" (1829), *Essays* 2:39; "Goethe's Works" (1832), *Essays* 2:390; and *On Heroes*, 11.2–6, where Carlyle repeats this passage from Novalis's *Fragmente*. This passage is an adaptation in part of I Corinthians 3:16: "Know ye not that ye are the temple of God; and *that* the Spirit of God dwelleth in you?"

177.4. English Johnson: Samuel Johnson (1709–1784), scholar, critic, poet, and essayist, who it is said once out of courtesy bowed to an archbishop.

177.5. shovel-hat: Compare 155.6.

177.6–7. Temple . . . Divinity: Compare Genesis 1:26–27: "And God said, Let us make man in our image, after our likeness: . . . so God created man in his *own* image."

177.13–15. Shells . . . Husks . . . Cast Clothes: Clothes that have been abandoned by nature and humankind, hence secondhand clothes.

Cast also has the sartorial meaning of warp or twist yarn. Compare also "empty Masks," 174.10–11.

177.16. **frogged**: Having an ornamental looped braid or cord with a button or knot for fastening the front of a garment.

177.17. **straddling animal with bandy legs**: Compare 44.35.

177.25. **free course**: 2 Thessalonians 3:1: "[P]ray for us, that the word of the Lord may have *free* course, and be glorified."

177.25–26. **Hindoo . . . Pagoda . . . God**: Hinduism, predominant in northern India, embraces a philosophy, culture, and religion characterized by a belief in reincarnation and in a supreme being found in many forms in nature. A pagoda is a Hindu or Buddhist temple in India or China. Compare Richter's "Life of Quintus Fixlein," *German Romance* 2:207, where Fixlein takes off his "hat before the empty windows of the Castle: houses of quality were to him like persons of quality, as in India the Pagoda at once represents the temple and the god."

177.30. **King *Toomtabard* . . . John Balliol**: Toomtabard, from old Scots; *Toom* means "empty" and *tabard* is a gown without sleeves worn over a knight's armor, hence "empty gown." John Balliol, or John de Baliol (1249–1325), King of Scotland (1292–1296). In a *Journal* entry, September 7, 1830, Carlyle records that he has been reading Scott's *History of Scotland* (1829–1830) which is "no more a *History* of Scotland than I am the Pope of Rome," and then adds, "One inference I have drawn from Scott: that the people in those old days had a singular talent for nicknames: King *Toom-Tabard* . . . &c. &c." (*Two Note Books*, 168–69).

177.37. **goose-speech**: Inane, stupid speech.

178.4. **carking Cares**: *Cark*, old Scots *kiaugh*, i.e., weary, vexatious, grinding. Compare Robert Burns, "The Cotter's Saturday Night" (1786), *Selected Poetry and Prose*, 51, lines 25–27: "The *lisping infant*, prattling on his knee, / Does a' his weary *kiaugh* and care beguile, / An' makes him quite forget his labour and his toil."

178.5. **Pegasus**: The winged horse of the Hippocrene fountain. He sprang from the blood of Medusa when her head was struck off by Perseus and helped Bellerophon conquer the Chimera. On his ascent to heaven, Bellerophon fell back to earth, but Pegasus continued on to dwell among the stars. He is associated with the Muses.

178.5. **skyey Messenger**: The language here is similar to that of Shelley's "Ode to the West Wind," lines 7, 15–20, where the "wingèd seeds" are blown by the "steep sky's commotion," and where the "Loose clouds" become "Angels [Messengers] of rain and lightning." Also, a possible adaptation of Jesus's words that John the Baptist is the "messenger" sent to prepare the way; compare Matthew 11:10; Mark 1:2; and Luke 7:27. Perhaps also Mercury, the messenger of the gods.

178.7–8. **monstrous Tuberosity . . . Capital of England**: London. Carlyle first visited London in June of 1824, and the description here is remarkably similar to that written in a letter to his brother Alexander, December 14, 1824: "Of this enormous Babel of a place I can give you no account in writing: it is like the heart of all the universe. . . . O that our father sey [saw] Holborn in a fog! with the black vapour brooding over it, absolutely like fluid ink. . . . No wonder [William] Cobbett calls the place a Wen [cyst]! It is a monstrous Wen!" (*Letters* 3:218–19).

178.9–10. **Spartan broth**: In an effort to curb luxury and to promote discipline, Lycurgus ordered that all citizens of Sparta eat common food together at public tables. See Plutarch's Liv*es*, "Lycurgus," chapters 10, 12.

178.10. **grinding**: Compare "carking," 178.4 above.

178.12. **Monmouth Street**: Noted for its secondhand clothes shops, near Seven Dials in central London.

178.13. **Sanhedrim**: Now normally *Sanhedrin* ("The incorrect form *sanhedrim* . . . has always been in England (from the 17th c.) the only form in popular use" *OED*, s.v. "Sanhedrim, sanhedrin."), the highest judicial and ecclesiastical council of the Jews in the period of the

Second Temple. The council of "the high priest" and "all the chief priests and the elders and the scribes" who "sought for witness against Jesus to put him to death" in Mark 14:53–59 has been taken to be a reference to the Sanhedrin.

178.16. **the Prison men call Life**: Compare "Life and Writings of Werner" (1828), *Essays* 1:109, where Carlyle translates from the drama *Die Söhne des Thals* (*The Sons of the Valley*, 1803–1804): "'And when the Lord saw Phosphoros his pride, / Being wroth thereat, he cast him forth, / And shut him in a prison called LIFE.'"

178.18–20. **Jewish Highpriest . . . Pope**: According to Flavius Josephus, *Antiquities of the Jews* in *Works of Josephus*, 90: "The high priest's mitre . . . was a golden crown polished, of three rows." The tiara of the pope is surrounded with three crowns which represent his temporal, spiritual, and purgatorial sovereignty.

178.19. **Angel of Doom . . . four winds**: Compare Revelation 7:1–2: "I saw four angels standing on the four corners of the earth, holding the four winds of the earth . . . to whom it was given to hurt the earth and the sea."

178.22–24. **sounds forth . . . trumpet . . . Judgment**: An adaptation of Revelation 1:10: "I was in the Spirit of the Lord's day, and heard behind me a great voice, as of a trumpet"; and 4:1: "[A] door *was* opened in heaven: and the first voice which I heard *was* as it were of a trumpet talking with me."

178.30. **Field Lane**: An alley leading to Saffron Hill, off Holborn, in London; later described by Charles Dickens in *Oliver Twist* (1837–1838), Chapter 26, as a "narrow and dismal alley" near Holborn Hill where "the clothesman, the shoe-vamper, and the rag-merchant display their goods." In the "filthy shops are exposed for sale huge bunches of second-hand silk handkerchiefs of all sizes and patterns; for here reside the traders who purchase them from the pick pockets."

178.31. **Dionysius' Ear**: Dionysius the Elder (405–367 B.C.), the tyrant of Syracuse, constructed a rock cave in the form of an ear, from which he was able to overhear the complaints of his political prisoners.

178.35. **Mirza's Hill**: Compare Addison's "The Visions of Mirzah," *Spectator*, no. 159 (September 1, 1711), where Mirzah, while contemplating the "Vanity of human life," is led by a shepherd to the "highest Pinnacle" and is permitted to see in the valley beyond the "Vale of Misery" and the "Tide of Eternity," and in consequence learns that humankind was not "made in vain."

178.38. **Bedlam**: Compare 112.10.

179.4–5. **money-changers**: Compare Matthew 21:12 and Mark 11:15: "Jesus went into the temple . . . and overthrew the tables of the moneychangers."

179.7. **middle-state**: Perhaps Indifference. Throughout, Teufelsdröckh protects himself from the fringes of paradox, often deciding it is easier if not more economical to remain aloof from life's apparent contradictions.

179.11. **eyes in a fine frenzy**: Compare *A Midsummer Night's Dream* 5.1.12–13: "The poet's eye, in a fine frenzy rolling, / Doth glance from heaven to earth, from earth to heaven."

179.12. **Delphic avenue**: An allusion to the oracle of Apollo that was housed in the great temple at Delphi from the sixth century B.C. The messages of the oracle were spoken by a priestess who sat on a golden tripod and uttered sounds in a frenzied trance, the meanings of which were then interpreted by a priest.

179.13. **Whispering-gallery**: A gallery running round the dome of St. Paul's Cathedral in London, across which a whispered word may be distinctly heard at a distance of 143 feet. Compare "Life of Quintus Fixlein," *German Romance* 2:252: "Two lovers dwell in the Whispering-gallery, where the faintest breath bodies itself forth into a sound."

179.15. **tympanum**: The eardrum.

179.15–16. **hearest the grass grow**: Heimdall, the watchman of the Norse gods, had such sharp hearing that he could hear the grass grow in the meadows.

179.24. **dawned**: Compare "Aurora," 176.5 above.

179.28. **Egg of Eros**: In Greek myth Eros, said to be the oldest of the gods, sprang from the cosmic egg laid by Night in the abyss of Chaos.

NOTES TO CHAPTER VII. ORGANIC FILAMENTS

title. ORGANIC FILAMENTS: An expression which permits Carlyle to indulge in the paradox of destruction and renewal, followed again by destruction. As soon as the Phoenix is reborn, it has already begun its spiral toward eventual death, followed by yet another rebirth. There is no sense of stasis in the expression "Organic Filaments." To Carlyle the filaments (threads) must continually unravel in order to be resewn: *Sartor* (filaments) *Resartus* (respun). Like Herder, *Über den Ursprung der Sprache* (*On the Origin of Language*, 1772), Carlyle viewed history as the spontaneous language of cultures, infinite filaments of fiction (metaphor) that have no beginning and no end and that are perpetually woven into past, present, and future. In "Voltaire" (1829), *Essays* 1:399, Carlyle asserts, "[H]uman society rests on inscrutably deep foundations; which he is of all others the most mistaken, who fancies he has explored to the bottom. Neither is that sequence, which we love to speak of as 'a chain of causes,' properly to be figured as a 'chain' or line, but rather as a tissue, or superficies of innumerable lines, extending in breadth as well as in length, and with a complexity, which will foil and utterly bewilder the most assiduous computation."

180.1. **World-Phœnix**: Compare 171–75 above.

180.11. **Creation and Destruction**: The paradox of rebirth through death dates from the earliest Asian and Indo-European philosophy, yet the language here is similar to that of Shelley's "Ode to the West Wind," lines 13–14, where the Wind is called "Destroyer and preserver." The "melodious Deathsong" in Shelley's poem becomes a "melodious Birthsong" which makes "mighty harmonies" as the Wind drives his "dead thoughts over the universe / Like withered leaves to quicken a new birth!" (lines 59, 63–64).

180.22–181.5. **Hatred . . . Sympathy . . . Love**: Compare "Voltaire" (1829), *Essays* 1:424: "[O]ur fellow-man is no steam-engine, but a man; united with us, and with all men, and with the Maker of all men, in sacred, mysterious, indissoluble bonds, in an All-embracing Love"; and "Goethe's Works" (1832), *Essays* 2:388–89, where Carlyle quotes Teufelsdröckh: "'Deny it as he will . . . man reverently loves man, and daily by action evidences his belief in the divineness of man. . . . Of a truth, men are mystically united; a mystic bond of brotherhood makes all men one . . . a heartfelt indestructible sympathy of man with man? Hatred itself is but an inverse love.'"

181.9. **Glass-bell**: Compare *Wilhelm Meister* 1:418, where Meister escapes the "glass bell, which shut me up in the exhausted airless space: One bold stroke to break the bell in pieces, and thou art delivered! . . . I drew off the mask, and on all occasions acted as my heart directed"; and "Signs of the Times" (1829), *Essays* 2:81, where the metaphor of the glass-bell is repeated.

181.11. **four winds**: Compare 178.19.

181.15–18. **Heart . . . circulation**: Compare 80.6–7.

181.22. **blesses or curses**: Compare James 3:10: "Out of the same mouth proceedeth blessing and cursing."

181.25. **Lake Winnipic**: Lake Winnipeg in south central Manitoba, Canada.

181.27–28. **pebble . . . Universe**: Compare Newton's *Principia*: Law 3: "To every action there is always opposed an equal reaction" (13–14); Corollary 4: "For the progressive motion, whether of one single body, or of a whole system of bodies, is always to be estimated from the motion of the centre of gravity" (19–20). In other words, the center of gravity is altered by the action and reaction of the forces created by the motion of the pebble.

181.36. **Stillschweigen and Company**: Compare 6.22.

181.36. **Cadmus of Thebes**: In Greek legend the founder of Thebes who is said to have introduced into Greece from Phoenicia or Egypt an alphabet of sixteen letters.

181.36. **Faust of Mentz**: See note at 30.20–21 above.

182.1. Mœsogothic Ulfila: Ulfilas, or Wulfila (311?–383?), "Little Wolf," Bishop of the Arian Visigoths and translator of the Bible into Gothic. Ulfilas is said to have invented the alphabet that he used in the translation. Mœsogoths: Goths from Moesia, an ancient region in Bulgaria. See *Letters* 5:105.

182.2. Tubalcain: Compare Genesis 4:22, where Tubalcain is described as "an instructor of every artificer in brass and iron"; also mentioned at 128.30.

182.15. cloud of witnesses: Those who have faith. Compare Hebrews 12:1, where the world is "compassed about with so great a cloud of witnesses." Also, a possible allusion to a book about Scottish Covenanters, *A Cloud of Witnesses for the Royal Prerogatives of Jesus Christ; or, the Last Speeches and Testimonies of Those Who Have Suffered for the Truth in Scotland, Since the Year 1680* (1714), which Carlyle recommends as "most notable" to John Stuart Mill in a letter, November 19, 1832 (*Letters* 6:260).

182.16. *Communion of Saints*: A part of the Apostles' Creed. In a letter to d'Eichthal, August 9, 1830, Carlyle discusses the Communion of Saints within the context of Saint-Simonianism: "I have long felt that only in Union could Religion properly exist; that this deep, mystic, immeasurable Sympathy, which man has with man, is the true element of Religion; that indeed the Communion of Saints, spoken of in the Creed, is no delusion, but the highest fact of our destiny" (*Letters* 5:137).

182.25–26. Newton . . . Kepler: Isaac Newton, English mathematician and natural philosopher; Johannes Kepler (1571–1630), German astronomer. The allusion here is to Kepler's laws of planetary motion which held that the sun controlled the orbits of the planets. In the *Principia*, Newton refined Kepler's unification theory in his law of universal gravitation which predicts the small forces the planets exert on each other although each is subject to the dominant force of the sun. Carlyle's interest in astronomy was peaking at the writing of *Sartor Resartus*, and in December of 1833 he approached Francis Jeffrey to ask for his support in application for a post in the Edinburgh Astronomical Observatory. Jeffrey's support was not forthcoming, and Carlyle marked this as an end to their eventful friendship. See *Reminiscences*, 378.

182.27. higher points of vision: In his *Opticks* (1704), Newton developed his corpuscular theory which held that light was made up of particles, a theory that was replaced in the early nineteenth century by the electromagnetic wave theory. Both theories were later combined to form part of quantum theory, hence fulfilling Carlyle's own theory of "perpetual metamorphoses." Newton's theory was vigorously disputed by Goethe in *Zur Farbenlehre* (*Toward a Theory of Colors*, 1810).

182.28. Hebrew Lawgiver: Moses. Compare John 1:17: "For the law was given by Moses, *but* grace and truth came by Jesus Christ."

182.28–29. Apostle of the Gentiles: Paul. Compare Romans 11:13: "For I speak to you Gentiles inasmuch as I am the apostle of the Gentiles."

182.31–32. Luther . . . Pope's Bull: In his *Address to the Christian Nobility of the German Nation* (1520), Martin Luther (1483–1546), an Augustinian friar, assailed the papacy for its corruption, disputed the papal claim of authority over secular rulers, denied that the pope was the final interpreter of the Scriptures, and appealed for national control over church matters. The pope in turn threatened excommunication and forwarded a papal bull (edict) condemning Luther's appeal for reforms and demanding contrition. In Wittenberg, on December 10, 1520, Luther publicly burned the bull, was therewith excommunicated, and the Reformation was assured.

182.32. Voltaire: Compare 144.15. Voltaire's animus toward traditional religion was expressed in his celebrated slogan, "*Écrasez l'infâme!*" (Crush the abomination!).

182.33–35. Whig . . . Radical . . . Rebuilder: Compare 9.8.

183.1. swan-song: Compare Plato, *Phaedo* 84e–85a, where Socrates is quoted: Swans, when they "realize that they have to die, sing more, and sing more sweetly than they have ever sung before, rejoicing at the prospect of going into the presence of that god whose servants they are"; *King John* 5.7.21–22, where Prince Henry says: "I am the cygnet to this pale faint swan, / Who chaunts a doleful hymn to his own death"; and *Othello* 5:2:247–48, Desdemona's death scene: "I will play the swan, / And die in music."

183.5–7. **Titles . . . Fighting**: In a *Journal* entry, February 7, 1831, Carlyle writes, "Earl (*Jarl, Yirl*), Count, Duke, Knight, &c. &c. are all titles derived from *fighting*: the honour-titles, in a future time, will derive themselves from *knowing* and well-*doing*. . . . This is a prophecy of mine" (*Two Note Books*, 185). In "Goethe's Works" (1832), *Essays* 2:435, Carlyle identifies Goethe as the hero who resolves contradiction: "That in Goethe there lay Force to educe reconcilement out of such contradiction as man is now born into, marks him as the Strong One of his time; the true *Earl*, though now with quite other weapons than those old steel *Jarls* were used to! Such reconcilement of contradictions, indeed, is the task of every man."

183.7–8. *Herzog . . . Dux*: *Herzog*, German for duke; *Dux*, Latin for leader or ruler.

183.8. *Jarl*: "An old Norse or Danish chieftain or under-king" (*OED*, s.v. "Jarl").

183.8. **Marshall**: From Old High German *marahscalc*, "horse-keeper," and Old French *mareschal*, "farrier" or "shoeing-smith."

183.9–10. **Millennium . . . prophesied**: Compare Revelation 20:6: "Blessed and holy *is* he that hath part in the first resurrection: . . . they shall be priests of God and of Christ, and shall reign with him a thousand years."

183.14. *König . . . Könning*: The etymology here is somewhat faulty. *König* is Modern German for king and is from the Old High German *Chuning*. In Anglo-Saxon the word is *cyning*, literally "a man of good birth." *Cyn* is a tribe, kin, or race, from the Old High German *chunni*. *Könning* is from the Old High German *chnaan* and the Modern German *können*, "to know or to understand." Cunning is from the Middle English *conning* which is from the Anglo-Saxon *cunnan*, perhaps derived from Icelandic *kunna*, "to know."

183.18. **King rules by divine right**: In a *Journal* entry, February 7, 1831, Carlyle writes, "Kings *do* reign by divine right, or not at all. The King that were God-appointed, would be an emblem of God, and could *demand* all obedience from us" (*Two Note Books*, 185). Carlyle is presenting here his theory of hero-worship. In *On Heroes*, 169.4–11, Carlyle says the king is "the most important of Great Men.

He is practically the summary for us of *all* the various figures of Heroism. . . . He is called *Rex*, Regulator, *Roi:* our own name is still better; King, *Könning*, which means *Can*-ning, Able-man."

183.20. **King Popinjay**: A popinjay (originally a parrot, especially a parrot tied to a pole as an archery target) is a fop, a supercilious figure-head of no value except as a target for ridicule.

183.32. **Necropolis**: Literally, "city of the dead," i.e., cemetery. Here London, the seat of Parliament where agitation for reform was at its zenith in 1831 during the composition of *Sartor Resartus.*

183.34. **Film**: A haze or mist.

184.3–4. **deep . . . Radicalism**: Compare 12.15.

184.6–11. **Elective Franchise . . . Ballot-Box**: The Reform Bill of 1832 addressed the problem of "pocket boroughs" (constituencies controlled by the crown or aristocracy) and "rotten boroughs" (constituencies where the population had declined) by redistributing the seats in Parliament and by extending the franchise to those who occupied premises that had an annual value of £10. The result was that the electorate was increased by about 50%; even so the new distribution of seats still allowed the rural areas to maintain an advantage.

184.17. **To rebuild . . . from the top downwards**: Compare Goethe's *Dichtung und Wahrheit* (*Poetry and Truth*, 1811–33), his *Autobiography*, 1.1.9–10, where Goethe recalls his father rebuilding their house from the "bottom upwards."

184.20–21. **knit up my chains into ornamental festoons**: Compare "Goethe's Works" (1832), *Essays* 2:441, where Carlyle says that "*Freedom*" is "a thing much wanted" and then translates from Goethe's *Epigramme Venedig* (*Venetian Epigrams*, 1795): "Is the world, then, itself a huge prison? Free only the madman, / His chains knitting still up into some graceful festoon?" Also used as the epigraph to volume 2 of *The French Revolution.*

184.22–23. **Peace Society**: Founded in London in 1816 by the Society of Friends.

184.33-34. **inferior of nothing . . . superior of nothing . . . equal of nothing**: The use of mathematical language to define the quality of life is found throughout Carlyle's text; compare, for example, 142.25-27.

184.38-39. **bowing down . . . himself exalted**: Compare Matthew 23:12: "And whosoever shall exalt himself shall be abased; and he that shall humble himself shall be exalted"; Luke 14:11; 18:14.

185.2-3. **Fear . . . Reverence**: Compare 77.4. Compare also "Count Cagliostro" (1833), *Essays* 3:249: Carlyle through his narrator Sauerteig draws the relationship between Fear and Reverence in Aristotelian terms and concludes that the "'highest Reverence,' and most needful for us: [is] 'Reverence for oneself.'"

185.12. **corner-stone of living rock**: Compare Isaiah 28:16, where God lays "a precious corner *stone*, a sure foundation"; Luke 6:48: "He is like the man which built an house, and digged deep, and laid the foundation on a rock: and when the flood arose, the stream beat vehemently upon that house, and could not shake it: for it was founded upon a rock"; and 1 Peter 2:4-6, where God is the "living stone" who lays a "chief corner stone." Compare also Psalms 118:22; Matthew 21:42; Mark 12:10; Luke 20:17; Acts 4:11; and Ephesians 2:20.

185.16. **Paris and Voltaire**: On February 10, 1778, at the age of eighty-four, after an enforced exile of some twenty-eight years, Voltaire returned in triumph to Paris, an event described in *The French Revolution* 1:42: "Sneering Paris has suddenly grown reverent; devotional with Hero-worship. Nobles have disguised themselves as tavern-waiters to obtain sight of him: the loveliest of France would lay their hair beneath his feet." In "Voltaire" (1829), *Essays* 1:436-37, Carlyle describes Voltaire's return as "a strange half-frivolous, half-fateful aspect; there is . . . a sort of dramatic justice in this catastrophe, that he, who had all his life hungered and thirsted after public favour, should at length die by excess of it." Compare also *On Heroes*, 13.35-14.22 and *Frederick the Great* 3:187.

185.20. **laid their hair beneath his feet**: Compare John 12:3, where Mary "anointed the feet of Jesus, and wiped his feet with her hair."

185.23–24. **dry tree . . . green**: Compare Ezekiel 17:24, where "I the Lord . . . have dried up the green tree, and have made the dry tree to flourish"; and Luke 23:31, where Jesus says to the Daughters of Jerusalem, "For if they do these things in a green tree, what shall be done in the dry?"

185.26. *Hortus Siccus*: Literally "dry garden," dried plants collected for study. In *Reveries of the Solitary Walker*, Fifth Walk, Rousseau describes his penchant for botany, particularly the study of dried plants and flowers, which resulted from his self-imposed exile brought on by the rejection suffered at the hands of his peers. Richter alludes to Rousseau's activities in "Life of Quintus Fixlein," *German Romance* 2:226: "I nowise grudge J. J. Rousseau his *Flora Petrinsularis*; but let him also allow our Quintus his *Window-flora*."

185.27. **Gumflowers**: Scots for artificial flowers.

185.27. **virtue could come out**: Compare 159.8.

186.1–2. **Preaching Friar . . . Newspaper**: Preaching Friars, also called Black Friars, were evangelical mendicants from the Dominican Order established in Spain in 1216. Here, the editors of newspapers and popular journals. Compare "Signs of the Times" (1829), *Essays* 2:77: "The true Church of England, at this moment, lies in the Editors of its Newspapers. . . . It may be said too, that in private disposition the new Preachers somewhat resemble the Mendicant Friars of old times: outwardly full of holy zeal; inwardly not without stratagem, and hunger for terrestrial things"; also *On Heroes*, 140.22–24: "I many a time say, the writers of Newspapers, Pamphlets, Poems, Books, these *are* the real working effective Church of a modern country."

186.13–14. **knit up this ravelled sleeve**: Compare *Macbeth* 2.2.33–34: "'Macbeth does murder sleep'—the innocent sleep, / Sleep that knits up the ravell'd sleave of care."

186.15. **But there is no Religion?**: Compare "Novalis" (1829), *Essays* 2:43, where Carlyle translates from *Die Christenheit oder Europa* (*Christianity or Europe*) from *Fragmente*: "'As yet there is no Religion. . . . Think ye that there is Religion? Religion has to be made and produced . . . by the union of a number of persons.'"

186.25. Goethe: Compare 143.4.

186.27-28. where there is no ministering Priest, the people perish: Compare Proverbs 29:18: "Where *there is* no vision, the people perish."

186.32. *Miserere*: From the Vulgate Bible, Psalms 51:1: "*Miserere mei Deus*" ("Have mercy upon me, O God").

186.36. Men's History, a perpetual Evangile: An allusion to Novalis's famous formula: "*Die ganze Geschichte ist Evangelium*" (The whole of history is gospel). Compare also "Jean Paul Friedrich Richter" (1827), *Essays* 2:113n, where Carlyle translates from Richter that through "'All History . . . [we] can divine and read the Infinite Spirit.'" This idea that history (humankind) is in "perpetual metamorphoses" is specifically addressed in *Sartor Resartus* at 174.24.

186.37-38. Morning Stars sing together: Compare Job 38:4-7, where God questions Job: "Where wast thou when I laid the foundations of the earth? . . . Whereupon are the foundations thereof fastened? or who laid the corner stone thereof; When the morning stars sang together, and all the sons of God shouted for joy?" Compare also 185.4-7.

NOTES TO CHAPTER VIII. NATURAL SUPERNATURALISM

187.1. *Natural Supernaturalism*: Carlyle's "new mythus" or "new religion," which finds definition in Natural Law and confirmation in the Mystery of the Universe. The oxymoron contained in the expression becomes the paradox upon which *Sartor Resartus* is built. As dialectic, "Natural" can mean all things proved or capable of proof; "Supernatural" all things beyond empirical measure. Yet both are complementary, each an extension of the other. The proof of the supernatural is found in the natural. *Miracles* are extensions of truth, not a corruption of it. *Mysteries* are dimensions of science, not a repudiation of it. And *Wonder* is the foundation of logic, not an antagonist of it. Hence Carlyle is able to justify his new science (metamorphoses) in the face of the old religion (tradition). Physical science, he says, may extend explanation but can never conquer it. No matter how much is explained, there is always the inexplicable. Carlyle thus turns corporeal truths into mystical truth, and proves the existence of miracles (wonder, mystery) by proving that science cannot prove otherwise. This method of shifting the burden of proof enables him to cope philosophically with what Wordsworth calls in "Tintern Abbey" the "burthen of the mystery." He has in effect reshaped a dying Romanticism by rekindling its spirit in a manner adaptable to impending Victorianism. In this chapter "Sartor" becomes "Resartus." Carlyle is of course employing here a dialectic similar to that found in Kant's phenomenon-noumenon paradigm, although the meaning is controlled more by the absolutism of his Calvinist heritage than by any all-encompassing theological philosophy. Carlyle's doubt of ecclesiastical miracle, a doubt reinforced by his reading of Gibbon, is here translated into a belief in natural miracle, a belief nurtured by Goethe. "Natural Supernaturalism" is a system that transcends the sensoria of Locke (*Discourse on Miracles*, 1702) and the skepticism of Hume (*Enquiry Concerning Human Understanding*, Section 10, 1748). "Natural Supernaturalism" approximates a mystic's view of life in which the wonders and the mysteries of the universe (the ocean) are suggested in the emblem of humankind (the stream), a viewpoint anticipated in "Pure Reason," 49–53 above. On August 31, 1830, less than a month before beginning the writing of *Sartor Resartus*, Carlyle wrote to Goethe: "When I look at the wonderful Chaos within me, full of natural Supernaturalism, and all manner of Antideluvian [*sic*] fragments; and how the Universe is daily growing more mysterious as well as more august, and the influences from without more heterogeneous and perplexing, I see not well what is to come of it all; and only conjecture from the violence of the fermentation that something strange may come" (*Letters* 5:153–54). The immediate source for the title "Natural Supernaturalism" may be an article, "The Last of the Supernaturalists," *Fraser's Magazine*, 1 (March 1830), 217–35, which has been attributed to Carlyle. See Tarr, *Thomas Carlyle: A Descriptive Bibliography*, 466. Upon completing the writing of *Sartor Resartus*, Carlyle records in his *Journal*, July 21, [1832]: "A strange feeling of *supernaturalism*, of 'the fearfulness and wonderfulness' of life, haunts me, and grows upon me" (Froude, *First Forty Years* 2:229). In "Goethe's Works" (1832), *Essays* 2:389, Carlyle connects supernaturalism to worship, more specifically hero-worship: "Man always *worships* something; always he sees the Infinite shadowed forth in something finite. . . . Yes, in practice, . . . we are all Supernaturalists."

In his introduction to *Das Mährchen* (*The Tale*, 1832), *Essays* 2:449, Carlyle quotes from Goethe's Proem, where the emblematic river flows "between two worlds? Call the world, or country on this side, where the fair Lily dwells, the world of SUPERNATURALISM; the country on that side, NATURALISM, the working week-day world where we all dwell and toil." Further, in a consideration of the structure of *Sartor Resartus*, Natural Supernaturalism (Soul) represents the third cycle (Book III), following the first cycle (Book I), the Natural World (Vesture), and the second cycle (Book II), the Supernatural World (Body). For a discussion of the social and aesthetic vision found in this triadic structure, see *Carlyle's Unfinished History of German Literature* (1830), ed. Hill Shine, 4–6; and Tennyson's *"Sartor" Called "Resartus,"* 157–93.

187.2. **Seer**: In Wordsworthian terms, Teufelsdröckh achieves the "philosophic mind," as in "Ode: Intimations of Immortality," lines 190, 145, 159–60, a state where the "obstinate questionings" become "truths that wake, / To perish never."

187.3. **refractory**: In the sense of "obstinate" as well as "unmanageable."

187.5–6. **Imperial Mantles**: Compare 44.23, 51.14–15, 55.34, 141.1, and 212.30.

187.6. **Superannuated Symbols**: Outdated symbols trapped by custom and tradition. Compare 166.25–27.

187.8. **TIME and SPACE**: Compare 43.6.

187.10. **victoriously**: Compare 138.5.

187.12. **garnitures, have all melted away**: Compare 2 Peter 3:10, where the "day of the Lord will come as a thief in the night; . . . and the elements shall melt with feverent heat."

187.13. **Holy of Holies**: Compare 77.3, 138.35.

187.15. **Transcendentalism**: Compare 12.12.

187.15. **last leap**: Compare 117.19.

187.16. promised land: Compare Exodus 12:25: "And it shall come to pass, when ye be come to the land which the Lord will give you, according as he hath promised, that ye shall keep this service"; Deuteronomy 19:8; 26:9; 27:3, the land given by God to the Israelites that "floweth with milk and honey"; Joshua 23:5; and 196.2 below.

187.16. *Palingenesia*: Compare 160.21, 197.2.

187.18. Diogenes the First: Diogenes the Cynic, see note at 6.15 above. Diogenes Laërtius (early third century B.C.), *Lives of the Philosophers*, records that when Diogenes the Cynic was at the close of a long lecture he said: "Courage friends! I see land." Notably, Tennyson uses this expression in the opening line of "The Lotos-Eaters" (1832): "'Courage!' he [Ulysses] said, and pointed toward the land."

188.3. What specially is a Miracle: In a *Journal* entry, January 1830, Carlyle writes: "Miracle? What is a Miracle? Can there be a thing more miraculous than any other thing? I myself am a standing wonder" (*Two Note Books*, 151).

188.4. Dutch King of Siam: Compare Locke's *Essay Concerning Human Understanding* 2:367, where a Dutch ambassador told the disbelieving King of Siam that "the water in his country would sometimes, in cold weather, be so hard, that men walked upon it." Alluded to in Hume, *Enquiry Concerning Understanding*, 113–14n: "The Indian prince, who refused to believe the first relations concerning the effects of frost, reasoned justly. . . . Such an event [the freezing of water] may be denominated *extra-ordinary*, and requires a pretty strong testimony, to render it credible to people in a warm climate: But still it is not *miraculous*"; and in Scott's *The Talisman* (1825), 10, where the northern Christian knight explains the relativity of knowledge to the southern Saracen: "[In] my land cold often converts the water itself into a substance as hard as rock."

188.7. *open sesame!*: The magical words used to open the door to the cave in "Ali Baba and the Forty Thieves" in *The Book of a Thousand Nights and a Night: Supplemental Nights* 4:369–402.

188.10–11. Laws of Nature: Or Natural Law. Originating in Greek philosophy, the theory of Natural Law held that there are laws basic to human nature that can be discovered through human reason. This idea became the foundation of Roman legal theory, and was elaborated on by Aquinas, *Summa theologica* (1267–73), who argued that Natural Law was common to all peoples and served as one of the bases of Christian moral principles, a belief that was given full review in the rationalist philosophy of Spinoza, *Ethics* (1677), and Leibniz, *Nouveaux essais* (1765). Rousseau, *Du Contrat social* (1762) and *Émile* (1762), used the theory of Natural Law to argue that freedom and democracy were reasoned extensions of the general will founded upon the common good. To Carlyle, Natural Law is the opposite of Materialism.

188.12. **rising of one from the dead**: An allusion to the miracle of Lazarus, or to the resurrection of Jesus himself. Both stories are alluded to throughout the New Testament. For example, compare John 11:43–44, where Jesus says, "Lazarus, come forth. And he that was dead came forth"; and Matthew 28:7, where the angel of the Lord says to Mary, "And go quickly, and tell his disciples that he is risen from the dead." Carlyle seems to be responding to Hume, *Enquiry Concerning Human Understanding*, 116: "When anyone tells me, that he saw a dead man restored to life, I immediately consider . . . whether it be more probable, that this person should either deceive or be deceived." In a *Journal* entry, [August?] 1830, Carlyle responds: "Is anything more wonderful than another, if you consider it maturely? *I* have *seen* no men rise from the Dead; I have seen some thousands rise from Nothing: I have not force to fly into the Sun, but I *have* force to lift my hand; which is equally strange" (*Two Note Books*, 162).

188.14–15. **Spiritual Force . . . Material Force**: Compare 54.19.

188.17. **Iron swim**: Compare II Kings 6:6, where Elisha retrieved the lost ax-head from the lake: "And he cut down a stick, and cast *it* in thither; and the iron did swim."

188.18. **teach Religion**: Adapted from John 3:2, where Nicodemus acknowledges Jesus: "[W]e know that thou art a teacher come from God: for no man can do these miracles that thou doest, except God be with him."

188.25. **without variableness or shadow of turning**: Compare James 1:17: "Every good gift and every perfect gift is from above, and cometh down from the Father of lights, with whom is no variableness, neither shadow of turning."

188.36–37. **incomprehensible All**: In "Goethe's Helena," *Essays* 1:153, Carlyle says that *Faust* is the microcosm through which the reader can approach the "stupendous All, of which it forms an indissoluble though so mean a fraction." The argument here is taken from Job 38:4–6: "Where wast thou when I laid the foundations of the earth? . . . Who hath laid the measures thereof, if thou knowest? . . . Whereupon are the foundations thereof fastened?"

189.2–3. **without bottom as without shore**: Part of a Scottish proverb: "The love of God is without a bottom and without a shore."

189.4. **Laplace's Book**: Compare 3.13.

189.9. **Sirius and the Pleiades**: Compare 135.35.

189.10. **Herschel's**: William [Friedrich Wilhelm] Herschel (1738–1822), English astronomer, who constructed powerful reflecting telescopes and with them discovered the planet Uranus and two satellites of Saturn and catalogued the stars.

189.12. **Waybill**: A document containing a list of goods and shipping instructions.

189.14. **signless Inane**: Compare Shelley, *Prometheus Unbound* (1820), 3.4.204: "Pinnacle dim in the intense inane." Compare also 195.26–28.

189.21. **Epicycle**: In Ptolemaic cosmology, a small circle, the center of which moves on the circumference of a larger circle at whose center is the earth.

189.22. **accident**: Compare 4.19.

189.28. **immeasurable All**: Compare 188.36–37.

189.32. **Author and Writer is God**: Compare Hebrews 11:9–10, where Abraham "sojourned in the land of promise . . . and looked for a city which hath foundations, whose builder and maker *is* God."

189.36. **celestial hieroglyphs**: Compare 28.6.

189.38. **here a line and there a line**: Compare Isaiah 28:10; 28:13: "For precept *must be* upon precept, precept upon precept; line upon line, line upon line; here a little, *and* there a little."

190.10. **Custom . . . doth make dotards of us all**: An adaptation of *Hamlet* 3:1:83: "Thus conscience doth make cowards of us all." Carlyle is following the Romantic belief that custom is a yoke upon the soul and thus an enemy of wonder; compare Wordsworth's "Ode: Intimations of Immortality," lines 130–32: "Full soon thy Soul shall have her earthly freight, / And custom lie upon thee with a weight, / Heavy as frost, and deep almost as life!"

190.17. **Free-thinking**: An allusion to the Freethinkers, those in the eighteenth century who arrived at conclusions using the rules of reason and thereby rejected supernatural authority and ecclesiastical tradition. Freethinking influenced the philosophies of the Order of Freemasons. Compare 74.25.

190.24. **the Miraculous . . . ceases to be Miraculous**: Compare Coleridge, "Definition of a Miracle," *Omniana* (1812), 346: "It is not strictly accurate to affirm, that everything would appear a miracle, if we were wholly uninfluenced by custom, and saw things as they are:—for then the very ground of miracles would probably vanish, namely, the heterogeneity of spirit and matter." Compare also 44.19–20.

190.26–27. **kind nurse . . . foolish nurse**: An adaptation of Wordsworth's "Tintern Abbey," lines 109–11, where Nature is "The anchor of my purest thoughts, the nurse, / The guide, the guardian of my heart, and soul / Of all my moral being"; and "Ode: Intimations of Immortality," lines 81–82, where "The homely Nurse doth all she can / To make her Foster-child, her Inmate-Man."

190.34. **Steam-engine**: Compare 91.21.

190.36-37. **potency of Names**: Compare 67.27.

190.38-191.1. **Witchcraft . . . Demonology**: Carlyle's brother, Dr. John Carlyle, reviewed Walter Scott, *Demonology and Witchcraft* (1830) in *Fraser's Magazine* 2 (December, 1830), 507-19. Compare 35.3-4; *Letters* 5:215n.

191.1-2. **Madness . . . Nerves**: In a letter to Anna Montagu, October 1830, Carlyle says, "I could feel as if our old fathers who believed in witchcraft and Possession were nearer the truth than we. . . . [T]he man, that walked in the midst of us, is clutched, as it were by some unseen devil, and hurled into abysses of Despair and Madness, which lie closer than we think on the path of everyone" (*Letters* 5:182-83).

191.6-7. **Luther's Picture of the Devil**: Compare *Fraser's Magazine* 2 (December, 1830), 518, where Luther's account of his confrontation with Satan who entered his sealed bed chamber and caused him to recommit himself to God is given. Compare also *On Heroes*, 119.28-33: "Luther sat translating one of the Psalms; he was worn down with long labour, with sickness, abstinence from food: there rose before him some hideous indefinable Image, which he took for the Evil One, to forbid his work: Luther started up, with fiend-defiance; flung his inkstand at the spectre, and it disappeared!"

191.18-19. **warp and woof**: Compare 42.35.

191.19-22. **Illusions . . . look through**: The language and the meaning here are reminiscent of Shelley's "Sonnet: 'Lift Not the Painted Veil,'" lines 1-6: "Lift not the painted veil which those who live / Call Life: though unreal shapes be pictured there, / And it but mimic all we would believe / With colours idly spread,—behind, lurk Fear / And Hope, twin Destinies; who ever weave / Their shadows, o'er the chasm, sightless and drear."

191.23. **Fortunatus . . . Hat**: Compare 117.10.

191.36. **Fire-Creation . . . Fire-Consummation**: An allusion to Heraclitus (535?-475? B.C.), Greek philosopher of Ephesus, who argued that there was no permanent reality except that of change, and that permanence was an illusion of the senses. Heraclitus believed that fire was the underlying substance of the universe and that all other elements were transformations of it. Compare *The Cosmic Fragments*, 307 (fragment 30): "This (world–)order . . . always was and is and shall be: an everlasting fire, kindling in measures and going out in measures."

191.38. **Paul**: St. Paul (died *c.*64–67), the apostle to the Gentiles, who experienced a conversion on the road to Damascus (Acts 9:3–18).

191.38. **Seneca**: Lucius Annæus Seneca (3? B.C.–65 A.D.), Roman stoic philosopher, dramatist, and statesman; tutor and adviser of Nero.

192.6–8. **Earth-blinded . . . darkly**: Compare 1 Corinthians 13:12: "For now we see through a glass, darkly."

192.14. **universal HERE . . . everlasting Now**: Compare 43.4.

192.22–23. **whatever was . . . is . . . will be**: An allusion to the *Gloria Patri*: "Glory be to the Father . . . as it was in the beginning, is now, and ever shall be."

192.27. **Thought-forms, Space and Time**: An allusion to Kant's *Critique of Pure Reason* ("The Transcendental Aesthetic," A 22–49, B 37–73), in which it is argued that Time and Space are infinite intuitive representations of the mind rather than *a priori* independent realities.

192.37. **stretch forth my hand**: Compare Coleridge's "Definition of a Miracle," *Omniana*, 345: "To stretch out my arm is a miracle, unless the materialists should be more cunning than they have proved themselves hitherto. To reanimate a dead man by an act of the will, no intermediate agency employed, not only is, but is called, a miracle." This expression, in various forms, is found throughout the Bible; compare Exodus 7:19; 8:5; Job 11:13; Psalms 68:31; Matthew 12:13; and John 21:18. Compare also 188.10–15, 197.18.

193.2–3. **pound avoirdupois of weight**: Avoirdupois is a system of weights based on a pound of sixteen ounces.

193.5. **free Force**: Free will. Compare 55.8–9.

193.11–12. **Thaumaturgy**: Compare 91.16–17.

193.15. **Orpheus**: In Greek myth the celebrated poet who with his lyre, presented to him by his father Apollo, tamed the wild beasts and suspended the torments of the damned in Hades.

193.15. **Amphion**: In Greek myth the son of Zeus who played his lyre, presented to him by Hermes, with such magic skill that the stones were moved to form the walls of Thebes. Compare Horace, *Ars Poetica*, lines 391–96.

193.18. *Steinbruch*: German: "stonequarry."

193.18–19 **Troglodyte**: A prehistoric cave dweller.

193.19. **green-mantled pools**: Compare *King Lear* 3.4.133–34: "[He] drinks the green mantle of the standing pool."

193.20. **Doric and Ionic pillars**: Two orders of Greek columned architecture; the third is the Corinthian order.

193.20. **ashlar houses**: Houses made of dressed blocks of building stone.

193.23. **highest Orpheus . . . Judea**: Jesus, who preached in Judea, the southern section of ancient Palestine.

193.24. **sphere-melody**: An allusion to the Pythagorean notion that as the planets rotated they made music and thus created a harmony.

193.34. **far distant Mover**: In Aristotelian philosophy, the Prime Mover; in Christian theology, God.

193.34–36. **stroke . . . elastic balls . . . sent flying**: An allusion to the experiment involving the transmission of energy where three spheres on strings are at rest. When an outside sphere is drawn back and permitted to hit the middle one, the middle sphere remains stationary and the opposite outside one flies away. Compare Newton's *Principia* (Law 3, Corollary 6), 21–25.

194.3. City of God: Compare Saint Augustine (354–430), *De Civitate Dei* (*City of God*, c.412), an elaborate defense of Christianity in which Augustine creates two mystical cities, one for God and one for Satan, and concludes that humankind will eventually belong to one or the other. Compare also Richter's *Siebenkäs*, 255: "The broad heaven, with the streets of the City of God all lit with the lamps which are suns, drew them on . . . into the great spectacle hall of night, where we breathe the blue of heaven, and drink the east breeze. . . . We should conclude . . . by 'going to church' in that cool, vast temple, that great cathedral whose dome is adorned with the sacred picture of the Most Holy, portrayed in a mosaic of stars."

194.9. Ghost . . . English Johnson: See Boswell's *Life of Johnson*, 137, for the account of Samuel Johnson's futile search, in 1762, for a ghost in Cock Lane.

194.24–25. squeak and gibber: Compare *Hamlet* 1.1.115–16: "[T]he sheeted dead / Did squeak and gibber."

194.25. screech-owlish: The owl is traditionally a harbinger of death. Compare *III Henry VI* 2.6.56: "Bring forth that fatal screech-owl to our house"; and *Macbeth* 2.2.3: "It was the owl that shriek'd, the fatal bellman."

194.27. Dance of the Dead: An allusion to Hans Holbein the Younger (1497?–1543), religious painter of the northern Renaissance, who did a series of woodcuts called *The Dance of Death* (c.1523–26, published 1538).

194.27–28. scent of the morning-air: Compare *Hamlet* 1.5.58, where the Ghost says, "But, soft, methinks I scent the morning air."

194.29–30. Alexander of Macedon . . . Issus and Arbela: Compare 70.20. Alexander defeated the Persians at Issus in Turkey in 333 B.C., and again at Arbela in ancient Assyria in 331 B.C.

194.32–33. Napoleon . . . Moscow Retreats and Austerlitz Campaigns: On December 2, 1805, Napoleon defeated the combined forces of the Russians and the Austrians at Austerlitz; compare 154.14–15. On October 19, 1812, he began his retreat from Moscow; compare 42.15.

194.34. **Night hideous**: Compare *Hamlet* 1.4.51–54, where Hamlet asks the Ghost: "What may this mean, / That thou, dead corse, again in complete steel / Revisits thus the glimpses of the moon, / Making night hideous?"

194.35. **Ghosts**: In a *Journal* entry, September 1830, Carlyle writes, "What am I but a sort of Ghost? Men rise as Apparitions from the bosom of Night, and after grinning, squeaking, and gibbering some space, return thither. The earth they stand on is Bottomless; the vault of their sky is Infinitude; the Life-*Time* is encompassed with Eternity. O wonder!" (*Two Note Books*, 164).

195.4. **dust and shadow**: *Pulvis et umbra*. Compare Horace, *Odes* 4.7.14–16: "We, when we have descended" into Hades, "are but dust and shadow."

195.11–12. **plummet's sounding**: Compare *The Tempest* 5.1.54–57, where Prospero in his so-called farewell speech says: "I'll break my staff, / Bury it certain fathoms in the earth, / And deeper than did ever plummet sound / I'll drown my book."

195.15. **beginning . . . end**: An adaptation of Revelation 1:8; 21:6: "I am the Alpha and the Omega, the beginning and the ending."

195.17. **Cimmerian Night**: The Cimmerians were a mythic people who lived in perpetual night. Compare Homer's *Odyssey*, 11.10–18, where the "most unblest Cimmerianes" live in a land in which a "perpetuall cloud obscures [the sun] outright." Compare also "Goethe's Helena," *Essays* 1:178, where Carlyle translates from *Helena*: "There, backwards in the rocky hills, a daring race / Have fix'd themselves, forth issuing from Cimmerian Night."

195.19–20. **hunter-like . . . madly dashed in pieces on the rocks**: The language in this passage and to a certain extent the situation can be found in Byron's *Manfred*, Act 1, Scene 2, where the Chamois Hunter restrains Manfred, who wishes to commit suicide by jumping from the cliffs of Jungfrau to be "strewn upon the rocks" (line 105).

195.21–22. earthy Vesture . . . vanished Shadow: Compare 1 Chronicles 29:15: "For we *are* strangers before thee, . . . our days on earth *are* as a shadow"; Job 8:9: "[O]ur days upon the earth *are* a shadow"; Psalms 102:11; 109:23; 144:4; and Ecclesiastes 6:12; 8:13.

195.27. astonished Earth: Compare *The Life of Friedrich Schiller*, 129, where Carlyle translates from *Wallenstein* (1798–99): "'Our life was but a battle and a march, / And, like the wind's blast, never-resting, homeless, / We storm'd across the war-convulsed Earth.'"

195.34. from God and to God: Carlyle's affirmation of faith. Compare a letter to John Carlyle, December 2, 1832: "Man issues from Eternity; walks in a 'Time-Element' encompassed by Eternity and again in Eternity disappears. Fearful and wonderful! This only we know, that God is above it, that God made it, and rules it for *good*" (*Letters* 6:267). Compare also John 13:3: "Jesus knowing that the Father had given all things into his hands, and that he was come from God, and went to God"; and Romans 1:17: "For therein is the righteousness of God revealed from faith to faith: as it is written, The just shall live by faith."

195.35–37. We *are such stuff* . . . rounded with a sleep: Compare *The Tempest* 4.1.156–58. The quotation is verbatim, except that "made on" is changed to "made of" and the italics are added. Compare also "Jean Paul Friedrich Richter" (1827), *Essays* 2:154, where Carlyle points out the profound effect this passage had on Richter. The quotation was a favorite of Carlyle's and can be found throughout his writings.

NOTES TO CHAPTER IX. CIRCUMSPECTIVE

196.2. new promised country: As in the "promised land"; compare 187.16.

196.5–7. Woollen-Hulls . . . Flesh-Garments . . . Garments of his very Soul's Soul: The triad represented by Book I (Vesture), Book II (Body), and Book III (Soul). Compare 187.12.

196.10. glass darkly: Compare 1 Corinthians 13:11–12: "When I was a child, I spake as a child, . . . but when I became a man, I put away childish things. For now we see through a glass, darkly." Compare also 192.6–8. The expression also appears in Richter's "Preface" to *Hesperus* (1795), part of which Carlyle translated in his essay "Jean Paul Friedrich Richter (Again)."

196.11–12. **changeable divided from what is unchangeable**: Yields a fraction; compare 97.33–35, 142.25–27.

196.12. **Earth-Spirit's speech**: Compare 43.11.

196.15. **speech of the Magician**: The lines are spoken by Prospero, the quotation altered slightly though not significantly, in *The Tempest* 4.1.151–56. The lines immediately precede the often quoted "We are such stuff / As dreams are made on." Compare 195.35–37.

197.2–3. **Palingenesia . . . Phœnix Death-Birth**: Compare 160.21, 187.16, and Book III, Chapter V, "The Phœnix," 171–75.

197.5. **Bridge**: Compare 60.21–24. The idea here, that the bridge might be temporarily concluded and made "quite firm, passable even" but never fully completed, is fundamental to Carlyle's more-Romantic-than-Victorian philosophy that humankind is in a constant state of palingenesis ("perpetual metamorphoses") and thus can only hope to move forward but never to achieve a single end. The notion that a "bridge" can be "converted into firm ground" is satirized by Nathaniel Hawthorne in "The Celestial Railroad" (1843).

197.10. **zigzag**: A term used in the seventeenth century to describe cloth as well as erratic direction. Zigzag material was material reinforced through the pattern of stitching. To extend the metaphor, this passage could be seen as the bringing together of pieces of cloth (Sartor) which then by "passings and repassings" are "mended" into a quilt (Resartus).

197.11. **leaps**: Compare 117.19, 187.15.

197.17. **be of courage**: Compare 187.17.

197.20. **labour, each according to ability**: Compare Matthew 25:15, where the talents were given "to every man according to his several ability"; Acts 11:29, where "the disciples, every man according to his ability, determined to send relief unto the brethren"; and 1 Peter 4:11.

197.20. **New labourers**: A reiteration of the idea that social, hence spiritual palingenesis takes place through work; compare 137.6-7.

197.30-31. **hand should be held out**: Compare the theory of the miracle, 192.37.

198.1. **replenishing thy purse**: An adaptation of *Othello* 1.3.339-71, where Iago advises Roderigo to "Put money in thy purse." Carlyle may also have in mind the Utilitarian Bentham, whom he describes in a letter to Macvey Napier, January 20, 1831, as a "Denyer, he *denies* with a loud and universally convincing voice: his fault is that he can *affirm* nothing, except that money is pleasant in the purse and food in the stomach" (*Letters* 5:12).

198.4. **Horn-gate**: One of the gates of sleep. Compare Virgil's *Aeneid*, 6.1191-96: "There are two gates of Sleep: the one is said / to be of horn, through it an easy exit / is given to true Shades; the other is made / of polished ivory, perfect, glittering, / but through that way the Spirits send false dreams / into the world above."

198.5. **Land of Dreams**: Wahngasse, Weissnichtwo. Notably, the land of the Lotos-Eaters; compare Tennyson, "The Lotos-Eaters" (1832).

198.6. *Pierre-Pertuis*: A natural opening in a rock in the Bernese Alps, Switzerland.

198.8-9. **life is girt . . . based on Wonder**: Compare 52.4.

198.11. **literary Tea-circle**: Compare 96.11.

198.14-16. **Symbols . . . Clothes**: Compare 55.30 and Book III, Chapter III, "Symbols," 161-66.

198.16. **Magna Charta**: Or Magna Carta, "Great Charter," guaranteed that the feudal rights of the barons would not be usurped by King John, who under compulsion signed the document of sixty-three clauses at Runnymede on June 19, 1215. Isaac Disraeli (1766–1848), *Curiosities of Literature* (1791) 1:72, relates the anecdote of how Sir Robert Cotton (1571–1631), the celebrated antiquarian, rescued an original copy of Magna Carta from his tailor who was about to cut it up for measures.

198.18–19. **Worships (Worth-ships):** *Worship* is from the Anglo-Saxon *weorthscipe*, or "worth-ship."

198.19–20. **Thirty-nine Articles:** From the reign of Elizabeth I, the Articles, which are Calvinistic in theological emphasis, present the tenets of the Church of England, most notable among them the doctrine of royal supremacy. The Articles were conceived to give uniformity to Anglican dogma. They are placed in every Prayer-Book, and must be accepted by everyone who is ordained. At Oxford they had to be accepted before admission, and at Cambridge before taking a degree. Carlyle felt that their total acceptance, feigned by many clergy at ordination, was a Jesuitical suppression of truth. George Fox's religion, that of direct intervention by the Holy Spirit, stands in direct contrast to such corporeal mandate. Carlyle's liberal heterodoxy repeatedly came into conflict with Anglican certainty, as evidenced in the jingle written in his *Journal*, May 26, 1835, in contempt of F. D. Maurice and the Articles:

Thirty-nine English Articles,
Ye wondrous little particles,
Did God shape his Universe really by *you*?
In that case, I swear it,
And solemnly declare it,
This logic of M[aurice]s's is true.

See *Letters* 8:139–40n, 11:205; and *Collected Poems*, 58, 177–78.

198.23. **Codification:** An allusion to the efforts of Bentham to reform the English judicial system through, among other things, the codification of the laws.

198.25. **prophetic height looks down:** Compare 16.26.

198.36. **practical nature:** This is evidence of Carlyle's attempt to make practical the transcendental philosophy he espouses. Compare, for example, 161.11.

199.1-2. **architectural ideas**: Compare 27.14, 193.15-32.

199.5. **Habilatory Class**: Clothed Class; pun on *habit*, a distinctive dress or costume, here dandiacal rather than monastical.

199.9. **die that we may live**: Adaptation of the belief that Christ died that sinners might live; compare John 11:50-51; Romans 5:10; 1 Corinthians 15:3; and 2 Corinthians 5:15. Perhaps a pun on *dye*.

199.11-12. **live, move, and have their being**: Compare 4.15-16, 133.15, 164.16.

NOTES TO CHAPTER X. THE DANDIACAL BODY

200.6. **dress to live**: Compare Book I, Chapter V, "The World in Clothes," 27-32.

200.11. **Divine Idea of Cloth**: Here and throughout the whole of this chapter Carlyle is using satire to bring to light from still another perspective the socio-moral-philosophical principles raised previously. Compare 154.13-37.

200.15. **Idea an Action**: Compare 118.25.

200.18. **Huddersfield dyes**: Compare 157.6.

200.18-19. **Sonnet to his mistress' eyebrow**: Compare *As You Like It* 2.7.147-49, where Jacques says of humankind in his "All the world's a stage" speech, "And then the lover, / Sighing like furnace, with a woeful ballad / Made to his mistress' eyebrow."

200.19. *Clotha Virumque cano*: "Of clothes and the man I sing"; a parody of the opening line of Virgil's *Aeneid*, Book I: "*Arma virumque cano*" (Of arms and the man I sing). *Clotha* is not Latin, although *Clotho* is the Latin name of one of the three *Parcae*, or Fates. Clotho (*Klwqw*, "I spin") spins the web of life as Lachesis measures it out and Atropos cuts it.

200.20. **Macaronic verses**: Poetry containing a mixture of vernacular words with Latin words or with non-Latin words that are given humorous Latin terminations. A pun here on *macaroni*, a fashionable fop or dandy. Compare 45.19.

200.20. **he that runs may read**: Compare 172.21.

201.2. **Eternity with Time**: Compare 165.8–9.

201.8–9. **niggardly Law**: A difficult allusion, perhaps to the law of supply and demand, that is, laissez faire; or perhaps to the pending or already passed reform legislation. If read ironically, perhaps a reference to Natural Law which gives humankind life but does not guarantee sustenance.

201.14. **Siamese Twins**: An allusion to the conjoined twins Chang and Eng (1811–1874), born in Siam of Chinese parents, who were exhibited in London in 1829. The twins, surnamed Bunker, became naturalized Americans; and, although never separated, they married and fathered twenty-two children. They died within two hours of each other.

201.14. **wonderful wonder of wonders**: Compare *The Wonderful Wonder of Wonders* (1720), a burlesque on affectation and equivocation, generally attributed to Swift.

201.16–17. **no Anatomist dissects with care**: Compare Swift's *A Tale of a Tub*, 173, where it is observed while discussing madness that in "most Corporeal Beings . . . the *Outside* hath been infinitely preferable to the *In*. . . . I ordered the Carcass of a *Beau* to be stript in my Presence; when we were all amazed to find so many unsuspected Faults under one Suit of Clothes."

201.19. **Lord Herringbone**: A dandy; from a type of twilled fabric woven in a slanted design of alternating rows.

201.20. **it skills not**: "It matters not"; an Elizabethan expression.

201.21. **passes by . . . on the other side**: An allusion to the parable of the Good Samaritan; see Luke 10:31–32, where the priest and the Levite ignored the injured man and "passed by on the other side."

201.22. **age of Curiosity**: An allusion perhaps to Isaac Disraeli's *Curiosities of Literature*, published in six volumes, 1791–1834.

201.22–23. **Chivalry . . . gone**: Compare Edmund Burke, *Reflections on the Revolution in France* (1790), *Selected Writings and Speeches*, 457: "But the age of chivalry is gone!" In "The Diamond Necklace" (1837), *Essays* 3:337, Carlyle concludes, "The age of Chivalry is gone, and that of Bankruptcy is come."

202.7. **new metamorphosis**: Compare "perpetual metamorphoses," 55.21–22.

202.10. **moon-calves**: Monsters or freaks, thought to be caused by the influence of the moon. Compare *The Tempest* 2.2.111.

202.20–21. **Fetish-worships**: Compare 119.1.

202.21. **Hero-worships or Polytheisms**: Compare Hume, *Natural History of Religion* (1755), Section 5.

202.23. **Manicheism**: Or Manichaeism, a third-century dualistic philosophy which holds that there exists the realm of God (Light) and the realm of Satan (Darkness). The body belongs to Satan and the soul to God. Corporeal life is the eternal struggle to be free of darkness and to return to light.

202.23. **Gnostic**: Gnosticism, from *gnosis* (knowledge), a religious philosophy that reached its zenith in the second century, promising salvation through an occult knowledge revealed to Gnostics alone. Considered heretics by the Church, Gnostics rejected the Old Testament God as evil, believed Christ was the intermediary sent to restore the knowledge of humankind's origin, and argued that humankind is divided into three classes: hylic (flesh), those who have no chance of salvation; psychic (soul), Christians who can attain a lesser salvation through faith; and pneumatic (spirit), Gnostics whose salvation through the "divine spark" was assured. Manichaeism adopted many of the ideas of Gnosticism.

202.26. **Athos Monks**: A community of monks established in c.963 on Mount Athos in northeastern Greece, the "Holy Mountain" of the Greek Church. Compare Gibbon's *Decline and Fall* 6:506, where a monk from the eleventh century is quoted on the practice of asceticism: "When thou art alone in thy cell, . . . shut thy door, and seat thyself in a corner; raise thy mind above all things vain and transitory; recline thy beard and chin on thy breast; turn thy eyes and thy thoughts towards the middle of thy belly, the region of the navel; and search the place of the heart, the seat of the soul . . . and you will feel an ineffable joy." The story of this practice, which Gibbon thought "the production of a distempered fancy, the creature of an empty stomach and an empty brain," must have given inspiration to Teufelsdröckh's observation that Utilitarians believed that the "*Soul* is . . . a kind of *Stomach,*" and to Carlyle's subsequent repudiation that "Soul is *not* synonymous with the Stomach." Compare 90.18–19, 121.19.

202.31. *Self-Worship*: Compare "Self-love," 166.13.

202.31. **Zerdusht**: Zoroaster (628?–551? B.C.), teacher and prophet of ancient Persia, founder of Zoroastrianism, a religious philosophy originally formed on contemplation that evolved into a complex cosmogony which taught that the history of the universe is divided into four periods of 3000 years, the last being a period of salvation by fire for those who overcome evil.

202.31. **Quangfoutchee**: K'ung Fu-tzu, or Confucius (551–479 B.C.), Chinese teacher and reformer, founder of Confucianism, originally a moral and religious philosophy espousing a social order based upon *Jen* (filial sympathy and understanding) and *Li* (social etiquette and ritual).

202.32. **Mohamed**: Muhammad (570?–632), the prophet of Islam, originally a religion characterized by total submission to God, known as Allah. Muhammad is considered the last of the prophets to whom Allah made revelations, principally recorded in the *Qur'an*. In Islam faith is not distinguished from work and, like Christianity, Islam anticipates judgment and redemption.

202.35. **Ahrimanism**: Darkness or evil. In primitive Zoroastrianism, Ahriman is the leader of the *daevas* (evil spirits) who opposed Ormazd (sovereign knowledge), the only god.

203.2. **costume**: Compare 27.1–3.

203.4–5. *Lingua-franca*: Literally, the "Language of Franks," a mixture of Latin and Arabic words used in the eastern Mediterranean. Here, a parody and ridiculing of the corruption of language for effect, already anticipated in the "macaronic verses."

203.6. Nazarene: Probably a mistake for Nazarite, a Jew whose dedication to God was measured through strict vows of separation. Compare Numbers 6:2–21. It is possible, however, that Carlyle may be trying to draw a distinction between the biblical ("true") Nazarene and the so-called Nazarene artists of the early nineteenth century who attempted to revive Christian art while dedicating themselves to a monastic life.

203.6–7. unspotted from the world: Compare James 1:27: "Pure religion . . . is this, To visit the fatherless and widows, in their affliction, *and* to keep himself unspotted from the world."

203.9. *Almack's*: Fashionable assembly- and ball-rooms in King Street, St. James's, London, named after William Almack (died 1781) who opened the club in 1765. It is here that Carlyle delivered his six lectures on German literature, now lost, beginning in May of 1837. In "Fashionable Novels," *Fraser's Magazine*, 1 (April, 1830), 335, Almack's is described as a "register of fashionable life." This article has been attributed to Carlyle; see Tarr, *Thomas Carlyle: A Descriptive Bibliography*, 466.

203.12. Menadic: I.e., frenzied. In Greek myth Maenads were women followers of the orgiastic cult of Dionysus.

203.13. Eleusinian: The Eleusinian Mystery, a cult dedicated to Demeter and Persephone, celebrated an annual, secret, initiatory ritual at Eleusis, near Athens, from at least the sixth century B.C. to the fourth century A.D.

203.13. Cabiric: The Cabiri were nature deities of obscure origin, possibly Phoenician, who were associated with mysterious fertility rituals and later with the Greek goddess Demeter.

203.15. *Fashionable Novels*: A wide-sweeping generic codification of all novels published during the eighteen-twenties, but especially those published by the firms of Henry Colburn and Richard Bentley. In

"Fashionable Novels," *Fraser's Magazine*, 1 (April, 1830), 318, the novels are said to be made up "of cant and humbug,—of fraud, folly, and foppery,—of idle words, vast pretensions, no sense, and latent hollowness." Compare 204.13.

203.15. **Canon**: The books of the Bible officially recognized by the church as inspired by God.

203.25-26. **Jew's-harping**: A jew's-harp is a lyre-shaped musical instrument that is held between the teeth when played.

203.26. **scrannel-piping**: Compare Milton's *Lycidas*, lines 124-25, where the clergy with "their lean and flashy songs / Grate on their scrannel Pipes of wretched straw, / The hungry Sheep look up, and are not fed." According to the *OED* (s.v. "Scrannel"), *scrannel* means "Thin, meager. Now chiefly as a reminiscence of Milton's use, usually with the sense: Harsh, unmelodious."

203.27. **Magnetic Sleep**: Hypnotism, Mesmerism, sometimes referred to as "animal magnetism," named after the German physician Friedrich Anton Mesmer (1734-1815).

203.29. **deliquium**: *Deliquium* has two senses in Latin, both of which have been brought into English, and sometimes confused. One sense derives from *delinquere*, "to fail, to be lacking, to be at fault" (e.g., *deliquium solis*, "an eclipse of the sun"). The other derives from *deliquare*, "to make liquid, to melt, dissolve, liquefy."

203.33. **Fire-balls**: Compare Gibbon, *Decline and Fall* 2:459-60, where the failure of the Roman emperor Julian ("the Apostate," 331?– 363) to rebuild the temple of Jerusalem is described as a "præternatural event." Gibbon relates that, according to the historian Ammianus Marcellinus, the appearance of "'horrible balls of fire . . . rendered the place . . . inaccessible to the scorched and blasted workmen [and thus] the undertaking was abandoned.'" Gibbon comments that the authority of the historian "should satisfy a believing, and must astonish an incredulous mind," and calls the event a "specious and splendid miracle."

204.5. *Stillschweigen'sche Buchhandlung*: "Silence and Company Bookshop." Compare 6.22.

204.8–9. Mohamedan . . . waste paper: Compare Addison, *The Spectator*, no. 85 (June 7, 1711): "It is the custom of the *Mahometans*, if they see any printed or written Paper upon the Ground, to take it up and lay it aside carefully, as not knowing but it may contain some Piece of their *Alcoran*."

204.16. Pelham: An allusion to a novel by Edward Bulwer-Lytton (1803–1873) entitled *Pelham* (1828), a picture of fashionable society. The article is in *Fraser's Magazine*.

204.21. sparkle out: Compare 25.24.

204.22. Theogonies: Recitations of the origins and genealogy of the gods.

204.24. Confession of Faith: An allusion to the "Westminster Confession of Faith" (1645–1647), the credo of the Calvinists and the Presbyterians.

204.25. Whole Duty of Man: Compare 145.20–21.

204.27. Seven distinct Articles: The seven "Articles of Faith" on the requisites of fashion are taken almost verbatim from a long passage on the "rules of costume" from the first edition of *Pelham* (1828), Volume 2, Chapter 7. In the second edition of *Pelham*, also published in 1828, Bulwer-Lytton significantly revises this passage, turning it into twenty-two "Maxims" on how one should dress, claiming that his thoughts on clothes are "writ in irony." Carlyle apparently did not see the second edition, or chose to ignore it. The original "rules" are repeated in "Mr. Edward Lytton Bulwer's Novels; and Remarks on Novel-Writing," *Fraser's Magazine*, 1 (June, 1830), 517–18, which might also be Carlyle's source.

204.37. Hottentot: A pastoral people in southern Africa. The reference is no doubt more pointed, however. From 1810 until her death in 1815, *la Vénus Hottentotte* (the Hottentot Venus) created a sensation as she was exhibited throughout Britain and the Continent where people gathered to view her protruding buttocks and large genitalia.

205.17–19. *Drudge* Sect ... *White Negroes* ... *Ragged-Beggar.* Carlyle is following here the ironic lead of Swift's *A Modest Proposal* by presenting Ireland as the seat of poverty, both physical and spiritual, which extends itself by example to all parts of Great Britain.

205.20. *Hallan-shakers.* Beggars. *Hallan* is Scots for the partition in a cottage, between the "but" (outside room) and the "ben" (inside room), which was shaken by beggars seeking alms.

205.23. **parent hive:** Compare 16.26.

205.24. *Bogtrotters.* A person who lives in or frequents bogs, used disparagingly to describe the Irish.

205.24–25. *Redshanks.* Redlegs, Irish mountaineers.

205.25. *Ribbonmen.* A secret Irish Catholic society founded in 1808, whose members wore green ribbons in opposition to the Orangemen, a secret Protestant society founded in northern Ireland in 1795.

205.25. *Cottiers.* Peasants who rented their land directly from the owners, the rent having been fixed by public bidding. This system was called "rack-rent" because of the exorbitant prices realized from the bidding.

205.25. *Peep-of-day Boys.* A secret Protestant society in the late eighteenth century whose members raided Catholic households, usually at dawn, looking for weapons.

205.25. *Babes of the Wood:* Bands of young Irishmen from County Wicklow known for their general lawlessness.

205.25. *Rockites.* Irish insurrectionaries in the eighteen twenties who signed their revolutionary notes "Captain Rock."

206.3–4. **Monastic Vows:** Compare "Life of Quintus Fixlein," *German Romance* 2:260–61, where it is said of one of the "Monastic Vows": the "beautiful equality in Poverty, is so admirably attended to, that no man who has made it needs any farther *testimonium paupertatis.*"

206.6. **Nazarene**: Here clearly a mistake for "Nazarite." See note at 203.6 above.

206.15. **lappets**: Compare 19.20.

206.18. **thrums**: Compare 50.16.

206.18. **skewers**: Compare 177.19.

206.24. **University-cap**: Flat-cap or mortar-board.

206.25. **Slavonic**: From the Medieval Latin *sclavus*, Slav, which is the root of *slave*.

206.27. **Druidical**: Paganistic; druids were priests in ancient Gaul and Britain.

206.28. **Hertha**: Or Ertha, the Mother-Earth of Germanic mythology. Compare Tacitus, *Germania*, Section 40.

206.30. **private Oratories**: I.e., factories.

206.38. **wicker idols**: Compare Julius Caesar, *The Battle for Gaul*, 6.16, where the druidical ceremonies of sacrifice are described: "Some of them have enormous images made of wickerwork, the limbs of which they fill with living men; these are set on fire and the men perish, enveloped in flames."

207.2. **Rhizophagous**: Root-eating. Compare Diodorus Siculus (died after 21 B.C.), whose *History of the World*, Book 4, contains a lengthy account of the Ethiopian Rarofagians which is immediately preceded by a description of the Icthiofagorians.

207.2. **Ichthyophagous**: Fish-eating.

207.4–5. **Brahminical feeling**: Brahmins, the caste of Hindu priests, opposed the killing of all animals.

207.9. *Potatoes-and-Point*: Among Irish peasants, the custom of eating potatoes and pointing at other wished-for but unobtainable foods.

207.12. *Potheen*: Illicit Irish liquor, distilled from potatoes.

207.13. *Blue-Ruin*: Gin, so-called because of the color of the bottle.

207.17. **liquid fire**: Compare 153.12.

207.21. *John Bernard*: John Bernard (1756–1828), British actor and writer whose *Retrospections of the Stage* (London, 1830) 1:349–50, Carlyle quotes nearly verbatim. However, he does make a number of incidental changes as well as two substantive ones in Bernard's text: "whiskey noggin" becomes "Potheen Noggin," and "pot of 'paratees'" becomes "Pot of Potatoes." Carlyle also continues to quote from Bernard in the rest of the paragraph following the close-quotation mark at 208.6.

207.28. **Theogonist**: Compare 204.22.

207.33. **Caravansera**: From the Persian, an inn built around a large court to accommodate caravans.

207.34. **Noggin**: A small mug holding about one-quarter of a pint.

208.9–10. **young ones . . . ravens**: Compare Job 38:41: "Who provideth for the raven his food? when his young ones cry unto God"; and Psalms 147:9.

208.12. **Dandiacal Household**: The following quotation on the "Dandiacal Household" is taken nearly verbatim from Bulwer-Lytton's *The Disowned* (1828; 2nd ed., 1829), the Introduction, which is reproduced in "Mr. Edward Lytton Bulwer's Novels," *Fraser's Magazine*, 1 (June, 1830), 515. See note at 204.27 above.

208.22. **Buhl**: A style of furniture in which elaborate designs are inlaid with tortoiseshell, ivory, and metal of various colors. Named after the French woodcarver André C. Boule (1642–1732).

208.27. **cambric**: A finely woven white linen or cotton fabric.

209.10. **Communion of Saints**: Compare 182.16.

209.21. Potwallopers: *Potwaller* or *potwalloper* (literally, "potboiler"), "the term applied in some English boroughs, before the Reform Act of 1832, to a man qualified for a parliamentary vote as a householder (i.e. tenant of a house or distinct part of one) as distinguished from one who was merely a member or inmate of a householder's family; the test of which was his having a separate fire-place, on which his own pot was boiled. . . . [T]he test was at times abused by persons not householders, who in anticipation of an election and of receiving money for their vote, boiled a pot in the presence of witnesses on an improvised fireplace in the open air within the borough, and thus passed as potwallers" (*OED*, s.v. "Potwaller").

209.29. Buchan-Bullers: Buchan Ness, the name of a vertical well in the rocks of the coast near Petershead in Aberdeenshire, Scotland, characterized by its violent, whirlpool-like churning, called a buller. Carlyle may be recalling the following description from "Greek Drama," *Blackwood's Magazine*, 30 (August, 1831), 389: "It was like one of the Cauldrons of the Bullers of Buchan. They . . . are not always black, but always boiling, and the reason is, that day and night the abysses are disturbed by the sea."

209.34–210.5. Electric Machines . . . World-Batteries: Compare "Characteristics" (1831), *Essays* 3:20: "Wealth has accumulated itself into masses; and Poverty, also in accumulation enough, lies impassably separated from it; opposed, uncommunicating, like forces in positive and negative poles"; and Carlyle's translation of Goethe's Proem from *Das Mährchen* (*The Tale*, 1832), *Essays* 2:452: "Consider them [Lily and Prince] as the two disjointed Halves of the singular Dualistic Being of ours; a Being . . . the most utterly Dualistic; fashioned . . . out of Positive and Negative (what we happily call Light and Darkness, Necessity and Freewill, Good and Evil, and the like); everywhere out of *two* mortally opposed things, which yet must be united in vital love, if there is to be any *Life*. . . . [W]ere not *Life* perpetually there, perpetually knitting it [Being] together again!" Compare also 34.27–29.

210.7–9. Earth . . . Moon: The apocalyptic "Eternity of Night" suggested here is similar in tone to that found in Novalis's lamenting *Hymnen an die Nacht* (*Hymns to the Night*, 1800), Part 3, and Byron's prophetic poem "Darkness" (1816). Compare also *King Lear* 1.2.103–04: "These late eclipses in the sun and moon portend no good to us."

210.15–16. **tendency to Mysticism:** Compare 51.11.

210.17. **amaurosis-suffusions:** Amaurosis is a form of blindness.

NOTES TO CHAPTER XI. TAILORS

211.11. **Pelion on Ossa:** Pelion and Ossa are mountains in Thessaly. According to Greek myth, the Titans attempted to scale heaven by heaping Pelion on Ossa, and then Pelion and Ossa on Mount Olympus. Compare Virgil's *Georgics*, Book 1, lines 281–82: "Thrice they assayed to plant Ossa on Pelion, ay, and roll up leafy Olympus upon Ossa."

211.11. **Moloch:** The god of the Ammonites and Phoenicians to whom children were sacrificed by fire. Compare Leviticus 20:1–5, where God warns Moses about the evils of Moloch; I Kings 11:7, where Solomon builds a temple to the "abomination" Moloch; and II Kings 23:10, where the idols to Moloch are destroyed. In *Paradise Lost* 1.392–99, Moloch, a sun-god, is described as the "horrid King besmear'd with blood / Of human sacrifice."

211.12. **Michael:** An archangel. Compare Daniel 12:1, where Michael is called the "great prince," the deliverer of Daniel's children; and Revelation 12:7, where "Michael and his angels" fight the "war in Heaven" against the "great red dragon," Satan. In *Paradise Lost* 6.44, Michael is described as the "Celestial Armies Prince."

211.18–19. **fractional Parts of a Man:** An allusion to the Breton proverb: "Il faut neuf tailleurs pour faire un homme" (It takes nine tailors to make a man).

211.23–212.2. *Tailor's-Melancholy . . .* **Cabbage:** Compare Charles Lamb (1775–1834), "On the Melancholy of Tailors," who quotes from Burton, *Anatomy of Melancholy* 1:220, who claims that cabbage "causeth troublesome dreams, and sends up black vapours to the brain. . . . It brings heaviness to the soul." There is a pun on cabbage, which can mean "pieces of cloth," or "to pilfer" as in tailors who appropriate for their own use remnants of cloth given to them to make garments. Compare also the British ballad "The Country Maid's Lamentation for the Loss of Her Tailor," *Roxburg Ballads* 7:475–76: "When he had got all her cloath[e]s in his hand, he quitted his

Country baggage, / And run from his lodging which was in the *Strand* ; thus cleverly rub'd with his Cabbage: / And left the poor wench in such a bad state, who hardly believ'd he would fail her."

212.3. **Hans Sachs**: Hans Sachs (1494–1576), German poet and meistersinger of Nuremberg, whose song, *Der Schneider mit dem Panier* (*The Tailor with the Banner*), tells of a tailor who has stolen cloth and then has a nightmare about a banner made up of patches of the stolen cloth. In a *Journal* entry, December 1826, Carlyle writes, "Hans Sachs is a curious fellow; . . . full of humour, reading, honesty, good nature; of the quickest observation. . . . See the *Tailor with the flag*" (*Two Note Books*, 74).

212.5. ***Taming of the Shrew***: Compare *The Taming of the Shrew* 4.3.61–168, where the unnamed tailor makes a gown "According to the fashion and the time" (line 95). Tailors also appear in *I Henry IV*, *Cymbeline*, *King Lear*, *A Midsummer-Night's Dream*, *Macbeth*, and *Romeo and Juliet*.

212.6. **English Queen Elizabeth**: Elizabeth I (1533–1603); the source for these anecdotes about the Queen and her tailors has not been traced.

212.8. **virago**: Perhaps in the sense of a courageous as well as a domineering woman.

212.10. **Tailors on Mares**: In the reeling of yarn, a cross thread is referred to as a mare.

212.15. **sartorius**: Latin: *sartorious musculus* (tailor's muscle), so named because this thigh muscle (the longest in the body) allows one to sit in a cross-legged position, traditionally the position of a tailor at work. From the Latin *sartor*, "tailor," and *sartus*, "to be in good repair," which is from *sarcio*, "to mend, to patch, to repair." Hence the title: *Sartor Resartus* (Tailor Remended, Tailor Retailored, or Tailor Repaired). The possible sources for the cryptic title are endless: (1) from the Latin etymologies suggested above; (2) from the popular Scottish ballad "The Tailor Done Over": "I once was a tailor, I lived with great pleasure, / I cut all my cloth to my customer's measure; / Oh, I once was so lusty they called me Bill the Rover, /

But now I'm a skeleton fairly done over"; or (3) remotely from the Old Latin *reseratore* (to edit), as in "The Clothes Volume Edited." See note at 10.26–27 above.

212.21. Swift: An allusion to Swift's *A Tale of a Tub*, 2.77–79, the inspiration for the clothes metaphor of *Sartor Resartus*. The Tailor Sect "held the Universe to be a large *Suit of Cloaths*, which *invests* every Thing. . . . Look on this Globe of Earth, you will find it to be a very compleat and fashionable *Dress*. . . . [W]hat is Man himself but a *Micro-Coat*, or rather a compleat Suit of Cloaths with all its Trimmings? . . . Is not Religion a *Cloak*, Honesty a *Pair of Shoes*, . . . Self-love a *Surtout*, Vanity a *Shirt*, and Conscience a *Pair of Breeches*. . . ." Swift refines his metaphor by asserting that "Man [is] an Animal compounded of two *Dresses*, the *Natural* and the *Celestial Suit*, which [are] the Body and the Soul."

212.24. Franklin: Benjamin Franklin (1706–1790), who proved the existence of electricity in lightning by flying a kite in a thunderstorm. The quotation is from the motto that Anne Robert Jacques Turgot appended to a portrait of Franklin by Joseph S. Duplessis: "Eripuit coelo fulmen / Sceptrumque tyrannis." Carlyle's first publications were in admiration of Franklin: "On the Phenomenon of Thunder" and "On Thunder," *Dumfries and Galloway Courier* (June 6 and 20, 1815), pp. 3, 3–4.

212.34. Metaphorical Tailors: Carlyle's original intention was to write a book on metaphors. In a *Journal* entry, August [1829], he writes: "All language but that concerning *sensual* objects is or has been figurative. Prodigious influence of metaphors! Never saw into it till lately. A truly useful and philosophical work would be a good *Essay on Metaphors*. Some day I will write one!" (*Two Note Books*, 141–42). Compare 56.4–9.

212.35. Guild-Brother: Goethe. Compare *Wilhelm Meister* 1:114: "'Nay, if thou wilt have it, who but the poet was it that first formed gods for us; that exalted us to them, and brought them down to us?'"

213.6. Anchorite: A person who seeks seclusion for religious purposes.

213.6. **Fakir**: Mendicant, from the Arabic for one who is poor. Compare 186.5.

213.11-12. **Fraction . . . Integer**: Compare 142.25-27.

213.13. **Hierophant**: An interpreter of sacred mysteries.

213.15. **Mosque of St. Sophia**: Hagia Sophia ("Holy Wisdom"), originally a Christian church in Constantinople that became a mosque after the Turkish conquest in 1453. The Turks covered the Christian icons with coatings of plaster and painted ornaments.

213.16. **Four-and-Twenty Tailors**: Or possibly, an adaptation of the "Four-and-Twenty Blackbirds."

213.17. **Caaba of Mecca**: Or Ka'abah, the Moslem shrine in Mecca which houses a sacred black stone said to have been given to Abraham by the archangel Gabriel, toward which followers of Muhammad face while praying. Compare *On Heroes*, 43.21-44.5.

213.18-19. **Unholies . . . holy**: Compare 77.3.

213.24. **Sic Itur Ad Astra**: "Thus one rises to the stars." Compare Virgil's *Aeneid* 9.641; and *Letters* 2:429. Carlyle may have seen this expression in Edinburgh. It was inscribed on the Canongate front of the Tolbooth, once a prison, which was demolished in 1817.

NOTES TO CHAPTER XII. FAREWELL

214.2. **Scottish Haggis**: The national dish of Scotland; minced heart, lungs, liver, and other entrails of a sheep or a calf, mixed with suet, onions, oatmeal, and seasonings, and boiled in the stomach of the sheep or calf.

214.6. **wash our hands**: Compare Matthew 27:24: "When Pilate saw that he could prevail nothing, . . . he took water and washed *his* hands before the multitude, saying, I am innocent of the blood of this just person [Jesus]."

214.19. **lumber-rooms**: Rooms cluttered with different articles.

214.20. lost rings: An allusion to the ring of Brunhild stolen by Siegfried in the *Das Nibelungenlied*, the German epic poem of the early thirteenth century. Carlyle considered writing about the poem as early as March of 1830 (*Letters* 5:85); and he subsequently published a critical article in the *Westminster Review*, 15 (July, 1831), 1–45.

214.20. diamond-necklaces: An allusion to the scandal in France in which a diamond necklace was used to dupe Cardinal de Rohan into believing he was a confidant of Queen Marie Antoinette. The plot brought disfavor upon the Queen even though she was entirely innocent. Carlyle writes about the affair in "The Diamond Necklace" (1837), *Fraser's Magazine*, 15 (January–February, 1837), 1–19, 172–89. His interest in the subject dates from early 1832, although he did not begin serious research for his article until March of 1833. See *Two Reminiscences*, 69, and *Letters* 6:142, 352n.

215.1-2. piebald . . . style of writing: Compare Butler's *Hudibras*, 1.95–6, where it is said of pedantry: "It was a particolour'd dress / Of patch'd and pyball'd Languages."

215.5-6. whirlpool: Compare 209.29.

215.7-8. lesser . . . portion of the greater: Compare 142.25–27.

215.14. Cant: Compare 10.34.

215.14. Dilettantism: Compare 53.21.

215.17-18. Hannibal-like . . . warfare: Hannibal (247–183? B.C.), Carthaginian general whose hatred of Rome was inherited from his father and whose brilliant victories over the Roman armies during the Second Punic War (218–201 B.C.) are legend.

215.20. Polack Scythe-man: An allusion to the Nationalist Revival in Poland in 1830, called the November Revolution, in which the lightly armed Poles (some, it is reported, armed only with scythes) caused havoc for the Russian army which finally subdued the uprisings in 1831. See Archibald Alison, *History of Europe* 2:458.

215.23-24. Thoughts ... on the absurd: This represents one of Carlyle's many characterizations of *Sartor Resartus*. He once called it a book of "nonsense," a kind of "Didactic Novel," a "'Satirical Extravaganza on Things in General'" that is best read a "few chapters at a time," but whose result is a "deep religious speculative-radicalism" (*Letters* 6:396). These characterizations were encouraged by William Maginn, the editor of *Fraser's Magazine*, 7 (June, 1833), 706; he called Carlyle the "thunderwordoversetter" of Goethe. Satirizing as well as imitating the style of *Sartor Resartus*, Maginn found Carlyle's works (albeit translations) "Teutonical in raiment, in the structure of sentence, the modulation of phrase, and the round-about, hubble-bubble, rumfustianish (*hübble-bübblen, rümfustianischen*), roly-poly growlery of style, so Germanically set forth."

215.26. Necessity ... Choice: Compare 75.32.

215.30-32. Picture ... Foam: An allusion to Apelles (fourth century B.C.), the most celebrated painter of Greek antiquity, who was court painter to Alexander the Great. Tradition has it that Apelles, angered by his inability to paint foam coming from a horse, succeeded by dashing a sponge against the canvas. Carlyle is, in fact, describing here the trials associated with the writing of *Sartor Resartus*. In a letter to Goethe, June 10, 1831, he writes, "But for these last months, I have been busy with a Piece more immediately my own. . . . Alas! It is, after all, not a Picture that I am painting; it is but a half-reckless casting of the brush, with its many frustrated colours, against the canvas: whether it will make good Foam is still a venture." (*Letters* 5:289).

216.2-8. How were Friendship possible ... man can yield to man: A restatement of Novalis's belief that humankind is an extension of humankind, a "Community of Saints" linked in a mystic union by the past, present, and future. Compare Book III, Chapter VII, "Organic Filaments," 180-86.

216.9-14. Night of the world ... shallow Dream: An allusion to the prophecy of redemption found in Richter's "Preface" to *Hesperus*, a romance partly translated by Carlyle in "Jean Paul Friedrich Richter (Again)," *Essays* 2:154: "'But there will come another era . . . when it shall be light, and man will awaken from his lofty dreams, and find—his dreams still there, and that nothing is gone save his sleep.

The stones and rocks, which two veiled Figures (Necessity and Vice) . . . , are casting behind them at Goodness, will themselves become men. . . . Infinite Providence, Thou wilt cause the day to dawn. But as yet struggles the twelfth-hour of the Night: nocturnal birds of prey are on the wing, spectres uproar, the dead walk, the living dream.'" The philosophy contained in this passage was inspired, says Richter, by *The Tempest*: "We are such stuff / As dreams are made on." Compare "Characteristics" (1831), *Essays* 3:32, and 195.35–37.

216.19–20. flame . . . guided: An allusion to the "pillar of fire" that led the Israelites from Egypt (Darkness) to the Promised Land (Light). Compare Exodus 13:21–22; also 122.21.

216.20. wandering spirit: Compare "[Wandering in a Strange Land]," *Collected Poems*, 76: "Though wandering in a strange land / Though in the waste no altar stand / Take comfort, thou art not alone / While Faith hath marked thee for her own. / . . . The holy band of saints renowned / Embrace thee brotherlike around / Their sufferings and their triumphs rise / In hymns immortal to the skies." The theme of the "stranger in a strange land," the subject of the popular Methodist hymn, is found throughout the Old Testament; compare, for example, Exodus 2:22.

216.27. Watchman, what of the Night?: Compare Isaiah 21:11, where the watchman stands guard only in the day and is asked: "Watchman, what of the night? Watchman, what of the night?"

216.31–32. Population-Institute: Compare 167.2–3.

216.32. Paperbag Documents: Compare 59.13.

216.37. *Ew. Wohlgeboren*: A mode of address, such as "Your Honor" or "Esteemed Sir."

217.4. Lieschen: Teufelsdröckh's multi-talented housekeeper. Compare 18.36–38.

217.6. Privy Council: The body of advisers to the British monarch, in modern times largely honorary body, which through its Judicial Committee can serve, if called upon, as the final appellate court.

217.7-8. **Parisian Three Days**: Compare 4.31.

217.9. *Gans*: Compare 13.1-2.

217.22. *Saint-Simonian Society*: Compare 174.35.

217.26. **Man is still Man**: Compare 58.4.

217.29-30. **Bazard-Enfantin**: Saint-Amand Bazard (1791-1832), French socialist who founded *Les Amis de la vérité* (The Friends of Truth) in 1818, and who plotted unsuccessfully to overthrow the monarchy in 1821-1822. He and Barthélemy Prosper Enfantin (1796-1864), also a French socialist, organized and promoted the theories of Saint-Simon from 1825, and published together pamphlets under the general title *L'Exposition de la doctrine de Saint-Simon* (1828-1830), which were sent to Carlyle in 1830. Finally philosophical disagreements and governmental pressure led to the dissolution of the Society in 1832. Afterwards, Enfantin established a monastic-like order, based in part on the doctrines of Saint-Simon. Carlyle was not only kept abreast of the activities of the Society through Gustave d'Eichthal, but also through his brother John who, while in Paris in 1831, attended the meetings of the Saint-Simon Society, met both Bazard and Enfantin, and then wrote lengthy observations to Carlyle. See *Letters* 6:27, 48; and Fielding, "Carlyle and the Saint-Simonians," *Carlyle and His Contemporaries*, 35-59.

218.2. *Palingenesie*: Compare 160.21.

218.5. **Ignis Fatuus**: A phosphorescent light seen at night over marshes, thought to be caused by the decomposition of organic matter; also a will-of-the-wisp, someone who is foolish or misleading. The expression also appears in Richter's "Preface" to *Hesperus*, part of which Carlyle translated.

218.10. **May Time**: A play on words, as in May being the season of beginning.

218.13-14. **Teufelsdröckh . . . London**: Clearly autobiographical: Carlyle completed the manuscript of *Sartor Resartus* at the end of July or early August of 1831, and left for London on August 9, to arrange for its publication. This comment is either a projection of that trip, or is an example of one of the revisions that took place after the initial rejections of the manuscript by the London publishers (see Introduction).

218.16. **lay down his pen**: An allusion to the long tradition that Prospero's breaking his staff is an analogue for Shakespeare's farewell—the "laying down of his pen"—to the stage. Compare *The Tempest* 5.1.33–57.

218.23. **irritated readers**: The response to *Sartor Resartus* while in manuscript and while in early serial numbers was in general negative, a fact which Carlyle anticipates in the text. See Introduction. For example, in a letter to John Carlyle, January 21, 1834, Carlyle writes some eight months before the publication of the last number, "James Fraser writes me that Teufelsdreck meets with the most unqualified disapproval; which is all extremely proper" (*Letters* 7:81); and two months later in a letter to John, March 21, 1834, he says that "Fraser complains still that the world complains" (*Letters* 7:125); to Henry Inglis, April 28, 1834, he observes, "The public seems to receive him [Teufelsdröckh] with fixed ba[yonets.] Little wonder" (*Letters* 7:139); and to Jane Carlyle, May 21, 1834, he adds, "*Teufelk* beyond measure unpopular" (*Letters* 7:175). Later Carlyle was to deny altering the manuscript: "Not a letter of it altered; except in the *last* and the *first* page, a word or two!" (*Two Reminiscences*, 74).

218.23. **outstretched arms**: Compare 66:23.

218.25–26. YORKE and OLIVER . . . **Irish mirth and madness**: In a letter to John Carlyle, January 21, 1831, Carlyle says of the Irish-born poet and editor William Maginn: "Is not *Maginn* a good-natured good-for-little? He has fun, no humour; and talks horribly of *drink*" (*Letters* 5:217); and in a letter to his mother, June 25, 1833, he describes Maginn as "a mad rattling Irishman" (*Letters* 6:406). Compare 10.18.

218.27. **punch**: An allusion to Maginn's notorious difficulties with alcohol, and to his "Ruminations Round the Remains of a Punch-Bowl," *Fraser's Magazine*, 2 (December, 1830), 638–40.

WORKS CITED

(The following list identifies all works referred to by page number in this volume. Unless otherwise specified, citations of the Bible are to the King James Version, of classical authors to the Loeb Classical Library, and of Shakespeare to The Riverside Shakespeare, *ed. G. Blakemore Evans, Boston: Houghton, 1974.)*

WORKS BY CARLYLE

References to the following works of Thomas Carlyle are given to the pagination of the Centenary Edition, edited H. D. Traill (London: Chapman and Hall, 1896–99), the most widely available edition, unless otherwise indicated.

Chartism	*Chartism.* In *Critical and Miscellaneous Essays.* Vol. 4.
Collectanea	*Collectanea Thomas Carlyle 1821–1855.* Ed. Samuel A. Jones. Canton, PA: Kirgate Press, 1903.
Cromwell	*Oliver Cromwell's Letters and Speeches, with Elucidations.* 4 vols.
Edinburgh Encyclopædia	*The Edinburgh Encyclopædia.* Ed. David Brewster. Edinburgh: Blackwood, 1830. Carlyle wrote entries for Vols. 14–17.
Emerson and Carlyle	*The Correspondence of Emerson and Carlyle.* Ed. Joseph Slater. New York, NY: Columbia University Press, 1964.
Essays	*Critical and Miscellaneous Essays.* 5 vols.
Frederick the Great	*History of Friedrich II. of Prussia Called Frederick the Great.* 8 vols.
French Revolution	*The French Revolution: A History.* 3 vols.
German Literature	*Carlyle's Unfinished History of German Literature.* Ed. Hill Hine. Lexington, KY: University of Kentucky Press, 1951.

German Romance   *German Romance.* 2 vols.

Goethe and Carlyle   *Correspondence between Goethe and Carlyle.* Ed.
                          Charles Eliot Norton. London: Macmillan, 1887.

Guises   *The Guises.* Ed. Rodger L. Tarr. In *Victorian
                          Studies* 25.1 (Autumn 1981): 1–80.

Heroes & Hero-Worship   *On Heroes and Hero-Worship and the Heroic in
                          History.* Ed. Michael Goldberg. Berkeley, CA:
                          University of California Press, 1993.

Historical Sketches   *Historical Sketches of Notable Persons and Events
                          in the Reigns of James I and Charles I.* Ed.
                          Alexander Carlyle. London: Chapman and Hall,
                          1898.

History of Literature   *Lectures on the History of Literature.* Ed. J. Reay
                          Greene. New York, NY: Scribner, 1892. Also
                          Lectures on the History of Literature. Ed. R. P.
                          Karkaria. London: Curwen, Kane, 1892

Journey to Germany   *Journey to Germany Autumn 1858.* Ed. Richard
                          A. E. Brooks. New Haven, CT: Yale University
                          Press, 1940.

Last Words   *The Last Words of Thomas Carlyle.* New York, NY:
                          Appleton, 1892.

Latter-Day Pamphlets   *Latter-Day Pamphlets.*

Letters   *The Collected Letters of Thomas and Jane Welsh
                          Carlyle.* Ed. Charles R. Sanders, K. J. Fielding,
                          Clyde de L. Ryals, et al. 24 vols. Durham, NC:
                          Duke University Press, 1970–1995.

Life of Schiller   *The Life of Friedrich Schiller.*

Life of Sterling   *The Life of John Sterling.*

Love Letters   *The Love Letters of Thomas Carlyle and Jane Welsh.*
                          2 vols. Ed. Alexander Carlyle. London: Lane,
                          1909.

Hamilton Memoir	Ed. John Veitch. Edinburgh: Blackwood, 1869.
Montaigne	*Montaigne and Other Essays Chiefly Biographical.* Ed. S. R. Crockett. London: Gowens, 1897.
Past and Present	*Past and Present*
Poems	*The Collected Poems of Thomas and Jane Welsh Carlyle.* Ed. Rodger L. Tarr and Fleming McClelland. Greenwood, FL: Penkevill, 1986.
Reminiscences	*Reminiscences.* Ed. K. J. Fielding and Ian Campbell. Oxford, Eng.: Oxford University Press, 1997.
Rescued Essays	*Rescued Essays.* Ed. Percy Newberry. London: Leadenhall Press, 1892.
Ruskin	*The Correspondence of Thomas Carlyle and John Ruskin.* Ed. George Allan Cate. Stanford, CA: Stanford University Press, 1982.
Sartor Resartus	*Sartor Resartus.* All references are to the present volume.
Two Note Books	*Two Note Books of Thomas Carlyle: from 23d March 1822 to 16th May 1832.* Ed. Charles Eliot Norton. New York: Grolier Club, 1898.
Two Reminiscences	*Two Reminiscences.* Ed. John Clubbe. Durham, NC: Duke University Press, 1974.
Wilhelm Meister	*Wilhelm Meister's Apprenticeship and Travels.* 2 vols.
Wotton Reinfred	In *Last Words.*

464   WORKS CITED

WORKS BY OTHER AUTHORS

Abrams, M. H. *Natural Supernaturalism*. New York: Norton, 1971.

———. *Doing Things with Texts: Essays in Criticism and Critical Theory*. Ed. Michael Fischer. New York: Norton, 1989.

Addison, Joseph. *The Works*. Ed. Richard Hurd. Vol. 1. London: Bell and Daldy, 1871.

———, et al. *The Spectator*. Intro. and ed. Henry Morley. Vol. 1. London: Routledge, 1883.

Aiken, Susan H. "On Clothes and Heroes: Carlyle and 'How It Strikes a Contemporary.'" *Victorian Poetry* 13 (Summer 1975): 99–109.

———. "Bishop Blougram and Carlyle." *Victorian Poetry* 16 (1978): 323–40.

Alexander, Edward. "Thomas Carlyle and D. H. Lawrence." *University of Toronto Quarterly* 37 (April 1968): 248–67.

Alison, Archibald. 4 vols. *History of Europe*. New York: Harper, 1870.

Allingham, William. *Diary*. Intro. Geoffrey Grigson. Fontwell, Eng.: Centaur, 1967.

Altick, Richard D. "Browning's 'Transcendentalism.'" *Journal of English and Germanic Philology* 58 (January 1959): 24–28.

apRoberts, Ruth. *The Ancient Dialect: Thomas Carlyle and Comparative Religion*. Berkeley, CA: University of California Press, 1988.

———. "Carlyle and the Aesthetic Movement." *Carlyle Annual* 12 (1991): 57–64.

Apuleius, Lucius. *The Golden Ass*. Trans. William Adlington. Intro. Charles Whibley. New York: AMS, 1967.

Ariosto, Ludovico. *Orlando Furioso*. Trans. Guido Waldman. London: Oxford University Press, 1974.

Aristotle. *Ethics*. Ed. J. L. Ackrill. London: Faber and Faber, 1973.

———. *The Nicomachean Ethics*. Trans. and ed. J. E. C. Welldon. London: Macmillan, 1906.

———. *The Nicomachean Ethics*. Trans. D. P. Chase. London: Dent, 1930.

———. *The Nicomachean Ethics*. Trans. and intro. David Ross. London: Oxford University Press, 1966.

Asselineau, Roger. "Hemingway, or 'Sartor Resartus' Once More." *The Transcendentalist Constant in American Literature*. New York: New York University Press, 1980. 137–52.

Bacon, Francis. *Essays*. Ed. W. Aldis Wright. London: Macmillan, 1885.

———. *Essays*. Intro. and ed. Samuel Harvey Reynolds. Oxford, Eng.: Clarendon Press, 1890.

Baird, John D., and Charles Ryskamp, eds. *The Poems of William Cowper*. 3 vols. Oxford, Eng.: Clarendon Press, 1995.

Baker, Lee C. R. "The Open Secret of *Sartor Resartus*." *Studies in Philology* 83 (1986): 218–35.

Barbour, James, and Leon Howard. "Carlyle and the Conclusion of *Moby-Dick*." *New England Quarterly* 49 (June 1976): 214–24.

Baumgarten, Murray. *Carlyle and His Era*. Santa Cruz, CA: University of California Library, 1975.

———. "Mill, Carlyle, and the Question of Influence." *Mill Newsletter* 10 (Winter 1975): 4–9.

Behnken, Eloise M. *Thomas Carlyle: "Calvinist Without the Theology."* Columbia, MO: University of Missouri Press, 1978.

Bernard, John. *Retrospections of the Stage*. London: Colburn, Bentley, 1830.

Blake, William. *Complete Writings*. Ed. Geoffrey Keynes. Oxford, Eng.: Oxford University Press, 1969. 620–747.

Blondel, Jacques. "Vision et ironie dans *Sartor Resartus*." *Confluents* 2 (1975): 3–11.

The Book of the Thousand Nights and a Night. Trans. and ed. Richard F. Burton. New York: Heritage, 1962.

Boswell, James. *Life of Johnson.* 1791. Oxford, Eng.: Oxford University Press, 1966.

———. *Journal of a Tour to the Hebrides.* Ed. Frederick A. Pottle and Charles H. Bennett. New York: McGraw-Hill, 1961.

———. *A Tour to the Hebrides.* Ed. Frederick A. Pottle and Charles H. Bennett. New York: Viking, 1936.

Brantley, Richard E. *Coordinates of Anglo-American Romanticism.* Gainesville, FL: University Press of Florida, 1993.

Brookes, Gerry. *The Rhetorical Form of Carlyle's Sartor Resartus.* Berkeley, CA: University of California Press, 1972.

Browne, Thomas. *Religio Medici and Other Works.* Ed. L. C. Martin. Oxford, Eng.: Clarendon Press, 1964.

Bunyan, John. *The Pilgrim's Progress.* Ed. James Blanton Wharey. 2nd ed. Oxford, Eng.: Clarendon Press, 1960.

Burckhardt, John Lewis. *Travels of M. Burckhardt in Egypt and Nubia.* London: Phillips, 1819.

———. *New Voyages and Travels, v. 2, no. 5: Travels in Syria and the Holy Land.* London: Murray, 1822.

———. *Travels in Arabia.* London: Colburn, 1829.

———. *Notes on the Bedouins and Wahabys.* London: Colburn and Bentlet, 1831.

Burke, Edmund. *Selected Speeches and Writings.* Ed. Peter J. Stanlis. Gloucester, MA: Smith, 1968.

Burns, Robert. *Selected Poetry and Prose.* Ed. Robert D. Thornton. Boston, MA: Houghton Mifflin, 1966. 50–55.

Burton, Robert. *The Anatomy of Melancholy.* Ed. Hobrook Jackson. London: Dent, 1968.

Butler, Samuel. *Hudibras.* Ed. and intro. John Wilders. Oxford, Eng.: Clarendon Press, 1967.

Byron, George Gordon, Lord. *Poetical Works.* London: Oxford University Press: 1966.

Caesar, Julius. *The Battle for Gaul.* Trans. Anne and Peter Wiseman. London: Book Club Associates, 1980.

Campbell, Ian M. "Carlyle's Borrowings from the Theological Library of Edinburgh University." *Bibliotheck* 5 (1969): 165–68.

——. "Carlyle's Religion: The Scottish Background." *Carlyle and His Contemporaries.* Ed. John Clubbe. Durham, NC: Duke University Press, 1976. 3–20.

Carlyle, John. "Rev. of Demonology and Witchcraft, by Sir Walter Scott." *Fraser's Magazine* 2 (December 1830): 507–19.

——. "Carlyle's *Sartor Resartus.*" *Monthly Review* 147 (1838): 54–66.

Carroll, Alicia. "'The Same Sort of Pleasure': Re-envisioning the Carlylean in *The Mill and the Floss.*" *Carlyle Annual* 12 (1991): 45–55.

Cather, Willa. "Concerning Thomas Carlyle." *Nebraska State Journal* 21 (1 March 1891): 14.

Cazamian, Louis. *Le Roman social en Angleterre.* Paris, Fr.: Société nouvelle de libraire et d'édition, 1904.

Chaucer, Geoffrey. *The Works.* Ed. F. N. Robinson. 2nd ed. Boston: Houghton Mifflin, 1957.

Cicero, [Marcus Tullius]. *Cicero on Oratory and Orators.* Trans. and ed. J. S. Watson. Intro. Ralph A. Micken. Carbondale, IL: Southern Illinois University Press, 1970.

——. *de Officiis.* Trans. Walter Miller. Cambridge, MA: Harvard University Press, 1961.

——. *The Orations.* Trans. C. D. Yonge. Vols. 1, 3–4. London: Bohn, 1852.

Clubbe, John. "John Carlyle in Germany and the Genesis of *Sartor Resartus.*" *Romantic and Victorian.* Ed. W. Paul Elledge and Richard L. Hoffman. Rutherford, NJ: Fairleigh Dickinson University Press, 1971. 264–89.

WORKS CITED

———. "Introduction." In Froude's *Life of Carlyle*. Columbus, OH: Ohio State University Press, 1979. 1–60. See Froude.

Cluett, Robert. "Victoria Resarta: Carlyle Among His Contemporaries." *Prose Style and Critical Reading* (1976): 178–215.

Coleridge, Samuel Taylor. *Aids to Reflection*. London: Hurst and Chance, 1831.

———. *Omniana*. Ed. Robert Gittings. Carbondale, IL: Southern Illinois University Press, 1969.

———. *Poetical Works*. Ed. Ernest Hartley Coleridge. London: Oxford University Press, 1973.

———. *The Collected Works of Samuel Taylor Coleridge*. 16 Vols. Ed. Kathleen Coburn and Bart Winer. Princeton, NJ: Routledge, Kegan Paul, 1983.

Cowper, William. *Poetical Works*. Ed. H. S. Milford and Norma Russell. 4th ed. London: Oxford University Press, 1967.

Dante. *The Inferno*. Trans. John Ciardi. New York: New American Library, 1954.

———. *Paradise*. Trans. Dorothy L. Sayers and Barbara Reynolds. Harmondsworth, Eng.: Penguin, 1971.

———. *Purgatory*. Trans. Dorothy L. Sayers. Baltimore, MD: Penguin, 1969.

DeLaura, David J. "Arnold and Carlyle." *Publications of the Modern Language Association* 79 (March 1964): 104–29.

———. "Carlyle and Arnold: The Religious Issue." *Carlyle Past and Present*. Ed. K. J. Fielding and Rodger L. Tarr. London: Vision, 1976. 127–54.

Descartes, René. *Principles of Philosophy*. Trans. and ed. Valentine Rodger Miller and Reese P. Miller. Dordrecht, Neth.: Reidel, 1984.

Dickens, Charles. *American Notes*. London: Chapman and Hall, 1910.

Disraeli, Isaac. *Curiosities of Literature*. Ed. Benjamin Disraeli. New York: n.p., 1885.

Donne, John. *The Metaphysical Poets.* Ed. Helen Gardner. Baltimore, MD: Penguin, 1963. 72.

Drummond, William. *Notes of Conversations with Ben Jonson Made by William Drummond of Hawthornden.* Ed. G. B. Harrison. New York: Dutton, 1966.

Dryden, John. *Absalon and Achitophel.* Ed. Bernard N. Shilling. New Haven, CT: Yale University Press, 1961.

———. *All for Love; or, The World Well Lost. British Dramatists from Dryden to Sheridan.* Ed. George H. Nettleton and Arthur E. Case. Boston, MA: Houghton Mifflin, 1939. 73–114.

Dunn, Richard J. "'Inverse Sublimity': Carlyle's Theory of Humour." *University of Toronto Quarterly* 40 (1970): 41–57.

Dunn, Waldo H. "The Centennial of *Sartor Resartus.*" *London Quarterly Review* 155 (1931): 39–51.

D'Urfey, Thomas, ed. *Wit and Mirth; or, Pills to Purge Melancholy.* London: Tonson, 1719. New York: Folklore Library Publishers, 1959.

Earle, Peter G. "Unamuno and the Theme of History." *Hispanic Review* 32 (October 1964): 319–39.

Earnest, James D. "The Influence of Thomas Carlyle upon the Early Novels of Miguel de Unamuno." *Kentucky Philological Association Bulletin* (1984): 25–35.

Eliot, George. "Thomas Carlyle." *The Leader* 6 (1855): 1035. Rpt. in *Essays of George Eliot.* Ed. Thomas Pinney. London: Routledge, Kegan Paul, 1963. 213–14.

Emerson, Ralph W. "Preface" to *Sartor Resartus.* Boston, MA: Munroe, 1836. iii–v.

The Encyclopedia of Philosophy. 8 vols. New York: Macmillan, 1967.

Erasmus. *The Praise of Folly.* Trans. Hoyt Hopewell Hudson. Princeton, NJ: Princeton University Press, 1941.

[Everett, Alexander H.] "Thomas Carlyle." *North American Review* 41 (1835): 454–82.

Faverty, Frederic E. "The Brownings and Their Contemporaries." *Browning Institute Studies.* Ed. William S. Peterson. New York: Browning Institute, 1974. 161–80.

"Fashionable Novels." *Fraser's Magazine* 1 (April 1830): 318–35.

Fichte, Johann Gottlieb. *Die Bestimmung des Menschen.* Hamburg, Ger.: Meiner, 1962.

——. *The Popular Works.* Trans. William Smith. Vol. 2. 4th ed. London: Trübner, 1889.

——. *Science of Knowledge.* Trans. and ed. Peter Heath and John Lachs. Cambridge, Eng.: Cambridge University Press, 1982.

——. *The Vocation of Man.* Ed. Roderick M. Chisholm. Indianapolis, IN: Bobbs-Merrill, 1956.

Fielding, K. J. "Carlyle and the Saint-Simonians (1830–1832): New Considerations." *Carlyle and His Contemporaries.* Ed. John Clubbe. Durham, NC: Duke University Press, 1976. 35–59.

——. "Carlyle Among the Cannibals." *Carlyle Newsletter* 1 (1979): 22–28.

——. "Vernon Lushington: Carlyle's Friend and Editor." *Carlyle Newsletter* 5 (Spring 1987): 7–18.

——, and Rodger L. Tarr, ed. *Carlyle Past and Present.* London: Vision, 1976.

Findlay, L. M. "Paul de Man, Thomas Carlyle, and 'The Rhetoric of Temporality.'" *Dalhousie Review* 65 (Summer 1985): 159–81.

Finlayson, C. P. "Thomas Carlyle's Borrowings from Edinburgh University Library, 1819–1829." *Bibliotheck* 3 (1961): 138–43.

Fox, George. *The Journal.* Ed. John L. Nickalls. Intro. Geoffrey F. Nuttall. Cambridge, Eng.: Cambridge University Press, 1952.

F[rothingham], N[athaniel] L. "*Sartor Resartus.*" *Christian Examiner* 21 (September 1836): 74–84.

Froude, James, A. *Thomas Carlyle: A History of the First Forty Years of His Life, 1795–1835.* 2 vols. London: Longmans, Green, 1882.

——. *Thomas Carlyle: A History of His Life in London, 1834–1881.* 2 vols. London: Longmans, Green, 1884.

Fuller, Margaret. "A Picture of Mr. Carlyle." *Littell's Living Age* 12 (1847): 605.

Gautier, Alfred. "Essai historique sur le problème des trois." *Bibliothèque Universelle* (1817): 253–75.

Gibbon, Edward. *The Decline and Fall of the Roman Empire.* Ed. J. B. Bury. 7 vols. London: Methuen, 1896–1898

Goethe, Johann Wolfgang von. *The Autobiography.* Trans. John Oxenford. Intro. Gregor Sebba. New York: Horizon, 1969.

——. *Faust* Part I-II. 2 vols. Wiesbaden, Ger.: Lilien, 1982.

——. *Faust.* Trans. Stuart Atkins. Boston, MA: Suhrkamp/Insel, 1984.

——. *Maxims and Reflections.* Trans. Bailey Saunders. New York: Macmillan, 1893.

Goldberg, Michael. "The True Shekinah is Man." *American Notes and Queries* 3 (1964): 42–44.

——. *Carlyle and Dickens.* London: University of Georgia Press, 1972.

Goldsmith, Oliver. *The Miscellaneous Works.* Intro. David Masson. London: Macmillan, 1915.

Gravett, Sharon L. "Carlyle's Demanding Companion: Henry David Thoreau." *Carlyle Studies Annual* 15 (1995): 21–31.

Gray, Thomas. "Elegy Written in a Country Church-Yard." *English Romantic Poetry and Prose.* Ed. Russell Noyes. New York: Oxford University Press, 1956. 47-49.

"Greek Drama." *Blackwood's Magazine* 30 (August 1831): 350–90.

Greenberg, Robert A. "A Possible Source of Tennyson's 'Tooth and Claw.'" *Modern Language Notes* 71 (November 1956): 491–92.

Hamilton, William. "Philosophy of the Unconditioned." *Edinburgh Review* 1 (1819): 194–221.

———. *Discussions on Philosophy and Literature, Education and University Reform.* 3rd ed. Edinburgh, Scot.: Blackwood, 1866.

Haney, Janice L. "'Shadow-Hunting': Romantic Irony, *Sartor Resartus,* and Victorian Romanticism." *Studies in Romanticism* 17 (1978): 335–55.

Harris, Kenneth M. *Carlyle and Emerson: Their Long Debate.* Cambridge, MA: Harvard University Press, 1978.

Harrold, Charles Frederick. *Carlyle and German Thought: 1819–1834.* Hamden, CT: Archon, 1963 [1934].

———. "The Nature of Carlyle's Calvinism." *Studies in Philology* 33 (1936): 475–86.

Hartman, Geoffrey H. "Carlyle, Eliot, and Bloom." *Criticism in the Wilderness: The Study of Literature Today.* New Haven, CT: Yale University Press, 1980. 42–62.

Hazlitt, William. *Lectures on the English Comic Writers.* 1819. World's Classics 124. London: Cumberlege-Oxford University Press, 1951.

———. *The Spirit of the Age.* Ed. Catherine Maclean. London: Dent, 1960.

Helmling, Steven. *The Esoteric Comedies of Carlyle, Newman, and Yeats.* Cambridge, Eng.: Cambridge University Press, 1988.

Heraclitus. *The Cosmic Fragments.* Ed. G. S. Kirk. Cambridge, Eng.: Cambridge University Press, 1962.

Hesiod. *Theogony, Works and Days, Shield.* Ed. and trans. Apostolos N. Athanassakis. Baltimore, MD: Johns Hopkins University Press, 1983.

Holloway, John. *The Victorian Sage.* New York: Norton, 1965 [1953].

Homer. *The Iliad, The Odyssey, and the Lesser Homerica.* Trans. George Chapman. Ed. Allardyce Nicoll. 2 vols. New York: Pantheon, 1956.

Hooker, Richard. *Of the Laws of Ecclesiastical Polity.* Intro. Christopher Morris. Vol. 1. London: Dent, 1967.

Horace. [Quintus Horatius Flaccus]. *The Art of Poetry*. Trans. and intro. Burton Raffel. Albany, NY: State University of New York Press, 1974.

——. *The Complete Works*. Trans. and ed. Charles E. Passage. New York: Ungar, 1983.

——. *Horace for English Readers*. Trans. E. C. Wickham. London: Oxford University Press, [1953].

——. *Satires and Epistles*. Trans. Jacob Fuchs. Intro. William S. Anderson. New York: Norton, 1977.

——. *Odes*. In The Complete Works. Ed. Charles E. Passage. New York: Ungar, 1983.

——. *Satires*. Ed. and trans. François Villeneuve. Paris, Fr.: Société d'Édition "Les Belles Lettres," 1966.

Howells, Bernard. "Heroïsme, Dandysme et la 'Philosophie du Costume': Note sur Baudelaire et Carlyle." *Litterature Moderne e Comparte* 41.2 (April-June 1988): 131–51.

Hruschka, John. "Carlyle's Rabbinical Hero: Teufelsdröckh and the Midrashic Tradition." *Carlyle Annual* 13 (1992–93): 101–08.

Hughes, Keith. "*Sartor Resartus* and Nonsense." *Papers of the Carlyle Society* 7 (1993–1994): 14–23.

Hume, David. *Enquiries Concerning the Human Understanding and Concerning the Principals of Morals*. Ed. L. A. Selby-Bigge. 2nd ed. Oxford, Eng.: Clarendon Press, 1963.

Iser, Wolfgang. "The Emergence of a Cross-Cultural Discourse: Thomas Carlyle's *Sartor Resartus*." *The Translatability of Cultures: Figurations of the Space Between*. Ed. Stanford Budick and Wolfgang Iser. Stanford, CA: Stanford University Press, 1996. 245–64.

J., J. J. [Isaac Jewett]. "Thomas Carlyle." *Hesperian* 2 (November 1838): 5–20.

Jackson, Leon. "The Social Construction of Carlyle's New England Reputation, 1834–1836." *Proceedings of the American Antiquarian Society* 106 (April 1996): 167–90.

Jeffrey, Francis. "Alison on Taste" *Edinburgh Review* 18 (May 1811): 1–46.

Jenner, Thomas. *The Soules Solace.* London: n.p., 1626.

Jessop, Ralph. *Carlyle and Scottish Thought.* London: Macmillan, 1997.

Johnson, Samuel. "Cowley." *Lives of the Poets.* Ed. George B. Hill. Vol. 1. Oxford, Eng.: Oxford University Press, 1905.

Josephus, Flavius. *The Works of Josephus.* Trans. William Whiston. Peabody, Mass.: Hendrickson, 1987.

Juvenal, et al. *The Satires of Juvenal, Persius, Sulpicia, and Lucilius.* Trans. and ed. Lewis Evans and William Gifford. London: Bohn, 1852.

Kant, Immanuel. *Critique of Pure Reason.* Trans. Lewis W. Beck. Chicago, IL: University of Chicago Press, 1949.

———. *Critique of Pure Reason.* Trans. F. Max Müller. Intro. Ludwig Noiré. London: Macmillan, 1881.

———. *Text-Book to Kant: The Critique of Pure Reason.* Ed. and trans. James Hutchinson Stirling. Edinburgh, Scot.: Oliver and Boyd, 1881.

Kaplan, Fred. *Thomas Carlyle: A Biography.* Ithaca, NY: Cornell University Press, 1983.

Keats, John. *Poetical Works.* Ed. H. W. Garrod. London: Oxford University Press, 1970.

Kegel, Charles H. "Carlyle and Ruskin: An Influential Friendship." *Brigham Young University Studies* 5 (Spring 1964): 219–29.

Laërtius, Diogenes. *Lives of the Philosophers.* Trans. A. Robert Caponigri. Chicago, IL: Regnery, 1969.

Lamb, Charles. *The Complete Works and Letters.* Intro. Saxe Commins. New York: Modern Library, 1935.

"The Last of the Supernaturalists." *Fraser's Magazine* 1 (March 1830): 217–35.

Leibnitz, Gottfried Wilhelm. *New Essays Concerning Human Understanding.* Trans. Alfred Gideon Langley. 3rd ed. LaSalle, IL: Open Court, 1949.

Le Sage, Alain René. *The Adventures of Gil Blas of Santillane.* Trans. Tobias Smollett. Intro. William Morton Fullerton. London: Routledge, [1913].

Levine, George. "*Sartor Resartus* and the Balance of Fiction." *Victorian Studies* 8 (1964): 131–60.

Locke, John. *An Essay Concerning Human Understanding.* Ed. Alexander Campbell Fraser. 2 vols. New York: Dover, 1959.

———. *Two Treatises of Government.* Ed. Peter Laslett. Cambridge, Eng.: Cambridge University Press, 1960.

———. *The Works.* Vol. 9. Aalen, Ger.: Scientia, 1963.

Machen, Meredith R. "Carlyle's Presence in *The Professor's House.*" *Western American Literature* 14 (1980): 273–86.

Macnish, Robert. "The Philosophy of Burking." *Fraser's Magazine* 5 (1832): 52–65.

Macpherson, James. *The Poems of Ossian.* Boston, MA: Phillips, Sampson, 1855.

[Maginn, William]. "Gallery of Literary Characters. No. XXXVII. Thomas Carlyle." *Fraser's Magazine* 7 (June 1833): 706.

———. "Ruminations Round the Remains of a Punch-Bowl." *Fraser's Magazine* 2 (December 1830): 638–40.

Marlowe, Christopher. *Doctor Faustus. Elizabethan and Stuart Plays.* Ed. Charles R. Baskervill, et al. New York: Holt, Rinehart, Winston, 1963. 349–73.

Marshall, George O. "An Incident from Carlyle in Tennyson's 'Maud.'" *Notes and Queries* 204 (February 1959): 77–78.

Martineau, Harriet. *History of England during the Thirty Years Peace, 1816–1846.* 2 vols. London: 1849–1850.

Mason, D. G. "Woolf, Carlyle, and the Writing of *Orlando.*" *English Studies in Canada* 19.3 (September 1993): 329–38.

Masson, David. *Carlyle Personally and in His Writings.* London: Macmillan, 1885.

Massinger, Philip. *The Unnatural Combat.* Ed. Philip Edwards and Colin Gibson. Oxford, Eng.: Oxford University Press, 1976.

Mellor, Anne K. "Carlyle's *Sartor Resartus:* A Self-Consuming Artifact." *Romantic Irony.* Cambridge, MA: Harvard University Press, 1980. 109–34.

Meyer, Maria. *Carlyles Einfluss auf Kingsley.* Weimar, Ger.: Wagner, 1914.

Miller, J. Hillis. "'Hieroglyphical Truth' in *Sartor Resartus:* Carlyle and the Language of Parable." *Victorian Perspectives.* Ed. John Clubbe and Jerome Meckier. Newark, DE: University of Delaware Press, 1989. 1–20.

Milton, John. *The Student's Milton.* Ed. Frank A. Patterson. Revised ed. New York: Appleton-Century-Crofts, 1961.

Moore, Carlisle. "Carlyle: Mathematics and 'Mathesis.'" *Carlyle Past and Present.* Ed. K. J. Fielding and Rodger L. Tarr. London: Vision, 1976. 61–95.

——. "Thomas Carlyle and Fiction: 1822–1834." *Nineteenth Century Studies.* Ithaca, NY: Cornell University Press, 1940. 131–77.

"Mr. Edward Lytton Bulwer's Novels; and Remarks on Novel-Writing." *Fraser's Magazine* 1 (June 1830): 509–32.

Newton, Sir Isaac. *Sir Isaac Newton's Mathematical Principles of Natural Philosophy and his System of the World.* Trans. Andrew Motte. Ed. Florian Cajori. Berkeley, CA: University of California Press, 1934.

——. *Principia.* Ed. Florian Cajori. Berkeley, CA: University of California Press, 1934.

North, Christopher. [John Wilson]. *Noctes Ambrosianæ.* Ed. John Skelton. New York: Lovell, n.d.

Novalis. *Werke / Briefe Dokumente*. Ed. Ewald Wasmuth. 4 vols. Heidelberg, Ger.: Schneider, 1957.

———. *Werke*. Trans. and ed. Hermann Friedmann. 4 vols. in 2. Berlin, Ger.: Bong, [1908].

Oakman, Robert L. "Carlyle and the Machine: A Quantitative Analysis of Syntax in Prose Style." *Bulletin of the Association for Literary and Linguistic Computing* 3 (Summer 1975) : 100–14.

Oddie, William. *Dickens and Carlyle: The Question of Influence*. London: Centenary, 1972.

Omans, Glen. "Browning's 'Fra Lippo Lippi.'" *Victorian Poetry* 7 (Spring 1969): 56–62.

Ormond, Richard. Intro. *Daniel Maclise*. London: Arts Council of Great Britain, 1972.

Pascal, Blaise. *Pensées*. Trans. and intro. A. J. Krailsheimer. Baltimore, MD: Penguin, 1968.

Peckham, Morse. *Beyond the Tragic Vision*. New York: Braziller, 1962.

———. *Victorian Revolutionaries*. New York: Braziller, 1970.

"The Philosophy of Apparitions." *Fraser's Magazine* 2 (August 1830): 33–41.

"The Philosophy of Pottery." Fraser's Magazine 1 (April 1830): 287–91.

Pindar, Peter. [John Wolcot]. "The Apple Dumplings and a King." *Peter Pindar's Poems*. Ed. P. M. Zall. Columbia, SC: University of South Carolina Press, 1972. 32.

Plato. *The Apology of Socrates*. Ed. Adela Marion Adam. Cambridge, Eng.: Cambridge University Press, 1964.

———. *Phaedo*. Trans. and intro. R. Hackforth. Indianapolis, IN: Bobbs-Merrill, 1955.

———. *The Republic*. Trans. and ed. Allan Bloom. New York: Basic, 1968.

Plutarch. *Consolation of Apollonius.* Ed. Leonardus Usterius. Turici, It.: Orelli, Fuesslini, and Sociorum, 1830.

———. *Lives.* Ed. John Langhorne and William Langhorne. Baltimore, MD: Neal, 1836.

———. *Life of Themistokles.* Ed. Hubert A. Holden. London: Macmillan, 1884.

———. *Moral Essays.* Trans. and intro. Rex Warner. Harmondsworth, Eng.: Penguin, 1971.

Poe, Edgar A. "Marginalia." *Democratic Review* 18 (April 1846): 268–72.

Pope, Alexander. *The Dunciad.* Ed. James Sutherland. 2nd ed. London: Methuen, 1953.

———. *Poems.* Ed. John Butt. London: Methuen, 1953.

———. *Essay on Criticism.* Ed. and intro. Frederick Ryland. London: Blackie, 1900.

———. *An Essay on Man.* Ed. Maynard Mack. London: Methuen, 1970.

———. *The Prose Works of Alexander Pope.* Ed. Rosemary Cowler. Vol. 2 of The Major Works, 1725–1744. Hamden, CT: Archon, 1986.

———, et al. *Memoirs of the Extraordinary Life, Works, and Discoveries of Martinus Scriblerus.* Ed. Charles Kerby-Miller. New Haven, CT: Yale University Press, 1950.

Rabb, J. Douglas. "The Silence of Thomas Carlyle." *English Language Notes* 26.3 (1989): 70–81.

Rabelais. *Gargantua and Pantagruel.* Trans. Jacques Le Clercq. New York: Modern Library, 1936.

Renner, Stanley. "*Sartor Resartus* Retailored? Conrad's *Lord Jim* and the Perils of Idealism." *Real* 3 (1985): 185–222.

Richardson, Samuel. *Clarissa.* Ed. George Sherburn. Boston, MA: Houghton Mifflin, 1962.

Richardson, Thomas C. "John Murray's Reader and the Rejection of *Sartor Resartus*." *Carlyle Newsletter* 6 (Spring 1985): 38–41.

Richter, Jean Paul Friedrich. *Flower, Fruit, and Thorn Pieces*. Trans. Edward Henry Noel. Vol. 1. Boston, MA: Ticknor, Fields, 1863.

——. *Flower, Fruit, and Thorn Pieces*. Trans. Alexander Ewing. London: Bell, 1888.

——. *Hesperus, or, Forty-Five Dog-Post-Days*. Trans. Charles T. Brooks. 2 vols. London: Trübner, 1865.

Robinson, Henry Crabb. *Diary, Reminiscences, and Correspondence*. Ed. Thomas Sadler. 3 Vols. 2nd ed. London: Macmillan, 1869.

Rosenberg, Philip. *The Seventh Hero*. Cambridge, MA: Harvard University Press, 1974.

Rousseau, Jean-Jacques. *The Confessions*. Intro. S. W. Orson. 4 vols. London: Gibbings, 1897.

——. *The Miscellaneous Works of Mr. J. J. Rousseau*. London, 1767.

——. *The Reveries of a Solitary Walker*. Trans. Peter France. Middlesex, Eng.: Penguin, 1986.

The Roxburghe Ballads. Ed. J. Woodfall Ebsworth. Hertford, Eng.: Austin, 1890.

Ryals, Clyde de L. "The 'Heavenly Friend': The 'New Mythus' of *In Memoriam*." *Personalist* 43 (Summer 1962): 383–402.

Saint Augustine. *The Basic Writings*. Ed. and intro. Whitney J. Oates. Vol. 1. New York: Random House, 1948.

Saint-Simon, Henri Comte de. *Selected Writings*. Ed. and trans. F. M. H. Markham. New York: Macmillan, 1952.

Sanders, Charles R. "Carlyle and Tennyson." *Publications of the Modern Language Association* 76 (March 1961): 82–97.

——. "The Byron Closed in *Sartor Resartus*." *Studies in Romanticism* 3 (Winter 1964): 77–108.

"Sartor Resartus." *Edinburgh Review* 68 (1838): 266.

"Sartor Resartus." *The Globe* 14 September 1838.

"[Sartor Resartus]." *Sun* 1 April 1834: 2.

"Sartor Resartus." *Metropolitan Magazine* 23 (1838): 1–5.

"[Sartor Resartus]." *Tait's Edinburgh Magazine* 5 (1838): 611–12.

Schelling, Friedrich W. J. *The Method of Academic Studies.* Ed. Norbert Guteman. Trans. E. S. Morgan. Athens, OH: Ohio University Press, 1966.

——. *On University Studies.* Trans. and ed. Norbert Guterman. Athens, OH: Ohio University Press, 1966.

Schiller, Johann Christoph Friedrich von. *Werke.* Vol. 20. Ed. Helmut Koopmann. Intro. Benno von Wiese. Weimar, Ger.: Böhlaus, 1962.

——. *Wilhelm Tell.* Trans. and ed. William F. Mainland. Chicago, IL: University of Chicago Press, 1972.

Schlegel, Friedrich. *Kritische Schriften.* Munich, Ger.: Hanser, 1964.

——. *Lucinde and the Fragments.* Trans. and intro. Peter Firchow. Minneapolis, MN: University of Minnesota Press, 1971.

Schwarzbach, F. S. "Dickens and Carlyle Again: A Note on an Early Influence." *Dickensian* 73 (September 1977): 149–53.

Scott, Sir Walter. *The Journal.* Ed. John Guthrie Tate. Edinburgh, Scot.: Oliver and Boyd, 1950.

——. *The Talisman.* London: Adam and Black, 1899.

——. *Old Mortality.* Boston, MA: Houghton Mifflin, 1912.

Shaw, Robert. *An Exposition of the Confession of Faith of the Westminster Assembly of Divines.* Philadelphia, PA: Presbyterian Board of Publication, [1846].

Shelley, Mary. *Frankenstein.* Ed. and intro. Diane Johnson. New York: Bantam, 1991.

Shelley, Percy Bysshe. *Poems.* Ed. Thomas Hutchinson. London: Oxford University Press, 1965.

——. "'A Defence of Poetry.'" *English Romantic Poetry and Prose.* Ed. Alfred Noyes. New York: Oxford University Press, 1956. 1097–1112.

Shine, Hill. *Carlyle and the Saint-Simonians: The Concept of Historical Periodicity.* Baltimore, MD: Johns Hopkins University Press, 1941.

——. "Carlyle's Early Writings and Herder's *Ideen.*" *Booker Memorial Studies.* Chapel Hill, NC: University of North Carolina Press, 1950. 3–33.

——. *Carlyle's Early Reading to 1834.* Lexington, KY: University of Kentucky Press, 1953.

[Simms, William G.?]. "Carlyle's *Sartor Resartus.*" *Southern Literary Journal* 1 (March 1837): 1–8.

Smith, Adam. *The Wealth of Nations.* Ed. Edwin Cannan. New York: Modern Library, 1965.

Smollett, Tobias. *Count Fathom.* Ed. George Saintsbury. New York: Nottingham Society, n.d.

Sophocles. *Philoctetes.* Trans. Kenneth Cavander. Intro. Edmund Wilson. San Francisco, CA: Chandler, 1965.

——. *The Women of Trachis and Philoctetes.* Trans. Robert Torrance. Boston, MA: Houghton Mifflin, 1966.

Southey, Robert. *The Complete Poetical Works.* New York: Appleton, 1848.

Spenser, Edmund. *The Complete Poetical Works.* Ed. Neil Dodge. Boston, MA: Houghton Mifflin, 1936.

Spinoza, Baruch. *Principles of Cartesian Philosophy.* Trans. Harry E. Wedeck. New York: Philosophical Library, 1961.

Starnes, De Witt T. "The Influence of Carlyle upon Tennyson." *Texas Review* 6 (July 1921): 316–36.

Sterne, Laurence. *The Life and Opinions of Tristram Shandy, Gentleman.* 3 vols. Ed. Melvyn New and Joan New. Gainesville, FL: University of Florida Press, 1978.

Sterling, John. "Carlyle's Works." *London and Westminster Review* 33 (1839): 52–39.

[Stirling, James H.]. "The Poetical Works of Robert Browning." *North British Review* 49 (1868): 353–408.

Stowell, Sheila. "Teufelsdröckh as Devil's Dust." *Carlyle Newsletter* 9 (1989): 31–33.

Sutherland, J. A. *Victorian Novelists and Publishers*. London: Athlone, 1976.

Swanson, Donald R. "Ruskin and His 'Master.'" *Victorian Newsletter* 31 (Spring 1967): 56–59.

Swift, Jonathan. *The Complete Poems*. Ed. Pat Rogers. New Haven, CT: Yale University Press, 1983.

——. *Gulliver's Travels*. Ed. Robert A. Greenberg. New York: Norton, 1961.

——. *A Tale of a Tub*. Ed. A. C. Guthkelch and D. Nichol Smith. 2nd ed. Oxford, Eng.: Clarendon Press, 1958.

Tacitus, Cornelius. *Complete Works*. Ed. Moses Hadas. New York: Modern Library, 1942.

Tarr, C. Anita. "Getting to the Lighthouse: Thomas Carlyle and Virginia Woolf." Unpublished lecture. Carlyle at 200: Bicentenary Conference, St. John's Newfoundland. 13 July 1995.

Tarr, Rodger L., and Anita Clayton Tarr, eds. "'Carlyle in America': An Unpublished Short Story of Sarah Orne Jewett." *American Literature* 54 (March 1982): 101–15.

Tarr, Rodger L. "Emerson's Transcendentalism in L. M. Child's Letter to Carlyle." *Emerson Society Quarterly* 58 (1970): 112–15.

——. "Thomas Carlyle's Libraries at Chelsea and Ecclefechan." *Studies in Bibliography* 27 (1974): 249–65.

——. *Thomas Carlyle: A Bibliography of English-Language Criticism, 1824–1974*. Charlottesville, VA: University of Virginia Press, 1976.

———."Dorothea's 'Resartus' and the Palingenetic Impulse of *Middlemarch.*" *Texas Studies in Literature and Language* 20 (Spring 1978): 106–18.

———. "'Fictional High-Seriousness': Carlyle and the Victorian Novel." *Strouse Lectures on Carlyle & His Era.* Ed. Jerry D. James and Charles S. Fineman. Santa Cruz, CA: University of California Library, 1982. 27–44.

———. *Thomas Carlyle: A Descriptive Bibliography.* Pittsburgh, PA: University of Pittsburgh Press, 1989.

———. "The Manuscript Chronology of *Sartor Resartus.*" *Carlyle Annual* 11 (1990): 97–104.

Tasso, Torquato. *Jerusalem Delivered.* Trans. and intro. Joseph Tusiani. Rutherford, NJ: Fairleigh Dickinson University Press, 1970.

Templeman, William D. "Tennyson's 'Locksley Hall' and Thomas Carlyle." *Booker Memorial Studies.* Chapel Hill, NC: University of North Carolina Press, 1950. 3–33.

Tennyson, Alfred Lord. *Poetical Works.* New York: Crowell, n.d.

Tennyson, G. B. "'The True Shekinah is Man.'" *American Notes and Queries* 3 (1964): 58.

———. *"Sartor" Called "Resartus."* Princeton, NJ: Princeton University Press, 1965.

———. *Carlyle and the Modern World.* Edinburgh, Scot.: The Carlyle Society, 1971.

———. "The Carlyles." *Victorian Prose: A Guide to Research.* Ed. David J. DeLaura. New York: Modern Language Association, 1973. 96–100.

———. "Carlyle as Mediator of German Language and Thought." *Thomas Carlyle 1981.* Ed. Horst Drescher. Frankfurt, Ger.: Lang, 1983. 263–79.

———. "The Editor Editing, The Reviewer Reviewing." *Carlyle Studies Annual* no. 14 (1994): 43–54.

Thoreau, Henry D. "Thomas Carlyle and His Works." *Graham's Magazine* 30 (March-April 1847): 145–52, 238–45.

Thrall, Miriam M. H. *Rebellious Fraser's: Nol Yorke's Magazine in the Days of Maginn, Thackeray, and Carlyle.* 1934. New York: AMS, 1966.

Tillotson, Kathleen. "Matthew Arnold and Carlyle." *Proceedings of the British Academy* 42 (1956): 133–53.

———. *Novels of the Eighteen-Forties.* 1954. London: Oxford University Press, 1961.

Timko, Michael. "Carlyle, Sterling, and the Scavenger Age." *Studies in Scottish Literature* 20 (1985): 11–33.

———. *Carlyle and Tennyson.* Iowa City, IA: University of Iowa Press, 1988.

Trevelyan, G. M. *English Social History.* London: Longmans, Green, 1943.

Vance, William S. "Carlyle in America before *Sartor Resartus.*" *American Literature* 7 (1936): 363–75.

Vanden Bossche, Chris R. *Carlyle and the Search for Authority.* Columbus, OH: Ohio State University Press, 1991.

Vaughn, C. E., ed. *English Literary Criticism.* Port Washington, NY: Kennikat, 1970.

Vida, E. M. *Romantic Affinities: German Authors and Carlyle: A Study in the History of Ideas.* Toronto, Can. University of Toronto Press, 1993.

Vijn, J. P. *Carlyle and Jean Paul: Their Spiritual Optics.* Amsterdam, Neth.: Benjamins, 1982.

Virgil. *The Aeneid, Eclogues, and Georgics.* Trans. J. W. MacKail. Intro. William C. McDermott. New York: Modern Library, 1950.

———. *The Aeneid.* Trans. Allen Mandelbaum. Berkeley, CA: University of California Press, 1971.

Voltaire. *Candide.* Trans. Robert M. Adams. New York: Norton, 1966.

——. *The Complete Works.* Ed. Pierre Augustin Caron de Beaumarchais. Vol. 36. Kehl, Fr.: Societe Litteraire-Typographique, 1784.

Watkins, Charlotte C. "Browning's 'Red Cotton Night-Cap Country' and Carlyle." *Victorian Studies* 7 (June 1964): 359–74.

Wesley, Samuel. *An Epistle to a Friend Concerning Poetry.* London: Harper, 1700. Augustan Reprint Society. Vol. 1. 1967.

Whitehead, William. *An Essay on Ridicule.* London: Millar, 1753. 2:67–82.

Whitman, Walt. "The Dead Carlyle." *The Literary World* 12 (12 February 1881): 57.

——. "Death of Carlyle." *The Critic* 1 (1881): 30.

Willey, Basil. *Nineteenth Century Studies.* 1949. New York: Harper, Row, 1966.

Wilson, David A. *The Life of Carlyle.* [Variously titled]. 6 vols. London: Kegan Paul, Trench, Trubner, 1923–1929.

Wither, George. "'Tobacco's but an Indian weed.'" *Wit and Mirth; or, Pills to Purge Melancholy.* Ed. Thomas D'Urfey. London: Tonson, 1719.

Wordsworth, William. *Poetical Works.* Rev. ed. Ernest de Selincourt. Oxford, Eng.: Oxford University Press, 1969.

Xenophon. *The Works.* Trans. H. G. Dakyns. Vol. 1, 3. London: Macmillan, 1897.

Young, Edward. *The Complete Works: Poetry and Prose.* Ed. James Nichols. Vol. 1. Hildesheim, Ger.: Olms, 1968.

——. *The Poetical Works.* Vol. 2. Westport, CT: Greenwood, 1970.

TEXTUAL APPARATUS

EMENDATIONS OF THE COPY-TEXT

ALL departures of the present edition from the *Fraser's Magazine* copy-text are listed below, except the global reversal of single and double quotation marks (see Note on the Text, pp. cv–cvii).

All variant readings found in the authorized versions of the text are reported in the Historical Collation beginning on page 541 below. Because the two lists serve distinct purposes, the variants reported below in the list of emendations are repeated in the Historical Collation.

In both lists, each item is keyed to the text by the number of the page and line on which the variant begins. The top line of each item gives the copy-text reading, followed by "33," the symbol of the copy-text. In the list of emendations, the second line in each item gives the variant reading adopted in the present edition, followed by the symbol of the version in which that reading first appeared. Because variants that first appeared simultaneously in both the 1846 American edition and the 1849 British edition have been accorded increased authority for that reason (see the Note on the Text, pp. cxvi–cxvii), such variants are marked in this list "46 & 49." In the Historical Collation, the other lines of each item give the complete record of variant readings in chronological order. In both lists, variant readings adopted in the present edition are printed in **boldface**, and items treated in the Discussion of Editorial Decisions (pp. 503–534) are marked with an asterisk. The symbol "¶" indicates that a new paragraph begins at that point.

Symbol	Version
33	The serialization in *Fraser's Magazine* between November 1833 and August 1834.
34	The bound reprint from the *Fraser's Magazine* typesetting. London: James Fraser, 1834.
38	The first British trade edition. London: Saunders and Otley, 1838.
41U	The initial typesetting of the 1841 Second Edition in uncorrected proofsheets.
41R	Carlyle's autograph corrections and revisions marked on the 1841 proofs.
41	The "Second Edition" as published. London: James Fraser, 1841.
46	The authorized American edition. New York: Wiley and Putnam, 1846.
49	The "Third Edition." London: Chapman and Hall, 1849.
58	Volume 6 (1858) of the Uniform Edition. 16 vols. London: Chapman and Hall, 1857–58.
69	Volume 1 (1869) of the Library Edition. 30 vols. London: Chapman and Hall, 1869–71.
71	Volume 1 (1871) of the People's Edition. 37 vols. London: Chapman and Hall, 1871–74.

489

3.13*	for ever;	33
	forever;	58
4.12*	Science—the	33
	Science,—the	38
5.7*	"By geometric scale	33
	'By geometric scale	38
5.9	vigorously enough thrashing	33
	vigorously thrashing	69
6.23	1833:	33
	1831.	38
6.33*	*(derben*	33
	(derben	38
6.33*	*derben*	33
	derber	58
6.33*	*Kerndeutscheit*	33
	Kerndeutschheit	38
6.33*	*Menschenliebe);*	33
	Menschenliebe);	38
8.1	If for a	33
	IF for a	38
8.4	Calendar.	33
	calendar.	41R
8.19	Clothes	33
	Clothes,	41R
8.19	such Philosophy	33
	such Philosophy,	41R
9.7	the whole Parties of the State	33
	all party-divisions in the State	69
9.8	the whole Journals	33
	all the Journals	69
11.24*	internecive	33
	internecine	38
12.1	To the Author's	33
	To the Author's	38
13.1	*Zum Grünen Ganse,*	33
	Zur Grünen Gans,	58
13.15	*steckt der*	33
	steckt doch der	69
15.30	*Grünen Ganse,*	33
	Grüne Gans,	58
16.26*	"I look	33
	'I look	Strouse
16.26	bee-hive,"	33
	bee-hive,'	Strouse
16.27	"and witness	33
	'and witness	Strouse
16.30	down to the low	33
	down the low	38
17.14*	no more." ¶ "*Ach,*	33
	no more.' ¶ '*Ach,*	Strouse
17.15*	*Leiber!"*	33
	Lieber!"	46 & 49
	Lieber!'	Strouse
17.16	talk, "it	33
	talk, 'it	Strouse
17.19*	Bootes	33
	Boötes	41U
17.29*	praying—on	33
	praying,—on	38
18.20	Stars."	33
	Stars.'	Strouse
18.36	Leischen	33
	Lieschen	58
19.5	*Erdbebungen*	33
	Erdbeben	58
19.8	for ever,	33
	forever,	49
19.9	Leischen	33
	Lieschen	58
19.19	Leischen	33
	Lieschen	58
20.6*	*Gemuth*	33
	Gemüth	46 & 49
20.7	*Schicksals-gunst;*	33
	Schicksals-Gunst;	58
20.8	"He	33
	'He	Strouse
20.10	half-congealed."	33
	half-congealed.'	Strouse

22.1	It wère a	33		37.16*	which especially,	33
	IT were a	38			which, especially	49
23.28	wesand,	33		37.19	an ell-long,	33
	weasand,	41R			an ell long,	41R
24.8	*Sanconiathon*	33		37.21*	ell (and	33
	Sanchoniathon	41R			ell, and	38
24.30	ever, with	33		37.21*	tags);	33
	ever with	41R			tags;	38
25.4	some remote echo	33		37.29	Cleopatras	33
	some echo	38			Cleopatras,	46 & 49
25.16*	terrestial	33		38.2	welts:	33
	terrestrial	38			welts;	41R
25.32	Heaven-kissing	33		38.37	Despreaux	33
	heaven-kissing	41R			Despréaux	69
27.2*	*Loix,*	33		40.1	If in the	33
	Lois,	69			IF in the	38
27.3*	*Coutumes* we	33		40.1*	his Volume,	33
	Coutumes, we	38			this Volume,	38
27.6*	Modes	33		41.9	too, must we	33
	Modes,	46 & 49			also, we have to	46 & 49
27.6*	endeavours	33		41.22*	stands	33
	endeavours,	46 & 49			stand	38
28.15*	well nigh	33		41.30	Integuments	33
	well-nigh	41R			integuments	41R
29.1	has filled	33		41.35	*Cogito*	33
	have filled	41R			*Cogito,*	41R
29.15*	chlamides,	33		43.19*	fire of the Living:	33
	chlamydes,	49			fire of Living:	58
31.8	(*Hanthierendes*	33		43.24	thereof?'	33
	(*Handthierendes*	49			thereof?	41R
33.1	One of the	33		45.1	Let no courteous	33
	ONE of the	38			LET no courteous	38
34.3	(*Teufels-schmeide*)	33		47.14*	Red, hanging-individual,	
						33
	(*Teufels-schmiede*)	38			Red hanging-individual	
34.6*	tucked in	33				38
	tucked-in	46 & 49		48.27	nay, perhaps	33
36.1	Happier is our	33			nay perhaps,	41R
	HAPPIER is our	38		49.1	It must now	33
36.14	Paullinus's	33			IT must now	38
	Paulinus's	38		49.5	'Bladders	33
36.14	*Zeitkurzende*	33			'bladders	41R
	Zeitkürzende	58				

49.5	Peas.'	33		64.6	*nenn 'ich*	33
	peas.'	41R			*nenn' ich*	41R
50.3*	Serbonian Bogs	33		64.6*	there	33
	Serbonian Bog	69			There	46 & 49
50.6	rivetting	33		64.12	at least	33
	riveting	41R			at heart	38
50.23	jacketted	33		64.17*	Büsching's Geography,	33
	jacketed	41R			Büsching's *Geography,*	69
51.11	every where	33		65.4	*schwerem*	33
	everywhere	41R			*schweren*	46 & 49
53.13	a (delirious) Mystic;	33		65.10	wife	33
	a delirious Mystic;	41R			wife,	41R
54.1	The Philosophy of	33		66.2	himself,	33
	THE Philosophy of	38			himself	41R
54.17	Thou too,	33		66.27	too must repel	33
	Thou thyself,	69			too had to repel	46 & 49
55.8	far stronger Force	33		67.13	Ostrich must leave	33
	far stranger Force	41R			Ostrich hadst to leave	
56.12*	does she not?	33				46 & 49
	does not she?	69		68.6*	*Clothes.'* ¶'Meanwhile	33
57.1*	external	33			*Clothes.* ¶'Meanwhile	
	External	38				Strouse
57.28	(*Gesnüth*),	33		69.8*	Tombuctoo	33
	(*Gemüth*),	38			Timbuctoo	58
58.7	(*menschlich-anecdotisch*)	33		70.1	'Happy season of	33
	(*menschlich-anekdotisch*)				'HAPPY season of	38
		69		70.5	(*umgäukelt*)	33
59.2*	and rot,	33			(*umgaukelt*)	58
	and to rot,	69		70.18	Arnauld, must say	33
59.30	delineations,	33			Arnauld, wilt have to say	
	delineations;	41R				46 & 49
59.37*	washbills	33		70.19	rest in?	33
	wash-bills,	46 & 49			rest in?"	38
61.1	Health,	33		71.13	Linden,	33
	health,	41R			Linden,'	38
61.1	Life,	33		71.33	(*Schaffenden*	33
	life,	41R			(*schaffenden*	58
64.4*	*Schweig Du Hund*	33		71.38	Co-operation,	33
	"*Schweig Hund*	69			Cooperation,	41R
64.5	hound!) before	33		72.19	for the cattle	33
	hound)!" before	41R			for cattle	38

72.20*	"a certain	33
	'a certain	Strouse
73.12	all but	33
	all-but	41R
73.37	Incredible	33
	Incalculable	41R
74.36	be-ribanded;	33
	beribanded;	41R
75.10	parti-coloured	33
	particoloured	41R
75.29	nay,	33
	nay	41R
76.12	every where	33
	everywhere	41R
76.28	well-meant.	33
	well-meant,	41R
76.32	Andreas, too,	33
	Andreas too	41R
78.1	Hitherto we see	33
	Hitherto we see	38
80.5*	here,	33
	here	41R
80.11	and the mystery	33
	and mystery	38
80.25	Burough,	33
	Borough,	41R
82.3	manufactured, at Nürnberg,	33
	manufactured at Nürnberg	41R
82.24	would not,	33
	would there not,	46 & 49
82.24	class, a certain	33
	class, perhaps a certain	46 & 49
82.29	boundless Abyss,	33
	bottomless Abyss,	38
82.32*	mother	33
	Mother	46 & 49
83.17*	family,	33
	Family,	46 & 49

83.19	add	33
	add,	41R
83.32	that in my Life	33
	which in my Life	46 & 49
84.15	that has passed	33
	who has passed	41R
84.19	yet nowise with	33
	yet never or seldom with	69
85.13	walled in	33
	walled-in	41R
86.30	omni-patient	33
	omnipatient	41R
86.31	lit lemechanism;	33
	little mechanism;	34
86.38	so	33
	so,	41R
87.8	sort must soon end	33
	sort had soon to end	46 & 49
87.32*	Manipulation,	33
	Manipulation	38
89.27	had been as yet those	33
	had as yet been those	46 & 49
91.1	'Thus nevertheless,' writes	33
	'Thus nevertheless,' writes	38
92.15	coronation ceremony	33
	coronation-ceremony	41R
92.36	ever new expectation, ever new	33
	ever-new expectation, ever-new	41R
93.4	not one that one	33
	not that one	38
93.14	(Brodtzwecke),	33
	(Brodzwecke),	58
93.27	embodyment	33
	embodiment	41R

94.17	Law Examination	33	
	Law-Examination	41R	
95.21	no where	33	
	nowhere	41R	
95.29	'there is ever Life for the		
	Living,'	33	
	'there is always life for a		
	living one,'	46 & 49	
96.1	forbearing	33	
	forbearing,	41R	
96.28	must serve	33	
	were to serve	46 & 49	
96.37*	*Journalistic*),	33	
	Journalistik),	41U	
97.14	unison;	33	
	harmony;	58	
97.29	will	33	
	will,	41R	
97.29	smallest	33	
	smallest,	41R	
98.1	passage,	33	
	passage	41R	
98.1	does there not	33	
	does not there	69	
98.13	to Move, to Work,	33	
	to move, to work,	41R	
98.20	Time-Element;	33	
	Time-Element,	41R	
98.23	for	33	
	for,	41R	
99.14	there;	33	
	there,	41R	
100.24	QUÆRIS	33	
	QUÆRIS,	41R	
102.4	(*Personlichkeit*)	33	
	(*Persönlichkeit*)	58	
102.19*	nor	33	
	nor,	41R	
102.19*	foliage,	33	
	foliage	38	
102.19*	Garden	33	
	Garden,	41R	

102.21	lovelier	33	
	lovelier,	41R	
103.24	must one day,	33	
	would one day,	46 & 49	
104.3	flesh,	33	
	flesh	41R	
105.37	(*ahnungsvoll*),	33	
	(*ahndungsvoll*),	41R	
108.5	mountain tops,	33	
	mountain-tops,	41R	
108.9*	dusk	33	
	dust	38	
108.26	case,	33	
	case	41R	
108.28	Actual,	33	
	Actual	41R	
108.34	a-day;	33	
	a day;	41R	
109.25	Eolean	33	
	Æolean	41R	
110.12	Kitchen	33	
	kitchen	41R	
110.26*	enough,	33	
	enough	46 & 49	
111.5*	'Farewell, then, Madam!		
		33	
	'"Farewell, then,		
	Madam!"	41R	
111.13	Universe,	33	
	Universe	41R	
112.1	We have long	33	
	WE have long	38	
112.13	enough:	33	
	enough;	41R	
114.3	feeling is it that	33	
	feeling it is that	41R	
114.21*	take but one	33	
	take only one	69	
115.11*	suit better:	33	
	suit thee better:	69	
115.12	shadows?"	33	
	shadows."	41R	

116.18*	view-hunting.	33		123.29	yet as	33
	View-hunting.	38			**yet, as**	41R
116.27	envelopement	33		123.35	all too-cruelly	33
	envelopment	41R			**all-too cruelly**	41R
116.32	must stumble	33		124.38	enough:	33
	has to stumble	46 & 49			**enough?**	41R
117.10	whole too	33		125.15*	whom He finds	33
	whole, too,	41R			**whom _he_ finds**	38
118.21*	of Epictetus	33		125.24	Jaws	33
	of Epictetus	46 & 49			**jaws**	41R
119.6	Teufelsdrockh!	33		125.24	Monster,	33
	Teufelsdröckh!	38			**monster,**	41R
119.7	Chace	33		125.28	Rue Saint Thomas de	
	Chase	41R			l'Enfer,	33
119.13	must write	33			_Rue Saint-Thomas de_	
	had to write	41R			_l'Enfer,_	41R
119.15	'to escape from	33		125.33	for ever	33
	to escape 'from	41R			**forever**	58
119.28	cannon-vollies,	33		126.3	for ever.	33
	cannon-volleys,	41R			**forever.**	58
120.1	Under the strange	33		126.7	_Ewige_	33
	UNDER the strange	38			**_ewige_**	41R
120.5	new Pilgrimings,	33		126.15	for ever	33
	mad Pilgrimings,	38			**forever**	41R
120.20	sieze	33		127.12	_Saint Thomas_	33
	seize	38			**_Saint-Thomas_**	41R
121.23*	Wordlings	33		127.21	nay that will	33
	Worldlings	58			**nay who will**	41R
121.32	meaning:	33		128.3	outwardly,	33
	meaning;	41R			**outwardly**	41R
122.4	even	33		128.14	mysterions	33
	ever	38			**mysterious**	38
122.14	things which _he_	33		128.24*	required	33
	things _he_	46 & 49			**acquired**	58
122.16	Thus must	33		129.8	Arsenals; their	33
	Thus has	46 & 49			**Arsenals; then**	38
122.16	Wanderer stand,	33		129.14	Field, but	33
	Wanderer to stand,				**field, but**	41R
		46 & 49		129.14	Field: like	33
122.22	what recks it	33			**field: like**	41R
	what boots it	38		129.14	Tree,	33
122.23	_thuts_)?'	33			**tree,**	41R
	thut's)?'	58				

129.17	Leaves	33	140.29	'Foreshadows,	33
	leaves	41R		'Fore-shadows,	41R
130.2	aye,	33	140.36	eyes too	33
	ay,	41R		eyes, too,	41R
130.19	lies as a desolate,	33	141.1	Royal	33
	lies a desolate,	38		royal	41R
131.22	us!'"	33	141.1	Beggar's	33
	us!'	38		beggar's	41R
132.15	have I not witnessed?	33	141.3	Brother! why	33
	have not I witnessed?	69		Brother, why	41R
132.31	did I not,	33	141.4	eyes.	33
	did not I,	69		eyes!	41R
133.35	Death,'	33	143.12	too honoured	33
	death,'	41R		also honoured	41R
134.3	cloth of gold;	33	143.26	thereof, opened	33
	cloth-of-gold;	41R		thereof, founded	41R
134.31	at least,	33	143.32	remark	33
	at last,	38		remark,	41R
135.5	Mannikins	33	143.32	them,	33
	Manikins	41R		them	41R
135.31	pity	33	144.15	Heart a	33
	pity,	41R		heart, a	41R
137.1	'Temptations in the	33	144.20*	will	33
	'TEMPTATIONS in the	38		will,	69
137.12	must there not be	33	144.30	internecive	33
	must not there be	69		internecine	38
138.23	So that	33	145.6	be "to	33
	So that,	41R		be, "to	41R
138.23	also	33	145.13	only,	33
	also,	41R		only	41R
138.25	his, were	33	145.14	Experience,	33
	his were	41R		Experience	41R
138.29	*me*	33	146.17	To-day,	33
	me,	41R		Today,	41R
138.30	*Apage Satanas?*	33	147.1	Thus have we,	33
	Apage, Satana?	41R		THUS have we,	38
139.18	(*Sebst-tödtung*),	33	148.28*	"SOCIETY	33
	(*Selbst-tödtung*),	49		'SOCIETY	41R
139.24	him? Were it not	33	148.29*	*Gesellschaft*),"	33
	him? If it were not	38		*Gesellschaft*),'	41R
140.26	thou not the "Living	33	149.6*	Napoleon,	33
	not thou the "Living	69		Napoléon,	69

149.17	*Liferent,*	33	159.12	Church Clothes	33	
	Life-rent,	41R		**Church-Clothes**	41R	
149.21	Boa Constrictors?	33	159.23	*muthes).*	33	
	Boa-constrictors?	41R		**Muthes).**	41R	
150.4	humouristico-satirical	33	159.24	the Church Clothes	33	
	humoristico-satirical	41R		**the Church-Clothes**	41R	
150.32	(*Pfüscher*):	33	159.25	as Church Clothes,	33	
	(*Pfuscher*):	58		**as Church-Clothes,**	41R	
152.13	mountain summits,	33	160.4	the Church Clothes,	33	
	mountain-summits,	41R		**the Church-Clothes,**	41R	
152.26	themselves	33	160.6	same Church Clothes	33	
	themselves,	41R		**same Church-Clothes**		
152.27	Shows or Vestures	33			41R	
	Shows, or Vestures,	41R	160.21	*Palinginesia,*	33	
152.28	Things even	33		**Palingenesia,**	41R	
	Things, even	41R	160.28	Church Clothes!	33	
154.10	this as heretofore	33		**Church-Clothes!**	41R	
	this, as heretofore,	41R	161.1	Probably it will	33	
155.8*	racketting,	33		**PROBABLY it will**	38	
	racketing,	41R	162.13	Shame the	33	
155.23	Want! Want!	33		**Shame (*Schaam*) the**	69	
	Want, want!	41R	162.35	embodyment	33	
155.27*	perrennial	33		**embodiment**	41R	
	perennial	38	162.39	every where	33	
156.7	Rag-fair,	33		**everywhere**	41R	
	Ragfair,	41R	163.6	embodyment	33	
156.9	height:	33		**embodiment**	41R	
	height;	41R	163.14	played	33	
156.28	did we not see	33		**played,**	41R	
	did not we see	69	164.32	every where;	33	
157.17	Distinctions re-			**everywhere;**	41R	
	established?	33	166.2	Indian Wau-Wau	33	
	Distinctions be re-			**Indian Pawaw**	41R	
	established?	41R	166.5	me	33	
158.1	Not less questionable	33		**me,**	41R	
	NOT less questionable	38	166.10	thing however	33	
158.1	on *Church Clothes,*	33		**thing, however,**	41R	
	on *Church-Clothes,*	41R	166.21*	English* Coronation	33	
158.4	'By Church Clothes,	33		**English Coronation***	38	
	'By Church-Clothes,	41R	166.23	must offer	33	
158.7	Church Clothes are,	33		**has to offer**	46 & 49	
	Church-Clothes are,	41R	166.28	every where,	33	
				everywhere,	41R	

166.foot	* *Now* last but one—ED.	
		33
	* **That of George IV.—**	
	ED.	38
167.1	At this point	33
	AT **this point**	38
168.19	thy body like thy soul	33
	thy body, like thy soul,	
		41R
168.28	Thinker, that	33
	Thinker, who	41R
168.31	Light and Guidance;	33
	Light, have Guidance,	38
169.6	athirst,	33
	athirst;	41R
169.10	is that	33
	is, that	41R
169.11	but, only	33
	but only,	46 & 49
169.12	Indignation. Alas,	33
	Indignation bear him	
	company. Alas,	46 & 49
169.15	God:	33
	God;	41R
169.19	which united	33
	which our united	41R
171.1	Putting which four	33
	PUTTING **which four**	38
172.4	your guidance,	33
	your **guidance,**	46 & 49
172.5	eat your wages,	33
	eat you your wages,	
		46 & 49
172.6	'must an observant	33
	'does an observant	
		46 & 49
172.6	every where	33
	everywhere	41R
172.28	every where	33
	everywhere	41R
173.14	every where known	33
	everywhere known,	41R

173.21	he,	33
	he;	41R
174.7	every where,	33
	everywhere,	41R
174.9	hard crashing	33
	hard-crashing	41R
174.27	mechanisms;	33
	mechanisms	41R
174.36	*L'age*	33
	'*L'âge*	58
174.36	*d'or*	33
	d'or,	41R
174.37	*passé*	33
	passé,	41R
174.37	age	33
	age,	41R
174.38	Past	33
	Past,	41R
174.38	us.—But	33
	us.'—But	41R
175.4	moths,	33
	moths	41R
175.16	we find	33
	we to find	69
175.25	*Utriusque*	33
	utriusque	41R
175.29	Trust	33
	trust	41R
176.6	London smoke	33
	London-smoke	41R
176.20	art thou not	33
	art not thou	69
177.6	Is he not	33
	Is not he	69
178.16	Prison called Life."	33
	Prison men call Life."	
		46 & 49
180.1	For us, who	33
	FOR **us, who**	38
181.11	but must drop	33
	but have to drop	46 & 49

181.27*	centre of gravity	33
	centre-of-gravity	
		46 & 49
182.1	Mæsogothic	33
	Mœsogothic	41R
182.1	Shakespeare,	33
	Shakspeare,	41R
182.8	flow on	33
	flow-on	41R
182.22	made	33
	made,	41R
185.2	for ever	33
	forever	46 & 49
185.8	for ever rooted	33
	forever rooted	46
185.11	for ever exist,	33
	forever exist,	49
185.27*	what is it to be	33
	what is to be	41U
187.1	It is in	33
	It is in	38
188.24	ancient,	33
	ancient	41R
189.12	Zodaical	33
	Zodiacal	38
190.7	will, in this wise, one day,	
		33
	will in this manner one	
	day	41R
190.15	for ever	33
	forever	46 & 49
191.1	Demonolgy,	33
	Demonology,	38
191.8	Soul,	33
	Soul	41R
192.14	Everlasting	33
	everlasting	41R
192.17	must be left	33
	had to be left	46 & 49
192.23	for ever.	33
	forever.	46 & 49
192.24	ponder,	33
	ponder	41R

192.29*	imagings (not	
	imaginings),—seems	33
	imagings or	
	imaginings,—seems	38
192.31	farthermore,	33
	furthermore,	41R
193.1	Baby,	33
	baby,	41R
193.15	Orpheus built	33
	Orpheus, or Amphion,	
	built	38
194.18	Spirits, shaped	33
	Spirits, that are shaped	
		46 & 49
194.24	do we not squeak	33
	do not we squeak	69
194.33	Spectre-Hunt;	33
	Spectre-hunt;	41R
194.36	earth	33
	Earth	41R
196.12*	*Faust:*	33
	Faust,—	58
196.16*	Shakespeare:	33
	Shakspeare:	46
	Shakspeare,—	58
197.6*	conclude,	33
	conclude	46 & 49
197.16*	few,	33
	few!	38
197.16*	Friends,	33
	Friends!	38
197.17*	courage!	33
	courage.	38
198.2	reader,	33
	Reader,	41R
199.1	Science:	33
	Science;	41R
199.6*	whereso much	33
	where so much	38
200.1	First, touching Dandies,	
		33
	First, touching Dandies,	
		38

201.12	world, that	33
	world, which	46 & 49
201.13	boon; that	33
	boon; which	46 & 49
201.30	regretted however that, here	33
	regretted however that here,	41R
201.33	tendency,	33
	tendency;	41R
202.4	yet must it	33
	yet does it	46 & 49
203.1	nature though	33
	nature, though	41R
203.9*	*Almacks,*	33
	Almack's,	41U
203.28	yield, came	33
	yield, there came	58
203.34	prodigies, that,	33
	prodigies, which,	41R
204.7	(*macalatur-bläter*),	33
	(*Maculatur-blätter*),	58
204.16	mystagogue,	33
	Mystagogue,	41R
204.28	shape,	33
	shape	41R
204.31*	'"ARTICLES	33
	'ARTICLES	38
204.36	licence	33
	license	41R
205.7*	All	33
	'All	38
206.7	irrevocably enough consecrated	33
	irrevocably consecrated	46 & 49
206.14	seemed indescribable.	33
	did not seem describable.	38
207.17*	me—indeed,	33
	me,—indeed,	38
207.20*	An Irish	33
	'An Irish	38

207.30*	First,	33
	'First,	38
207.31*	original: [italics through 208.6] '*The*	33
	original: [centered title] *Poor-Slave Household.* [no italics] ¶'"The	58
208.6*	*with.*' [end of italics]	33
	with." [no italics]	38
208.12*	But now,	33
	'But now,	38
208.15*	abode: [italics to line 31] '*A Dressing-room*	33
	abode: [centered title] *Dandiacal Household.* [no italics] ¶'"A Dressing-room	58
208.26*	*Author* (our Theogonist in person), *obsequiously*	33
	Author," our Theogonist in person, "obsequiously	38
208.28	*Apron.*' [end of italics]	33
	Apron." [no italics]	38
209.34*	"Machinery of Society"),	33
	"Machinery of Society"),	38
210.17	amaurosis suffusions	33
	amaurosis-suffusions	41R
211.1	Thus, however, has	33
	THUS, however, has	38
212.4	Shakespeare,	33
	Shakspeare,	41R
212.16*	Debt? is	33
	Debt? Is	38
213.28	for ever	33
	forever	58
214.12	being now done	33
	having now done	38
215.6	so must the lesser	33
	so has the lesser	46 & 49

215.7	instance, become	33		217.35	emissaries:	33
	instance, been forced to				**emissaries;**	**41R**
	become	**46 & 49**		218.5*	darker.—So	33
215.26*	been	33			**darker. ¶So**	**38**
	been,	**46 & 49**		218.18	likewise, it is	33
215.31	dashes his brush,	33			**likewise, this is**	**38**
	dashes his sponge,	**38**		218.20	digestion, not	33
216.11	as blotted	33			**digestion; and indicate**	
	as if blotted	**46 & 49**			**so much, not**	**46 & 49**
216.37	*Wohlgebohren*	33		218.22*	ought he not	33
	Wohlgeboren	58			**ought not he**	**58**
217.4	Leischen	33		218.25	that namest thyself	33
	Lieschen	**58**			**who namest thyself**	
217.9	*Ganse*	33				**46 & 49**
	Gans	58		218.29	have we not lived	33
217.12	*Wohlgebohren*	33			**have we not existed**	**41R**
	Wohlgeboren	58		218.30*	quarrel?	33
217.23	*Ganse*	33			**quarrel? [centered**	
	Gans	58			**paragraph] ¶THE END.**	**38**

DISCUSSION OF EDITORIAL DECISIONS

FOLLOWING are discussions of the editorial decisions made with respect to problematic variants. For an explanation of the symbols used, see the Historical Collation below, p. 541.

3.13	for ever;	33
	forever;	58 → 71

We have followed the editions of 1858 and after in consistently spelling the compound as one word, Carlyle's explicit preference, as expressed in the marginal note in the 1841 proofs. See Note on the Text, p. cxiii–cxv above.

3.21	*apples*	33
	Apples	38 → 58

Analysis of the 41U variants shows that that typesetter added capitals ten times, none of which was corrected in proof, while lower-casing existing capitals 32 times, one of which was corrected in proof, one more in 49, and one more in 58. Of the ten capitalizations that we know were introduced by the 1841 typesetters, only three approach this one in inexplicability (at 9.6, 14.21, and 190.37), the other seven being explainable as regularizations or eyeskips. But those three demonstrate that a typesetter *might* have done this, so we follow copy-text.

4.11	*Tissue,*	33
	Tissue,	38 → 71

A change from roman to italic would *prima facie* have to be authorial, since no typesetter could change fonts accidentally, unless the context suggests a possible regularization (e.g., the italicization of a book-title, as at 64.17, see discussion below). But a change from italic to roman may well be the result of inadvertence.

4.12	Science—the	33
	Science,—the	38 → 71

This comma-dash combination is typical of Carlyle, as we decided in editing *On Heroes* (see "Discussion of Editorial Decisions," *On Heroes*, p. 437).

5.7	"By geometric scale	33
	'By geometric scale	38 → 71

We have removed all further examples of 1838 quote variants, both from the Historical Collation and from the List of Emendations (where they would otherwise all appear), as long as they follow the rule (double to single, single to double). Elsewhere in the apparatus, all quotation marks are given in their 1838 forms, except in reporting the small number of cases (ten between 16.26 and 20.10, never corrected, and two at 148.28–29, corrected by Carlyle in 41R) in which the 1838 typesetter failed to make the change correctly (see discussions at 16.26 and 148.29 below), and a few other places where variants in quotation marks occur.

| 5.33 | the stinted condition | 33 |
| | the stunted condition | 69 71 |

The *OED* cites this sentence (dated "1831," and obviously taken from some edition earlier than 69), as an exemplum of "stinted" (and provides other instances of Carlyle's use of "stint" and its inflections). It seems at least as probable that the change was a typographical error as that an error in the 33 text was not corrected until 1869, or that Carlyle changed his mind.

6.33	*(derben Kerndeutscheit*	33
	*(derben **Kerndeutschheit***	38 → 49
	*(**derber** Kerndeutschheit*	58 → 71

As explained in the Note on the Text, p. cxxii above, we have adopted all variants in German spelling and usage, since these represent either corrections of errors that we do not believe to have been deliberate or authorial revision for whatever reason.

The italic parentheses in 33 we take to be an example of *Fraser's* house style. They are not logical as punctuation; the italics are for words in a foreign language, whereas the parentheses are not part of the foreign phrase.

| 11.24 | internecive war | 33 |
| | **internecine war** | 38 → 71 |

Although the *OED* gives three examples of "internecive," dated between 1819 and 1853, the editors characterize these collectively as "a (scribal) var. of . . . INTERNECINE," that is, as typographical errors. Carlyle used "internecine" in other works, but we have no examples of his use of "internecive" elsewhere. The 33 spelling was repeated at the word's only other occurrence in *Sartor*, at 144.30, where it was also corrected in the 38 edition.

| 13.38 | woof! ¶How | 33 |
| | woof! [extra leading between paragraphs] ¶How 69 71 |

We take it that printers took some degree of liberty to add or subtract these extra leadings when necessary to solve difficult problems of page layout. In the absence of evidence that any of these changes were authorial, we have followed the 33 text in these cases.

| 16.21 | showing | 33 |
| | shewing | 41u → 49 |

In editions of both *Sartor* and *On Heroes* before 1858, both "shew" and "show" appeared, more or less randomly (see "Note on the Text," *On Heroes*, xciii). The proportion of the two spellings varied from edition to edition in both works, until all instances in both were made consistent as "show" in 1858 (*On Heroes*, c). Oddly for a book on clothes, the word in either spelling occurs only about half as often in *Sartor* as in *On Heroes*, 25 times as against 48. Of these 25, the *Fraser's Magazine* text used the "shew" spelling thirteen times, the 1838 text twelve times. But the 1841 typesetter used "shew" nineteen times. Carlyle made no changes in either direction in the 1841 proofs, and both the 1846 American and 1849 British editions, somewhat surprisingly, follow the 41u spellings exactly.

The evidence does not allow us to infer a preference or pattern in Carlyle's use of these two spellings. The fact that the first printings of both works contain both spellings may mean no more than that the vowels were hard to distinguish on Carlyle's autograph manuscripts. As with *On Heroes*, however, we have no basis for departing from the distribution of the two spellings found in the earliest extant version.

16.25	for most part	33
	for the most part	38 → 71

"For most part" occurs six times in *Sartor* other than here; "for the most part" does not occur elsewhere in the text, in any edition. It is therefore more likely that this variant represents a typesetter's error than authorial revision.

16.26	"I look	33 → 71
	'I look	Strouse

There are ten points, all between here and 20.10, where double inverted commas ought to have been changed to singles in 1838 but were not changed, either then or later. Since we have accepted the system of quotation marks used in the 1838 and later editions, and since, according to that system, these ten ought to have been changed, we have undertaken to correct them.

The fact that all these unchanged quotation marks are clustered together within four pages may be significant, but it is not the case that all quotation marks in this four-page passage were left unchanged. The eight quotation marks at 18.32, 19.28, 19.29, 20.1, and 20.2 were correctly changed from double inverted commas to singles in 1838, and are therefore not reported in the Historical Collation.

17.6	lose it;	33
	lose it,	46 → 71

As explained in the Note on the Text (p. cxvii above), the question to be asked when considering variants that appear in both the 1846 American and 1849 British editions is "whether the best explanation for the correspondence of the two texts is the coincidental independent activity of the New York and London typesetters or rather whether the improbability of such a coincidence means that the revision in question must have been ordered by Carlyle in the parallel printer's copies" that he prepared for the two editions. This instance is a case where the improbability of the coincidence is not compelling to us.

17.15	*Leiber!*	33
	Lieber!	46 → 71

This example, unlike the preceding one, seems improbably coincidental, but rather to be evidence of Carlyle correcting, in the parallel printer's copies, an unintended but previously undetected German spelling error.

17.19	Bootes	33
	Böotes	38
	Boötes	41u → 71

In "Boötes," a transliteration of the Greek name of the constellation, Βοωτης, the diaeresis is not strictly required, but is traditional. All three of the *OED*'s citations for "Boötes," from the seventeenth, eighteenth, and nineteenth centuries, have the diaeresis on the second *o* (though the nineteenth-century citation is this same sentence from *Sartor*, obviously taken from an edition later than 1838). The placement of the diaeresis on the first *o* in 1838 is clearly wrong, but is a step toward the traditional spelling. Its correction in 41u must be credited to the 1841 typesetters, but we believe the correct traditional spelling was what Carlyle intended.

17.27	coverlid of vapours,	33
	coverlet of vapours,	38 → 71

We believe it to be at least as likely that this change was made by the 1838 typesetter, either accidentally or as a "correction" of a perceived misspelling, as that Carlyle preferred the later reading. Both versions of the word were current, and the *OED* cites Carlyle using "coverlid" ("Under a coverlid of London Fog") as late as volume 4 of *Frederick the Great* (1864).

17.30	praying—on	33
	praying,—on	38 → 71

See discussion at 4.12 above.

17.33	its lair	33
	his lair	38 41u

We call attention to this variant as an example of Carlyle's not infallible proofreading skills. He corrected the 1838 mistake in the 1841 proofs, but had missed it when he proofread in 1838. This is also a good example of what a typesetter can do by mistake.

18.10	position;	33
	positions;	71

In view of the lack of evidence that Carlyle participated at all in the Library Edition, this is most probably merely a pedantic regularization by a typesetter or proofreader.

18.36	Blücher Boots	33
	Blucher Boots	38 → 41

The *OED* informs us that the boots are named for one Blücher, but are called Blucher boots, except that the first citation given is this passage in *Sartor*, dated 1831 (but apparently taken from an edition later than 1841), with the umlaut. Another citation has "blucher," lower-cased. Although the citation from *Sartor* is the only one with an umlaut, we have no reason to think that the omission of the umlaut in 1838 represented authorial revision, especially as the umlaut was restored in both the 1846 American and 1849 British editions, presumably marked in the two "precisely identical" printer's copies prepared by Carlyle in 1846.

| 20.6 | *Gemuth* | 33 |
| | *Gemüth* | 46 → 71 |

Note that this umlaut was also added in both the 1846 American and 1849 British editions.

| 22.17 | inaptitude; | 33 |
| | ineptitude; | 38 → 71 |

To the extent that the *OED* recognizes a difference in meaning between these two words, or two spellings of the same word, the context favors the 33 reading over that of the later editions. We think it likely that the 1838 typesetters, confronted with an unfamiliar word, thought they were modernizing a spelling or correcting a typographical error.

| 23.14 | smiths' | 33 |
| | smith's | 38 → 71 |

This is the sort of change that a typesetter might make; it is a regularization (one stithy, therefore one smith), but a pedantic one, ignoring the possibility that more than one smith might take shifts at one stithy and work on the same implement, and also ignoring Carlyle's fondness for plurals.

| 25.16 | terrestial | 33 |
| | **terrestrial** | 38 → 71 |

All editions have "terrestrial" at the fourteen other places where the word occurs. "Terrestrial" is etymologically correct, though the *OED* notes that "-tial(l)" is a common error, formed by analogy with "celestial." So someone made a common mistake in the *Fraser's Magazine* text at this point. Since Carlyle's preferred spelling is clear from the other fourteen instances, since his preferred spelling is more correct, and since this one misspelling was corrected at the earliest opportunity, we have followed the correction, as an expression of authorial intention.

| 27.2 | *Esprit des Loix,* | 33 |
| | *Esprit des Lois,* | 69 71 |

"*Lois*" is the correct plural of "*Loi*," and the correct spelling of Montesquieu's title. Therefore, following our policy regarding corrections of German and French material, we have accepted the correction as the fulfillment of authorial intention. However, in the next lines, "*Esprit de Coutumes*" and "*Esprit de Costumes*" perhaps ought to be "*Esprit des Coutumes*" and "*Esprit des Costumes*," but since they were never corrected in any edition, we do not feel obliged to emend them ourselves.

| 27.3 | Esprit de *Coutumes* | 33 |
| | *Esprit de Coutumes,* | 38 → 71 |

In contrast with the apparent error of "*de*" instead of "*des*," the lack of this comma in the *Fraser's Magazine* text does seriously impair the intelligibility of this sentence, and the lack was repaired at the first opportunity. We have therefore adopted the correction.

| 27.6 | all his Modes and habilatory endeavours | 33 |
| | **all his Modes, and habilatory endeavours,** | 46 → 71 |

These two commas are not required by any rules of punctuation, yet both were added in both of the editions based on the two "precisely identical" printer's copies that Carlyle prepared in 1846. The coincidence is too great to permit any other explanation than authorial revision marked in both copies.

| 28.15 | well nigh | 33 |
| | **well-nigh** | 41ʀ → 71 |

The phrase, with or without the hyphen, occurs seven times in *Sartor*. At two of those occurrences (80.11 and 190.6), the hyphen was present in 33 and all subsequent editions. The fact that Carlyle added the hyphen here in 1841 does not commit us to adding it in the four other places where it was added later (at 194.15 in 1858; at 6.29, 58.12, and 166.26 in 1869).

| 29.12 | waggons | 33 |
| | wagons | 41ᴜ → 71 |

This spelling change happened four times in *Sartor*, twice in 41ᴜ (at 29.12 and 49.16) and twice in 41ʀ (130.11 and 132.29), the only four loci of either spelling in the book (other than two instances of the German "*Postwagen*"). According to the *OED*, "waggon" was the normal eighteenth-century spelling. While the word does not occur in *On Heroes*, it does occur in Carlyle's essay on "Mirabeau" (1837), where it is consistently spelled "waggon." In the first edition of *The French Revolution* (1837), "waggon" and "wagon" each appear three times.

We believe it significant that the 1841 typesetters made the first two of these four spelling changes, but left the latter two as in the printer's copy; Carlyle's marking of the remaining two instances can therefore be seen as expressions of his editorial intention to achieve consistency, rather than of a changed authorial spelling preference. In other words, we believe that Carlyle's marks at 130.11 and 132.29 were motivated by the earlier changes by the typesetters, and would not have been made on his own initiative, and so we have followed the copy-text reading at all four places.

| 29.15 | chlamides, | 33 |
| | **chlamydes,** | 49 → 71 |

We have emended here on the ground that "chlamides" is not a possible spelling. Upsilon is never transliterated as an *i*, always as a *y*; the *OED* records no instance with an *i*; and Carlyle has used the Greek plural (the singular is "chlamys"), so one could not argue that he was intending to coin an English word with his own spelling.

| 30.27 | was it in | 33 |
| | it was in | 38 → 71 |

The inversion of two words, as here, is obviously a change in the wording of the text, and presumably would not have been undertaken *deliberately* by printers on their own authority, but such transposition is a recognized category of typographical or scribal error. In 41u we find one clear-cut example of such an error ("every with" for "with every" at 6.28, corrected by Carlyle in 41R), one less-obviously erroneous example ("in all darkness" for "all in darkness" at 109.35, never corrected), and two other examples that would be plausibly authorial revisions if we had not concluded that all 41u new readings are non-authorial (*"This thou shalt do"* for *"This shalt thou do"* at 123.3 and "So true it is" for "So true is it" at 142.25, the former persisting in all later editions, the latter inverted back to the original order in 1869). On the other hand, Carlyle ordered one inversion in the 41R proofs ("it is" for "is it" at 114.3), and a pattern in the Library Edition of ten inversions of "not" and the subject pronoun in negative questions is obviously deliberate, and thus in these cases probably authorial (see the Note on the Text, pp. cxxiii–cxxiv above).

In other cases, such as the present example, where the inversion is not part of a pattern of similar revisions in the relevant edition, we have no basis for choosing between typographical error and authorial revision as an explanation for the change, and we have therefore followed the copy-text reading. All of these undecidable cases (e.g., at 50.34, 163.14, 166.25, 174.30, and 218.1) involve changes from a more unusual to a more normal word order, such as would be expected in inadvertent transposition, but so does the one demonstrably authorial inversion in 41R.

| 34.6 | tucked in | 33 |
| | **tucked-in** | 46 → 71 |

Although we have decided to accept none of the hundreds of verb-preposition linking hyphens that appear in the 1858 Uniform Edition of both *Sartor* and *On Heroes*, they were not unprecedented in Carlyle's usage. We have two such added hyphens in Carlyle's hand in 41R at 85.13 and 182.8. This one has the authority of appearing in both the 1846 American and 1849 British editions, an inconceivable coincidence if it had not been marked in their "identical" printer's copies.

37.16	which especially,	33
	'which especially,	41u
	which, especially	49 → 71

Comma placement is often optional, but this is an extreme case. The punctuation of 49 is so much preferable here that we have decided that it fulfills Carlyle's original intention and emended. Carlyle might have fixed it himself in 41R, had he not been distracted by the misplaced left quote in 41u. It is also possible that the change was marked in at least the London version of the "identical" 1846 printer's copies.

37.21   ell (and laced on the side with tags);   33
ell, and laced on the side with tags;   38 → 71

These clearly deliberate changes, though strictly speaking a matter of punctuation, seem fairly substantial and arbitrary for typesetters to undertake on their own authority, so we have accepted them as authorial. Carlyle made two changes in parentheses in 41R (at 53.13 and 64.5), whereas the typesetters made none in 41U.

37.23   Farther,   33
Further,   41U → 71

To the *OED*, this is more than just a spelling change, since "farther" is (semantically, though not etymologically) the comparative of "far," while "further" is the comparative of "fore" or "forward." However, as Fowler observed, "hardly anyone uses the two words for different occasions; most people prefer one or the other for all purposes, & the preference of the majority is for *further*" (*Modern English Usage*, s.v. "farther, further"). At least in *Sartor*, Carlyle (or *Fraser's Magazine*) did *not* observe the *OED*'s proposed semantic distinction, and preferred "farther." "Further" does not occur at all in 33, except in compounds like "furthermore" or "furtherance." "Farther" occurs eighteen times, in thirteen of which it should be "further" if the semantic distinction were in force. But of those thirteen, only two were ever changed in a British edition: this one, declared by its provenance to be a typographical error, and the one at 152.15, changed in 38 (46 changed the one at 60.5, but 49 did not). Presumably if the preference for "farther" had been *Fraser's* house style, Carlyle would have corrected more of them in oblique editions. The question is settled by the fact that *On Heroes* also contains only "farther," in all editions, never "further" except in compounds.

37.35   their mothers' headgear   33
their mother's headgear   38 → 71

It seems unlikely, though not impossible, that all the maidens had the same mother. Sense as well as our principle of relying on the copy-text in ambiguous cases favor the 33 reading. But the reason for the fidelity to this apparent typographical error in subsequent editions remains a mystery.

40.1   his Volume,   33
this Volume,   38 → 71

The phrase "this Volume" is frequent in *Sartor*, both before and after this point (e.g., "this remarkable volume" at 9.2; "this surprising Volume" at 21.2; "this remarkable Volume" at 21.13, 26.24, and again at 179.27; "this Clothes-Volume" at 153.2; "this unpretending Volume" at 181.34; "this Volume" at 203.3 and 212.18; etc.). The 1846 American, but not the 1849 British, edition changes "this" to "his" at 153.2, thus proving that such errors could be and were sometimes committed, but otherwise this is the only example of such a change. Although the phrase "his Volume," while less frequent, could also be documented elsewhere in the text, and might be thought to make slightly better sense in the context of this variant, we think this is more likely to be a correction by Carlyle of an error in the 33 typesetting than to be itself an error.

| 40.20 | limbos, | 33 |
| | limboes, | 38 → 71 |

Although Carlyle apparently did not object to this change, if he did not make it himself, the fact remains that the plural is Carlyle's coinage. There are no examples of a plural in the *OED;* "limbo" is the ablative of *limbus,* Englished from the Latin phrase *in limbo.* The manuscript was undoubtably copied accurately here: it is not conceivable that Carlyle wrote "limboes" in the manuscript but the *Fraser's* printer set "limbos." Both forms are potentially slightly confusing ("limbos" might be a Greek second-declension nominative singular, though a plural is signaled by the absence of a preceding article; "limboes" might be more than one limboe, whatever that is). For our purposes, it is enough that we are fairly sure that Carlyle wrote "limbos" in the manuscript, whereas we are not at all sure that the revision in 38 was his idea.

| 41.21 | canvass | 33 |
| | canvas | 58 → 71 |

The *OED* lists "canvass" as an alternative spelling of the noun. The rule that makes the noun "canvas" and the verb "canvass," neat as it may be, is more recent than the *OED* and it would be an anachronism to apply it retroactively here, or at 42.35 where the same change is at issue.

| 41.22 | stands | 33 |
| | **stand** | 38 → 71 |

We take it that this is a deliberate change to the subjunctive (most likely a return to the correct manuscript reading) rather than a typographical error, and if deliberate, then probably authorial.

| 43.19 | The fire of the Living: | 33 |
| | **The fire of Living:** | 58 → 71 |

The German original will apparently support either version of this variant in what is presumably Carlyle's own translation. We take it to be of a piece with the other corrections in German in 1858. Since we have accepted these as authorized, if not authorial, we have decided to follow the revised reading here.

| 43.25 | foredone | 33 |
| | fordone | 58 → 71 |

According to the *OED,* these are simply alternate acceptable spellings of the same word. We therefore follow copy-text.

| 47.14 | Red, hanging-individual, | 33 |
| | **Red hanging-individual** | 38 → 71 |

The *Fraser's* typesetter is unlikely to have invented these two unfortunate commas—they were probably in the manuscript—and any alert typesetter might have been responsible for deleting them in 1838 without needing to ask authorial permission. However, we cannot allow an uncritical fidelity to the copy-text to force on us a reading that is so nearly indecipherable. We emend on the ground that the change is expressive of Carlyle's intention.

| 50.3 | Serbonian Bogs | 33 |
| | **Serbonian Bog** | 69 71 |

The reference is to *Paradise Lost* 2.592 (see Notes), where "Serbonian bog" is singular. The later reading is therefore more correct, and most likely authorial, unless we are to imagine a printer who had Milton by heart.

| 50.36 | Know, to Believe; | 33 |
| | know, to believe; | 46 → 71 |

As described in the Note on the Text, there is a trend in every oblique edition toward the lower-casing of Carlyle's irregular capitalizations. The evidence of the 1841 proofs tells us that some of the lower-casings in the 1841 edition were made, accidentally or deliberately, by typesetters, while others were ordered by Carlyle in proof, and we assume that the same is true for other editions when Carlyle prepared copy or read proof. In the case of parallel lower-casings appearing in both the 1846 American and the 1849 British editions, we have to decide whether the coincidence of the parallel changes compels the inference that they were among the revisions marked by Carlyle in the two "precisely identical" printer's copies that he prepared in 1846. There are thirteen such parallel lower-casings in the two editions (and three parallel capitalizations). Perhaps significantly, eight of these parallel lower-casings occur between 50.36 and 53.17, including these two at 50.36 and four on lines 53.16–17. On the other hand, there are 35 lower-casings in the 1846 New York edition that are not paralleled in the 1849 London edition (and three non-parallel capitalizations), and there are 34 lower-casings (and two capitalizations) in the 1849 edition not found in the 1846 edition.

It follows, we believe, that some but not all of the parallel changes of case in the two editions were ordered by Carlyle, while some were a purely coincidental intersection of the set of the American lower-casings with the set of the British lower-casings. We observe that "Know" and "Believe" are verbs, whose capitalization is even more irregular than that of nouns (and that two of the four changes in the "cluster" at 53.16–17 are likewise verbs, "Born" and "Die"); that if one had decided to lower-case one of the verbs in each of these pairs, the decision to lower-case the other would be automatic; that the two nouns lower-cased at 53.16 are another obvious pair, "Cow" and "Bull." We observe further that Carlyle in 1868 objected, in a letter to his printer (the same printer who was responsible for the 1849 and all British editions later than 1838), to "[t]hat abolition of Capitals . . . abolition quasi-total, which in many places considerably obscures the sense." It is clear to us that one of the subnarratives in the textual history of Sartor is a lifelong conflict between Carlyle's desire to retain his irregular capitals and his printers' resistance to them, in which Carlyle continually compromised under pressure. Not being under the same pressure to modernize and regularize our text, we have decided to reject all lower-casings except those ordered in his own hand by Carlyle in the surviving 1841 proofs. We accordingly also reject these parallel lower-casings, albeit possibly authorial, from the 1846 and 1849 editions.

54.14 Whole: 33
whole: 38 → 41

Interestingly, here we see both the 1846 and 1849 (and subsequent) editions returning to the capitalization of the copy-text reading.

55.34 are Emblematic, 33
are emblematic, 69 71

On the 1841 proofs, Carlyle marked the E to be lower-cased, then scratched out the marginal notation, indicating that he had changed his mind. Note that the capitalized word here is an adjective rather than a noun, and that "Emblems" was lower-cased four lines above in 1849 (but not 1846) and thereafter.

56.12 does she not? 33
does not she? 69 71

This is the first of the ten inversions of "not" and the subject pronoun in negative questions in the Library Edition, discussed in the Note on the Text, pp. cxxiii–cxxiv, and in the discussion at 30.27 above. The other instances are at 98.1, 132.15, 132.31, 137.12, 140.26, 156.28, 176.20, 177.6, and 194.24.

57.1 external 33
External 38 → 71

Although we are loath to accept changes of case from any edition—given the evidence of the 1841 proofs in which the typesetters lower-cased 32 words, and capitalized nine others, on their own authority or by accident— we make an exception in this instance, judging this capitalization to be most probably authorial, as well as more expressive of the sense of the passage.

57.12 Scottish Hamburgh Merchant, 33
Scottish Hamburg Merchant, 58 → 71

Although this might be considered a correction of a German spelling, such as it is our general policy to accept, there is also the possibility that a "Scottish Hamburgh Merchant" might be a merchant who trades, with portmanteau, between Hamburg and Edinburgh, a possibility that we are unwilling to lose by making the obvious emendation.

59.2 and rot, 33
and to rot, 69 71

We take this to be an example of the minor revisions Carlyle made throughout the Library Edition, as well as an improvement in sense.

59.7 Clothes stand 33
Clothes stands 38 41u
Clothes will stand 41r → 71

Clearly the 41r revision was a response to the 38 variant, which is of doubtful authority. It seems probable that the 33 copy-text accurately represented the manuscript. The 38 reading was probably an error, because the context demands some kind of future tense ("will draw ... and so ... [will] stand"; the elision of the parallel auxiliary is typically Carlylean). In 1841, Carlyle saw that the present tense "stands" was wrong but did not restore the original reading. Since the 41R revision might well not have been made but for the error in 38, we have retained the original, copy-text reading.

59.37	washbills	33
	wash-/bills	41U → 41
	wash-bills,	46 → 71

The new comma, appearing, without any obvious contextual necessity, in both the 1846 American and 1849 British editions, is presumably authorial, and we have accepted it. On the other hand, both 46 and 49 misinterpreted the line-end hyphen in "wash-/bills" in their 41 printer's copies.

64.4	*Schweig Du Hund*	33
	"*Schweig Du Hund*	38
	"*Schweig, Du Hund*	41U
	"*Schweig' Du Hund*	41R 41
	"*Schweig' Hund*	46 → 58
	"*Schweig Hund*	69 71

The 41U typesetter introduced a comma after "*Schweig*" and Carlyle changed it to an apostrophe in 41R, inexplicably. In 69 (not in 58) the apostrophe was removed; it seems never to have been necessary. The "*Du*" was removed in both 46 and 49, presumably by Carlyle.

64.6	there	33
	There	46 → 71

This could be seen as a regularization (the German sentence begins with a capital, so its translation also needs to begin with a capital), but it is not so obviously necessary as to provide an alternative explanation for its parallel appearance in both 46 and 49. More likely it was ordered by Carlyle in the two printer's copies.

64.17	Büsching's Geography,	33
	Büsching's *Geography*,	69 71

The evidence of the 1841 proofs generally supports the idea that typesetters did not make changes in italics. The only italics change found in 41U is the extension of italics from one word to two, at 118.34. Since the change from roman to italic type involved the change to a different font (literally a different drawer-full of type), it is impossible to imagine that printers could italicize by accident, and difficult to imagine that they would italicize unless they felt obliged to do so. Although there is a rule of style that says that titles of books must be italicized, we think this is probably an example of Carlyle's minor revisions throughout the Library Edition.

68.6   *Clothes.*' ¶'Meanwhile   33
          Clothes? [extra leading between
          paragraphs] ¶'Meanwhile   69 71
          Clothes. ¶'Meanwhile   Strouse

There is no reason for a closing, single quotation mark at the end of this paragraph. It is evidently an error that was never detected because it occurs at the end of an italicized passage that is syntactically a quotation, though neither it nor the other parallel italicized passage earlier in the sentence was ever otherwise marked as such. (Both passages, since they are embedded in the long quotation from 66.37 to 68.32, would have needed double rather than single quotation marks.) Another such superfluous end-of-paragraph close quote mark was introduced at 126.6 in 38 and copied in 41u, but it was deleted by Carlyle in 41R.

69.8   Tombuctoo   33
          Timbuctoo   58 → 71

It is difficult to decide whether the earlier form represents an error that was not corrected until 58 or an acceptable contemporary alternative spelling, but on the whole we are inclined to the former opinion, and we have accordingly emended. See Notes.

72.20   "a certain   33
          a 'certain   38 → 71
          'a certain   Strouse

We have changed the double quotation mark to a single one, according to our policy of following the 38 system, but the movement of the quotation mark in 38 and after has no particular claim to authority.

73.32   gray, austere,   33
          grey austere,   38 → 41
          grey austere   46 49
          gray austere   58 → 71

The loss of the comma after "gray/grey" in 38 was presumably a mistake, and the loss of the other comma after "austere," in both 46 and 49, was obviously an attempt to deal with the confusing punctuation that was brought about by that mistake. Whether the 46 and 49 variant was ordered by Carlyle on the two "identical" printer's copies or was a coincidentally identical solution to the same problematic punctuation is a question we need not decide, since we see no reason to depart from the copy-text reading.

78.23   For the shallow-sighted, Teufelsdröckh is   33
          For the shallow-sighted Teufelsdröckh is   41u 46

It is extremely puzzling that this essential comma was omitted in two unrelated typesettings. We call attention to the fact as a warning against making too much depend upon the improbability of a coincidence.

80.5	here,	33
	here	41R

The deletion of this comma was ordered by Carlyle in the 1841 proofs, but the change was not made in correcting the 1841 type, nor in any subsequent edition until the present.

82.4	any thing;	33
	anything;	46 → 71

Although strictly a change of wording in both 46 and 49, we take this to be a coincidental modernization of no significance.

82.32	mother	33
	Mother	46 → 71

83.17	family,	33
	Family,	46 → 71

In contrast to the variant at 82.4 discussed above, these two capitalizations, while not strictly irregular, seem too much of a coincidence not to have been ordered by Carlyle in the two printer's copies for 46 and 49.

85.34	What monies,	33
	What moneys,	46 → 71

85.38	said monies,	33
	said moneys,	46 → 71

The fact that this spelling modernization was repeated in both 46 and 49 does not prove that it was ordered in the two printer's copies.

86.6	place and wages	33
	place of wages	69 71

This we judge to have been a typographical error in 69.

87.32	Manipulation,	33
	Manipulation	38 → 71

The omission of this comma changes the sense of the sentence. Did Carlyle mean that it was the whole "vain jargon of controversial Metaphysic, Etymology, and mechanical Manipulation" that was "falsely named Science," or was it only the "mechanical Manipulation" that was "falsely named Science"? We think the latter reading, without the comma, better represents Carlyle's intention.

93.17	forward and forward,	33
	forward and forward;	46 → 71

We do not believe that this is enough of a coincidence to compel the inference that it was ordered on the two printer's copies for 46 and 49.

96.37 *Journalistic*), 33
Journalistik), 41u → 71

As explained in the Note on the Text (p. cxi above), this correction of a German spelling does not prove that Carlyle revised the text prior to the 1841 typesetting, merely that the typesetter had some knowledge of German. We accept it in accordance with our policy of accepting all German corrections.

97.5 many things, besides "the
Outrooting of Journalism," 33
many things besides "the
Outrooting of Journalism," 46 49
many things besides 'the
Outrooting of Journalism' 58 → 71

The sense of the passage requires either both of these commas or neither. But while the first was deleted in both 46 and 49, the other was not deleted until 58, which argues against any authority that the first variant might derive from its parallel appearance in 46 and 49.

97.15 Victory is only possible by Battle.' 33
Victory is only possible by battle.' 41u
victory is only possible by battle.' 41R → 71

The lower-casing of "Victory" in 41R is clearly a response to the lower-casing of "Battle" in 41u, which has no authority.

100.26 PRIMUM 33
PRIMÙM 46 → 58

100.26 POSTREMUM 33
POSTREMÙM 46 → 58

These two accent marks, if that is what they are, appearing in both the 46 and 49 editions and persisting in the British stemma through 58, were clearly deliberately introduced by Carlyle. Just as clearly, there is no possible justification for them in the rules of Latin. Carlyle often used a circumflex accent mark (ˆ) instead of a macron (ˉ) to indicate long vowels in Latin (e.g., "*bonâ fidê*" in *On Heroes* at 57.4), but these *u*'s are not long vowels. There is no Latin suffix *-um* in which the *u* is long. Also, these marks are neither circumflexes nor macrons, but clearly grave accents, and of course neither grave nor acute accent marks are used in Latin. It would seem either that Carlyle made an inexplicable mistake or that he introduced these errors deliberately—perhaps as a further development of his joke about the surprising "Latinity" of the inscription—but it must be said that neither of these explanations is easily credible. Fortunately, we are relieved of this editorial conundrum by the fact that the accents were both deleted in 69, a change that we hasten to attribute to authorial revision.

| 102.19 | nor | 33 |
| | nor, | 41R → 71 |

| 102.19 | foliage, | 33 |
| | **foliage** | 38 → 71 |

| 102.19 | Garden | 33 |
| | **Garden,** | 41R → 71 |

We could argue that the two commas that Carlyle introduced on this line in 41R were a response to the loss of the comma after "foliage" in 38, which may not have been authorial. But we prefer to argue that, whether or not the change in 38 was authorial, it left a passage whose punctuation required and obviously received Carlyle's detailed attention in his 1841 proofreading. Therefore the solution he then adopted must be followed, which requires accepting the 38 variant as well as the two from 41R.

| 103.7 | whereso | 33 |
| | wheresoever | 69 71 |

The same kind of change was made twice more in the 69 edition ("whatsoever" for "whatso" at 114.10 and 125.37). While these might be thought to be more examples of the pattern of minor revisions that Carlyle seems to have made throughout the Library Edition, they are well within the range of modernization or regularization of which we know the 69 printers to have been capable. In the Library Edition of *On Heroes*, a printer in the same shop changed the word "euphuism" to "euphemism" at all four of its occurrences, obviously under the erroneous impression that this was merely modernizing or correcting a spelling. We accept, for example, the ten inversions of word order in 69 (discussed at 56.12 above), because they are changes away from normal word order toward an idiosyncratic word order that we do not believe a printer would have deliberately introduced. But here the change is from a less to a more familiar form of the same word, and we are far from confident that Carlyle was responsible for it.

| 106.4 | specially | 33 |
| | especially | 41U → 71 |

Given our conviction that none of the variants in the 41U uncorrected proofs is authorial, this must be considered a typographical error (perhaps an erroneous modernization) that was never corrected. The same change was made in 41U at 200.2, corrected by Carlyle in 41R, and at 22.13 in 71, though instances of both forms can be found throughout the text that were never changed.

| 108.9 | dusk and darkness; | 33 |
| | **dust and darkness;** | 38 → 71 |

Either the 33 reading was an error which was then corrected by Carlyle during the 38 publication process, or the 38 reading was an error that persisted undetected through all subsequent lifetime editions. Superficially, the sense of the sentence rather strongly favors the earlier reading. However, we reason as follows: The two words would have been difficult to distinguish in Carlyle's autograph manuscript; it is easier to believe that the 33 typesetter misread the manuscript than that the 38 typesetter misread the printed "foul copy," the 34 reprint. Also, a mistake in 33 would have been in the direction of the expected word, and such a mistake is generally more probable than one that changes a more-expected into a less-expected word, as a mistake in 38 would have done. A further consideration is that if the 38 reading were an error, there were at least three opportunities for Carlyle to have corrected it (when reading the 38 or 41 proofs or when preparing the "identical" printers' copies for 46 and 49). Finally, there is the evidence of Carlyle's use of the phrase "dust and shadow" at 195.4, an echo of Horace's *pulvis et umbra* (see Notes).

109.5	yet all in darkness:	33
	yet in all darkness:	41u → 71

As we said at 30.27 above, we believe this to be a typographical error, never corrected.

110.26	enough,	33
	enough	46 → 71

There seems no better explanation for the parallel deletion of this comma in the 46 and 49 editions than that it was ordered on both printer's copies.

111.5	'Farewell, then, Madam!	33
	"'Farewell, then, Madam!"	41R 46 → 71
	"Farewell, then, Madam!"	41

In his revisions marked in the 1841 proofs, Carlyle attempted to add internal quotation marks (double inverted commas, in the British system used in 38 and thereafter) before and after these three words. However, in correcting the type the printer *substituted* the left double quote for the left single quote, rather than inserting the double after the single as ordered. The correction was made in both the 46 and 49 editions.

114.10	whatso	33
	whatsoever	69 71

See the discussion at 103.7 above.

114.21	take but one	33
	take only one	69 71

While the 69 typesetters might well have decided that "whereso" and "whatso" were not, or were no longer, acceptable words, they could have had no such excuse for this level of intervention in the text. It seems much more likely that this change is one of Carlyle's minor revisions of the Library Edition.

115.11	suit better:	33
	suit thee better:	69 71

This is a good example of the kind of change that, however minor its effect on the sense of the passage, can only have been initiated by the author.

116.6   postilions   33
          postillions   58 → 71

The French word has two *l*'s, but the *OED* prefers one, while allowing two. The change of spelling in 58 has no special authority. Note that the same word was spelled with one *l* in *On Heroes* at 14.18 until the Library Edition doubled the *l*.

116.18   view-hunting.   33
          View-hunting.   38 → 71

The point of this sentence depends upon making a parallel between the two diseases of "Small-pox," which was capitalized in every edition, and "View-hunting," which was capitalized in every edition beginning with 38. Although we have generally preferred not to accept changes of case from any edition, except those ordered by Carlyle in the 41R proofs (see the discussion at 3.21 above), too strict an adherence to this rule in this instance "considerably obscures the sense (or comprehensibility in reading)," as Carlyle complained of attempts to abolish his irregular capitals.

118.21   "*Enchiridion* of Epictetus   33
          '*Enchiridion of Epictetus*   46 → 71

If this change had occurred in a single edition, we might take it as someone's idea of a necessary regularization, or even as a mistake (compare the erroneous italics committed in 41U and corrected in 41R, coincidentally on the same page at 118.34), but the same change on two continents strongly suggests that it was marked in the copies Carlyle revised in 1846. He might have considered that *Enchiridion* is a generic title meaning "Manual," so that the author's name is properly part of the title: not the *Dialogues* of Plato, but the *Dialogues of Plato*.

119.9   Jew, save   33
          Jew,—save   69 71

Although we have elsewhere accepted this comma-dash combination as typically and distinctively Carlylean (e.g., at 4.12 and 17.30 above), in this case a printer or editorial assistant may have felt that the dash later in the sentence, after "guilt," required an opening dash here to set off the parenthetical phrase.

120.9–10 the Eagle, when he moults, is   33
          the Eagle when he moults, is   41U
          the Eagle when he moults is   41R → 71

In these two variants, Carlyle's 41R deletion of the comma after "moults" was a response to the 41U omission of the comma after "Eagle." The sense requires either both commas or neither. Since 41U has no authority, and Carlyle's change in 41R would not have been necessary without the 41U mistake, we prefer the copy-text reading.

121.15   goes   33
           grows   49 58

Our decision as to whether this variant represents a mistake or authorial revision in 49 is influenced toward the former alternative by the fact that it did not appear in the 46 American edition (and we have no reason to believe that Carlyle participated further in the 49 British edition after preparing the printers' copies in 1846). The matter is settled by the fact that the 49 innovation was reversed in 69.

121.23   Wordlings   33
           Worldlings   58 → 71

We have accepted this emendation, on the consideration that either word is unusual enough that a printer would have slowed down and taken care, so in this case the change must have been both deliberate and authorial. It also seems a considerable improvement in sense. The 33 copy-text, or perhaps the manuscript, must have been in error.

121.38   that   33
           who   41u → 71

Since we know by its provenance that this change was not initiated by Carlyle, the only question is whether it is required for the comprehensibility of the text and should therefore be considered a necessary expression of authorial intention. The answer is that while the change might seem to be called for by the rules of pronoun usage, the copy-text reading is far from impossible. We note but are not swayed by the fact that Carlyle did make the same kind of change three times in 41R (at 84.15, 127.21, and 168.28), where we of course follow his revisions, nor by the speculation that he might have done the same here if he had not been preempted by the printer.

123.3   *shalt thou*   33
           thou shalt   41u → 71

See discussion at 30.27 above.

124.11   round   33
           around   38 → 71

This is a mistake that we find in 46 (but not 49) at 42.6, 64.20, 121.8, and 140.19, so although it is strictly speaking a change of wording in an authorial edition, we are not convinced that it is not also a mistake here.

124.13   In midst   33
           In the midst   69 71

Like the change from "for most part" to "for the most part" at 16.25 in 38, we believe that this change could well be attributed to the typesetter, either as the accidental substitution of a more familiar for a less familiar phrase, or as a deliberate if ill-advised regularization.

| 125.15 | whom He finds | 33 |
| | **whom *he* finds** | 38 → 71 |

It is much harder to imagine a scenario in which a printer might have done this deliberately than to accept it as an authorial revision, and it is quite impossible to imagine a printer switching from one type-drawer to another absent-mindedly.

| 125.37 | whatso | 33 |
| | whatsoever | 69 71 |

See discussion at 103.7 above.

| 128.24 | required | 33 |
| | **acquired** | 58 → 71 |

Whoever actually made the correction in 58, we judge that the copy-text reading was an error (perhaps present in the manuscript) and that the revision is necessary.

| 129.30 | Desart, | 33 |
| | Desert, | 38 → 71 |

The *OED* observes that "desart . . . was the regularly accepted spelling of the 18th century" for this sense of the noun.

130.11	Ammunition-waggons,	33
	Ammunition-waggons	41U
	Ammunition-wagons	41R → 58
	Ammunition-wagons,	69 71

See discussion at 29.12 above.

| 131.14 | Deutschland, | 33 |
| | Deutchsland, | 41U → 49 |

It is perhaps worth noticing that this typographical error passed undetected through Carlyle's 1841 proofreading and also his revisions for 46 and 49.

| 131.17 | Smollett, | 33 |
| | Smollet, | 41U → 71 |

As with the previous item, it is of some interest that this error in 41U was never subsequently corrected.

132.29	waggon-load	33
	wagon-load	41R 41
	wagonload	46 → 71

As explained at 29.12 above, we do not feel obliged to follow the change from two *g*'s to one, marked here by Carlyle in the 41R proofs. Although the deletion of the hyphen may also have been ordered by Carlyle, since it occurs in both 46 and 49, we cannot know whether he would have made the change in 1846 had he not accepted the printer's modernization of spelling in 1841. Since we are reverting to the copy-text for the spelling "waggon," it seems best to do so with respect to the hyphen as well.

| 133.19 | Evangile, | 33 |
| | Evangel, | 38 → 71 |

The earlier spelling is given as an acceptable alternative by the *OED*, which however cites this sentence using the "1858" edition and the later spelling. The word itself is said to have been archaic in England by the seventeenth century, "but in Scotland it remained in current use . . . until a still later period."

133.23	Backwoods-man,	33
	Backwood's-man,	41U
	Backwoodsman,	41R → 71

Using the same argument employed at 132.29 above, we see Carlyle here, confronted with a spelling he was not responsible for, judging it incorrect and making further changes. Since we cannot tell whether in 1841 he would have felt the need to delete his own earlier hyphen if he had been presented with his own earlier spelling of the compound, we prefer to revert to the copy-text form.

134.23	say:	33
	say	38 41U
	say,	41R → 71

Clearly Carlyle in 1841 saw a need for punctuation before the quote, but rather than restoring his original colon, which he cannot be expected to have remembered, he inserted a comma. Since we take the loss of the colon in 38 to be an error, and since we are correctly more interested in restoring Carlyle's original punctuation than he was, we have followed copy-text here.

| 135.7 | specialities, | 33 |
| | specialties, | 49 → 71 |

The *OED* cites this sentence, dated "1831" but with the later spelling (we have observed that the *OED* seems to have used a copy of the Uniform Edition for its citations from *Sartor*), as its most recent exemplum of "specialty" in the sense, "6. A special or particular matter, point, or thing." However, the first sense given for "speciality," "1. A special, particular, or individual point, matter, or item; freq. *pl.* particulars, details," seems at least as apposite to this context. Also, the rhetorical parallel Carlyle is making with "generality" favors "specialities." Finally, the change is not found in the 46 American edition, but first occurred in the 49 British edition which we do not generally believe is authorial where it is not supported by a parallel 46 variant. In sum, we believe the later spelling to be mistaken, despite whatever authority it derives from its appearance in the *OED*.

139.15	doubtless,	33
	doubtless	46 69 71

Although the sense seems clearer without the comma, its deletion in 46 but not 49 has no authority, and we cannot be confident that Carlyle was responsible for its deletion in 69. Nor do we feel justified in accepting the emendation as a *necessary* expression of authorial intent, though we may feel that it expresses that intent better than the copy-text reading.

140.26	of God?'	33
	of God?,	34
	of God"?	69 71

140.27	HE, then,	33
	HE' then,	34
	HE then	38 → 58

These two variants were at consecutive line-ends in 34. Evidently the comma after "HE" and the right single quote after "God?" were accidentally reversed.

142.25	true is it,	33
	true it is,	41u → 58

See discussion at 30.27 above.

144.20	will	33
	will,	69 71

Unlike the comma change discussed at 139.15 above (also made in 69), we cannot feel that this comma is optional if the reader is to have any chance of parsing this sentence without undue effort.

146.13	pitifullest	33
	pitifulest	41R → 49

As explained in the Note on the Text, p. cxiii above, and like the case of "waggon/wagon" discussed at 29.12 above, we believe Carlyle's changes, in the 41R proofs, of the spelling of the fourth (this one) through seventh of the seven instances in the text of adjectives in *-fullest* (at 83.31, 102.8, 123.15, 146.13, 152.25, 167.18, and 203.26), were prompted by his observation that the first and second instances had been spelled "-fulest" in the 41u typesetting, and by a desire to achieve consistency, rather than by a spontaneous change in his own preferred spelling. Because these four are marked revisions in 41R that we are *not* accepting, we have included them in this list.

148.26	doing it	33
	doing, it	49 → 71

This is another example, like those discussed at 139.15 and 144.20 above, of a comma change that, while unquestionably helpful to the reader, is of doubtful authority. We have decided that the copy-text should be followed in such cases unless the emendation is necessary for the coherence of the sentence, which in this case it is not.

| 148.28 | "Society | 33 |
| | 'Society | 41R → 71 |

| 148.29 | Gesellschaft)," | 33 |
| | Gesellschaft),' | 41R → 71 |

The anomaly of these two variants is that the double quotation marks were not changed to singles along with all the others in 1838, but remained doubles until Carlyle corrected them in the 41R proofs. Note that while Carlyle noticed these two, he failed to correct the ten similar mistakes between 16.26 and 20.10, discussed at 16.26 above.

| 149.6 | Code Napoleon, | 33 |
| | Code Napoléon, | 69 71 |

The word order signals that this is the French name for what is usually called the Napoleonic Code in English. The corrected French spelling is therefore appropriate. Like the German variants discussed in the Note on the Text (p. cxxii) and at 6.33 above, we believe that Carlyle either made this correction himself or authorized someone else to do so.

| 150.7 | Mystification! | 33 |
| | mystification! | 46 → 71 |

As we explained in the discussion at 50.36 above, we have decided not to accept any of the parallel changes of case from the 46 and 49 editions, as here, though at least some of them may have been authorial.

| 151.28 | toilsome diggings | 33 |
| | tiresome diggings | 41U → 71 |

"Tiresome" is a much more familiar word than "toilsome," and "toilsome" is better in context, a combination of considerations pointing to a typographical error. The provenance of the variant is further evidence supporting this decision.

152.15	Nay farther,	33
	Nay, further,	38 → 58
	Nay further,	69 71

See discussion at 37.23 above.

| 152.25 | fearfullest | 33 |
| | fearfulest | 41R → 46 |

See discussion at 146.13 above.

| 155.8 | racketting, | 33 |
| | racketing, | 41R 46 → 71 |

This spelling change was ordered by Carlyle in the 41R proofs, but the type was not corrected; the 1841 edition was published with the earlier spelling intact. It seems probable that he ordered it again on both of the printer's copies he prepared in 1846. The case can be distinguished from "waggon/wagon" and "-fullest/-fulest" discussed at 29.12 and 146.13 above, since in this instance Carlyle is not responding to the same spelling change imposed by the typesetters earlier in the book. Compare "riveting" at 50.6 and "jacketed" at 50.23, also altered by Carlyle in 41R.

| 155.27 | perrennial | 33 |
| | **perrennial** | 38 → 71 |

We take the spelling "perrennial" in 33 to be a mistake; there is no record in the *OED* that "perennial" was ever spelled with two *r*'s.

| 155.34 | hindrances | 33 |
| | hinderances | 38 → 41 |

Note that both 46 and 49 return to the copy-text spelling.

| 160.5 | man. | 33 |
| | men. | 49 → 71 |

Given that this variant occurred in 49 but not in 46, we believe it to be more likely a specious typographical error than an authorial revision.

| 162.11 | right hand know what thy left hand doeth! | 33 |
| | left hand know what thy right hand doeth! | 58 → 71 |

Since these two changes move the passage into conformity with Matthew 6:3, there are too many possible scenarios in which the change was neither made nor authorized by Carlyle. It is possible that one of Carlyle's "editorial assistants" had this verse by heart. It is even possible that the 58 typesetter accidentally reversed the words, which only fortuitously made the reference more accurate. In our judgment, the copy-text version sufficiently conveys the reference, while preserving whatever interest there may be in the fact that the early editions misquoted it.

| 162.27 | doubled | 33 |
| | double | 58 → 71 |

We are not convinced that this minor change, though strictly speaking a change of wording, was more likely authorial than erroneous.

| 163.14 | has man | 33 |
| | man has | 49 → 71 |

The inversion in 49, not paralleled in 46, was most probably inadvertent.

| 165.26 | matter, | 33 |
| | manner, | 41U → 71 |

Surprisingly, for a pair of words that are often used as opposites, the context gives little guidance as to which of these we ought to prefer. Fortunately, our well-established conclusion that none of the 41U variants was ordered by Carlyle allows us to decide that the copy-text reading is correct, the later reading an error.

166.21	English* Coronation	33
	English Coronation*	38 → 49
	English Coronation[1]	58 → 71

Both versions of the footnote refer to "Coronation" rather than to "English." Therefore the position of the asterisk in 33 was a mistake and needed to be emended, whoever was responsible for noticing this. On the other hand, the change of reference symbol in 58 from an asterisk to a superscript numeral could have any number of explanations other than a change in Carlyle's preference.

| 166.25 | have we | 33 |
| | we have | 38 → 71 |

See the discussion at 30.27 above.

| 167.5 | for sake of | 33 |
| | for the sake of | 38 → 71 |

Like "for the most part" at 16.25 (also in 38) and "In the midst of" at 124.13 (in 69), this change from a less to a more familiar form does not convince us of its authority.

| 167.18 | frightfullest | 33 |
| | frightfulest | 41R → 46 |

See discussion at 146.13 above.

| 169.14 | stupified, | 33 |
| | stupefied, | 58 → 71 |

According to the *OED*, "The spelling with i (cf. liquify) was common until the latter half of the 19th c. 'This word should . . . be spelled *stupefy*; but the authorities are against it' (Johnson)."

| 173.5 | far in rear of | 33 |
| | far in the rear of | 38 → 71 |

"In rear of" may sound more questionable to us than "for most part," "In midst of," or "for sake of," but the *OED* (s.v. "Rear," sense 4.c) tells us that the phrase "In the rear of" *was* used "occas. without *the*" and gives an example from 1815.

| 174.30 | has it two | 33 |
| | it has two | 38 → 71 |

See the discussion at 30.27 above.

| 174.34 | loom-treaddles? | 33 |
| | loom-treadles? | 38 → 71 |

The *OED* has several citations of "treddle" from various centuries including the nineteenth, but no example of "treaddle." However, it seems likely that the copy-text accurately represents Carlyle's manuscript spelling, the copy-text spelling is no less comprehensible than the conventional later spelling, and it is far from certain that Carlyle was responsible for such an obvious modernization in 38. Given all this, we have retained the copy-text spelling.

177.30	Balliol, reign	33
	Baliol, reign	49 → 71
177.31	Balliol being	33
	Baliol being	49 → 71

Webster's *New Biographical Dictionary* prefers one *l* for the name of the family, though it accepts two *l*'s as an alternative spelling. The name of the Oxford college that this John's father founded has two *l*'s. Since this change was not paralleled in the 46 American, it has no special authority. We therefore follow the copy-text spelling.

| 181.8 | with even | 33 |
| | within | 38 → 71 |

Although the change from "with even" to "within" was plausible enough in this context to survive through all lifetime editions, one has only to consider the alternatives to see that the copy-text reading makes sense, while the reading in 38 and later editions does not.

| 181.27 | centre of gravity | 33 |
| | **centre-of-gravity** | 46 → 58 |

The coincidence of the addition of this pair of hyphens in both 46 and 49 can best be explained on the assumption that Carlyle ordered them on the two printer's copies. Certainly the coincidence cannot be explained as independent regularization. The phrase "centre of gravity" does not occur elsewhere in *Sartor*, and the phrase "Centre of Indifference," with which both the 46 and 49 typesetters might conceivably have analogized it, was never hyphenated. On the other hand, the deletion of the hyphens in 69 has much less authority than their parallel appearance in 46 and 49.

| 185.27 | what is it to be | 33 |
| | **what is to be** | 41U → 71 |

This is obviously a correction of a mistake in the manuscript or in 33. Since it is a necessary correction, we adopt it, although it must be credited to the 41U typesetter rather than to Carlyle.

192.29	imagings (not imaginings),—seems	33
	imagings or imaginings,—seems	38 → 58
	imagings or imaginings, seems	69 71

The 33 reading must be a mistake, though it is hard to see how it could have happened. The passage is distinctly Kantian, and Kant certainly included "imaginings" among the forms of thought conditioned and determined by Space and Time. And however that may be, we cannot imagine typesetters undertaking both to delete the parentheses and to reverse the negation, either on their own authority or by accident.

| 193.30 | by the Music | 33 |
| | by the music | 46 → 71 |

See discussion at 50.36 above.

196.12	*Faust:*	33
	Faust:	38
	Faust,—	58 → 71

There seems no explanation for this change and the corresponding one at 196.16 except a change of authorial preference.

| 196.15 | thousand-times-repeated | 33 |
| | thousand-times repeated | 46 → 71 |

The loss of this hyphen in both 46 and 49 does not seem to us a coincidence that requires the hypothesis of identical printer's copies to explain it.

196.16	Shakespeare:	33
	Shakspeare:	46
	Shakspeare,—	58 → 71

As we explained in the Note on the Text (p. cxviii, note 48), either the 46 typesetters alertly corrected this on their own initiative, or it was marked in the two printer's copies but missed by the 49 typesetter, or it was marked in the American printer's copy but Carlyle failed to transcribe the change into the British printer's copy. Based on the uniform spelling in all editions of *On Heroes*, as well as the two other occurrences in *Sartor* (at 182.1 and 212.4) that Carlyle corrected in 41R, there can be no question about Carlyle's preferred spelling of "Shakspeare" after 1841. For the comma-dash substitution in 58, see the discussion at 196.12 above.

| 197.6 | conclude, | 33 |
| | **conclude** | 46 → 71 |

The deletion of the comma in both 46 and 49 we take to be evidence of a revision marked in both printer's copies.

197.16–17	Happy few, little band of Friends,	
	be welcome, be of courage!	33
	Happy few! little band of Friends!	
	be welcome, be of courage.	38 → 71

These three variants in punctuation in two lines, all involving changes in exclamation marks, are hard to explain as either errors or typographer's emendations. The most reasonable explanation is authorial revision.

| 198.10 | worth, | 33 |
| | worth; | 46 → 71 |

As we did not accept the change in the other direction, from semi-colon to comma, at 17.6 (see discussion above), so we are not convinced that this change from comma to semi-colon must be authorial, in spite of its parallel appearance in both 46 and 49.

199.6   whereso much   33
          where so much   38 → 71
We take this to have been a mistake in 33.

201.20   undecerning   33
          undiscerning   41u → 71

This, we learn from the *OED*, could actually be seen as a change of wording, since there is a verb "decern" that was used in "Scottish judicature" to mean "decide, decree." As between these two different words, "undiscerning" is clearly what was always meant here. However, given the possible Scottish connection, and since the *OED* recognizes this variation as a common confusion "in earlier times," we prefer to call it a modernization of spelling and to retain the copy-text form.

203.9   *Almacks,*   33
          Almack's,   41u → 71

Since the reference is to a ballroom built by one William Almack, we have accepted the emendation of the 41u typesetter, which was perhaps based on local knowledge.

203.26   frightfullest   33
          frightfulest   41R → 49

See discussion at 146.13 above.

204.14   from the Secular   33
          from a Secular   69 71

Surely the Secular Sect can have only a single point of view, so the definite article makes better sense. Also, the familiarity of the formula "from a . . . point of view" might have tempted the 69 typesetter into error. We are not convinced that this is necessarily an example of Carlyle's minor revisions throughout the Library Edition.

204.31   "'ARTICLES   33
          'ARTICLES   38 → 71

This title is evidently Teufelsdröckh's, not part of the quotation from the "Original" printed sheets. Therefore it is not an internal quote, and the 38 punctuation is correct. The use of quotations and quotation marks in this chapter is so complicated that we feel obliged, for the sake of the reader, to adopt whatever variant readings of them seem most correct.

205.7   All   33
          'All   38 → 71

Each new paragraph within the "long Extract from Professor Teufelsdröckh" (201.28) that began at 201.35 ought to begin with a left single quotation mark. Most are thus marked in all editions, but the 33 text failed to mark four such new paragraphs within the quotation (here and at 207.20, 207.30, and 208.10). We have accepted the emendations of these quotation marks from 38.

206.25	name, Poor-Slaves,	33
	name- Poor-Slaves,	46
	name Poor-Slaves	49 → 71

The hyphen after "name" in 46 is obviously a typographical error, but it was more likely intended to be a comma than intended to be nothing. So probably the loss of the comma after "name" in 49 should not be considered a parallel 46 and 49 variant.

| 207.17 | me—indeed, | 33 |
| | **me,—indeed,** | 38 → 71 |

We are generally accepting these comma-dash combinations, as characteristically Carlylean.

| 207.20 | An Irish | 33 |
| | **'An Irish** | 38 → 71 |

See discussion at 205.7 above.

| 207.30 | First, | 33 |
| | **'First,** | 38 → 71 |

See discussion at 205.7 above.

207.31	original: [italics to line 58] *'The*	33
	original: [no italics] "The	38 → 49
	original: [centered title] *Poor-Slave*	
	Household. **[no italics] ¶'"The**	58 → 71

We have accepted the added title. The loss of the italics through 208.6 in 38 and thereafter also seems most likely authorial; certainly it is a gain in legibility. Deciding on the correct quotation-mark usage here is fairly complicated. If one tries to make an analogy with the treatment of "ARTICLES OF FAITH" at 204.31, which was punctuated, in 38 and after, as a new paragraph within the "long Extract," there ought to be a left single quote before "*Poor-Slave Household*" here and also before "*Dandiacal Household*" at 208.12, but no edition used that punctuation. On the other hand, the analogy with "ARTICLES OF FAITH" is not very strong, and is further weakened by the different typographical treatment of the titles (small caps versus italics). We think that the 58 edition was the first to arrive at an acceptable arrangement. The internal double quotes before "The furniture," first supplied in 58, are certainly necessary, especially if the italics are lost. The external (originally double) quotes in 33 at this point were clearly a mistake, following from the failure to mark the paragraphs at 207.20 and 207.30 as continuations of the "long Extract."

208.1   *mother at bottom,*   33
          mother at the bottom,   58 → 71

The somewhat redundant but certainly predictable article could have been added by the 58 typesetter, deliberately or perhaps even accidentally.

208.2   *each side of a large oaken Board*   33
          each side, of a large oaken Board,   58 → 71

These commas may seem to be linked to the addition of the definite article in the previous variant; they are similarly somewhat redundant, certainly predictable, and not necessarily authorial.

208.6   *with.'* [end of italics]   33
          with." [no italics]   38 → 71

Here again, as at 207.31, the external (originally double) quotes in 33 were a mistake. This is the end of an internal quotation (calling for double quotes in the 38 system), not of an external one.

208.12   But now,   33
          'But now,   38 → 71

See discussion at 205.7 above.

208.15   his abode: [italics to line 31] "*A Dressing-room*   33
          his abode: [no italics] "A Dressing-room   38 → 49
          his abode: [centered title] *Dandiacal*
          Household. [no italics] ¶"A Dressing-room   58 → 71

This is obviously parallel with the situation at 207.31 above, and here again we have adopted the solution first offered in 58.

208.26   *Author* (our Theogonist in person), *obsequiously* 33
          Author," our Theogonist in person,
          "obsequiously   38 → 71

The added quotation marks here in 38 and thereafter were made necessary by the decision in that edition not to use italics in this passage.

209.34   "Machinery of Society"),   33
          "Machinery of Society"),   38 → 41 49 → 71
          "Machinery of Society,"),   46

Note that according to *Fraser's Magazine* house style, 33 should have had internal (single) quotes here, but had external (double) quotes instead. The internal (double) quotes in 38 and thereafter are correct.

211.22   *Schneidermässig* (Tailorlike)   33
           Schneidermässig (Tailor-/like)   41u → 41 49
           Schneidermässig (Tailor-like)   46
           schneidermässig (tailor-like)   58 → 71

These two lower-casings in 58 were clearly not accidental, proven by the fact that both the German and its translation were lowered. On a strict application of the rules of German style (and what other kind of application would be appropriate?), this could be considered a necessary correction, since in German all nouns and no adjectives must be capitalized, and "*schneidermässig,*" like its translation "tailorlike," is an adjectival form. On the other hand, the same rule of style (i.e., to capitalize all nouns and only nouns) was observed in some eighteenth-century English prose, but Carlyle in *Sartor* capitalized all parts of speech when he was moved to do so. If we do not hold him to the rule in English, it seems overly pedantic to enforce it on his German.

212.16   Debt? is   33
           Debt? Is   38 → 41
           debt? Is   46 → 71

The lower-case "is" in 33 looks like a typographical error, so we have accepted the 38 emendation of it. On the other hand, the lower-casing of "Debt," although paralleled in both 46 and 49, might be a coincidental regularization of an irregular capital.

215.3   men! as it might   33
           men! As it might   38 → 71

In contrast to the previous item, here the capitalization of "as," though apparently required if the exclamation mark is read as a full stop, would result in a sentence fragment much shorter than usual for Carlyle.

215.26   been   33
           been,   46 → 71

We have generally found that the parallel introduction or deletion of commas in both 46 and 49 seem too coincidental not to have been ordered on the two printer's copies, and this instance is not an exception to that pattern.

217.19   pacificated.—To   33
           pacificated.— ¶'To   58 → 71

We found new paragraph breaks in *On Heroes* in the Library Edition that we decided were not authorial, but rather introduced by the typesetter to solve problems with page layout. This new paragraph in the Uniform Edition might have been created for the same reason, or an editorial assistant might have felt that it was needed.

218.1   must his archives,   33
           his archives must,   58 → 71
See discussion at 30.27 above.

218.5   darker.—So   33
           darker. ¶So   38 → 71

We distinguish this case from that discussed at 217.19 above because it occurred in 38, when Carlyle was more personally involved in the editing of the text, rather than in 58, and because, unlike 217.19 where the dash was left intact, this new paragraph break involves a simultaneous change of punctuation.

218.22   ought he not   33
           ought not he   58 → 71

Unlike the pattern of ten similar inversions of the "not" and the subject pronoun in negative questions discussed and listed at 56.12 above, this one occurred in 58 rather than 69. Like those, on the other hand, this also represents a change from a more normal to a more idiomatic word order (unlike those discussed and listed at 30.27 above), increasing the likelihood that it was an authorial, rather than an editorial or typographical, emendation.

218.30   quarrel?   33
           quarrel? [centered paragraph] ¶THE END.   38 → 41 49

All editions of *On Heroes* had "THE END" at the end. We assume that its absence from the 33 *Sartor* text was due to *Fraser's Magazine* house style. Similarly, it was probably absent from 58 because in 58 *On Heroes* followed *Sartor* in the same volume, and it was absent from later editions because no one restored it after 58.

LINE-END HYPHENS IN THE COPY-TEXT

The following are the editorially established forms of possible compounds that were hyphenated at the ends of lines in the *Fraser's Magazine* copy-text. A slash (/) indicates the position of the line-break in the copy-text where this is not obvious.

4.27	deep-thinking	34.28	Fountain-/of-Motion
4.32	watch-tower	34.36	Broad-sheet
5.4	goose-hunting	38.3	well-starched
8.8	sea-wreck	38.7	*zusammen/gekleistert*
9.13	Waterloo-Crackers	38.13	bushel-breeches
14.8	birth-place	38.37	bed-tester
16.26	wasp-nest	42.1	thousand-figured
17.34	*Rouge-et-/Noir*	42.34	master-colours
18.3	supper-rooms	43.4	ever-lasting
18.9	two-legged	43.7	light-sparkles
18.18	smoke-counterpane	43.32	man-milliner
18.36	bed-maker	43.33	court-suit
19.29	little-wisdom	44.21	lifetime
19.32	stalking-horses	44.23	russet-jerkined
20.31	Dalai-Lama	45.4	Sansculottist
22.9	self-activity	45.9	new-comer
22.17	mine-shafts	45.13	man-kind
23.8	God-created	47.19	Drawing-rooms
24.20	full-formed	49.4	Cloth-rags
24.28	nine-tenths	49.14	draught-cattle
25.27	self-secluded	50.19	Sansculottists
25.32	world-Mahlstrom	50.32	Deep-hidden
26.2	ever-young	50.34	sky-woven
26.15	everlasting	51.30	cloth-webs
26.27	subdivisions	51.37	Digestive-apparatus
26.32	nondescript	52.12	workshop
27.11	bell-girdles	52.23	wider-spreading
27.14	Later-Gothic	52.27	Logic-choppers
28.29	cabalistico-sartorial	53.8	Handlamp
29.9	mankind	54.9	Hell-on-/Earth
30.8	snow-/and-rosebloom	54.12	all-confounding
30.15	self-perfecting	55.2	dark-growing
30.17	ever-working	55.4	horse-shoe
30.32	out-miracled	55.34	King's-mantle
30.36	sixpence	56.1	all-powerful
31.8	Tool-using	56.27	show-cloaks
31.19	Tool-using	57.22	long-winded
31.34	Flint-ball	58.22	burial-aisle
32.5	five-/and-thirty	58.25	stair-steps
33.9	wire-drawing	58.27	Old-Clothes
33.15	housewife	58.32	road-companions
33.19	Smelt-furnace	59.24	Steam-engine

60.12	gaseous-chaotic	93.9	thenceforth
60.13	aqueous-chaotic	93.26	foreshadowed
60.23	Hell-gate	93.36	stone-walls
60.38	nervous-system	95.1	deeper-seated
63.19	pruning-hook	97.24	mankind
63.20	Cincinnatus-like	97.27	self-indulgence
64.1	Schoolmaster	98.12	Time-impulse
64.14	Regiment's-School/master	98.19	Time-Spirit
64.22	grenadier-cap	99.9	so-called
64.25	evergreens	101.20	Calypso-Island
64.25	many-coloured	102.34	many-coloured
65.17	green-silk	103.9	Air-maiden
65.31	coach-/and-four	103.21	Gunpowder
67.7	Name-catalogues	105.32	wide-opened
67.13	offspring	106.15	Heaven-angels
67.33	over-shadowing	107.14	self-secluded
69.9	Basket-bearing	108.28	Archimedes'-lever
70.13	day-moth	109.24	Morning-Star
70.21	eyelids	110.25	sand-bags
71.2	frostnipt	111.1	Air-sailor
71.3	bitter-rinded	113.17	Ocean-waters
71.25	Harvest-Home	114.34	tree-shaded
72.34	Swineherd	115.26	sunwards
72.35	discoloured	116.7	wedding-favours
73.4	double-barrelled	116.8	marriage-evening
73.20	short-clothes	116.29	basilisk-glance
73.25	ever-streaming	117.19	mad-foaming
74.7	slow-rolling	118.32	horse-tail
74.35	Nutbrown	119.31	Clothes-Philosopher
78.19	every-way-/excellent	121.8	earthquake
79.10	Class-books	121.20	well-being
82.2	Gerund-grinder	121.38	Motive-grinder
82.38	sunshine	122.17	Sibyl-cave
83.7	wide-scattered	123.2	Handwriting
83.8	monster-bearing	123.5	Motive-grinders
85.30	all-over/topping	123.6	Profit-and-/Loss
85.35	Shoeblacking	125.11	unvisited
86.11	Game-Preserver	125.19	Arch-Devil
87.19	ever-motionless	126.9	God-created
87.20	winter-seasons	127.1	Fire-baptism
87.21	nobler-minded	127.6	fire-baptised
87.23	safe-lodged	130.4	Egg-shells
88.16	Self-help	130.5	mould-cargos
88.30	charnel-house	130.7	corn-bearing
89.16	likewise	130.15	a-swoon
90.21	Dinner-guests	130.18	hedgerows
91.2	Somewhat	130.21	Powder-Devilkins
91.18	henceforth	130.28	upshot
92.28	*fac-simile*	133.6	Tara/kwang

133.23	unpenetrated		173.19	World-kennel
135.25	Shadow-hunter		174.4	diabolico-angelical
137.10	clay-given		174.17	foot-shackles
137.23	handwriting		175.3	high-eddying
138.1	all-subduing		176.4	sunlight
138.15	fallow-crop		176.5	rainbow-dyed
138.32	Paperbags		176.10	Good-breeding
139.27	guitar-music		177.38	Coat-arm
139.28	fore-court		178.37	farce-tragedy
139.37	straw-roofed		179.4	money-changers
140.12	love-makings		180.14	Whirl/wind-Element
140.22	grim-white		181.9	Glass-bell
140.35	godlike		181.15	venous-arterial
143.17	deep-seated		181.17	World-tissue
146.4	wild-weltering		182.8	main-currents
147.9	new-attained		183.14	*Könning*
147.22	Papin's-Digester		184.28	Hero-worship
149.12	mankind		185.7	Godlike
149.18	Catchpoles		185.7	fellow-man
149.28	Property-conserving		185.21	Hero-Worship
150.8	so-called		186.10	God-ordained
151.7	Paperbags		186.24	rag-burning
151.19	spray-vapour		186.30	brother-like
154.11	light-spots		187.5	Cobwebs
154.25	paste-horns		187.6	Superannuated
155.11	Leather-parings		187.20	all-illuminating
156.4	World-worship		189.19	square-miles
156.5	swimmer-strokes		190.1	thick-crowded
156.17	Heavenward		190.6	well-nigh
156.33	underhand		190.17	Free-thinking
157.4	close-fitting		191.9	Demon-Empire
159.29	Craft-Guilds		191.19	all-embracing
161.21	unstrategic		192.6	Earth-blinded
162.3	Frenchman		192.10	Time-Element
163.13	Motive-Mill/wrights		192.18	Milestone
163.39	heavenward		193.10	Time-annihilating
166.16	Prometheus-like		193.17	sandstone
166.27	superannuated		194.28	morning-air
167.14	fixed-idea		195.24	long-drawn
168.11	besoiled		196.8	Mankind
168.13	Hardly-entreated		196.12	Earth-Spirit's
168.17	god-created		197.3	Death-Birth
169.19	mankind		198.35	Clothes-Philosophy
169.27	thickly-peopled		202.31	Quang/foutchee
170.19	war-chariot		204.6	printed-sheets
171.9	Pericardial		204.8	Clothes-Philosopher
171.10	Life-essence		205.1	swallow-tail
171.18	Lodging-house		206.37	outbreakings
172.8	Overwork		207.10	Cookery-Book

208.9	sun-browned	212.32	co-operating
208.13	often-mentioned	213.16	Four-/and-Twenty
208.17	full-length	215.12	much-inflicting
208.20	mother-/of-pearl	215.16	Time-Prince
208.34	Demon-worship	216.17	Clothes-Volume
209.8	rallying-point	216.18	Pitchpan
209.21	Pot/walloppers	218.26	all-too
209.29	Buchan-Bullers		
211.23	*Tailor's-Melancholy*		

LINE-END HYPHENS IN THE PRESENT TEXT

In quotations from the present edition, no line-end hyphens are to be retained except the following:

11.27	door-lintels	79.21	pocket-money
12.13	Didactico-Religious	80.10	well-nigh
14.4	best-informed	82.22	instructing-tool
16.27	poison-brewing	83.7	wide-scattered
17.21	chariot-wheels	86.25	fairy-money
17.34	voice-of-destiny	86.35	undershot-wheel
18.18	smoke-counterpane	97.11	too-unfurnished
20.7	*halb-zerrüttet*	99.9	so-called
22.5	double-vision	103.9	Air-maiden
25.32	heaven-kissing	108.29	Heaven-gate
26.4	long-continuing	110.24	air-navigator
27.14	Later-Gothic	110.32	fire-heart
27.16	high-flaming	110.35	dusky-red
30.15	self-perfecting	111.1	Air-sailor
31.31	pipe-clay	113.25	tear-dew
32.6	fifty-eight	116.14	*Clothes-Volume*
37.18	Gothic-arch	118.1	world-pilgrimage
37.29	silk-cloth	123.5	Motive-grinders
38.3	Ruff-mantles	124.31	broken-heart
41.28	paper-hangings	124.33	mud-bespattered
42.2	God-written	127.12	*Saint-Thomas*
42.25	Air-castles	129.4	Cloud-image
43.8	air-image	130.31	able-bodied
44.11	tightly-articulated	132.29	too-stupid
48.4	*Staats-Action*	133.6	Water-roses
49.4	turkey-poles	133.31	World-promontory
50.9	soul's-seat	135.2	Non-extant
51.14	Charlemagne-Mantle	138.15	fallow-crop
52.11	chink-lighted	139.12	life-weary
52.27	treble-pipe	140.12	scandal-mongeries
54.8	yellow-burning	143.11	God-inspired
56.8	light-particle	148.5	solid-seeming
56.34	Time-vesture	149.1	Owndom-conserving
58.20	spoon-meat	149.18	fall-traps
59.23	Metaphysico-theological	149.20	meat-devouring
60.17	*cursiv-schrift*	152.13	rock-strata
61.5	new-coming	157.5	train-gowns
63.20	Cincinnatus-like	159.8	thick-plied
68.28	spoon-meat	160.3	all-important
71.25	Harvest-Home	164.7	colour-giving
72.29	Village-head	164.10	market-cross
74.7	slow-rolling	165.12	god-inspired
75.15	skating-matches	168.13	Hardly-entreated

HISTORICAL COLLATION

EACH item is keyed to the present edition by the number of the page and line on which the variant begins. For each item, the top line gives the copy-text reading followed by "33," the symbol of the copy-text. The other lines of each item report all variant readings in chronological order. The present edition follows the 33 copy-text reading at each crux, unless another reading is given in **bold face**, signalling an emendation. A separate list of emendations is given on pp. 489–501 above.

Each variant reading is followed by the symbols of all versions in which that reading occurred, as given in the table below. An arrow between two such symbols (e.g., 46 → 71) signifies that the reading in question is found in all intervening versions. Any version not accounted for in this way agrees with the copy-text reading.

With a few exceptions, all double quotation marks in 33 became single quotation marks and vice versa in 38 and thereafter. Changes according to this rule are not reported, though the exceptions are. To avoid confusion, all quotation marks are given in the system adopted in 1838 and after, unless it is a variant in quotation mark usage that is being reported. In other words, all 33 and 34 quotation marks are represented as their opposite (doubles for singles, and vice versa) where the variant does not involve the quotation mark. Where it does, all quotation marks are of course reported as they were.

Double brackets ([ ]) signify that one character or punctuation mark is absent at that point in the indicated version, but that extra blank space is found at that point, suggesting broken type. When relevant, the symbol "¶" indicates a new paragraph and the symbol "/" indicates the end of a line.

Variants marked with an asterisk are explicated in the Discussion of Editorial Decisions, pp. 503–534 above.

Symbol	Version
33	The serialization in *Fraser's Magazine* between November 1833 and August 1834.
34	The bound reprint from the *Fraser's Magazine* typesetting. London: James Fraser, 1834.
38	The first British trade edition. London: Saunders and Otley, 1838.
41U	The initial typesetting of the 1841 Second Edition in uncorrected proofsheets.
41R	Carlyle's autograph corrections and revisions marked on the 1841 proofs.
41	The "Second Edition" as published. London: James Fraser, 1841.
46	The authorized American edition. New York: Wiley and Putnam, 1846.
49	The "Third Edition." London: Chapman and Hall, 1849.
58	Volume 6 (1858) of the Uniform Edition. 16 vols. London: Chapman and Hall, 1857–58.
69	Volume 1 (1869) of the Library Edition. 30 vols. London: Chapman and Hall, 1869–71.
71	Volume 1 (1871) of the People's Edition. 37 vols. London: Chapman and Hall, 1871–74.

3.3	five thousand	33
	five-thousand	58 → 71
3.5	Rush-lights	33
	Rush-lights,	38 → 41
	Rust-lights	46
	Rush-/lights,	49 71
	Rushlights,	58 69
3.13*	for ever;	33
	forever;	58 → 71
3.15	water-transport	33
	water transport	38
3.20	Dumpling;	33
	dumpling;	69 71
3.21*	*apples*	33
	Apples	38 → 58
4.11*	real *Tissue,*	33
	real Tissue,	38 → 71
4.12*	Science—the	33
	Science,—the	38 → 71
4.13	Cloth;	33
	cloth;	38 → 71
4.17	owl's-glance	33
	owl's glance	38 → 49
5.2	Finance,	33
	Finance	58
	finance	69 71
5.7*	"By geometric scale	33
	'By geometric scale	
		38 → 71
5.8	ale,'	33
	ale.'	38
	ale;'	41u → 71
5.9	vigorously enough	
	thrashing	33
	vigorously thrashing	
		69 71
5.12	Steppe has Tumuli	33
	steppe has tumuli	38 → 71
5.16	fingerpostsx	33
	finger-/posts	38
	finger-posts	41u → 71
5.16	impassable	33
	impassible	46

5.22	outlying,	33
	out-/lying,	
		41u → 41 49 58
	out-lying,	69 71
5.28	Night!	33
	Night?	38 → 58
5.31	listed. [extra leading	
	between paragraphs]	
	¶Perhaps	33
	listed. ¶Perhaps	46
5.33*	stinted	33
	stunted	69 71
6.16	subject;	33
	subject,	58 → 71
6.21	*Kleider*	33
	Kleider,	41u → 71
6.23	1833:	33
	1831.	38 → 71
6.25	which,	33
	which	46
6.26	Weissnichtwo: issuing	33
	Weissnichtwo. Issuing	
		38 → 71
6.28	with every	33
	every with	41u
6.29	defiance.' * * * 'A	33
	defiance.' * * * * 'A	
		38 → 71
6.29	well nigh	33
	well-nigh	69 71
6.32	Philanthropy	33
	Phi[ ]/lanthropy	46
6.33*	*(derben*	33
	(derben	38 → 71
6.33*	*derben*	33
	derber	58 → 71
6.33*	*Kerndeutscheit*	33
	Kerndeutschheit	38 → 71
6.33*	*Menschenliebe);*	33
	Menschenliebe);	38 → 71
6.35	ranks	33
	rank	46

6.36	Temple-of-Honour.'	33
	Temple of Honour.'	
		38 → 71
7.1	Presentation Copy	33
	Presentation-copy	
		41ᴜ → 71
8.1	If for a	33
	Iꜰ for a	38 → 71
8.2	Ideas,	33
	ideas,	41ᴜ → 71
8.4	Calendar.	33
	calendar.	41ʀ → 71
8.13	Character,	33
	character,	38 → 71
8.16	Proselytising	33
	proselytising	69 71
8.19	Clothes	33
	Clothes,	41ʀ → 71
8.19	such Philosophy	33
	such Philosophy,	
		41ʀ → 71
8.21	nation?	33
	Nation?	58 → 71
8.23	Truth.	33
	truth.	69 71
9.2	volume,	33
	Volume,	38 → 71
9.5	revealed	33
	revealed,	69 71
9.6	treated of	33
	treated of,	69 71
9.6	circulation	33
	Circulation	41ᴜ → 58
9.7	the whole Parties of the	
	State	33
	the whole parties of the	
	State	38 → 58
	all party-divisions in the	
	State	69 71
9.8	the whole Journals	33
	all the Journals	69 71
9.22	shut out	33
	shut-out	58

9.28	more surprising,	33
	mor esurprising,	41ᴜ
10.2	West;'	33
	West:'	34 → 71
10.2	Work	33
	work	69 71
10.14	arrangement;	33
	arrangement:	38 → 71
10.32	acumen,	33
	acumen	49 → 71
10.32	Meditation	33
	meditation	69 71
10.34	Prejudice,	33
	prejudice,	69 71
10.34	Cant;	33
	cant;	69 71
10.36	insignificant:*	33
	insignificant:¹	49 → 71
10.37	* With	33
	¹ With	49 → 71
11.1	Voice	33
	voice	41ᴜ → 71
11.2	ears	33
	ears,	69 71
11.10	Logical	33
	logical	69 71
11.11	nowise	33
	no wise	46
11.11	apprehended	33
	apprehended,	38 → 71
11.17	gods,	33
	Gods,	46
11.17	when	33
	when,	69 71
11.20	measure!	33
	mea-/ure!	46
11.22	we hope,	33
	we hope	41ᴜ → 71
11.23	with whom	33
	with whom,	41ᴜ → 71
11.24	LDarkness	33
	LDarkness,	41ᴜ → 71

11.24*	internecive	33
	internecine	38 → 71
11.25	Puffery	33
	puffery	69 71
11.25	Quackery	33
	quackery	69 71
11.27	door-lintels,	33
	door-lintels	69 71
12.1	To the Author's	33
	To the Author's	38 → 71
12.6	indeed;	33
	indeed:	38
12.7	Refutation	33
	refutation	58 → 71
12.12	high	33
	high,	38 → 71
12.18	any thing	33
	anything	58 → 71
12.21	forever	33
	for ever	38 → 49
12.22	*Gukguk,**	33
	Gukguk,[1]	49 → 71
12.23	* Gukguk	33
	[1] Gukguk	49 → 71
12.23	Beer.	33
	beer.	38 → 71
13.1	stood up	33
	stood-up	58
13.1	coffeehouse	33
	coffee-house 38 → 41 49	
	coffee-/house	46 58
13.1	*Zum Grünen Ganse,*	33
	Zur Grünen Gans,	
		58 → 71
13.3	Intellect,	33
	Intellect	49 → 71
13.7	Poor	33
	Poor,	69 71
13.12	cloudcapt	33
	cloud-capt	69 71
13.12	broke up,	33
	broke-up,	58
13.13	*Spass- und*	33
	Spass-und	38 46
13.15	*steckt der*	33
	steckt doch der	69 71
13.23	eyes,	33
	eyes	41u → 71
13.25	half fancied	33
	half-fancied	58 → 71
13.26	spinning-top?	33
	spinning top?	38 46
13.26	there as	33
	there as,	41u → 71
13.27	in loose, ill-brushed,	33
	in loose ill-brushed	69 71
13.33	deepseated	33
	deep-/seated	69
	deep-seated	71
13.38	putting in	33
	putting-in	58 → 71
13.38*	woof! ¶How	33
	woof! [extra leading	
	between paragraphs] ¶How	
		69 71
14.5	Teufelsdröckh was	33
	Teufelsdröckh waa	41u
14.6	Stranger	33
	stranger	69 71
14.8	birth-place,	33
	birthplace,	49 → 71
14.8	prospects	33
	prospects,	38 → 71
14.8	Curiosity	33
	curiosity	69 71
14.21	which Thing	33
	which thing	38
14.31	ruins: that	33
	ruins: That	38 → 71
15.17	Re-construction;	33
	Re-/construction;	38
	Reconstruction;	
		41u → 71
15.17	were, where	33
	were where	38 → 71

15.24	and, long	33		16.35	timber leg,	33	
	and long	46			timber-leg,	58 → 71	
15.30	*Grünen Ganse,*	33		16.37	tumbling in	33	
	Grüne Gans,	58 → 71			tumbling-in	58 → 71	
15.35	Coffeehouse	33		17.5	visible;	33	
	Coffee-/house	38			visible:	49 → 71	
	Coffee-house	41u → 71		17.6	shape,	33	
16.3	Fountain,	33			shape	38 → 71	
	fountain,	69 71		17.6*	lose it;	33	
16.5	indeed,	33			lose it,	46 → 71	
	indeed	46		17.6	pavement	33	
16.17	windows,	33			Pavement	49 → 71	
	windows	69 71		17.9	heels,	33	
16.18	Sitting-room	33			heels	58 → 71	
	sitting-room	69 71		17.10	To-day,	33	
16.19	(Bed-room)	33			Today,	58 → 71	
	(bed-room)	69 71		17.10	To-morrow;	33	
16.20	Kitchen,	33			Tomorrow;	58 → 71	
	kitchen,	69 71		17.13	will	33	
16.20	as it were,	33			wiil	46	
	as it were	46		17.14*	no more." ¶ "*Ach,*		
16.21*	showing	33				33 → 71	
	shewing	41u → 49			**no more.' ¶ '*Ach,*** Strouse		
16.25	*Treiben)*	33		17.15*	*Leiber!"*	33	
	Treiben),	38 → 71			***Lieber!"***	46 → 71	
16.25*	for most part	33			***Lieber!***	Strouse	
	for the most part			17.15	when we had	33	
		38 → 71			when he had	46	
16.26*	"I look	33 → 71		17.16	Coffeehouse	33	
	'I look	Strouse			Coffee-house	38 → 71	
16.26	bee-hive,"	33 → 71		17.16	talk, "it	33 → 71	
	bee-hive,'	Strouse			**talk, 'it**	Strouse	
16.27	"and witness	33 → 71		17.17	struggling up	33	
	'and witness	Strouse			struggling-up	58	
16.30	down to the low	33		17.19*	Bootes	33	
	down the low	38 → 58			Böotes	38	
16.34	bagged up	33			**Boötes**	41u → 71	
	bagged-up	58 → 71		17.19	Hunting Dogs	33	
16.34	leather:	33			Hunting-Dogs	58 → 71	
	leather;	46		17.20	Zenith	33	
16.35	rolls in	33			Zenith,	46	
	rolls-in	58 → 71		17.23	roofed in,	33	
					roofed-in,	58 → 71	

17.26*	coverlid	33
	coverlet	38 → 71
17.29	born;	33
	born:	46
17.29*	praying—on	33
	praying,—on	38 → 71
17.33*	its lair	33
	his lair	38 41u
17.35	Villains;	33
	Villians;	46
17.38	fear,	33
	fear	46
18.2	crowbars,	33
	crow-bars,	49 58
18.3	supper-rooms	33
	supper-rooms,	46
18.4	high-swelling	33
	high swelling	38
18.5	look out	33
	look-out	58 → 71
18.9	o' building.	33
	o'building.	46
18.9	five hundred thousand	33
	five-hundred-thousand	
		58 → 71
18.10*	position;	33
	positions;	71
18.16	crammed in,	33
	crammed-in,	58
18.16	fish,	33
	fish	69 71
18.17	Vipers,	33
	vipers,	69 71
18.18	others:	33
	other:	46
18.20	Stars."	33 → 71
	Stars.'	Strouse
18.27	silent,	33
	silent	41u → 71
18.34	aside:	33
	aside;	41u → 71

18.35	bread-crusts,	33
	bread crusts,	38
18.36*	Blücher	33
	Blucher	38 → 41
18.36	Leischen	33
	Lieschen	58 → 71
18.36	(Lisekin, 'Liza),	33
	(Lisekin,' Liza),	69
19.2	month,	33
	month	49 → 71
19.5	*Erdbebungen*	33
	Erdbeben	58 → 71
19.5	(Earthquakes),	33
	(earthquakes),	69 71
19.5	Teufelsdröckh	33
	Teufels-/sdröckh	41u
19.8	for ever,	33
	forever,	49 → 71
19.9	Leischen	33
	Lieschen	58 → 71
19.12	for Teufelsdröckh	33
	for Teufelsdröckh,	
		49 → 71
19.13	only	33
	only,	49 → 71
19.16	swept,	33
	swept	38 41u
19.19	Leischen	33
	Lieschen	58 → 71
19.30	ninety and nine	33
	ninety-and-nine	58 → 71
19.32	stalking-horses	33
	stalking horses	38
20.3	hope	33
	hope,	58 → 71
20.4	Nevertheless,	33
	Nevertheless	41u → 71
20.6*	*Gemuth*	33
	Gemüth	46 → 71
20.7	*Schicksals-gunst;*	33
	Schicksals-Gunst;	
		58 → 71

20.8	"He	33 → 71
	'He	Strouse
20.10	half-congealed."	33 → 71
	half-congealed.'	Strouse
20.11	this,	33
	this	38 41ʀ → 71
	tihs	41ᴜ
20.27	harangue	33
	harangue,	38 → 71
20.27	gurgled out	33
	gurgled-out	58 → 71
20.29	twanging, nasal	33
	twanging nasal,	69 71
20.31	of which	33
	of which,	38 → 71
20.32	Indifference,	33
	indifference,	49 → 71
20.35	domestic, physical,	33
	domestic, and physical,	
		46
20.37	perched up	33
	perched-up	58 → 71
20.37	watchtower,	33
	watch-tower,	41ᴜ → 71
21.7	curiosity	33
	curiosity,	41ᴜ → 71
21.7	such like	33
	suchlike	69 71
21.10	reporting,	33
	reporting	46
21.12	But on	33
	But, on	41ᴜ → 71
21.15	opinions namely	33
	opinions, namely,	
		41ᴜ → 71
22.1	It were a	33
	Iᴛ were a	38 → 71
22.2	Genius, like	33
	genius, like	69 71
22.3	Creation,	33
	creation,	69 71
22.4	Genius, has	33
	genius, has	69 71

22.13	specially	33
	especially	71
22.17*	inaptitude;	33
	ineptitude;	38 → 71
23.2	speaks out	33
	speaks-out	58 → 71
23.3	dictionary names.	33
	dictionary-names.	
		41ᴜ → 58
23.6	or-molu,'	33
	or-moulu,'	38 → 58
23.7	such Drawing-room	33
	such Drawing room	46
23.10	pearl-bracelets,	33
	pearl bracelets,	41ᴜ → 58
	pearl bracelets	69 71
23.14*	smiths'	33
	smith's	38 → 71
23.28	wesand,	33
	weasand,	41ʀ → 71
23.31	through.	33
	through?	49 → 71
23.32	silent	33
	silent,	41ᴜ → 71
23.33	unconscious	33
	unconscious,	41ᴜ → 71
23.37	sheers	33
	shears	71
24.8	*Sanconiathon*	33
	Sanchoniathon	41ʀ → 71
24.9	*Korans,*	33
	Korans	38
24.10	*Céleste,*	33
	Céleste	46
24.14	indeed,	33
	indeed	49 58
24.19	vigour,	33
	vigor,	46
24.19	inspiration:	33
	inspiration;	41ᴜ → 71
24.19	Thoughts	33
	thoughts	69 71

24.20	Words,	33
	words,	69 71
24.21	splendour	33
	splendor	46
24.21	idiomatic	33
	idiamotic	41U
24.29	buttressed up	33
	buttressed-up	58 → 71
24.30	ever, with	33
	ever with	41R → 71
24.31	sprawl out	33
	sprawl-out	58 → 71
24.31	sides	33
	sides,	38 → 71
24.34	its keynote	33
	his keynote	46
25.4	some remote echo	33
	some echo	38 → 71
25.8	ethereal Love burst forth from him, soft wailings of infinite Pity; he could clasp the whole Universe into his bosom,	33
	ethereal / Pity; he could clasp the whole Universe into his / Love burst forth from him, soft wailings of infinite / bosom,	41U
25.8	Love	33
	love	69 71
25.8	Pity;	33
	pity;	69 71
25.11	shews	33
	shows	38 58 → 71
25.16*	terrestial	33
	terrestrial	38 → 71
25.18	street-sweepings,	33
	street sweepings,	46
25.18	whirled;	33
	whirled,	38 → 71
25.22	mountain-pool,	33
	mountain pool,	46

25.32	world-Mahlstrom	33
	World-Mahlstrom	
		38 → 71
25.32	Heaven-kissing	33
	heaven-kissing	41R → 71
25.34	Death!	33
	death!	69 71
26.2	radiant	33
	radiant,	71
26.3	Tattersall's,—tears	33
	Tattersall's—tears	49
26.9	any thing,	33
	anything,	38 → 71
26.26	shew	33
	show	58 → 71
27.2*	*Loix,*	33
	Lois,	69 71
27.3*	*Coutumes* we	33
	***Coutumes,* we**	38 → 71
27.6*	Modes	33
	Modes,	46 → 71
27.6*	endeavours	33
	endeavours,	46 → 71
27.9	flow	33
	flows	46
27.10	tower up	33
	tower-up	58 → 71
27.11	swell out	33
	swell-out	58 → 71
27.11	starched	33
	starch	46
27.11	stuffings	33
	stuffings,	49 → 71
27.15	Anglo-Dandiacal.	33
	Anglo-Dandical.	46
28.1	Cause-and-effect	33
	Cause-and-Effect	
		38 → 71
28.9	any thing!	33
	anything!	58 → 71
28.15	take in	33
	take-in	58 → 71

28.15*	well nigh	33	30.18	(says one)	33	
	well-nigh	41R → 71		(says one),	41U → 71	
28.17	glance over	33	30.24	pestle	33	
	glance-over	58 → 71		pestel	46	
28.25	Literature?'	33	30.26	Courage	33	
	Literature'?	69 71		courage	41U → 71	
28.37	say	33	30.27*	was it in	33	
	say,	58 → 71		it was in	38 → 71	
29.1	has filled	33	30.33	Sovereign	33	
	have filled	41R → 71		sovereign	69 71	
29.3	But quitting	33	30.34	Cooks	33	
	But, quitting	69 71		cooks	69 71	
29.11	Learning:	33	30.35	Philosophers	33	
	learning:	49 → 71		philosophers	69 71	
29.12*	waggons	33	30.35	Kings	33	
	wagons	41U → 71		kings	69 71	
29.15*	chlamides,	33	30.37	Security,	33	
	chlamydes,	49 → 71		Security	49 → 71	
29.15	trunk hose,	33	31.7	of us. (¶'But) on the	33	
	trunk-hose,	41U → 71		of us. (¶'But,) on the		
29.19	part too	33			69 71	
	part, too,	69 71	31.8	(*Hanthierendes*	33	
29.20	tumbled down	33		(*Handthierendes*		
	tumbled-down	58 → 71			49 → 71	
29.25	Clothes,	33	31.10	half square-foot,	33	
	clothes,	46		half-square foot,	69 71	
29.31	wild fruits;	33	31.12	Steer	33	
	wild-fruits;	58 → 71		steer	69 71	
30.1	leaves,	33	31.19	remark	33	
	leaves	46		remark,	58 → 71	
30.5	is Decoration;	33	31.19	Tool-using Animal,)		
	is Decoration,	38 → 71		appears to	33	
30.6	civilised	33		Tool-using Animal)		
	civilized	41U → 46		appears to	58 → 71	
30.8	Highness;	33	31.21	but do not	33	
	Highness:	46		but not	41U	
30.10	which indeed,	33	31.26	to Cook,	33	
	which, indeed,	41U → 71		to cook,	38 → 71	
30.10	she is,—has	33	31.28	stowing up	33	
	she is—has	46		stowing-up	58 → 71	
30.18	to-day	33	31.28	marmot,	33	
	today	58 → 71		marmot	46	

31.32	But on	33
	But, on	69 71
31.33	show	33
	shew	41u → 49
31.36	Tool-using animal,'	33
	Tool-using Animal,'	
		58 → 71
32.3	digs up	33
	digs-up	58
32.4	Earth,	33
	earth,	49 → 71
32.5	*me,*	33
	me	41u → 71
32.5	*luggage,*	33
	luggage	49 → 71
32.6	six hundred	33
	six-hundred	58 → 71
32.8	*hunger, and sorrow,*	33
	hunger and sorrow,	
		41u → 49
	hunger and sorrow	
		58 → 71
33.1	One of the	33
	ONE of the	38 → 71
33.2	*on Aprons.* What	33
	on *Aprons.* What	41u → 71
33.2	Gao	33
	Gao,	41u → 71
33.6	Husband's	33
	husband's	41u → 71
33.7	Bishop;'	33
	bishop;'	38 → 71
33.14	Emblem	33
	emblem	69 71
33.14	beatified	33
	beautified	41u
33.14	Ghost	33
	ghost	69 71
33.15	highest-bred	33
	highest bred	41u
33.19	Smelt-furnace,	33
	smelt-furnace,	41u → 71

34.3	(*Teufels-schmeide*)	33
	(*Teufels-schmiede*)	
		38 → 71
34.4	Episcopal,	33
	Episcopal	41u → 71
34.6*	tucked in	33
	tucked-in	46 → 71
34.7	shadow forth	33
	shadow-forth	58
34.18	choke up	33
	choke-up	58 → 71
34.21	Fire	33
	fire	41u → 71
34.23	meanwhile,	33
	mean while,	38 58 → 71
34.23	five million	33
	five-million	58 → 71
34.25	printed on,	33
	printed-on,	58 → 71
34.28	Fountain-of-Motion,	33
	Fountain-of-motion,	
		41u → 71
34.28	Social	33
	Soeial	41u
34.31	us	33
	us,	38 → 71
34.33	meet	33
	met	38
35.8	Witchfinder	33
	Witchfinder,	46
36.1	Happier is our	33
	HAPPIER is our	38 → 71
36.3	Costume.	33
	costume.	46
36.9	every way	33
	everyway	58 → 71
36.10	thrown out	33
	thrown-out	58 → 71
36.14	Paullinus's	33
	Paullinus's	38 → 71
36.14	*Zeitkurzende*	33
	Zeitkürzende	58 → 71

36.14	*Lust* (II. 678)	33
	Lust (ii. 678)	41U → 71
36.17	smile;	33
	smile;:	41U
36.22	under ground.	33
	underground.	58 → 71
37.2	filled up	33
	filled-up	58 → 71
37.7	buff-belts,	33
	buff belts,	46
37.10	signpost	33
	sign-/post	41U → 41
	sign-post	46 → 71
37.15	walks	33
	walks,	49 → 71
37.16*	which especially,	33
	'which especially,	41U
	which, especially	
		49 → 71
37.19	an ell-long,	33
	an ell long,	41R → 71
37.21*	ell (and	33
	ell, and	38 → 71
37.21*	tags);	33
	tags;	38 → 71
37.22	noses:	33
	noses;	46
37.23*	Farther,	33
	Further,	41U → 71
37.24	*Gesäss*	33
	Gesœs [*a*, without umlaut,	
	set upside down]	41U
37.29	Cleopatras	33
	Cleopatra	41U
	Cleopatras,	46 → 71
37.35*	mothers'	33
	mother's	38 → 71
38.2	welts:	33
	welts;	41R → 71
38.4	(*Kragenmäntel*).	33
	(*Kragenmnätel*).	41U
38.10	Humour	33
	humour	49 → 71

38.14	shoes,	33
	shoes	46
38.15	him;	33
	him:	49 → 71
38.24	dyed	33
	died	46
38.26	swollen out	33
	swollen-out	58 → 71
38.31	wheat-dust;	33
	wheat-dust:	38 41R → 71
	wheat dust:	41U
38.34	History!	33
	History?	58 → 71
38.37	Despreaux	33
	Despréaux	69 71
39.9	alluded to	33
	alluded-to	58
39.11	cut off	33
	cut-off	58 → 71
39.12	effected,	33
	effected	38 → 71
40.1	If in the	33
	IF in the	38 → 71
40.1	Portion of	33
	portion of	58 → 71
40.1*	his Volume,	33
	this Volume,	38 → 71
40.4	Speculative-Philosophical	
		33
	Speculative-	
	Philosophical,[?]	41U
40.4	Portion, which	33
	portion, which	58 → 71
40.4	*Wirken,*	33
	Wirken	46
40.7	chaos;	33
	chaos:	38 41U
40.14	interests	33
	interests,	41U
40.20*	limbos,	33
	limboes,	38 → 71
41.5	whereby	33
	whereby,	38 → 71

41.7	yet,	33
	yet	46
41.9	too, must we	33
	also, we have to	
		46 → 71
41.14	wide enough	33
	wide-enough	58 → 71
41.21*	canvass	33
	canvas	58 → 71
41.22*	stands	33
	stand	38 → 71
41.27	*nennt*)?	33
	nennt)?	46
41.28	and, through	33
	and through	46
41.30	Integuments	33
	integuments	41R → 71
41.33	it,	33
	it	46
41.35	*Cogito*	33
	Cogito,	41R → 71
41.36	enough,	33
	enough	46
42.6	flit round	33
	flit around	46
42.30	only	33
	only,	58 → 71
42.33	brother	33
	brother,	41U → 49
42.35	Canvass	33
	Canvas	58 → 71
43.4	Now?	33
	Now?	41U 69 71
43.19*	fire of the Living:	33
	fire of Living:	58 → 71
43.24	thereof?'	33
	thereof?	41R → 71
43.25	thereof? [extra leading	
	between paragraphs] ¶'It	
		33
	thereof? ¶'It	38 → 71
43.26*	foredone	33
	fordone	58 → 71

43.31	spinner:	33
	spinner;	69 71
43.33	court-suit	33
	court suit	46
43.37	Good	33
	good	38 → 71
44.1	beasts;	33
	breasts;	38
44.6	brushed off	33
	brushed-off	58 → 71
44.14	and, by	33
	and by	38 → 71
44.19	nose:	33
	nose;	58 → 71
45.1	Let no courteous	33
	LET no courteous	
		38 → 71
45.12	been,	33
	been	69 71
45.15	apprised	33
	apprized	46
45.16	pudding cheek,	33
	pudding-cheek,	
		41U → 71
45.17	handsel,	33
	hansel,	46
46.1	moveable	33
	movable	38 → 71
46.4	mudboots,	33
	mud-/boots,	69
	mud-boots,	71
46.6	though	33
	thongh	41U
46.11	whirlpool:	33
	whirlpool;	46
46.17	best:	33
	best;	46
46.21	indeed?'	33
	indeed'?	69 71
46.23	fell?'	33
	fell'?	69 71
46.29	Adamite:	33
	Adamite;	49 → 71

46.30	age	33
	age,	46
47.1	noosed up,	33
	noosed-up,	69 71
47.9	so is it done:	33
	so it is done:	46
47.12	Secondly,	33
	secondly,	58 → 71
47.14*	Red, hanging-individual,	
		33
	Red hanging-individual	
		38 → 71
47.14	squirrel skins,	33
	squirrel-skins,	
		46 58 → 71
47.15	plush gown;	33
	plush gown:	38 → 41
	plush-gown;	49 → 71
47.26	fly off	33
	fly-off	58 → 71
48.4	*Haupt- und*	33
	Haupt-und	46
48.5	Pickleherring-Farce	33
	Pickleherring Farce	46
48.7	Civilised	33
	Civilized	41u → 46
48.8	wails	33
	wails,	46
48.14	every body,	33
	everybody,	46
48.15	carved?'	33
	carved?	46
	carved'?	69 71
48.16	Fate	33
	fate	69 71
48.16	St. Stephen's,	33
	St Stephen's,	41u
48.19	Unhappy	33
	Un[ ]/happy	58
48.22	goaded on	33
	goaded-on	58 → 71

48.23	re-impart	33
	re-/impart	58
	reimpart	69 71
48.27	nay, perhaps	33
	nay perhaps,	41R → 71
48.31	him.' * * ¶* * 'O	33
	him.' * * * * * * 'O	41u
48.33	market:"	33
	market;"	46
49.1	It must now	33
	It must now	38 → 71
49.1	be	33
	bə[e set upside down]	
		41u
49.5	'Bladders	33
	'bladders	41R → 71
49.5	Peas.'	33
	peas.'	41R → 71
49.12	Life-tackle	33
	life-tackle,	69 71
49.16	waggon-science,	33
	wagon-science,	41u → 71
49.20	every where	33
	everywhere	49 → 71
49.22	pictured out	33
	pictured-out	69 71
50.1	World	33
	world	41u → 71
50.3*	Serbonian Bogs	33
	Serbonian Bog	69 71
50.6	rivetting	33
	riveting	41R → 71
50.9	soul's-seat,	33
	soul's seat,	58 → 71
50.12	For though	33
	For though,	69 71
50.20	unparalleled	33
	unparaleled	41u
50.21	Transcendentalism	33
	Transcendentalism,	
		41u → 71
50.23	jacketted	33
	jacketed	41R → 71

50.24	gods.	33
	Gods.	49 → 71
50.27	Soul,	33
	soul,	41u → 46
50.28	there lies,	33
	therel ies,	41u
50.33	swathed in,	33
	swathed-in,	58 → 71
50.34	overshrouded:	33
	over-/shrouded:	
		41u → 41
	over-shrouded:	49 → 71
50.34	yet is it	33
	yet it is	38 → 71
50.34	sky-/woven,	33
	skywoven,	38 → 71
50.36*	Know, to Believe;	33
	know, to believe;	
		46 → 71
51.3	fellow man?'	33
	fellow-man?'	69 71
51.6	flood:	33
	flood;	46
51.11	every where	33
	everywhere	41R → 71
51.22	bright?'	33
	bright'?	69 71
51.30	cloth-/webs	33
	clothwebs	38 → 71
51.32	Imagination?	33
	imagination?	71
51.35	Bank-paper	33
	Bank-paper,	46
51.35	Clothes), into	33
	Clothes) into	69 71
52.3	universal Wonder,	33
	universal Wonder;	
		38 → 71
52.5	reign of Wonder	33
	reign of wonder	38 → 71
52.16	Head alone,	33
	head alone,	38 → 71

52.17	basin,	33
	basin	69 71
52.18	prosecute	33
	persecute	46
52.22	Cookery	33
	cookery	46 → 71
53.8	Hand-/lamp	33
	Hand-lamp	38 → 41
	hand-lamp	46 → 71
53.8	Attorney Logic;	33
	Attorney-Logic;	
		41u → 71
53.10	recognises	33
	recognizes	46
53.13	a (delirious) Mystic;	33
	a delirious Mystic;	
		41R → 71
53.14	Handlamp,	33
	hand-lamp,	46
	Hand-/lamp,	49
	Hand-lamp,	58
	hand-lamp,	69 71
53.16	Cow	33
	cow	46 → 71
53.16	Bull	33
	bull	46 → 71
53.17	Born,	33
	born,	46 → 71
53.17	Die?	33
	die?	46 → 71
54.1	The Philosophy of	33
	The Philosophy of	
		38 → 71
54.1	predicted	33
	predicated	46
54.9	Hell-on-Earth?	33
	Hell-on Earth?	58
54.14*	Whole:	33
	whole:	38 → 41
54.17	Thou too,	33
	Thou thyself,	69 71
54.20	to-morrow	33
	tomorrow	58 → 71

54.21	already,	33	56.34	Time-vesture	33	
	already	69 71		Time vesture	41U	
54.23	Force,	33	57.1	done,	33	
	Force	46		done	46	
55.4	cut off	33	57.1*	external	33	
	cut-off	58 → 71		**External**	38 → 71	
55.5	universe;	33	57.9	gray,	33	
	Universe;	38 → 71		gray	38 → 46 58 → 71	
55.8	far stronger Force	33		grey	49	
	far stranger Force		57.9	half-light,	33	
		41R → 71		half light,	58	
55.10	about:	33	57.12*	Hamburgh	33	
	about;	49 → 71		Hamburg	58 → 71	
55.13	Dingy	33	57.26	Life-Philosophy	33	
	dingy	69 71		Life Philosophy	46	
55.20	together with all; is borne 33		57.28	(*Gesnüth*),	33	
	together with all:[?] is borne	41U		(*Gemüth*),	38 → 71	
55.21	shoreless	33	57.31	short,	33	
	shoreless,	38		short	38 → 71	
55.25	Earth	33	57.33	'Nay,' adds	33	
	earth	69 71		'Nay, adds	38	
55.30	Emblems;	33	57.36	shaped out	33	
	emblems;	49 → 71		shaped-out	58 → 71	
55.34	King's-mantle	33	57.36	and, either	33	
	King's mantle	38 → 71		and either	38 → 71	
55.34*	are Emblematic,	33	58.6	Autobiography;	33	
	are emblematic,	69 71		Auto-Biography;		
56.12*	does she not?	33			49 → 71	
	does not she?	69 71	58.7	(*menschlich-anecdotisch*)		
56.15	recognised; still	33			33	
	recognised: still	46		(*menschlich-anekdotisch*)		
56.17	Flesh-garment, Language,	33			69 71	
	Flesh-Garment, Language,		58.10	'By this time, *mein*	33	
		38 → 71		'By this time *mein*	41U	
56.22	hunger-bitten,	33	58.12	well nigh	33	
	hunger-bitten	58 → 71		well-nigh	69 71	
56.28	woollen	33	58.12	'by this time, you	33	
	woolen	46		'by this time you		
56.33	written	33			38 → 71	
	written,	41U → 71	58.13	(*vertieft*)	33	
				(*verteift*)	41U → 49	
			58.29	public	33	
				Public	46	

58.32	road-companions;	33
	road companions;	58
59.2*	and rot,	33
	and to rot,	69 71
59.6	insight;	33
	insight:	41u → 71
59.7*	Clothes stand	33
	Clothes stands	38 41u
	Clothes will stand	
		41r → 71
59.8	England;	33
	England,	34 → 71
59.13	PAPER-BAGS,	33
	PAPER-BAGS,	
		41u → 41 49 → 71
	PAPER BAGS,	46
59.15	sealed Bags,	33
	sealed Bags[ ]	38
	sealed Bags	41u → 71
59.17	scarce-legible	33
	scarce legible	
		41u → 46 69 71
59.17	*cursiv-schrift;*	33
	cursiv-schrift;;	41u
59.20	manner!	33
	manner.	49 → 71
59.21	here	33
	here,	69 71
59.22	person	33
	person,	69 71
59.25	or	33
	or,	38 → 71
59.30	delineations,	33
	delineations;	41r → 71
59.32	'P. P.	33
	'P.P.	41u → 71
59.33	order	33
	order,	58 → 71
59.36	Oration	33
	Oration,	41u → 71
59.37	Doctor's-Hat,'	33
	Doctor's-Hat,	41u
	Doctor's Hat,'	46

59.37*	washbills	33
	wash-/bills	41u → 41
	wash-bills,	46 → 71
60.5	farther	33
	further	46
60.6	Paper Bags	33
	Paper-Bags	38 → 71
60.8	Autobiography	33
	autobiography	46
60.10	shadowy,	33
	shadowy	41u → 71
60.10	unheard-of efforts,	33
	unheard-of-efforts,	46
60.11	intellect	33
	intellect,	38 → 71
60.25	leading	33
	leading,	41u → 71
60.26	fished up	33
	fished-up	58 → 71
60.28	beneath:	33
	beneath;	46
61.1	Health,	33
	health,	41r → 71
61.1	Life,	33
	life,	41r → 71
61.6	already-budding	33
	already budding	46
61.9	sharest with us,	33
	sharest with us;	69 71
63.20	which he,	33
	which, he	46
64.3	him,	33
	him	46
64.4*	*Schweig Du Hund*	33
	"*Schweig Du Hund*	38
	"*Schweig, Du Hund*	41u
	"*Schweig' Du Hund*	
		41r 41
	"*Schweig' Hund*	46 → 58
	"**Schweig Hund**	69 71

64.5	hound!) before	33
	hound!)" before	38
	hound)!" before	
	41R 49 → 71	
	hound)! "before	46
64.6	*nenn 'ich*	33
	nenn' ich	41R → 71
64.6*	there	33
	There	46 → 71
64.7	exclaim: "but	33
	exclaim: but	41U
64.12	at least	33
	at heart	38 → 71
64.14	Regiment's-Schoolmaster	
		33
	Regiment's Schoolmaster	
	41U → 71	
64.17*	Büsching's Geography,	33
	Büsching's *Geography*,	
	69 71	
64.20	round him,	33
	around him,	46
	round him	49 → 71
64.20	housemother	33
	house-mother	46
64.23	environment where,	33
	environment, where	
	38 → 71	
64.23	honour,	33
	honour	38 → 71
64.24	gay:	33
	gay;	46
64.25	forest-trees,	33
	forest-trees.	46
64.26	struggling in	33
	struggling-in	58 → 71
64.28	seats,	33
	seats	41U → 71
64.29	smoke	33
	smoke,	38 → 71
65.4	*schwerem*	33
	schweren	46 → 71

65.4	*zurückgefordert,*	33
	zurückgefordert.	
	41U → 71	
65.8	back."	33
	back"	46
65.8	forever	33
	for ever	38 41U
65.10	wife	33
	wife,	41R → 71
65.17	green-silk	33
	green silk	38 → 58
65.21	there,	33
	there	46
65.22	but	33
	but,	69 71
65.24	Friedrichs,	33
	Friedrichs	46
65.26	document	33
	documents	46
66.2	himself,	33
	himself	41R → 71
66.4	faculty,	33
	faculty	69 71
66.7	General.'	33
	General.	46
66.16	(*sehnsuchtsvoll*),	33
	(*sehnsuchtsvoll*,)	46
66.24	Alas!	33
	Alas,	69 71
66.27	regard:	33
	regard;	46 58 → 71
66.27	too must repel	33
	too had to repel	
	46 → 71	
66.32	pap-fed	33
	pap-/fed	41U
67.2	the Name	33
	the name	46
67.9	Again,	33
	Again	41U → 49

67.10   Basket-bearer   33
        Basket-/bearer
                41ᴜ → 41 49
        Basketbearer   58

67.10   intend,   33
        intend   46

67.11   shadow forth   33
        shadow-forth   58 → 71

67.13   Ostrich must leave   33
        Ostrich hadst to leave
                46 → 71

67.18   shot at   33
        shot at,   49 → 71

67.18   handfettered,   33
        hand-fettered, 38 → 71

67.19   bedevilled,   33
        bedevilled   69 71

67.20   seared   33
        seered   49 → 69

67.26   indeed   33
        indeed,   58 → 71

67.28   Earth-visiting   33
        earth-visiting   69 71

67.33   seed-grain   33
        seed-/grain 41ᴜ → 41 49
        seedgrain   58 → 71

67.33   all over-shadowing   33
        all-overshadowing   46
        all overshadowing   71

67.35   Clothings,   33
        clothings,   46

68.1   be the (Appearances)
        exotic-vegetable, organic,
                                 33
        be the (appearances)
        exotic-vegetable, organic,
                                 46

68.4   *one a (thief) and he*   33
        one a (thief,) and he
                41ᴜ → 71

68.4   almost similar (sense,) may
        we   33
        almost similar (sense) may
        we   69 71

68.5   *one Diogenes*
        (Teufelsdröckh) and he 33
        one Diogenes
        (Teufelsdröckh,) and he
                41ᴜ → 71

68.6*   *Clothes.'* ¶'Meanwhile 33
        Clothes?' [extra leading
        between paragraphs]
        ¶'Meanwhile   69 71
        Clothes. ¶'Meanwhile
                Strouse

68.9   sprawling out   33
        sprawling-out   58 → 71

68.10   Sixth   33
        sixth   46

68.11   half awakened   33
        half-awakened   41ᴜ → 71

68.14   his progress;   33
        his his progress;   46

68.15   the miracle   33
        the the miracle   46

68.16   formless,   33
        formless;   46

68.18   Sensation,   33
        Sensation   69 71

68.24   gave out   33
        gave-out   58 → 71

68.26   birth-land;   33
        birthland;   69 71

68.31   Time   33
        time   38 → 71

68.31   cut out   33
        cut-out   58 → 71

68.32   whimpering.' [extra
        leading between
        paragraphs] ¶Such,   33
        whimpering.' ¶Such,
                49 58

68.38   undercurrents   33
        under-/currents   38
        under-currents 41ᴜ → 71

69.4   Sheets,   33
        sheets,   41ᴜ → 71

69.5	Circulating-Library,	33
	Circulating Library,	
		49 → 71
69.8*	Tombuctoo	33
	Timbuctoo	58 → 71
69.9	Basket-bearing Stranger,	
		33
	Basket-bearing stranger,	
		38 → 58
	basket-bearing Stranger,	
		69 71
70.1	'Happy season of	33
	'Happy season of	
		38 → 71
70.5	(*umgäukelt*)	33
	(*umgaukelt*)	58 → 71
70.8	Free.	33
	free.	58 → 71
70.12	downrushing	33
	down-/rushing	
		41u → 49
	down-rushing	58 → 71
70.18	Arnauld, must say	33
	Arnauld, wilt have to say	
		46 → 71
70.19	rest in?	33
	rest in?"	38 → 71
71.2	frost-/nipt,	33
	frostnipt,	38 → 71
71.2	grow	33
	grows	46
71.8	on, with	33
	on with	49 → 71
71.13	Linden,	33
	Linden,'	38 → 71
71.14	towered up	33
	towered-up	58 → 71
71.16	old men	33
	old man	46
71.20	Sun	33
	Sun,	69 71
71.21	Taskmaster	33
	Taskmaster,	69 71

71.21	gold-purple	33
	gold-purpled	41u
71.22	fire-clad bodyguard	33
	fire-/clad bodyguard	58
	fireclad body-/guard	69
	fireclad body-guard	71
71.30	Linden?'	33
	Linden'?	69 71
71.33	(*Schaffenden*	33
	(*Schaffeden*	38 41u
	(*schaffeden*	41r → 49
	(*schaffenden*	58 → 71
71.34	*Trieb*):	33
	Trieb):	41u
71.35	to Work.	33
	to work.	58 → 71
71.36	pengun,	33
	pen-/gun,	41u → 41 69
	pen-gun,	46 → 58 71
71.38	Co-operation,	33
	Cooperation,	41r 41 49
	Coöperation,	58 → 71
72.5	short-cloth,	33
	short cloth,	38 → 49
72.10	carry forth	33
	carry-forth	58 → 71
72.11	out of doors.	33
	out-of-doors.	58 → 71
72.11	Orchard-wall,	33
	Orchard wall,	46
72.12	set up	33
	set-up	58 → 71
72.13	pruning-ladder,	33
	pruning ladder,	49
72.19	for the cattle	33
	for cattle	38 → 71
72.19	poultry'	33
	poultry,'	41u → 49
72.20*	"a certain	33
	a 'certain	38 → 71
	'a certain	Strouse
72.21	Nature:'	33
	Nature;'	46

72.24	hungry, happy	
	quadrupeds, were	33
	hungry happy quadrupeds	
	were,	38 → 71
72.25	sides	33
	sides,	38 → 71
72.26	them,	33
	them	58 → 71
72.26	marching in	33
	marching-in	58 → 71
72.28	trotting off	33
	trotting-off	58 → 71
72.31	Ham:	33
	Ham;	38 → 71
72.34	who were	33
	who, were	58 → 71
72.35	discoloured tin	33
	disco-/coloured tin	41U
	discoloured-tin	58 → 71
73.2	close-folded	33
	close-/folded	58
	closefolded	69 71
73.6	crushed down	33
	crushed-down	58 → 71
73.8	'With	33
	With	71
73.12	all but	33
	all-but	41R → 71
73.14	wide-shadowing	33
	wide shadowing	58
73.15	edible, luxuriant,	33
	edible, luxuriant	46
	edible luxuriant	58 → 71
73.16	note down	33
	note-down	58 → 71
73.19	now-a-days	33
	nowadays	
		38 → 41 49 → 71
	now-adays	46
73.20	short-clothes	33
	short clothes	46
73.25	Sights,	33
	Sighs,	46

73.30	stirred up,	33
	stirred-up,	58
73.32*	gray, austere,	33
	grey austere,	38 → 41
	grey austere	46 49
	gray austere	58 → 71
73.33	"Much-enduring	33
	"much-enduring	69 71
73.35	hearth:	33
	hearth;	58 → 71
73.37	Incredible	33
	Incalculable	41R → 71
74.4	World;	33
	World:	46
74.7	(Stage-Coach),	33
	(Stage-coach),	69 71
74.9	truly,	33
	truly	46
74.10	year,	33
	year	49 → 71
74.10	Postwagen	33
	Postwagon	46
74.18	far Africa	33
	fair Africa	46
	far Africa,	49 → 71
74.22	bracket,	33
	bracket	58 → 71
74.24	them.	33
	them,	38
74.26	police?	33
	policy?	46
74.29	activity	33
	activity,	49
74.33	poured down	33
	poured-down	58 → 71
74.35	hurly-burly.	33
	hurly-/burly.	69
	hurlyburly.	71
74.36	be-ribanded;	33
	beribanded;	41R → 71
74.37	possible,	33
	possible	46

75.1	skullcaps,	33
	scull-caps,	38 → 41 49
	skull-caps,	46 58 → 71
75.2	oxgoads;	33
	ox-goads;	38 46
	ox-/goads;	41U → 41
75.2	half-articulate	33
	half-articulated	41U
75.10	ground-and-lofty tumbling,	33
	ground-and-lofty-tumbling,	41U
75.10	parti-coloured	33
	particoloured	41R → 71
75.10	Andrew;	33
	Andrew,	34 → 71
75.11	itself. [extra leading between paragraphs] ¶'Thus	33
	itself. ¶'Thus encircled	49 → 71
75.14	waited on	33
	waited-on	58 → 71
75.16	Christmas carols,	33
	Christmas-carols,	58 → 71
75.19	World:	33
	World;	58
75.25	'Nevertheless	33
	'Nevertheless,	41U → 71
75.29	nay,	33
	nay	41R → 71
75.30	overshadowed	33
	over-shadowed	49 → 71
75.32	Necessity,	33
	Necessity	49 → 71
75.32	begirt:	33
	begirt;	38 → 71
75.36	there. ¶'For	33
	there. [extra leading between paragraphs] ¶'For	69 71
76.7	Power	33
	Power,	41U

76.7	hemmed in;	33
	hemmed-in;	58 → 71
76.12	every where	33
	everywhere	41R → 71
76.23	nay,	33
	nay	69 71
76.24	upbringing!	33
	upbringing.	69 71
76.25	every way	33
	everyway	58 → 71
76.26	Earnestness,	33
	earnestness,	38 → 71
76.28	well-meant.	33
	well meant,	38
	well-meant,	41R → 71
76.32	Andreas, too,	33
	Andreas too	41R → 71
76.33	parade-duty,	33
	parade duty,	46
76.34	received:	33
	received;	41U → 71
77.7	two and thirty	33
	two-and-thirty	58 → 71
78.1	Hitherto we see	33
	HITHERTO **we see**	
		38 → 71
78.3	workshop;	33
	workshop,	69 71
78.6	Hitherto accordingly	33
	Hitherto, accordingly,	
		69 71
78.7	abstract:	33
	abstract;	58 → 71
78.10	least,	33
	least	38 → 71
78.14	how	33
	how,	69 71
78.19	nay,	33
	nay	69 71
78.19	so well-fostered	33
	so well fostered	38 → 49
	so-well-fostered	58

78.19	every-way-excellent	33
	every-way excellent	
	38 → 49	
	everyway-excellent	58
	everyway excellent	69 71
78.22	after-days,	33
	after days,	69 71
78.23*	shallow-sighted,	33
	shallow-sighted	41u 46
79.1	No-man;	33
	No man;	58
79.7	endeavour. [extra leading	
	between paragraphs]	
	¶Among	33
	endeavour. ¶Among	
	38 → 71	
79.10	man of letters,	33
	man-of-letters,	58
79.15	learn;	33
	learnt;	46
79.15	stored by	33
	stored-by	58 → 71
79.22	laid out	33
	laid-out	58 → 71
79.22	stall-literature;	33
	stall-literature:	38 41u
	stall literature;	46 49
79.27	as yet	33
	not yet	46
79.28	well	33
	well,	41u → 71
79.31	thoughtful,	33
	thoughtful[ ]/	46
79.34	stumbled,	33
	stumbled	41u
79.35	much,	33
	much	38 41u
80.2	Cæsar,	33
	Cæsar	46
80.3	Eurotas,	33
	Eurotas	38 → 71
80.5*	here,	33
	here	41r

80.5	Vein or Veinlet	33
	vein or veinlet	41u → 71
80.7	Arteries,	33
	arteries,	41u → 71
80.8	Art	33
	art	49 → 71
80.9	six thousand	33
	six-thousand	58 → 71
80.11	and the mystery	33
	and mystery	38 → 71
80.14	Gymnasic	33
	Gymnastic	46
80.19	when	33
	when,	69 71
80.20	hope,	33
	hope	69 71
80.21	Eight),	33
	Eight)	38 → 71
80.22	moving in	33
	moving-in	58 → 71
80.24	tin kettle	33
	tin-kettle	58 → 71
80.25	creature loud-jingling	33
	creature, loud-jingling,	
	38 → 41 49 → 71	
	creature, loud jingling,	46
80.25	Burough,	33
	Borough,	41r → 71
80.28	tin kettle	33
	tin-kettle	58 → 71
80.29	which,	33
	which	58 → 71
80.31	World,	33
	world,	46
80.38	deerherd	33
	deer-herd	69
	deer-/herd	71
81.2	admits	33
	admits,	58 → 71
81.4	result,	33
	result	38
81.4	as would	33
	as it would	46

81.5	(for,	33
	(for	38 → 71
81.5	seasons,	33
	seasons	69 71
81.9	war-element,	33
	war element,	46
81.11	Teufelsdröckh's	33
	Teufelsdröck's	46
81.12	degree,	33
	degree	38 → 71
81.15	burst forth	33
	burst-forth	58 → 71
81.16	Stormfulness	33
	stormfulness	69 71
81.19	reedgrass,	33
	reed-/grass	58
	reed-grass	69 71
81.20	forced,	33
	forced	69 71
81.21	sickly	33
	sickly,	38 → 71
81.23	called	33
	call	46
81.30	has	33
	had	46
81.32	shews	33
	shows	58 → 71
81.36	nature	33
	nature,	49 → 71
82.3	manufactured, at Nürnberg,	33
	manufactured at Nürnberg	41R → 71
82.4*	any thing;	33
	anything;	46 → 71
82.6	like a Spirit,	33
	like a spirit,	69 71
82.8	burnt out	33
	burnt-out	58 → 71
82.10	Syntax	33
	syntax	69 71
82.11	acted on	33
	acted-on	58 → 71

82.12	birch rods.	33
	birch-rods.	58 → 71
82.13	every where,	33
	everywhere,	41U → 71
82.14	Hodbearing;	33
	hodbearing;	69 71
82.18	Field-marshals	33
	Fieldmarshals	69 71
82.20	Soldier	33
	soldier	46
82.23	nay,	33
	nay	46
82.24	would not,	33
	would there not,	46 → 71
82.24	class, a certain	33
	class, perhaps a certain	46 → 71
82.29	boundless Abyss,	33
	bottomless Abyss,	38 → 71
82.31	generations	33
	generations,	69 71
82.32	showed	33
	shewed	41U → 49
82.32*	mother	33
	Mother	46 → 71
82.34	pent up	33
	pent-up	58 → 71
82.34	Nevertheless,	33
	Nevertheless	49 → 71
82.35	strong,	33
	strong;	38 → 71
82.37	cypress forest,	33
	cypress-forest,	41U → 71
83.2	Cypress tree;	33
	Cypress-tree;	41U → 71
83.4	penalties,	33
	penalties	49 → 71
83.7	weep for	33
	weep-for	58
83.10	THERE,	33
	THERE,	38 → 71

83.17*	family, **Family,**	33 46 → 71	
83.17	traced back traced-back	33 58	
83.19	add **add,**	33 41ʀ → 71	
83.25	abundant abandoned	33 46	
83.25	disclosure, discolsure,	33 41ᴜ	
83.26	nature: nature;	33 46	
83.30	*other;* *other:*	33 46	
83.31	frightfullest frightfulest	33 38 → 49	
83.31	Tendencies, tendencies,	33 69 71	
83.32	that in my Life **which in my Life**	33 46 → 71	
84.5	shew show	33 58 → 71	
84.6	Sibylline: Sibylline;	33 46	
84.6	College Exercises, College-Exercises,	33 58 → 71	
84.7	Testimoniums, Testimonials,	33 46	
84.15	that has passed **who has passed**	33 41ʀ → 71	
84.16	vigorously vigourously	33 46	
84.17	vocables,' vocables.	33 46	
84.19	yet nowise with **yet never or seldom with**	33 69 71	
84.28	Thus Thus,	33 69 71	

84.29	of Time, of Time	33 69 71
84.31	eagerness eagerness,	33 69 71
84.34	Paperbag, Paper-/bag, Paper-bag,	33 58 71 46 69
84.38	fall in fall-in	33 58 → 71
85.3	however, I however, I,	33 38 → 71
85.4	no wise nowise	33 49 → 71
85.8	limit; limit:	33 38 → 71
85.11	ditch: ditch;	33 46
85.12	led lead	33 71
85.12	any where anywhere	33 38 → 71
85.13	walled in **walled-in**	33 41ʀ → 71
85.14	eleven hundred eleven-hundred	33 58 → 71
85.16	years; years:	33 41ᴜ → 71
85.18	admission-fees, admission fees,	33 38
85.24	costlier apparatus, costlier apparatus	33 49 → 71
85.27	any thing anything	33 58 → 71
85.34*	What monies, What moneys,	33 46 → 71
85.35	realised realized	33 46
85.37	incomings incoming	33 38 41ᴜ
85.38*	said monies, said moneys,	33 46 → 71

86.1	infinitely complected	33
	infinitely-complected	
		58 → 71
86.6*	place and wages	33
	place of wages	69 71
86.6	Performance:	33
	Performance;	46
86.22	I mean	33
	I I mean	46
86.27	together,	33
	together	69 71
86.30	omni-patient	33
	omnipatient	41R → 71
86.31	lit lemechanism;	33
	little mechanism;	
		34 → 71
86.35	strong, brisk-going,	
	undershot-wheel,	33
	strong brisk-going	
	undershot-wheel,	38 → 58
	strong brisk-going	
	undershot wheel,	69
	strong, brisk-going	
	undershot wheel,	71
86.38	accord,	33
	accord	38 → 71
86.38	so	33
	so,	41R → 71
87.5	degree,	33
	degree	49 → 71
87.5	Mysticism:	33
	Mysticism;	38 → 71
87.8	sort must soon end	33
	sort had soon to end	
		46 → 71
87.10	Self-conceit,	33
	Self-conceit	38
87.10	to all	33
	toa ll	41U
87.13	longdrawn Systole and	
	longdrawn Diastole,	33
	longdrawn systole and	
	longdrawn diastole,	69
	long-drawn systole and	
	long-drawn diastole,	71

87.18	endeavour,	33
	endeavour	49 → 71
87.22	awake,	33
	awake	69 71
87.22	if	33
	if,	69 71
87.25	slumber through,	33
	slumber-through,	
		58 → 71
87.30	'looked up	33
	'looked-up	58
87.31	east wind.	33
	east-wind.	58 → 71
87.32*	Manipulation,	33
	Manipulation	38 → 71
87.34	eleven hundred	33
	eleven-hundred	58 → 71
88.1	fishing up	33
	fishing-up	58 → 71
88.4	subjects,	33
	subjects	49 → 71
88.11	recognised	33
	recognized	38 → 46
88.12	experiments,	33
	experiments	49 → 71
88.15	wild desert,	33
	wild desert	49 → 71
88.22	prayers,	33
	prayers	69 71
88.28	pass:	33
	pass;	41U → 71
88.38	struggling up	33
	struggling-up	58 → 71
88.39	flame?	33
	flame.	46
89.4	stretching out	33
	stretching-out	58 → 71
89.5	on him.	33
	upon him.	46
89.5	dreary enough	33
	dreary-enough	58
89.5	humour,	33
	humuor,	41U

89.20	shewed	33
	showed	58 → 71
89.20	impassivity	33
	impassivity,	38 → 71
89.21	fury	33
	fury,	38 → 71
89.27	had been as yet those	33
	had as yet been those	
		46 → 71
89.31	turned out	33
	turned-out	58 → 71
89.32	chins,	33
	chins	38 → 71
89.34	Head	33
	head	38 → 71
89.36	Attorney Logic!	33
	Attorney-Logic!	58 → 71
89.37	but, at	33
	but at	41u → 71
90.2	faculty,	33
	Faculty,	38 → 71
90.3	not bad	33
	no bad	41u
90.5	*zu, Bruder!*	33
	zu Bruder!	46
90.9	looked out	33
	looked-out	58 → 71
90.13	Towgood,	33
	Towgood	69 71
90.25	dived under,	33
	dived-under,	58 → 71
91.1	'Thus nevertheless,' writes	
		33
	'Thus nevertheless,'	
	writes	38 → 71
91.8	Does	33
	does	38 → 71
91.15	one	33
	oue [n upside down]	41u
91.16	learned or begun learning	
		33
	learned, or begun	
	learning,	38 → 71

91.21	mention:	33
	mention;	46
92.6	Wisest.	33
	Wisest?	41u → 71
92.14	(*Zeitfürst*),	33
	(*Zeitfurst*),	46
92.15	coronation ceremony	33
	coronation-ceremony	
		41R → 71
92.17	similitude,	33
	similitude	69 71
92.19	way?'	33
	way'?	69 71
92.29	Capability	33
	Capabilitiy	46
92.30	unfriended,	33
	unfriendly,	46
92.33	work,	33
	work	69 71
92.36	ever new expectation, ever	
	new	33
	ever-new expectation,	
	ever-new	41R → 71
93.1	side;	33
	side:	41u → 71
93.1	threescore and ten,	33
	threescore-and-ten,	
		58 → 71
93.4	not one that one	33
	not that one	38 → 71
93.10	Capability,	33
	Capability	38 → 71
93.14	Professions,	33
	professions,	46
93.14	(*Brodtzwecke*),	33
	(*Brodzwecke*),	58 → 71
93.14	preappointed	33
	pre-/appointed	49
	pre-appointed	58
93.16	Bread-artist	33
	Bread artist	58
93.17	still fancying	33
	till fancying	46

93.17* forward and forward, 33
forward and forward;
46 → 71

93.17 realise 33
realize 46

93.20 neck-halter, 33
neck halter, 58

93.21 broke it off. 33
broke it. 46

93.22 World 33
world 49 → 71

93.23 strength or cunning, 33
strength of cunning, 46

93.27 embodyment 33
embodiment 41R → 71

93.31 'breaks off 33
'breaks-off 58 → 71

93.32 rigourously 33
rigorously 38 → 71

93.33 fenced in. 33
fenced-in. 58 → 71

93.36 stone-walls, 33
stone walls, 41U → 49

94.1 way; 33
way: 46

94.3 Freedom 33
Freedom, 69 71

94.3 Scarcity 33
Scarcity, 69 71

94.4 sweetness. 33
sweetness[ ] 58

94.4 thrown up 33
thrown-up 58 → 71

94.10 *Rest;* 33
Rest: 41U

94.11 work through 33
work-through 58

94.13 'neck-halter' 33
'neck halter' 58

94.15 Capital, 33
capital, 58 → 71

94.17 Law Examination 33
Law-Examination
41R → 71

94.17 come through 33
come-through 58

94.21 connexions 33
connexions, 38 → 71

94.25 shewed 33
showed 58 → 71

94.32 and, what 33
and what 41U → 71

94.36 Perhaps too 33
Perhaps, too, 69 71

94.38 brag of; 33
brag of: 41U

95.3 Independence, 33
independence, 49 → 71

95.6 had 33
have 46

95.10 genius;' 33
genius:' 41U → 71

95.11 Papers 33
Papers, 38 → 71

95.15 cheated 33
cheated, 58 → 71

95.16 copper.' 33
copper. 46

95.18 meanwhile, 33
mean while,
38 → 41 49 → 71

95.21 no where 33
nowhere 41R → 71

95.29 'there is ever Life for the
Living,' 33
**'there is always life for a
living one,'** 46 → 71

95.37 tied down 33
tied-down 58 → 71

96.1 forbearing 33
forbearing, 41R → 71

96.7 THEE, 33
THEE 58 → 71

96.10	comes,	33	97.29	smallest	33
	comes	46		**smallest,**	41R → 71
96.19	good will	33	97.32	every where	33
	good-will	58 → 71		everywhere	58 → 71
96.27	soft,	33	97.32	simple	33
	soft	46		simply	46
96.28	must serve	33	97.33	Rule of Three:	33
	were to serve	46 → 71		Rule-of-Three:	58 → 71
96.30	dexterously she fitted on,		97.36	found out,	33
		33		found-out,	58 → 71
	dextrously she fitted-on,		97.38	of.'	33
		58 → 71		of.	58
96.33	His	33	98.1	passage,	33
	his	41U → 71		**passage**	41R → 71
96.33	Count),'	33	98.1	does there not	33
	Count)'	41U		**does not there**	69 71
96.37	Journalism	33	98.4	Alas!	33
	Journalism,	41U		Alas,	58 → 71
96.37*	*Journalistic*),	33	98.8	threescore and ten	33
	Journalistik),	41U → 71		threescore-and-ten	
97.3	him.'	33			58 → 71
	him.	46	98.13	to Move, to Work,	33
97.5*	things,	33		**to move, to work,**	
	things	46 → 71			41R → 71
97.5*	Journalism,'	33	98.17	thus	33
	Journalism'	58 → 71		thus,	41U → 71
97.9	Universe,'	33	98.20	Time-Element;	33
	Universe,	46		**Time-Element,**	
97.14	unison;	33			41R → 71
	harmony;	58 → 71	98.20	that, only	33
97.15*	Victory	33		that only	69 71
	victory	41R → 71	98.21	moments,	33
97.15*	Battle.'	33		moments	69 71
	battle.'	41U → 71	98.23	for	33
97.27	self-indulgence;	33		**for,**	41R → 71
	self-indulgence:	46	98.32	eat into	33
97.28	vainglorious;	33		eat-into	58
	vain-/glorious;	41U → 49	98.35	circumstance,	33
	vain-glorious;	58 → 71		circumstance	49 → 71
97.29	forward.	33	99.4	any thing,	33
	forward[]	46		anything,	58 → 71
97.29	will	33	99.8	divine,	33
	will,	41R → 71		divine	69 71

99.12	buckram-case, buckram case,	33 38 → 71		102.8	pitifullest pitifulest	33 41U → 49
99.13	envelope envelop	33 58 69		102.14	flames forth flames-forth	33 58 → 71
99.14	there; there,	33 41R → 71		102.19*	nor nor,	33 41R → 71
99.16	have, long since, have long since	33 69 71		102.19*	foliage, foliage	33 38 → 71
99.21	name, name	33 49 → 71		102.19*	Garden Garden,	33 41R → 71
99.28	one one,	33 38 → 69		102.21	lovelier lovelier,	33 41R → 71
99.28	*anzuschliessen*)?' *anzuschliessen*)'?	33 69 71		102.22	flaming sword Flaming Sword	33 38 → 71
99.33	uncholeric' un[ ]/choleric'	33 58		102.24	Shame shame	33 38 41U 49 → 71
99.37	grand principle grand spirit	33 41U		103.1	(*Holden*)—*Ach* (*Holden*) *Ach*	33 46
100.3	which, which	33 69 71		103.4	all sceptical all-sceptical	33 69 71
100.9	ZAEHDARMI COMES, ZAEHDARMI COMES,	33 69 71		103.4	Angels, Angels	33 38 → 71
100.18	SERVOS SERVOS	33 69 71		103.6	Skyborn, Sky-born,	33 38 → 71
100.24	QUÆRIS QUÆRIS,	33 41R → 71		103.7*	whereso wheresoever	33 69 71
100.26*	PRIMUM PRIMÙM	33 46 → 58		103.14	burst forth, burst-forth,	33 58 → 71
100.26*	POSTREMUM POSTREMÙM	33 46 → 58		103.22	blaze up? blaze-up?	33 58 → 71
101.11	steers off, steers-off,	33 58		103.24	must one day, would one day,	33 46 → 71
101.17	shorter, shorter	33 41U → 71		103.26	flamed off flamed-off	33 58 → 71
101.17	Northwest North-west	33 46		103.29	burnt out; burnt-out;	33 58 → 71
101.18	rover, rover	33 46		103.29	relieved, relieved	33 49 → 71
102.4	(*Personlichkeit*) (*Persönlichkeit*)	33 58 → 71		103.36	'Crater 'crater	33 38 → 71
102.7	burns out burns-out	33 58 → 71		104.1	Philosopher, philosopher,	33 49 → 71

104.2	franticly	33	
	frantically	49 → 71	
104.3	flesh,	33	
	flesh	41ʀ → 71	
104.3	loved once;	33	
	loved once:	41ᴜ	
104.11	myrtle garland.	33	
	myrtle-garland.	58 → 71	
104.17	specialties	33	
	specialities	46	
104.18	blazes off.	33	
	blazes-off.	58 → 71	
104.27	Pre-established	33	
	Preëstablished	69 71	
104.37	highborn,	33	
	highborn	46	
104.37	spirit;	33	
	spirits;	46	
105.1	not too gracious	33	
	not-too-gracious	58	
105.2	monied	33	
	moneyed	69 71	
105.10	write;	33	
	write,	69 71	
105.13	Sunbeams,	33	
	sunbeams,	38 → 71	
105.14	Dorado,	33	
	Doredo,	46	
105.15	Hills:	33	
	Hills;	58 → 71	
105.23	handed in	33	
	handed-in	49 → 71	
105.26	cavaliers;	33	
	cavaliers:	58 → 71	
105.30	rose-clusters,	33	
	roseclusters,	41ᴜ	
105.31	thousand	33	
	thousaud	41ᴜ	
105.37	(*ahnungsvoll*),	33	
	(*ahndungsvoll*),41ʀ → 71		
106.4*	specially	33	
	especially	41ᴜ → 71	

106.5	damosels,	33	
	damosels	49 → 71	
106.10	wide,	33	
	wide	41ᴜ → 71	
106.13	Friend	33	
	friend	49 → 71	
106.14	blooming,	33	
	blooming	38 → 71	
106.17	light	33	
	light,	46	
106.23	on him,	33	
	on him;	69 71	
106.23	speak	33	
	speak,	69 71	
106.33	painful,	33	
	painful	49 → 71	
106.34	Future	33	
	Future,	38 → 71	
106.37	shrouded up	33	
	shrouded-up	58 → 71	
106.37	tremours	33	
	tremors	49 → 71	
107.4	Shew	33	
	Show	58 → 71	
107.5	forever	33	
	for ever	38 → 41 49	
107.7	and, borne	33	
	and borne	49 → 71	
107.17	bodies forth	33	
	bodies-forth	58 → 71	
107.21	pouring forth	33	
	pouring-forth	58 → 71	
107.29	nay,	33	
	nay	69 71	
107.30	tremour	33	
	tremor	49 → 71	
107.36	circle:	33	
	circle;	41ᴜ → 71	
108.5	mountain tops,	33	
	mountain-tops,		
		41ʀ → 71	
108.9	man's	33	
	Man's	41ᴜ → 71	

108.9*	dusk	33
	dust	38 → 71
108.14	whisper:	33
	whisper,	69 71
108.21	art magic,	33
	art-magic,	69 71
108.26	case,	33
	case	41R → 71
108.27	Sight;	33
	sight;	41U → 71
108.28	Actual,	33
	Actual	41R → 71
108.28	Archimedes'-lever,	33
	Archimedes-lever,	
		41U → 71
108.31	(*Zeitbühne*),	33
	(*Zeitbühne*)	46
108.34	a-day;	33
	a day;	41R → 71
108.36	Alas,	33
	Alas!	41U → 71
109.1	'highsouled	33
	'high-souled	
		38 → 46 58 → 71
	'high-/souled	49
109.1	Earth	33
	earth	71
109.2	one,	33
	one	41U → 71
109.5*	yet all in darkness:	33
	yet in all darkness:	
		41U → 71
109.7	Withdrawn,	33
	Withdrawn	46
109.8	fastnesses;	33
	fastnesses:	46
109.17	Music:	33
	Music;	46
109.24	Morning-Star;	33
	morning-Star;	46
109.25	Eolean	33
	Æolean	41R → 58
	Æolian	69 71

109.26	rosy-finger	33
	rosy finger	38 → 71
109.28	bloomed up	33
	bloomed-up	58 → 71
109.28	Past,	33
	past,	49 → 71
109.35	it must	33
	ti must	41U
109.37	Feeling	33
	feeling	46
110.1	bosom,	33
	bosom	69 71
110.2	cut asunder	33
	cut-asunder	58 → 71
110.2	bonds.'	33
	bounds.'	46
110.4	meagre,	33
	meagre	49 → 69
110.12	Kitchen	33
	kitchen	41R → 71
110.13	shews	33
	shows	58 → 71
110.15	Love-mania,	33
	Love mania,	58
105.21	view,	33
	view	46
110.26*	enough,	33
	enough	46 → 71
110.29	reader	33
	reader,	38 → 71
110.30	himself;	33
	himself:	41U → 71
111.1	they	33
	They	41U → 71
111.5*	'Farewell, then, Madam!	
		33
	'"Farewell, then,	
	Madam!"	41R 46 → 71
	"Farewell, then, Madam!"	
		41
111.7	eyes:	33
	eyes;	69 71

111.13	Universe,	33
	Universe	41R → 71
112.1	We have long	33
	WE have long	38 → 71
112.2	that, in	33
	that in	41U → 71
112.11	blow out	33
	blow-out	58 → 71
112.13	enough:	33
	enough;	41R → 71
112.13	lion-bellowings	33
	lion bellowings	58
112.17	(Pilgrim-staff),	33
	(Pilgrim-stafl),	41U
112.17	wound up;'	33
	wound-up;'	58 → 71
112.19	Globe!	33
	globe!	46
112.20	feeling;	33
	feeling,	69 71
112.22	Thus	33
	Thus,	41U → 71
113.5	rush out	33
	rush-out	58 → 71
113.8	it;	33
	it:	46
113.12	Hope,	33
	hope,	41U → 71
113.13	Life:	33
	life:	46
113.14	passed over	33
	passed-over	58
113.17	waste Ocean-waters:	33
	waste-Ocean-waters:	38
113.20	quite	33
	quiet	49 58
113.21	paroxysm	33
	proxysm	69
113.23	weather,	33
	weather	69 71
114.1	Paperbags	33
	Paper-/bags	69
	Paper-bags	71

114.3	feeling is it that	33
	feeling it is that	
		41R → 71
114.10*	whatso	33
	whatsoever	69 71
114.10	love:	33
	love;	38 → 71
114.19	birthland,	33
	birth-land,	46
114.21*	take but one	33
	take only one	69 71
114.22	elsewhither?	33
	elsewhither.	58
114.23	Nature;	33
	Nrture;	41U
114.26	noteworthy:	33
	note-/worthy:	38
	note-worthy:	41U → 46
114.32	gray	33
	grey	49
114.33	shoots up	33
	shoots-up	58 → 71
115.11*	suit better:	33
	suit thee better:	69 71
115.12	shadows?"	33
	shadows."	41R → 71
115.13	outwards:	33
	outwards;	38 → 71
115.14	closes in	33
	closes-in	58 → 71
115.15	water-worn	33
	water-/worn	38 69
	waterworn	41U → 58
115.21	together;	33
	together:	38 → 71
115.22	look down	33
	look-down	58
115.24	little	33
	little,	69
115.25	inaccessible	33
	inaccessible,	38 → 71
115.31	deluge	33
	Deluge	38 → 71

116.6	barouche-and-four:	33	117.32	character,	33
	Barouche-and-four:	69 71		character	38 → 71
116.6*	postilions	33	117.35	present:	33
	postillions	58 → 71		present;	58 → 71
116.7	wedding-favours:	33	118.5	blotted out;	33
	wedding favours:			blotted-out;	58
		49 → 69	118.7	alone! alone!	33
116.8	marriage-evening!	33		alone, alone!	38 → 71
	marriage evening!		118.9	had that,	33
		38 → 71		had, that	69 71
116.9	*Himmel!*	33	118.9	fever-thirst,	33
	Himmel!	38		fever-thirst	69 71
116.9	slight,	33	118.12	Events:	33
	slight	38 → 71		events:	41U
116.16	Small-pox	33	118.14	deserts	33
	Small-Pox	58		deserts,	41U → 71
116.18*	view-hunting.	33	118.19	*Gott!*	33
	View-hunting.	38 → 71		*Gott,*	38 → 71
116.18	date,	33	118.19	a Son	33
	date	41U		aSon	41U
116.27	envelopement	33	118.21	elsewhere:	33
	envelopment	41R → 71		elsewhere;	46
116.29	basilisk-glance	33	118.21*	of Epictetus	33
	Basilisk-glance	41U → 71		*of Epictetus*	46 → 71
116.29	withered up	33	118.29	housetop,	33
	withered-up	58 → 71		house-top,	41U → 71
116.32	must stumble	33	118.32	earthen-kettle	33
	has to stumble	46 → 71		earthen kettle	69 71
116.35	world-pilgrimage	33	118.33	wild eggs	33
	world-piligrimage	41U		wild-eggs	58 → 71
117.6	God,	33	118.34	Vienna	33
	God	49 → 71		*Vienna*	41U
117.9	wishing-carpet,	33	118.35	Living	33
	wishing carpet,	41U → 58		living	46
117.10	whole too	33	119.6	Teufelsdrockh!	33
	whole, too,	41R → 71		**Teufelsdröckh!**	38 → 71
117.13	that	33	119.7	Chace	33
	that,	38 → 71		**Chase**	41R → 71
117.16	Biography!	33	119.9*	Jew, save	33
	Biography:	38 → 71		Jew,—save	69 71
117.29	Public	33	119.13	must write	33
	public	38 → 71		**had to write**	41R → 71

119.15	'to escape from	33
	to escape 'from	
		41R → 71
119.16	Shadow!'	33
	Shadow'!	69 71
119.18	things:	33
	things,	41U → 71
119.21	Idle,	33
	idle	41U → 71
119.28	cannon-vollies,	33
	cannon-volleys,	
		41R → 71
120.1	Under the strange	33
	UNDER the strange	
		38 → 71
120.1	Professor	33
	Profesor	41U
120.5	new Pilgrimings,	33
	mad Pilgrimings,	
		38 → 71
120.7	evolve	33
	evolves	41U
120.9*	Eagle,	33
	Eagle	41U → 71
120.10*	moults,	33
	moults	41R → 71
120.10	dash off	33
	dash-off	58 → 71
120.12	motions	33
	motions,	38 → 71
120.13	raging within;	33
	raving within;	46
120.13	flash out:	33
	flash-out:	58
120.16	pray for	33
	pray-for	58
120.20	sieze	33
	seize	38 → 71
120.21	Alas!	33
	Alas,	69 71
121.1	runs over,	33
	runs-over,	58

121.1	hisses over	33
	hisses-over	58
121.3	justness	33
	justice	71
121.5	What then	33
	What, then,	69 71
121.7	shut out	33
	shut-out	58 → 71
121.8	round	33
	around	46
121.10	shut out	33
	shut-out	58 → 71
121.11	For	33
	For,	69 71
121.13	that,	33
	that	46
121.15*	goes	33
	grows	49 58
121.19	Stomach;	33
	stomach;	38 41U
121.22	and, without	33
	and without	46 69 71
121.23*	Wordlings	33
	Worldlings	58 → 71
121.23	puke up	33
	puke-up	58 → 71
121.23	suicide,	33
	suicide	46
121.25	every thing.	33
	everything.	58 → 71
121.27	Friendship,	33
	Friendship	69 71
121.28	heart	33
	heart,	41U → 71
121.30	absentee	33
	abseentee	46
121.32	meaning:	33
	meaning;	41R → 71
121.33	made up	33
	made-up	58 → 71
121.34	Celestial-Bed?	33
	Celestial-bed?	46

121.35	of an	33	122.29	him!'	33	
	o an	34		him?'	58 → 71	
121.38	Word-monger,	33	122.31	Servants	33	
	Word-monger			servants	38 → 71	
	38 → 41 49		123.1	Apostacy."	33	
	Word-/monger	58		Apostasy."	58 → 71	
	Wordmonger	69 71	123.3	me,	33	
121.38*	that	33		me	38 → 71	
	who	41u → 71	123.3*	shalt thou	33	
122.2	out Virtue	33		thou shalt	41u → 71	
	outVirtue	41u	123.5	Fire!	33	
122.3	unregenerate Prometheus			Fire.	58 → 71	
	Vinctus	33	123.11	Heaven-written	33	
	reungenerate			heaven-written	38 → 71	
	PrometheusVinctus	41u	123.15	painfullest	33	
122.4	even	33		painfulest	49	
	ever	38 → 71	123.16	ever,	33	
122.9	Happiness	33		ever	46	
	Happíness	41u	123.25	work at.	33	
122.12	Cookery	33		work-at.	58	
	Cookery,	58 → 71	123.26	net result	33	
122.13	fryingpan,	33		net-result	58 → 71	
	frying-pan,	49 → 71	123.29	yet as	33	
122.14	things which he	33		yet, as	41R → 71	
	things he	46 → 71	123.32	Alas!	33	
122.16	Thus must	33		Alas,	69 71	
	Thus has	46 → 71	123.35	all too-cruelly	33	
122.16	Wanderer stand,	33		all-too cruelly	41R → 71	
	Wanderer to stand,		123.36	me:	33	
	46 → 71			me;	46	
122.17	Sibyl-cave	33	123.38	cast out.	33	
	Sybil-cave	38 41u		cast-out.	58	
122.18	once fair	33	124.7	vain,	33	
	once-fair	58 → 71		vain	58 → 71	
122.19	wild beasts,	33	124.7	too-hungry	33	
	wild-beasts,	58 → 71		too hungry	38 → 49	
122.22	what recks it	33	124.7	souls,	33	
	what boots it	38 → 71		souls	58 → 71	
122.23	thuts)?'	33	124.11*	round	33	
	thuts)?'	41u		around	38 → 71	
	thut's)?'	58 → 71	124.11	Figures;	33	
122.26	Unbelief:	33		Figures:	46	
	Unbelief;	38 → 71				

124.13*	In midst	33		125.24	Monster,	33
	In the midst	69 71			**monster,**	41R → 71
124.13	streets,	33		125.27	Dogday,	33
	streets	69 71			Dog day,	34
124.19	Downpulling	33		125.28	Rue Saint Thomas de	
	Down-/pulling	69			l'Enfer,	33
	Down-pulling	71			*Rue Saint-Thomas de*	
124.20	pulled down,	33			*l'Enfer,*	41R → 71
	pulled-down,	58		125.33	for ever	33
124.22	immeasurable	33			**forever**	58 → 71
	immeasurable,	38 41U		125.36	will,	33
124.22	rolling on,	33			will	58 → 71
	rolling-on,	58		125.37*	whatso	33
124.23	O the	33			whatsoever	69 71
	O, the	69 71		126.3	for ever.	33
124.25	Why if	33			**forever.**	58 → 71
	Why, if	69 71		126.6	Defiance.	33
124.32	Practice;	33			Defiance.'	38 41U
	practice;	69 71		126.7	*Ewige*	33
124.35	foredone	33			*ewige*	41R → 71
	fordone	58 → 71		126.9	stood up,	33
124.38	enough:	33			stood-up,	58
	enough?	41R → 71		126.14	Me	33
124.38	after-shine	33			ME	46
	after-/shine	58		126.15	for ever	33
	aftershine	69 71			**forever**	41R → 71
125.11	dew-drop,	33		127.1	THOUGH, after this	33
	dewdrop,	38 → 71			Though, after this	34
125.14	*Siegesglanze*	33		127.5	hopeless	33
	Sieges-glanze	46			hopleless	69
125.15*	whom He finds	33		127.12	*Saint Thomas*	33
	whom *he* **finds**	38 → 71			*Saint-Thomas*	41R → 71
126.16	Destiny	33		127.15	howl-chauntings,	33
	destiny	46			howl-chantings,	38 → 71
125.17	Hope,	33		127.16	gnashings	33
	hope,	38 → 71			gnashing	46
125.17	definite Fear,	33		127.16	meanwhile,	33
	definite fear,	38 → 71			mean while,	38 → 71
125.21	pining Fear;	33		127.18	scrutinize	33
	pining fear;	38 → 71			scrutinise	49 → 71
125.24	Jaws	33		127.21	nay that will	33
	jaws	41R → 71			**nay who will**	41R → 71

128.3	outwardly, **outwardly**	33 41R → 71	129.30*	Desart, Desert,	33 38 → 71
128.6	look upon look-upon	33 58	129.31	three thousand three-thousand	33 58 → 71
128.11	put down, put-down,	33 58	129.34	Wagram; Wagram:	33 46
128.11	two thousand two-thousand	33 58 → 71	129.37	Marchfeld Marchfield	33 46
128.14	mysterions **mysterious**	33 38 → 71	129.38	dead men deadmen	33 41U
128.14	put down put-down	33 58	130.2	aye, **ay,**	33 41R → 71
128.18	looking out looking-out	33 58	130.3	crammed down crammed-down	33 58 → 71
128.23	Cloth-habits Cloth-Habits	33 41U → 58	130.5	mould-cargos mould-cargoes mould cargoes	33 38 69 71 41U → 58
128.24*	required **acquired**	33 58 → 71	130.7	Marchfeld, Marchfield,	33 46
128.26	lock and key, lock-and-key,	33 58	130.10	Highways, highways,	33 46
128.36	there, there	33 69 71	130.11*	Ammunition-waggons,	33
128.37	Where then Where, then,	33 69 71		Ammunition-waggons	41U
129.7	reckon up reckon-up	33 58 → 71		Ammunition-wagons	41R → 58
129.8	Arsenals; their **Arsenals; then**	33 38 → 71		Ammunition-wagons,	69 71
129.11	last-invented, last invented,	33 69 71	130.17	torn up torn-up	33 58 → 71
129.12	City city	33 41U → 71	130.17	trampled down; trampled-down;	33 58 → 71
129.14	Field, but **field, but**	33 41R → 71	130.18	pleasant dwellings, pleasant-dwellings,	33 38
129.14	Field: like **field: like**	33 41R → 71	130.19	blown away blown-away	33 58 → 71
129.14	Tree, **tree,**	33 41R → 71	130.19	lies as a desolate, **lies a desolate,**	33 38 → 71
129.17	Leaves **leaves**	33 41R → 71	130.20	Place-of-Sculls. Place of Sculls.	33 38 → 71
129.29	Pyramids pyramids	33 41U → 71	130.22	shrouded in, shrouded-in,	33 58 → 71

130.23	Marchfeld	33
	Marchfield	46
130.23	nay	33
	nay,	46
130.26	Living!	33
	Living.	46
130.27	net purport	33
	net-purport	58 → 71
130.28	upshot	33
	usphot	49
130.28	War?	33
	war?	38 → 71
130.29	five hundred	33
	five-hundred	58 → 71
130.33	them; she	33
	them: she	49 → 71
130.34	them to crafts,	33
	them up to crafts,	46
130.38	two thousand	33
	two-thousand	58 → 71
131.1	now,	33
	now	38 → 71
131.1	spot	33
	spot,	69 71
131.4	juxta-position;	33
	juxtaposition;	49 → 71
131.6	given;	33
	given:	41u → 71
131.12	fallen out;	33
	fallen-out;	58 → 71
131.14*	Deutschland,	33
	Deutchsland,	41u → 49
131.17*	Smollett,	33
	Smollet,	41u → 71
131.20	faces,	33
	faces	46
131.20	gives in:	33
	gives-in:	58
131.22	us!'"	33
	us!'	38 → 71
131.32	Sights	33
	sights	38 → 71

131.34	Knowledge	33
	knowledge	49 → 71
131.38	Samarcand:	33
	Sarmacand:	38 41u
132.3	Geographics,	
	Topographics	33
	Geographies,	
	Topographies	46
132.7	meted out	33
	meted-out	58 → 71
132.9	Scenes,	33
	Scenes	69 71
132.12	palm-trees	33
	Palm-trees	58 → 71
132.13	grey	33
	gray	58 → 71
132.14	shows	33
	shews	41u → 49
132.15	have I not witnessed?	33
	have not I witnessed?	
		69 71
132.15	sweated down	33
	sweated-down	58 → 71
132.16	Customhouse-officers;	33
	Customhouse-Officers;	
		58 → 71
132.17	World well lost;	33
	world well lost;	46
132.17	hundred thousand	33
	hundred-thousand	
		58 → 71
132.29*	waggon-load	33
	wagon-load	41r 41
	wagonload	46 → 71
132.31	Thus,	33
	Thus	38 → 71
132.31	did I not,	33
	did not I,	69 71
133.13	doors,	33
	doors	46
133.15	moved,	33
	moved	69 71

133.16	divine	33
	Divine	38 → 71
133.19*	Evangile,	33
	Evangel,	38 → 71
133.19	Liberty	33
	liberty	49 → 71
133.23*	Backwoods-man,	33
	Backwood's-man,	41U
	Backwoodsman,	
		41R → 71
133.32	Brine,	33
	Brine	41U
133.33	stirred,	33
	stirred	46
133.35	Death,'	33
	death,'	41R → 71
134.3	cloth of gold;	33
	cloth-of-gold;	41R → 71
134.9	porch-lamp.	33
	porch-lamp?	49 → 71
134.10	moment,	33
	moment	69 71
134.13	brevity,	33
	Brevity,	38 41U
134.23*	say:	33
	say	38 41U
	say,	41R → 71
134.26	sidles off;	33
	sidles-off;	58
134.27	suicidal,	33
	suicidal	38 → 71
134.31	at least,	33
	at last,	38 → 71
134.35	Two little	33
	Too little	46
134.36	insecure enough	33
	insecure-enough	58
135.3	Deuce	33
	Deuse	46
135.3	(*verdammt*)! The	33
	(*verdammt*), the	
		38 → 71

135.5	Mannikins	33
	Manikins	41R → 71
135.7*	specialities,	33
	specialties,	49 → 71
135.30	*Gott!*	33
	Gott,	38 → 71
135.31	looked down	33
	looked-down	58 → 71
135.31	pity	33
	pity,	41R → 71
135.34	swallowed up	33
	swallowed-up	58 → 71
136.1	who then	33
	who, then,	69 71
136.4	Too heavy-laden	33
	Too-heavy-laden	
		58 → 71
136.6	free,	33
	free	58 → 71
137.1	'Temptations in the	33
	'TEMPTATIONS **in the**	
		38 → 71
137.4	Necessity;	33
	necessity;	49 58
137.5	Force:	33
	Force;	41U → 58
137.6	Battle.	33
	battle.	38 → 71
137.7	Promethean,	33
	Promethean	69 71
137.11	time,	33
	time	41U → 71
137.12	must there not be	33
	must not there be	69 71
137.13	upper?	33
	upper.	41U
137.18	nought,	33
	naught,	46 58 → 71
137.19	choose;	33
	choose:	41U → 71
137.20	natural Desart	33
	natural Desert	38 → 71

137.20 populous, moral Desart
                                    33
        populous moral Desert
                        38 → 71

137.22 not!   33
        not.   46

137.23 hand-/writing   33
        hand-writing   38
        handwriting   46 58 → 71

138.2   lights;   33
        lights: 38 → 71

138.17 Unbelief;   33
        Unbelief,   49 → 71

138.21 Doubt):   33
        Doubt);   41u → 71

138.23 So that   33
        So that,   41R → 71

138.23 also   33
        also,   41R → 71

138.25 his, were   33
        his were   41R → 71

138.28 turning point   33
        turning-point   58 → 71

138.29 *me*   33
        me,   41R → 71

138.29 *shreds,*   33
        shreds;   69 71

138.30 *Apage Satanas?*   33
        Apage Satanas?   38 41u
        Apage, Satana?
                        41R 41 49 58
        Apage Satana?   46 69 71

138.33 innuendoes,   33
        inuendoes,   38 → 46

138.35 passes in the   33
        passes int he   41u

138.36 afar off   33
        afar-off   58 → 71

138.37 Unspeakable?'   33
        unspeakable?'   38 → 71

139.5   Harmattan-wind   33
        Harmattan wind   69 71

139.5   out;   33
        out: 46

139.11 too, haggard   33
        too haggard   46

139.12 here; for   33
        here: for   38 → 71

139.12 life-weary;   33
        life weary;   46

139.14 in that   33
        in the   46

139.15* doubtless,   33
        doubtless   46 69 71

139.18 (*Sebst-tödtung*),   33
        (*Selbst-tödtung*),
                        49 → 71

139.19 mind's   33
        minds'   46

139.24 him? Were it not   33
        him? If it were not
                        38 → 71

139.25 than   33
        thon   38

139.26 expected.   33
        expected!   38 → 71

139.27 dancing,   33
        dancing   38

139.29 entire: 33
        entire.   69 71

139.32 Dome;   33
        Dome,   38 → 71

139.33 azure flowing   33
        azure-flowing   49 → 71

139.33 azure Winds,   33
        azure winds,   58

139.35 Castles   33
        Castles,   46

139.36 flower-lawns,   33
        flower lawns,   38 → 49

140.1   folded up   33
        folded-up   58 → 71

140.3   which,   33
        which   46

140.7	housewives,	33
	housewives	41u → 71
140.19	round	33
	around	46
140.23	elaboratest,	33
	elaboratest	46
140.25	what is Nature?	33
	what is nature?	46
140.26	thou not the "Living	33
	not thou the "Living	
		69 71
140.26*	of God?"	33
	of God?,	34
	of God"?	69 71
140.27*	HE, then,	33
	HE' then,	34
	HE then	38 → 58
140.29	'Foreshadows,	33
	'Fore-shadows,	
		41R → 71
140.31	ah!	33
	ah,	69 71
140.33	too exasperated	33
	too-exasperated	58 → 71
140.34	Evangile.	33
	Evangel.	38 → 71
140.35	spectres;	33
	spectres:	46
140.36	eyes too	33
	eyes, too,	41R → 71
140.36	fellow man;	33
	fellow man:	69 71
141.1	Royal	33
	royal	41R → 71
141.1	Beggar's	33
	beggar's	41R → 71
141.3	Grave.	33
	grave.	46
141.3	Brother! why	33
	Brother, why	41R → 71
141.4	eyes.	33
	eyes!	41R → 71

141.5	which,	33
	which	46
141.6	one:	33
	one;	58 → 71
141.11	Brother.	33
	brother.	46
141.13	ways,	33
	ways	69 71
141.24	comes out	33
	comes-out	58 → 71
141.35	two;	33
	two:	69 71
141.36	Stomach;	33
	Stomach:	41u → 49
142.3	Ophiuchus!	33
	Ophiuchus:	38 → 71
142.7	the most	33
	'the most	41u
142.8	black	33
	'black	41u
142.8	the *Shadow*	33
	'the *Shadow*	41u
142.14	complaint:	33
	complaint;	49 → 71
142.24	to die in hemp.	33
	to in hemp.	41u
142.25*	true is it,	33
	true it is,	41u → 58
142.26	*Numerator,*	33
	Numerator	38 → 71
142.36	cared for?	33
	cared-for?	58 → 71
143.7	preach forth	33
	preach-forth	58 → 71
143.12	too honoured	33
	also honoured	
		41R → 71
143.14	O thank	33
	O, thank	69 71
143.18	engulphed,	33
	engulfed,	49 → 71
143.20	solved;	33
	solved:	69 71

143.25	Knowest	33
	'Knowest	41u
143.26	*Sorrow?*"	33
	Sorrow"?	69 71
143.26	thereof, opened	33
	thereof, founded	
		41ʀ → 71
143.32	remark	33
	remark,	41ʀ → 71
143.32	them,	33
	them	41ʀ → 71
143.36	'true Priests,	33
	true 'Priests,	41u
143.38	fractions,	33
	fractions	46
144.15	Heart a	33
	heart, a	41ʀ → 71
144.20*	will	33
	will,	69 71
144.21	tear out	33
	tear-out	58 → 71
144.22	such like:	33
	suchlike:	69 71
144.28	Or	33
	Or,	58 → 71
144.30	Life,'	33
	life,'	49 → 71
144.30	internecive	33
	internecine	38 → 71
144.36	Alas!	33
	Alas,	69 71
145.4	wantest;	33
	wantest:	46
145.6	be "to	33
	be, "to	41ʀ → 71
145.13	only,	33
	only	41ʀ → 71
145.14	Experience,	33
	Experience	41ʀ → 71
145.17	ground too	33
	ground, too,	58 → 71

145.25	revealed,	33
	revealed	46
145.27	nowhere?"	33
	nowhere"?	58 → 71
145.31	Impediment	33
	impediment	49 → 71
145.33	out of:	33
	out of;	46
145.33	sort or of that,	33
	sort or that,	41u → 71
146.4	be Light!	33
	be light?	46
146.6	even, as	33
	even as,	38 → 71
146.7	least?	33
	least.	41u → 71
146.11	Heaven-encompassed	33
	heaven-encompassed	
		49 → 71
146.13*	pitifullest	33
	pitifulest	41ʀ → 49
146.14	produce it	33
	produce it,	69 71
146.15	thee;	33
	thee:	49 → 71
146.15	with it	33
	with it,	69 71
146.17	To-day,	33
	Today,	41ʀ 41 49
	Today;	58 → 71
146.17	cometh	33
	cometh,	58 → 71
147.1	Thus have we,	33
	Tʜᴜs **have we,**	38 → 71
147.7	Modern	33
	modern	49 → 71
147.8	Conversion: instead	33
	Conversion; instead	
		58 → 71
147.14	here then	33
	here, then,	69 71

147.15	'Work in Welldoing,' 'work in well-doing,'	33 41u → 71	149.9	all but faded away all-but faded-away all-but faded away	33 58 69 71
147.17	for, for	33 69 71	149.11	every where everywhere	33 38 → 71
147.20	itself, itself	33 46	149.11	behoved, behoved	33 46
147.21	power-loom, power-loom	33 69 71	149.12	deliration, deliration	33 46
147.21	head; head:	33 49 → 71	149.16	*Bodies,* *Bodies*	33 46
147.23	something; something:	33 58 → 71	149.17	*Possession,* *Possession*	33 49 → 71
148.1	*do.*—Tools? *do.* Tools?	33 46	149.17	*Liferent,* **Life-rent,**	33 41R → 71
148.5	so solid-seeming so-solid-seeming	33 58	149.17	looked for? looked-for?	33 58
148.17	seedfield seed-/field seed-field	33 46 58 69 71	149.19	keep down keep-down	33 58
148.24	stretching out stretching-out	33 58 → 71	149.19	vermin: vermin;	33 69 71
148.26*	doing it doing, it	33 49 → 71	149.21	Boa Constrictors? **Boa-constrictors?**	33 41R → 71
148.26	Idea in some Idea, in some	33 38 → 71	149.29	Journal, Journal	33 49 → 71
148.26	Head Head,	33 38 → 71	149.31	when, when	33 38 → 71
148.28*	"SOCIETY 'SOCIETY	33 41R → 71	149.31	Newspaper leaf, Newspaper-leaf,	33 58 → 71
148.29*	*Gesellschaft),*" *Gesellschaft),*'	33 41R → 71	149.32	Paperbags! Paper-bags!	33 69 71
148.31	Paperbags? Paper-/bags? 41u → 41 49 58 Paper-bags?	33 69 71	149.33	whimsicalities, whimsicalities	33 69 71
148.35	pour in pour-in	33 58	149.35	fast and loose fast-and-loose	33 58 → 71
149.2	and, and	33 49 → 71	149.36	us? [extra leading between paragraphs] ¶Here, us? [two lines of extra leading between paragraphs] ¶Here,	33 58
149.6*	Napoleon, **Napoléon,**	33 69 71	149.38	suspicion suspicion,	33 69 71

150.1	enthusiasm,	33
	enthusiasm	69 71
150.4	humouristico-satirical	33
	humoristico-satirical	
	41R → 71	
150.5	humours,	33
	humours	49 → 71
150.6	suspicion,	33
	suspicion	46
150.7	Auto-/biographical	33
	Auto-biographical	38
	Autobiographical	
	41U → 69	
150.7*	Mystification!	33
	mystification!	46 → 71
150.11	shadowing forth	33
	shadowing-forth	
	58 → 71	
150.18	Editor and Hofrath,	33
	Editor and Hofrath	
	69 71	
150.19	covered ways	33
	covered-ways	58 → 71
150.23	slip,	33
	slip	46
150.24	all but	33
	all-but	58 → 71
150.26	above all,	33
	above all	49 → 71
150.26	stringing together	33
	stringing-together	
	58 → 71	
150.27	The Man	33
	The man	38 → 58
150.32	(*Pfüscher*):	33
	(*Pfuscher*):	58 → 71
150.34	Reptile.'	33
	reptile.'	69 71
151.3	Suspicion	33
	suspicion	69 71
151.4	unfounded,	33
	unfounded	46

151.7	Paperbags,	33
	Paper bags,	38
	Paper-bags	69 71
151.10	revolution, of importance,	
		33
	revolution of importance	
		46
151.10	looked for.	33
	looked-for.	58
151.11	Psyche;	33
	Psyche:	41U → 71
151.15	clothes herself	33
	clothes himself	46
151.16	task;	33
	task,	41U → 71
151.20	Enough that	33
	Enough that,	46
151.21	direction:	33
	direction;	58 → 71
151.23	rained down	33
	rained-down	58 → 71
151.25	matter	33
	matter,	69 71
151.28	meanwhile	33
	meanwhile,	46
151.28*	toilsome diggings	33
	tiresome diggings	
	41U → 71	
151.29	If now,	33
	Ifnow,	41U
151.37	calculate.	33
	calculate:	41U → 71
151.38	Teufelsdröckh:	33
	Teufelsdröckh;	41U → 71
152.5	Nature; the	33
	Nature, the	58 → 71
152.7	a-weaving	33
	aweaving	69 71
152.7	Time:'	33
	Time;'	46 58 → 71
152.9	Remark too	33
	Remark, too,	69 71

152.9	man,	33		153.13	complete	33
	Man,	58 → 71			complete,	38 → 71
152.11	obscurity,	33		153.14	Civilised	33
	obscurity	41u → 58			Civilized	46
152.13	loom forth,	33		153.14	to;	33
	loom forth	38 41u			to:	46
	loom-forth,	58		153.21	evolved	33
152.13	mountain summits,	33			evolved,	49 → 71
	mountain-summits,			153.22	shew	33
		41r → 71			show	58 → 71
152.15*	Nay farther,	33		153.23	dig out	33
	Nay, further,	38 → 58			dig-out	58 → 71
	Nay further,	69 71		154.6	stand out	33
152.17	man,	33			stand-out	58 → 71
	man	46		154.8	judgement,	33
152.22	Solitude,	33			judgment,	38 → 71
	Solitude	46		154.10	this as heretofore	33
152.23	task:	33			**this, as heretofore,**	
	task;	46				41r → 71
152.25*	fearfullest	33		154.17	others;	33
	fearfulest	41r → 46			others:	38 → 71
152.25	destruction:	33		154.18	Suit	33
	destruction;	46			suit	41u → 71
152.26	themselves	33		154.22	souls:	33
	themselves,	41r → 58			souls;	46
152.27	looking through	33		154.26	had nevertheless	33
	looking-through	58 → 71			had, nevertheless,	69 71
152.27	Shows or Vestures	33		154.31	Hundred,	33
	Shows, or Vestures,				hundred,	58 → 71
		41r → 71		154.33	hammering,	33
152.28	Things even	33			hammering	38 → 71
	Things, even	41r → 71		155.4	beer,	33
153.2	this Clothes-Volume,	33			beer	71
	his Clothes-Volume,	46		155.6	shovel-hats	33
153.7	visible:	33			shovel-hat	41u
	visible;	46		155.6	scooped out,	33
153.8	every where	33			scooped-out,	58 → 71
	everywhere	38 → 71		155.6	girt on;	33
153.11	Mysticism.	33			girt-on;	58 → 71
	mysticism.	69 71		155.8*	racketting,	33
153.12	such	33			**racketing,** 41r 46 → 71	
	such,	38 → 71		155.19	hemmed in,"	33
					hemmed-in,"	58

155.23	Want! Want!	33
	Want, want!	41R → 71
155.26	wild berries	33
	wild-berries	58 → 71
155.27*	perrennial	33
	perennial	38 → 71
155.27	Suit	33
	suit	41U → 71
155.29	Oil-painting,'	33
	Oil-painting,)	41U
155.30	shall I not	33
	shall not	41U
155.31	canvass.	33
	canvas.	58 → 71
155.33	threatened	33
	threat[ ]/ened	58
155.33	engulph	33
	engulf 38 → 41 49 → 71
155.34*	hindrances	33
	hinderances	38 → 41
155.37	spreads out	33
	spreads-out	58 → 71
155.37	cow-hides	33
	cowhides	58 → 71
156.7	Rag-fair,	33
	Ragfair,	41R → 71
156.7	Liberty;	33
	liberty;	46
156.9	height:	33
	height;	41R → 71
156.10	Surely,	33
	Surely	58 → 71
156.13	Moderns;	33
	Moderns,	69 71
156.21	abroad:	33
	abroad;	46
156.22	Love.'	33
	Love.	46
156.28	did we not see	33
	did not we see	69 71
156.31	than meets	33
	that meets	71

156.31	time,	33
	time	41U
157.5	frills,	33
	frills	38 → 71
157.6	second-skin	33
	second skin	38 41U
157.13	realized.	33
	realised.	38 → 71
157.14	highborn	33
	high-born	71
157.14	step forth	33
	step-forth	58 → 71
157.15	shamoy:	33
	shamoy;	46
157.17	Distinctions re-established?	33
	Distinctions be re-established?	41R → 58
	Distinctions be reëstablished?	69 71
158.1	Not less questionable	33
	NOT less questionable	
		38 → 71
158.1	on *Church Clothes,*	33
	on *Church-Clothes,*	
		41R → 71
158.4	'By Church Clothes,	33
	'By Church-Clothes,	
		41R 41 58 → 71
158.4	premised,	33
	premised	69 71
158.7	Church Clothes are,	33
	Church-Clothes are,	
		41R → 71
158.15	together"	33
	together,"	49 → 71
158.16	indestructible	33
	indestructible,	69 71
158.18	Communion	33
	Communion,	38 → 46
158.20	heavenward: here	33
	heavenward; here	46
159.1	gains	33
	gaius	41U

159.2	thereof!"	33
	thereof"!	69 71
159.8	thick-plied	33
	thick plied	41u
159.9	hulls	33
	hull	46
159.10	Me is,	33
	Me, is,	49
159.12	Church Clothes	33
	Church-Clothes	
	41r → 71	
159.14	perhaps	33
	perhaps,	49 → 71
159.22	chaunting,	33
	chanting,	49 → 71
159.23	on	33
	on,	38 → 71
159.23	*muthes*).	33
	Muthes).	41r → 71
159.24	the Church Clothes	33
	the Church-Clothes	
	41r → 71	
159.25	as Church Clothes,	33
	as Church-Clothes,	
	41r → 71	
159.27	outward skin	33
	outward Skin	69 71
159.30	osseous Tissues	33
	osseous Tissues, 41u → 46	
159.31	such skin),	33
	such Skin),	69 71
159.35	the skin	33
	the Skin	69 71
160.4	the Church Clothes,	33
	the Church-Clothes,	
	41r → 46	
	the Church-Clothes	
	49 → 71	
160.5*	man.	33
	men.	49 → 71
160.6	same Church Clothes	33
	same Church-Clothes	
	41r → 71	

160.7	out at elbows:	33
	out-at-elbows:	58 → 71
160.10	Mask	33
	mask	49 → 71
160.11	generation and half	33
	generation-and-half	
	69 71	
160.16	(*Scheinpriester*)	33
	(*Schein-/priester*)	
	41u → 41 49	
	(*Schein-priester*)	
	46 58 → 71	
160.16	basest:	33
	basest;	58 → 71
160.21	*Palinginesia,*	33
	Palingenesia,	41r → 71
160.22	Re-texture	33
	Re-/texture	58
	Retexture	69 71
160.24	Work	33
	work	49 → 71
160.28	Singular Chapter	33
	singular chapter	38 → 71
160.28	Church Clothes!	33
	Church-Clothes!	
	41r → 71	
161.1	Probably it will	33
	Probably it will 38 → 71	
161.10	Paperbags	33
	Paper-bags	69 71
161.21	forbore	33
	forebore	38
162.1	purposes,	33
	purposes	49 → 71
162.3	shut out!	33
	shut-out!	58
162.11*	right hand know	33
	left hand know	58 → 71
162.11*	left hand doeth!	33
	right hand doeth!	
	58 → 71	
162.13	Shame the	33
	Shame (*Schaam*) the	
	69 71	

162.13	manners, manners	33 69 71	
162.15	Sun shine sun shine	33 38 → 71	
162.15	nay, nay	33 69 71	
162.18	over-wreathe, overwreathe,	33 69 71	
162.18	example, exemple,	33 41u	
162.20	and, with and with	33 71	
162.21	shews shows	33 58 → 71	
162.22	Printing Press Printing-Press	33 58 → 71	
162.26	here, here	33 69 71	
162.27*	doubled double	33 58 → 71	
162.30	stands out stands-out	33 58	
162.35	embodyment **embodiment**	33 41R → 71	
162.37	were attainable, were, attainable	33 38 → 71	
162.39	every where **everywhere**	33 41R → 71	
163.2	nay, nay	33 69 71	
163.4	Force force	33 49 → 71	
163.6	embodyment **embodiment**	33 41R → 71	
163.10	cut short cut-short	33 58 → 71	
163.11	'man is 'Man is	33 69 71	
163.11	Perhaps too Perhaps, too,	33 46 69 71	
163.13	actually existing actually-existing	33 58	

163.14*	has man man has	33 49 → 71	
163.14	played **played,**	33 41R → 71	
163.20	age, age	33 49 → 71	
163.27	these these,	33 38 → 71	
163.32	went on went-on	33 58 → 71	
163.32	"Motives?" "Motives"?	33 69 71	
163.34	perhaps perhaps,	33 46	
164.3	existence, existence	33 49 → 71	
164.4	two) two),	33 58 → 71	
164.4	gleams in gleams-in	33 58 → 71	
164.8	five hundred five-hundred	33 58 → 71	
164.9	crows' meat, crows' meat crows'-meat	33 49 58 → 71	
164.14	value, value	33 49 → 71	
164.23	Shoe Shoe,	33 38 → 71	
164.23	Peasants peasants	33 46	
164.30	category category,	33 69 71	
164.31	coats-of-arms; Coats-of-arms;	33 38 → 71	
164.32	every where; **everywhere;**	33 41R → 71	
164.37	Nay, Nay	33 69 71	
165.4	Time-Figure Time-figure	33 46	
165.6	divineness. divinenesss.	33 41u	

165.11	three thousand	33
	three-thousand	58 → 71
165.12	heroic,	33
	heroic	41ᴜ → 71
165.23	body forth	33
	body-forth	58 → 71
165.24	Godlike:	33
	Godlike;	46
165.26*	matter,	33
	manner,	41ᴜ → 71
165.28	Christianity	33
	Christianity,	46
166.2	Mumbo-Jumbo,	33
	Mumbo-Jumbo	49 → 71
166.2	Indian Wau-Wau	33
	Indian Pawaw	
		41ʀ → 71
166.5	me	33
	me,	41ʀ → 71
166.6	gilt wood;	33
	gilt-wood;	
		38 → 41 49 → 71
166.10	thing however	33
	thing, however,	
		41ʀ → 71
166.12	Heart;	33
	Heart:	46
166.18	matters	33
	matter	46
166.21*	English* Coronation	33
	English Coronation*	
		38 → 49
	English Coronation¹	
		58 → 71
166.23	must offer	33
	has to offer	46 → 71
166.25*	have we	33
	we have	38 → 71
166.26	well nigh	33
	well-nigh	69 71
166.27	Ragfair	33
	Rag-/fair	38
	Rag-fair	41ᴜ

166.28	every where,	33
	everywhere,	41ʀ → 71
166.28	hoodwink,	33
	hood-wink,	41ᴜ
166.30	suffocation!'	33
	suffocation.	38 41ᴜ
	suffocation.'	41ʀ → 49
	suffocation?'	58 → 71
166.foot	* *Now* last but one—Eᴅ.	
		33
	* **That of George IV.—**	
	Eᴅ.	38 → 49
	¹ That of George IV.—	
	Eᴅ.	58 → 71
167.1	At this point	33
	Aᴛ this point	38 → 71
167.5*	for sake of	33
	for the sake of	38 → 71
167.6	Teufelsdröckh's	33
	Teufelsdröch's	69
167.7	in their right	33
	in the right	46
167.18*	frightfullest	33
	frightfulest	41ʀ → 46
168.4	Tract,	33
	Tract	69 71
168.4	following,	33
	following	38 → 71
168.12	Oh,	33
	O,	69 71
168.19	Labour;	33
	Labour:	58 → 71
168.19	thy body like thy soul	33
	thy body, like thy soul,	
		41ʀ → 71
168.23	but the Bread	33
	but the bread	58 → 71
168.25	this, by act	33
	this by act,	46
168.28	Thinker, that	33
	Thinker, who	41ʀ → 71
168.30	return	33
	return,	38 → 71

168.31   Light and Guidance;   33
         Light, have Guidance,
                          38 → 71
168.37   any where   33
         anywhere   49 → 71
169.4   stealing)   33
         stealing),   38 → 71
169.6   athirst,   33
         athirst;   41R → 71
169.8   envelopes   33
         envelops   58 → 71
169.10   is that   33
         is, that   41R → 71
169.11   but, only   33
         but only,   46 → 71
169.12   Indignation. Alas,   33
         **Indignation bear him
         company. Alas,**   46 → 71
169.14* stupified,   33
         stupefied,   58 → 71
169.15   God: 33
         God;   41R → 71
169.15   Earth   33
         earth   38 → 71
169.16   Ignorant   33
         ignorant   49 → 71
169.19   which united   33
         which our united
                          41R → 71
169.23   hunted down   33
         hunted-down   58 → 71
169.26   standing armies,   33
         standing-armies, 58 → 71
169.30   nay,   33
         nay   69 71
169.37   two hundred   33
         two-hundred
                   38 41U 58 → 71
170.7   Gold-Hofrath!'   33
         Gold-Hofrath,'   38 → 71
170.7   'Too crowded indeed. 33
         'too crowded indeed!
                          38 → 71

170.12   Platform   33
         Plat form   49
170.16   still glowing, still
         expanding   33
         still-glowing, still-
         expanding   58 → 71
170.17   enlist   33
         enlist,   49 → 71
171.1   Putting which four   33
         PUTTING **which four**
                          38 → 71
171.6   Gregarious   33
         gregarious   49 → 71
171.9   all, for   33
         all for   49 → 71
171.9   Peri-/cardial   33
         Peri-cardial   38
         Pericardial   41U → 71
171.11   smote at   33
         smote-at   58 → 71
171.14   life,   33
         life;   38 → 71
171.18   common, over-crowded
                               33
         common over-crowded
                          58 → 71
172.4   *faire;*   33
         faire;   34 → 71
172.4   your guidance,   33
         your **guidance,**   46 → 71
172.5   eat your wages,   33
         eat you your wages,
                          46 → 71
172.6   'must an observant   33
         'does an observant
                          46 → 71
172.6   every where   33
         everywhere   41R → 71
172.9   Overgrowth.   33
         Over-/growth.   46 49
         Over-growth.   58 → 71
172.12   Once sacred   33
         Once-sacred   49 → 71

172.16	Practical men,	33
	practical men	49 → 71
172.20	Society'	33
	Society,'	38 41U
172.23	name	33
	name,	38 → 46
172.24	for Superiors,	33
	for Superiors	38 → 46
172.28	every where	33
	everywhere	41R → 71
172.33	chaunting	33
	chanting	49 → 71
173.5*	far in rear of	33
	far in the rear of	
		38 → 71
173.6	Sect	33
	sect	38 → 71
173.6	co-operative	33
	coöperative	46 58 → 71
173.14	every where known	33
	everywhere known,	
		41R → 71
173.15	workshop-intellect	33
	workshop intellect	
		49 → 71
173.16	workshop-strength	33
	workshop strength	
		49 → 71
173.21	he,	33
	he;	41R → 71
173.24	beleaguered	33
	beleagured	41U
173.33	watch-coat	33
	watchcoat	49 → 69
	watch-/coat	71
173.34	Job's news	33
	Job's-news	69 71
173.36	wheel-spokes	33
	wheelspokes	49 → 71
174.7	raining down	33
	raining-down	58 → 71
174.7	every where,	33
	everywhere,	41R → 71

174.9	*sic-vos-non-vobis*	33
	sic vos non vobis	69 71
174.9	pressure,	33
	pressure	49 → 71
174.9	hard crashing	33
	hard-crashing	41R → 71
174.10	so hateful	33
	so-hateful	58
174.11	glaring out	33
	glaring-out	58
174.12	glass-eyes,	33
	glass eyes,	49 → 71
174.16	UTILITARIA,	33
	UTILITARIA,	69 71
174.18	tread down	33
	tread-down	58
174.19	Temples,	33
	Temples	69 71
174.23	shuffled off,	33
	shuffled-off,	58 → 71
174.25	developement,	33
	development,	41U → 71
174.27	mechanisms;	33
	mechanisms	41R → 71
174.30*	has it two	33
	it has two	38 → 71
174.34*	loom-treaddles?	33
	loom-treadles?	38 → 71
174.36	*L'age*	33
	"L'age	38 41U
	'L'age	41R → 49
	'L'âge	58 → 71
174.36	*d'or*	33
	d'or,	41R → 71
174.37	*jusqu' ici*	33
	jusqu'ici	38 → 71
174.37	*passé*	33
	passé,	41R → 71
174.37	age	33
	age,	41R → 71
174.38	Past	33
	Past,	41R → 71

174.38	us.—But	33
	us."—But	38 41u
	us.'—But	41r → 71
175.2	flying?	33
	flying!	41u → 71
175.4	moths,	33
	moths	41r → 71
175.11	three hundred	33
	three-hundred	58 → 71
175.13	require	33
	require,	38 → 71
175.14	Mankind	33
	Mankind,	49 → 71
175.16	we find	33
	we to find	69 71
175.20	(alas!	33
	(alas,	69 71
175.23	Indicator,	33
	Indicator	46
175.25	*Utriusque*	33
	utriusque	41r → 71
175.27	kind),	33
	kind)	38 → 49
175.29	Trust	33
	trust	41r → 71
175.31	scot and lot	33
	scot-and-lot	58 → 71
176.1	Sansculottist,	33
	sansculottist,	49 → 71
176.3	Politeness;	33
	Politeness:	46
	politeness;	49 → 71
176.4	vagaries;	33
	vagaries:	46
176.4	sun-/light,	33
	sun-light,	38 → 71
176.6	nay,	33
	nay	69 71
176.6	London smoke	33
	London-smoke	
		41r → 71
176.15	any thing	33
	anything	58 → 71

176.17	Peasant, could	33
	Peasant could	38 → 71
176.18	with than	33
	with, than	38 → 71
176.20	art thou not	33
	art not thou	69 71
176.21	one Temple	33
	one temple	69 71
176.22	that Temple	33
	that temple	69 71
177.6	Is he not	33
	Is not he	69 71
177.16	men do reverence;	33
	men do reverence:	
		38 → 71
177.16	broad-cloth,	33
	broad-/cloth,	46 58
	broadcloth,	69 71
177.18	Who ever	33
	Whoever	49
177.18	blanket,	33
	blanket	49 → 71
177.22	Falsehood,	33
	falsehood,	49 → 71
177.28	Man:	33
	Man;	46
177.30*	Balliol, reign	33
	Baliol, reign	49 → 71
177.31*	Balliol being	33
	Baliol being	49 → 71
177.34	gesture;	33
	gesture:	41u → 71
178.3	Sense,	33
	sense,	38 → 71
178.4	Cares and foul Vices	33
	cares and foul vices	
		38 → 71
178.7	Tuberosity	33
	tuberosity	41u → 71
178.7	Civilised	33
	Civilized	46
178.10	Soul	33
	soul	69 71

178.16	Prison called Life."	33	
	Prison men call Life."		
		46 → 71	
178.17	Old Clothes	33	
	old Clothes	41u → 49	
178.17	Watch	33	
	Watch,	41u → 71	
178.18	Highpriest,	33	
	High-/priest,	69	
	High-priest,	71	
178.21	hand,	33	
	hand	49 → 71	
178.21	Wings,	33	
	wings,	41u → 71	
178.23	fateful note,	33	
	fearful note,	46	
178.25	Ghosts: he	33	
	Ghosts he	46	
178.26	Oh! let	33	
	O, let	69 71	
178.33	cast out	33	
	cast-out	58 → 71	
178.34	Darkness,	33	
	Darkness	58 → 71	
179.4	broken in	33	
	broken-in	58	
179.4	money-changers,	33	
	money-changers		
		49 → 71	
179.7	middle-state,	33	
	middle state,	69 71	
179.10	Figure,	33	
	figure,	41u → 71	
179.10	loose-flowing	33	
	loose flowing	38 → 71	
179.17	time,	33	
	time	41u → 46	
179.17	Paperbag	33	
	Paper-bag	69 71	
179.17	Documents,	33	
	Documents	38 → 71	
179.18	Work,	33	
	work,	49 → 71	

179.27	shot forth	33	
	shot-forth	58	
180.1	For us, who	33	
	FOR us, who	38 → 71	
180.8	burn out,	33	
	burn-out,	58 → 71	
180.10	start up	33	
	start-up	58 → 71	
180.13	themselves;	33	
	themselves:	38 → 71	
180.14	Whirlwind-Element,	33	
	Whirlwind-Element		
		49 58	
	Whirlwind-element		
		69 71	
181.2	Lies	33	
	lies	69 71	
181.6	once,	33	
	once	41u → 71	
181.6	myself,	33	
	myself	46	
181.8	covered up	33	
	covered-up	58 → 71	
181.8*	with even	33	
	within	38 → 71	
181.10	only,	33	
	only	46	
181.11	but must drop	33	
	but have to drop		
		46 → 71	
181.14	hand;	33	
	hand:	49 → 71	
181.16	fallen out	33	
	fallen-out	58 → 71	
181.17	darned up	33	
	darned-up	58 → 71	
181.19	going out	33	
	going-out	58	
181.19	coming in,	33	
	coming-in,	58	
181.20	eye:	33	
	eye;	46	

181.27*	centre of gravity centre-of-gravity	33	183.38	inevitably-coming inevitably coming	33 69 71
		46 → 58	184.12	worst, worst	33 46
181.36	Company: Company;	33 58 → 71	184.20	knit up knit-up	33 58 → 71
182.1	Mæsogothic Mœsogothic	33 41R → 71	184.34	equal of nothing. equal of notning.	33 41U
182.1	Shakespeare, Shakspeare,	33 41R → 71	185.2	for ever forever	33 46 → 71
182.3	court suit court-suit	33 58 → 71	185.2	cast away cast-away	33 58
182.7	Individual, Mankind, Individual Mankind,	33	185.2	lower; lower:	33 38 41U
		38 → 71			
182.8	flow on flow-on	33 41R → 58	185.5	obey he obey, he	33 49 → 71
182.9	Polities, Politics,	33 46	185.7	shewed showed	33 58 → 71
182.13	Heart, heart,	33 69 71	185.8	for ever rooted forever rooted	33
182.13	Eye eye	33 69 71			46 58 → 71
182.20	toilsome Mankind; toilsome Mankind:	33	185.8	nay, nay	33 69 71
		58 → 71	185.11	for ever exist, forever exist,	33 49 → 71
182.22	made made,	33 41R → 71	185.11	mayst mayest	33 38 → 71
182.36	Find Mankind Find mankind	33 46	185.12	living rock, living-rock,	33 38 → 71
183.8	Marshall Marshal	33 41U → 71	185.15	exclaims: exclaims,	33 38 → 71
183.14	Könning, Könning	33 38 → 49	185.21	Hero-Worship; Hero-worship;	33 41U → 71
183.17	Theologians: Theologians;	33 46	185.23	tree, tree	33 41U
183.26	Teufelsdröckh's Teufelsdrockh's	33 46	185.24	man's Man's	33 38 → 71
183.35	radiances, radiances	33 49 → 71	185.27	out of it: out of it;	33 38 → 71
183.36	light-beams, light-beams	33 49 → 71	185.27*	what is it to be what is to be	33 41U → 71
183.37	Indifference, indifference,	33 38 → 71	185.27	looked for looked-for	33 58

185.31	holding. Shew	33
	holding. Show	58 → 71
185.32	clodpole, shew	33
	clodpole, show	58 → 71
185.32	Higher	33
	higher	49 → 71
185.35	worship.' [extra leading between paragraphs] ¶Organic	33
	worship.' ¶Organic	34 → 71
185.39	but,	33
	but	58 → 71
185.39	hast thou	33
	has thou	46
186.4	every where	33
	everywhere	41u → 71
186.9	mark out	33
	mark-out	58
186.13	Perhaps, also,	33
	Perhaps also	58 → 71
186.13	knit up	33
	knit-up	49 → 71
186.18	nay,	33
	nay	41u → 71
186.19	point out.	33
	point-out.	58
186.33	boundless,	33
	boundless	58 → 71
186.36	Evangile?	33
	Evangel?	38 → 71
187.1	It is in	33
	Iᴛ is in	38 → 71
187.5	Cob-/webs,'	33
	Cobwebs,'	38
	Cob-webs,'	41u → 71
187.10	asunder.	33
	asnnder. [u set upside down]	46
187.11	till	33
	till,	38 → 71
187.12	garnitures,	33
	garnitures	38 → 71

187.12	and now	33
	and now,	38 → 71
187.12	vision	33
	vision,	38 → 71
187.12	interior,	33
	interior	38 → 71
187.13	Holies,	33
	Holies	38 → 71
187.14	Here therefore	33
	Here, therefore,	49 → 71
187.19	long,	33
	long	38 → 71
187.20	but	33
	but,	49 → 71
187.20	contrary	33
	contrary,	49 → 71
188.5	phial	33
	vial	69 71
188.6	Horse	33
	horse	46
	Horse,	69 71
188.7	"open	33
	"Open	38 → 71
188.23	nay, I too	33
	nay I, too,	69 71
188.24	ancient,	33
	ancient	41ʀ → 71
188.28	rules. And	33
	rules, And	41u
188.28	you too	33
	you, too,	69 71
188.32	man's Experience?—Was man	33
	man's Experience?—Was Man	41u → 49
	Man's Experience?—Was Man	58 → 71
188.34	dived down	33
	dived-down	58
188.35	every thing	33
	everything	49 → 71
188.36	ground-plan	33
	groundplan	69 71

188.38 Alas,   33
        Alas!   46

189.1   handbreadths   33
        handbreaths   71

189.10 Fifteen thousand   33
        Fifteen-thousand
                             58 → 71

189.12 Zodaical   33
        Zodiacal   38 → 71

189.12 Waybill;   33
        Way-/bill;   41u → 41 49
        Way-bill;   58 → 71

189.14 from us   33
        from us,   49 → 71

189.17 centuries,   33
        centuries   49 → 71

189.18 square-miles.   33
        square miles.   46

189.19 to us;   33
        to us: 38 → 71

189.27 man;   33
        Man;   58 → 71

189.35 spread out   33
        spread-out   58

190.2   pick out,   33
        pick-out,   58

190.3   dextrous   33
        dexterous   38 → 49

190.6   Domestic-Cookery   33
        Domestic Cookery   46

190.7   will, in this wise, one day,
        33
        **will in this manner one
        day**   41R → 71

190.7   in this wise, one day,   33
        in this manner one day
                            41R → 71

190.12 air-raiment   33
        airy raiment   46

190.14 workshops;   33
        work-/shops;
                        41u → 41 69
        work-shops;   49 58

190.15 for ever   33
        forever   46 → 71

190.16 every thing   33
        everything   49 → 71

190.22 legerdemain tricks   33
        legerdemain-tricks
                             58 → 71

190.23 these   33
        these,   49 → 71

190.28 nurselings, when,   33
        nurslings, when   46

190.30 two hundred, or two
        million   33
        two-hundred, or two-
        million   58 → 71

190.34 Cotton   33
        cotton   69 71

190.37 Custom-woven,   33
        custom-woven,   69 71

190.38 garments.   33
        Garments.   41u → 71

191.1   Demonolgy,   33
        Demonology,   38 → 71

191.4   boiling up   33
        boiling-up   58 → 71

191.8   Soul,   33
        Soul   41R 41 49 → 71
        soul   46

191.18 canvass,   33
        canvas,   58 → 71

191.24 he was There.   33
        he was there.   46

191.32 To clap on your felt,   33
        To clap-on your felt,
                             58 → 71

191.33 you were Any*where*,   33
        your were Any*where*,   46

191.33 to clap on your other   33
        to clap-on your other
                             58 → 71

192.3   thou,   33
        thou   49 → 71

192.4   non-extant,   33
        non-extant   46

192.9	curtains of To-morrow	33	193.1	Baby,	33	
	curtains of To-/morrow			**baby,**	41R → 71	
	41U → 41 49		193.4	stretch forth	33	
	curtains of Tomorrow			stretch-forth	58	
	46 58 → 71		193.7	practises	33	
192.9	Yesterday and To-morrow			practices	46	
	33		193.10	put on	33	
	Yesterday and Tomorrow			put-on	58	
	49 → 71		193.15	Orpheus built	33	
192.10	Time-Element,	33		**Orpheus, or Amphion,**		
	Time-element,	58 → 71		**built**	38 → 71	
192.14	Everlasting	33	193.17	who	33	
	everlasting	41R → 71		Who	38 → 71	
192.17	must be left	33	193.17	summoning out	33	
	had to be left	46 → 71		summoning-out	58	
192.23	for ever.	33	193.20	houses,	33	
	forever.	46 → 71		houses	49 → 71	
192.24	mayst	33	193.23	Man?	33	
	mayest	69 71		man?	46	
192.24	ponder,	33	193.23	eighteen hundred	33	
	ponder	41R → 71		eighteen-hundred		
192.29*	imagings (not			58 → 71		
	imaginings),—seems	33	193.26	Accompaniments,	33	
	imagings or			accompaniments,	69 71	
	imaginings,—seems		193.29	two million?	33	
	38 → 58			two-million?	58	
	imagings or imaginings,		193.30*	by the Music	33	
	seems	69 71		by the music	46 → 71	
192.31	farthermore,	33	193.32	glories in	33	
	furthermore,	41R → 71		glories-in	58	
192.34	nay,	33	193.33	Time:	33	
	nay	69 71		Time;	38 → 71	
192.37	I stretch forth my hand,		193.34	far distant	33	
	33			far-distant	71	
	I stretch-forth my hand		193.35	was it less	33	
	58			was it it less	46	
	I stretch forth my hand		193.36	Oh,	33	
	69 71			O	69 71	
192.38	daily stretch forth my		194.8	any thing	33	
	hand,	33		anything	49 → 71	
	daily stretch-forth my		194.9	life,	33	
	hand	58		life	46	
	daily stretch forth my					
	hand	69 71				

194.11	tapped on	33
	tapped-on	58
194.15	well nigh	33
	well-nigh	58 → 71
194.16	sweep away	33
	sweep-away	58
194.17	three-score	33
	three-/score	
		38 → 41 49 58
	threescore	46 69 71
194.18	Spirits, shaped	33
	Spirits, that are shaped	
		46 → 71
194.19	fade away	33
	fade-away	58
194.19	air,	33
	air	49 → 71
194.24	do we not squeak	33
	do not we squeak	69 71
194.25	gibber	33
	jibber	69 71
194.26	bodeful,	33
	bodeful	46
194.28	morning-air	33
	morning air	69 71
194.30	battle-shouts	33
	battle-shouts,	46
194.33	Spectre-Hunt;	33
	Spectre-hunt;	41R → 71
194.35	thousand million	33
	thousand-million	58 → 71
194.36	earth	33
	Earth	41R → 71
195.5	wherein,	33
	wherein	46
195.8	Force dwells	33
	force dwells	38 → 71
195.13	ago	33
	ago,	49 → 71
195.13	while and	33
	while, and	49 → 71
195.17	mission,	33
	mission	38 → 71

195.22	vanished	33
	Vanished	46
195.31	foot-print	33
	footprint	58 → 71
195.31	stamped in;	33
	stamped-in;	58 → 71
195.36	Dreams	33
	dreams	71
195.37	sleep!'"	33
	sleep!"	38
	sleep!'"	41U → 71
196.1	HERE then arises	33
	Here then arises	34
	HERE, then, arises	
		46 69 71
196.5	Woollen-Hulls	33
	Woolen-Hulls	34
	Woollen Hulls	46 69 71
196.8	spiritual,	33
	Spiritual,	38 → 58
196.12*	*Faust:*	33
	Faust.	38
	Faust,—	58 → 71
196.14	see'st him	33
	see'st Him	58 → 71
196.15*	thousand-times-repeated	
		33
	thousand-times repeated	
		46 → 71
196.16*	Shakespeare:	33
	Shakspeare:	46
	Shakspeare,—	58 → 71
196.20	inherit,	33
	inherit	46
197.3	things,	33
	Things,	38 → 71
197.6*	conclude,	33
	conclude	46 → 71
197.16*	few,	33
	few!	38 → 71
197.16*	Friends,	33
	Friends!	38 → 71
197.17*	courage!	33
	courage.	38 → 71

197.21	built:	33		199.13	asserted without scruple	
	built;	41u → 71				33
197.31	held out;	33			asserted, without scruple,	
	held-out;	58				38 → 58
198.2	reader,	33			asserted without scruple,	
	Reader,	41R → 71				69 71
198.10*	worth,	33		200.1	First, touching Dandies,	
	worth;	46 → 71				33
198.11	Tea-circle,	33			**FIRST, touching Dandies,**	
	Tea-circle	49 → 71				38 → 71
198.13	Nay, farther	33		200.2	specially	33
	Nay, farther,	41u → 58			especially	41u
	Nay farther,	69 71		200.2	Clothes-wearing Man,	33
198.15	Sense,	33			Clothes-wearing man,	46
	sense,	49 → 71		200.3	office,	33
198.18	(Worth-ships)	33			office	69 71
	(Worth-/ships)	69		200.4	purse,	33
	(Worthships)	71			purse	69 71
198.20	wearing apparel	33		200.9	sprung up	33
	wearing-apparel	69 71			sprung-up	58
198.25	nay,	33		200.9	Dandy,	33
	nay	69 71			Dandy	69 71
198.25	looks down	33		200.10	genius:	33
	looks-down	58			genius;	38 → 71
198.27	consecrate,	33		200.15	shows himself,	33
	consecrate	71			shews himself,	41u → 49
198.27	often	33			shows himself	69 71
	often,	41u		200.15	guise,	33
198.32	Portion	33			guise	69 71
	portion	49 → 71		200.16	Worth	33
199.1	Science:	33			worth	69 71
	Science;	41R → 71		201.12	world, that	33
199.2	ideas'	33			**world, which**	46 → 71
	ideas,'	69 71		201.13	boon; that	33
199.4	glance,	33			**boon; which**	46 → 71
	glance	38 → 71		201.18	the Dandy,	33
199.6*	whereso much	33			the Dandy	58 → 71
	where so much	38 → 71		201.20*	undecerning	33
199.11	move,	33			undiscerning	41u → 71
	move	38 → 71		201.22	is indeed,	33
					is, indeed,	46

201.30   regretted however that,
         here   33
         regretted however that
         here,   41R → 46
         regretted, however, that
         here,   49 → 71

201.33   tendency,   33
         tendency;   41R → 71

201.36   driven out   33
         driven-out   58

202.4   yet must it   33
         yet does it   46 → 71

202.4   indestructible,   33
         indestuctible,   71

202.10   Heat,   33
         Heat   38 41U

202.18   one: 33
         one;   58 → 71

202.25   not inconsiderable   33
         not-inconsiderable
                           58 → 71

202.31   *Self-Worship;*   33
         Self-worship;   49 → 71

203.1   nature though   33
         nature, though
                           41R → 71

203.9*   *Almacks,*   33
         Almack's,   41U → 71

203.22   nought.   33
         naught.   46 58 → 71

203.23   utmost: 33
         utmost;   41U → 71

203.25   unsufferable   33
         unsufferable,   49 → 71

203.26* frightfullest   33
         frightfulest   41R → 49

203.28   yield, came   33
         yield, there came
                           58 → 71

203.29   deliquium:—till   33
         deliquium: till   38 → 71

203.32   forbore.   33
         forebore.
                    38 → 41 49 → 69

203.34   prodigies, that,   33
         prodigies, which,
                           41R → 71

203.35   scared back   33
         scared-back   58 → 71

204.3   dilemma,   33
         dilemma   49 58

204.4   held out   33
         held-out   58

204.7   (*macalatur-bläter*),   33
         (*macalatur-blätter*),
                           38 → 49
         (*Maculatur-blätter*),
                           58 → 71

204.9   waste paper,   33
         waste-paper,   58 → 71

204.11   stray sheet,   33
         stray-sheet,   58 → 71

204.14* from the Secular   33
         from a Secular   69 71

204.15   individual,   33
         individual   49 → 71

204.16   mystagogue,   33
         Mystagogue,   41R → 71

204.21   sparkle out,   33
         sparkle-out,   58

204.23   mixed),   33
         mixed)   38 → 71

204.26   Confession, or   33
         Confession or   41U → 71

204.28   shape,   33
         shape   41R → 71

204.29   Observe,   33
         Observe   58 → 71

204.31* '"ARTICLES   33
         'ARTICLES   38 → 71

204.36   licence   33
         license   41R → 71

205.6   trowsers   33
         trousers   69 71

205.7*   All   33
         'All   38 → 71

205.7	Propositions,	33
	Propositions	38 → 71
205.11	every where	33
	everywhere	41u → 71
205.18	*White-Negroes;*	33
	White Negroes;	38 → 71
205.20	*Stook-of-Duds* Sect;	33
	Stook of Duds Sect;	69 71
205.21	named *Stook-of-Duds*	33
	named *Stook of Duds*	
		69 71
205.25	*Peep-of-day*	33
	Peep-of-Day	41u → 71
205.25	*Babes of the Wood,*	33
	Babes in the Wood,	46
205.26	*Poor-Slaves;*	33
	Poor-Slaves:	41u → 71
205.32	characteristics,	33
	characteristics	46 69 71
205.36	Universe, and Man,	33
	Universe, and the Man,	
		46
206.4	Vows, of Poverty	33
	Vows of Poverty	46
206.7	irrevocably enough	
	consecrated	33
	irrevocably consecrated	
		46 → 71
206.14	seemed indescribable.	33
	did not seem	
	describable.	38 → 71
206.15	lappets,	33
	lappets	69 71
206.18	thrums,	33
	thrums	49 → 71
206.21	freedom:	33
	freedom;	46
206.22	valve crown;	33
	valved crown;	71
206.25*	name, Poor-Slaves,	33
	name- Poor-Slaves,	46
	name Poor-Slaves	
		49 → 71

206.30	shut up	33
	shut-up	58 → 71
206.31	looking up	33
	looking-up	58 → 71
206.37	out-/breakings	33
	out-breakings	38
	outbreakings	46 → 71
207.10	drink	33
	drink,	49 → 71
207.16	oils;	33
	oils:	46
207.17*	me—indeed,	33
	me,—indeed,	38 → 71
207.20*	An Irish	33
	'An Irish	38 → 71
207.26	so precious	33
	so-precious	58
207.26	sheet,	33
	sheet	58 → 71
207.30*	First,	33
	'First,	38 → 71
207.31*	original: [italics through	
	208.6] *'The*	33
	original: [no italics] "The	
		38 → 49
	original: [centered title]	
	Poor-Slave Household.	
	[no italics] ¶"'The	
		58 → 71
208.1	*dinner:*	33
	dinner;	46
208.1*	*mother at bottom,*	33
	mother at the bottom,	
		58 → 71
208.2*	*side*	33
	side,	58 → 71
208.2*	*Board*	33
	Board,	58 → 71
208.3	*scooped out*	33
	scooped-out	58 → 71
208.3	*Trough,*	33
	trough,	58 → 71
208.6	*knives,*	33
	knives	49 → 71

208.6*   *with.'* [end of italics]   33
          with." [no italics]
                         38 → 71
208.7   Poor-Slave   33
          Poor Slave   38
208.10   Philosophical,   33
          Philosophical   69 71
208.12*   But now,   33
          'But now,   38 → 71
208.15*   abode: [italics to line 31]
          '*A Dressing-room*   33
          abode: [no italics) "A
          Dressing-room   38 → 49
          abode: [centered title]
          Dandiacal Household.
          [no italics] ¶"'A
          Dressing-room 58 → 71
208.16   *furnished:*   33
          furnished;   38 → 71
208.22   *which being*   33
          which, being   49 → 71
208.23   *open*   33
          open,   49 → 71
208.25   *back-ground.*   33
          back-/ground.   58
          background.   69 71
208.26*   *Author* (our Theogonist in
          person), *obsequiously*   33
          Author," our
          Theogonist in person,
          "obsequiously
                         38 → 71
208.28   *Apron.'* [end of italics] 33
          Apron." [no italics]
                         38 → 71
209.7   union: 33
          union;   46 58
          union;   69 71
209.8   best,   33
          best   69 71
209.8   co-operate   33
          coöperate   58 → 71
209.12   look down on   33
          look-down on   58 → 71

209.20   sweeping up   33
          sweeping-up   58 → 71
209.21   Pot-/walloppers,   33
          Potwallopers,
                    38 → 46 58 → 71
          Pot-/walloppers,   49
209.23   broken out   33
          broken-out   58 → 71
209.25   cover in;   33
          cover-in;   58 → 71
209.26   widening;   33
          widening: 58 → 71
209.27   boil up   33
          boil-up   58 → 71
209.28   crumbling in,   33
          crumbling-in,   58 → 71
209.31   away;   33
          away: 58 → 71
209.34*   "Machinery of Society"),
                                       33
          "Machinery of Society"),
                    38 → 41 49 → 71
          "Machinery of Society,"),
          46
209.37   nation   33
          Nation   46
210.2   sputters: 33
          sputters;   46
210.5   bottled up   33
          bottled-up   58 → 71
210.8   Doom's-thunder-peal; 33
          Doom's-thunderpeal;
                         38 → 71
210.10   liken'——— ¶Oh!   33
          liken'——— ¶O,   69
          liken'— ¶O,   71
210.16   every thing   33
          everything   58 → 71
210.16   scenting out   33
          scenting-out   58 → 71
210.17   amaurosis suffusions   33
          amaurosis-suffusions
                         41ʀ → 71

210.22	of doubt.	33		212.15	sartorius?	33
	of doubt.	41U			sartorious?	71
210.23	meanwhile,	33		212.16*	Debt? is	33
	mean while,	58 → 71			**Debt? Is**	38 → 41
211.1	Thus, however, has	33			debt? Is	46 → 71
	THUS, **however, has**			212.19	Nay,	33
		38 → 71			Nay	69 71
211.5	Volume;	33		212.20	Inquiries	33
	Volume,	58 → 71			Inquiries,	49 → 71
211.5	to whom therefore	33		212.27	new-created	33
	to whom, therefore,				new created	38 41U
		49 → 71		212.31	Nations,	33
211.12	Martyrs,	33			nations,	41U → 71
	martyrs,	38 → 71		212.32	co-/operating	33
211.17	Error,	33			co-operating	38 → 46
	error,	38 → 71			cooperating	49
211.18	but fractional	33			coöperating	58 → 71
	but but fractional	46		212.33	Poets,	33
211.22*	*Schneidermässig*				Poets	69 71
	(Tailorlike)	33		212.35	Guild-Brother	33
	Schneidermässig (Tailor-/				Guild-brother	41U → 71
	like)	41U → 41 49		212.36	"Nay,	33
	Schneidermässig (Tailor-				"Nay	69 71
	like)	46		213.2	Shop-board,	33
	schneidermässig (tailor-				Shopboard,	38 → 71
	like)	58 → 71		213.3	much injured	33
212.1	opprobrious	33			much-injured	41U → 71
	opprobious	41U → 41		213.4	noble	33
212.3	speak	33			nobler	46
	speaks	69		213.5	ancle-joints	33
212.4	Shakespeare,	33			ankle-joints	58 → 71
	Shakspeare,	41R → 71		213.9	Day.	33
212.7	a: Good	33			day.	46
	a "Good	38 → 71		213.13	Hierophant,	33
212.7	both!	33			Hierophant	69 71
	both!"	38 → 71		213.26	deliverance;	33
212.9	injured:	33			deliverance,	69 71
	injured;	58 → 71		213.28	for ever	33
212.11	acted on	33			**forever**	58 → 71
	acted-on	58		213.30	rent,	33
212.12	Whether	33			rent	46
	whether	41U → 71		213.32	Clothes;	33
212.14	bones,	33			Clothes:	41U → 71
	bones	58 → 71				

214.1	Plumpudding,	33
	Plum-/pudding,	58
	Plum-pudding,	69 71
214.3	pick out	33
	pick-out	58
214.12	being now done	33
	having now done	
		38 → 71
214.14	shorter? [extra leading	
	between paragraphs] ¶Of	
		33
	shorter? ¶Of	71
214.19	nay,	33
	nay	69 71
214.21	Censure	33
	censure	38 → 71
215.3*	men! as it might	33
	men! As it might	38 → 71
215.4	Teufelsdröckh's	33
	Teufeldröckh's	69
215.6	so must the lesser	33
	so has the lesser	
		46 → 71
215.7	instance, become	33
	instance, been forced to	
	become	46 → 71
215.8	time,	33
	time	38 → 71
215.9	effort,	33
	effort	38 → 71
215.10	shows	33
	shews	41u → 49
215.15	be; and	33
	be: and	46
215.16	'Time-Prince,'	33
	'Time-prince,'	71
215.16	nay,	33
	nay	69 71
215.20	Scythe-man,	33
	Scythe-/man,	38 58
	Scytheman,	41u → 49
215.26*	been	33
	been,	46 → 71

215.31	dashes his brush,	33
	dashes his sponge,	
		38 → 71
215.32	canvass,	33
	canvas,	58 → 71
215.35	It is	33
	It is,	49 → 71
216.11	as blotted	33
	as if blotted	46 → 71
216.11	Fantoms,	33
	Phantoms,	49 → 71
216.12	Gowle,	33
	Gowl,	58 → 71
216.14	shallow	33
	Shallow	58
216.20	disconsolately wandering	
		33
	disconsolately-wandering	
		58
216.26	Beaconfire	33
	Beacon-/fire	38
	Beacon-fire	41u → 71
216.29	Space!	33
	space!	58 → 71
216.30	ago	33
	ago,	38 → 71
216.30	Hofrath	33
	Hof[ ]/rath	71
216.32	Paperbag	33
	Paper-bag	69 71
216.36	paragraph: [extra leading	
	between paragraphs]	
	¶'Ew.	33
	paragraph: ¶'Ew.	
		38 → 71
216.37	*Wohlgebohren*	33
	Wohlgeboren	58 → 71
216.37	seen,	33
	seen	69 71
217.2	nay,	33
	nay	69 71
217.4	Leischen	33
	Lieschen	58 → 71

217.8	every ear	33
	very ear	38
217.9	*Ganse*	33
	Gans	58 → 71
217.11	Shortly	33
	'Shortly	41U
217.12	*Wohlgebohren*	33
	Wohlgeboren	58 → 71
217.13	Nor did there	33
	For did there	46
217.14	Alarmists,	33
	Alarmist,	46
217.17	perhaps, through	33
	perhaps through	
		49 → 71
217.19*	pacificated.—To	33
	pacificated.— ¶'To	
		58 → 71
217.21	For example,	33
	'For example,	41U
217.23	*Ganse*	33
	Gans	58 → 71
217.23	lamentation,	33
	lamentation	69 71
217.24	evening,	33
	evening	69 71
217.28	Post Director,	33
	Post-Director,	38 → 71
217.34	spirited away	33
	spirited-away	58
217.35	emissaries:	33
	emissaries;	41R → 71
217.36	with them,	33
	with them	71

217.37	living:	33
	living;	49 → 71
218.1*	must his archives,	33
	his archives must,	
		58 → 71
218.3	reposited.' [extra leading between paragraphs]	
	¶Thus	33
	reposited.' ¶Thus	58
218.5*	darker.—So	33
	darker. ¶So	38 → 71
218.7	perhaps,	33
	perhaps	49 → 71
218.11	also.	33
	also!	41U → 71
218.18	likewise, it is	33
	likewise, this is	
		38 → 71
218.20	digestion, not	33
	digestion; and indicate	
	so much, not	46 → 71
218.22*	ought he not	33
	ought not he	58 → 71
218.25	that namest thyself	33
	who namest thyself	
		46 → 71
218.26	all-too	33
	all too	46
218.28	eternity,	33
	Eternity,	38 → 71
218.29	have we not lived	33
	have we not existed	
		41R → 71
218.30*	quarrel?	33
	quarrel? [centered	
	paragraph] ¶THE END.	
		38 → 41 49

INDEX

INDEX

The subject entries in bold are those from the index of the Uniform Edition (1858), authorized by Carlyle. The page numbers are to the present edition, and the number of page citations has been expanded.

Compositor: Zoë Sodja, University of California, Santa Cruz
Text: Galliard 10/13, PageMaker 4.2 and 6.5
Display: Galliard 24/36, Galliard 16/auto
Printer: Malloy Lithographing, Inc.
Binder: Malloy Lithographing, Inc.